The
MX Book
of
New
Sherlock
Holmes
Stories

Part I: 1881-1889

THE MX BOOK OF NEW SHERLOCK HOLMES STORIES

PART I · 1881-1889

SOUTHAMPTON STREET

359

EDITED
By
David
Marcum

OFFICES

TRADITIONAL HOLMES
ADVENTURES
COMPILED FOR THE
BENEFIT OF THE
RESTORATION OF
UNDERSHAW

ISBN 9781780928241 Hardback
ISBN 9781780928258 Paperback
ePub ISBN 9781780928265
PDF ISBN 9781780928272

Published in the UK by MX Publishing
335 Princess Park Manor, Royal Drive,
London, N11 3GX
www.mxpublishing.co.uk
Cover design by www.staunch.com

CONTENTS

PART I: 1881-1889

(Continued on the next page . . . .)

(Continued on the next page . . . .)

These additional adventures are contained in
The MX Book of New Sherlock Holmes Stories
PART II: 1890-1895

. . . and PART III: 1896-1929

COPYRIGHT INFORMATION

The following contributions appear in
**The MX Book of New Sherlock Holmes Stories
Part II – 1890-1895 *and* Part III – 1896-1929**

Editor's Introduction:
The Whole Art of Detection
by David Marcum

Part I: *The Great Watsonian Oversoul*

According to Merriam-Webster, a *pastiche* is defined as a literary or artistic work that imitates the style of a previous work. Almost from the time that the first Sherlock Holmes stories began to appear in print, there were Holmes pastiches as well, side by side with the official sixty tales that are known as *The Canon*. Some from that period are more properly defined as parodies, but a few were written to sincerely portray additional adventures featuring Our Heroes, Holmes and Dr. John H. Watson,

I personally discovered pastiches at around the same time that I found the original Holmes stories, and began reading them just as eagerly as I did the material found in The Canon. In my mind, a well-written pastiche, set in the same correct time period as the originals, was as legitimate as anything written by the first – but definitely *not* the only! – of Watson's literary agents, Sir Arthur Conan Doyle. In the past, I've described the whole vast combination of Canon and pastiche as *The Great Holmes Tapestry*, with each providing an important thread to the whole, some brighter or thicker than others perhaps, but all contributing to the big picture. Perhaps another comparison would be to say that the union of Canon and pastiche forms a *rope*, with the Canonical adventures serving as the solid wire core, while all the threads and fibers of the additional pastiches bound around it provide greater substance and strength, with the two being indivisible.

I believe that pastiches have contributed immensely to the ever-increasing popularity of Holmes and Watson throughout the years. Additional cases and adventures only serve to feed the Sherlockian Fire, and ideally refocus interest back to the original narratives. There are some Sherlockian scholars who want nothing at all to do pastiches, and there are others who don't even want to classify all of the original sixty stories as being authentic, stating in various essays and books that this or that Canonical tale is spurious. I cannot agree with them.

In my essay, "In Praise of the Pastiche" (*The Baker Street Journal*, Vol. 62, No. 3, Autumn 2012), I argue that just sixty original stories relating incidents from Holmes's career are simply not enough. There must be more *about* the world's greatest consulting detective to justify that he *is* the world's greatest consulting detective, rather than just a few dozen "official" stories that leave too much unanswered. Pastiches fill in the gaps and cracks.

In "The Adventure of the Abbey Grange", Holmes tells Watson that ". . . I propose to devote my declining years to the composition of a textbook, which shall focus the whole art of detection into one volume." The vast amount of stories that make up the combination of both Canon and pastiche may not be – in fact, it certainly isn't! – what Holmes had in mind, but it is the closest we'll get to seeing and observing that overall tapestry of his life and work, the *Whole Art of Detection*.

Over the years, an incredible number of people have added to the body of work initially introduced by Watson's first literary agent. Sometimes, people discover lost manuscripts, usually written by Watson, but occasionally narrated by someone else – a Baker Street Irregular perhaps, or a client, or Mycroft Holmes, or a passing acquaintance, or maybe even by Sherlock Holmes himself. On a regular basis, an adventure is discovered in one of Watson's Tin Dispatch Boxes – and there must have been several of those to hold so many tales! These stories may be narrated in first person, or they may have a third-person omniscient viewpoint. No matter how they are found or transcribed, I believe that each of the "editors" of these later discovered adventures has tapped into what I like to call *The Great Watsonian Oversoul*.

When I was in high school, my award-winning English teacher, (who sadly never ever taught anything at all about the literary efforts of one Dr. John H. Watson, leaving that joyful task for me to capably take care of for myself,) introduced us to the concept of an "oversoul" – she was using it in relation to how it influenced some poet. Essentially – and I am no doubt remembering this somewhat incorrectly – the idea is that we are all tiny pieces of a greater entity, split off for a time from it, out here in the darkness and trapped in our own heads, before returning at some later point to the protection, warmth, goodness, and omnipotence of the greater whole. I, however, appropriated the idea to describe the overall source of the Holmesian narratives.

To my way of thinking, all of the traditional Canonically-based Sherlock Holmes stories are linked back eventually to this same basis of inspiration, no matter how the later "author" accesses it. Since the mid-1970's, I've read and collected literally thousands of adventures concerning the activities of Mr. Sherlock Holmes, and since the mid-1990's, I've been organizing all of them – both Canon and pastiche – into an extremely detailed day-by-day chronology, now covering hundreds of pages and literally thousands of narratives. Among the things that have become apparent to me over the years are: 1) There can *never* be enough good Holmes stories, relating the activities of the *true, correct,* and *traditional* Holmes of the Victorian and Edwardian eras; and, 2) The people who bring these stories to the public, no matter how they go about it, or whether they even realize it, are all somehow channeling Watson.

So one way or another, the spark of imagination that sets these narratives in motion originates in the *Great Watsonian Oversoul.* That's not to say that a lot of authorial/editorial blood, sweat, and tears doesn't go into all of these "discovered" stories, and these efforts should not be negated at all. These works don't simply appear as finished products – even the ones that are found essentially complete in Tin Dispatch Boxes. It takes a lot of work to first make contact with the Watsonian Oversoul, and then to transcribe what is being relayed in such a way that the public can understand and enjoy it. Sometimes the person relaying the story might misunderstand a fact or two along the way, leading to an odd discrepancy, or the "editor" channeling the tale may weave some little thing from his or her own agenda onto Watson's original intentions that isn't quite consistent with the big tapestry. But if the writer listening for that still small Watson voice within is sincere, the overall sense of the Sherlockian events that are being revealed within the story remains true.

Part II: *The MX Book of New Sherlock Holmes Stories*

This collection of new Sherlock Holmes adventures came about by listening to that still small voice. One Saturday morning in late January 2015, I popped awake, several hours earlier than I had intended, having just had a full-fledged and vivid dream about a new Holmes anthology. Now, I've tapped into the Oversoul and "edited" a few of Watson's works myself, but I hadn't tried anything like this before. If I'd rolled over and gone back to sleep, the idea would probably have disappeared. But it had grabbed me by then, so I quietly got up and started making a wish list of "editors" of Watson's works that I already knew and admired, in order to see if they would be willing to go through the effort to come up with some more new adventures

I emailed Steve Emecz of MX Publishing, and he enthusiastically liked the idea. Early on, we agreed that the author royalties for the project would be used to support Undershaw, the home where Sir Arthur Conan Doyle was living when both *The Hound of the Baskervilles,* as well as some of the later Holmes adventures, were written. MX Publishing has supported this effort in the past, so this decision was an easy one.

The same morning that I had the idea, I began to email authors, and I immediately started receiving positive responses. I was then emboldened to start asking still more people, and quickly the whole thing escalated. I reached out to friends to help me track down some authors in England that could only be reached by the old-fashioned mail. People already participating suggested still more folks who might also want to tap into the Oversoul and contribute a story to the anthology. It quickly grew to the point where it obviously needed to be two volumes, and sometime after that, it became three. (If it hadn't been split into multiple books, the whole thing would have become so fat that the book spines would have cracked apart.) It was always important to me that this collection, although finally presented under three covers, be considered as *one unified anthology*. As such, it is the largest collection of new Sherlock Holmes stories assembled in the same place.

These volumes have contributors from around the world: the U.S. and Canada, all over Great Britain, India, New Zealand, and Sweden. There are a couple of British expatriates who were living in Asia at the time they made their contributions, and two American ex-pats in London and Kuwait as well. Early on, I let all of the participants know that, since we had contributors from all around the globe, the format and punctuation of the books would be uniformly consistent, but they could use either British or American spellings in their finished works. Therefore, if you see some stories with *color* and others with *colour*, for example, that's why.

The contributors to these anthologies come from a wide variety of backgrounds. Some are professional best-selling authors. Others, like me, write for fun, but have day jobs elsewhere. A few are noted fan-fiction authors, taking this opportunity to write for a wider and different kind of audience. (I've always felt that some of the best Holmes writing has appeared as fan-fiction, and that a great Holmes story doesn't have to be found in a published book.)

There are several here who are writing a Holmes story for the first time. In the case of a few of these, I specifically invited noted Sherlockians who have worked long and hard to promote the World of Holmes but haven't written a pastiche before, with the idea that someone – and I can't think of who – once said that every Sherlockian should write at least one pastiche in their lives. This was their chance, and they did a great job with it.

A number of our authors have not been previously associated with MX. Welcome to the MX family! I'm aware that a few of these authors have already caught the Holmes-adventure-writing bug and are working on additional stories for future MX books of their own. I can't wait to read them!

Early on, I decided to arrange the stories chronologically, extending from 1881, when Holmes and Watson first met, to 1929, the year of Watson's death. This allowed for a logical arrangement of the stories, covering the entire period of Holmes and Watson's friendship and professional partnership. I was greatly influenced by that wonderful volume edited by Mike Ashley, *The Mammoth Book of New Sherlock Holmes Adventures* (1997). He also arranged the stories within by date, and as a hard-core chronologist, I have a great appreciation for that method.

My conditions for participation in the project were very basic. First and most important, as the editor of this collection I was very firm that Holmes and Watson had to be treated with respect and sincerity, and as if all involved were playing that fine old Sherlockian tradition, *The Game*. For those unfamiliar with this idea, Holmes and Watson are treated as if they were living, breathing, historical figures, and as such they *cannot* be transplanted to other eras, or forced to do something that is completely ridiculous for the time period in which they existed, such as battling space aliens. The stories had to be set in the correct time periods, ideally from 1881 to 1929. There could be no parody, nothing where Holmes was being used as a vampire-fighting Van Helsing, and nothing where he was incorrectly modernized, as if he is some version of Doctor Who to be reincarnated as whatever version of hero the current generation needs him to be.

Additionally, the stories had to be approximately the same length as the original short stories, with no novellas, and no fragments, such as something along the lines of "The Return of the Field Bazaar" or "How Watson Learned Another Trick". Also, I initially stated that the submitted tales all had to be narrated by Watson. However, there were a few that showed up in my email (t)in-box that stepped away from the Watsonian viewpoint – specifically, a case narrated by Wiggins, a couple by Professor Moriarty, one by a passing acquaintance of Holmes during The Great Hiatus, and two about the Professor told in third person. These provided valuable insight, they were set within the correct Holmesian world, and they were simply too good to miss.

Another goal that I set was to make use of completely new stories for the collection, in one format or another. With this in mind, I was *almost* completely successful . . . but not quite, if you wish to be technical about it. I must admit that, by way of a tiny bit of Watsonian Obfuscation, a few of the items herein have appeared in other locations or in other mediums, although they have never been published in this format before. One story was previously in a rather obscure local publication, and I believe that it is almost completely unknown to the larger audience, and might not be read by a lot of people otherwise. (In fact, with all my pastiche collecting, this was one that I didn't know about until it was submitted for this anthology.) A couple of the submissions have previously been on the internet for a short time, and two of the submissions are in the form of scripts that were previously used for radio broadcasts in the U.S. and the U.K. This their first appearance as text in book form.

As a side note, mentioning the scripts reminds me to acknowledge this volume's unintended but happy association with Imagination Theatre, which broadcasts traditional radio dramas weekly throughout the U.S., and has recently passed 1,000 broadcasts. As part of their rotating line-up, they feature a series of original tales, *The Further Adventures of Sherlock Holmes* – as of this writing numbering 117 episodes – and they are also in the process of broadcasting adaptations of the original Holmes Canon as *The Classic Adventures of Sherlock Holmes.* Currently, they are close to completing radio dramatizations of all sixty original Holmes stories featuring the same actors as Holmes and Watson throughout, John Patrick Lowrie and Lawrence Albert respectively, and with all adaptations by the same scriptwriter, Matthew J. Elliott. One of the scripts in this collection, never before in print, is by Imagination Theatre founder Jim French. A number of other Imagination Theatre writers besides Mr. French have contributed to this collection, including Matthew Elliott, Matthew Booth, John Hall, Daniel McGachey, Iain McLaughlin and Claire Bartlett, Jeremy Holstein, J.R. Campbell, and me (David Marcum) – that's a sizeable chunk our authors!

Part III: *With many sincere thanks . . . .*

Throughout the process, everyone that I've contacted about writing a story has been more than gracious, either by immediately stepping up and offering to provide one, or – when he or she couldn't join the party due to other obligations – continuing to offer support in numerous other ways. As the editor, being able to read these new adventures straight out of the Tin Dispatch Box is an experience not to be missed. Having never before tried to put together such a diverse Sherlock Holmes anthology, I must say that the whole thing has quickly become addictive, and I cannot promise not to do another one, although one of this size and scope, which was truly jumping into the deep water and *then* learning to swim, is unlikely.

6

Of all the people I'd like to thank, I must first express my gratitude as a whole to the authors – or "editors", if you will – of these new adventures from the Great Watsonian Oversoul. You stepped up and provided some really great stories that didn't previously exist. You also put up with my reminders, nudges, and story suggestions when I had to don my Editing Deerstalker. Along the way, as I was able to read these fine stories, I also met some really nice new people.

More specifically, I'd like to thank the following:

- My wife Rebecca and my son Dan, who mean everything – and I mean *everything*! – to me. They constantly put up with my Sherlockian interest, my ever-increasing pastiche collection, and my tendency to wear a deerstalker as my only hat for three-quarters of the year.
- Steve Emecz, publisher extraordinaire and the hardest working man in show-biz. Thanks for the constant support and for always listening!
- Bob Gibson of *staunch.com* – an amazing graphic artist, who let me keep tinkering with the cover, which became two covers, and then three . . . .
- Joel and Carolyn Senter. Years ago, my family knew to start my birthday and Christmas shopping with Joel and Carolyn's "Classic Specialties" catalogs. Later, when the original version of my first Holmes book was published, they enthusiastically got behind it and were responsible for selling almost every copy that was sold. They've encouraged me at every step, and I'm so glad that they could be a part of this anthology.
- Roger Johnson, who is so gracious when my random emails arrive with Holmesian ideas and questions. Visiting with him and his wife, Jean, during my Holmes Pilgrimage to England in 2013 was a high point of my trip. More recently, he located some wonderful pictures of Holmes and Watson for use in these books. In so many ways, I thank you!
- Bob Byrne, whom I first "met" by emailing him a question about Solar Pons – if you don't know who Solar Pons is, go find out! – and then we ended up becoming friends.
- Derrick Belanger, who hadn't specifically channeled Watson before, and is now on his way to becoming one of the best. Thanks for the friendship, the back-and-forth discussions upon occasion, and the support.

7

- Marcia Wilson, an incredible author and friend who received my first fan letter, long before I ever started thinking about writing anything myself. I've always said that, with her complex tales of Lestrade and his associates, she's found *Scotland Yard's* Tin Dispatch Box.

- Denis O. Smith, who was at the top of my pastiche wish list. I'm so glad that I was able to track him down, and I've really enjoyed the ongoing e-discussions we've had along the way since then;

- Lyndsay Faye, who said yes the very first day that I invited her to submit a story, and who also educated me about contracts.

- Bert Coules, for his advice and contributions, and for helping put together the Holmes and Watson that I hear in my head, Clive Merrison and Michael Williams.

- Carole Nelson Douglas, who – among many things – gave me some invaluable advice about foreign editions.

- Les Klinger, who spent part of a Sunday afternoon in a cross-country phone call, giving me some really valuable advice.

- Otto Penzler, who helped me several times when I pestered him for advice, and who wisely told me that "editing anthologies isn't quite as easy as drawing up a wish list and signing up stories".

- Chris Redmond, who jumped in early, and for all that he does, and just for having that incredible website, *sherlockian.net*.

- Kim Krisco, whom I met (by email) along the way, and was a never-ending source of encouragement.

- Tim Symonds, also an email friend with a lot of great ideas and support. I look forward to catching up with you at Birling Gap someday.

- John Hall, whose books – both pastiches and scholarship – I've enjoyed for years.

- Andy Lane – Thanks for the clever back-and-forth emails. I'm sorry I couldn't make it to New York when you were over here. I'll catch you next time!

- James Lovegrove, who corresponded with me way-back-when about the *true* location of Holmes's retirement villa on the Sussex Downs. (You know where I mean.) I'm very jealous of where you live.

- Steven Rothman, editor of *The Baker Street Journal*, for always responding so nicely whenever one of my emails drops in from out of the blue.

8

- Matthew Elliott, for all that he's done, and also for helping with the description of what he's accomplishing at Imagination Theatre.
- Maxim Jakubowski, who introduced me to a great new set of people.
- Mark Gagen, who gave me permission to use that absolutely perfect picture of Holmes on the back cover.
- And last but certainly *not* least, Sir Arthur Conan Doyle: Author, doctor, adventurer, and the Founder of the Feast. Present in spirit, and honored by all of us here.

This collection has been a labor of love by both the participants and myself. Everyone did their sincerest best to produce an anthology that truly represents why Holmes and Watson have been so popular for so long. This is just another tiny piece of the Great Holmes Tapestry, which will continue to grow and grow, for there can never be enough stories about the man whom Watson described as "the best and wisest . . . whom I have ever known."

David Marcum
August 7th, 2015
163rd Birthday of Dr. John H. Watson

Questions or comments may be addressed to David Marcum at
thepapersofsherlockholmes@gmail.com

9

Study and Natural Talent
by Roger Johnson

Greenhough Smith, editor of *The Strand Magazine*, hailed Arthur Conan Doyle as "the greatest natural storyteller of his age". Over a century on, Conan Doyle's genius keeps us reading, and, because many of us feel that sixty adventures of Sherlock Holmes just aren't enough, we write as well. The original tales are exciting and often ingenious; they're intelligent without being patronising, and they're never pretentious. The characters of Holmes and Watson – the apparently contrary forces that actually complement each other like Yin and Yang – stimulate our imaginations. Surely every devotee believes that the world needs more stories of Sherlock Holmes, and as, barring a true miracle, there'll be no more from his creator's fondly wielded Parker Duofold pen, we should provide at least one or two ourselves. We know the originals inside-out, or we think we do; we have a grand idea for a plot, and the style seems to be – well – elementary. How hard can it be?

In fact it's a sight harder than most of us think. Believe me: I know! To set a story convincingly in late Victorian or Edwardian London can require a fair deal of research just to avoid simple anachronisms and similar errors of fact. There are aspects of personality that may need careful attention – not just Holmes and Watson, but other established characters such as Messrs Lestrade and Gregson, and Mrs. Hudson (who really *was* the landlady at 221B, and *not* the housekeeper). Vocabulary and speech-patterns are important . . . .

Some will say, of course, that it's impossible to replicate the Doyle-Watson style. Nevertheless, there are writers who have come acceptably close to the real thing. Edgar W. Smith declared that *The Exploits of Sherlock Holmes* by Adrian Conan Doyle and John Dickson Carr should be re-titled *Sherlock Holmes Exploited*, but it is actually a remarkably good collection. Nicholas Meyer, L. B. Greenwood, Barrie Roberts, and Michael Hardwick are other names that come to mind, of authors who have, as Holmes himself said in a different context, applied both study and natural talent to the writing of new Sherlock Holmes adventures. For the current monumental collection, conceived and published for the benefit of the house that saw the rebirth of the great detective, David Marcum has coaxed stories from the best of today's generation of Holmesian chroniclers. Some of the contributors are famous, and some perhaps are destined for fame, but all of them bring intelligence, knowledge, understanding and deep affection to the task – and we are the gainers.

Roger Johnson, BSI, ASH
Editor: *The Sherlock Holmes Journal*
August 2015

Foreword
by Leslie S. Klinger

The urge to write new stories about Sherlock Holmes is not new. The first parody appeared in November 1891, after only a handful of Watson's tales had been published in the *Strand Magazine*. The public was fascinated by Holmes and wanted *more*. Parodies, an exaggerated version of a writer's style, written with humorous intent are exempt from the copyright laws, and so the author of the genuine Sherlock Holmes stories said nothing when these appeared. Pastiche, however, a reproduction of a writer's style without humorous intent, has long been restricted, as it should be, by the copyright laws granting the original author the right to control the use of his or her own characters.

Klinger v. Conan Doyle Estate Limited did not make new law. It merely recognized what the Estate had tried so hard to deny, that many of the elements of the characters of Sherlock Holmes, Doctor Watson, and their milieu, including not least the character names, had passed into the "public domain" throughout the world. This book celebrates the possibilities of that freedom, as creators tell their own stories about the beloved characters. Some may find it ironic that the celebration is dedicated to preserving the memory of Arthur Conan Doyle, whose heirs so bitterly fought the loss of their control of the characters. But, in the words of John Le Carre, "No one writes of Holmes and Watson without love."

Leslie S. Klinger, BSI
August 2015

Undershaw:
An Ongoing Legacy
for Sherlock Holmes
by Steve Emecz

Undershaw
Circa 1900 *(Source: Wikipedia)*

The authors involved in this anthology are donating their royalties toward the restoration of Sir Arthur Conan Doyle's former home, Undershaw. This building was initially in terrible disrepair, and was saved from destruction by the *Undershaw Preservation Trust* (Patron: Mark Gatiss). Today, the building has been bought by Stepping Stones (a school for children with learning difficulties), and is being restored to its former glory.

Undershaw is where Sir Arthur Conan Doyle wrote many of the Sherlock Holmes stories, including *The Hound of The Baskervilles*. It's where Conan Doyle brought Sherlock Holmes back to life. This project will contribute to specific projects at the house, such as the restoration of Doyle's study, and will be opened up to fans outside term time.

You can find out more information about the new Stepping Stones school at *www.steppingstones.org.uk*

15

Sherlock Holmes (1854-1957) was born in Yorkshire, England, on 6 January, 1854. In the mid-1870's, he moved to 24 Montague Street, London, where he established himself as the world's first Consulting Detective. After meeting Dr. John H. Watson in early 1881, he and Watson moved to rooms at 221b Baker Street, where his reputation as the world's greatest detective grew for several decades. He was presumed to have died battling noted criminal Professor James Moriarty on 4 May, 1891, but he returned to London on 5 April, 1894, resuming his consulting practice in Baker Street. Retiring to the Sussex coast near Beachy Head in October 1903, he continued to be involved in various private and government investigations while giving the impression of being a reclusive apiarist. He was very involved in the events encompassing World War I, and to a lesser degree those of World War II. He passed away peacefully upon the cliffs above his Sussex home on his 103rd birthday, 6 January, 1957.

Dr. John Hamish Watson (1852-1929) was born in Stranraer, Scotland on 7 August, 1852. In 1878, he took his Doctor of Medicine Degree from the University of London, and later joined the army as a surgeon. Wounded at the Battle of Maiwand in Afghanistan (27 July, 1880), he returned to London late that same year. On New Year's Day, 1881, he was introduced to Sherlock Holmes in the chemical laboratory at Barts. Agreeing to share rooms with Holmes in Baker Street, Watson became invaluable to Holmes's consulting detective practice. Watson was married and widowed three times, and from the late 1880's onward, in addition to his participation in Holmes's investigations and his medical practice, he chronicled Holmes's adventures, with the assistance of his literary agent, Sir Arthur Conan Doyle, in a series of popular narratives, most of which were first published in *The Strand* magazine. Watson's later years were spent preparing a vast number of his notes of Holmes's cases for future publication. Following a final important investigation with Holmes, Watson contracted pneumonia and passed away on 24 July, 1929.

PART I: 1881-1889

In 1874, while visiting the home of a University friend (see "The Gloria Scott"*), Sherlock Holmes realized that his life's calling was to become a Consulting Detective. Moving to Montague Street in London, he commenced his career. A few years later, John H. Watson received his Doctor of Medicine degree and eventually joined the Army. After being wounded at the Battle of Maiwand, he returned to England, where he was introduced to Sherlock Holmes on New Year's Day, 1881. They agreed to take rooms at 221b Baker Street. Within months, Watson was assisting Holmes on his various investigations. In the mid-1880's, Watson married his first wife, about whom only limited facts are available. Although now wed, Watson often found time to assist in his friend's adventures. Following the death of his first wife in late 1887, Watson returned to 221b, where he lived until his second marriage to more well-known Mary Watson (née Morstan) in mid-1889. This volume covers this earlier period from soon after Holmes and Watson's first meeting through the early months of Watson's second marriage. During this time, Holmes was building his practice, and Watson did not publish any narratives of Holmes's cases until late 1887. Thus, Holmes was still somewhat unknown at this point. It was during this interval that the two first became friends, and then* "brothers, not in blood, but in bond."*

*From the film Sherlock Holmes (2009)

Sherlock Holmes of London
A Verse in Four Fits
by Michael Kurland

If you've a missing heir to locate, or a bank you have to guard,
There's only one detective, and he's not from Scotland Yard.
When the duke has lost his coronet or the treaty's gone astray,
It's Sherlock Holmes of London who's called in to save the day!

What the dog did in the night-time only Sherlock Holmes can hear.
He knows why the boot was missing from the doorway of the peer.
You may find him considering where redheads can be found
Or lost in thought while studying the footprints of a hound.

In the frigid nights of winter when the fog swirls in the street
And the gas light from the street lamp don't illuminate your feet,
And you hear the steady clopping of a hansom down the mews,
Why it's Sherlock Holmes of London out following his clews.

Queen and Wolfe and Wimsey and a host of private 'tecs
Along with Marple and Millhone and the others of their sex
And Gregson and Lestrade – all of them have their place,
But it's Sherlock Holmes of London who we trust to solve the case.

The Adventure of the
Slipshod Charlady
by John Hall

Y ou may well surmise that following that first case in which I was associated in some small way with Mr. Sherlock Holmes, and which I have called *A Study in Scarlet*, I followed Holmes's work with some considerable interest, and even ventured to hope that I might again at some point, and in some humble capacity, be able to join with him in the chase. I was, as you may recall, sharing rooms with Holmes at the time, and I had no real occupation or interests of my own, so I clutched eagerly at any opportunity for diversion. Holmes, however, was then, as always, somewhat reluctant to encourage confidences, and I had to wait several weeks after the conclusion of that first sensational problem before he allowed me to share in another investigation.

It was late spring, and the weather was showing every promise of improvement after what had been a very dreary fortnight. I had risen a little before my usual hour, and was somewhat surprised to find that Holmes, so often a late riser himself, had already breakfasted. Before I could remark upon this, or do more than wish him good morning, he said, "Well, Watson, and how does your writing progress?"

"Pretty much finished, Holmes. And if I do say so myself, a very promising little tale. I have great hopes for both its publication, and its reception by the reading public."

"It will, I trust, be instructive? Scotland Yard could well use a proper textbook of detective procedure!"

I laughed. "I fear it will hardly be that, Holmes, although you may be sure that I have given full attention to your remarkable methods. But the public taste is both fickle and demanding, insisting upon entertainment, diversion, some degree of imagination, as well as mere dry and dusty factual exposition."

He groaned, and lit a cigarette.

"But surely you would not deny the power, and utility, of imagination?" I protested. "Had you not been able to imagine what had taken place in that dreadful house, then – "

He raised a hand. "That was hardly imagination, Doctor," he said in that pedantic tone which he sometimes adopted. "A purely scientific reconstruction of events, as the French put it, based solely upon observation and deduction."

23

"H'mm," said I, not wishing to argue the point before I had finished my breakfast egg. Then, recognising an opportunity, I went on, "And have you any small problems in hand just now which might call for your unique talents? Having finished my own account of that horrid and most puzzling case, I confess that I am at somewhat of a loose end, and would welcome some mental stimulus, even vicariously."

He smiled ruefully, and shook his head. "There is nothing of similar moment just now. It is true that I have one or two insignificant matters in hand, but they are mainly pedestrian enough, scarcely likely to appeal to your Epicurean palate." He paused. "However – "

"Well?" said I, eagerly.

"Well, then, there is one small problem that I cannot immediately solve. Tell me, Watson, why would a manservant spend all day in the cellar of his master's house?"

"H'mm. To avoid being asked to do some uncongenial work?"

Holmes laughed. "Practical as ever, Doctor! But it can scarcely be that, for the master is absent from the house all day, and there is no wife who might bustle about the place and give the man unwelcome orders."

"Well, then. Rats? Or perhaps he is helping himself to the master's wine?"

"There is, as far as I am aware, no wine. And no rats – and if there were, there is a useful and practical body of men known as 'rat catchers' who will solve that particular problem cheaply and effectively." He thought for a moment in silence. "I confess, Watson, that Mrs. Bradley's little problem has given me much difficulty, though doubtless the real explanation will prove to be as prosaic as your own very practical suggestions."

"Mrs. Bradley? Do I – "

"You have never been formally introduced, but I fancy you will recollect the lady. Some sixty years of age, or perhaps a trifle more, of the working class, usually somewhat down at heel?"

"Ah, yes! I noted her appearance down when I was writing up the study in scarlet which began our association." I glanced at the old notebook which lay upon the table by my elbow. "Here we are – 'a slipshod elderly woman' was my rather ungallant depiction. I recollect that my first thought was 'bunions!' I did wonder if my professional services might be called upon."

Holmes laughed. "It is true you might be helpful in that regard," said he. "But it was the wish to consult upon detective, and not medical, problems that originally brought Mrs. Bradley to Baker Street about a month ago, and I must confess that I have nothing in the way of advice to offer."

"Perhaps if you were to lay the facts before me, it might help you to arrange them in a way which would prove capable of explanation?" I suggested tentatively.

"You are right, it does sometimes help to lay out the problem methodically. Very well, then. Mrs. Bradley is what is politely called a 'daily' or 'domestic,' or more vulgarly a 'charlady,' that is, she makes a slender living by cleaning floors, polishing furniture, and similar unskilled but necessary household tasks."

"Not – and no offence to her, or to others of her profession – but not the sort of person to have a problem which would require your services?" I ventured to suggest.

"You would hardly think so, but you would be wrong, Watson. Indeed, I have asked her to call in here this very morning before she goes to work."

Rather surprised I pulled out my watch. "So late? Late, that is, to begin daily work of that sort."

"Mrs. Bradley informs me that she begins work at ten in the morning, and finishes at three in the afternoon. Her employer is, as I say, absent from the house all day on business, so there is no question of her interfering with his activities by mopping the floor whilst he is at his desk writing letters, or some such task."

"I see. That in itself makes sense, but is somewhat unusual."

Holmes nodded. "It is one odd aspect among several. A curious household, I gather. Ah!" he said, as there was a ring at the front door, "I believe that's the lady herself. Please remain, Doctor, for I should be pleased to have your views on the matter."

A moment later, Mrs. Bradley was shown into our little sitting-room, and I escorted her to a chair, into which she sank with an audible sigh of relief. I had already remarked upon her dilapidated shoes – indeed, slippers would be nearer the mark – but now I took the opportunity to cast her a surreptitious glance, and observe her general appearance more closely. She was perhaps some sixty years of age, stout, with a mop of untidy grey hair escaping from beneath the frayed brim of an unfashionable hat. Darned stockings, and an ancient coat with a slightly greasy collar of fur from some unidentifiable species, completed the picture. Altogether you could scarcely expect to find a more typical, if timeworn, example of the class to which she so clearly belonged.

"Now, Mrs. Bradley," said Holmes in his most soothing voice, "this gentleman is Doctor John Watson, and I have told him something of your worries, but perhaps you would be so kind as to begin at the beginning, for his benefit, and pray omit no detail."

25

"Well, sir," said Mrs. Bradley, "I hardly know what to tell you, it all seems something and nothing, like."

I may add by way of parenthesis that her speech was the purest Cockney, with many a dropped "h" and the like. I shall not endeavour to reproduce it at all accurately here, as the reader will doubtless be able to imagine it.

Holmes, with an obvious effort of will, prompted her, "Pray allow us to be the judges of that, madam. Now, you began your employment some six weeks ago, is that not correct?"

"That it is, Mr. Holmes, and I rue the day! What with that Naylor sneaking about the place, and telling outright lies into the bargain! Why – "

"You forget, Mrs. Bradley, that the good doctor here knows nothing of the matter," said Holmes, with just the merest hint of asperity.

"Oh, to be sure! Well then, Doctor, and you, Mr. Holmes, though you've heard this already – well, then, six weeks or so ago I applies for this job with the colonel – Colonel Fanshawe, that is, and such a nice gentleman, what I would call a real gentleman, if you follow me – anyway, I applies for the job, the hours being so good, and the colonel, him being away all day at his office, and making no trouble and all."

"You got the job," said Holmes, "and entered upon your duties at once. There were, I understand, no other servants kept, save only the manservant, this Naylor whom you mentioned?"

"That's right, sir. And a proper little sneak he is, at that!"

"In what way?" I asked, intrigued.

"Well, sir, you'd be doing your floors, and that, and you'd look up, and there 'e is, standing in the doorway, or wandering about the corridors."

"I see. I must confess I see nothing particularly objectionable in that," I said.

"No, sir. Not in itself, as you might say. But then, a week after I started, the colonel, he says to me, 'Mrs. B. – ' and 'e always calls me that, nice and pleasant as you please, and no edge to 'im at all – 'Mrs. B., there will be some workmen in for a few weeks or so, down in the cellar. Some small repairs to be done, nothing to worry about, so pray do not be alarmed if you hear them banging and crashing,' something to that effect."

"And they duly arrived," Holmes supplied.

"They did, sir. Or 'e did, for there was only one of 'em, a nice young fellow. I saw Naylor – Mr. Naylor, 'e likes to be called, I don't think! – anyway, Naylor let 'im in, showed him to the cellar. Now, I – "

"One moment," said I. "Have you ever been into the cellar yourself?"

"Very good, Watson!" Holmes exclaimed.

"No, sir, I 'aven't what you'd call been down there," said Mrs. Bradley. "But I did – not to be sneaky, or anything of that – but one day when I'd the 'ouse to myself I took a peep in."

"And?"

Mrs. Bradley shook her head. "Nothing, Doctor! Just an old brick cellar. Nothing down there at all, excepting some old bits and pieces of furniture, and them very much the worse for wear, all banged about and that."

"No wine rack? No sign of rats?" asked Holmes, with a sidelong glance at me.

"No wine rack, sir, certainly. As for rats – why, if I'd even suspected such a thing I'd 'ave given my notice at once!"

"To be sure," said Holmes. "But thus far, with the exception of your dislike for the manservant Naylor, you have given the doctor no indication as to what it is which so perturbs you."

"Indeed I 'aven't, sir. Well, then, like I was saying, I seen the young fellow come, but I never seen 'im go, being s 'ow I'd left before 'e'd finished. Now, that's all well and good, but the next day, Naylor, 'e tells me the young chap is already down in the cellar, and wasn't to be disturbed. Well, as the day wore on, I could 'ear some banging and that down there, and so I knew the young chap, 'e was 'ard at work, so after an hour or so I looks for Naylor to ask if I should make a cup of tea for the young man, that being only right and proper and expected, 'im being a tradesman and that. But Naylor now, 'e was nowhere to be seen, so I knocks on the cellar door, and calls out, did I ought to make a cup of tea."

"Well?" I asked.

"You may well say, 'Well,' sir! Well, it was Naylor 'imself who called out from the cellar, "Thank you, Mrs. Bradley, that won't be necessary." Now, what d'you think of that?"

"Why, that Naylor was down there, perhaps making sure the job was properly done?" I said. "Or perhaps the young man had asked him for a hand with some heavy work?"

"'Eavy work!' Mrs. Bradley found the notion amusing. "Not 'im, sir! No. no, you mark my words, Doctor, 'e's up to no good. And I've noticed that there ain't no young tradesman – no, nor old one neither! – around the place. But yet there's still somebody – and it's Naylor, that I do know for a fact – messing about in that same cellar, day after day. And what I'd *like* to know, Mr. 'Olmes, is what you might be able to do

27

about it? Only I'll be ever so grateful if you could set my mind at rest." And this was said with such an evident and honest sincerity that I leaned over and patted her arm.

"I confess," said Holmes, "that your problem is indeed a curious one. And I fear that I have little to offer in the way of advice from your last visit. Perhaps, Watson, you have some words of wisdom."

Put thus suddenly on the spot, as it were, I struggled for words. "Ah – is the matter then so distressing, Mrs. Bradley, that you really cannot see your way to remaining in the house? There are surely other openings for you?"

"Now, Doctor! Isn't that just what I've been thinking myself?" said Mrs. Bradley. "But you see, the hours is so good, and the pay is so good – it's only the nagging worry, as you might call it." She hesitated, obviously waning to say more.

"Well, Mrs. Bradley?" said Holmes.

"Well, sir, there's two things. First – " and again came that hesitation.

"Well?" asked Holmes a second time, with a little more impatience in his tone.

"Well, sir, you might just think that it's an old lady's fancy, but I'm sure that little sneak Naylor followed me 'ere. And if you was to go to the door with me, and keep an eye open, I can promise you that you'll see 'im."

"And why should he follow you, do you think?" asked Holmes, evidently puzzled.

"Why, bless you, sir! To see if I've been 'ere to talk to you, like."

"H'mm, I see. You said there were two things?"

"Ah, yes. You see, sir, Naylor, 'e let on that 'e 'as some urgent business errands to do for the master, this very afternoon. Now, suppose you was to call round, I could let you 'ave a look in the cellar, easy as anything. That way you might be able to tell me what you think, even if it's to say there's nothing to worry about."

"I see." Holmes glanced at me. "What say you, Doctor?"

"An excellent notion," said I.

"Very well then. I have a note of the address," said Holmes, "and we shall call at, say, two o'clock. Is that satisfactory?"

"That it is, sir, and it'll set my mind at rest," said out visitor, clambering to her feet.

I rose to see her out.

"By the way, Watson," said Holmes in his languid fashion, "you might just stand at the door a moment, and see if Mrs. Bradley is indeed being followed."

"Very well."

"Oh, and Mrs. Bradley – how did you come to hear of me? I do not believe you mentioned that to Watson."

"Well, sir, it was a friend of the colonel's, a young chap 'e was, came to call on the colonel one day, only 'e was out. The young man, proper gent, he looks very forlorn, says he's come a long way, and wouldn't mind a cup of tea and that. So I makes him one, and somehow we got to talking – 'e 'ad no sort of edge to 'im, talked as nice as you like, and somehow – don't you never ask me just 'ow – he gets me to tell him wha's been bothering me, and then 'e says: "You should talk to Mr. Sherlock 'Olmes, he's the man to solve this problem," and 'e gives me your address, writes it down on a bit of paper. And so 'ere I came," she finished with a note of triumph.

"I see. Very well. Watson?"

"Ah, yes. This way, madam." I led the way to the street door, and saw Mrs. Bradley off, but I did not return at once. Instead, I partly closed the door, and looked keenly out through the slit which remained. To my surprise – for I had put Mrs. Bradley's suspicions down to mere fancy – I saw a man lurk from out of the shadows, for all the world like some villain of melodrama, and take the same direction as Mrs. Bradley. My first instinct was to accost him, or at the very least to follow him, but then it occurred to me that we already knew his, and Mrs. Bradley's, destination. To follow would perhaps spoil Holmes's plans, and so, albeit reluctantly, I made my way back up the stairs, and told Holmes what I had seen.

"Ah. It shows that Mrs. Bradley's suspicions were correct in at least one regard," said Holmes. "Let us see if her other concerns are equally well founded."

It was with some considerable impatience that I set myself to wait until two o'clock in the afternoon. I tried one of Clark Russell's collections, *In the Middle Watch,* but could not concentrate on it as it deserved, and it was with great relief that I heard Holmes saying, "We have twenty minutes to keep our appointment, Watson."

We left our cab at a busy crossroads on the outskirts of the City, and headed eastwards. Our road did not take us into very fashionable surroundings, and I observed as much to Holmes.

"Indeed," said he, "a military man, with an important occupation, and – what did our client say? Ah, yes, 'a real gent,' I believe. Such a man might be expected to have a more elegant establishment. Ah, but here we are. Hum! The house seems as faded as the street."

In this, Holmes was quite correct. I looked somewhat askance at the slightly dusty windows, the faded green paint on the door, the general air of neglect. Holmes rang the bell, and the door was opened at one by Mrs. Bradley, who had evidently been expecting us, and was in a state of some excitement.

"Oh, Mr. 'Olmes," she began, "am I pleased that you've come! As I said, Naylor – the little rat – 'e's just gone out, says he'll be an hour or two. Now, if you'll step this way, sir, and I'll show you the cellar."

She was as good as her word, taking us to a plain wooden door which gave onto a flight of stone steps. "I won't go down there, sir, if you don't mind," said Mrs. Bradley, "I'd be that frightened of what we might find."

"That is very well," said Holmes, "Watson and I will manage well enough. Do you have a candle, or – ah!" as Mrs. Bradley produced a lantern and matches. "Excellent! You are an ideal client! Now, Watson, let us proceed."

I followed Holmes into the cellar. It was, as Mrs. Bradley had told us, a perfectly ordinary cellar, with brick walls. A few bits of old furniture and the like stood about, or lay, rather, for the detritus was scattered all over the floor: and old chair, the remains of a kitchen table, much battered, a hammer, and the like, were among the useless items which I noticed.

Holmes had gone over to one wall, one which I knew was the innermost wall of the house. He held up the lantern. "Ah!"

I looked where he pointed, and saw that several of the bricks had been removed, as if someone were trying to break through the wall into the adjoining premises. The bricks themselves were stacked neatly on the floor.

"Not the common or garden attempt at robbery, surely, Holmes?" I protested, the disappointment in my voice plain enough even to my own ears. But then I *was* disappointed, I admit it frankly. The case which had seemed to be possessed of some interesting points was nothing more than a trite robbery, or attempt at a robbery! And I could see that Holmes, too, felt let down. Let down, and perhaps even puzzled.

Now that the thought occurred, there was something not quite right about all this. Oh, I do not mean the attempt at theft, or anything of that kind. No, it was something else that nagged at me, though I could not have put into words just what it was.

"There is nothing more to be seen here, Doctor," said Holmes abruptly. "Let us regain the outer air and see what may be on the other side of this wall."

We left Mrs. Bradley mumbling something about what a relief it was to have us looking into the matter, and went out into the street. The corner was at no great distance, and Holmes paced it out carefully before turning into the road, somewhat broader than the one we had just left, which backed onto the colonel's house. I could see Holmes count out the steps as he walked briskly along, before coming to a halt in front of a fairly ordinary looking shop. I glanced up, to see a sign reading: "T. Dudley – Curios and *Objects d'Art.*"

"I had half expected a bank, at the very least!" said I, somewhat ruefully.

Holmes laughed. "As did I. although Mr. Dudley does have some interesting, and indeed quite valuable, objects. I myself am amongst his clients."

I glanced into the dusty window, which was crowded with every imaginable object. Old coins, medals from long-forgotten campaigns, something which looked like the dried paw of some monkey, and at the back, in the shadows, what looked like one of the hideous shrunken heads of South America. I shuddered, and wondered in a vague sort of way what it was Holmes had last bought here!

"Not," I ventured, "the sort of swag dreamed of by your average burglar?"

"Sadly, no. but then – "

"But then why the tunnel, or beginnings of one?" I prompted him.

"Just so. And more particularly since Mr. Dudley does not keep anything of value in his cellar, but stores it at his bank." Holmes shrugged his shoulders. "It requires thought, Doctor. Thought, and tobacco." And off he went, leading me back to Baker Street.

Back in our old familiar surroundings, Holmes proceeded to curl up in his chair, and pack his old clay pipe. I myself found a decent cigar, and was just about to light it when a thought occurred to me. "You know, Holmes," I ventured, "to say that Mrs. Bradley contacted you some time ago, the tunnel does not seem very far advanced. Indeed, although I was at the outset inclined to call this 'The Case of the Slipshod Charlady,' it might equally well be called 'The Case of the Slipshod Villains'!"

Holmes stared at me for a long moment, then laughed in his peculiar silent fashion. "Or yet again, 'The Case of the Slipshod Detective,' for I have been most remiss. The so-called 'tunnel' is nothing of the sort. It is a good old-fashioned red herring."

"We watch – or the official police do – the shop, and all the time the real crime takes place elsewhere?"

"Just so, Watson. But where? And equally important, when? More, what is the nature of the proposed crime?" Holmes shook his head. He rose to his feet. "I fear my consideration of the matter must wait. I need to consult – someone who may know just what is to take place in the near future which may interest a criminal."

31

"Lestrade, perhaps?"

"Ah – indeed, Lestrade may also be of use." And without saying more he took his coat and hat, and left me alone.

You may be sure that I pondered the matter over my cigar, and a touch of brandy and water. It did not seem to me that we had got very far. After all, we had learned merely that a robbery, or some villainy at any rate, was planned in London, at some indefinite time in the future! The rawest recruit to the police force could have told us as much. If we knew where, or if we knew when, then we might progress.

Perhaps, though, the matter was not entirely incapable of some logical analysis? After all, I had studied Holmes's methods pretty closely in that awful business of Drebber and Jefferson Hope, and should be able to apply them here. First, then, if the villains were not tunnelling into the old curiosity shop, then were they tunnelling elsewhere? It seemed unlikely, for here appeared to be only two men concerned, the colonel, if such he was, and Naylor – oh, and perhaps the obliging young man who had directed Mrs. Bradley to Holmes in the first place. Now, if Naylor were down in the cellar pretending to dig, that left but one, possibly two, to dig elsewhere. Add to that the fact that they must find convenient premises, and that theory seemed unlikely.

Then was it robbery face-to-face, so to speak? A gang holding up an individual, or perhaps breaking into a private house, an hotel room? That seemed more to meet the facts as I saw them. But again, when, and where? Or, who? Who was the potential victim?

My reverie was interrupted by a tap on the door, and our landlady looked in. "Mr. Holmes is out, is he not? Well, Doctor, would you see to this – lady?" and there was a slight but perceptible pause. "In a right taking, she is, sir."

"Show her in," said I. Mrs. Hudson did so, and to my astonishment the visitor was none other than Mrs. Bradley, and all too clearly in that 'right taking' of which Mrs. Hudson had spoken.

"Come in, Mrs. Bradley," I said, endeavouring to emulate Holmes's suave manner. "Pray take a seat and tell me your troubles. Perhaps, Mrs. Hudson, a pot of your delicious strong tea?"

"Thank you, sir," said Mrs. Bradley, "but there's no time for that. The fact is, sir, I've 'ad something of a shock, as you might say."

"Oh?"

"Yes, indeed. You may recall as 'ow I said I'd thought of giving in my notice? Yes, well, now I won't need to, for the colonel, 'e's 'ad me into 'is study this very afternoon, and given me my notice! Says as how he 'as to go away, and the place is to be shut up, or let out, or some such."

It took a while for me to realise the importance of this. Then, "You mean to say that the colonel is leaving the house? When is this to happen?"

"Next Tuesday, sir."

"Indeed? That seems a trifle abrupt, does it not?

"Came right out of the blue, sir. Mind you," said Mrs. Bradley, "the colonel has paid me – handsomely, too – for the short notice. But you see, sir, with things being as they are, I thought Mr. Holmes should know at once."

I thanked her, and, after some lengthy reiteration of her statement, Mrs. Bradley allowed herself to be escorted out by our landlady, and I settled down to a reconsideration of the problem with a lighter heart.

If the house were to be closed on Tuesday of next week, then it was obvious that the pretended robbery of the curio shop would be that day, or possibly on the Monday. We, that is the official forces and Holmes, would be watching the curio shop, whilst the gang were – what?

It was that last question which brought me to a halt. But then, I had already determined that the actual crime was not to be directed against a bank or shop, whether humble or grand, but against an individual. Now, there is little point robbing a poor man! The crime, then, would be against someone worth the robbing. I picked up the illustrated papers, which Holmes always took, though seldom read, and began to peruse the "society" columns.

After an hour or so, Holmes returned, the disappointment evident in his face. In answer to my unspoken question he shook his head. "The matter is as dark as ever," he said, throwing himself into a chair.

"Perhaps not," I answered, with perhaps just a touch of pardonable pride. I went on to tell him of Mrs. Bradley's surprising news, and of my own thoughts on the matter.

Holmes listened intently, and when I had almost done, he clapped his hands. "Upon my soul, Watson, you have analysed the matter remarkably!"

"Is there anything amiss with my reading of it?"

"None that I can see. Sadly, all your reasoning does not narrow it down sufficiently."

"I am in hopes that it may, Holmes," I answered, and threw the latest of my society papers across to him. "There are notes in there of three foreign visitors due to arrive in London on Tuesday. It is my guess – my opinion, that is to say – that one of them is the intended victim."

"H'mm." Holmes did not look entirely convinced. "It is an interesting line, Doctor, but still it may be that none of these – "

"But what is there to lose? You yourself have said that the field is too wide for your own brand of analysis. Even if none of the three is correct, we have lost nothing by watching them, or asking Lestrade to watch them."

"You are right," said Holmes. He opened the paper at the page whose corner I had turned down. "Well, then, what are your selections?"

"A Russian prince – "

Holmes held up a hand. "His name is known to me. His family is a good one, but financially negligible."

"There is an American heiress, coming to England to marry an earl – "

The hand went up again. "Her father disapproves of the match, and will assuredly disinherit her should she follow her heart."

"Indeed? I had not heard as much, nor have the writers of that paper."

Holmes laughed. "It is not widely advertised. Next?"

"Next, and last, I fear. The South African diamond magnate, Barney Granato, is coming to London on business."

Holmes nodded. "He is a more likely candidate, I agree. But he has the reputation of carrying a couple of pearl-handled revolvers with him, and of travelling in company with his bodyguards, a half-dozen former prize-fighters."

"H'mm," I said ruefully. "A formidable army for any crook to face!" I reflected a moment. "And besides, I was reading just the other day that diamonds are transported not by Mr. Granato, but by very ordinary, perhaps rather drab, individuals, so as not to draw unwelcome attention to them. I – " And here I broke off, for Holmes was staring into space with that curiously abstracted expressing which he sometimes wore. "Holmes?"

"I beg your pardon, Watson. You know," he said, rising to his feet, "I think you may have hit the nail on the head. But I must make further enquiries." And before I could ask him anyone of the half-dozen questions which rose to my mind, off he went, and I did not see him again that night.

Nor did I see him at all the next day, which was Saturday. You may be sure that I pestered Mrs. Hudson for any word of him, but she knew as little as did I. I racked my brains, but could not see what it was that Holmes must have seen. The day passed in some frustration.

By Sunday, I was irritable, and when I saw Holmes, which was late in the day, he refused to say anything, beyond asking if I might be free to join him on Tuesday!

I shall not write of my state of mind on the Monday. Fortunately Holmes was absent most of the day, or Lestrade might have been obliged to arrest me for assault and battery.

By Tuesday, all my impatience was gone. I was merely eager to follow wherever Holmes led. And he led me first to Scotland Yard, where we collected Lestrade and a silent lady dressed in some sort of black uniform, after which we all four went to Victoria train station.

At the first opportunity I steered Lestrade to one side and indicated the black-clad lady. "Oh," said the official detective, "that's one of our police matrons. Useful in these cases, Doctor."

Before I could ask what "these cases" might be, Lestrade grabbed my arm and pulled me into the shadows. "This is our train," he hissed in my ear. "Or it is if Mr. Holmes has the matter right."

The train from France pulled in, and the usual throng disembarked. Lestrade indicated one man, a tall gentleman in heavy furs. The man stopped on the platform, looked round. A couple of men moved towards him, evidently expecting him. Behind them walked a middle-aged lady, well-dressed, handsome enough, but with something about her which seemed familiar to me. There were greetings and handshakes all round.

I was about to question Lestrade, when the little group on the platform moved towards the exit, and the cab rank. They made no attempt to join the queue waiting for a cab, though, but moved a little to one side, as if waiting for something. Then a carriage pulled up, and they all made to get into it.

It was then that Lestrade blew his police whistle. And then events moved so fast that I could scarcely follow them. A whole crowd of men seemed to appear from thin air, and seized the two men who had met the tall passenger from the train. The tall man himself seemed to be helping with the seizing business, while the police matron did a similar service for the middle-aged lady. And for good measure, the driver of the carriage had whipped up his horse and was trying to get away, while Lestrade, showing considerable courage, grabbed the reins and bridle and tried to stop him!

In less time than it takes to write, the whole thing was over. A couple of closed police vans appeared from the shadows, and the two men plus the lady and the driver of the carriage, were all driven away.

Lestrade, looking somewhat dishevelled but very proud of himself, accompanied Holmes and me back to Baker Street, where my first task was to address the brandy and soda. "I assume that was the Russian prince?" I asked, as nonchalantly as I could.

Holmes nodded. "Or, rather, one of Lestrade's men impersonating him, the real prince being detained for his own safety at Dover."

"But I thought you said he had nothing worth stealing?"

"Nothing of his own. But you gave me the clue, Watson, when you mentioned that diamond couriers are so often colourless individuals, not wishing to attract attention. The prince was acting on behalf of a Russian lady who wishes – discreetly – to dispose of some jewellery, without her husband being troubled in the matter. The prince was to have been met at the Savoy Hotel, but the gang turned up here, and said there was a change of plan."

"Ah!" Then I frowned. "You know, Holmes, that lady on the platform looked a bit like a younger Mrs. Bradley."

Holmes and Lestrade laughed out loud. Lestrade said, "She was, Doctor! That is, she was a lady known variously as Miss Skeffington, Miss Wells, Mrs. Lamont – "

"And Mrs. Bradley," Holmes finished.

"She started off as a lady's maid," said Lestrade reminiscently, "more years ago than I care to think. Joins the household, gets to know the house, and the family, then – you name it, robbery, blackmail, anything. Oh, yes, a long record, your Mrs. Bradley."

"The scheme was not without merit," said Holmes. "And it does illustrate the advantages of being an accomplished artist in make-up and disguise, something I have already noted, and indeed used."

"So the whole story of noises in the cellar was a sham?" I asked. "And the story of the young man who suggested your involvement?"

Holmes nodded. "Designed merely to arouse our – my – interest, and set me on a false scent, as they feared I might somehow discover their scheme independently. Still, I think, Lestrade, you will not be too unhappy with the result?"

"Indeed not, Mr. Holmes! Thanks for the brandy, Doctor, but I must be on my way." And he rose to his feet. "It's all worked out very nice, and nothing too complicated about it, not like some of your theories, Mr. Holmes."

"True. Unless, Watson, there are any small points you would wish cleared up?"

"No, all very straightforward, Holmes. Although I do just wonder how the American heiress will get on with her English lord."

"Ah, for that you will have to consult next week's illustrated papers!" said Holmes. "No doubt it will be a case of *omnia vincit amor.* Though for me," and he waved a hand at the morning's post, which contained the usual appeals from puzzled clients, "for me it must, I fear, be always a matter of *labor omnia vincit.*"

The Case of the
Lichfield Murder
by Hugh Ashton

Note by Dr. Watson: The case of Henry Staunton, in which my friend Sherlock Holmes became involved, was one of the more remarkable crimes of that year, though the true story never reached the ears of the public. Holmes himself expressed his wish that I should withhold the details until such occasion as he considered the time to be ripe. Since that occasion never transpired, I have kept the details in my dispatch-box, safe from the curious eyes of the present, but where they may possibly be discovered by generations and readers as yet unborn. Here, then, I present the remarkable events that transpired in the city of Lichfield in the year 188-.

Originally, I used pseudonyms to denote the personalities and locations of this case, but have restored the originals, all the principals now being deceased.

At the time that the events of which I am writing began, Sherlock Holmes was unengaged on any case. He had recently returned from the Continent, where he had been occupied with a matter of some delicacy regarding the ruling family of one of the minor German principalities, and now found time to hang idle on his hands.

He was amusing himself by attempting to discover a link between the Egyptian hieroglyphic system of writing, and that of the ancient peoples of the central American continent. This attempt, incidentally, proved to be fruitless, and the results of his researches never saw the light of day.

The rain was falling, and few cabs and even fewer pedestrians were on the street, as I stood in the window of our rooms in Baker Street observing the scene below. "Halloa!" exclaimed Holmes, who had laid down his pen with a gesture of impatience, and joined me at the window. "A client, if I am not mistaken."

The corpulent man approaching our house certainly seemed to bear all the distinguishing marks of those who sought the assistance of Sherlock Holmes. The vacillation in his movements, and the nervous glances at the numbers displayed on the front doors of the houses of

37

Baker Street, had by now become almost as familiar to me as they were to Holmes.

As we watched, he glanced upwards, and caught sight of us standing in the window, as we in turn observed him. Hurriedly ducking his head downwards, he quickened his pace, half-running to the door, and within a matter of seconds we heard the pealing of the bell.

We returned to our seats as Mrs. Hudson announced the arrival of our visitor, presenting Holmes with his card.

"A somewhat uninspiring choice of name," he announced, after examining the card, briefly presenting it to his long aquiline nose, and presenting it to me, where I read simply the name "Henry Taylor" and the title "Merchant". "No matter," he continued, "the truth will eventually come out. Show him up, if you would, Mrs. Hudson."

The man who presented himself a few minutes later was clearly in the grip of a powerful emotion, in which fear appeared to be mingled with grief.

"Sit down, please, Mr. Taylor," Holmes invited him. "You have come far today, and no doubt you are tired."

"Why, yes, Mr. Holmes, indeed I am." The words were uttered in an accent that betrayed our visitor as hailing from one of our more northern counties. He seated himself in the armchair usually occupied by Holmes's clients, and I was able to observe him more closely.

Clad in a tweed suit, more fitted for the country than the town, his large frame was still heaving with the exertion of having climbed the seventeen steps to our rooms, and to my professional eye, this, combined with his over-ruddy complexion, indicated some problems with his health. His left hand gripped a stout blackthorn, and the corner of a sheaf of papers peeked out from beneath his coat. His eyes were reddened, as though he had been weeping.

"Forgive my impertinence," Holmes said to him after about a minute had passed in silence, "but is your visit here connected with your recent loss?"

I myself had, naturally, remarked the mourning band attached to his right sleeve.

For answer, Taylor raised his head, which had sunk to his breast, and answered in a lugubrious tone, "Yes, Mr. Holmes, that is indeed the case." Another silence ensued, broken only by the wheezing emanating from our visitor as he slowly regained his composure. At length, he spoke again, in a voice heavily charged with emotion. "Gone, Mr. Holmes. Gone. Struck down in the full flower of her beauty by a fell hand."

38

"Murder, you say?" exclaimed Holmes in a tone of some excitement. The news seemed to arouse him from his languor. "How very fortuitous – I mean to say that it is fortuitous that I have no other cases on hand, of course. The police . . . ?"

"The police have their suspicions as to who may have committed this foul crime, but I believe them to be in error," replied the other. "This is why I have come to you. I wish to seek justice for my dear wife, Martha."

"Tell me more," Holmes invited him, leaning back in his chair and regarding our client with that curious hooded gaze of his. "Watson, take notes, if you would be so kind."

"I am a merchant of cloth and other such goods," began our visitor. "Some years ago, my first wife died of consumption, leaving me with two young children. As a busy man of business, I found I was unable to care for them as they deserved, and I thereupon lodged them with my sister in the town of Burton upon Trent, and made due financial provision for their support. Though my sister is a good woman, and took excellent care of them, I nonetheless felt that my children deserved to be with their father and his wife. In addition, living alone was irksome to me, and I therefore cast about for a wife. When I moved to the city where I currently reside, my eye was caught by Martha Lightfoot, the daughter of a neighbour, and after a brief courtship, we married, and my children, Stephen and Katie, returned to my home." He paused, and I took the opportunity to offer him a glass of water, which he accepted gratefully. "Well, sir, it seems I could not have made a better choice for a wife. Martha was devoted to my children as if they had been her own, and they, for their part, appeared to adore her in return."

"Excuse me," Holmes interrupted him. "May I ask the ages of the principals in this case?"

Our visitor smiled, for the first time since he had entered our room. "I suppose that some would term our marriage – our late marriage, that is – a December and May affair. When we married, some two years ago, I was fifty-three years of age, and Martha twenty-two. Stephen was at that time twelve years old, and Katie ten." He paused and mopped his brow with a none-too-clean handkerchief. "We were a happy family, in so far as my work would allow it."

"What do you mean by that?" Holmes asked him sharply.

"Well, Mr. Holmes, my work involves a good deal of travel, and obliges me to be away from home for considerable periods of time. I considered it to be somewhat of an imposition on Martha for her to care alone for two youngsters, but as I mentioned, she and the children appeared to have a harmonious life together. That is," he sighed, "until the events of a month ago."

"Pray continue," Holmes requested, as our visitor seemed to have sunk into some kind of reverie.

"I came back from an extended trip that had lasted for a week, and discovered my Stephen in an uncharacteristically sulky mood, and with what appeared to be a bruise upon his face. I assumed that he had received a blow while scuffling with his playfellows, as lads will, but on my questioning him, he informed me that the blow had been struck by my wife. He refused to give the reason for this event, simply referring me to Martha. When I questioned her, and confronted her with the accusation, she admitted to striking the child, but claimed it had not been a deliberate action."

"No doubt she was able to give reasons for this assertion?"

Taylor sighed. "Yes. She informed me that she had observed Stephen taking money from the maid's purse. A small sum, to be sure – a few pence only – but theft is theft, no matter what the amount, do you not agree, Mr. Holmes?"

"Indeed so," answered my friend, with a half-smile.

"She remonstrated with him, and an argument ensued, during the course of which she attempted to retrieve the money, and struck the lad in the face. She swore to me with tears in her eyes that it was an accident, and she had never had any intention of doing him harm. He, when I questioned him later, admitted that he had taken the money in order to purchase some trifle, but claimed that Martha had deliberately delivered the blow to his face."

"And which one did you believe?"

Taylor sighed. "I believed my wife, Martha. Much as I love my Stephen, he has proved himself to be less than truthful in the past, and I have had cause to admonish him. I fear that the sojourn at my sister's did nothing to improve his character. She is a woman whom some might term over-kind, and she indulged his whims while he was living there, at the expense of his character."

"I take it that relations between your wife and your son deteriorated from that time?"

"Indeed so, Mr. Holmes. As I mentioned, I am often compelled to be away from home, and so it was for this past month. However, on recent occasions when I returned from my travels, it was painfully obvious to me that my wife and my son were on poor terms with each other. I confess that I was completely ignorant of any way in which this breach could be mended, and was forced to endure the spectacle of those whom I love in a state of mutual enmity. Mealtimes were a particular torment, where each seemed to find every opportunity to insult and belittle the other. If one could be banished from the table, peace would have prevailed, and as master of the house, I could remove one of the sources of conflict. But which one was to be removed, Mr. Holmes? I ask you, for I could not resolve that riddle." He paused, as if for effect. "And then, Mr. Holmes, we come to the events of yesterday."

"It was last night that your wife died?"

"Indeed it was only yesterday. I returned home to find Martha lifeless, stretched out in her own blood on the drawing-room floor. She had suffered a series of stab wounds to the body."

"And your son?"

"I discovered him in the scullery, with a bloody kitchen knife. He was cleaning bloodstains off his clothes in an almost frantic manner. The water in the basin in which he was washing his hands and garments was a scarlet mess, Mr. Holmes. I never want to see the like again."

"And his story?"

"He told me that he had discovered my Martha in the room, with the knife beside her. Despite his recent dislike of her, he is not at heart a bad lad. He believed that she was not dead, but severely wounded, and attempted to move her to make her more comfortable. It was during this operation that he determined that she was, in fact, dead, and it was at this time that his hands and clothing became covered in blood. He picked up the knife – "

"Why did he do that?" I asked.

Taylor shrugged. "Who can tell?"

"The mind causes us to act strangely and without rational motive under unusual conditions," remarked Holmes. "I can think of several similar cases in my experience. Go on, Mr. Taylor."

"He picked up the knife, as I say, and carried it with him into the scullery, where he started to wash his hands and to clean the blood from his clothes. When I encountered him, I immediately ordered him to cease what he was doing, and to come into the street with me, where I gave him over to a passing constable. It gave me little pleasure to do so, but I felt that justice must be served."

"Quite so, quite so," murmured Holmes, but his words seemed to me to lack conviction.

"I felt in my heart that it was impossible that he had committed such a base deed, but what other explanation could be given?"

"You mentioned a maid," said Holmes. "Where was she while this was going on?"

"It was her afternoon off."

"I see. And your daughter?"

41

"She was visiting a schoolfellow. My son and my wife were the only two people in the house when I returned."

"When you returned, was the house door to the street locked?"

"The police asked me the same question. Yes, it was. The door leading to the back yard was also locked."

"And there was no sign of entry through any other aperture? A window, for example?"

"To the best of my knowledge, there was no such sign."

"And the police?"

Taylor spread his hands. "What can they do, but believe that my son is guilty? What other explanation could there possibly be for these events? They are confining him, and I fear he will hang."

"Even if he is guilty, it is not likely he will be hanged," Holmes informed him, not without a certain sympathy in his manner. "The courts often show clemency to younger offenders, even in the case of serious crimes. However, I take it you will wish me to establish his innocence?"

"Of course, Mr. Holmes. But may I ask your fee? I am not a wealthy man, and I fear that I may be unable to afford your services."

"My fees never vary, save on those occasions when I remit them altogether," smiled Holmes. He scribbled a few lines on a card and handed it to Taylor. "I advise you to return to Euston and take the fastest train available back to Lichfield. Do you happen to know the name of the police agent in charge of the case?"

"An Inspector Upton, I believe, of the Staffordshire Constabulary."

"Excellent. Pray give him this message, and inform him that I will be arriving soon. Thank you, Mr. Taylor. We will join you at your house. Where may we find it?"

"Dam Street, on the way from the marketplace to the Cathedral. Number 23."

"We will find it, never fear."

Our visitor picked up his hat, and bidding us farewell, departed.

I turned to Holmes in astonishment. "How on earth did you know that he lived in Lichfield?"

"Elementary. When I see that not only his hat bears the label of a tailor in that city, but that his stick also bears the mark of a merchant there, I am forced to conclude that most of his purchases are made in Lichfield. Since he describes himself as a merchant who travels extensively, I consider it unlikely that he lives in a village, since Lichfield is a city well served by two railway stations. Lichfield therefore presents itself to me as his city of residence. In addition, today's weather being wet, I would have expected his boots and his stick to display splashes of mud if he lived outside the city. It is obvious, therefore, since

42

they did not display such signs, that his journey on foot was conducted along paved thoroughfares. Hence my conclusion that he lives in the city."

"And you remarked that his name was uninspired. Surely a man has no choice regarding his name."

"Under certain circumstances, he may well be able to choose," answered Holmes, but did not expound further on this somewhat enigmatic pronouncement. "Did you not remark that the card he presented to us still smells strongly of printer's ink, thereby signifying that it has been produced very recently? Not only that, but the initials marked in ink inside the hat were not HT, but HS? Mr. Taylor, or whatever his true name may be, does not strike one as the kind of man who borrows others' hats."

"You see more than I do," I remarked.

"On the contrary, Watson, you see all that I do. I merely draw logical inferences from what I see, and you fail to do so."

"And those papers he was carrying inside his coat. What were they? I had assumed that they had some relevance to his query."

"I, too," confessed Holmes. "Many of them appeared to be letters, from the little I could observe, and I fancy that at least one of them was a will."

"His late wife's?" I asked. Holmes shrugged.

"Who can tell with certainty? But we may assume so, I think. In any case, we must move fast, before the heavy boots of the local constabulary remove all traces of evidence from the scene. As you know, I have little faith in the abilities of our Metropolitan Police, and even less in those of the provincial forces." He rang the bell for Billy, our page, and wrote and handed him another note, to be sent as a telegram to the police inspector in Lichfield.

"You are prepared to stay in the Midlands for a few days?"

"It is the work of a minute for me to be ready," I answered him.

"Good. If I recall correctly, there is an express train from Euston at fifty-three minutes past the hour, which will bring us to the Trent Valley station before the day is too far advanced. Be so good as to confirm it in Bradshaw."

I did so, and reported this to Holmes. "I confess that I am confused regarding our client's motives," I said to Holmes. "On the one hand, he appears to love his son with true parental feeling by approaching you in an attempt to establish his innocence. On the other, he seems keen to blacken his name, as shown by his confession that the child is not always truthful. Also, by immediately giving his son in charge to the police,

43

Taylor seems to have assumed that he was indeed the culprit, without bothering to make detailed enquiries."

"Indeed, there are several mysteries about this aspect of the matter, which I think we can only clear up by means of a visit to the scene. Come, Watson, let us make our way to the fair city of Lichfield."

We alighted from the train at Lichfield Trent Valley station, a mile or so from the centre of the city, and hailed a cab to take us to the market square. From there, we walked along Dam Street until we reached number 23, close to the Cathedral. A police constable was standing outside the door.

Holmes introduced himself to the constable, and requested permission to speak to the Inspector in charge of the case.

"I've read of you in the newspapers, sir," replied the policeman, "and I am sure that you will be welcome, but I have to talk to Inspector Upton first before I allow you inside, if you don't mind, sir." He went inside the house, and re-emerged a minute or so later, followed by a uniformed officer, who identified himself as the inspector.

"Mr. Holmes, sir, welcome to Lichfield. A pleasure to make your acquaintance, though I fear there will be not much for you to do here. We are pretty certain that the young 'un is the culprit."

"You received my telegram?" Holmes asked him.

"Why, yes sir, we did indeed, and Taylor has presented your card to me. You'll be happy to know that the room is not significantly changed from when Taylor entered it and discovered his wife there, though of course we have removed the body. As I say, there is really no doubt that the lad did it. Shocking case. I can't remember anything like this happening here in the past. This way, sir."

He led the way into the front room of the house, which had been furnished in a good, if provincial style. Holmes stood in the doorway, and surveyed the room's contents, which included a desk by the window, and a chair lying on its side beside it. Some dark stains marked the carpet and the bearskin rug beside the desk.

"The front and back doors of the house were both locked, Taylor told us," we were informed by Upton. "All the windows appeared to be shut, and there was no other means of entrance into the house."

"Unless the murderer came down the chimney, or through the coal-chute, assuming there to be such a thing in this house."

"True enough, Mr. Holmes, as regards the coal-chute, but no such apparatus exists here."

"The case against the boy certainly seems strong, then."

"Strong enough, Mr. Holmes. It's a pity, as he seems like a nice lad. Just a sudden flash of temper, and – " The inspector shrugged.

"Where was the body located?" Holmes asked.

By way of answer, the police officer started to step forward to point out the spot, but was restrained by Holmes. "Please, Inspector," he implored the other, "let us not disturb any further the remaining evidence that will help us determine the murderer, faint as it may be by now."

"Very well, then," replied Upton. "Mrs. Taylor was discovered by Taylor lying on her back, over there by the desk, with her head nearest the chair."

"And yet she had been sitting at the desk, had she not, and the chair was overturned in the struggle with her murderer," mused Holmes to himself. "Strange. Taylor told me that the son, Stephen, had moved the body, but did not provide any details," addressing the policeman once more. "Do you know more?"

"According to the son's statement, he discovered his mother – rather, his step-mother – lying on her side, and merely moved her onto her back, and at that time determined that she was dead."

"I see," said Holmes. "And where was the knife discovered, according to this statement?"

"Beside the body, on the floor."

Holmes said nothing, but stood in silence for a moment before dropping to his hands and knees, and pulling out a lens from his pocket, with which he proceeded to examine the floor, crawling forward towards the desk as he did so. At one point he paused, and appeared to be about to retrieve something from the rug, but checked his movements and continued his appraisal of the carpet. The policeman and I watched him from the doorway for the space of about five minutes.

At length he stood up, and dusted his garments, before turning to the desk and using his lens to scrutinise its surface, and the inkwell which still stood open, as well as the pen and the blotter and other objects that lay upon it. "Your men have been busy," he said to Upton, "and have almost, but not completely, destroyed the traces of the events that took place. Nonetheless, many points of interest still remain. May we view the body of Mrs. Taylor?"

"She is at a local Inn, the Earl of Lichfield Arms, in Conduit Street by the market square," replied the inspector. "Though I fail to see that there is much to be learned from a further examination."

"There may well be more than you imagine," answered my friend. "May I advise you that no-one is to enter this room until I have finished my investigation?"

I could see that the police officer resented this usurpation of his authority, but he assented to Holmes's request, and instructed the constable at the door to prevent any entrance to the chamber.

The inspector accompanied Holmes and myself on the short walk to the inn, where we were shown to an upstairs room, which had been cleared of all furniture save a deal table on which lay the body, covered by a sheet.

"There has as yet been no autopsy, of course?" Holmes enquired.

On receiving the information that this was the case, he requested and received permission to draw down the sheet and examine the body. There were several wounds to the abdomen, obviously inflicted with a sharp instrument.

"In my opinion," I said to Holmes, in answer to a query of his, "this wound here could well have reached the heart. Of course, without a post-mortem examination, it will be impossible to say with certainty that this is the case, but my experience with bayonet wounds leads me to this belief. Even without the other wounds, this alone could be the cause of death. Shock and loss of blood would also be a factor in the cause of death."

"Thank you, Watson," Holmes said. "As you rightly point out, this cannot be confirmed until an autopsy is performed, and it would be premature to certify this as the cause of death. But, dear me, this murder was committed in a frenzy of passion, was it not? I count at least five major wounds, and several grazes where the weapon has almost, but not completely, missed its mark." He bent to examine the ghastly wounds more closely. "Watson. Your opinion on the nature of these? Specifically, how they were delivered."

I, in my turn, bent to the cadaver. "Delivered to the front of the body, with the blade entering from the right and above for the most part."

"That was also my conclusion," said Holmes. "Mrs. Taylor appears to have been quite a tall woman, Inspector. Can you confirm that?"

"I believe she was some five feet and seven inches in height." Holmes made some notes in his pocket note-book.

"And the boy?"

"He is somewhat small for his age. I would put him at a little under five feet."

"And it would take considerable strength, would it not, Watson, to cause these wounds?"

"Indeed so," I confirmed. Holmes bent to the body once more, and eventually stood straight and addressed Upton again.

"What was the state of the boy's mind when the constable took him in charge, Inspector?"

"According to the constable's report, he was shaking. The constable judged him to be in a state of fear."

"That is hardly surprising," Holmes commented. "And he has not confessed to the murder?"

"He continues to insist that he entered the room and discovered his step-mother lying in her own blood. As to the knife, he says that he has no idea why he picked it up and carried it with him to the scullery where he washed his hands and clothing."

"Those in such a condition often are unaware of their actions," answered Holmes. "I think we may attach little importance to this. You are satisfied, of course, that the knife discovered with the boy is indeed the murder weapon?"

"Why, what else could it be?" asked Upton in surprise. "You may see it for yourself at the station. I take it you will wish to interview the boy?"

"If that is permitted."

"Surely," replied the inspector. "Though I fear you will be wasting your breath if you are attempting to establish his innocence."

"We shall see," answered Holmes. "By the by, where is Taylor now? He did not seem to be in evidence at the house."

"He has left the city for the day. He told me that he had urgent business in Birmingham to which he must attend, and I allowed him to go there."

"I have a feeling that you may never again set eyes on Mr. Henry Taylor," Holmes told him.

"Why, what can you possibly mean?" asked Upton in surprise and dismay. "Do you mean that he means to do away with himself in despair? Have I let him go to his self-inflicted death?"

"By no means," smiled Holmes. "The truth will prove to be at once simpler and more complex than that."

"You have me scratching my head," said Upton in puzzlement, and led the way to the police station, where he produced for our inspection the knife that had been discovered by the body.

Holmes produced his lens, and examined the blade, covered with now-dried blood, closely. "It is impossible to say with any certainty without knowing the exact position and location of the knife when it was found," he announced at length, "but it seems to me that this knife was not the murder weapon. Has it been identified, by the way?"

"Yes, Taylor recognised it as one of the knives used in the kitchen for preparing food. The maid, Anne Hilton, likewise identified it, as indeed does the boy, Stephen. But why do you say that it is not the murder weapon. Surely it is obvious?"

"Too obvious," retorted Holmes. "Two factors lead me to this conclusion, which, as I said, must remain tentative for now. Firstly, the blade, as you will observe, is almost triangular in shape, with a narrow point, and widening towards the hilt."

"That is a common design," answered Upton, "and I fail to see how you can make anything of that."

"Ah, but the wounds on the body were performed using a narrower blade. Either that, or this knife was not inserted to its full depth."

"In which case, it could not have reached the heart, as I surmised," I interrupted.

"Precisely, Watson," he confirmed. "And in that event also, the blade near the hilt would not have been coated with blood, at least not to the even degree that blade exhibits. To me, this has all the appearance of a knife that has been deliberately smeared with blood, possibly not even human blood, and left beside the body, while the actual murder weapon is still missing."

"But no other weapon was found in the room or indeed in the house," protested the policeman.

"And there was no-one else in the house other than the boy and his step-mother, according to the boy's story, and that of Taylor," Holmes added. "And the boy never left the house, it would appear."

"You continue to produce puzzles, Mr. Holmes. Do you wish to see the boy now?"

"Thank you, yes."

I will not dwell for long on the exchange between the poor child and Holmes. The boy was clearly in a wretched state, and though he freely admitted the bad feeling that had recently sprung up between him and his late step-mother, and confirmed the story that had been told to us by Taylor, he emphatically denied her murder. The only new detail he added that we had previously not heard was his account of having heard some noises, as of something heavy falling, a few minutes before he entered the drawing-room. He appeared to be a somewhat nervous youth, of somewhat slender build, and undersized for his age.

Holmes produced his notebook, and asked the lad to draw a rough sketch of the room and the position of the body and the knife when he discovered them. Examining the diagram, he complimented the boy on his skills, for which he received a faint smile from the youth.

"And there were no papers on the desk or lying around the room?" he asked the boy by way of concluding the interview.

Stephen Taylor shook his head. "Nothing like that, sir," he answered.

48

"Thank you," Holmes told him. "I am confident," he added, to Upton's obvious astonishment, "that you will be out of here very soon."

"What in the world did you mean by raising the boy's hopes with false promises like that?" Upton asked Holmes, almost angrily, when we were walking back to the inspector's office. "That was indeed a cruel jest to play on the poor lad, was it not?"

"No jest," Holmes told him. "I believe that we can have this whole matter cleared up in a matter of hours. May I make a request that you send word to Sutton Coldfield police station, and ask them to send a Mr. Henry Staunton to you for questioning in connection with this matter? A house in Victoria Road, I believe, will find him."

"In the name of all that's good, Mr. Holmes!" exclaimed the policeman. "What on earth can you want with such a person? And how do you come to know of him?"

"I feel that he will be most germane to your enquiries," Holmes answered him. "As to how I have knowledge of him, why, the answer stood as clearly before you as it did to me."

"Very well. If this request had come from any other source, I would have regarded it as the ravings of a madman, but your reputation, Mr. Holmes, precedes you, and I will do as you ask, though I fail to comprehend your reasoning on this matter."

"While we are awaiting the arrival of Mr. Henry Staunton," Holmes said to Upton, "we will find lodgings. I doubt if we will wish to be accommodated in the Earl of Lichfield Arms. I have heard The George spoken well of by an acquaintance who passed through this city once."

"The George is indeed a pleasant hostelry. I will send for you there once Staunton, whoever he may transpire to be, arrives here."

"Come, Watson," Holmes said to me, and we passed through the pleasant streets of this old city to the George, where we secured a most comfortable room, and bespoke an early dinner, anticipating the arrival of Staunton.

Over the course of our meal, I attempted to interrogate Holmes regarding what he had discovered, and the conclusions he had drawn, but much to my chagrin, he refused to be drawn, and discoursed instead on the life of Doctor Samuel Johnson, a native of the city that we were currently visiting. I could follow his reasoning with regard to the knife, and was forced to agree that the knife that had been discovered by the body was in all probability not the murder weapon. It also seemed to me that the boy was unable to have inflicted the wounds that had caused the death of Mrs. Taylor, by reason of his under-developed physique.

We had just finished our meal when a uniformed constable entered the dining-room, much to the consternation of the hotel waiters, and informed us, with a strange smile, that Mr. Henry Staunton from Sutton Coldfield was now at Lichfield police station.

"Inspector Upton's compliments to you, Mr. Holmes," he added with a broad grin. "He thanks you for your discovery of Mr. Staunton, sir."

We followed the countable to the police station, where we encountered the inspector who wore the same smile as his constables. "Mr. Staunton is in the next room," he told us, and opened the door – to reveal Mr. Henry Taylor!

"What is the meaning of this?" I asked. "Are Henry Staunton and Henry Taylor one and the same person?"

"Indeed so."

Our client's face had turned red with anger. "How the devil did you discover all this?" he demanded of Holmes.

"You thought that by removing and destroying the letter that your second wife had written to your first wife, informing her of Mrs. Taylor's new-found knowledge of Mrs. Staunton, you had removed any possible evidence of a motive, did you not? But you failed to notice that she had blotted the envelope. Your true name and address were clearly visible on the blotter, reversed, naturally."

"My God!" Staunton sank back in his chair.

"Bigamy, eh?" said Upton. "Well, my lad, we can have you for that."

"And add to that the murder of Martha Taylor, as I suppose we must call her," said Holmes, "though I fear her actual marital status must be in some doubt."

"I never meant to kill her – " cried Staunton, and bit off the words as they came out of his mouth.

"Oh, but I think you did indeed kill her, and then worse," said Holmes. "In my whole career, I have hardly ever encountered such a cold-hearted diabolical piece of treachery."

"Your proof?" taunted the other.

"It would be easy to prove to a jury that the blows that killed Martha Taylor were not inflicted by the knife found beside her body. The blows that killed her could only have been inflicted by a stiletto blade, as any wide blade would have been stopped by the ribs. Once that doubt had been established, your son would walk free. No other possible weapon was discovered in the house. You may have thought you were being clever by killing with one weapon and leaving another, more plausible instrument to implicate an innocent party – your very son – but you ignored elementary anatomy."

"That might prove my son's innocence, but it hardly establishes my guilt," protested Staunton defiantly.

"True," agreed Holmes. "However, there is the matter of the missing seal from your watch chain, the empty clasp of which I noticed when you visited us in Baker Street." Staunton looked aghast and grabbed at the chain in question with a look of horror on his countenance. "No, it did not fall off somewhere else. It is currently pressed into the bearskin rug in the front room of the house in Dam Street. Did your men overlook this, Inspector? Pressed in there by the weight of a body lying on it, and covered with blood. It is impossible that in that state it was ever there before Martha Taylor was struck down.

"Let me reconstruct the events for you, gentlemen. Mr. Staunton took a fancy to have more than one name, and more than one family. It happens to some men. I am myself not that way inclined, but I regard this aberration with an amused tolerance. As Mr. Taylor, he was widowed, and he removed himself to Lichfield, where he cast about for a new partner. Mrs. Staunton is obviously not suited as the ideal sole helpmeet and companion of his life – "

"Leave her out of this, damn you!" exclaimed Staunton, angrily.

"By all means," answered Holmes with an equable air. "In any event, Miss Martha Lightfoot fitted the bill, and she appears to have been a good match, and an excellent parent to the two children of the first Mrs. Taylor."

"The best," sighed Staunton, with what seemed to be genuine regret.

"But she became suspicious of her husband's frequent absences, which were not always as concerned with his supposed business as she had first thought. Somehow, perhaps by means of a private detective, or some other method, she discovered that her supposed beloved husband was maintaining another establishment in neighbouring Sutton Coldfield, and she decided to confront her husband with the knowledge. At this time, a coolness developed between her and Staunton's son.

"She told Staunton that she was about to reveal his double life, and confront his other wife with the knowledge of her existence. Frightened that he was about to be ruined, and quite possibly be prosecuted, for his duplicity, he returned home and saw his wife writing at the desk. He immediately guessed what she was about. He quietly let himself into the house and went to the kitchen for a knife. Entering the drawing-room, he confronted his wife, who was indeed writing the fatal missive. A violent argument ensued, during which he produced the kitchen knife, and in defence, she snatched up the long paperknife that lay in its holder on the desk. You really should have taken better note of that empty knife-holder, Inspector."

"Since we believed the murder weapon had already been discovered, it seemed to be of no importance," answered the abashed police agent.

"Well, well. Be that as it may. In the ensuing struggle, which took place in near-silence, the kitchen knife was dropped, and the stiletto paperknife passed from Martha Taylor to Henry Staunton, who in his blind fury used it to kill the unfortunate woman. It was at about this time that the seal was ripped from the watch-chain. The fastening is twisted on both the chain, and the seal itself, and I have no doubt that you will easily find a perfect match there, Inspector.

"You will remember Doctor Watson's characterisation of the fatal wounds, and also note the fact that Staunton here is left-handed. His son is right-handed, as I ascertained when I asked him to sketch the scene of the murder. The wounds could only have been inflicted either by standing behind the victim and stabbing her by reaching over her shoulder, stabbing downwards – a most awkward way of delivering the blows, and one which is contradicted by the position of the body's head relative to the chair – or alternatively if the victim was standing, by stabbing with the murderer facing his victim, using an overhand grip – less effective, perhaps, than the underhand grip, but ultimately fatal. Am I correct so far, Staunton?" He received no answer, other than a silent, grim-faced nod, and continued.

"Being faced with the undisputed fact that he was now the killer of the woman with whom he shared his house, his principal object now was to avoid detection. He quickly snatched up the fatal letter in its envelope, which had only just been addressed and blotted before he entered the room. He knew his son was in the house, and his twisted mind instantly conceived a way in which he could escape blame, and transfer it to his own flesh and blood."

"A foul and heinous act," growled Upton.

"He secreted the stiletto, and smeared the kitchen knife with blood before letting the chair fall with a crash, to alert the boy and to draw his attention, before letting himself out of the front door and silently re-locking it. He disposed of the murder weapon, and I have no doubt that if you drag the Minster Pool at the end where Dam Street runs close by, you will discover it there. The rest you know."

"I never meant to kill her!" wailed the unfortunate Staunton. "It was my intention only to prevent her from sending the letter."

"That's as may be," replied Inspector Upton in stony tones. "But instead of confessing to your guilt like a man, you attempted to fasten the crime on a poor defenceless young man – your own flesh and blood at that."

"I never meant him to go to the gallows," cried Staunton, in an agony of distress.

"Maybe you did not," answered the police agent. "But I will make every effort to ensure that you make that trip yourself. Thank you, Mr. Holmes. You have saved a young man's life, and prevented a grave miscarriage of justice."

"All I ask," replied Holmes, "is that my name not be mentioned in connection with this case. Inspector Upton shall take all the credit for the observations and deductions, and the bringing to justice of Mr. Henry Staunton. Come, Watson, our task is done, and I think that we shall sleep well tonight at the George before our return to London on the morrow."

"But why in heaven's name," I could not refrain from asking Holmes as we made our way from the police station, "did Staunton ask you to clear the boy's name, given that this inevitably would lead to the proof of his own guilt?"

Holmes shook his head. "He believed that he had committed the perfect crime, and that suspicion would never fall on him," he said. "We may see his retaining me as an act of bravado and cocking a snook at the police. After all, who would believe that a man who had hired the foremost man in his field to clear his son's name would himself be guilty of any wrongdoing? Unfortunately for Mr. Henry Staunton, he underestimated my abilities, as have so many others in the past. It is their loss."

"And the world's gain," I added.

Holmes's only answer was his familiar sardonic smile.

The Kingdom of the Blind
by Adrian Middleton

It was during the late autumn of our first year together that my relationship with Sherlock Holmes, the celebrated detective, took on the semblance of a routine. He had, for some months, continued to conduct his affairs without my assistance, mentioning only a handful of his cases and excusing his often lengthy disappearances with little or no explanation. On several occasions I had stumbled upon him coming and going in a number of rudimentary disguises. Each of these, he later explained to me, was put to use in different parts of the city.

"The secret to good intelligence," he had said upon his return to our apartment in the early hours of the morning, "is establishing a long and unremarkable presence in those parts of the city where crime, and potential clients, frequent. If I can pick up the rudiments of the different trades at the same time well, that improves the accuracy of my deductive reasoning."

"And the bruises?" I enquired, noting that many of his forays resulted in personal injury which he was, invariably, loathe to discuss.

"Rough and tumble is a way of life on the streets, Watson. The giving and taking of beatings is a matter of note that fixes my characters in the memories of those from whom I obtain my information; and it is a safer alternative to thievery and intemperance."

"I have no need to practice my medical skills, Holmes," I retorted. "You should take better care of yourself."

"I can assure you that it is only superficial – the London criminal relies more on reputation than skill, and as long as he *thinks* he has the upper hand there is little danger. I avoid the hardened sloggers for the best part."

"Except when your hubris gets the better of you."

"And have you seen that happen?" He challenged. "Control and discipline are bywords for professionalism. I know my limits."

"Indeed," I harrumphed, unconvinced. "You can at least rely on me to attend when you exceed them."

"Do you know, I believe that I can," he said, shaking away the traces of Fuller's Earth that had greyed the hair of his latest disguise, before making a fresh pot of coffee as I set about collecting the morning papers.

Upon my return, Holmes had changed into his dressing gown and was standing at our window, observing the beginning of the day's intercourse while I settled into my armchair to read the *Illustrated London News*. While my attention was focused on news of troops returning from Afghanistan, Holmes's continued to observe, occasionally glancing at his fob as if noting the time of those events which transpired on the streets beneath.

"We have a visitor, Watson," he said, gesturing towards the street below. "A friar of the Dominican Order – possibly Dutch – recently returned from Rome."

Joining Holmes at the window, I glanced across the street where the man who had attracted his attention paused, waiting to cross as a hansom passed him by. He was a young and portly man, with a great black overcoat and a wide brimmed hat, which I conceded gave him the air of a clergyman.

"Are you sure he's for us, Holmes?"

"His gaze was directed upon this very window, Watson, and his choice of crossing place is similarly specific. See? He crosses now so that he will arrive at our door."

"How can you be sure he is a friar?" I asked.

"I am occasionally called upon to carry out interventions on behalf of the Vatican. In doing so I have had the opportunity to study certain aspects of ecclesiastical society. For example, the weather is fine, and the cassock is the usual form of street dress. That our visitor wears a *capello romano* hat shows he has no fear of being identified as a Catholic, so the heavy coat may only suggest that he does not wish his order to be identified. While the hat is without distinguishing features, suggesting a deacon or a seminarian, the hairstyle suggests that it covers a tonsure. Hence a friar."

"That still doesn't explain why he might be Dominican, or Dutch," said I.

"He carries beneath his arm two rare books of Dutch origin, and the Blackfriars are the most studious, the most surreptitious, and the most well-travelled of the Catholic orders."

"And Rome?"

Holmes merely smiled, asking if I would be so kind as to attend to the door. Returning to his chair, he was perfectly composed by the time we heard the knocking that announced our guest.

"Come," said Holmes loudly as I opened the door.

The friar entered the room silently, his piercing blue gaze scouring it as he removed his hat, revealing, as Holmes had predicted, that the top of his head had been shaved.

"Mister Holmes?" he said, with an unmistakably Dutch accent, "I am Brother Pius Augustus of the Order of Preachers, *rector pro tempore* to the Catholic University in Kensington."

"A Dominican?" Holmes smiled at me, making no effort to conceal his triumph. "This is my associate, Doctor Watson."

Acknowledging the man, who placed his hat and the two volumes he carried upon a side table while I closed the door and withdrew to take a comfortable spot by the window.

"Please," Holmes continued, "be seated, and tell me what matter brings you directly from the Apostolic Palace?"

The young friar took the seat opposite Holmes, pausing to look in my direction. For a moment our eyes locked and it felt as if he was looking directly into my soul. I withered, breaking away as the friar turned his gaze towards my friend, who met it with an equally steely look of his own. It was suddenly as if I were not present, and that these two powerful minds were locked in some invisible test of strength from which, I had no doubt, Holmes would emerge victorious.

"How could you tell from whence I came?"

"While both of those books were recently bound in the ecclesiastical province of Utrecht in the Netherlands, they have since been returned to Rome."

"How could you possibly know this?"

"The uppermost volume bears a seal. *Archivum Secretum Apostolicum Vaticanu.* Stamped on a new binding, it confirms you were in the Vatican compound quite recently. Furthermore, your coat has been weathered by your journey, suggesting you are presently returned to these shores."

"I am impressed," said the friar. "You have been to the Holy See yourself?"

"On several occasions," my friend confirmed. "While there I gained some understanding of Catholic binderies – I had intended to turn my notes into a monograph, but the subject was so specialised that I dismissed its usefulness. It seems the knowledge found a purpose after all."

"Then you are, indeed, the man to consult."

"Indeed? Then you had best state your case."

"It is a matter of the gravest importance, Mr. Holmes. The fates of the Roman Church and of all forms of Christian worship, rest upon it."

"Hmm." Holmes sunk into his chair, his fingers steepled. "I must have the truth, and all of it, sir. It seems unusual that you would visit me at this time of the morning."

"Why do you say this?"

56

"I presume that you are a devout follower of the Liturgy of the Hours, and therefore you do not conduct meetings without careful timing. A planned appointment would have to take place between early and mid-morning prayer, and yet here you are, in my office, at the very time you should be observing *terce*. Your visit is therefore an unscheduled one."

"That is so," said Pius, slumping a little at Holmes's deduction. "I will tell you all. You have heard of the philosopher Empedocles?"

Holmes nodded. "Not just a philosopher. A political activist and a fraudster."

"Fraudster? Why do you say that?"

"As I recall, Empedocles was meant to have certain . . . powers. Similar to those of Jesus Christ, if I am not mistaken."

"So the histories would tell us, but why would that make him a fraudster?"

"I hardly think the Catholic Church would be interested in canonizing him. He claimed to be a god."

"I can assure you that his miracles were genuine. It was Empedocles who established that the four elements of earth, air, fire and water make up the structures in the world. His powers were derived from an understanding of the divine, and they directly inspired the works of Saint Albertus Magnus."

"Albertus the Dominican?"

"Quite so, Mr. Holmes. The works of Empedocles were recorded in the *Index Librorum Prohibitorum*, and held in the Vatican Secret Archive until the sixteenth century, when they disappeared."

"So they are both sacred texts *and* banned?"

"The Church has been attempting to recover them ever since. Imagine, Mr. Holmes, such secrets falling into the wrong hands. Miracles performed by heathens would undermine the very foundations of the church."

"You seriously think this book can enable the performance of miracles?" I asked. "Are we talking about medical miracles like making the blind see and the lame walk, or those of the biblical variety, like summoning plagues or walking on water? It's preposterous."

"No more preposterous than our own saints performing such miracles, Doctor?" said Holmes, gently chiding my interference.

"Well . . . .." I realised I was on tricky ground, not wanting to offend the church.

"We are talking about real power, gentlemen, and we believe that power may fall into the wrong hands. Whilst travelling through Europe I learned that certain . . . terms, first used by Empedocles and later

Albertus Magnus, have started to emerge here in London. These terms could only have come from the lost papyri, and I can only conclude that these heretics have access to them."

"Who are these heretics?"

"They are Freemasons, of the Rosicrucian Society of England. Dr. William Westcott and Dr. William Woodman. Woodman is the Supreme Magus of his Order, and they are expanding quickly into all of England and Europe."

"I know of them," said I. "Woodman is a retired police surgeon, and Westcott is a Deputy Coroner in the East End."

"So he is," said Holmes, "and you are sure these men are a danger? Surely a formal approach – "

"Out of the question. The Catholic Church must have nothing to do with them. The Holy Father has been quite specific on the matter. It is his belief that the sect of the Freemasons are determined to bring the Holy Church into ruin."

"And what would you have me do? Expose the Order in some fashion, or simply retrieve the lost texts?"

"Retrieve the texts, if you can. I am told that Woodman has a translation, and that a German Countess, Frau Sprengel, holds the originals."

"Told by whom?"

"A fellow priest that I met upon my travels. As you can see from what I carry, my interest in books is notable."

"I see. I am sure you will understand that burglary is not a service that I provide. All that I can offer is to negotiate on your behalf. Anonymously, of course. Is there, perhaps, a sum that the Church would be willing to pay for the retrieval of such documents?"

"Absolutely not! I ask only that you confirm the existence and whereabouts of these papers. This will enable . . . further action to be taken."

"Very well, Brother Pius, I shall look into these Freemasons to determine true origin of this manuscript. If it exists, I shall confirm its location to you."

"That seems a most acceptable arrangement, Mr. Holmes. If you need me, I shall be at Abingdon House."

With that the friar rose, retrieved his hat and books, and left.

"Well, Watson?" said Holmes once our guest had departed. "What say you?"

"Clerical mumbo-jumbo if you ask me," said I. "Miracles indeed."

"It is not what *we* believe that makes this case of interest, but what the friar believes."

"The friar? Surely he is just a messenger."

"Hardly. Upon closer examination, I observed a number of characteristics that disturbed me. The books, for example. There is a reason that he keeps them close. No volume bearing the seal of the secret archive may be removed. They are considered to be the Pope's personal property."

"Are you suggesting that he stole it?"

"That may be a strict interpretation, but I suspect he believes his actions are both legitimate and justified. Did you observe the title of the uppermost book?"

"I did not," said I. "I do recall the second had a word upon its spine. *Empto*. Probably Emptor, or buyer. A catalogue or index of book for sale?"

"Well spotted, Watson, but the title of the uppermost book was *Logicae Seu Philosophiae Rationalis Elementa*."

"The elements of logical or rational philosophy?"

"I have no doubt that his story was otherwise true, but on whose behalf is he pursuing miraculous powers? Brother Pius is following a most personal agenda."

"To become a miracle worker? There is little chance of – Holmes, his eyes!" I said, recalling the piercing gaze. "There was something about his eyes."

"Indeed. He is a student of mesmerism. I am pleased that you noticed."

"Don't be quite so surprised," said I. "I'm not a complete bumbler."

"Of course you aren't. One day you might even learn the trick that turns observed fact into logical deduction."

The Georgian town house that William Woodman kept in Stoke Newington was a grand affair, far beyond the meagre salary of a retired police surgeon. According to Holmes, diligence and a good inheritance had left him with the means to keep both his London home and a country garden in Exeter. Even before we reached the main door there was evidence of his horticultural prowess, with tall exotic plants obscuring its frontage with a display of variety and colour that would not have gone amiss at Kew.

The butler – a short and stocky man, with a thick grey beard and scarcely any hair – was so poorly blessed that his features brought to mind the philosopher Socrates, renowned for his ugliness. Perhaps the talk of Empedocles had brought this thought to mind, or perhaps it was the stark atrium that greeted us, alternately lined with exotic succulents and the marble busts of diverse philosophers in the manner of a public building rather than a private home.

"Impressive," said Holmes as we were escorted up the grand staircase that led us to the doctor's private rooms. "It would seem that Dr. Woodman receives a good number of guests here, and on a regular basis."

The butler remained silent at Holmes's observation, but the implication was clear – that Woodman conducted masonic rites at his home. Atop the stair, we were guided past a portrait of Woodman himself, dressed in full masonic regalia – something which drew an irritated tut from my companion. He looked quite regal adorned by the signs and symbols of his office, made more so by the splendid bifurcated beard that dominated his face.

Moments later, with our presence announced and the servant withdrawn, we stood at the heart of an impressive library. Its walls were lined with mahogany shelves that stretched from the floor to the ornate alabaster coving that skirted the ceiling. On the floor was spread a plush Turkish carpet, its chequered pattern broken up by a variety of motifs – compasses, levels, skulls, stars, and crosses – reflecting its owner's passions. The shelves were well-ordered, with travelogues separated from historical and religious volumes. On the far wall I saw an impressive selection of Latin and Greek volumes – mostly *esoterica* and books of philosophy. Enough to momentarily draw my attention away from our host, with whom Holmes seemed to be making firm friends. Woodman was much like his painting, but portlier and thinner of hair, with bold white flecks peppering his beard. He dressed plainly, but well, and carried beside him an ornate cane which, somewhat garishly, was carved from ivory and topped with a silver skull and crossed bones.

Their handshake lingered, just enough for me to note its purpose, and I wondered if I would be aware had I not already been told of the doctor's interests.

"Mr. Sherlock Holmes," the doctor greeted us warmly. "I have heard good things about you. Are you here to – "

"I shall not dwell on niceties, Dr. Woodman," said Holmes. "We are here on a delicate matter, concerning a rare text believed to be in your possession."

"Oh?" Woodman's jaw dropped, clearly shaken by the statement. Composing himself, he stepped away from us, gesturing toward the shelves of his impressive collection. "As you can see, I own many books. Perhaps you can pick out the volume concerned."

"This particular volume is not here," said Holmes, perusing its contents. "Not in this room at least. Perhaps next door . . . ."

"Next door? There is no adjoining room."

"On the contrary, Doctor. While there are no visible doors, you appear to have chosen to adapt one of your shelves so that it may function as the entrance to the study that lies beyond. The shelf containing philosophy, I'll venture."

"How can you know that, Holmes?"

"Pile direction, Watson. A simple enough deduction."

"I'm sorry?" I did not follow.

"The carpet. When one is cleaning carpets it is usual for dirt to be brushed in a single direction – towards the door, where it can be easily swept and collected. In this room, with but a single door, the direction of the carpet pile moves *away*, and one can see the cleaning strokes have created a unique pile direction, showing that dirt was swept towards a single point on the opposite side of the room – towards the door concealed behind 'philosophy'."

"Forgive me, Mr. Holmes," said Woodman, his pleasant demeanour giving way to irritation. "While I commend your powers of observation, I fail to see how such impertinence can be excused. I welcome you as a guest, and in return you request – no, you *demand* – to be shown into a private part of my house. It is unbecoming of a brother – "

"Or of a gentleman. Indeed, Doctor, I must apologise. It is natural for a man of my profession to assert himself when he is being misdirected, and no offence was intended. If the text concerned is not available for examination or, indeed, for acquisition, then a polite refusal would suffice. I had assumed you would be more interested in negotiation."

"Of course. I, too, apologise. I believe I know the text of which you speak, and I should indeed have declined your request."

"Might I ask the name of the text?" Holmes asked.

"I'm sorry."

"My client failed to name it. I was given such information as to confirm its identity on sight, but he neglected to reveal its title."

"The black friar. Well, he is a persistent fellow, though I am surprised that compensation might be offered. His last attempt to obtain it involved harsh demands and the threat of eternal damnation."

"No, I am not negotiating on behalf of the clergy." That was news to me. Assuming it to be some subterfuge on Holmes's behalf, I held my counsel. "*My* client merely wishes to keep the original safe. I take it that Frau Sprengel is a fiction, and that you own both the original document and its translation?"

"The Countess? Ha, I see. She is real enough. I was in her company when the friar last approached me. It was she who had the text translated."

"On the Continent?"

"She operates out of Nuremberg," Woodman confirmed, "but before we talk further, I must ask who it is you represent, Mr. Holmes?"

"I am not at liberty to say, other than that my client has held certain records since the dissolution of the monasteries during the time of Henry VIII."

"So," Woodman's mood lightened, "am I to understand that you wish to acquire the book, but *not* for the friar?"

"You keep mentioning this friar," said Holmes, bald-faced, "but who is he?"

"A client of Frau Sprengel, like myself."

"A *regular* client?" Holmes pressed.

"Regular enough that I've seen him twice – once abroad and once here, in London."

"Excuse me," said I, desperate to catch up. "Why would a Latin-speaking friar need an English translation?"

"He seeks either edition," said Woodman. "The Frau is a businesswoman with many clients. Her services are highly sought after, especially since – "

" – since the Italian Unification?"

"Quite so, Mr. Holmes," said Woodman, turning his attention to the bookshelf and activating a concealed catch. "Please observe my rules. This is my private collection, and many items are of great personal value. I trust you have no interest in my translation?"

"It is yours to keep, Doctor, although I suggest you make another copy at the soonest opportunity. I suspect your friar will not give up its pursuit so easily."

Swinging away from us, the concealed door opened onto a near identical room to the first, with equally full shelves. The singular difference was the floor. In place of carpet was polished parquet, and in the centre of the room sat a large table surrounded by chairs, suggesting that the chamber doubled as a private meeting room. A pile of books rested on the table, and it was to these that Woodman gravitated. Among them, wrapped within a velvet cloth, sat a hefty volume. Sliding it carefully across the table, the doctor gingerly eased back the covering to expose a large weathered binding, heavily dog-eared, with its spine barely holding it together.

"This," said Woodman, "is the *Ars Philosophica* of Empedocles, itself a Latin translation from lost papyri."

Holmes drew a magnifying glass from within the folds of his coat, leaning forward to examine the cover in more detail.

"There is an Index mark," he said, "barely visible and of great age, but it confirms from whence the book came. Might I see the translation?"

Woodman gestured towards a second volume, and Holmes and I could see that it was a freshly bound copy of the original. Not just a documented translation, but a facsimile in which the Latin had been replaced with English."

"So, Frau Sprengel is herself a bookbinder?"

"Of the highest quality. You did not know this?"

"I had my suspicions," said Holmes. "Now, let us discuss terms on the original."

Our hansom journey back to Baker Street was one filled with questions. Having held my tongue throughout our visit to Stoke Newington, I could barely contain my curiosity.

"Well played, Holmes," said I, congratulating my friend on his acquisition, "but why did you purchase the book when the friar asked only for its whereabouts? And what was all that about another client?"

"It was no deception, Watson." Holmes smiled thinly, patting his velvet-wrapped prize as he spoke. "I do indeed have a second client. Two in fact."

"So Brother Pius Augustus – "

"Shall be told the whereabouts of the translation in due course, but he shall not know that we have the original document. We shall visit him presently."

"How did you know Woodman had both copies?"

"I didn't, but it follows that if you pay for a document to be translated you may have acquired that document first. When I realised that our friar had attempted to secure the book whilst in Europe, several of my suspicions were confirmed. What I *can* be certain of is that Brother Pius Augustus has no Papal approval."

"How – "

"My work for the Vatican has been most discrete and, more importantly, could only be surmised from the various enquiries I have made in and around the secret archive. The Holy Father and I have a . . . *personal* understanding."

"Great Scott, Holmes. You're saying that the Pope himself is your client?"

"He is *a* client. Several years ago I travelled in Europe, and paid a visit to Rome. It was a difficult time. Tensions between Italy and the prisoner in the Vatican were strained, and my request to receive access to the *Index Prohibitorum* was unusual. Nevertheless, I was received by Cardinal Pecci, the Camerlengo of the Holy Roman Church, and we discussed my requirements at length. It turned out that he had been something of a detective himself. During his time as provincial governor of Benevento, he had rooted out an entire criminal conspiracy. Quite the policeman; and so he already had knowledge of me when my name crossed his desk.

"We struck up quite a friendship, and after three weeks we struck a bargain. I would receive an entry card to the secret archive, along with a retainer from the Cardinal, in exchange for certain services. These I perform sporadically, and in due course Cardinal Pecci became Pope Leo XIII."

"So you acquired the book on his behalf?"

"After a fashion. The service I render is one of detection and retrieval, but – as I explained to Dr. Woodman – the book is not to be returned to the Vatican. Not yet, at least. Books have been disappearing from the archive for many years, but in 1870 the seizure of the Papal States saw many documents and works of art disappear, and Cardinal Pecci believed that an underground trade was in operation, and that the Vatican was no longer safe. A *détente* has been negotiated between the Anglican and Roman churches. Britain, as the dominant world power, is better placed to protect the world from those forces that might otherwise challenge the status quo, and has agreed to the secure storage of whatever papal treasures I uncover."

"And the Freemasons?

"I have no view on the matter. It is true that Pope Leo has spoken out against them, but that is not my concern. I shall fulfil my obligation to the friar, and also my duty to the Pope. For now, Frau Sprengel of Nuremberg beckons, and I suspect I shall be gone for a number of weeks. If Woodman's information is correct, she lies at the heart of the smuggling conspiracy, and I may enjoy some success in my continuing service to Rome."

Upon our return to Baker Street, Holmes and I carefully packaged his prize, arranging for its delivery to a private establishment in Westminster. At the time, I attached no significance to the gentlemen's club with which I would become acquainted in the years to come. Holmes then turned his attentions to some research and other correspondence, asking that I turn my own attentions to an account of our day thus far. It was not until after we had taken tea that, with the evening drawing close, we summoned a cab and paid a visit to Brother Pius Augustus.

"Why so late in the day?" I had asked.

"The Liturgy of the Hours, Watson. The habits of the clergy are quite strict, and I have timed our arrival to coincide with the commencement of Evening Prayers. That should give us a good half hour."

We arrived at what appeared to be an abandoned premises in the heart of South Kensington. Abingdon House, the former Catholic University College. It had been bought up some years ago, having become an ivy-covered ruin, but the new owner, Monsignor Thomas Capel, had great plans, convincing the Archbishop of Westminster that it could provide a fee-paying education to those seminarians of wealthy families whose entry into Oxford and Cambridge had been forbidden by papal decree. Staffed by an eclectic mix of lay tutors ranging from the eccentric genius to the ethically corrupt, the experiment was a dismal failure. Beset by financial irregularities and scandals concerning the moral values of his students, Capel was removed as Rector in '78. Its tarnished reputation saw the College emptied of its remaining students. Whatever purpose it had since been put to, the building again looked sad and derelict, the ivy overgrown and a strange miasma infused the air around it.

"What is that awful smell?" said I as we passed through the gate.

"Fish-glue, I would hazard" said Holmes, sniffing the air cautiously, "and pickle liquor. Certainly nothing produced by decay or neglect."

As we reached the threshold, Holmes struck three times upon a galvanized knocker, stepping back to wait on a response. It wasn't long before we detected movement within, and the door was answered by a dishevelled youth dressed in a simple black *soutane*. I noticed that his nose was red and swollen, as if he had been in a fight.

"Hullo?" he said, staring vacantly into the air between us. "Welcome to the kingdom of the blind."

Turning before we had acknowledged him, the youth disappeared into the house, pausing briefly to beckon us inside. Holmes and I exchanged glances before stepping into the dim atrium that lay within.

"I am Christopher," said our guide, calling to us from the shadows. "You will excuse the darkness, I will light some candles."

"Thank you," said Holmes, calling ahead, "we are here for Brother Pius Augustus, I understand he is your rector."

"Indeed, forgive me," said Christopher, pausing to address us. "They are all at vespers. I was excused on account of my . . ." he indicated his face, ". . . accident."

"What happened?" Asked Holmes.

"Nothing," said Christopher, feeling for a Lucifer and striking it. "I stumbled. We are all blind here, I'm afraid."

"Why are you *all* blind? Is this seminary just for those who cannot see?"

"Indeed," said the youth, as his candle flickered into life. "Our sightlessness is punishment for our sins, sir. Bad boys, we were, and now we're doing our penance, hidden away from the eyes of those who would judge us."

"What was your sin?"

"Bad science," he joked, ushering us further into the house. "Please, sir, take the lantern, and I shall lead you to the rector."

"What do you mean, bad science?" I asked.

"We didn't do a very good job of distilling spirits," explained Christopher. "We made some nasty liquor. It was a bad batch – methanol instead of ethanol – and it took our sight. The ones who weren't blinded moved elsewhere, leaving we, the afflicted, behind. The church needs our money, so here we stay to complete our studies in the dark."

"Forgive me," said Holmes, "but you don't sound very committed to your calling."

"Oh, this is our best chance," said the youth. "The rector tells us so. We were too young and reckless to be held to account, so *indults* were issued permitting us to pursue ordination in spite of our . . . disability."

"And you can study the bible without seeing?" I asked.

"Not exactly," Christopher grinned at the space between us, his pupils flicking uncertainly from side to side. "We are versed in the Braille system, but there are so few embossed books available. We get some sent over from America, and the rector provides the rest."

As Christopher spoke, Holmes had studiously opened each door that we passed. We peered in as we slowly followed our guide. To the left-hand side were the classrooms, while to the right we saw rooms stacked with books, metal plates and mechanical equipment.

"You bind your own books, I see."

"The rector believes we need more funds than our donors provide. We're hoping to get a Braille press soon."

Christopher brought us to a large, well-lit conservatory, overlooking the unkempt grounds of what had once been known as Cheniston Gardens. Here, he indicated that we sit and await our host, before returning to whatever duties lay within the bowels of the house.

"Thank you, Christopher," said Holmes, "but before you go, would you answer one last question?"

"If I can," the boy said helpfully.

66

"Explain to me why all the books I have seen are banned volumes listed as missing from the *Index Prohibitorum*?"

The boy's face fell, and he withdrew with haste.

Rather than await our host, Holmes rose from his seat, gesturing for me to follow. Christopher moved quickly through the empty house, and we were careful to make as little sound as we could. The faint drone of distant evensong aided our stealthy pursuit of the boy, but on more than one occasion he paused to listen out for us. Each time we froze, holding our breath steady and awaiting his continued movement.

Passing through the kitchen, Christopher stepped out into the overgrown gardens, carefully picking his way along a well-trodden path that led us to the sound of the singing voices. As we closed upon a small chapel hidden well within the grounds, Holmes steadied me, allowing Christopher to put some distance between us.

"Do you hear those words?" whispered Holmes.

"A musical chant in Latin. A psalm?"

"I distinctly heard them sing the praises of something *other* than God. Where *Deum* should have been, I heard *Satanam*!"

"Surely not," said I, aghast at the implications.

"With me, Watson!"

Holmes sprinted forwards, catching up to the cautious Christopher and dashing past him. Close behind, I paused to stop the boy, who called out as I ran on, following in my friend's footsteps.

I was at Holmes's heel, passing through the great oak door that led us into the chapel where the Satanic Vespers was in full sway. At first it looked no different from a Christian ceremony, but there were symbolic differences. The smoke that drifted from censers didn't bear the rich smell of incense, but something more . . . exotic. Holmes would later refer me to the rituals of the Wixárica Indians of Mexico, and the heads of wild cacti that they cultivate and use to dull pain and encourage hallucinations. Sure enough, their very presence was to affect my judgement in the coming hours.

As the seminarians knelt in prayer, Brother Pius Augustus stood at the head of the chapel, his robes a parody of the Catholic faith. Embroidered golden pentacles adorned the cope that he wore over his cassock. Over these was draped a great chain of office, at the centre of which was mounted an inverted pectoral cross. Behind him, set over the altar, was a decidedly unchristian carving, replacing the traditional crucifix. Instead, it was a tree in the form of a tau cross, from which a dying man – decapitated and suspended upside down – hung. I was uncertain of the meaning, but it quickened my resolve. Drawing my service revolver from my coat pocket, I held it aloft and discharged a round, its booming echo bringing an end to the sound of corrupted voices praising the depths of spiritual evil. As I did so, the dozen youths knelt in prayer lifted their faces upwards, their blind eyes seeing only the twisted visions induced by the foul stench that filled the chamber.

"Brother Pius Augustus!" Holmes barked, "I believe you may have overstepped your authority in this matter."

The priest's hate-filled eyes looked coldly upon us, with no acknowledgement of shock or surprise whatsoever.

"By what authority do you enter these premises, Mr. Holmes?" he snapped.

"You invited me to report at my convenience. I did come to share my discoveries, but I can see that you are otherwise engaged in the corruption of innocent souls."

"On the contrary, Mr. Holmes, I draw my power from them. Behold!"

For the second time I witnessed the friar's mesmeric gaze, but this time in a different context, and a chill swept through my bones as I could feel my own resolve begin to weaken. Sherlock Holmes, however, simply tilted back his head and laughed, and as he did so, the penetrating gaze subsided, and the friar's shoulders slumped.

My friend, meanwhile, reached into his coat and withdrew a leaf of carbon-printed paper. "This," he explained, "is a copy of the missive I dispatched to his Holiness in Rome this afternoon."

Holding it forth for Brother Pius Augustus to snatch from his hands, Holmes continued. "It outlines your activities, smuggling books from Rome under the pretext of binding, and of how you trade some books on the black market in return for books more appropriate to your needs. I shall be travelling to Nuremberg presently, where I hope to confront Frau Sprengel to obtain her testimony. It was unwise of you to try and use me to deal with your rivals."

"How did you know this?" Pius Augustus demanded.

"The second book you carried into my rooms. The word *Empto* was imprinted upon its spine. This can surely only be *Liber officiorum spirituum, seu liber dictus Empto Salomonis, de principibus et regibus demonorium*. A legendary book of spirits thought lost in the sixteenth century. A treasure to those who pursue the dark arts, and it was enough for me to construct an argument convincing enough to see you excommunicated."

"Boys . . ." Holmes called upon the dozen blind seminarians, "you should consider yourselves lucky that my letter was posted before I learned you were complicit in this abhorrence. We shall return to the House, whereupon you shall prepare yourselves for a visit from the

Archbishop of Westminster, whom I believe has jurisdiction in this matter."

With those words, he turned upon his heel and we marched from the chapel, a column of blind seminarians marching in our wake. As we headed towards the house, I paused for a breath of air, quite giddy from the heady infusion that had filled my lungs. As I did so, glancing up, I saw something – a sign – I hope never to see again.

"Holmes!" I cried. "The Moon! See how large it is, and see how it is bleeding."

"I see it, Watson," he replied, "and I see that you are much better at administering strong drugs than you are at inhaling them."

The Adventure of the Pawnbroker's Daughter
by David Marcum

"I appreciate the gesture," said my friend, Sherlock Holmes, that spring morning, "but I do not foresee a happy conclusion. Still," he continued, reaching for his pipe on the mantel, "if you persist in going forward with this plan, perhaps you would allow me to suggest a title?"

I turned from my desk, where I had been pursuing my labors in solitude for quite some time. As was often the case when some pressing matter did not result in his rising early, Holmes had slept late, and had just entered the sitting room from his adjacent bedroom. Without a glance toward the coffee pot on the table, he made his way toward the fireplace, where he proceeded to pack his pipe with all of the plugs and dottles accumulated and dried from the previous day. A disgusting habit, to be sure, but by this time, after having shared rooms with Holmes for a little over a year, an unsurprising one.

"A title?" I asked. "How on earth do you know that my work here needs a title? Perhaps I am simply constructing a list of items to purchase when I go out for a walk."

"Clearly you are not working on such a list," he said, teeth clenched around the stem of his pipe, working to get the tobacco scraps burning. "The journal you have open before you would not be used for that sort of thing. Rather, you are certainly constructing something of greater importance than the list that you have suggested. Obviously, you have been referring to some of the documents that are also arrayed on your desk. I will not insult you by referring to the other indications that point in the same direction. Therefore, the probabilities are that you will need a title."

"Perhaps," he continued, dropping into his chair, "you already have one in mind, but I truly fear as to what it might be. Might I suggest, instead, something along the lines of '*Some Notes Upon the Tracing of Homicidal American Cab Drivers Residing Within the Capital, as Related to Particularly Vicious Revenge Crimes and Long-Standing Mormon-Associated Feuds, with Associated Documentation Concerning the Use of Chance When Selecting Obscure Water-Soluble Poisons.*'"

He was nearly out of breath by the time he finished this recital, but there was a twinkle in his eye and a trace of a smile upon his lips, and I realized that, even though he obviously knew about the subject of my morning's work, he was not seriously advising that I denominate it as he had suggested.

"In what way did you ever – ?" I started to ask how he had guessed, before I remembered that Holmes never did that.

Seeing that I was aware of my near-error, he replied, "Last night, before you went up to your room, you appeared to be giving thought to some matter or other, with regular glances toward your desk, and your journals kept therein. Finally, upon standing up, you walked to the mantelpiece, where you took a moment to finger the wedding ring, still lying there over a year after the fact, that was found with the body in that house in the Brixton Road. Clearly you were considering adding to the work that you threatened a year ago to write and publish, recounting our first investigation together. When I entered this morning and found you writing, the confirmation was complete."

I nodded. I had been trying to progress toward a published version of that occasion when I had first been privileged to observe Holmes's methods, involving the capture of Jefferson Hope. I have long kept journals, and my lack of the need for a surfeit of sleep, especially after the events of the Afghan campaign, had often let me write deep into the night. I regularly made extensive notes of Holmes's cases. But this matter, referred to by Holmes as involving "the scarlet thread of murder" and "the finest study I ever came across: a study in scarlet," was different, in that I wanted it to be polished for presentation to the public. It had been something over a year since the events had occurred, and I had felt the stirrings once again to have the thing published. And yet, I was still having difficulties in determining how to write the larger portion of Jefferson Hope's own tale, which explained those events of so long ago that had served as the motivation for the crimes. Perhaps something would suggest itself at some time in the future. Looking down at what I had already accomplished that morning, I decided that my labors were sufficient unto the day, and stood, whereupon I moved to my chair to the left of the fireplace, across from Holmes in his.

In those days, Holmes still tried to maintain the idea that he was capable of, for the most part, conducting his practice from his armchair. He had described for me, on the day when he first explained his profession, that he was consulted by a great number of people, and that he was generally able, simply from hearing their description of the facts, to set them on the right scent. Sometimes, however, he was forced to rise and go forth to examine things first hand. "Now and again," he had said, "a case turns up which is a little more complex. Then I have to bustle about and see things with my own eyes."

I did not realize it then, in the spring of 1882, that when Holmes was attempting, as often as possible, to reach his solutions from his armchair, he was no doubt trying to emulate his older brother, Mycroft, who functioned in much the same way for the government from his regular haunts within Whitehall and Pall Mall. In those early days, I did not yet know of Mycroft's existence, and simply thought that Holmes was trying to perfect his methods in order to show that, with the correct information, and also by drawing educated and experienced conclusions, an armchair reasoner could do better than any Scotland Yarder who was physically on the scene of a crime. Little did I realize that I would soon see a demonstration.

Having recently been rewriting the portion of my manuscript dealing with this very aspect of Holmes's practice, I led with a question regarding some of his more recent clients, most of whom had required a certain amount of investigation in the field. From there, Holmes and I had settled into a discussion of other facts related to the Jefferson Hope case, and I suddenly realized with a mixture of amusement and concern that Holmes did not seem inclined to notify Mrs. Hudson that he was up and about. His pipe would apparently be serving as his breakfast this day, as it had on so many other mornings.

I was considering whether to ring for more hot coffee for my own benefit when we perceived the bell at the front door. In a moment, we heard the sound of movement coming up the steps.

"Lestrade," said Holmes. "Unmistakable. And he has someone with him. A girl, I think, from the lighter tread. Young enough to take the steps quickly, as compared to the inspector's more seasoned and steady gait. Do you hear how she takes three steps to his two, and then waits for just a moment as he catches up, the scuff on the stairs from his boots as regular as clockwork? And of course that inward twist of his foot is the same as if he had called out his presence."

A knock on the door proved that Holmes was correct. It was our friend, the inspector, with a girl of no more than twenty, and possibly younger. She was dainty, a pretty thing, and looking quite small, even next to the short, wiry policeman. Her blonde hair was pulled back rather severely and pinned beneath a small hat, but that fact could not hide either its luster or curls, and only served to accentuate the fresh healthy color of her complexion.

Lestrade showed the girl forward toward the basket chair, before comfortably making himself at home in front of the settee. As we stood, he introduced her as Miss Letitia Porter. "Of Limehouse," he added.

"How do you do?" said Miss Porter.

Holmes turned his head and gave a speculative glance. "Surely not originally from Limehouse?" he said. "I fancy somewhere more to the east."

She looked startled for a moment, and then said, "I grew up with my mother in Clacton-on-Sea. I only returned to live here with my father two years ago."

Holmes nodded. He gestured for her to sit. When she had done so, the rest of us followed.

"How did you know?" she asked. "Where I grew up?"

Holmes crossed his legs and said, "I have made something of a study of various accents. It is a little specialty of mine to identify most of the manners of speech in the different London districts, although I have not yet carried my researches to the point where I can identify specific streets. On a larger scale, I can delineate a number of regional dialects. Yours, from the eastern coast, was mere child's play."

As the girl glanced toward Lestrade, who looked as surprised as she, Holmes said, "How may we help you today?"

The girl dropped her eyes, and then twisted slightly to defer to Lestrade, who was leaning forward with his arms resting on his knees, hat grasped in one hand. He cleared his throat, sat back, and placed the hat beside him. "Miss Porter dropped in today at the Yard seeking our assistance. She fears that her father, who owns a pawn shop in Limehouse, is in some sort of danger, although she cannot precisely define its nature. After hearing her story, I thought that this matter might be of interest to you, Mr. Holmes, and we wasted no time in coming around."

Holmes's eyes cut toward the Lestrade, and the two shared a knowledgeable look which went over my head. Holmes then turned his attention back to the girl, who had not seemed to notice the quick exchange between the consulting detective and the Inspector. Holmes made a small come-along gesture to her as he wished for her to commence her explanation.

Clearing her throat, she twined her small hands and began to speak. "I was born here in London, an only child. My father owns a small pawnbroker's shop in Limehouse, at the southwest corner of Commercial Road where it meets Bekesbourne Street. It was where we lived when I was very small, in the rooms upstairs. When I was but two years old, my mother, who had never been comfortable here in the rough life of London, returned to her people by the sea, taking me with her. My parents remained legally married, but had no further contact with one another, except by way of the occasional letter.

"My father continued to reside above his shop, making a living, and seemingly content to get by, year after year. I grew up with my mother's family, aware of my father, but never communicating with him, in respect of my mother's wishes. Two years ago, when I was sixteen, my mother passed away from a short illness. My grandparents, with whom we had lived since moving back to Clacton-on-Sea, had died a few years earlier, and I was left living in the house where I grew up, but with it now under the ownership of my uncle and his wife.

"I may say that my aunt-by-marriage and I did not get along very well, and I began to feel that I must seek a life elsewhere. While disposing of my mother's possessions, I came across many of her old letters from my father, written both when they were courting, and later, after their separation. While they had never seen each other again after we left London, it seemed that that they may have, in truth, had some lasting feelings for one another. Father had expressed a genuine interest in my progress and well-being, and it occurred to me that it might be a good thing if I were to return to London, the idea of which had never seemed unpleasant to me, as it had to my mother.

"To relate the matter in as short a manner as possible, I wrote to my father, expressing my interest in joining him, and he was very amenable to the plan. I left the house by the seaside where I grew up, moved back to the capital, and soon settled into the routine of being a pawnbroker's daughter."

"And that was two years ago, you say?" interrupted Holmes.

"Nearly," the girl replied.

"Go on."

"I must admit that I seem to have some skills in the working of the business. My father and I quickly became the best of friends, and he had no compunction regarding me learning the trade. I am rather proud to admit that I have an eye for spotting little treasures here and there, and in the time since I've returned, I've become adept at dealing with the public as well. Quite frankly, my father's business has more than doubled since I have started assisting him.

"About three months ago, we had become so busy that we found it necessary to hire an assistant. I was involved in the selection, and we were fortunate enough to employ a man named Floyd Willis. He is tall and strong, quite handsome actually, and as willing to take orders from a woman as he is my father, which is an important aspect to our arrangement. It should come as no surprise, then, that the two of us, thrown together so frequently, should fall in love. We are to be married later in the spring." She held out her hand, showing a modest engagement ring.

We murmured our congratulations, although Holmes's best wishes were more perfunctory, as he obviously desired for the story to continue, the scene now having been set. However, to the girl's surprise, he leaned in for a closer look at the ring. "May I?" he said, surprising her as he took her hand and proceeded to turn it this way and that, studying it for a moment before releasing her and leaning back in his chair. "Please go on," he said.

She took a breath and said, "We now come to the matter which led me to seek assistance, in spite of my father's wishes that the entire affair should be ignored. A couple of months ago, not long after the new year began, Father and I went downstairs one morning to discover a sheet of paper lying in plain sight on the countertop in the main shop. The front door was still locked, and there was no indication of how anyone could have gained entrance to our building. We were both certain that there was no sheet of paper there when we had closed up and gone upstairs the night before. Even before unlocking the shop that morning, we made sure that the building was still secure, and that no one had remained hidden inside from the night before. I insisted upon it."

"And this note?" asked Holmes. "What did it say? Do you still have it?"

"No, Mr. Holmes. After reading it, my father burned it. But I still remember quite vividly what it said: *'Your days are numbered, as are the grains of sand within the glass. You shall pay for your sins.'* "

"What sort of writing was it? What of the paper?"

"It was quarto sized," she said, looking to her right, over Holmes's head, as she seemed to visualize it. "It was yellowish, and peculiarly thick."

"Was the writing small, or did it fill the page?"

"Oh, it filled it from top to bottom and side to side."

"And the writing itself? Was is practiced, or crude?"

"Crude, I should say. The letters were quite square, and the ink had bled into the paper."

"Black ink?"

"Yes, I believe that it was. I only saw it for a moment before Father dashed it into the fireplace."

"Did your father have any explanation of the matter?"

"He gave none. I was obviously concerned, due to both the threatening nature of the words, and the fact that the note had been placed into our shop, which was securely locked."

"And what of his reaction?" asked Holmes. "Was he concerned as well?"

"He did not seem to be. Rather, he seemed angry, although he did not lose his temper." She glanced to the side, frowning. "He did say something along the lines of 'So that's his game, is it?' or something to that effect." She returned her gaze to Holmes. "I cannot quite recall."

"And there have been other warning letters as well?"

"Yes, two that I know about, but I was unable to read them, as Father destroyed them as soon as he found them. I believe that he started rising earlier than usual to make sure that he entered the shop first."

"So there could have been other letters in addition to the ones that you have seen?"

"Yes," she said.

"How was it that you saw the other two, and yet you were unable to read them?"

"On those occasions, I heard Father rise early and make his way downstairs. I slipped down behind him and saw him retrieve the letters from the counter. They seemed to be the same type of paper, and were lying in the same place. As soon as he read them, he threw them in the fire."

"And there was already a fire going in the shop on those mornings?"

"We have a stove there that we leave banked from the night before. The remaining coals were enough to burn the letters."

"Why did you not go down early on your own on some mornings to get a look at one of the letters?"

"Quite honestly, Mr. Holmes, I was afraid. I did not want to encounter whoever might have found a way into the shop, in case he should be discovered in the process of leaving the notes."

"Having only read the one letter, why do you assume that the others, both observed and inferred, were warnings?"

"Wouldn't that be obvious?" interrupted Lestrade. "If the others that she saw were of the same type of paper, and her father was moved to burn them, then surely they were also warnings." He glanced at Miss Porter. "Tell him the rest."

She lowered her eyes for a moment, and then, glancing over toward the window, she said, "There has been a tension growing between my father and Floyd. That is, Mr. Willis. It began around the time that the first letter was discovered, about a month after Mr. Willis first joined us. At first, I made no connection. But a week ago, after I saw Father hurl one of the sheets into the stove before I could stop him, he paced like a caged animal until Mr. Willis came to work. Then they went into the back, shutting the door. I heard much angry whispering, as if they did not want me to understand their words, but they could not entirely contain their emotions. When they came out a quarter-hour later, my father was

76

as white as a ghost, while Mr. Willis could not contain a gleam of triumph in his eyes. It was quite unattractive, and the first time I had ever seen such an expression on his face. His attitude was most unusual, and very different from his regular agreeable and deferential self.

"From that day on, Father has moved as if in a dream, or rather like in a waking nightmare, while Mr. Willis has behaved with a new and rather unpleasant confidence."

"Have you asked Mr. Willis if he can shed any light on the matter?"

"No. I had hoped at first that their argument was about some other topic entirely, and I did not want to make it my business. In hindsight, I'm sure that I should have said something."

"To your knowledge, have there been any further warnings since their conversation?"

"None that I have seen. Since then, I *have* made an effort to get up early in order to follow my father down, but he has not gone down early as he did before, and I have seen nothing."

"I take it, then, that Mr. Willis does not live in the shop?"

"No."

"But he does have a key?"

"Yes. We gave him one after he had worked there for several weeks, and we knew that he was a reliable employee. And yet, I have never known him to use it."

"During the course of his business duties, you mean," said Holmes. "Surely you realize that the direction of your story implies that Mr. Willis may in fact be the man who is, or was, leaving the threatening notes."

She lowered her gaze to her intertwined fingers. "I have come to believe that this might be so," she said softly.

"Have you asked Mr. Willis for an explanation of these events? As your fiancé, surely he would be willing to take you into his confidence."

She did not lift her eyes. "I cannot ask him, Mr. Holmes. I am afraid that he might lie and that I would be foolish enough to believe him."

Holmes shook his head. "Is there any indication that these two men had any previous acquaintance prior to Mr. Willis's employment?"

"None that I know of," said Miss Porter. "There was certainly no mention of such when Mr. Willis interviewed for the position."

"And what of your father? Is there some secret in his past that could have come back to haunt him?"

"Again, I am not aware of any such aspect to his past, but you must remember, Mr. Holmes, that I've only really known him for two years. I believe him to be a simple pawnbroker. There was certainly nothing in his letters to my mother which might indicate anything questionable, or that might explain the circumstances that I have seen."

"Why did your mother leave him? Did she have any knowledge that you have gleaned through conversations or correspondence that might give any hint of unsavory activities in your father's background?"

"Nothing, Mr. Holmes. Their letters were simply news about each other's lives, and about me. And my mother was never open to discussing my father with me while she was alive."

Holmes was silent for a moment, and then said, "Your visit to Scotland Yard this morning. What did you hope to accomplish?"

She seemed at a loss for just a moment. "To be frank, I am not certain. The situation has become increasingly intolerable, due to the tension within the shop. It was worse this morning, between my father and Mr. Willis. Finally, I resolved that I could stand it no longer, and I set out to seek help. Without telling either of them, I quietly left and walked to Scotland Yard."

Holmes raised his eyebrows. "You walked? Surely not! That was quite a distance to traverse, from Limehouse to Whitehall."

"Not nearly as far as you would think, Mr. Holmes," said Miss Porter. "In truth, I wanted to use some of the time to think. I need help, but I also did not want to do something which might cause more trouble. In all honesty, I was afraid that I might inadvertently expose some secret of my father's, or of Mr. Willis's. But at the same time, if Mr. Willis is in fact the kind of man that is threatening my father, then I wish to know the truth before our betrothal progresses any further."

"Quite," said Holmes. "As I'm sure Inspector Lestrade would tell you, the situation as you have so far described it does not fall within the purview of the police. No actionable crime has been committed, and the victim of whatever persecution that is occurring, your father, has made no effort to secure any assistance, official or otherwise."

Miss Porter opened her mouth to object. Before she could speak, Holmes continued. "However," he said, "I do see some points of interest, and I would be happy to look further into the matter." He stood abruptly. "May I see you into a cab? Limehouse is simply too far to return by foot."

The girl looked confused, glancing from Holmes to Lestrade and back. Lestrade stood, more slowly, and said, "You will be in good hands with Mr. Holmes, miss. Let me see you down to that cab." He glanced at Holmes, and then back to her. "I need to stay and discuss another matter with these gentlemen, but I will look in on you in a day or so, if that will be all right."

"Yes, yes, that will be fine, I suppose." She nodded good morning to Holmes and me, and then let Lestrade guide her downstairs.

As I heard the front door opening, I started to ask Holmes a question, but he simply raised a finger and stepped over to his scrapbooks, held on the shelves to the left of the fireplace. At that time, Holmes's scrapbooks were not nearly as extensive as they would grow to be over the years. Yet, even in those days, they were formidable. They were not so much actual books as albums, filled with loose sheets and newspaper clippings, some carefully glued into their well-ordered places, while others were arranged in a cabalistic pattern that only Holmes could identify. And then there were the leaves of paper that were simply stuffed in between pages, threatening to flutter to the floor, or – heaven forbid! – into the nearby fireplace if each volume were not opened with great care.

When Holmes and I first agreed to share the Baker Street rooms in early January '81, I had obviously had no idea what I was getting myself into. I had moved my things around from my hotel the very evening we entered into the agreement, and Holmes had arrived the next morning from his former lodgings in Montague Street, depositing a number of boxes and portmanteaus into the center of the sitting room. For a day or two, we busied ourselves in the unpacking and arranging of our possessions. I quickly noted that Holmes had a great deal more than I, and also that he needed more space in which to lay it out. This was understandable, as I had only been back in England for a little over a month, following my return from overseas service. I did not begrudge the extra space needed for Holmes's various possessions, except in one instance.

I had spotted early on that set of shelves to the left of the fireplace. I thought it would be just the place for the few volumes that I had acquired and wished to show off to their best advantage – some Clark Russell sea stories, a set of Dickens books that I had found very cheap in Charing Cross Road. However, before I could claim the shelves for my own, Holmes dragged over several boxes, opened the first he came to, and started loading down the shelves with his scrapbooks.

I had simply sighed and changed my plans. My health was still quite fragile in those days, and I objected to rows of any sort. It was not worth the trouble to ask him to share even a little of the shelf space. Now, many months later, I couldn't imagine anything in that spot but the scrapbooks. Time and again, they had proved their usefulness when Holmes needed to refer to some note that he had made, or to verify an obscure fact that might make all the difference in one of his investigations.

As I watched, Holmes walked to the middle of the room, flipping from page to page and humming tunelessly to himself. Lestrade returned to the sitting room and stopped inside the door. Seeing what Holmes was doing, he laughed, bent, and slapped his knee. "There's no getting past you, is there, Mr. Holmes?" he cried. Holmes glanced up, a twinkle in his eye.

"Is this the matter that you wished to stay behind and discuss?" he asked, raising the book.

"The very same," replied the inspector.

I cleared my throat. "I find myself at a loss," I said.

"It is simple, Doctor," said Lestrade, dropping into the basket chair before the fire, so recently vacated by our new client. "The lady's father, Lyton Porter, is one of the biggest criminals still unprosecuted."

"Tut, tut, Lestrade," said Holmes. "Innocent until proven guilty. You do not want to slander the man."

"Then tell me what *you* think, Mr. Holmes," said Lestrade. "Tell me what libelous statements you have in your magical book, there."

Holmes glanced up with a smile and said, "In spite of the risk of committing myself in front of witnesses, I *will* tell you. I have noted here, in my very own handwriting, that Mr. Porter is, in fact, quite notable for being one of the most notorious fences currently operating in the East End."

"Exactly," said Lestrade. "That's partly why I wanted to bring the girl to you, when she showed up this morning with her story." He turned to me. "I wanted to find out what Mr. Holmes's notes on the man said." Twisting in his chair so that he could see Holmes, he said, "Those books have been useful once or twice in the past. Why, I remember back when you lived in Montague Street, I stopped by one night. The City and County had just been robbed, and I – "

"Water under the bridge," said Holmes moving to his own chair and sitting. "What is your own knowledge of Mr. Lyton Porter?"

"As you said, the man is a fence. We know it, but so far we have left him to his own devices. He's useful in his own way right now, and it's just a matter of time until he stumbles. Perhaps this affair with the threats, ostensibly from the fiancé, is just the thing to start chipping away at him."

"It may interest you to know," said Holmes, "that I have recorded that Lyton's meteoric rise to his position as king of the Limehouse fencers only began two years ago." He paused knowingly, and Lestrade simply looked puzzled, but I thought that I dimly understood.

Finally, Lestrade said, "I fail to see the significance of that, except that the man's daughter returned to live with him two years ago. Are you saying that he increased his criminal activity in order to obtain more income, now that he needed to maintain a larger household? Or did the arrival of his daughter somehow make him more careless, so that we became aware of him for the first time, when in fact he had been operating for much longer than that? And did this man Willis move in on him, and is now trying for a piece of the business?"

"I'm not saying anything yet," replied Holmes. "It is simply a fact to be documented and considered."

Lestrade wondered if there were any other relevant notes concerning Lyton Porter. Without comment, Holmes turned the book toward Lestrade, who leaned in for a look. I stood in order to see as well. There was one word, written in the margins in Holmes's careful fist: *Manipulated.*

Lestrade glanced at me with his eyebrows raised questioningly. He turned the same glance back towards my friend, who had closed the book and was in the process of replacing it on the shelf. When Holmes offered nothing else, the inspector appeared to be disappointed, and soon thanked us and departed, promising to return soon to discuss any new developments in the case.

"So much for that," said Holmes, dropping into his chair. "I must smoke a pipe or three to decide how to proceed in this matter."

"You apparently saw more in our client's story than I did," I said.

"Not so much in her story, but rather in her appearance and her actions."

"Her actions? She did nothing but sit on that chair and relate her story to you."

"Ah, Watson, there were so many other cues, if only you had known how to interpret them. Alone, they might mean nothing. Together, they told me a completely different story from what her mouth was saying. That was what interested me enough to take further interest in the case."

He reached for his pipe, intending to think in silence, but I wanted to know more. "Tell me, then. Tell me this different story that you heard from what Lestrade and I heard."

"It was not anything that could be heard, Watson. It had to be seen, and once seen, it had to be understood." He packed some fresh shag into the pipe – the clay, I was happy to see, and not the disputatious cherrywood – and said, "She was lying, Watson. Although it certainly wouldn't be the first time that a client has done that. The question is, why?" And he lapsed into silence.

I went about my own business for the next hour or so. I had planned to take a walk, but decided to remain, in case something of interest were soon to present itself.

It was approaching eleven o'clock when a ringing of the bell startled me. Holmes glanced up and met my gaze. "Are you expecting another visitor?" I asked.

He laughed. "Indeed, Watson. I *am* expecting a visitor later today, a rather important one, but not yet, and I doubt that Lord Carlington will ring the bell with such fervor when he arrives. No, this is undoubtedly something unexpected."

This proved to be the case. A heavy tread climbed the stairs, and in a moment our door was opened to reveal a constable, bearing a missive. "From Inspector Lestrade," the man rumbled. Holmes quickly read the note, and then moved to his desk, where he retrieved a sheet of his stationery from the drawer and proceeded to write a series of short sentences. Then, folding his reply, he handed it to the constable, with instructions to relay it to the inspector with all possible speed. With a touch to his helmet, the constable turned and departed, as solid as when he had arrived.

Only then, noticing my curiosity, did Holmes say, "It is murder, Watson. I must admit, that I did not expect anything to happen quite so soon."

"Murder?" I repeated, half rising from my chair. "Who has been murdered? Should we have accompanied the constable?"

"I cannot leave at the moment," said Holmes. "Lord Carlington is arriving with the documents that he stole from his father, the Duke. I must be here to receive them, and swap them for the documents that are now in my possession, or I may never get another chance. It's been a pretty three day's work to get all the pieces in place, and if I walk away now, the whole game might fall apart. And I may tell you," he lowered his voice, "the fee that I have received from the Duke to manage this business will more than cover my share of the rent for both this month and the next, and I'm sure you wouldn't want me to give up on that unnecessarily."

"But murder, Holmes!" I cried. "Surely Lestrade needs you? Who has been killed?"

"Miss Porter's fiancé," he said blandly. "It seems that Miss Porter returned to find that her father had beaten Mr. Willis to death, and then in remorse over what he had done, turned a gun upon himself."

I was aghast. "What else did Lestrade's letter say?"

"Hmm? Here, read it for yourself. I will get the documents for Lord Carlington." And he walked into his bedroom, while I glanced through Lestrade's note.

The inspector wrote in choppy, succinct sentences that shortly after he had returned to the Yard, a message had arrived for him, sent by officers in Limehouse, and summoning him to Porter's pawnshop. Upon arrival, he had discovered the police in possession of the premises, and Miss Porter in a faint at a neighbor's house, being attended by a local doctor.

In the main shop area were the bodies of the two men in question. Willis had received a single terrible blow at the back of the skull, caving it in completely. The wound had bled profusely across much of the floor. The murder weapon, a heavy brass pot, had been dropped beside the body.

Nearby, lying behind the shop counter, was the girl's dead father. He had been shot with a small-caliber bullet through the right temple. There were powder burns on the wound, and the man was right-handed. A pistol matching the size of the bullet rested beside him, partly gripped in his right hand. On the counter was a single sheet, a pencil lying beside it. The pencil had obviously been used to write the one word on the message: *Sorry*

According to Lestrade's note, the girl had been returned by cab from Baker Street to the pawnshop. She had walked across the sidewalk and opened the shop door while the cab driver was still there. As soon as she had opened the door and observed the scene inside, she had begun to scream. The cab driver had jumped down to run to her assistance, and he was joined by several passers-by as well. At first they could not see what was causing her distress. Miss Porter had collapsed in the doorway, and the interior of the shop, with its cluttered windows facing north, was very dark. Eventually it became obvious what had caused the girl to react in so dramatic a fashion, and the police were summoned.

Lestrade concluded the note by stating that he knew Holmes would want to be informed, and asking if he would be joining the investigation in Limehouse. As I read those lines and looked up, imagining the scene that the girl had found, Holmes walked back into the room and sat down across from me. In his hand was a stack of letters, tied with a single red ribbon. Even from across the bearskin rug I could smell the perfume which was so liberally doused on the documents.

"I gave Lestrade a few questions to answer," said Holmes, placing the packet on the table beside him. "I don't believe that there is any need to go there right now, even if I had the time. But," he added, standing back up again, "I suppose tying up another loose thread will help us to have a complete case by the time Lestrade comes back later this afternoon."

Without seeming to notice my obvious confusion, Holmes threw open the door and bellowed for Mrs. Hudson. Then he sat down at his desk once again and dashed off a telegram. While he was in the midst of this activity, Mrs. Hudson climbed the stairs and entered, drying her hands on her apron, and wearing a barely concealed look of peeved irritation.

Holmes finished, and turned with a charming smile. As usual, Mrs. Hudson could not stay upset with him for very long, and she graciously took the telegram, promising that the boy in buttons would dispatch it immediately. Expressing thanks, Holmes followed her to the door, closing it behind her and then returning to his chair, where he picked up his pipe and resumed his silent considerations.

Lunch came and went, but I ate alone as my friend pondered. Finally, long after Mrs. Hudson had cleared the table, and much later in the afternoon, Holmes stood and began tidying, something that he did only irregularly, and usually when he expected a visitor.

He glanced at the clock on the mantel and said, "We still have a few minutes before our visitor arrives. Do you have any questions regarding the case?"

"All that I have are questions. Do you mean the matter of the murder and the suicide, or about those letters for Lord Carlington there beside you?"

"Oh, the deaths in Limehouse, of course. The affair of the letters must simply take its course. I can see that you are puzzled about my refusal to join Lestrade at the scene."

"I am. You seem as if you already know what happened."

"I fancy that I do, although I have asked Lestrade to obtain a few confirmatory facts before absolutely establishing the truth."

"Speaking of truth," I said, "I meant to ask earlier about when you said that Miss Porter had lied, but you clearly did not want to discuss it then. How did you know that?"

"Ha!" said Holmes with a grin and a slap on the arm of his chair. "Good old Watson! You have put your finger on the very heart of the matter!" He leaned forward, with his elbows on his knees. "Tell me a story, Watson," he said, suddenly making no sense at all. "Tell me about the first time you were ever on a train!"

I looked at him in surprise, but he wiggled a finger and urged me to comply. I closed my eyes for a moment, casting back for the memory. Then, I opened them and looked up above the fireplace as the details emerged before me. "It was on a trip from my parents' home to that of my grandmother. I was only a wee lad – "

"That's enough," he said, interrupting me. "And now, tell me what you would do if you found a wallet on the street containing a thousand pounds?"

I thought to question these mad and random instructions, but I knew by now that Holmes had a purpose for this, although I could not fathom at all how it related to the deaths of the poor girl's father and fiancé. I ordered my thoughts before replying, "I suppose that I would attempt to find the owner. Perhaps the wallet would contain some sort of – "

"That's enough, Watson," Holmes said, interrupting me once again. "Did you realize what you were doing?" he asked.

I laughed. "No," was my simple reply, instead of elaborating on the fact that his requests had made no sense whatsoever. "I suppose you'll explain to me how these questions are somehow relevant to the matter."

"Quite." He settled back in his chair, and – with another glance at the clock – said, "Years ago, I happened to notice a curious behavior in myself. Once aware of it, I could not ignore it. To explain it simply, whenever I thought about something that had happened before, an actual event that I had witnessed, I would cast my eyes up and to the left as I visualized it in my head. Even being aware of this trait did not stop me from doing it whenever I would consider a memory. Conversely, when I would picture something that was completely imaginary, such as what I would do if I found a wallet with a great deal of money inside, I would glance up and to the right.

"I found that something similar happened when thinking of sounds. Remembered sounds would make my eyes glance in a more lateral direction to the left, and if I were to construct or imagine a conversation, for instance, I would find that my eyes were resting in a lateral direction toward the right.

"Having noticed this trait in myself, I began to study if it was present in my fellow man. To my amazement, it was. Time and again, during a conversation, people would frequently glance up to the right or left while they told me something or other. Less rarely did I observe the lateral glances indicating remembered or fabricated sounds, but that happened as well.

"Oh, it doesn't always work, mind you, and if a person is left-handed, it sometimes works in reverse. But on the whole I have found it quite reliable. Before long, I was able to tell with a fair degree of accuracy who was telling the truth and who was lying. I can assure you, such a skill, properly cultivated, is quite useful in my profession."

I was amazed, and with a laugh, I replied, "I should think so."

He smiled. "I suppose that, like a magician, I should not easily explain what is in my bag of tricks. When I asked you to recall our first train ride, you glanced without thought to your left, up toward the mantel. I asked about an imaginary situation, and you glanced to the right, above our dining table. As an indicator, it has proved itself useful time and again. It is not absolute, you understand, but as an overall compass needle, it is quite effective."

"And you determined that today, based upon her reactions while telling her story, Miss Porter was lying about something."

"More specifically, about nearly everything of importance," said my friend. "When she was telling about her parents' separation and the move to the seashore with her mother, she either made direct eye contact, or glanced up and to the left, indicating that she was seeing real memories. The same was true when describing her success at learning the pawnbroking business, and when and why Mr. Willis came to work at the shop. But I believe from her actions while describing it that her engagement to Mr. Willis was a fiction."

A light dawned. "You made a point of looking at her ring."

"I did. And her finger underneath it showed no signs whatsoever of long-term wear, as evidenced by a person who wears a ring daily for extensive periods. I suspect she simply picked up a ring from a tray in the shop to add credence to her story.

"Of course, when she reached the part of her tale regarding the threatening notes and the subsequent argument between her father and his assistant, she was – without fail – fabricating the entire business. I am certain of it."

"But to what purpose?" I asked. "And how does that relate to the events in the pawnshop?"

"Ah, the knowledge that she was lying, as well as one or two other trifling observations made while she was here in our sitting room, made me suspicious of her. Although I suspected that something was going to happen at some point in the future, I had no idea that the crime would reveal itself so soon. The fact that the murders *did* happen almost immediately makes the whole thing quite clear to me."

I felt some exasperation, as I did not yet see the greater picture that he was slowly revealing. But before I could ask any further questions, the bell rang, and within a few moments, Lord Carlington was shown into our presence.

There is no need to relate here the extensive and seamy details of the precise and final deconstruction of that man's threadbare character on that day. The story has since played out in the press, to the great embarrassment of his father, the unfortunate Duke, and further picking at that wrecked man's reputation will serve no useful purpose. Suffice it to say, the situation could have been much worse, especially for the Duke, and Holmes's handling of the situation was masterful. When he showed Lord Carlington the documents that he possessed, the others that he had been hired to retrieve were quickly placed into his possession. At the

86

conclusion of the matter, Lord Carlington rose to his feet, looking even more gaunt than when he had arrived, tottering on his feet as if he were being stretched too thin. He didn't seem to notice the bell when it rang from the street, and he made no acknowledgement to either Lestrade, Miss Porter, or the accompanying constable when he passed them coming in as he bolted for the steps. Sadly, the man would be dead within a fortnight.

Lestrade and Miss Porter found the same seats as before, while the stolid constable placed himself with his back to the door. Almost immediately, however, a knock behind him caused him to step aside, revealing Mrs. Hudson, with a telegram in hand. She passed it to Holmes, glanced around at the room's assembly, and departed. The constable resumed his post. Lestrade had arrived with a Gladstone bag, and he carefully placed it by his feet.

"Excellent," murmured Holmes as he read the telegram, and then placed it without comment on the octagonal side table beside his chair, where the packet of letters had so recently rested. Looking at Lestrade, he asked, "Did you find it?"

Lestrade nodded, and Holmes glanced toward Miss Porter who appeared puzzled.

"This telegram," he said, "is a reply to an inquiry that I set in motion not long ago. I had not expected an answer quite so soon, but sometimes things work out. I have an associate in Clacton-on-Sea, a man named Garren that I once helped out of a pesky little problem. I had thought that my question for him might need some extra time, in order for him to complete a more thorough investigation, but it seems that the answer is fairly common knowledge out that way. And after all, it is not a very large town, is it?"

"Clacton-on-Sea?" asked Miss Porter. "What did you want to know about that? I could have told you whatever you wished."

"I suspect," said Holmes, "that you would *not* have wanted to tell me this particular story. I wished to determine if you had left there for London for any reason other than the one that you told us."

Without moving or changing expression in the slightest, Miss Porter appeared to go rigid for an instant. Perhaps it was an unconscious pause in her breathing, before she seemed to force herself to exhale. Then she said, "Whatever can you mean? I told you that I did not get along with my aunt, and I knew that my father would take me in if I came back to him."

"Ah, but why did you not get along with your aunt?" He lowered his arm and tapped a long finger on the telegram. "There is the matter of your aunt's younger brother, whom you influenced into robbing a manor house. He acted alone during the actual robbery, and was sadly wounded during the attempt. He later died without implicating you to the police, but not before he told the story to his sister, your aunt-by-marriage, of how you pushed him into it. She has made it her business to make sure that your involvement, although unprosecuted, is common knowledge in those parts. It was no wonder that you felt the need to hie yourself to a place where you could start over."

He steepled his fingers in front of his face. "That, in itself, is simply a minor confirmatory fact, helping to paint in the background of the picture. It is interesting, however, in that it shows you have a history of being someone who can manipulate others to your will."

I saw Lestrade's eyes widen fractionally with sudden understanding as he recalled the single word, written by Holmes, in the margin of his scrapbook in relation to Porter's pawn shop, and the increased success of the business over the last couple of years. Since the time, in fact, that Miss Porter had moved to London to learn the trade.

"You probably did not realize that the pawnshop's less legal activities have been known to the police for quite some time," said Holmes. Again, the girl did not move, but now she suddenly seemed to look wary and dangerous without changing her expression at all.

"The police, and myself as well, I might add, already knew about the fencing that has been carried out there, in ever increasing amounts over the last couple of years. However, until you decided to put your plan in motion this morning, including a visit to the police, no one had ever suspected your complicity."

Miss Porter still made no comment as Holmes continued. "More than complicity. I should say, your supervision. For it was your vision that changed your father's small steady pawnbroking business into the leading place to fence stolen items in the East End. My only question is did your father knew from the start, or did he only learn of it recently."

The girl's eyes narrowed, and her nostrils flared, as if she were taking in extra oxygen in preparation for flight. She glanced at both the constable against the door, and the tall windows looking out over the street, as if weighing her chances at escape. Evidently she was not provoked to the point of leaping through the glass quite yet, as instead she said, "You are mad, Mr. Holmes. My father and I never did anything illegal. If there was something going on of that sort, it must have been done in secret by Floyd Willis, behind our backs. After all, he was obviously threatening Father."

"No, that won't do," said Holmes. "The fencing first became known two years ago, and it has increased steadily since that time. What you could not realize is that the police will often let such an activity continue for a while, taking place as it is in a known location. They know that by closing it immediately, it would soon reestablish itself somewhere else, and they would have to find it anew. Also, by leaving it in place, they can keep track of who goes in and out, identifying other related criminals. You stated that Mr. Willis has only been an employee for three months. That is long after the fencing was first known.

"This is what happened, then, in general terms," continued Holmes. "I would hope that you might correct me in the small particulars where I go wrong, but of course I don't expect it. You moved back to London, after having escaped any official connection to the crime at the coast. You were welcomed to some degree or other by your father, and began to learn the business. I'm not sure to what level he was involved in the fencing as you found your way into it, but I suspect that he was blissfully ignorant for some period of time. Eventually that part of the business started to become very successful indeed, and you became used to the income that you were salting away. It was probably around this time that your father became aware of it. Possibly he wanted his own share. Or perhaps he urged you to stop.

"I'm not certain of this part, but in either case it would explain why you determined that you had to kill him, and also why you chose to involve an innocent dupe, Mr. Willis. I'm aware, never mind how, that your entire story from this morning, regarding the warning letters and the conflict between your father and your supposed fiancé, was a complete fabrication. I say supposed fiancé, as I know that your engagement was false, and that Mr. Willis was simply hired to have a ready-made victim on hand.

"This morning you set your plan in motion. You met Mr. Willis when he arrived at work, and, stepping behind him, hit him in the head, killing him instantly with the brass pot. It would not take as much effort as one might think for a small woman such as yourself to inflict a deadly force on an unsuspecting victim. Then, when your father came down and stood staring at the corpse, you stepped up and shot him in the head. The inspector's letter to me mentioned that it was a small caliber weapon, and you counted on the fact that the sound would not be noticed or commented upon at that busy time of the morning.

"You went upstairs and changed out of the bloody dress, no doubt spattered from when you killed one or the other, or both. Placing an easily forged and simple suicide note on the counter, you then left up the shop and took a cab to Scotland Yard. It is obvious that you have not walked any great distance today, despite your earlier statement that you made your way on foot from the shop all the way to Whitehall. Another lie, as your dress is too fresh. We know you have ridden in cabs since you left here, both from here back to the shop where you revealed the bodies, and then from the shop back to here with Inspector Lestrade.

"Your plan was to go to the Yard, after supposedly walking for an extended period of time while the two men were involved in the fabricated disagreement. You would tell your story and lay the groundwork of mysterious threats and a falling out between your father and Willis. Then you would return to the shop, and in front of witnesses, find the bodies, if they hadn't already been discovered, posed to look as if your father had killed Willis and then himself. Your trip to Scotland Yard went according to plan. But the one thing that you hadn't counted on was that Inspector Lestrade would then bring you around to Baker Street, ostensibly to share the story with me, but also to look at my scrapbooks to see if my facts matched what the police already knew about the fencing operation.

"You returned to the shop as planned and found the bodies, preparing to play the grieving daughter for a few days before resuming your work and increasing the fencing activities, but now as sole owner and without the interference of your father. What you did not know was that I already knew you to be the likely manipulator who had taken your father's innocent business and turned it criminal, and also that I was aware that your entire story this morning was a lie.

"When word came of the two murders, I instantly realized what your plan must have been, and I sent a wire to my agent in Clacton-on-Sea, and instructions to Lestrade." He turned to the inspector. "You say that you found it?"

"I did. It was pushed down in some other dirty clothes."

He opened the Gladstone bag by his feet and pulled out a yellow dress, spattered with blood.

The girl gasped, the first sign that I had seen of any sort of reaction. I think it was only then that she realized she was well and truly caught.

"As you wrote in your note, she must have been spattered when she killed Willis – it was a very messy murder – and then after she killed her father, she went back upstairs and changed to her current dress before going to the Yard."

Holmes gestured with a finger toward the dress in Lestrade's hand. "It must have been very messy indeed. You verified that she never went back into the shop after opening the door, finding the bodies, and fainting, as observed by the cabbie and other passers-by?"

"That is correct," said Lestrade.

"Then," Holmes said, shifting his finger to now point at the hemline of the girl's current dress, the same that she had worn during her morning visit, "she probably obtained that small spot of blood along the hemline there when she passed through the shop after changing clothes," said Holmes. "She was certainly careful, but not careful enough. I had noticed the spot on her dress when she was here the first time, at the same time that I was observing she had not walked to Whitehall as claimed. If she had truly walked, there was always the chance she could have received the spot on some street. But we know she did not walk. At the time I noticed that stain, I simply filed it away. Later it gained a great deal more importance."

"That it did," agreed Lestrade, raising his head from where he had bent to see the bloodstain. Then he stood up, and the constable moved forward, sensing what was going to happen next. "Miss Letitia Porter, I place you under arrest for the murder of your father and Floyd Willis." He continued the formalities, but she did not seem to hear. She was physically turned toward Holmes, but her face was staring up at the mantel to her left.

"Do you see, Watson?" Holmes asked. "Do you see it? She is remembering what she did this morning, trying to think if she could have done anything differently."

Her eyes then cut sharply to Holmes, and then, after a long moment while Lestrade continued to speak, they drifted up to the right, just for a second. "And now," Holmes added, "she's imagining the various possibilities of how to escape this predicament."

She looked back at Holmes again, and then with an unexpected shriek, she lunged at him. But before she could sink her nails into Holmes's face, Lestrade had her arm, spinning her around and into the approaching constable. Within moments she had been bundled out of the sitting room and downstairs.

"They are never to be trusted, Watson," said Holmes softly. "Not the best of them, and certainly not this pawnbroker's daughter."

Later that evening, Lestrade returned to let us know that the girl had made a full confession. He inquired how Holmes had known that she was lying, but Holmes did not choose to explain his knowledge regarding the way that people behaved when visualizing real or constructed memories. Instead, he gave a vague answer concerning his deductions about the girl's engagement ring, the dress and its slight bloodstain, and his determination that she had ridden in a cab when she said that she had walked, resulting in his questioning all of her statements. This seemed to satisfy our friend the inspector, and he departed soon after.

"After all, Watson," said Holmes when the man had gone, "my ideas about this sort of involuntary action are not thoroughly researched or proven. It would not be a good idea – in fact it might be dangerous in the wrong hands – to present it as otherwise until more data has been established. Should you ever publish a monograph about these little cases of mine, you must be sure not to mention this trick."

I laughed. "As a matter of fact, you simply don't want to give an advantage to the criminals. Or to your rivals at the Yard, I'd wager."

Holmes smiled in agreement. "Perhaps you are right. Possibly someday. But right now, a poor consultant needs every advantage that he can get."

"Then I thank you, Holmes," I said, "for letting me in on one of your many secrets."

"Ah, Watson," he replied, "you are an equal partner in this agency now, and as such you need to be fully equipped with every tool in your toolbox. Yet, I despair, as you still so often see but do not observe. While you did not yet know the method that I used to read the girl's glances during her story today, you *should* have seen that her dress was far too fresh to have walked so great a distance across London. Surely, there were seven different indicators – "

He could see my reaction to that statement, so he quickly changed the subject and suggested a dinner at Simpson's, which was a rare treat indeed in those days, as a way to celebrate the recent fee from the Duke. We both knew that his two-month's share of the rent that he had just earned would be somewhat depleted from such a meal, and that a new case would be necessary in order to replace the spent funds, but that night, with the memory in both our minds of the trapped girl's suddenly vulpine face as she was led away by the constable, seemed to require some sort of special reward to counter the unpleasantness of it all.

By way of an epilogue, I would like to mention the small encounter that led me to recall these events. Just the other day, I was down by the south end of the new Tower Bridge, standing where Jacobson's Yard used to be located. It had all been torn down when the bridge was built a few years ago. I still remembered that night, not quite seven years earlier, when the signal had come, in the form of a waved white handkerchief, letting us know that Mordecai Smith's boat, *The Aurora,* was departing from its hiding place at Jacobson's to begin that mad and dangerous dash down the river, pursuing Jonathan Small, the last of the Four. Holmes, Athelney Jones, and I were waiting on a similar steam launch across the river, hugging the shore by the Tower, little realizing what the rest of the night would bring.

Now, I was pretending to look over toward the Tower itself, shining in the morning sun on the far side of the Thames. The tide was in, and the wind was raising a gray chop on the water's surface. I say that I was pretending to look at that old historic pile, but in reality, I was glancing to my right, towards the bridge, to see for sure that a certain man carried out his instructions and exchanged one package for another. This went as planned, and I then gave the signal, a touch to the brim of my hat with my left hand, to a small, dirty lad sitting on a nearby barrel, eating an apple. Without acknowledgement, he jumped down and scampered toward the bridge. He was, of course, one of Holmes's Irregulars, and he was carrying word that the next phase of the complicated investigation had commenced.

It was then that I saw an expensive carriage stop nearby. While the horse skittishly took a step or two forward and back, the door opened, and a woman stepped down. She was clearly one of those impoverished unfortunates who prey and are preyed upon throughout the East End. The attention that the area had received back in '88 had done very little to alleviate their terrible circumstances.

As the woman found her footing, she turned back to the carriage, and a man's arm, covered in a sleeve of very rich-looking fabric indeed, flipped her a coin, which she tried to catch, but dropped. The carriage door slammed shut, and I heard the sound of a stick knocking inside. The driver, thus alerted, gigged the horse into a trot and departed into the first advances of an impending fog.

I glanced across the river to see that the Irregular was now to the west of the Tower, and conversing with another very similar-looking lad. The second one nodded, and took off running toward the north, into the City, while the first put his hands on his knees to catch his breath. Looking away from them, I found my gaze wandering back to the unfortunate woman as she unbent from retrieving the coin.

As she straightened, her eyes locked with mine, and I was shocked to realize that I knew her. It had been thirteen years since her arrest and conviction, and except for her eyes, I do not think that I could have identified her. She was only in her early thirties now, but time in prison had wasted her. Gone was the pretty girl with the lustrous curls. In spite of Holmes's testimony and her own confession, she had escaped a life sentence, due to somehow charming the jury, and had instead served only ten hard years. But what years they must have been.

I could see that she recognized me as well. Miss Letitia Porter, if miss she still was, glared at me with a raw hatred. It lasted only a second, before her gaze drifted off to the right. Then, with a grim smile, she shifted her eyes back to mine, and making an abrupt turn, she walked away from the river, into a rat's warren of streets.

It was an unsettling experience, and I can only imagine what she was thinking when she smiled. It cannot have been a good thing, whatever she was picturing then, either for Holmes or myself . . . .

The Adventure of the
Defenestrated Princess
by Jayantika Ganguly

I have often remarked on the variety and oddity of clients who sought
the aid of my friend, Mr. Sherlock Holmes, at our shared quarters. More
often than not, our visitors would be accompanied by an aura of drama
and intrigue. An especially dramatic entrance sprung to my mind when I
last visited Holmes in Sussex Downs, and he finally gave his assent to
reveal the details of the case. The parties involved are beyond human
reach now, and the only sufferer of this narration would be Holmes's
own perception of his sentimentality – or rather, the lack thereof.

It was towards the end of autumn in the year 1882, and in the
months that I had known Holmes by then, I was truly convinced that he
was as coldly logical and unfeeling as he projected himself to be. He had
been generous enough to permit me to accompany him on several of his
cases, and I was as much in awe of his genius as I was appalled at his
apparent lack of empathy. While he was mostly polite to his clients, and
unfailingly gentle with the fairer sex, I had come to realise that he did not
much care for their plight; it was the puzzle which appealed to him. I
know better now, of course, but in those early days, Holmes and I were
not as close, and he kept much of his thoughts to himself.

This particular case began with a gunshot at the ungodly hour of
three in the morning. The terrible noise roused me from my sleep. I
hurriedly threw on my dressing gown, pocketed my bull pup and rushed
downstairs to find Holmes similarly dressed and armed.

"What happened?" I enquired, my voice barely a whisper.

"From the sound, I can only tell you that a .476 calibre Enfield Mk I
revolver has been fired within twenty yards of our abode, Watson,"
Holmes replied grimly. "I intend to step out to investigate further."

"I should like to keep you company, if you do not object," I offered.

"Thank you, Doctor. Your assistance may be invaluable. I suspect
we shall have an injured person at hand shortly."

We passed an anxious Mrs. Hudson in the hallway. Insistent
knocking, growing increasingly desperate with each passing moment,
beckoned us to the front door. Holmes waved Mrs. Hudson away to
safety, and gestured at me to take up a discreet position, so I could assist
him if our late-night guest bore intentions of assault. The detective threw
open the door.

94

A raggedly-dressed young man stood outside, one hand still raised towards the knocker and the other clutching his abdomen.

"Mr. Holmes?" he whispered hoarsely.

To my surprise, Holmes pulled him in immediately and closed the door. The boy leaned against the wall, breathing heavily. His dark eyes were wide as he stared at Holmes.

"Oh, but you are more beautiful than I was told to expect, Mr. Holmes," the boy sighed dreamily. "May I paint you?"

I was rendered speechless. Holmes appeared embarrassed and flabbergasted in equal measures. Then the boy collapsed and I noticed the dark blood coating his fingers, realising he had been delirious with pain.

"Get your medical kit ready, Watson," Holmes said urgently. "I will bring up our visitor."

I rushed upstairs and grabbed my bag and some clean linen. We might not have the antiseptic environment of a hospital, but I would not let an infection take my patient. But where could I perform the required surgery? Our living room did not offer a surface large enough.

"My bed should suffice," Holmes said, walking in with the boy in his arms.

Wordlessly, I followed him to his bedroom and spread the clean linen on his bed. With as much care as a mother would display for her injured child, Holmes laid our visitor on the bed. He proceeded to turn up all the lights.

In the well-lit room, I could see the beauty of that young, smooth, golden face and felt a wave of fury sweep through me. The boy could not have been more than fourteen. How dare a ruffian harm a child?

Holmes's soft voice broke through my anger. "How may I assist you, Watson?"

"Cut away his clothes, if you would, Holmes. I need to see the bullet wound," I told him, pouring alcohol on both our hands.

Holmes nodded and carefully removed a strip of the boy's blood-stained shirt.

"It might be better if you removed the shirt completely," I suggested.

Twin spots of colour appeared on my friend's pale cheeks. "I am afraid that may not be prudent, Doctor," he said. "Our client is a lady."

I could only stare at him in shock. However, as I turned my eyes back to my patient, I realised he was right. The figure under those ragged-boy clothes could only belong to a woman.

As it turned out, she was a rather fortunate young lady. Once I had cleaned the blood, it appeared that the bullet had passed cleanly through her side without touching any vital organ, and there was nothing for me to do except clean up the wound and bandage it. She would be fine. Holmes heaved a sigh of relief when I informed him. He laid a set of spare clothes on the chair and we left the girl to rest. We would get her story when she awoke. I was quite exhausted myself, but curiosity gnawed at me.

"A foreign lady," I said to Holmes.

He nodded. "Indeed, Watson. I was not able to deduce much, but it appears she is from our Indian colonies, belongs to a royal family – or at least a very affluent one, studies at the University of London, is a voracious reader, dabbles in art and the violin, seems to be good at horse-riding, fencing and shooting – and is presently caught in a web of international politics. She was abducted recently, but either escaped or was rescued soon."

"How could you possibly know that?" I asked, amazed. "She asked if she could paint you, so I can understand her affinity for art, but how could you know the rest?"

Holmes gave me a small smile. "Look at her boots and jewellery, Watson – custom made, extremely expensive. Also, the soil is clearly from Gower Street. From the dents on her nose, she regularly uses eye glasses, even at this young age – clearly reads a lot. So, a young, studious and rich foreigner in Gower Street – could it be anyone other than a student at the University College London?"

I nodded, following his observations. "You mentioned she plays the violin, rides, fences and shoots."

"Riding boots, calluses and gun-powder residue," he replied. "And if I am not mistaken, that is an 1874 Chamelot-Delvigne in her pocket."

"Abduction? Did you deduce that from the rope-burns on her wrists and ankles?"

"Bravo, Doctor."

"But why on earth is she dressed as a man, Holmes?"

"I suspect it was to foil an assassination attempt," he remarked. "I shall know more upon an investigation of the contents of her coat pocket and satchel."

My face must have betrayed my thoughts, for Holmes laughed. "Do not worry, my good doctor, I assure you that I have our client's permission." He regarded me thoughtfully. "I suggest you rest while you can, Watson – I shall wake you if your patient has any need of you."

I was too tired to argue, so I took his advice. As it turned out, our visitor did not wake until Mrs. Hudson was sent to help her out of bed. One look at the apparel Holmes had laid out for the young woman and our landlady was kind enough to bring up some of her own laundered clothes. Finally seeing the girl dressed in feminine attire, I realised what an utterly beautiful woman she would be in a few years. Even though the dress was plain and ill-fitting, I could easily believe Holmes's conjecture that she was a princess.

"Good morning, your Highness," Holmes greeted her, and almost simultaneously, I asked, "How do you feel?" when Mrs. Hudson and my patient appeared at the breakfast table. I noted absently that Holmes seemed to be observing the princess rather intensely.

"Much better, thank you, Doctor Watson, Mr. Holmes," she replied softly. "You have all been very kind. And please, you must call me Ada – everyone does. I am afraid my Indian name is not conducive to the British tongue, but 'Ada' is quite close to the shortened version."

I was surprised to note she spoke with an upper-class British accent. She smiled at my surprise.

"I have mostly been educated in Europe," she said. "My father is uncharacteristically modern, and I have been rather fortunate for it."

Mrs. Hudson had thoughtfully set up a third place for breakfast, and Holmes invited our client to join us. She took up the chair gratefully and we ate together in silence.

The Princess was the first to speak when we took up chairs near the fireplace.

"Did you have a chance to look through my papers, Mr. Holmes?" she asked quietly.

"Indeed," Holmes replied.

"And what do you make of it?" she enquired.

"I prefer not to hypothesise until I have adequate facts, your Highness," Holmes told her. "I must confess myself stupefied, though, at the absence of any symptoms of poisoning."

Ada laughed. "Oh, you are right, Mr. Holmes, I have been poisoned. However, in my family, we are inured to most varieties of venom, and for anything more potent, we have a *vaidya* – I suppose you could say doctor – at hand. I have not been seriously harmed."

Holmes nodded, but did not look very convinced. "It might be best for you to give us the facts first," he said instead.

Ada smiled ruefully. "Of course, Mr. Holmes, I shall do as you say. I suppose I was hoping to see your skills of deduction first-hand. Victor was always rather verbose about your talents. And when your . . . ." She paused and glanced at me. "Well, M suggested that I consult you at the earliest."

Holmes frowned and the Princess smiled again. She really did have a rather fetching smile. The M she had spoken of, I learnt several years later, was none other than Mycroft Holmes.

"I apologise, Mr. Holmes, Doctor Watson – my brains are still rather addled. Let me narrate the events that have led me here in chronological order." She paused again. "I am afraid it is a rather long tale, but I shall endeavour to make it as brief as possible."

"My father is the King of Terai, a small Indian territory. Incidentally, Mr. Holmes, your friend Victor has lived in our kingdom for several years now, and I have been friends with him since I was a child. It was he who first spoke of you." She smiled fondly. "But I digress. My father is a great believer in education, gentlemen, and at his insistence, all his children – there are six of us – have been thoroughly educated in various parts of the world. This has also helped us further our international relations. Consequently, our little kingdom has prospered even more. Lately, however, my father has not been keeping very well and desires to see all his children married. My brothers and sisters are significantly older, and therefore, already well-settled. While I would prefer to complete my graduation before I wed, my father's plight does not allow for such delay. As it is, I am sixteen, which makes for a rather old bride in traditional families. It was initially believed that there would be a dearth of suitors for my hand . . . now, however, it appears that the problem is quite the reverse." She paused and smiled sardonically. "I do have a rather significant dowry to my name."

"Currently, I have four perfectly fine men willing to take me for a wife. One has been chosen by my father and our mutual acquaintance M, and the rest by my siblings. The first, Sir Norbert, is a British nobleman of impeccable heredity, tragically impoverished. The second, Rajkumar Vikramaditya, is an Indian prince from a neighbouring eastern state. The third, Prince Pierre, is the heir to the throne of an African kingdom. The fourth, Dokter Diederik, is also a European gentleman of Dutch origin, not titled, but immensely rich. I have met each one, Mr. Holmes, and they are all wonderful gentlemen . . . and I am unable to choose. Ordinarily, I would blindly follow my father's advice, Mr. Holmes – he is the wisest man I have ever known, but recent events have made me wary. The warning letters in my bag started pouring in a fortnight ago. There have been three assaults on my person and two break-ins at my London residence in the last week. I am reluctant to bother my father with this, so I have consulted with M, who has been akin to a guardian to me since I arrived in this country. I intended to visit you at a decent hour last evening, but I was cornered in my apartment by a gang of ruffians. My guards fought them off bravely, allowing me to escape in disguise, while my maid dressed herself in my clothes and fled in another direction as a decoy. The man who followed and shot me on Baker Street must have taken me for a messenger sent to seek your assistance."

"You were abducted two days ago," Holmes said.

She nodded.

"Did you know your captor? How did you escape?" I asked.

"Faithless man," she said quietly. "It was one of my friends from the university. Fortunately, my men caught up with the carriage I was in."

"Where was he supposed to take you?" Holmes asked.

"I do not know, Mr. Holmes. He killed himself before we could take him to the police."

"Are you quite certain you do not have any lingering effects of poisoning? Watson may be able to help."

"Thank you. That is very kind of you."

"May I enquire if any your suitors or their assistants bear the initials K.O.?" Holmes asked.

The Princess stared at him in shock. "None," she said eventually.

"But you are – or were – close to someone with those initials," Holmes said, watching her keenly.

"Yes. Kaarle Olivier is my best friend," she replied defiantly.

"Why did you not go to the police?" Holmes asked.

"M advised against it."

"Does he have any ideas?"

She looked away. Holmes frowned, but before he could question the princess further, Mrs. Hudson appeared with the newspapers. It was unusual for her to bring them up herself; obviously she desired to check up on Ada, whom she now considered to be under her wing.

Holmes pounced upon the papers. The front page declared, "Defenestration in London!" Holmes quickly passed the paper to me and I read out loud:

> *Late last night, a young woman was thrown out of her third-floor apartment window at Gower Street. The girl, who was killed upon impact, has been identified as Her Royal Highness, Princess Advyaitavadini, youngest daughter of the Indian King Abhayananda of Terai. Her entire entourage, consisting of six trained guards, three male servants and three female servants, has also been found to be killed in a violent fight while defending the princess. The deceased, known to her friends as Ada, was well-liked amongst her fellow students at the University. Her friends have confessed that the princess had been threatened and attacked previously as well, but had refused police assistance. This brutal massacre of thirteen people, however, is being investigated by Scotland Yard, under the able leadership of*

*Inspector G. Lestrade, whom the public may remember from the
Jefferson Hope case.*

Ada had lost all colour and tears poured down her cheeks. Her
hands shook, portraying her distress, and I was reminded that she was
still barely more than a child.

"I must go to the university at once, Mr. Holmes," she cried,
pushing herself off the chair with some effort. "This news must not travel
to my father at any cost."

She staggered towards the door but faltered halfway. Fortunately,
Mrs. Hudson caught her.

"Now you listen here, young lady," Mrs. Hudson scolded. "You are
to stay here and rest. Mr. Holmes and Dr. Watson will take care of your
troubles."

"But . . . ."

"No buts. Look at the state of you, all pale and trembling! What you
need is a cup of good, strong tea," our landlady said firmly, and
proceeded to press a cup into the girl's hands.

Holmes took a seat next to the traumatised girl and said gently, "I
shall attempt to contain the news, barring which, I shall ensure that news
of your survival accompanies any notification from the university.
However, you must stay hidden here until I return. Watson and Mrs.
Hudson will look after you. Do you understand?"

She nodded tearfully.

Holmes turned to me. "Watson, no one must see her. If we have any
visitors not accompanied by myself, escort her to my room. I expect
Lestrade shall come by at some point. Be ready."

"Certainly, Holmes," I promised, understanding his warning to be
armed and prepared.

"Mr. Holmes," Ada called softly. "My people . . . they have to be
cremated, and their ashes sent home to be scattered in the holy river. I do
not know who the thirteenth person is, but if she is Christian, she ought
to be buried here. If you require me to identify my people, I shall
accompany you."

Holmes's grey eyes glittered like diamonds as he turned back to the
girl.

"Who knew the specific number of people in your entourage?" he
asked.

She frowned. "I am not sure. It was not exactly a secret."

"Do you have any idea who the unknown woman might be?"

"It could be the milkmaid, the charwoman or the laundry girl – they
were friendly with my staff and often visited socially. In fact, Jane – the

100

laundry girl, and Satyanand – one of my guards, were hoping to marry when we returned to Terai." Ada pursed her lips, eyes bright with unshed tears. "You will find out who did this, won't you, Mr. Holmes?"

"I shall certainly endeavour to do so," Holmes replied.

Ada nodded, visibly assured. "Please spare no expense. No price is too dear to me to avenge the murder of my people!"

Holmes nodded his assent. "How many of your suitors are presently in London?"

"All of them."

"One last question, before I leave," Holmes said quietly. "Could you describe Sir Norbert and Dokter Diederik?"

Ada smiled. "I can do better. I can give you their pictures." She fetched a small album from her dress pocket and handed it to Holmes, pointing out each of her suitors.

Holmes appeared pleased. "Thank you," he said. "I shall be back soon."

Holmes was away for several hours. I changed the dressing on Ada's wound, and then looked through the papers Holmes had spent the night poring over. There were fifteen envelopes, several of which bore stamps from exotic cities. Each contained an insult, scrawled on a torn piece of foolscap in an untidy hand with scarlet ink:

> *Vile <u>worm</u>, thou wast o'erlook'd even in thy birth.* (London)

> *You are not worth another <u>word</u>, else I'd **call** you knave.* (London)

> *I wonder that you will still be talking. <u>Nobody</u> marks you.* (Madrid)

> *Here, thou incestuous, murderous, damned Dane, <u>Drink</u> off this potion!* (Helsinki)

> *Dissembling harlot, thou art <u>false</u> in all!* (London)

> *I shall laugh myself to <u>death</u> at this puppy-headed monster!* (London)

> *Thou unfit for any **place** but hell.* (London)

> *Away! Thou'rt <u>poison</u> to my blood.* (Calcutta)

More of your conversation would <u>infect</u> my brain. (Cairo)

***Away**, you mouldy rogue, away! I am <u>meat</u> for your master.*
(Havana)

*O <u>faithless</u> coward! O dishonest wretch! Wilt thou be made a
<u>man</u> out of my vice?* (Milan)

*<u>Take her away</u>; for she hath lived too long, To fill the world **with**
vicious qualities.* (Hamburg)

***I** shall cut out your tongue. 'Tis no matter, I shall <u>speak</u> as much
wit as thou <u>afterwards</u>.* (London)

*O you <u>beast</u>! I'll so maul you and your toasting-iron, That you
shall think the <u>devil</u> is come from hell.* (Krakow)

Heaven truly knows that thou <u>art false</u> as hell. (Odessa)

I stared at the scraps in disbelief. When I looked up at Ada, she was smiling sadly.

"Shakespeare. I thought the first few were a joke," she said, her voice quiet.

There was also a small diary filled with neat, feminine handwriting, meticulously noting down the date and time of receipt of each letter, and the Shakespearean play each message was taken from – *The Merry Wives of Windsor, All's Well that Ends Well, Much Ado about Nothing, Hamlet, The Comedy of Errors, The Tempest, Richard III, Cymbeline, Coriolanus, Henry IV, Measure for Measure, Henry VI, Troilus and Cressida, King John,* and *Othello.* Ada had also noted down the bold and underlined words separately.

The underlined words read: "*worm word Nobody Drink potion false death poison infect meat faithless man Take her away speak afterwards beast devil art false*" and the bold words read "*call place Away with I*". Even I could see the barely concealed warning in the papers and the missive to call India. I wondered what else Holmes had deduced from these. How was it even possible to deliver these letters so regularly from such different locations?

Ada had also made a list of her staff members, including the local hires and their contact details. Similarly, she had also listed the London addresses of her suitors.

I recognised the English nobleman immediately. He was at least thirty years older than our young princess! When I made a remark, Ada simply smiled and said, "They all are; at forty seven, your bachelor Englishman is in the younger half. The Indian is the youngest at thirty five – and I am to be his fifth wife. The African is fifty two, and I shall be the second wife; the first died recently. The Dutch is seventy, a famed misogynist until now."

"Would you not prefer to wed someone close to your own age?" I enquired, curious.

She smiled sadly, her bright eyes dimmed. "I have a duty to my kingdom, Dr. Watson; I do not have the luxury of love."

I had a sudden thought. Could it be that the warning disguised as threats were the work of a rejected admirer from a failed love-affair? I did not realise I had spoken out loud until I saw the stricken expression on her face.

"M thinks so, too – in fact, I made the notes under his instructions," she said unhappily. "But I know Kaarle would never do so!"

"I am glad you think so, *ma mie*," came a soft voice from the door.

Ada jumped out of her seat with a cry of "Kaarle!"

Monsieur Olivier strode in and engulfed her in his arms. She sobbed quietly on his shoulder.

I took a moment to regard the rather striking blue-eyed, dark-haired young man before Holmes, who had followed the young man in, cleared his throat delicately.

The young pair sprang apart immediately.

"*Je suis désolée, mon trésor*," Ada said quietly. She turned to Holmes. "How did you find him, Mr. Holmes?"

"From the letters," Holmes replied. "You had, rather helpfully, written down the Shakespearean references. All foreign places started with the same letter as the play's title, and the bold words were followed by such letters of the alphabet. 'Call MH. Place CCH. Away for MH. I KO.' I paid a visit to the Charing Cross Hospital and found him in the morgue, looking for you. Child's play."

The princess directed her flashing dark eyes at the young Frenchman. "It was you," she spat. "You sent those letters! You killed my people!"

Monsieur Olivier winced. "*Non, ma mie, non*," he pleaded. "I merely attempted to warn you. There is a great conspiracy afoot. You are in grave danger, *ma mie*."

Ada glared.

"He was with M," Holmes said gently.

Ada turned her furious gaze back to the boy. "How do you know M?" she demanded.

"That ought to be a story for another time," Holmes interrupted impatiently. "We have more pressing concerns."

Ada stepped back, gathered herself and reclaimed her seat. "You are right, of course, Mr. Holmes. My apologies."

Holmes gestured for the young man to take a seat as well. He lit his pipe and I offered cigarettes to the boy.

"Cremation and transit of the ashes have been arranged," Holmes said, his voice quiet and soft. "Notice of your safety is also en route to your family."

"Thank you," Ada whispered. Her eyes shone with grateful tears.

"The additional victim appears to be Jane Miller, your laundry girl," Holmes continued. "She is the only person unaccounted for. Requisite funeral arrangements have been made."

Ada nodded.

"News of your survival has been contained so far. I would like to keep it thus until we are able to locate the perpetrator." Holmes blew out a long spiral of smoke. "Monsieur Olivier has been trying to warn you of imminent danger for the last two weeks. M and I agree with him."

"But why would anyone want to kill me? No one stands to gain anything from my death. Once I am married, my death would undoubtedly benefit my husband, but till then, I am pretty useless." Ada frowned and glared at her young friend. "How do *you* know?"

Kaarle winced. "After we parted in Geneva, I went to meet my father. I accidentally stumbled upon a conspiracy involving Terai. Your father is not on his deathbed. Each of your suitors is a political plant. The British, Dutch and Indian represent their own, and the African is a French agent."

"But Terai is neutral!" Ada exclaimed. "We have always been peaceful."

Kaarle shook his head. "Terai is rich, independent, and possesses a powerful military force. It is strategically located and impossible to avoid for any trade route through Asia. You are surrounded by British, French and Dutch colonies, as well as rebellious Indian states. It is no secret that you are the favourite daughter of your father, and unlike most kingdoms where the crown automatically passes down to the eldest son, your family has been known to be eccentric enough to choose a successor deemed worthy. Your father himself was the fourth son, was he not? And your grandfather the second son-in-law?"

Ada nodded, her eyes wide.

"Your husband would be in the race for the crown of Terai, a most desirable object for each of your neighbours. The French and the Dutch would gain a strong foothold in the east, and will be able to wrest control of several states from the British. The British would become invincible if they won Terai. Any Indian state that has your unconditional support would gain not only a great army, but also a political advantage against European intruders. Also, even though your father is non-aligned, some of your siblings are very involved in the Indian independence movement. You have been known to sympathise."

The Princess lifted her chin defiantly. "I advocate peace, like my father before me. However, if you saw the brutalities heaped upon my countrymen, you would feel the need to rebel, too. Terai is only safe because we are powerful enough."

"Nonetheless," I interjected. "This does not explain why anyone would wish to harm Ada. Surely it is in the interest of these men to keep her alive and happy with them, so they could win her hand?"

Holmes smiled. "You have cut straight to the heart of the matter, my dear doctor," he said. "While the British, French, Dutch and Indians stand to win, others stand to lose. As such, eliminating the princess is a good way of reducing the risk. One less contender to the throne."

Ada sprang from her seat. "Are you implying my relatives are involved, Mr. Holmes?"

"I do not theorise without adequate data," Holmes replied calmly.

"But you suspect?"

"It is only logical."

"No," Ada declared. "Please cease your investigations. I shall return to my homeland immediately."

"Are you out of your mind?" Kaarle cried. "You will be killed on the way!"

The princess remained stubbornly silent.

Holmes turned his raptor gaze upon the young woman. "There is no dignity in death by betrayal," he said quietly. "If a member of your family is indeed responsible for this assault, would their next move not be to eliminate your father and other dissenting members of your family?"

She staggered. Holmes caught her gently and led her back to her chair. I had always known Holmes to be chivalrous, but he usually disliked women. In this instance, however, I could see genuine concern for the girl in his eyes. Was it because she was barely more than a child, or could it be that Holmes's projection of machine-like imperturbability was false?

105

"Do not exert yourself, Ada," Holmes said softly. "You have been poisoned, abducted and shot at; you require rest."

Kaarle's eyes widened in shock. "But I warned you! Did you not heed my words?"

"I did," Ada said softly. "I was prepared for the wormwood in the wine and hemlock in the quail."

"Correct me if I'm wrong, your Highness, but were you with one of your suitors each time you were attacked?" Holmes asked.

She nodded. "I had wine with the African prince; it was one of his special vintages from his vineyard in Bordeaux. Quail was served for dinner with your British peer. I was taken from the street right outside the Indian prince's hotel, and the attack last night happened just after I returned from dinner with the Dutch gentleman."

"What happens to your dowry if you die?" I asked.

She shrugged. "I suppose it reverts to my father's treasury." She looked straight at Holmes. "My relatives would not care about that. It is not a significant sum of money for my family."

Holmes nodded.

I turned to the boy and asked, "Who is beast devil?"

"I am unsure," Kaarle replied. "As I said, I overheard two men talking of Terai. I sent out whatever information I had through mail to warn Ada – in parts, so that they would not be intercepted, and *prima facie* nonsensical, so that they would be dismissed as innocuous. I had the two agents arrested and made my way to London immediately. I arrived at Charing Cross last evening."

The bell rang.

Holmes quickly sent our young guests to his bedroom with strict instructions to stay out of sight.

"I have been expecting you, Lestrade," Holmes said, greeting our visitor.

Inspector Lestrade shook his head sombrely. "It's an unholy mess, I tell you, Mr. Holmes. Some foreign princess got herself killed, and the Prime Minister descended upon us." He smiled. "We know who did it, but we need your help to find the fellow."

Holmes arched an eyebrow.

"The princess left everything in her will to a Kaarle Olivier; she was sweet on him in Switzerland, her friends say. We know Olivier arrived in London yesterday. Probably wanted to marry the girl, but she was to wed someone of her own class – must have killed her in a jealous fit."

"And her entourage?" Holmes asked.

"Died protecting her, didn't they?"

"Do you honestly think one man could have killed thirteen people single-handed?" I interjected hotly.

"Accomplices."

"Tell me, Inspector, are you familiar with the brothers Zvíře and Ďábel?" Holmes enquired.

"Beast and devil!" Lestrade exclaimed. "Are they involved?"

"It is likely." Holmes took in my befuddled expression. "Mercenaries, my dear doctor, named for their looks. These two make a most vicious pair of criminals. Their origins are unknown, and they are fluent enough in at least six languages to disguise themselves as natives. I believe they are wanted by several nations."

Lestrade groaned.

"I believe we may be able to capture them," Holmes told the policeman. "However, I shall need full cooperation of Scotland Yard."

"By all means, Mr. Holmes." Lestrade's beady eyes glinted with excitement. "What do you need?"

A devious smile appeared on Holmes's thin face, and, for a moment, I was reminded of a bloodhound catching a scent. "We shall lay a trap, my dear Inspector, and I need bait."

"What bait?"

"I believe you are aware of the shooting here last night?"

Lestrade nodded.

"I would like Scotland Yard to publicly state that valuable information on the perpetrators has been found at Baker Street, and an eye-witness has survived. The police have a solid lead and shall arrest the culprits soon."

"Now, look here, Mr. Holmes, I can't put out false information."

"It is true."

"What?"

Holmes smiled. "We have an eye-witness who was shot by Zvíře last night, presently under the care of Dr. Watson."

"I need to see him," Lestrade said stubbornly.

Holmes glanced at me.

"I'm afraid my patient is not in a state for visitors at the moment, Inspector," I replied. "However, we may be able to set up a meeting later today."

"Rest assured, Inspector, once we have the thugs, your eye-witness will testify if required. Also, as always, I would like you to keep my name out of it." Holmes's demeanour was sombre. Even at that young age, he was quite masterful. Lestrade agreed reluctantly and departed.

"Now we wait, Watson," Holmes sighed.

Lestrade kept his word. The evening papers carried the bait.

Barely an hour later, Sir Norbert, Ada's British suitor, appeared at our doorstep. He looked much younger than his forty-seven years, and was unusually handsome. His long fingers clutched the evening *Times*.

"Mr. Holmes," he said softly. "You must find my Ada; I know in my heart that she is alive."

"What makes you so sure?" Holmes asked sharply.

"This." The nobleman held up the newspaper. "I knew each man and woman that looked after Ada, Mr. Holmes. If only one person survived, it is she. These Indians – *Rajput*, they are called – would protect their charge at any cost. If Ada perished, the rest would commit suicide."

"Interesting," Holmes remarked.

Sir Norbert's response was cut off by the entry of a rather large elderly gentleman.

"Where is *het meisje*?" he demanded.

"Interesting," Holmes repeated. "Dokter Diederik, I assume?"

"*Ja*. Where is she? We will go to Maastricht and be safe."

"Why do you assume she is alive?" I asked.

"I believe it is more surprise than assumption, my dear Watson," Holmes drawled. "After all, our guest here is an excellent shot."

Instantly, in a coordinated move, Diederik grabbed me and held a gun to my head, while Sir Norbert drew a sword from his cane and rested the tip on Holmes's throat.

Holmes appeared indifferent. "It is a .476 calibre Enfield Mk I. I was right after all, Watson. I can confess to a monograph on the subject."

"Clever, aren't you, Holmes?" the Englishman spat. "Now, where is the girl?"

Holmes shrugged nonchalantly. "How would I know?"

The sword pressed in. I could see droplets of blood beading on Holmes's pale neck.

"Would you like me to shoot your friend?" Diederik growled.

Holmes's eyes flashed silver with contained rage. "If you harm Watson, Zvíře, I promise you and Ďábel shall not leave this room alive."

I finally understood. Zvíře and Ďábel had been posing as Ada's suitors!

Ďábel laughed. "You are hardly in a position to threaten," he mocked. "Now tell me where she is and I might let you live." He jabbed the blade further.

Holmes ignored him.

A door opened. "Stop," Ada commanded. "Let them go."

"Do not come out!" Holmes shouted.

The princess stepped out of Holmes's bedroom. Her hand was steady as she aimed her pistol at the scoundrels.

"Now, Watson!" Holmes cried.

Pandemonium ensued. Two shots rang out, followed by a cry of pain and the sound of shattering glass. Holmes knocked the sword off Ďábel and delivered a swift left hook. Simultaneously, I brought up my good leg in a brutal kick and Zvíře staggered, giving me ample time to pistol-whip him. Kaarle dived at Ada and both hit the floor. Kaarle moved quickly to shield her. Lestrade and a dozen policemen burst in.

Holmes and I stepped back, allowing the policemen to handcuff the two rogues. Zvíře was hit in the arm by Ada's shot and his bullet had shattered the framed painting behind her head. Kaarle had saved her life.

"Now, gentlemen, would you care to enlighten us regarding the identity of your employer?" Holmes asked cheerfully, holding his handkerchief to the cut on his neck.

"Go to hell," Zvíře growled.

"What are you willing to offer us in return?" Ďábel asked at the same time.

"That would depend on how valuable your information is," Holmes replied. "If it is good enough, we may forget that you assaulted and attempted to murder the princess."

Lestrade protested, but Holmes held up a hand to silence him.

"The money came from India. We heard references to a Ranjit Singh."

Ada paled. "The royal counsel. We must inform my father."

Holmes nodded. "And who is your British contact?"

"We do not know the principal. He is simply referred to as the professor. We only met with one of his agents, a university student named Horace Bloomington."

Holmes turned to Ada. "Your abductor?"

"Yes," she said softly.

"Very well," Holmes said. "Assault and attempted murder charges will be dropped."

The criminals smirked.

"However," Holmes continued, "You will be charged with the murders of the real Sir Norbert and Dokter Diederik as well as thirteen innocent men and women."

"You cheat!" Ďábel cried, lunging at Holmes. He was restrained by two able-bodied policemen.

"Congratulations, Lestrade, on a case well-solved," Holmes told the shocked policeman. "You will find the murder weapons on your prisoners, and bodies of the two gentlemen at the Highgate cemetery, close to a birch tree, judging from the mud on their shoes. Also, the charred end of Zvíře's sleeve and the soot on Ďábel's trousers betray their presence at the crime scene last evening. I have no doubt that you will be able to extract the names of their accomplices hired for the act."

Lestrade thanked Holmes effusively and departed.

"Thank you, Mr. Holmes," Ada whispered. "You have brought peace to the souls of my fallen compatriots."

"How did you know?" Kaarle enquired.

"It was elementary," Holmes replied. "Zvíře and Ďábel had to be in close proximity to the princess, which indicated the suitors. Fortunately, I recognised them from their pictures. They may not remember, but we have crossed paths before." He looked up at our curious faces. "It had best be discussed over dinner."

After Holmes regaled us with his tales over a lavish dinner at Simpson's, I asked Ada about her future.

"I suppose I shall have to marry either Vikram or Pierre," she said sadly.

I noticed the stricken expression on Kaarle's face. Before I could say anything, though, Holmes announced that he had an errand to run and requested Kaarle to accompany him. Ada and I returned to Baker Street.

Unable to bear the aura of misery surrounding my companion, I finally asked her the question which had been plaguing me. "Is there no way you could escape this unwanted marriage? Your father is not ill, you may be able to buy some time."

"It does not matter, Dr. Watson," she wept. "I would never be permitted to marry Kaarle, even if I renounced my husband's claim to contend for the throne of Terai. We need the political support. If I did not have a duty to my kingdom, I would have happily taken this chance to be presumed dead."

I could only offer her a warm beverage in consolation. Exhaustion crept in upon her, and I sent her to bed. I waited up for Holmes, but at the stroke of midnight, I found myself too drowsy to sit and retired to my chambers.

Holmes and Kaarle finally appeared at breakfast. It was obvious that they had been up all night. Kaarle's cerulean eyes were red-rimmed, as were Ada's. A wave of sympathy coursed through me at the plight of the young couple.

Holmes rested a hand on the boy's shoulder. "Ada," he called gently. "Kaarle would like to have a few words."

Ada looked up apprehensively.

110

Kaarle winced. "I may not have been entirely truthful about my origins in the past," he began, eyes downcast. "I am not French, though my mother was. I am the crown prince of a small island nation off the coast of Nice. I have been in exile for several years, but I have now been reinstated – and finally in a position to ask for your hand in marriage." He knelt before her and held out a solitaire ring. "*Advyaitavadini,*" he pronounced carefully. "*Ma belle, ma petite, ma bichette, ma mie - je t'aime, veux-tu m'epouser?* Would you do me the honour of being my wife? *Kya aap hamari ardhangini banengi?*"

Ada stared at him. "When did you learn Hindi?" she whispered.

"You learnt my language for me, the least I could do was to learn yours," the crown prince muttered, his cheeks aflame. "I should also tell you that I have M's blessing, and I have sought your father's approval through him, which, I am assured will be forthcoming. My father sends his regards as well." He looked up at her hopefully. "So . . . will you?"

A beatific smile spread across our young princess' visage. "Yes," she whispered shyly. "*Oui. Haan.*"

The ring was slipped on. The euphoric groom-to-be picked her up and twirled about the room, both of them giggling like schoolchildren.

Holmes and I exchanged an amused glance.

"Mr. Holmes, Dr. Watson," Ada said breathlessly, as Kaarle finally released her. "Would you be our witnesses?"

Kaarle nodded enthusiastically. "Without you, we would be dead. Without you, we would have been torn apart. We owe you our life and our happiness. The traditional ceremonies in our respective kingdoms would be arduous, but we would like to have a small church wedding in London before we depart, and we would be very honoured if you would be our witnesses."

Holmes had a strange look on his face. For an instant, I was afraid he would reply in the negative. He glanced at me and I nodded slightly.

"It would give us great pleasure," Holmes said quietly.

Much to our embarrassment, the young couple flung themselves at us. I patted the boy's back awkwardly while Holmes turned an alarming shade of red in the girl's arms. Then Ada embraced me and Kaarle enveloped Holmes. When we were finally released, the prince laughed.

"*Désolé,*" he said, smiling. "We forget how reserved the British are." He took his fiancée's hand. "We shall be in touch, gentlemen. *Au revoir.*"

The young royals departed with a spring in their steps.

I could not contain my curiosity any longer. "Holmes, did you mete out romantic advice to the boy last night? Did you take him to this M you all keep talking about?"

Holmes nodded and refused to meet my eyes. I smiled to myself, preparing to tease my friend.

"Not a word, Watson!" he shook his head. "It was only logical."

He turned dramatically, his greatcoat bellowing behind him like a cape, and, for the want of a better word, *fled* – quite possibly to delete all traces of sentimentality from his brain-attic!

The Adventure of the
Inn on the Marsh
by Denis O. Smith

In glancing over the records I kept during the time I shared chambers with my eminent friend, the renowned detective, Mr. Sherlock Holmes, I am struck by the many occasions on which what appeared at the outset to be but a trivial affair became, in the end, a deadly serious investigation. Not infrequently, too, a case which began in London would oblige us to travel far beyond the capital and deep into the countryside in search of a solution. The case associated with The Wild Goose of Welborne, which I shall now recount, provides a good illustration of both of these points.

It was a pleasant, breezy day during the first week of September, 1883, the sort of weather that seems to freshen the air after the heat of the summer, and freshen, too, one's own energies and aspirations. Holmes and I had both spent the morning endeavouring to tidy and bring order to the sheaves of papers and documents which had built up on every surface during the previous months. We were about to take lunch, satisfied with our morning's work, when a ring at the doorbell announced a visitor. A moment later, our landlady ushered a young couple into our sitting-room, announced as Mr. and Mrs. Philip Whittle.

"I am sorry to intrude if you are eating," the young man said in an apologetic tone, "but this was the only time I could get away from work to see you."

"Not at all," returned Holmes affably, putting down his knife and fork and standing up from the table. "One can eat at any time. I had much rather hear what it is that has brought you here to see us."

"We have had a very odd experience," said the young man, as he and his wife seated themselves on the chairs I brought forward. "We cannot think what to make of it."

"The details, if you please," said Holmes.

"It is soon enough told. We stayed recently for a few days at an old inn, The Wild Goose, which lies in the marshland near the north Norfolk coast. It is the second time we have stayed there. The first time was at the beginning of June, when we stayed there for a week."

"Upon the occasion of your honeymoon, no doubt."

The young man looked surprised. "Yes, it was, as a matter of fact," said he, "but how did you know?"

Sherlock Holmes chuckled in that odd, noiseless fashion which was peculiar to him. "Since your wife removed her gloves, she has been displaying two very fine rings upon the third finger of her left hand. One is undoubtedly a wedding ring, and the other, with a sparkling stone in it, is no doubt an engagement ring. They both appear relatively new and shiny, and, moreover, the wedding ring is still a little loose, as is apparent when your wife touches it with the fingers of her other hand, which she has done several times already. It demands no great leap of logic to surmise that your wedding took place not very long ago, and that your week's holiday in Norfolk constituted your honeymoon."

The young lady flushed to the roots of her hair.

"I apologize for alluding to your personal circumstances," said Holmes quickly in an urbane tone. "It is a little hobby of mine – trifling and no doubt silly – to deduce facts about people from their personal appearance."

"That is perfectly all right," said Mrs. Whittle with a little smile.

"Such a hobby may prove useful in this case, if it helps you get to the bottom of the matter," remarked Whittle. "We were married at the very end of May, and immediately took a week's holiday in Norfolk, as you surmised. One or two of my married friends had spent their honeymoons at the sea-side, at Margate, Brighton and places like that, but my fancy was for somewhere a little quieter, and Prudence agreed. When we heard from a cousin of mine of The Wild Goose, on the Welborne Marsh in Norfolk, it sounded ideal. It is a wild and beautiful spot, very popular with bird-watchers, I understand, as it is a haven for birds of all kinds. We spent most of the week there, in walks over the countryside or by the sea, and when we moved to Cromer, for the last two days of our holiday – even though Cromer itself is a quiet, charming and select sort of seaside town – it seemed to us very noisy and bustling compared with where we had been staying.

"We had enjoyed our stay at The Wild Goose so much that when the opportunity arose recently to take another brief holiday, both Prudence and I at once thought of returning there. We therefore travelled down to Norfolk last Friday, and stayed until Monday morning. However, the pleasure of being there, which we had been looking forward to so much, was marred by one odd little circumstance. As I was entering our details in the register, I turned the pages back to see the entries for the beginning of June, with Prudence looking over my shoulder. You will appreciate, no doubt, that the occasion of our honeymoon meant a lot to us both, and the urge to see 'Mr. and Mrs. Whittle' written somewhere for the first time was irresistible. Imagine our astonishment and dismay, then, to see that on the week in question there was no trace of our names whatsoever!

114

Of course, I looked on the page before and the page after, but we were not there. Our names had simply vanished from the book completely, as if our visit to The Wild Goose had never taken place!"

Holmes rubbed his hands together in delight, a look of interest on his face.

"Did it appear to you that a page had been removed from the book?" he asked.

Whittle shook his head. "Perhaps it had, but if so, it must have been done very neatly, for I didn't notice anything of the sort. Besides, there were other names written in on the dates we had stayed there. It was not that everyone's name had disappeared from that week, just ours."

"Did you recognize any of these other names?"

"No, but I scarcely knew the name of anyone else that was staying there. We rather kept ourselves to ourselves, if you know what I mean, when we were there in June. As a matter of fact, it was very quiet then, anyway; there were very few other people staying there. I understand it gets much busier during the wild-fowling season. But the register now shows that a Miss Stebbing, a Mr. and Mrs. Williams, and a Mr. and Mrs. Myers were staying there at the same time as we were, and I don't remember any of those people."

"Did you mention the matter to anyone at the inn?"

"I certainly did. I mentioned it to the girl who was attending us as we signed in. But she said she had only worked there for a month and didn't know anything about it. 'If you've got any questions,' she said, 'you'll have to ask Mr. Trunch.'"

"He being the landlord?"

"Exactly. I raised the matter with him that evening. He said he couldn't remember as far back as June. 'I have lots of visitors coming and going all the time,' he said. 'You can't expect me to remember everyone.' I pointed out to him that his memory was not the issue. Rather, it was the disappearance of our names from his register. He then suggested that we must be mistaken. 'I don't think you were ever here at all,' he said, and suggested that we had, rather, stayed at The Old Duck, which lies about three miles distant, across the marsh. Of course, it is ridiculous to suppose that a man could forget in three months where he had spent the very first holiday with his wife, but when I pointed that out to him, he became very irritable and almost abusive, and I had to let the matter drop. I must say his manner quite spoiled our memory of our previous visit there."

"It is certainly an odd experience," remarked Sherlock Holmes after a moment, "but there may be some rational explanation for it. Perhaps, for instance, a jug of water was accidentally spilled onto the register, rendering some of the pages illegible, including the one on which your names were written. Then, perhaps in attempting to rewrite the page from memory, someone has simply failed to recall your name. It may be that the 'Mr. and Mrs. Williams' which is now written in the book was someone's attempt to remember your name. Of course, that would not explain the landlord's unpleasant manner towards you. One would imagine that if such an explanation were the case, he would simply have informed you of the fact. But perhaps he has an unusually poor memory, and is embarrassed about it. Perhaps he drinks heavily. If so, he wouldn't be the first landlord of a remote country pub to consume all the profits in liquid measures, and I understand that excessive drinking has a very detrimental effect on the memory. Or is there something else?" he enquired, eyeing the young man closely.

Whittle nodded. "There has been a further development, which we have both found very upsetting, and for which such simple explanations cannot account."

"Very well. Pray proceed."

"We returned to London on Monday, having enjoyed our few days away despite the inauspicious beginning. Yesterday morning, however, this letter arrived by the first post." As he spoke, the young man took an envelope from his inside pocket and passed it to Holmes, who took from it a single sheet of paper which he unfolded upon his knee and studied intently for a few moments.

"What do you make of it, Watson?" said he, as he passed the letter to me and turned his attention to the envelope. The note, which was not signed, was a brief one, written in black ink in the centre of an oddly square-shaped sheet of paper, and ran as follows:

> *Asking many questions can be a dangerous course. Keep out of matters that do not concern you, and mind your business. This is a warning to you.*

"What a very unpleasant and menacing letter!" I remarked to Whittle. "I am not surprised it has upset you both."

"It was posted in central London," said Holmes, "so it is unlikely to have come directly from the landlord of The Wild Goose himself. But the information that you have been 'asking questions' must surely have come from him, so he is evidently in communication with someone in London. The paper is unusually thick and heavy, but is an odd size. I wonder – "

He took his lens from the shelf and examined the letter closely through it. "Something has been cut off the top of the sheet," he said,

116

"probably a printed heading which included an address. It has been carelessly done, though: there are a couple of tiny black marks at the top edge, where the scissors have clipped the bottom of a row of printed letters. There seems something familiar about it. Let me see – "

He sprang from his chair and began rummaging through the piles of old letters on his desk, which he had spent the morning putting in order. Presently he selected one and held it up beside the letter Whittle had received. "This is a letter of thanks I received from a client to whom I had been of service a few months ago," he said. "I think it is the same. Yes, undoubtedly it is the same. See," he continued, passing the sheets to our visitors. "The type of paper is a precise match, and the little traces of a line of printing that the scissors have left correspond exactly to this line on the other sheet."

"But that letter is from the German embassy!" I cried in astonishment, as I leaned over to verify his observations. "I cannot believe the German embassy would send such a crude threatening letter to Mr. and Mrs. Whittle! And why should they, anyway?"

Holmes nodded. "The Germans may be a forceful people, but – in my experience, at least – they like things to be done in a legal and proper manner. There is evidently nothing official about this letter. I imagine that someone employed at the embassy, acting on his own initiative, and without official sanction, has simply used a sheet of official notepaper as it was to hand, having cut the top couple of inches off to preserve, as he hoped, his anonymity."

"Then it is of no help to us in solving the problem."

"I should not say that, Watson. It confirms, after all, our suspicions that the writer of the note is probably a foreigner, as suggested by his incorrect rendering of the common idiom, 'mind your own business'. Can you recall, Mr. Whittle, if there were any foreigners staying at The Wild Goose at the time of your first visit there?"

"Yes," replied Whittle. "Now you mention it, I do recollect that there were two men there who I thought were probably foreign. One was middle-aged, with close-cropped sandy hair and a very large moustache, the other was a young fellow, about my own age, a little on the plump side. They kept very much to themselves and never spoke to us, but I overheard them talking once or twice. Sometimes they spoke in English, but with very strong accents, and sometimes in a foreign language. It may have been German for all I know – I am not familiar with that language, so I can't say."

"We thought they were probably keen bird-watchers," added Mrs. Whittle. "The landlord had told us that people come from all over Europe to study the birds on the Welborne Marsh."

"One evening when we were eating," Whittle continued, "a third man arrived and joined them at their table, a tall man with a bald head, and they all talked together very quietly. Later that evening, when we were in bed, I heard what sounded like a quarrel developing downstairs – raised voices and so on – and I remember wondering if it was these foreigners, but I fell asleep and heard no more."

"Nor me," added Mrs. Whittle. "Later in the night, though, I was abruptly awakened by a strange loud cry, as of pain or fear, and thought at first that it had come from downstairs. But when I mentioned it to the landlord in the morning, he said it was probably an owl, or one of the marshland birds, some of which have very strange cries that can sound almost human, he said."

"Anyway," continued Whittle, "the two foreign gentlemen left the next day, soon after breakfast. We didn't see the third man at all, so we presumed he'd left earlier, before we got up."

Holmes nodded his head and sat in silent thought for some time.

"I shall look into the matter for you," said he at length, addressing his visitors, "and let you know what I discover. As for the unpleasant letter you have received, I should not worry too much about it. It is a warning, after all, and not a direct threat, probably designed simply to deter you from asking any further questions. If you go about your daily business in your usual way, I don't think you will be troubled. However, it cannot hurt to observe due caution. Keep your eyes and ears open at all times, and avoid lonely places and dark alley-ways."

When Mr. and Mrs. Whittle had left, Holmes hurried through his lunch and went out immediately afterwards. He returned two hours later, but there was a look of disappointment on his features.

"I have been scouring the back issues of the daily papers," he explained to me as he threw himself into an armchair by the hearth and took his old clay pipe from the rack. "My reasoning was that as the menacing letter had been posted in London and written on a sheet of paper from the German embassy, then the mystery was as much connected with London as it was with Norfolk, and the solution might as well be found here as there. However, all my efforts have uncovered precisely nothing, which is a somewhat frustrating result, although not so uncommon as you may suppose when you are compiling those records you keep of my successes."

"I don't imagine it helped that you didn't really know what you were looking for."

"A perceptive remark," said my friend, nodding his head. "I have looked closely at all the newspapers that appeared in the last week of May and the first week of June without finding anything there which

118

refers in any relevant way to the German Empire, the Norfolk coast, German visitors to this country – whether to Norfolk or elsewhere – or anything else which might possibly have a bearing on the problem. However, I have learned one thing this afternoon."

"What is that?"

"That the Whittles were followed here earlier."

"How do you know?"

"Because I myself am now being followed. I observed the same man in three different places. I have no idea who he is, but he was clearly watching my every move."

"What will you do?"

"I think I shall run down to Norfolk and look into matters there. There are local papers there which may contain reports which did not reach the London Press. Perhaps I shall find some suggestive fact there. Unfortunately," he continued, with a glance at the clock, "although I could get down to Norwich this evening, it would be too late to do anything by the time I got there. I am thus obliged to sit here doing nothing until tomorrow, and I hate wasting time in this way."

I laughed, and my friend turned to me with a raised eyebrow. "I know what you are thinking, Watson," said he, "that you have never known a man waste time in as thorough-going a fashion as I do on occasion. It is true. I do not deny it. If a national championship in time-wasting were to be held, I should probably set a new all-comers record. But that is when I have no case to engage my brain. When I am on a case, it is a different matter, and it is infuriating not to be able to get on as quickly as I would wish."

"You could go down to Norwich this evening, anyway," I suggested after a moment. "You could lodge for the night somewhere in the city centre, and make an early start in the morning."

"Of course, you are quite right, old man. That is the sensible course of action. It is only tiredness and irritation that prevented my seeing it. I will take your advice, Watson, on one condition."

"What is that?"

"That you accompany me."

"I should be delighted to do so. I was thinking only the other day that it would be pleasant to get away from London for a day or two before the nights start closing in."

"Then it is settled," said he, putting his pipe down and springing from his chair with a renewed vigour, "although I can't promise that you will find our expedition the holiday you have been looking forward to, Watson." He pulled open the top drawer of his desk, and, taking out his revolver, began to examine the chambers, then he glanced my way. "Pack a bag, then, old fellow, and let us be off!"

We caught the early evening train, reached Norwich just before nine o'clock, and put up at a small hotel near the station. In the morning we rose early, took breakfast at the hotel, and were in the office of the local newspaper, the *Eastern Daily Press*, soon after it opened. There we learned that as well as the daily newspaper, several weekly papers were also published, containing news specific to particular parts of the county. Holmes selected the daily papers of late May and early June, while I looked through the weeklies. Most of the news was trivial, or of purely local interest, and I was beginning to doubt we should find anything even remotely relevant, when my companion abruptly stopped his rapid page-turning.

"Hello!" said he. "Here is something, Watson!"

I leaned over to see what had caught his eye, and read the following:

CROWN PRINCE VISITS SHOE FACTORY

Prince Otto von Stamm, crown prince of Waldenstein, has this week visited a shoe factory in Norwich, where he was conducted round the premises in the company of the Lord Mayor, and was said to be greatly impressed by the modernity and efficiency he saw displayed there. Waldenstein has long been a notable producer of hides, but most are simply exported, and Prince Otto is keen to establish a leather-working industry within the principality to help alleviate the problem of unemployment.

"That sounds harmless and banal enough," I remarked.

"Yes, Watson, but it gives us, if not a German, then a German-speaker at least, in the county of Norfolk at the relevant time. Do you know anything of Prince Otto von Stamm?"

"He appears in the Society pages of the *Morning Post* fairly regularly," I replied. "I have frequently read such references as 'Prince Otto seems to prefer London to his homeland', and 'We hear that Prince Otto has got himself into trouble again'. It is the usual sort of thing: a young foreign nobleman with more in his pockets than in his head. For some reason, London seems to act like a magnet to such people. I think he leads a fairly harum-scarum existence: visiting a shoe factory is the first sensible thing I've ever heard that he's done."

"Anything else?"

"Not really. I know he's fairly young – perhaps eight-and-twenty – but I know nothing else about him – and I know nothing whatever about Waldenstein, wherever that is."

"Waldenstein is one of those curiosities of European history," said Holmes. "It is one of the very few central European principalities which has not been swept up into the German Empire. It is very small – the population is probably not much greater than that of the town we are now in – and of no significance in itself. But its geographical position is a strategic one, lying adjacent as it does to both Germany and Austria. Its very existence creates a rivalry between the two great powers, both of which attempt to exercise an influence over it, and both of which would probably like to subsume it into their respective empires. Let us see if we can find anything else in these papers about Prince Otto's visit to Norfolk."

Our search for further reports on the young nobleman proved fruitless, but just as we were about to put the papers back in order, something caught my eye in one of the weeklies from the second week of June.

"This is a remarkable coincidence," I said.

"More on Prince Otto?"

"No, but a fellow-countryman of his, surprisingly enough." I folded the page over and read aloud the following report:

FOREIGN VISITOR PRESUMED LOST AT SEA

Franz Krankl, a visitor to Norfolk from the principality of Waldenstein, is missing, feared drowned, after a boat in which he had rowed out to sea on an angling expedition was found washed up on a beach near Sheringham. The owner of the boat, inn-keeper and part-time fisherman, Albert Trunch of Welborne, says he had warned Krankl of the dangerous currents off the north coast of Norfolk, but Krankl had insisted he was very experienced in small boats. Herr Krankl holds a senior position in the government of Waldenstein, but was apparently here alone on a private holiday, and had been out of touch with his relatives for some time. A statement issued by the coast guard makes the point that all visitors must be made aware that there is a very great difference between conditions on inland waters and those encountered at sea.

"That is it!" cried Holmes. "It must be! Whittle informed us that the landlord of The Wild Goose was called Trunch, and now here is Trunch again, connected to a mysterious disappearance."

"It is certainly a striking coincidence."

Holmes shook his head. "It cannot simply be coincidence, Watson. The odds against it are enormous. Rather, these separate events are all links in a long chain of cause and effect, which will lead us to the truth. Trunch is clearly a link, so is this man Krankl, and so, I believe, is Prince Otto von Stamm, for I feel certain that he was the younger of the two men that the Whittles saw at the inn. It is to conceal his presence there, I believe, that the register has been altered."

"But if you are right," I said as we left the newspaper offices, "and it is Prince Otto's presence at The Wild Goose that someone is trying to conceal, why should the warning note to the Whittles have come from the German embassy?"

"As I understand it," Holmes replied, "Waldenstein does not have its own diplomatic representation in London. I believe that the German embassy acts on Waldenstein's behalf when necessary, in an informal sort of way. But someone at the German embassy may also, of course, have his own reasons for keeping the truth concealed. Don't look now, old fellow, but I think we are being followed."

"Is it the same man you saw in London?"

"I believe so. Anyhow, I observed this one – a man with a large moustache – outside our hotel this morning, and now he is outside the newspaper office. Evidently he – or a confederate – followed us to the railway station in London yesterday evening."

"What shall we do?"

"Nothing – or, at least, nothing other than what we were going to do anyway, which is to catch a train to Cromer, and make our way along the coast to the Welborne Marsh. It will be interesting to see if he comes with us."

The short branch train was already standing at the platform when we entered the station. We took seats in the compartment nearest to the front of the train, and Holmes positioned himself by the window, so that he could see anyone that came onto the platform. For almost ten minutes, he had nothing to report, then, just as the guard walked past our carriage after a consultation with the engine driver, and it was evident he was returning to his position at the rear of the train to give the signal to start, Holmes gave the "view-holloa".

"There he is!" cried he. "He has just broken cover, run onto the platform carrying a large leather bag, and climbed into the last compartment! He is following us to the coast!"

122

We reached Cromer in a little over fifty minutes, and hurried from the train to make sure we secured the station fly. Of the man apparently following us, there was no sign.

"He is lying low in his compartment," said Holmes under his breath, as we rattled off along the road by the station. "I saw the crown of his hat through the window. He evidently has no idea we have seen him."

Our journey took us at first through undulating countryside, but presently descended to low-lying, marshy terrain, where the narrow road meandered like a snake past rivulets and creeks, never far from the mud-flats and the sea. From time to time we heard the sound of distant gunshots, and saw the little puffs of smoke rising up from the hollows where the wild-fowlers crouched, waiting for the birds to fly their way. At length, after about half-an-hour, we reached a small, isolated village, which I saw from a sign was Welborne. The wind was blowing sharply off the sea now, the clouds overhead were dark grey, and there were a few spots of rain in the air. Our driver did not pause, but passed right through the village and on towards the sea. Half-a-mile further on, we at last reached The Wild Goose. It was a low, spreading building, with grimy lime-washed walls and a weathered-looking thatched roof, and appeared as ancient as the ground upon which it stood.

"We don't yet have all the threads in our hands," said Holmes to me, when we had paid off our driver and stood before the weather-beaten front door of the inn, above which a painted sign depicting a flying goose swung and creaked in the wind. "We shall therefore have to approach the matter in an oblique way. If in doubt, just follow my lead."

He pushed open the door, and I followed him into the dark interior. After a moment, a young woman in an apron appeared through a doorway, but when Holmes asked if we might speak to the landlord, she informed us that he was out, and would not be back for another hour. We decided then to leave our bags at the inn and take a walk across the marsh towards the sea.

It was a wild, tempestuous day now, and the nearer we approached the sea, the stronger the wind became, and the more the gusts seemed to veer and shift about us. At length we surmounted a steep shingle bank, and there before us lay the broad, heaving expanse of ocean, the breakers pounding the shore with a boom and a crash, sending mountains of spray into the air which the sharp wind whipped into our faces. I opened my mouth to speak, but abandoned the attempt almost at once: the thunderous noise of the sea blotted out all other sounds. After we had stood shivering for a few minutes by this deafening maelstrom, Holmes plucked my sleeve and indicated that we should retire behind the shelter of the shingle bank.

123

"The sea is very rough today," said he as we crouched down in the lee of the bank. "I suppose you were reflecting on the conditions the unfortunate Herr Krankl may have encountered."

"Among other things, yes."

"I should not trouble yourself with that thought, Watson. As I read the matter, Krankl was never in a boat at all. I strongly suspect he lost his life at The Wild Goose, on the evening the Whittles heard a quarrel there."

"You believe he was the third man, the tall man who arrived one evening, but was nowhere to be seen the following morning?"

"That does seem to me the likeliest explanation. But, come, let us get back to the inn, and see if Trunch has returned yet."

At The Wild Goose, in answer to our query, Trunch himself appeared after a moment from some back room. He was an absolute giant of a man, a good six-foot-four if he was an inch, with a chest like an ox. For a moment he stood looking down upon us with an expression of disdain.

"Well?" said he at length.

"A friend of mine stayed here not long ago," Holmes began.

"What of it?"

"When he came again more recently, he found that his name had been removed from the register."

"Oh, *him!* A snivelling trouble-maker from London! If you're on the same errand, you can sling your hook!"

He made to turn away, but Holmes persisted:

"It is, of course, a criminal offence to fraudulently alter books used for accounting purposes. The authorities take a dim view of that sort of thing."

"Oh, do they? What is that to you, Mr. Know-all? Are you one of those blood-sucking tax-collectors yourself? No? Then listen, friend, and I'll tell you what my father told me when I was a young man. 'Mark my words, son,' he said to me: 'there's always some swine wanting money, and the best way of dealing with them is to tell them to go to Hell.'"

Sherlock Holmes remained unmoved. "Something else you may not be aware of is that to attempt to conceal something criminal is itself a crime. In attempting such concealment you also lay yourself open to being charged as an accessory to the original crime, even if you had nothing directly to do with it."

"Just what are you saying?" demanded Trunch. His voice was still loud and scornful, but there was a note in it now, too, of apprehension, and it was clear that Holmes's remarks had had an effect. Holmes

124

himself evidently perceived this, for he quickly pressed home his advantage.

"We know that Prince Otto von Stamm was here, and the other men."

"What if they were?" said Trunch defiantly, but the tone of bluster in his voice was rapidly ebbing away, and it was clear he was on the defensive.

"Whatever occurred here, you, as landlord, will be held responsible – "

"What humbug!"

" – especially as you helped conceal the truth by fraudulently altering the register."

"Someone else pulled out the page. I had to re-write it from memory. There's no crime in that. What else could I do?"

"But you didn't put all the names in again, did you? You deliberately omitted some."

Trunch's bullying manner had quite disappeared now. It is difficult to say what might have happened next, but we were interrupted by the re-appearance of the young serving-woman. She whispered something to the landlord and he nodded his head. "Come this way," he said to us, "and I'll tell you what happened."

We followed him through the doorway, along a corridor and into a back room. As we entered, I saw a large leather bag lying open on a side-table. Holmes evidently saw it, too, for I saw him glance that way and stop. But it was too late, the door slammed shut behind us. We turned, to see a man with a large, straggling moustache, who had been concealed behind the open door. In his hands was a large double-barrelled shotgun, which he pointed at us.

"Leave them to me, Trunch," he said in a strong, guttural accent. "I'll deal with them." He yanked open a back door and indicated we should go out that way.

"Now," said he, when we were outside in a small backyard, the cold wind whistling about our ears, "start walking." All about us as we left the yard, the Welborne Marsh stretched away as far as the eye could see.

"Don't be a fool," said Holmes over his shoulder, as we followed a muddy, winding track. "If it's your intention to murder us here on the marsh, you'll never get away with it."

"You forget, Mr. Busybody, that the wild-fowling season has now begun," returned our captor from behind me. Even as he spoke there came the sound of gunshots – one, two, three – from all about us on the marsh. "Your deaths will be ascribed to an unfortunate sporting accident. Sadly, such things do happen."

"You murdering swine," I cried. "Don't think we don't know about Krankl! Soon everyone will know the truth!"

For an instant he was silent, but it was only for an instant. "So," he cried, in a voice full of venom. "If you're so interested in Krankl, I can show you where he is lying, and then you can join him there! Keep walking!" he snarled, thrusting the shotgun sharply into my back. My mind reeled. There must be something we could do – we could not simply walk quietly to our deaths – but panic had seized me, and I could think of nothing.

Ahead of me, Holmes walked on steadily, his shoulders hunched against the cold wind, his hands thrust into his coat pockets, as we made our way deeper into the wilderness of the marsh. "Slippery path, this one, Watson," said he over his shoulder. "Mind you don't lose your footing!"

For a brief moment, I confess I was surprised that, in our desperate situation, Holmes should make such a banal remark. Next moment, I realized that he was telling me he wished me to slip and fall to the ground, perhaps as a distraction. How that would help us, I could not imagine, but if that was what he wanted me to do, then that is what I would do.

A short distance further on, as the path breasted a small rise and dropped away into a shallow dip, I saw my opportunity. I deliberately let my left foot slide away in the mud, and, with a loud cry, tumbled to the ground. At once our captor lowered his shotgun and pointed it at me, but in the same instant there came the sharp crack of a pistol-shot. Holmes's hands were still in his pockets, and I realized he had turned and fired his revolver through the fabric of his overcoat. There came a cry of pain from our captor, as the shot caught him on the left arm, and he raised the shotgun towards Holmes. With every ounce of energy in my body, I sprang up and threw myself upon him, forcing the barrels of his gun upwards and to the side. The movement evidently jerked his finger against the triggers, and both barrels discharged with a deafening roar into the open sky above us, then, with a force I would not have believed myself capable of, I swung my fist up and struck him on the chin with the most perfect uppercut I have ever delivered, sending him sprawling backwards into the mud. I quickly picked up the gun which he had dropped as he fell, as Holmes covered him, his revolver held rock-steady in his hand.

"Good man," said my friend to me. "Your swift action saved us all. Are you all right?"

"I think I may have depressed the knuckle of my third finger," I remarked as I examined my right hand, wincing with pain as I touched the spot. "It will probably need setting. I am not much used to fisticuffs."

126

There came a cry from behind us. I turned, to see a young man hurrying towards us down the path from The Wild Goose. "Stop! Stop!" he cried, waving his arms in the air. As he came nearer I recognized him from pictures I had seen in the illustrated London papers as Prince Otto himself. "Stop at once!" he cried as he came up to us, breathing heavily, his cheeks flushed with effort. "I want no more violence on my account, Schnabel. I have decided to make a clean breast of everything. After all, it *was* an accident."

"Be quiet, you fool!" said the other man in a harsh tone, as he struggled unsteadily to his feet. "How did you get here?"

"I learned late last night in London where you had gone, and caught the first train I could this morning."

"Tell us about the accident you referred to," said Holmes, covering both of them with his pistol. "It is, I take it, to do with Krankl, and Waldenstein's foreign policy."

"Don't tell them anything," said Schnabel quickly, but Stamm ignored him.

"You appear well-informed already," said he to us, "so you may be aware that my country has recently been in discussion with Austria, with a view to linking our future to theirs. This is the course long favoured by my father and his chief minister, Franz Krankl. However, Herr Schnabel here has been arguing on behalf of the German Empire that the better course is for us to favour his country. My father is frail and may not have much longer to live. When he dies and I succeed him, the decision will of course be mine, so it is something I must think about now.

"I was in this part of the country anyway, for some duty I had to perform, so Herr Schnabel and I arranged to meet for secret discussions at the most remote spot we could find, The Wild Goose. Unfortunately, Herr Krankl, who was also in England, got wind of what we had planned, and hurried here to try to dissuade me from this course of action. He arrived one evening and we quarrelled. I had had too much to drink, I admit, and was quite drunk. In the heat of the quarrel, I am ashamed to say, I lost my temper and struck out at him, he fell from his chair and hit his head so hard on the corner of the hearth that it killed him. Herr Schnabel here ushered me from the room – I was in no fit state to do anything sensible – and said he would deal with the matter. He disposed of the body somewhere on the marsh, and later bribed the inn-keeper, Trunch, to say that we had never been here, and that Krankl had hired his boat, put out to sea alone in it, and appeared to have been lost overboard."

"You have made a serious mistake," said Holmes.

"I know," returned Stamm. "I am ashamed of myself, both for being drunk, and for losing my temper with Krankl."

"That was not my meaning," said Holmes. "Your mistake was in permitting Schnabel to dispose of the body. Don't you see that that places you completely in his power? At any time in the future he could, by threatening to expose the truth, blackmail you into doing precisely what he wished you to do."

"Don't listen to him, your Highness," cried Schnabel.

"I imagine that that has been his intention all along," continued Holmes, ignoring the other man's outburst, "to have this hold over you, so that he could force you to do his bidding, as a puppet-master controls his puppets. On the night Krankl was here, he saw his chance and seized it."

"It's a lie!" cried Schnabel.

"You don't even know for certain that Krankl was really dead when you left the room." Holmes persisted. "Perhaps he was only stunned, and was finished off later by Schnabel, after you had gone to bed. It would of course suit his purposes perfectly to be rid of Krankl, who was a staunch proponent of the Austrian alliance."

"That's lie number two!" interrupted Schnabel, his voice hoarse, but Holmes's words had evidently plucked a cord in the young nobleman's memory.

"I had wondered about that," he said, "wondered if I had really killed him or not. For even in my shamefully drunken state, I had noticed that Krankl's wound did not appear to be bleeding at all, and nor was there any sign of blood on the floor the following morning."

Abruptly, the infuriated Schnabel attempted to launch an attack on Holmes, but the latter levelled his pistol at him and he gave it up at once.

"The only way to decide the matter is to examine the body," said Holmes. "Schnabel says it is buried out this way on the marsh. Will you show us where it is?" he asked, turning to the German.

"No. You can find it yourself," Schnabel responded.

"Your lack of co-operation is disappointing," remarked Holmes. "I had only permitted you to drag us out here in the hope that you would lead us to the remains of the unfortunate Herr Krankl. However, we shall find them soon enough. First, though, I think we'll all get back to the inn, and notify the authorities of what has occurred."

When we reached The Wild Goose, Trunch was nowhere to be seen, but his absence was soon explained, as the serving-girl informed us that he had gone to fetch the local constable, after declaring with great vehemence that he wished he had never become involved with these people. Just a few minutes later we heard a trap pull up outside the inn and Trunch entered, with a policeman who was almost as massive as Trunch himself. Holmes quickly explained to the policeman all that had taken place. This interview ended with Schnabel in handcuffs, and he and von Stamm going off with Trunch and the constable.

"I can't imagine what Mr. and Mrs. Whittle will think when they learn what you have discovered," I remarked to Holmes later that day, as we took lunch at a hotel in Cromer.

My friend chuckled. "Yes, it will certainly be strange for them to discover that as their honeymoon was taking its no doubt blissfully happy course, they were, all unaware, sharing a roof with international intrigue and murder!"

I heard later that the body of Franz Krankl had been recovered from a shallow grave on the marsh, but the medical examination and inquest which followed proved inconclusive. The cause of death was established with certainty as being the wound to the head, but the medical examiner stated that he could not be certain whether Krankl had been struck once, or more than once, and in the end a verdict of accidental death was recorded. Trunch, Schnabel and von Stamm were all convicted on their own admission of attempting to conceal the death, but taking various circumstances into account, and with no doubt half an eye on the diplomatic aspects of the case, the court took a lenient view and handed down relatively light sentences. Trunch therefore returned, no doubt a chastened man, to the inn on the marsh where he continued to cater for the needs of keen bird-watchers, and von Stamm and Schnabel returned to their homelands, and never, so far as I am aware, visited these shores again.

The Adventure of the
Traveling Orchestra
by Amy Thomas

My friend Sherlock Holmes, as I have observed on occasion, was at his best when investigations were at their zenith. With all of his senses and powers of observation engaged, he appeared lit from within, as if by some force neither known nor experienced by the rest of the world. In contrast, when too long a time elapsed in which a case had not presented itself – or, at least, no case possessing feature sufficient to keep his interest – that selfsame light was extinguished, progressively, until a dim shadow of the man remained, a repository of talent lacking an igniting catalyst. Such was Holmes's condition in the autumn of a year not many into our acquaintance.

We were partaking of dinner together in Baker Street, as was our usual custom, when a thought occurred to me. "Perhaps you might take up the violin tonight. Mrs. Hudson and I would be vastly amenable to a concert." I had observed the effect music had on my flatmate, a deeply calming one not unlike that of his seven-per-cent solution.

Holmes raised blank eyes to mine, his long, thin fingers closed around his glass. "I have no inspiration, Watson." Such was the exact source of my concern, for when his mind had reached that point, there was little else to expect but the drug. I fell silent, but fortunately, the lassitude was soon to be remedied.

As I finished my last morsel of sustenance, my friend rose abruptly from the table and went to the window, peering down into the darkening street. "If I am not mistaken, Watson, a client appears." His voice sounded hopeful for the first time in several weeks. I followed Holmes's gaze with my own and found it filled with the sight of a young man carrying an oblong object in his right hand.

"A musician," said my friend, and I realized that the object was of the size and shape of the sort of box that normally contains a small instrument such as a flute. Unlike many of our visitors, the man did not hesitate in the slightest to make his way to the entrance to the building.

Holmes already looked more vital than I had seen him in quite some time, and as we waited for the newcomer to join us, his energy only appeared to increase. Gone was the lethargy that had plagued him; it was instead replaced by the quickness of movement and glance that characterized the detective in his prime.

Within a moment or two, Mrs. Hudson admitted the young man to our dwelling. In the light, I could make out more of his appearance. He was tall but slight in build, of an age I put between twenty and thirty years, and possessed of dark brown hair. Now that he stood before us, he seemed no more tentative than he had previously. In fact, the air of confidence he conveyed made it seem as though his thin frame took up far more space than it actually occupied.

"Mr. Holmes?" His blue eyes passed across both my friend and myself.

"I have the honor to be thus addressed," said Holmes readily, motioning to the chair we kept for guests.

"I am Charles Green," he replied, before taking his seat, a smile on his lips. Rarely had I seen a client in such a perfect state of non-agitation.

"I see that you've come to me about the theft of your instrument," said Holmes, taking his seat opposite Green, his eyes on the instrument case that rested on our visitor's lap.

"How?" asked the young man simply. Far from appearing put out, he grinned broadly at the deduction of the missing contents of a hard-sided, closed case that did not seem to betray anything about its contents or lack of such.

"The theft wasn't a brutal one," my friend replied, "but I see signs of the center clasp, which normally locks, being pried open, an unlikely action for the owner of the instrument to perform." Green handed over the case, and upon closer inspection, I, too, could see evidence that something had bent the clasp and then bent it back.

"I also deduce from your manner," continued Holmes, "that this theft was, if not welcomed, at least not overly troubling."

Our guest smiled again and leaned forward excitedly. "It was stolen from a concert hall, along with every other instrument in the entire orchestra. If they're not recovered, or are recovered damaged, the hall will have to pay us for the lot of them. I liked my flute well enough, but the payout would furnish me with a better one. I haven't been with the orchestra for long, and my instrument is hardly worthy of it." It occurred to me to wonder, if this were true, why he had chosen to consult my friend at all. He must have realized how he sounded, for he added, "Not all of us were so fortunate. A few of the instruments were valuable enough to be irreplaceable. I've come to you on behalf of friends for whom the losses are far more catastrophically felt than my own."

"Were all the cases, like yours, left behind?"

"Yes," answered Green, nodding emphatically. "That's the strange part. They took the trouble of taking every one of the instruments and leaving each case exactly as they found it."

"Which was how?"

"We are a traveling orchestra," the young man replied. "Our members are usually responsible for their own instruments, but most of us had left them behind for a single evening of dining out. We are not wealthy, and our manager had promised us a night of rest and good food, not something we are normally afforded for free."

"The hall itself was left in the care of a guard, and we locked our instruments into a dressing room and thought little of it. The few who refused to do this are, of course, relieved and filled with the glow of justification."

"All right," said my friend, "let me ascertain the timeline of events. You and your fellow musicians arrived in London upon what day?"

"Yesterday morning," he answered promptly. "We traveled from Edinburgh to begin a series of engagements in England. We lodge at a boardinghouse near Dorrigan Hall, which is in – "

"I know where it is," said Holmes brusquely. "Continue."

"We arrived by train in the early morning hours, and had only long enough to deposit our personal belongings in sparsely-furnished rooms before we were spirited away to rehearse in the hall, a schedule we are accustomed to keeping. We observed our usual agenda of four hours of practice, then a half hour for dining, and back to the grindstone in the afternoon."

"What did you do with your instruments during your midday meal?" I was gratified that the same question my friend asked had also occurred to me.

"We kept them with us," answered Green. "Food was brought to us from a local public house."

"Very well. What of your evening entertainment?"

"Before we recommenced our rehearsal, our manager, Mr. Pike, informed us that we were all to be his guests last evening at the Hotel Durrants on George Street, a fact that was met with a great deal of excitement by most members of the orchestra, who are little accustomed to such luxury, especially at Pike's expense."

"It is unlike him, then, to offer such a gift," murmured Holmes.

Green nodded. "I don't mean to imply he's an unfair employer. He's scrupulously conscientious in his dealings and, I think, errs more on the side of leniency than severity in most instances; but he is not a rich man. He's in a better way than most of us, but he's far from truly wealthy, at least as far as any of us have ever seen in his person or manner of living."

"I see," answered Holmes.

132

"As I said previously," Green kept on, "most of us left our instruments in a large dressing room on the right side of the hall, with the assurance of a sturdy lock, a competent guard, and the hall's responsibility for their safekeeping. Musicians, as a rule, care for our instruments, but only a few of us are so particular as to require them with us at all times, especially considering how little most of them are worth."

"The theft was discovered, I take it, upon your return," said Holmes. I could tell that he was beginning to grow impatient with the repetitive part of Green's narrative.

"Yes," came the answer. "We returned to our boardinghouse after six hours of practice to prepare ourselves up for the evening. From there, we were taken by taxicab to Durrants, where we dined very well, drank good wine, and generally enjoyed ourselves. We returned in the late evening, determined to rehearse for one more hour, but we were greeted by a locked room of empty instrument cases and a guard who was at the other side of the building and claimed utter ignorance."

"Peculiar," said my friend. I hoped that this portended his willingness to take the case and finally escape from his recent malaise. "Why did you not consult me sooner?"

The young man sat back in his chair. "I had not – as you said before, I did not have the strongest incentive for approaching you. It was only after – "

"After the young woman with whom you are in love made her distress known to you." Green nodded wordlessly and did not ask for an explanation of Holmes's deduction.

After a moment of silence, he explained, "I became aware of your talents last year. I read about your exploits in the newspaper during our last trip to London, so when Doris – Miss Lake – told me of her distress over the loss of her viola, I spoke to Mr. Pike about consulting you."

"I'll admit – " He looked down at his interlaced fingers, "that I did not quite believe that you could be real or your reputation justified. However, Pike mentioned the idea of consulting you to Mr. Dorrigan, who owns the hall and will be out a great deal of money if our instruments remain lost, and he expressed great faith in you and tasked me with coming here straightaway to consult you about the matter."

"Very well," said Holmes. "Now I wish to see the scene of the robbery."

We engaged a taxi, and within minutes, found ourselves passing through the London streets toward a part of the city that might almost be called fashionable, except that the highest echelons of society were never seen there on account of it being too affordable for those they considered

133

irrevocably beneath them. In other words, it was a place of social passage between the low and the high, where those who wished to climb rubbed shoulders with those who had fallen.

After a brisk ride, we arrived in front of a large, solid building that clearly belonged to its place in the city: Dorrigan Hall. I had never attended there, but I had certainly seen theatrical entertainments and heard concerts in similar places. It was of a new style, constructed, I thought, within the past decade. Eight entrances opened it to the street, and the tall façade was impressive with its arched doorways and massive windows.

We entered in the deepening dark of evening and found ourselves in a large vestibule designed to accommodate large crowds of patrons before a show. It was, like the outside, functional rather than opulent, but there was an impressive quality to its newness and scrupulous cleanliness.

"You're back." A soft, feminine voice spoke to us as we passed through the low-lighted lobby. Holmes, Green, and I were alone, save for the owner of the voice, who quickly joined us. Miss Doris Lake was a small, pale young woman with a shy smile. As we spoke our greetings, I fancied I could understand her association with Green, whose open and confident temperament was so much the opposite of her own. Nevertheless, her voice was low and lovely, and she had striking blue eyes that made her otherwise ordinary face attractive. She took Green's arm as soon as she could manage it and clung to him as we made our way about the premises, which were much as I had expected, avoiding the appearance of extreme opulence or extreme tawdriness. We were still standing in the front room while Green explained the basic layout of the hall, when a short, round, and extremely fast-moving man entered from somewhere in the deeper environs of the building.

"Charles!" he said breathlessly, as if he'd been exerting himself, "I'm glad to see you. Who are these gentlemen?"

"This is Dr. Watson and Mr. Holmes, the detective I was sent to seek."

"Oh, thank goodness," the other man replied. "I've had nothing but questions from every quarter the entire time you've been gone. The Misses Blake are threatening to – to leave us, after all these years!"

Holmes cleared his throat. "Mr. Pike, I believe?"

"Oh, yes, sir," said the agitated man. "I'm so pleased you've come."

"Then please allow us to proceed on our tour of the premises," said my friend shortly, though I hardly blamed him. The man seemed harmless enough, but he was not in a helpful frame of mind.

Green, as calm as ever, picked up where he'd ceased and continued to explain the structure's simple design of main auditorium with wings on either side, the left of which contained practice rooms and the right dressing rooms, with offices in the back, behind the stage. The hall, while primarily concerned with musical entertainments, sometimes also hosted small dramatic productions, so its allotment of dressing rooms was greater than might be supposed necessary for an orchestra or an individual singer.

Once he'd finished his overview, Green led us through the vestibule and into the auditorium, which was illuminated but empty, save for a lone cellist who sat upon the stage and played his instrument without looking up as we entered. I thought that he had not heard us come in, so great was his concentration. It was curious, to my mind, that one of the remaining instruments was one so large and unwieldy. I tried to imagine him carrying it to a restaurant and had some difficulty in doing so.

"All right, Robert?" Once we were close enough to the stage to be heard, Green addressed the cellist in a loud voice. The auditorium held, by my estimation, about four hundred seats, so it did not take long for us to make our way down the center aisle to stand in front of the stage.

The man, who was white-haired and elderly, looked up and blinked, immediately ceasing his playing. "Aye, Charles. Can't get a moment of quiet in the wings. Everyone rushing this way and that. Came here to be alone."

"Ah, yes, yes, everyone's in a terrible roar," said Pike, who was trailing behind and seemed entirely ignorant of the fact that he was part of the commotion. Robert the cellist did not seem overly fond of his manager, for he did not answer and simply stared down at him from his place atop the stage.

I did, for a moment, wonder if the strange subversion of a flute player having more obvious authority than the manager of the orchestra was the normal way of things for this particular group, or if it had merely arisen out of the present circumstance.

Holmes was, as I would have expected, growing impatient by this time, and he simply strode toward the doorway on stage right, which opened into the left side hallway. Green, Pike, and I followed along, and as we turned, I heard Robert's cello begin again, eerie in the emptiness.

"The room where it happened is this way," said Green, leading us to the third door on the right. When we reached it, Holmes studied the lock for a moment. "No sign of any sort of tampering or forcing," he said.

"None at all," answered Green, "but both keys to the room were accounted for the whole time – one with Pike and the other with the guard."

I followed Holmes inside the practice room, which was a large, bare space with nothing but rickety wooden chairs, upon which and against which were balanced all manner of instrument cases. It looked, to all intents, like the players had left them moments before.

"Once the theft was discovered, we asked everyone to leave things exactly as they'd been before, or as nearly as they could remember," Green offered.

"I take it the police haven't been here," said Holmes dismissively. "It looks far too unmolested."

"That's correct," offered Pike. "Mr. Dorrigan, the owner of the hall, doesn't want to involve them unless it's absolutely necessary, in order to avoid the terms of contract that force him to pay for the instruments."

Holmes rounded on him. "I should think you'd have something to say about that."

The man blanched. "I – didn't think there was any harm in it. No one's moved anything, and we sent Green to consult you when we realized there wasn't a simple explanation, like a joke of some kind."

"No matter," said my friend, almost to himself.

As I had many times before, I watched Holmes do his work. First, he walked around the room, as if to gain an understanding of it from every angle. Then, he moved through the rows of chairs without touching anything. Finally, he began a systematic examination of every instrument case in the room.

Green, Pike, and I stood behind, not saying anything while he did his work. By this time, it was quite late in the evening, and our inactivity led to drooping eyes and flagging energy. I was certainly eager to hear Holmes's opinion on the matter, but I could little discern of his thoughts from his actions.

Finally, when we had been at loose ends for many minutes, Holmes looked up from somewhere on the right side of the room. "Were any instruments moved to a new position in the room after the discovery, any at all?"

"None, for I watched the entire exercise," boomed a voice from behind me, and I looked back to see a tall, broad-shouldered man in the doorway. His face wore a sour expression.

"Mr. Dorrigan?" Holmes came over and gazed on the man without revealing any of his thoughts.

"Oh, sir, here is the detective," said Mr. Pike quickly, like a mouse addressing an intractable elephant.

"So I see," said the newcomer, fixing his eyes on my friend as if he didn't much care for what he saw. "I hope you'll be able to make an end

136

of this ridiculous matter. Surely the theft of an entire orchestra's instruments is nothing but someone's idea of an unfortunate joke."

"Perhaps," said Holmes noncommittally. "Mr. Green informed us on the way here that the members of the orchestra are all on the premises. Please fetch the players of stringed instruments for me."

We were taken to another room, a slightly smaller space with a few tattered, cloth-covered chairs. "Would you like them sent in as a group or individually?" asked Green.

"One by one," answered Holmes. "Mr. Green, your assistance will not be required."

The first musician to enter the room was a middle-aged woman with long white hair, who slowly sat down opposite Holmes and me and smiled. "Come to find what's happened, have you?" she asked with a broadly northern accent.

"We hope to attempt it. Now, then, Mrs. Stoker, please tell me where your seat is in the orchestra and what instrument you play."

"If we go to the next room, I could show you," she said, inclining her head in the direction of the room we'd just exited.

"That will be unnecessary," said Holmes. "I am familiar with orchestral seating, and I have the room's layout stored in my memory."

"All right," she answered. "I'm a second violin. We're opposite the firsts. I'm third from the center."

Holmes wrote this down in a notebook he pulled from his jacket pocket. "That's all that will be necessary. Send in the next one." I looked over at my friend, mystified. Even I, with my limited powers of deduction, had surmised that if none of the instruments had been moved, Holmes really didn't need the musicians themselves to answer his questions. The evidence was already present, and surely Pike could have told him where they sat.

Nevertheless, I didn't have time to ask Holmes anything before we were joined by a middle-aged man with a slight limp. He took his seat and stared at the floor, a bit bleary, as if he'd been on the bottle.

Again, as before, Holmes asked incidental questions and was answered without issue. Finally, as the man prepared to leave the room, he turned back. "I hope you find my viola," he said.

This happened twice more, once with a young man of awkward disposition, and again with an elderly, emaciated male violinist. Each time, my friend asked the same questions and received simple answers. Each time, I was mystified as to his real purpose in asking.

Finally, after the fourth musician exited the room, there was a slight delay before the next entered, and I turned to my flatmate, who stared straight ahead in his uncomfortable chair and said nothing. "Holmes," I hissed, thinking we might be interrupted again at any second, "what on earth are you doing?"

He bent the full intensity of his gaze upon me and, unexpectedly, smiled, answering rapidly, "You're a medical man, Watson. I didn't think it could have escaped your notice."

"What do you mean?" I asked, but just then, Doris Lake entered the room. Compared to her fellow musicians, she was a burst of life, alert where they had been nearly somnambulant.

"Good evening, Miss Lake," said Holmes, smiling. "I apologize for the ceremony, but I didn't have a chance to ask you about your seating position in the orchestra. Mr. Green informed us of your instrument."

"In the chair right behind Mrs. Stoker's. You've already spoken to her, I believe."

"Yes," answered Holmes. "That's all I need from the string section. I would, however, like to speak to Mr. Pike and Mr. Dorrigan again."

Miss Lake nodded. "If you follow me, I'll take you to the office." I noticed as we exited that Green was nowhere to be found.

The girl took us past a few clusters of gathered orchestra members, who stared openly. I wanted to pity them; surely it must be distressing, I thought, for so many to have lost the sources of their livelihood. But their gazes were strange, unnerving, as if they weren't quite right.

We went through the hallway, past other small, empty rooms and back toward the dark area behind the stage, where Dorrigan's office was located. The area wasn't large, but it had enough room to contain an outer and inner sanctum. Miss Lake knocked on the door of the outer office. It was opened by a young, dark-haired man with a moustache and pock-marked skin.

"They weren't expected yet, Doris," he said sharply.

"Nevertheless," she answered meekly, "they're ready to see Pike and Dorrigan."

The secretary nodded and knocked on the inner door, which was soon opened by an irate Dorrigan, who frowned even more deeply than before when he saw us. "I had understood you as wanting to question members of the orchestra."

"So I have," said Holmes coolly, "and I am now finished."

"Pike isn't here," said the man tersely, "but if you'd like to speak to me, I suppose I can't prevent you."

"Just so," Holmes replied. "If I may, I would like to speak to you, Green, and Miss Lake together." Dorrigan's brows knitted together even more forcefully, but he nodded once and shouted for his secretary.

Miss Lake returned first, and it was another ten minutes before Green joined our awkwardly silent group. Upon entering the room, he immediately took the girl's hand. Dorrigan presided over his enormous wooden desk, and Holmes and I sat on its other side, with our chairs facing outward, toward the young people who stood before us.

"How long have you been obtaining opium for the members of Pike's orchestra, Miss Lake?" The girl's face went even paler than it usually was as the words of Holmes's question poured over her.

"I – we – Mr. Green is my fiancé. That is my only position of importance."

"No," said Holmes decidedly, though not cruelly, "he isn't. Or, if he is, that certainly isn't all he is, but you know the truth. I would like you to tell it to me now."

"How did you know?"

Holmes answered after contemplating her for a moment. "Your empty viola case was in the wrong section of the practice room. Every other instrument case in the orchestra was in its proper location; only yours was incorrect, obviously a signal of some kind. I could have attributed this to the confusion after the theft was discovered, but it wasn't a seat or two away from its place. It was in the middle of the woodwinds. Of course, when I first discovered the case, I had no idea whose it was, but that was easy enough to ascertain by questioning members of your section."

She shook her head and gave Dorrigan a desperate look. "He said – he said that you wouldn't know about that. He was afraid the police would bring in a musical expert of some kind, but he said one detective wouldn't know difference, so I mustn't risk anyone seeing me move it back."

"My musical talents are less renowned than my others," Holmes replied, "but I certainly know how an orchestra is arranged." The irony was not lost on me, for I was well aware, as was Holmes, that if they had called in the official force, the likelihood of anyone noticing a detail of that nature would have been nearly nonexistent. They had bet on one man, but he was entirely the wrong man.

Holmes added, "Every member of the orchestra whom I've met up to this moment shows the effects of opium – not the most acute effects; Pike wouldn't have allowed that, but I recognized its lingering presence in their lethargy. It was too coincidental to assume that your instrument signal was uninvolved in something so unusual. Now," he continued firmly, "the truth."

She nodded, resigned. "I met James Dorrigan two years ago, when our orchestra was first engaged here. It was a good time for us. Pike was delighted, because this hall represented a step up in the world, a foothold in London. Green hadn't joined us yet – of course." I did not know what she meant by this, but Holmes obviously did.

"The night of our first concert here, Dorrigan caught me bringing the opium to our members, something Pike had paid me to do for three years previously, using the placement of my viola case to signal the members that the drug was available. He recruits members from opium dens, supplies them with the drug, and then pays them nearly nothing, supposedly because they owe their wages to him as payment. He makes a profit, and they don't know they're being cheated." Her contempt was palpable. "The only reason I did his work of giving out the drug once he obtained it was that he threatened to put me out on the street if I didn't, and I had nowhere else to go – I'm not accomplished enough to join a more important orchestra, if one would even take a woman, which is extremely rare, and I had joined this one without realizing its true nature."

"The night Dorrigan found out, he threatened to terminate the contract and cancel our remaining three performances on account of the disgrace of it. This would have been disastrous. Pike had already put up what little collateral he had to transport us to London, under the promise of a large profit. I knew that he would blame me for being indiscreet, so I offered Dorrigan a deal – part of the profits from the opium in exchange for being quiet and letting things go on as they had been. The potential of making money far eclipsed any scruples he might have had."

"I had to tell Pike, but I waited until I had things arranged with Dorrigan. Pike is – he's not an utterly unkind man, and he took a more charitable view than I'd expected. He offered to divide the loss of Dorrigan's share with me, so the three of us were, effectively, in business together."

She stared daggers at the owner of the hall. "Of course, we'd have liked to get rid of Dorrigan as part of the equation, but he had the upper hand. He threatened to spread the news publicly of our orchestra's particular – interest and destroy our careers just as they were beginning to improve. That was the reason for the theft. Pike stole the instruments in order to force Dorrigan to either pay for them or agree to relinquish his share in the opium. If Dorrigan refused, Pike intended to go to the police and force him to honor his contract. By then, the instruments would have been long destroyed. It was Green's idea to go and see you and ascertain your likelihood of solving the case. He was only to bring you if he thought you would be easily deceived." Holmes smiled at this, and I realized that not only had Green been trying to fool us, but Holmes had also been fooling him all along, using flattery and simple deduction to look as if he esteemed his own abilities as much greater than they were.

At that moment, someone yelled. I realized, after my initial surprise, that it had sounded like a male rather than a female voice. Miss Lake and I stared at each other for a few seconds, but Holmes wasn't paralyzed by surprise. He was at the door in an instant and nearly collided with a white-faced Robert the cellist. "It's Pike. He's – dead."

Holmes swore under his breath. I followed him out of the room, dazed, and into the dressing room wing. Sure enough, Pike lay in the middle of a deserted room with his throat slashed. From the look of things, I surmised that he'd been dead for at least a quarter of an hour.

Holmes turned to Miss Lake and Green. "No one may leave this building. I'll have the murderer contained presently." I could tell that he had no intention of concealing his purpose from any of the orchestra members, who stood around the corpse with wide eyes and horrified faces.

"Where is Mr. Dorrigan's assistant?" my friend continued. "I have need of his abilities."

In that moment, Green tried to flee the room and was only caught by the resourceful Robert, the cello player, who pinned him to the floor easily.

"Mr. Green," said Holmes, giving him a hard stare. "Your disguise was a good one, but not good enough."

Doris Lake looked as shocked as I've ever seen anyone be in my life. "Charles, you – "

"You weren't the only one with secrets, Doris," said Dorrigan. "Didn't you notice that Green joined you just after my discovery of your arrangement? I sent him to you to make sure you and that fool Pike didn't cheat me. I didn't order him to do a stupid thing like killing Pike, though," he said, utterly disgusted.

"Neither Pike nor Miss Lake appears to have made the connection to your secretary," said Holmes, "but I believe you did." He indicated Robert, who was still sitting on Green with good cheer.

"He had me fooled at first," said Robert, "but it was just too ideal – the way he'd found the orchestra, settled in so easily. He did well to keep himself from being seen in his other guise, but he couldn't entirely avoid it."

Holmes nodded. "I recognized the connection between Miss Lake, Pike, and Dorrigan first, but then I realized Green's recent entry into the orchestra and swift courting of the lady couldn't be without significance. I didn't know what it portended until I saw that Dorrigan's secretary was the same man."

Robert the cellist smiled. "Most policemen don't get to use their musical talents. I suppose I should be grateful for the opportunity. I'm only sorry to have to go back to my usual duties after such a long and interesting digression. I'm also sorry, of course, that I didn't prevent Pike's death."

At this moment, Green, who had been silent, exploded. "I did it for Doris, to free her from this – imprisonment! No one was supposed to come to this wing. In the morning, when the body was discovered, Dorrigan would have been suspected."

"Contingent," said Holmes mildly, "on your identity as Dorrigan's secretary remaining undiscovered and on no one poking about the way Robert has. You wouldn't have come out of this well either way, but killing Pike was a fatal mistake, one I doubt you'd have made if you hadn't determined that I trusted you completely, as I intended you to believe when you visited my flat."

"My name is Williams," said the cellist, "Inspector Robert Williams, Scotland Yard. You may think little of us, Mr. Holmes, but one of my associates – Gregson – saw a pattern in the information he obtained from one of his informants in the opium business. I was tasked with joining this unfortunate group many months ago, and I have been trying to build a legal case against them for some time."

"Yes, Inspector Williams, you're free to give your report to Scotland Yard. Your competence has been, frankly, a welcome surprise. Pike's death is a pity, but it's not your concern to anticipate the actions of a mentally unstable and narcissistic criminal."

"I agree," the man answered with a grin.

In the end, none of the participants in the orchestral case faced retribution except Miss Lake, Dorrigan, and Green. The lady stood trial, but since her precise level of knowledge of the opium operation beyond her activities as intermediary could not be determined, she was allowed to go free, with her broken heart as her only punishment. Dorrigan, who had possessed extensive knowledge of both the legal and illegal aspects of Pike's involvement in the opium business, faced an unsympathetic jury who were plied with tales of ruined lives. He was given a prison sentence likely to outlast his earthly life. Green, his guilt easily proven through evidence and his own angry admission, was sentenced to hang. I cannot say that the thought of him being removed from the earth bothered me a great deal, but I did ask my friend why anyone would engage in such a blatantly ridiculous act as murdering someone when Sherlock Holmes was on the premises.

142

"I have seen it before," Holmes answered placidly. "Some criminals crave being caught and appreciated for their deeds. You saw the man when he first approached us. I've never met a more perfectly narcissistic personality. I believe he thought he could not fail in his plan to frame Dorrigan and free the lady, and all the better to have the satisfaction of knowing he'd done it under my nose. Barring that, he seemed to think Doris would love him more as a result of his the murder." I shook my head in disbelief.

"Still, this must be the most quickly-solved case of your career," I said. "Though the details are ugly, your investigation was not."

Holmes, who enjoyed praise far more than he liked to let on, smiled. "Thank you, Watson. The details and mistakes of the participants aligned to give me an excellent foothold, to say nothing of Williams's ingenuity, but I believe I did well enough with what I was given."

A month after the closing of the sordid case of Pike's orchestra, Mrs. Hudson and I were finally treated to the concert I'd suggested prior to Green's fateful evening visit. For once, however, my friend did not play alone. He was accompanied by a middle-aged policeman whose cello seemed to fill up the room. Williams was not as accomplished a player as Holmes, but then, few were. Still, I could tell by Holmes's expression when they played that he found the man's efforts satisfactory. I hoped, temporarily, that their shared interest might lead to my friend engaging more in society, but that was never his preference at any point in our acquaintance, and his first evening of musical partnership was also his last.

The Haunting of
Sherlock Holmes
by Kevin David Barratt

In the events that I have recorded elsewhere as "The Adventure of The Speckled Band", I wrote that the case had more singular features than any that I had encountered up to that time in the April of 1883. Six months passed and my days with Mr. Sherlock Holmes seemed to settle back into a familiar routine until the receipt of a letter in the October of that same year set off a train of events that brought the whole horrific episode back into my life once more.

I kept few secrets from Sherlock Holmes. Indeed, as he seemed able to glean facts from the littlest things that I said or did, I found it almost impossible to keep anything to myself. However, my family and its history were not subjects into which I wanted him to intrude, and until now I had succeeded in keeping them private. The letter that came was from my sister-in-law, who wrote to tell me that my brother, who was a gambler and a heavy drinking man, was currently in poor health because of his excesses and that she had reached her wits end with him. She begged for me to try and step in before he killed himself, or before one of his moneylenders did it for him. My brother had made and lost a substantial amount of money in the gold fields of Australia, and years back I had received a similar summons to the other side of the world to assist them in fleeing the country. They had now settled in Scotland, but a visit would mean being away from Baker Street for some time, and this was not a particularly good time to leave. Holmes had been behaving strangely of late. Cases had recently been in short supply and, knowing the ways that boredom affected him, I was convinced that his long-standing drug habits were again being employed, despite his attempts to hide them from me.

"You must go, Watson," Holmes declared, as I sat opposite him before the fire.

"Yes, I suppose that I must," I mumbled, lost in my thoughts. I then jerked myself back from them and said, "This habit of yours is beginning to get tiresome. How much have you deduced from my thoughts this time?"

"Very little," he admitted, "but it is obviously a summons for help from someone dear to you."

144

It was at this point that I told Sherlock Holmes a lie. "It is not from someone dear to me, actually, but from an old comrade from my university days who wishes me to spend some time in Scotland looking after his medical practice because he has to travel abroad on family business. I could be away for some time and, depending on the date of his return, I may not be able to get back to Baker Street in time for Christmas. That is why I am deep in thought."

If Holmes saw through my fabrications he was polite enough to not show it, but, as he had rightly said, I must go. I quickly made arrangements to travel as soon as possible. I left Mrs. Hudson with my brother's address in case she needed to contact me. I could hardly leave it with Holmes, now that I had lied to him, but I believed that I was not the only one keeping secrets. Holmes may have the greater intellect, but I have the greater medical skills, and I can spot the effects of drug misuse as easily as he can spot footprints.

My time in Scotland was spent in attempting to rehabilitate my poor brother and saving his marriage. His gambling and drinking had resulted in a spiralling descent into a sickness of body and mind such as to leave him unrecognisable as the loving husband and brother that I knew him to be. He had sunk so low into debt as to pawn our dear father's watch, a treasured heirloom that, as the oldest son, he had inherited some years ago. I believe that it was the death of our father that had first set him on this road to ruin.

By employing a generous amount of tender care and an equal portion of steely resolve, I succeeded in keeping my brother away from alcohol and gambling for two months. His spirits revived enough for him to recommence work and earn money again. As a sign of gratitude for his compliance and efforts, I presented him with a gift. I paid the pawnbroker for the return of our father's watch. My brother was so grateful that he broke down in tears and vowed never to return to his old ways. His wife was, of course, delighted, and she begged me to stay with them for Christmas. Despite my eagerness to return to Baker Street, I did not feel able to refuse her generous hospitality.

Unfortunately, I was soon forced to change my plans. A letter arrived from Mrs. Hudson and it was couched in words of distress. She expressed concern that Sherlock Holmes was ill. He was spending practically all his time indoors, forsaking company of any kind. She had tried to let in clients on a couple of occasions, only for Holmes to shout at her from the landing. Even Inspector Lestrade had been turned away. She wondered what it could all mean. I had an uncomfortable feeling that it meant trouble.

145

It also appeared that, despite Holmes's insistence on no visitors, he must have taken a new lodger into our rooms. The man who could go for days with little nourishment had suddenly taken to demanding more frequent and larger meals. He had also been heard shouting at someone, "You will not succeed with your plan, you devil! You will not!" This was often followed by the heavy sound of something being thrown at the wall. Things reached a head when Mrs. Hudson heard a fearful banging on our door. She reached the top of the stairs to find the door locked. When she called to Holmes, his voice screamed at her from the other side, "Help me! Find Watson! Please, find Watson!"

With a heavy heart I explained that I had to return home urgently. Feeling that I had done as much as I could for my brother, they both agreed with my plan to make a hasty return to London. I dare not begin to contemplate what I may find upon my return, but I was fearful for Holmes's safety from whomever, or whatever, now occupied our rooms.

It was Christmas Eve when I arrived back in the Metropolis. As I made my way from the train station back to Baker Street I saw shopkeepers and passers-by making the most of the festive season. Groups of singers stood on street corners, gloved and muffled against the cold. Everything appeared normal, in stark contrast to the thoughts running through my head. As I entered 221b, our landlady came running up to me, clearly in a state of distress. The anxious looks upon her face showed that she was both pleased and relieved that I had returned. Words tumbled from her, and I had to raise my hands to silence the torrent.

"Mrs. Hudson, please calm yourself. Firstly, let me thank you for sending for me. Secondly, I do not know what I will find, so I beg of you to return to your rooms until I have evaluated the situation."

She said, "Be careful, Doctor. Whoever this other person is, he must have some nasty hold over Mr. Holmes, or why hasn't he let me call the police and have him removed?"

With a promise to speak to our landlady later, I left my case and coat in the hall and ascended to our rooms. Each of the seventeen steps seemed to pull at my feet as if to prevent me from reaching the door. I was also aware that I was holding my breath, as if I was fearful to make a sound. However, I must have made some sound for, as I reached the landing, I heard the turn of a key, and our door was thrown open. Holmes stood on the threshold in his dressing gown.

Such a change had come over my friend. His face was grey, sweat stood out upon his forehead, and he had a look of intense horror upon his face. His voice came as a croaking rattle as he said, "Oh, Watson! Watson! Thank God you've come."

146

Grasping my coat sleeve, he pulled me inside and quickly closed and locked the door once more. He stood with his back against it, and I could see that he was shaking, as if in a considerable state of anxiety.

"Holmes, you are shivering," I said, my voice filled with concern.

"It is not cold which makes me shiver," Holmes said in a voice that seemed to come from a great distance. "It is fear. It is terror."

At these words, the hairs seemed to rise on the back of my neck, for I had heard these exact words before. In April, Helen Stoner of Stoke Moran had said the same in this very room before laying her story concerning the speckled band before us. Slowly, I approached Holmes, guided him to his armchair, and sat him down. I offered him a drink, but he made no reply.

As I poured him a large brandy, I looked around. The room was a mess, with a number of objects on the floor by the door to Holmes's bedroom, as if he had been throwing them at it and had left them where they fell. The table and sideboard were weighed down with a large number of dirty plates and dishes as if they had not been cleared for days. A strange thing was that it looked as if there had only been one diner. There was no fire in the hearth, and the whole room felt as cold as the grave.

I placed the glass to Holmes's lips and made him drink a little brandy. As he gave a choking cough a little colour seemed to return to his face. I poured myself a drink and sat across from him in my own chair.

"Holmes, you spoke just now of fear and terror. Fear and terror of your mysterious guest?"

"Guest, Watson? There is no guest. What is here has come uninvited."

"And what is here?" I asked quietly.

Holmes appeared to be looking over my shoulder towards his bedroom. When he spoke, although I recognised the voice, the words were not what I expected to hear from my friend.

"As you know, Watson, I am not a superstitious man, and logic tells me there are no such things as ghosts, and yet I say in all faith that I am being haunted by an evil spirit."

"Evil spirit? Surely – "

"An evil spirit with a name, Watson, and that name is Dr. Grimesby Roylott."

Despite the look of seriousness upon his face I had only one reaction to his announcement. I broke into a hearty laugh. As tears began to roll down my face, I saw tears of another sort roll down Holmes's face. I fell silent, and Holmes continued with words that again came from

147

Miss Stoner, spoken in a high voice with an intensity that sent a thrill down my spine.

"Oh, sir, do you not think that you could help me, and at least throw a little light through the dense darkness which surrounds me?"

It was not the lack of a fire that suddenly chilled me. I leaned forward and looked into Holmes's vacant eyes. My heart seemed to stop until I saw a light return to them. When I spoke, it was in a voice that showed him that I no longer doubted that he was a troubled man.

"Holmes, I swear to do everything that I can to help you through this."

"Thank you, my friend," he replied, and again I saw tears well up in his eyes.

After another mouthful of brandy, Holmes proceeded to explain the events that had brought him to this singular position.

"At first it began as a feeling that something was approaching. I forbade Mrs. Hudson to let anyone into the house, but as time went on I knew it was already here. I began to hear Roylott's voice coming from my bedroom."

I asked what the voice had said, but I feared I knew the answer. He became animated and began to shout, "Meddler! Busybody! Scotland Yard Jack-in-office!" As he settled down again, he said, "At all times of day I heard him, but no matter what I threw at him, he kept on returning to taunt me. He warned me that day when he came here to keep myself out of his grip. Well, now he has me in that grip, and matters are approaching a climax."

"What makes you think that?" I asked.

His voice took on a distant sound again and the pitch rose as he said, "Because during the last few nights I have always, about three in the morning, heard a low, clear whistle." I remained silent as he continued, "I sprang up and lit the lamp, but nothing was to be seen in the room." The light then returned to his eyes and he looked at me.

"Holmes, this is intolerable. If you truly believe that someone is whistling in the night and menacing you with a snake, how does the snake get in and out of your room? There are no vents, no bell-ropes."

"Spirit snakes do not require bell-ropes."

"And spirit snakes do not attack the living in their beds. For Heaven's Sake, Holmes, return to your senses before it is too late."

"If these things are but fancies of an addled brain, Watson, how do you explain this?"

He got up from his chair and went over to his desk. He opened the drawer and returned with our poker. It had been bent in half, just as Roylott had done on his visit. I sat in silence. I knew now that any answer I made would not appease him. Instead I asked him what he needed me to do.

His eyes glazed over once more and in a hushed voice he said, "There is a distinct element of danger. Your presence might be invaluable." Then he seemed to return to himself again as he added, "For goodness' sake let us have a quiet pipe, and turn our minds for a few hours to something more cheerful." Instead of reaching for his pipe, his hands clenched into fists, his eyes seemed to roll up into his head and he lapsed into unconsciousness.

As Holmes slept for what might have been the first time in days, I built up a fire and tidied the room a little. I collected up as many dirty plates as I could and carried them down to Mrs. Hudson. I took tea with her and assured her that I would take good care of Holmes. I asked her to trust me when I said that I was sure that he would soon be returned to his old self.

I returned to our rooms to find Holmes was still unconscious. I unpacked my case then, washed and refreshed, I took a Clark Russell sea story from the bookcase and settled in for a long night ahead. As I read, the adventure took me onto the high seas far away from my friend's troubles and spirit snakes. I became so engrossed in my book that I lost track of the time and it was soon eleven o'clock.

As the clock struck the hour, Holmes opened his eyes. "That is our signal," he said, springing to his feet just as he had done at the Crown Inn many months ago.

Lighting a lamp, he crossed the room and put his ear to his bedroom door, then silently motioned me to him. Making a trumpet of his hand, he whispered in my ear. "The least sound would be fatal to our plans." With the lamp before him he slowly opened the door and stepped into the room. Of course, it was empty.

Holmes returned to himself again. "Good. Roylott is unlikely to try anything until I am in bed, so this is what we must do. Watson, you must stay with me tonight, keeping watch. As we know from the events at Stoke Moran, the snake does not strike every time and the victim may escape for nights. I have been lucky so far, but eventually it will kill me. Therefore you must be ready to kill it first."

Holmes removed his dressing gown and hung it behind the door. I placed a heavy chair against the same in order to bar any means of entry or exit. I set tables at both sides on which I placed a drink, my book, a lighted candle, some matches, and a stout stick. As I settled into the chair, Holmes climbed into bed and extinguished his lamp, leaving the flickering flame of my candle as the only illumination. It cast strange shadows across his anxious face.

"Do not go asleep, your very life may depend upon it," he whispered, his voice taking on that far away quality once more. "Have your pistol ready in case we should need it."

"And risk shooting you in the dark? If anything should appear I am sure my stick will suffice."

No answer came. Holmes had lapsed into unconsciousness once more. I took up my Clark Russell in the hopes that the thrill of the tale might keep me awake, but with the strain placed on my eyes from the dim light and the tiredness of a long day, I am ashamed to say that I fell asleep.

A sibilant sound penetrated my mind, like the hissing of a kettle. I opened my eyes but could see little for my candle had burned down to a stump and was barely flickering. The hissing stopped, and as my eyes grew accustomed to the gloom I could make out Holmes, resting up on his elbows and looking down his body.

"You see it, Watson?" he yelled. "You see it?"

Fear gripped me for upon Holmes's chest there was something long and thin in the shape of a letter 'S'. I could not make out any details in the dim light, but it appeared to be trying to move towards Holmes's neck as if to strike at it.

With no thought for my own safety I leapt across to the bed, grabbed the vile thing and hurled it into the corner of the room. Taking up my stick I followed it and beat it, and beat it, and beat it, until I was certain that it must be dead.

Quickly I lit the lamp on Holmes's bedside table. He was now sat upright in bed, his face ashen, sweating profusely. His eyes were fixed on the corner of the room, his lips quivered. "The band! The speckled band!" Holmes whispered, and then his eyes closed. He sank back onto his pillow and was asleep once more.

Turning away from him I approached the corner of the room and could now make out the coiled object on the floor against the wall where it had fallen. I could barely believe what I saw lying there. It was the cord from Holmes's dressing gown.

It was Christmas Day, and all the churches around were ringing out their glad tidings. It was now late morning and I was sat before a roaring fire with a cheery drink and pipe. When Holmes's bedroom door opened he was dressed, and I had to admit that he looked more like his old self than he had done on the previous night. He certainly sounded like his old

150

self as he bellowed, "Merry Christmas, Watson, and the greetings of the season to you." Crossing to me, he handed me a box. As he stood warming himself before the hearth with a broad smile, I opened the box. Within it was the morocco case containing his syringe and bottles of drugs. I looked up at him.

"What does this mean, Holmes?"

"It means that it is all over," Holmes answered. As he prepared his first pipe of the day, he began to explain. "As you were aware before you left on your travels north, there had been little to stimulate my brain. As a result of this I began to use more and more drugs to counter the boredom that possessed me. Without your presence to keep me in check my intake grew to the point where I began to fear for my safety. One night I resolved to stop completely in order to surprise you with the news upon your return, and that is what I did. Unfortunately – "

I interrupted him. "Unfortunately, you suffered the consequences of your actions. As a medical man I have read much about the misuse of drugs and their effects upon the body, and I am well aware of the symptoms caused by sudden withdrawal from them. There is a growing feeling of agitation and much restless behaviour, and then paranoia sets in. This was why you began to believe that Dr. Roylott was haunting you, and explains why you shut yourself away from all visitors, even Lestrade. You became convinced that he was in your room, even believing that you could hear his voice. It was no wonder that Mrs. Hudson believed you had a new lodger, for as well as holding bizarre conversations, you were eating enough for two. An increased appetite is another symptom of sudden withdrawal. I think I am correct in saying that you began to suffer vivid and unpleasant dreams, and that during one of these dreams you walked in your sleep. Do you remember how, in April, you had the strength to straighten the poker again after Roylott had bent it?"

Holmes chuckled at the memory, but said nothing, to allow me to continue.

"It was you who bent the poker in half this time, and then returned to bed with no knowledge of your actions. Finally, we come to the events after my return. How long had it been since you last slept?"

Holmes lit his pipe and sank into the chair opposite me. "Two days, maybe three."

"And by that point you could not distinguish fantasy from reality. Hence, the drama that played out last night. I believe that you have been reading my notes on the Roylott case."

Holmes smiled. "How do you deduce that?"

"My notes are my memory of what was said and done, and thus may vary from the actual events. Yet, you quoted me word for word on many occasions."

Holmes gave a hearty laugh and clapped his hands. "Wonderful, Watson."

"Then the dressing gown cord arranged upon your chest to look like a snake, the hissing sound you made to waken me. Due to the flickering light of my guttering candle, I did think that I saw a snake slithering up your body, but I had been deceived. It was your conscience that created the entire illusion. You told me that you did not think that Roylott's death would weigh very heavily upon your conscience, but I believe that it had more of an effect upon you than you realise."

"Perhaps it did, but thanks to you, I hope to have finally defeated my demons. Hence, my gift to you."

I looked once more at the case before me. It appeared that not only had I saved my brother from the path of self-destruction, I had now assisted in saving Holmes from his personal demons. But, I wondered, in both cases, for how long?

"Holmes, I cannot accept this gift. I will accept you as a patient and help you as much as I am able, but you must appreciate that only you can ultimately conquer this thing."

"But we have conquered it," Holmes replied.

"Not yet, Holmes. You must understand that this might not be the end of your troubles, and that dark days and nights may still lie ahead for the both of us."

"Nonsense, Watson. The ghost of Dr. Grimesby Roylott has been well and truly exorcised." As Holmes puffed on his pipe, he paused to add, "But there is one detail, however, that appears to have been overlooked within your theory."

"And that is?"

"The dressing gown cord."

"I have explained that," I replied.

Holmes shook his head. "Not at all, my friend. Consider this. How could I have got up from my bed, crossed the room, and taken the cord from my dressing gown without waking you? Remember, you were sat against the door and my dressing gown, with tables at both sides blocking my approach. It would have been impossible to reach without moving either a table or yourself, and what is it that I try to impress upon you? When you have eliminated the impossible, whatever remains, however improbable, must be the truth. Don't you agree, Watson?"

The Allegro Mystery
by Luke Benjamen Kuhns

As I glance over my notes between '82 and '90, I fondly remember those early years. I, having returned to London from my Afghan campaign with a Jezail bullet as a souvenir in my limb, was by no means ready for civilian life. I will always be grateful to Stamford for introducing me to that strange bohemian man, Sherlock Holmes, whose powers of observation and deduction continue to astonish for nearly quarter of a century.

It was in the autumn of 18– when one of the strangest cases found its way to the doorstep of 221b. While the story received some press, a proper and accurate account of the event has yet to reach the public. I feel, also, that the parties concerned in the matter have reached a time of life where these events would be nothing more than a thrilling story of their youth. A wound long since healed as opposed to a freshly bandaged scrape.

"I have put her away for good, Watson. I have put her away for good!" said Sherlock Holmes with a sweeping entrance into the study. I folded the paper.

"Who have you put away?" I asked.

"Miss Susan Sutherland, my dear fellow! For months she's plagued chapels, music halls, theatres and busy streets, pick-pocketing any inattentive fool."

"Well, this is the first I have heard you mention her, Holmes."

"Yes, well, you have had your own matters to attend to of late. Though I deduce you aren't friendly with Miss Edwards any longer."

"Good heavens, Holmes!" I barked. He smiled.

"She has kept you from our work the past few months, but looking at the state of your hair, the longest it's been since you met her, and the state of your whiskers, your personal grooming says there is no one to impress."

"Not that it is any of your business, but you are, as always, correct." I rubbed my face, my whiskers had become rather unruly and were in need of a good trim. "Tell me about this Miss Sutherland."

"Right!" Holmes began as he continued through the study and fell into his chair. "Sutherland, quite the villain I should say." Holmes picked up his pipe and filled it with tobacco from his Persian slipper. "I got word that men and women were being robbed in church services across

London. And don't give me that look, Watson. The robbery was not the minister collecting the tithe. The robberies were from individual pockets and handbags. Change, watches, bracelets, and even rings were slipped off. Raptured away! I discovered that each of the robberies were on the person's right side. So, I was looking for a left-handed crook. Of course the difficult thing was finding the person hiding in plain sight. I had to find the disguise among the general public façades in the crowd."

"How on earth did you catch them, then?"

"Accessories, Watson. It all came down to simple muff."

"A muff?"

"Correct." Holmes took a deep inhale of his pipe before exhaling and continuing. "This is where I found Susan Sutherland. She always kept her left hand inside her muff."

"I thought you said the thief was left handed." Holmes raised his finger to me.

"So I planned my trick to take place at one of her places of worship. Having disguised myself splendidly as an old woman with a monstrously huge bag ripe for the plucking, I sat and waited. Soon enough, she sat by me, just to my right and her left. Then I felt it!" Holmes said slapping his hand upon his knee. "Her hand was inside my bag. I peered over to see her left hand still in her muff. My assumptions were correct. I, too, had a similar plan. As she reached into the bag what she did not expect to find was my hand inside. I grabbed hers, threw off my disguise, and exposed her. Then one of Scotland Yard's finest came to cart her off to a cell." Setting down his pipe and pressing his fingers together, he leaned his head back and a smile of satisfaction stretched across his face. "Though, there is no guarantee that any or all the stolen belongings will ever be recovered. Most are likely lost to the pawnbrokers."

I clapped my hands together.

"Well done, Holmes!" I paused a moment. "And I am sorry for my absence of late. I pray you won't hold it against me?"

"Watson, all matters of love I leave in your hands. While I haven't the time or energy for such commitment, I can, at the very least, understand the game you play. For love is a game, maybe the most dangerous game of them all."

There was a ring on the bell followed by the sound of hurried steps up the stairs. A woman, my God, a woman burst into the study. I turned quickly, Holmes slowly lifted his head. The fairest creature I had ever seen stood there, pale faced and gasping for breath. There was a familiarity about her, I thought, as I marvelled at her tall slender frame. She wore a long green dress and large floral hat. Her dark blonde hair had fallen loose from under her hat. This porcelain woman, with striking rosy cheeks, darted her blue, gem-like eyes between myself and Holmes.

"I am looking for Mr. Sherlock Holmes," the woman asked in a French accent.

"I am he," Holmes returned

"Then you must help me, sir!" she pleaded, still standing in the doorway panting.

"My dear, won't you have a seat. You are flush," I said. She looked at me with a blank stare before nodding quickly. She glided across the floor, her green dress flowing with every step. I called for Mrs. Hudson to bring us some tea.

"Mademoiselle Dipin," Holmes said, "what can the West End's shining star need with my services?"

"You know me?'

"I know you are rising star, with a one-off stint at Her Majesty's Theatre performing an exotic ballet. No paper in London has missed the show."

"It is a beautiful story," Mademoiselle Dipin began. It seemed that whatever concerns she had upon entering our rooms vanished as her mind turned back to her art. "The movements, the music, oh it's . . . ." She pressed her fingers to her soft lips and kissed them.

"So I've heard, though yet to see," said Holmes.

"And you might never get the chance." Her face turned to stone. "I cannot say how much longer I'll survive the show."

"Is your life in danger?" I asked. She looked at me, her eyes piercing.

"For the last two-and-a-half months we performed and all seemed fine, but it began with letters."

"Tell me all from the beginning. Leave no detail out, no matter how trivial you might think it," said Holmes.

"Then, to tell you of recent events, I need to tell you about my past. My stage fame has inspired many devoted followers. They attend more shows than the lead actor or actress themselves, it seems. They wait outside the stage door, they bring you flowers, chocolates, many different gifts. If you miss a show they send you a card. It's quite remarkable what the fanatics will do for you. A mutual appreciation for the art brings people together.

"I love these types of people, Mr. Holmes, those who love the art and can discuss the art. But some," she paused and clasped her hands, and nervously twiddled her thumbs, "they see you as the embodiment of art, and assume you are the final authority on it, rather than one of the

155

many channels by which one can demonstrate it's beauty. Back in France I had many admirers. Some were harmless. Some were more . . . forceful.

"There was a man named Jean Javet. He believed he was in love with me. He started by offering flowers after performances. I thought nothing of it at the time. I graciously accepted his gifts. That was my first mistake. Next, he started sending letters. In the beginning, they spoke of his love for my art and how passionate my movements were. Saying how he'd never seen such marvellous style and superb technique.

"From time to time I would write very gracious letters in return, thanking him for his compliments and coming to see the performances. I started to become a concerned after a rather poor review was published in one of the local papers. The critic called our performance a disgrace, scandalous, and said it should be ended now. One never forgets a terrible review. I did my best to put it to the back of my mind. Some people will always hate your art.

"A few days after that the review, I received a letter. Monsieur Javet took great offence on my behalf for the review. He ranted about how terrible they were for saying such harsh things, and that the paper should know the error of their ways. I replied saying it was no issue and that we must move forward in our art. He replied with a single letter, 'Our art will be beautiful. I will make sure no one speaks of you and our art that way again.'

"I was slightly haunted by this response. What he meant I did not know, at the time. A few days later the paper that published the review was set on fire and burnt down! There was no evidence, no clues at all as to who started it or how it happened. It was passed off as an accident. Javet wrote me again, this time he said, 'Our art is saved'. I knew what he meant. I knew he was responsible, but I did not know if I should turn the letter over to the authorities. Would they believe me?

"I waited, foolishly. Mr. Holmes, I waited! That very night after my performance, I was the last to leave the theatre. When I left, Javet was outside the stage door. He rushed me and took me in his arms. He raved about our art and love. I pleaded with him to let me go. He continued to speak of our love and what love does to art. He said he loved me and forced a kiss on me. I was confused, frightened, and alone. I said I had no feelings for him.

"This angered him. He pushed me against the wall. My breath was taken from me. I tried to regain composure, but he held me gently and caressed my hair saying, 'No, no, you do love me, you do. I know it. We are both artists, and we'll make beautiful art.' I dug my nails into his face and tore his skin. He fell back holding his face, which began to drip with blood. I ran, he chased. Thankfully, a policeman was nearby and heard

156

my cries. He stopped Javet and arrested him. He was tried and sentenced to jail for the fire and assault. That was three years ago this last July."

She paused a moment. "This brings me to now. At the end of the first week's performance here in London, I received a letter." The ballerina took out a piece of paper and handed it to Holmes. He took it and quickly read it before handing it over to me. It read thus:

My beautiful Mademoiselle, How I've missed your art. How I've missed your movements.

How I've missed your touch. I am excited to see you on stage in London very soon.

Keep a watchful eye, I will be there.

J

"I have been frightened terribly by this. I did not keep this letter a secret, but I was assured measures would be taken to ensure my, and the entire cast's, safety. During my second week's performance I got another letter. It was from Javet. He said how wonderful the show was and how I am the light of London. He promised he'd see more performances, and that I'd never be out of his sight again." Her eyes began to well and her lower lip quivered. But she remained strong. She straightened herself and fought back the tears.

"Two nights ago, I believe I saw him in the audience. He was not seated. He was standing in a doorway. He made a nod and hand gesture at me, like an American salute. It was the only time during a performance that I have ever stumbled! The next day he wrote again, saying how pleased he was to get that reaction. Then, last night on my way home, I was followed. A man, of similar stature to Javet, followed me from the theatre, through Leicester Square. It was heavily crowded and I took the opportunity to hurry my pace and get away. I made haste to Soho where I have lodging while I am here in London. Before I entered, I looked and took no notice of anyone else. I sat at my table and looked at the newspaper. An article in it spoke of you and your assistance to the Yard. I looked you up and thought if anyone could help me, it would be you!"

Holmes looked at the woman a few moments. "Well, well. You fear, then, that this Javet has escaped or been set loose from his cell in France and is here in London to watch you perform, and possibly more. Have you made enquiries with the France police to see if he is still there?"

"I have not, no," she admitted. Her cheeks flush with embarrassment.

"No need to blush. These are enquires I will make on your behalf. If this man is in London, and intends to cause you torment, I assure you he will be found and his deeds exposed."

"Mr. Sherlock Holmes!" she cried. "So you will help me?"

"I will." Holmes handed the woman a slip of paper. "Please write your address on here. Continue life as usual. Please know I might call upon you at various times and places if need be." She nodded excitedly as she scribbled down her address and handed it back to him. "Tell me, the letters you received here in London, have you kept them?"

"Yes, I have."

"Good. Then I will send Watson here to fetch them and bring them back to me," Holmes looked at me. "That is, if you have nothing else pressing, my good fellow."

"Indeed, I do not! I would be happy to get them." I passed a friendly smile at the ballerina. She smiled. The out-of-breath and frightened creature was gone. The woman who sat before us now was different, more confident, more enticing. It was no wonder she had driven a man to lunacy.

"And you won't mind if I keep this letter until the others arrive?" Holmes asked, holding up the document which she had presented to us.

"It is yours. I never wish to see it again."

"The last thing I would like to know, what does Javet look like?"

The woman swallowed and jutted her chin slightly. "He is Lucifer," she said.

"Ah, but my dear woman, Lucifer, according to the holy text, is a beautiful being," interjected Holmes.

"Then Javet is a troll who belongs under a bridge," she returned.

"Let us not get carried away with bitterness. I want straight facts."

"Forgive me, Mr. Holmes." My friend nodded and motioned for her to continue. "He is about your height, but stalky. Broad chest and thick skinned. He is not a fat man, though. He, last I saw, had thick whiskers on his cheeks, but his chin and upper lip were clean. He will now have the scars from three scratch marks on his left cheek from me. His hair is dark, black or dark brown. I've only seen it from under his hat and at night. I do remember him having a thin upper lip and a dot in the centre of his chin. He is a very strongly built man, Mr. Holmes."

"Thank you, Mademoiselle." Holmes turned to me.

"Shall I retrieve those letters?" I asked.

"Yes, we can take a cab," replied our guest.

158

"If you will bind the letters with a thread and set it just outside your door, Watson will wait in in the cab collect them once you have set them out, I don't want anyone to see him go inside," said Holmes.

We were off in a hurry. I sat next to our alluring client. The crisp autumn air filled the cab as we bounced down the streets. I peered, causally, out the window to see if we had been followed. Nothing out of the ordinary caught my attention. Mademoiselle Dipin sat calm and quiet, keeping her face away from the windows. I would ask her questions about the show, but her responses reminded me of Holmes when he was busy with thought. Short and vague. We passed through Soho Square before coming to a stop a few yards behind the ballerina's door. I watched as she darted out, looking back and forth, before vanishing into her building. I stepped out of the cab just as the door opened enough for me to catch a glimpse of her dainty hand leaving a bundle of letters bound together. Putting them safely into my pocket, I returned to my cab and ordered the driver to return to Baker Street. When I did, Holmes was nowhere to be found. A note had been left which said he had gone to enquire about Javet and would return later. I did not see Holmes the remainder of the day. What exploits he had engaged himself with were not learned until I woke the next morning.

I found my friend lying on the floor on our bear rug. He gazed intensely at the ceiling. At his feet lay scraps of paper, and to one side lay the letters I had retrieved. I bade him good morning. He was, as on several occasions, unresponsive. I glanced the room for any sign of his cocaine usage, which had, at times, been the cause for his silence.
"Fret not, good fellow," he said. I turned to look at him. He remained unmoved except one hand extended into the air. Grasped between his index finger and thumb hung one of the letters. "I have been in engaged with this. I seek solace in cocaine when there is nothing to stimulate my mind." I rose an eyebrow at him. He finally turned his head slightly to look at me.
"What have you done?" I asked.
"Look at the floor and make a deduction," he encouraged.
"It seems like you've created a mess," I said sarcastically.
"Beyond the most obvious, Watson," his tone became stern, which I found surprising.
"It looks like you have been comparing papers to the letters, given the different makes you've laid out."
"Well done!" He said cheerfully. "After I sent a message to the Continent to learn the whereabouts of Javet, I came back to find these

letters. I immediately rushed back out, after having thoroughly examined then. The letters are all written in the same hand, of that I have no doubt, even the ink is the same, as was the pen that was used. The paper, dear Watson, on which our man scribbled, is not all the same. So I scoured the city to see where these types of papers are relatively found."

"What was your conclusion?" I pressed.

"The paper is off poor quality. Sold primarily through street vendors. Most vendors won't give you what you pay for and you run out of your sheets soon."

"So our culprit is new to town and grabbed cheap paper, which is why you know this man used it so quickly?"

"The ink, Watson, is a fine ink. Expensive to obtain. He is buying cheap paper from street vendors in order to avoid being recognised in more well established retailers. How I know he's using it quickly: On two of these letters there are three droplets of ink that correspond when the pages are placed together. The man dipped his pen in the ink and it splatted and stained both pages. What I do believe is that our man has set himself up in Islington, somewhere near Angel."

"How did you come to this?"

"Street vendors!" He exclaimed and shot up from the bear rug. He rifled through the paper and the letters. He matched the letters to the blank sheets of paper. I stood over him and looked down. Written on the new sheets at the top left corner was the name of the vendor and a street where they were sold. "It took me most of the day and into the evening but I found them all. There are three vendors who sell these papers in the Angel area. I took their information, and once I learn about Javet from the French authorities, I will go retrace that avenue if need be."

"When do you expect to hear back?"

"I sent a message to Monsieur Dubuque of the Paris police," Holmes was interrupted by a knock on the door.

"A message for you," said Mrs. Hudson, poking her head around the door. Taking it from her, I handed it to Holmes. In a single thrust he leapt to his feet from the floor.

"Come, Watson! The game is afoot!"

Silently we sat in the cab. My heart raced with excitement and curiosity. Mademoiselle's apartment had been ransacked during the late morning, between nine and eleven a.m., and Inspector Lestrade of the Metropolitan Police had called for our assistance. When we arrived, two police officers stood outside. They waved Holmes and me through.

The apartment was a devastating mess. Cabinets where toppled over, clothing was scattered and torn, pillows were thrown here and there.

Shreds of paper were under every step. Inspector Lestrade stood in the middle of a small lounge near Mademoiselle Dipin. Her face was buried in her hands for a moment before running them through her extraordinary hair, pulling it back away from her beautiful face. When she saw Holmes and me, she stood up and approached.

"I am so glad to see you, Mr. Holmes," she said.

"Yes, good of you to come in such a hurry," said Lestrade.

"What do you know?" Holmes asked making no time for pleasantries. Lestrade nodded at the lady.

"Nothing seemed out of the ordinary. I did not notice myself being followed or feel that someone was watching me. I've been about my daily business. I spent most of the morning at the theatre. I came home to relax for a few hours and freshen up before I returned this evening. When I got home, I found the place like this!"

"The lady here has told us about this Javet character. He seems a good suspect," said Lestrade.

"Yes, but we are not certain where he is at present," returned Holmes.

"He's certainly in London!" Lestrade said with a chuckle. "The girl told me about the letters and everything."

There was a commotion outside; officers were shouting. We could hear the sound of several feet thumping up the stairs.

"Where is she? Where is my daughter?" echoed the voice of a strong woman. She stood in the shadow of the doorway, majestic, towering some six feet tall. Glowing golden hair was fashionably tied up and styled on top of her head. She was certainly a woman who, in her prime, would have been stolen the hearts of every man. While still very handsome, she was the type of woman who now preferred softly lit rooms. Tucked under her arm was small box which she clung to tightly.

"*Mere!*" cried Mademoiselle Dipin. Her expression was of utter horror. "What are you doing here?"

"I have come to speak with you, and when I do, I find you caught up in a mess!" the matriarch returned. "Tell me what has happened!"

"It seems your daughter has caught some unwelcome attention by an enthusiast for her art," said Lestrade. Her mother scoffed. "We believe he's the one behind it all."

"It's Javet, *Mere*."

"That man?" she roared. "This is why I come here, to beg your return to Paris at once."

"I won't leave, *Mere!*"

"But can't you see, this is punishment? Holy judgement for pursuing such an unholy profession!"

161

"You're wrong!" Mademoiselle Dipin yelled.

"Come now, ladies," Inspector Lestrade chimed in. "Let's just calm down." The tension between the two women slowly eased.

"What are you doing here?" Holmes asked our new arrival.

"I am here to see my daughter," she replied.

"Yes, but why?" he pressed.

"To beg my daughter's return. Are you deaf, sir?" She rolled her eyes. "I would do anything to get her to come home where it is safe!" The ballerina's cheeks began to turn red.

"Do you know about Javet?" Holmes asked. The woman shook her head.

"Why do you have such a fervent aversion to her performing?" I asked.

"Look at it, already! She was stalked and attacked in Paris, now her home has been vandalised." She turned towards Lestrade. "And what you are doing to keep my girl safe? Scribbling in your notebook! "

"*Mere*, please. I beg you, stop!" asked Mademoiselle Dipin.

"Ladies, calm down, shall we?" said Lestrade. "I assure you, Madam, that we will do our best to find the one responsible," assured Lestrade. Holmes let out a sigh.

"Have you questioned any of the *corps de ballet*?" the girl's mother asked. "It wouldn't be the first time an up-and-coming tried to push the *Prima* out!" Lestrade turned back towards the ballerina.

"I . . . I don't know."

"Have you noted any peculiar behaviour?" Lestrade asked.

"I have not, well . . . no. It was nothing." Mademoiselle Dipin trailed off, her face blank as if she recalled something.

"Very well, then," said Lestrade. "We will get to work on this Javet character. Mr. Holmes, a word outside, please."

We left the mother and daughter in the apartment and stood outside in the cool air. The mother had made the room warm with unease. I found the brisk air refreshing.

Lestrade stated, "What do you make of it?"

Holmes replied, "The mother is an odd character."

"I shouldn't wonder if it was her who has done all this," said Lestrade. "What with coming here like this all the sudden, wanting her daughter to leave. She's probably organised it all."

"Javet is very much a possibility," said I.

"We won't know until later," said Holmes.

"The young girl said you were currently looking for this Javet. Any leads?" Lestrade asked.

"Nothing that I can reveal."

162

"Holmes! You aren't you're own authority," snuffed Lestrade.

"Do remember, I am not employed by the Yard. It was the girl who hired me. My duty is to her and her safety. If there is any information that is beneficial to both parties, I will share. Presently there is not. I will keep you updated, Lestrade." Just then the girl's mother rushed out the front door and jumped into a cab. Her elegant face was distorted by a horrid expression of anger and grief. Her daughter followed, holding the box which her mother had held earlier. She only saw the back of the cab pull away. "Your mother has quite the temper, dear girl."

"She does. She hates my work, my art," she returned.

"Has she always hated it?" I asked. She nodded.

"She has, yes."

"What did she give you?" I pressed, looking at the box. She opened it to show us two ballet shoes tucked inside.

"For someone who hates your art, I'm a little surprised by her choice of gift," said I.

"She said she picked them up from the theatre. A gift." I nodded.

"Might I have a solitary word?" asked Holmes to the ballerina. The two walked off a moment. I stood there, Holmes's back to me, watching our client answer whatever mysterious questions he posed to her.

"He's bloody brilliant, but he boils my blood sometimes," scoffed Lestrade. Holmes and the girl turned and came back towards us.

"For now, Watson and I must go. We have other business to attend." I gave Holmes an inquisitive look. Without so much as a nod or wink he took off in a fast walk. I jogged behind a moment to catch up, leaving Lestrade and Mademoiselle Dipin behind.

Holmes and I arrived that Her Majesty's Theatre and walked inside. During our cab ride, Holmes told me about the brief conversation had with Mademoiselle Dipin. He, too, noticed her uneasy expression when her mother asked about the *Corps*. The girl admitted that one of the fellow dancers, Esther Daines, who would be first in line to replace her, should anything happen, ducked out of a rehearsal about two hours before she came home. Mademoiselle Dipin said that she hadn't been close to Miss Daines and didn't pay her much attention, but noted her acting uneasy before she left.

"If ever there was a motivation, Miss Daines would have it, Holmes," said I, as we walked the backstage halls of the theatre. "Mademoiselle Dipin is a remarkably handsome and elegant woman. I'm sure jealously follows her wherever she treads."

"Jealously, Watson. A waste of an emotion. It spurs people and drives them to ludicrous decisions that never reveal a positive outcome.

163

Look at David and Bathsheba, jealous for another man's wife, so he sends that man to the frontline of war, and he's slain."

"It is a monstrous emotion, but do you mean to tell me you do not feel it?" Holmes did not reply. "Truly, Holmes?"

"I suppose I have had my experiences with it, yes." Holmes stopped. "Ah," said he tapped his knuckles repeatedly upon a closed door. It swung open and a short girl with big bold green eyes and dark brown hair greeted us.

"May I help you?" she asked. He voice was mouse-like.

"I am Mr. Sherlock Holmes, and this is my friend and colleague, Doctor Watson. Aren't you Miss Daines?

"I am, yes . . . ."

"We are professional enthusiasts for your art, and we hoped to speak with you," Holmes continued.

"Well, I, uh . . . are you sure you mean me and not Dipin?"

"No, no! We mean you." I stood there and watched Holmes. I smiled and nodded at the girl, who reluctantly allowed Holmes and me into the dressing room. As we followed, Holmes continued to converse with her about the ballet. I noticed no one was around. She sat at a table littered with cosmetics and large mirror at the back. Holmes pulled a seat over and they continued talking.

"I feel you should be the lead!" said Holmes. Miss Daines blushed.

"But Dipin is a master," she replied.

"Wouldn't you like to lead?"

"Of course, it is my dream."

"Rumour has it Mademoiselle Dipin is being stalked again. Rumour has it some people aren't keen on her being here, and they want her out of town." Miss Daines frowned and laid her hand on the table. "Maybe you can take over?"

Miss Daines moved her hand, knocking over bottle of perfume. She frantically tried to pick it up. Holmes reached over and caught the bottle before it rolled over the side. "Yes, I've heard that, but well," she said, as Holmes handed the bottle back to her. "No. Of course I don't want her to go." She seemed startled and uneasy.

"Sorry if I have crossed a line. I mean no offence," said Holmes.

"It's quite alright."

"We really must be going," said Holmes, "but thank you ever so much for letting a couple of excited fanatics a chance to speak with you."

"Well, at least one of you spoke. Your friend here seems shy." Miss Daines smiled her perfect smile at me.

"I am just pleased to be here . . . ." I said. She extended her hand and I kissed it. Holmes tapped my shoulder and we left.

164

"What was all that about?" I asked as we walked down several narrow corridors.

"I wanted to see if Miss Daines did have any aggression towards Mademoiselle Dipin."

"You couldn't have possibly learnt anything from that maskarade!"

Holmes pushed a door open and we came outside. "As a matter of fact I did. Miss Daines has been writing letters!"

We walked back to Baker Street. My friend became a silent companion was we made our way through Piccadilly, over Oxford Street, and up Baker Street. Upon our return there was a letter from the Continent. Holmes ripped it open and read out.

Mr. Holmes, I have looked into the whereabouts of Monsieur Javet.

He was jailed but served his sentence. Has taken a lodgings outside the city.

I confirm he has not crossed the channel, nor hasn't in some years.

I cried, "My God, Holmes, he isn't here?"

"Seems not. I have a few things to look over the rest of the day. I shall come to you when I need a companion." Holmes walked into his room and shut the door gently.

The next day, I was awakened by a sudden jerk. Holmes had his hand pressed to my shoulder.

"Did I wake you?" he asked.

"You did, yes."

"As you are awake, might you do me a kindness?"

"Name it," I returned.

"I need you to go to Mademoiselle, tell her to end all her performing, and leave at once for the Continent by the morning."

"Is her life in danger?"

"Go to her now!"

I went off immediately to find our ballerina and relay Holmes's instruction. It was not unlike Holmes to keep his plans to himself. As much as he criticised my apparent romanticising of his adventures, he, too, had a flair for the dramatic when he drew a case to a close. This was

165

no exception. Holmes was playing this so very close to his chest. But his reasons were always valid. Holmes was an endless enigma. His methods were strategic but unpredictable. What the game was rolled over in my mind again and again as I made haste to our client.

Arriving at the theatre, I found Mademoiselle Dipin. She was in mid-rehearsal. The stage was full of ballerinas in tutus, their legs bound by white stockings. They bent and twirled this way and that with impeccable timing. They flowed together, and everything was natural, like the movements of the oceans as tides comes and go. Mademoiselle Dipin was glorious. She wore her outfit with pride and seduction. She was a magnificent sight to behold! Everything about her was a masterpiece. She eyes lit when she looked out into the auditorium and saw me. She waved her hands and the productions stopped. She floated towards me.

"Doctor Watson, what brings you here?"

"Holmes has sent me with word," said I. Her expression suddenly tensed. "He's said the game is over. It is best for your safety that you stop performing and leave the show."

"I demand a reason. What is happening?" she snapped.

"He hasn't informed me. He's just told me to come and tell you at once. He's asked that you pack and leave by morning." The woman look at me with horror. Her breathing increased. Was it panic or anger? I could not fully tell, perhaps a combination of the two. Watching this fine artist be told she must abandon her art for her safety – when has an artist done such a thing truly?

"No!" she roared. "I won't go. I won't do it. This is what my mother wants. This is what the villain who is chasing me wants, to ruin my life." She stormed off. I began to follow her. She darted onto the stage again. She called Miss Daines over. Our sweet ballerina looked at Miss Daines and instructed her to do something. She snapped her fingers and Miss Daines went off. I was taken aback by this. The woman, so gentle before, seemed tense and fierce. Miss Daines returned, looking most unhappy. She carried a pair of ballet shoes.

"I've brought these like you asked," I heard her say. Mademoiselle Dipin took them into her hands, slipped off her old shoes and put the new on. She looked at them a moment and balanced herself momentarily. She clapped her hands then the rehearsal began. She began to move and glide across the stage. She was picked up and twirled. The soft shuffle of feet could be heard against rhythm of the orchestra. She began to twirl furiously around, the clicking of her shoes echoed as she balanced between spins. Suddenly she slipped, her legs buckled and she fell, letting out a cry of pain. I stood. A crowd rushed around her. She was

166

escorted off stage and taken to her dressing room. As I followed, I caught a glimpse of Miss Daines, who looked to be smirking. I found Mademoiselle Dipin in her private room with her leg propped up. Her shoes were on the floor. I examined her leg and foot. She has sprained her ankle, at least several day's rest would be in order.

"I should have left," she said to me.

"What happened?"

"A problem with the shoe." She turned her head towards them. I picked them up.

"Heeled? Unusual."

"I wanted to try them. They are like the shoes of old."

"Looks like the heel broke," I observed. I examined it closely and sniffed the heel. I attempted to put Holmes's own power of deduction to use. I ran my finger along the broken edge. "Who gave you these shoes?" I asked.

"My mother. She said they were left for me here."

"By who?"

"Miss Daines got them as a gift."

"Excuse me," came a mouse-like voice from behind. It was Miss Daines. She looked at me with surprise. In her hand she held a letter. "Don't I know you?" she asked.

"I believe we met," I returned.

"Yes, the shy man. Your friend was very talkative."

"What do you want?" Mademoiselle Dipin snapped.

"I wanted to say sorry. The shoes. I was told they were strong, I didn't know they would do that." She fiddled with a slip of paper in her hands.' "

"What is that?" I asked.

"This came for her just now." She handed her the letter, which was read immediately. Mademoiselle Dipin looked at me with despair.

"Miss Daines, leave us please." When the girl had gone I looked over the letter.

I hope the shoes fit

J

"It's him," she said, with an exhale.

"I must let Holmes know what has happened." She looked at me longingly as if to say, "Don't leave me alone here." I put my hand on the lady's hand. "I will make sure no more harm befalls you. Give me a moment." Leaving the shoes, I spoke with a young stage hand and asked him to stand watch outside her rooms and see that she went nowhere. As I walked through the theatre, I saw Miss Daines. She was with a tall, dark-haired man. Tears ran down her face and he embraced her. A man wearing flat cap with a bucket and mop shuffled past the two, bumping into them.

"Watch where you're going, geezer!" the dark-haired man shouted.

"My apologies, my apologies," the old man echoed, shuffling past me. I exited the theatre and found a police officer outside. I begged his assistance and told him to go inside and watch over the ballerina. When I said I was working with Sherlock Holmes, he did not hesitate. We both rushed inside, but when we got to her dressing room she has vanished. The young man who I instructed to watch her was unconscious on the floor. We revived him, but he had no recollection of what happened. On her table was a note the said she was leaving and not returning. My heart sank. I needed Holmes. I looked for the broken ballet shoes but they were nowhere to be found! I took my leave and raced to Baker Street.

When I arrived, I ran up the stairs and into the study. I called out for my friend. Holmes came out his room, quickly shutting the door behind him. He held a rag and was wiping his face. I took a moment to catch my breath.

"Sit down, man," he said to me.

"We have a problem," said I. "At the theatre, Mademoiselle was hurt. The shoes her mother brought to her . . . ."

"They were tampered with. The heel was weak and bound by cheap glue, with the intent of causing physical harm to our dear ballerina," Holmes finished. I look upon him with utter amazement.

"Holmes! You are magician! How can you know?" He picked something up from his chair and tossed it over to me. It was a flat cap. "That was you?" I asked. "Tell me what you know!"

"Let the night play out, Watson. I have a few things left to arrange. Tomorrow morning all will be revealed. Tonight, though, you and I will attend the ballet."

We did just as Holmes said. The crowed was buzzed with excitement. Murmurs of Mademoiselle's departure was talked about by almost everyone we passed. Miss Daines had finally slipped into the lead. As for the performance began, she was elegant and graceful with her movements. Watching, one would think she had always been the lead. Holmes watched the stage, not as a spectator, but like a hawk. He disappeared after intermission, leaving me to watch the remainder on my own. After the show, as I made my way through the lobby, my arm was grabbed. It was Holmes.

"Where have you been?"

"Putting the final pieces in place," he smirked.

"You are enjoying this too much, Holmes!"

"Well, aren't you the detective who was meant to look after my daughter?" I looked to see Madam Dipin.

"I am," said Holmes.

"And now she's vanished, abandoned all. I hear she's even sustained a sprain."

"And why aren't you looking for her?" I interjected.

"I told that girl this life would end her, and so it has. And I wanted to see how her replacement did."

"Some might think you ended it for her," said I. The woman's eyes blazed with anger. She puffed her cheeks and stormed off.

"Come now, Watson," said Holmes. I gave him a curious look. "Oh, dear boy, she's not our culprit."

"The shoes though, she could have tampered with them!"

"I know who tampered with them. It wasn't her," Holmes confirmed. "I've dropped the net, and now we pull our catch in! Come and watch." I followed my friend outside the theatre and around the back. There was a police Maria and two officers. Lestrade had Miss Daines cuffed and was escorting her into the carriage. I couldn't believe my eyes. I thought back to when Holmes and I met with her. The mouse-like girl. Then I remembered her smirk when the injury occurred.

"This church-mouse of a girl is responsible for such horrible acts, fueled solely by jealousy."

"Come, let's return to Baker Street. We don't have much time."

Holmes told me to take a seat upon entering. He darted into his bedroom quickly shutting the door behind him. I heard a murmur as if he was speaking to himself. There was as sudden beat upon the door. Holmes shot out of his room. I stood. The door swung open and a dark haired man stood there. It was the same man who I saw hugging Miss Daines.

"I got your note, Mr. Holmes!"

"Why don't you take a seat and explain yourself?" Holmes asked.

"Why don't you explain why you framed my darling sister!"

"Don't make threats unless you have solid evidence," Holmes said coolly. The man pressed forward.

"You have no evidence against her. She's done nothing!" The man's face turned beet red.

169

"Your sister wanted the spotlight and she got it, at a high price I might add."

"She is a saint! She deserves that light, not some French *Prima Donna*!" The man lashed out and charged at Holmes. With a swift and graceful movement Holmes took hold of the man's extended arm spun him around and tossed him into a chair. He sat there shocked to have not caught his prey. Holmes motioned for me to stay back, but I remained ready to come to his aid.

"You will admit the truth, or you sister will suffer," said Holmes.

"Admit what?"

"This is no time to play games." Then Holmes gave three taps on the floor. His bedroom door opened and there stood Mademoiselle Dipin! Her presence only inflamed the man's rage. He shot from his chair and Mademoiselle Dipin held her hand up. Grasped in it were the letters. Suddenly the man's rage withdrew and his face turned white with panic.

"I suppose you know what's in her hand?" Holmes asked. He shook his head.

"It's . . . nothing."

"It's everything," she said. The man fell back into the chair.

"I . . . it was all done for my sister," he said.

"Miss Daines?" I questions. He nodded.

"I got carried away. It was meant to be harmless."

"You tried to run me out of town! You tried to foil my work! You send me letters pretending to be Javet. You followed me, you destroyed my apartment! How is any of that harmless you . . . you beast!"

"This isn't over, Mr. Holmes. You have yet to prove a single thing. This is all conjecture and blackmail!" The colour began to return to his face.

"Shall I lay it out so that even you can understand?" Holmes said sharply. "You might have got away with the entire operation should you have done one thing differently." The man looked at Holmes. "Typed out the letters." Holmes paused a moment, and Mr. Daines suddenly looked sheepish. "Being familiar with the study of the written hand, when I spoke with your sister I noticed on her dresser that there was a letter on her table. I recognised the hand which had written it. I was able to take a quick glimpse at the letter," which Holmes withdrew from his pocket. "It was an invitation from you for her to join you for dinner." Holmes walked over to Mademoiselle Dipin and took a letter from her. "It's the way you swoop your L's and looped your E's that gave it all away initially when I examined the papers.

"So, I followed your sister to her dinner date. I watched you like a hawk. I found where you live, a nice place in Angel. Inside your house, I

170

found papers bought from local sellers, all of whom remember selling to you. Types of paper that match the letters received by Mademoiselle Dipin. I also noticed a particular brand of ink on your desk which happens to be the exact ink on the letters, and a particular pen which was used to script the letters." Holmes looked at the man who now cowered in the chair. "Harmless, you say? Was it harmless when you sent the shoes to Mademoiselle Dipin with a weak heel? Your sister already said how you gave them to her, to try and win favour with Mademoiselle. Or when you placed the final letter at the front desk for her about the shoes? Oh, don't look surprised. You might remember an 'old geezer' who was mopping the floors. Yes, that was me. Give it up, Mr. Daines, the game is over." There was a ring at the bell, and Lestrade came in with Miss Daines. She look horrified to see her brother standing there.

"Darling, I'm sorry," he said to his sister, as tears welled in her eyes.

"I didn't want to believe them, brother!"

"Lestrade, we have your man," said Holmes. Mr. Daines looked confused, as all his elaborate planning to see his sister take the spot lot foiled around him. In the coming months, not only would his actions end up ruining his life, but they would also ruin her career simply by association.

"Come now, Mr. Daines, you're coming with us," said Lestrade, taking them man by the arm and escorting him out of 221b Baker Street. His sister followed sobbing behind.

"Mr. Holmes, I can't thank you enough," said Mademoiselle Dipin.

"It was my pleasure to assist."

"As to your fee . . . ." she insisted.

"Why don't you treat Watson and me to your next performance, when your foot has healed." She smiled and nodded cheerfully. She grabbed Holmes by the hands and squeezed.

"Until next time," said I. She touched my arm and made her way out. When she had left, Holmes walked over to the window and looked out at the street below.

"You surprise me, Watson," said he.

"Why is that?"

"She was a splendid woman, as far as women go. I gave you plenty of opportunities to be in her presence without me."

"I don't understand?" said I.

"I thought you would have invited her for meal. I liked her better than the last."

"Good gracious, man. Were you trying to arrange something between us then?" He smiled, reached for his pipe and lit it. A few puffs and smoke lifted from the cherrywood pipe.

"Maybe we'll find you a wife with one of these cases."

The Deadly Soldier
by Summer Perkins

Someone was trying to kill him. Of that, Professor James Moriarty was certain. For three nights now he'd seen the shadow of a man standing outside his Conduit Street residence. The man stood just out of the way of the gas lamps that lined the street, so only the long silhouette of him was discernable in the light.

When a carriage passed by, it disrupted the play of light on the cobblestones, throwing the shadow into long contrast against the walkway to Moriarty's home, as if the shadow itself was an insidious beast, lengthening and reaching out to take Moriarty within its grasp.

However, Moriarty was a scientist and believed in nothing of the terror to be found in beasts and shadows. He was rational above all else, and though his pursuer had been careful to keep his face well hidden, his unmoving, attentive posture was that of an army man.

Moriarty had no personal quarrels with Her Majesty's Army, nor had he recently done business with anyone who had a bone to pick with a man from the service, which made him conclude that this man had been hired by someone else altogether.

While in the practice of thinking, and especially when puzzling over some incredibly intricate piece of mathematics or trying to decide in just such a way how he would deliver a certain client's request, he had taken to pacing long, sure strides along the floor of his library. The movement of his legs helped energise his brain, and occasionally his fingers would twitch about the window coverings, pulling them back to view the city's comings and goings.

It was a pity that the gas lamps gave off too much light to accurately see the stars; the view of such a thing would have settled his mind much more than watching the scurrying to-and-fro of the citizens of London as they rode by in hansom cabs or walked arm in arm as lovers – all inconsequential to him, like so many ants upon a hill.

Yet, the stars were obscured from him, so he contented himself with stalking his rooms, thinking and watching. It was during just such an evening days ago that he'd first noticed that shadow of the man standing too still and purposefully ensconced in darkness.

The sight had amused Moriarty; for if the man had been sent to watch him, he'd have a long evening ahead of himself indeed, as the professor had no plans to leave his home that evening.

By the time he'd risen the next morning, the spot on the sidewalk where the man had stood was vacant, and while not putting the situation out of his mind, he filed it away carefully to be recalled if need be, though he had far more important things to think about than mysterious men standing on sidewalks.

Yet the long shadow of the man was back the very next night, and then again the next. Moriarty had noticed him again in one of his pacing turns about his library when he'd pulled aside the curtain to imperiously view his little spot of earth.

As he stood with black silk curtains still grasped in one hand and in full view of the window, he imagined the man must be stalking him, and perhaps compiling information upon his whereabouts to present to a third party. Then Moriarty noticed the silver glint of a gun as it was aimed and *oh*, wasn't that just the thing to spice up a dreary evening?

Moriarty was a tall man, nearing fifty, though slender as a matchstick with viper-fast reflexes. The very sight of the gun had sent off the impulse in him to duck before his conscious mind had caught up, and rightly so – his pursuer fired once, then twice, straight through the window.

The glass gave way with a powerful crack and shatter, raining down upon him in slivers like razor-sharp snowflakes. Moriarty, flat on his stomach, face pressed into the dull pattern of the Persian rug that carpeted his library, pulled himself away from the window, not risking raising his head to look out. He scuttled further into the room to reach his own weapon.

Despite being a man of books and cunning, it would be folly of him to not carry a piece for these such very reasons. In the decade since he'd got into his particular brand of criminal acts, he'd made a laundry list of enemies, and attempts on his life had run the gamut from poisoned tea to an attempted kidnapping. Though the latter had been botched from the start and ended rather abruptly when, having been tied to a chair and threatened with the red hot tip of a fire poker, he calmly inquired to the man holding if it he was going to attempt to burn the soul from him. He'd wondered aloud if such a thing were possible if he were lacking a soul to begin with.

Whether it was his perfectly calm demeanor at the question, as if they were discussing something of no more importance than the weather over tea, or the fact that the pupils of Moriarty's eyes were coal black and betrayed no fear, he found the poker being dropped and his kidnapper backing away, muttering something about "This ain't worth it – the crazy bastard," under his breath. At the time, he'd laughed.

174

He laughed again, crawling across his floor three hours after sunset with broken glass crunching under his knees and the elbows of his jacket. The laugh was a low, unholy rumble, mad and lacking in any real mirth. It was a laugh that cautioned *you'll be sorry.* He got to his knees when he reached his piano, deft fingers feeling across the wooden seat, finding the catch underneath. Once opened, he lifted up the false bottom to unearth an opening the length of the seat in which he kept a loaded rifle.

Outside he heard voices. There had been shrieks at the shot and the tramping of feet – probably someone running to call a constable. He lived in too respectable a neighbourhood not to warrant the concern of the police when something as alarming as gunshots occurred.

How disappointing. I'd have liked to deal with him himself, Moriarty mused from his crouched position; his long spindly fingers still wrapped around the handle of the gun aimed directly at his window. He only stood once he'd heard an authoritative voice call, "Is there anyone inside?" with the accompanying light from a shining torch.

He rose in a fluid, near-serpentine movement, lowering his gun slightly – though not all the way in case the soldier was only pretending to be police – and took stock of his own countenance. His jacket and trousers were rumpled from his abrupt movements and a fine layer of white dust coated the dark garments. This he immediately tried to brush from his clothing, disliking the way it marred the fabric.

His features, too, he schooled into the look of bewildered apprehension he assumed the situation called for, his brow furrowing, eyes widening slightly. His lips, already a rather thin slash in his face, going even thinner with faux fear. By the time the constable peered in at him through the window, Moriarty was playing his part quite well.

"Alright in there, sir?" the constable inquired, reaching in through the broken glass of the window with his torch to widen the gap in the curtains. As his ruddy looking face came further into view, Moriarty lowered his gun completely and abandoned it on the closed piano bench, giving a nod.

"Quite alright now," he assured the policeman. "Though those gunshots were indeed a shock. Would you like to come in?"

The officer nodded his agreement and Moriarty crossed the room to let him in the front door. He showed the man into the library where the assault had taken place.

After a cursory glance around the room, both men's eyes followed the trajectory of the bullets, both of which were lodged into the spines of books upon Moriarty's shelf opposite the window. One had even pierced the spine of his own work, *Dynamics of an Asteroid*, and *oh*, whoever this shooter was would pay dearly for that.

"Do you have any idea who might want you dead?" the constable inquired, head tilted up to look into Moriarty's eyes.

Moriarty pretended to pause momentarily, as if to consider the question before replying in the negative. "I'm afraid not. I don't have any enemies as far as I'm aware. I suppose this means you weren't able to apprehend the suspect?"

The constable shook his head. "The ruffian must've fled the scene before I arrived."

"Pity, that."

Again, the constable glanced around, taking in the opulence of the room. Though Moriarty's upper-class residence wasn't out of place in Westminster, he did own rather a large collection of both ancient and new texts, not to mention a nice looking piano and a telescope in the corner of the room.

"Could be a thwarted robbery," the constable mused. "That wouldn't be uncommon in a neighbourhood like this. Thieves prey upon the wealthy."

Moriarty suppressed an eye roll. A thief, this assailant was not, nor could he imagine there being much call for astronomy books and scientific apparatuses to fence on the black market.

His gaze once again drew to the bullet holes. Judging by their relative height, the first shot would've struck him square in the chest had he not ducked, and the second was likely the assailant's second attempt to get him before he hit the floor. The fact that the man had got off two quick shots in succession like that spoke of his experience, which further bolstered Moriarty's suspicion that the man responsible had a military background.

The constable pulled him out of his musings by speaking once more. "I could have some of my boys do a patrol of your street if you'd like, to make sure he doesn't come back."

"No, no," Moriarty waved the suggestion away. "I'm sure I'll be perfectly alright here." He did have use for a police officer, but he'd already had one in his employ who understood the sort of business he conducted. "If I have further need for the police, I'll speak with Inspector Turner at the CID."

The constable's brows rose nearly to his hairline at the mention of the name. "Oh sure, of course, sir. I didn't know you were friends with the higher ups."

Moriarty just gave him a tight nod, growing bored and impatient with the constable's dull, bumbling presence, and crossed the room, opening his front door swiftly for him in an effective dismissal.

176

That night Moriarty was unable to sleep. The boarded up window marred the perfection of his library, looking crude and out of place, like a scar marring otherwise perfect skin. He shut the curtains to block it from view, but even having retired to his bedroom, he still could not rest for knowing it was there, so back down to the library he went, resuming his pacing. Upon every turn of his heel he glared at the window, eyes narrowed and full of simmering fury that doubled with each passing hour.

At the first light of dawn, he decided he could wait no longer to leave the house. He'd go to Clapham and see Andrew Turner right away.

Turner had been a former client of his. At the time, the up and coming constable had been aiming for the job of detective and it had come down to he and another man in the end. The other man, a Mr. Charles Woodlite, had at least a decade in age on Turner, and had been working as a constable a handful of years longer. That was where Moriarty had come in. At Turner's behest, Moriarty had arranged for Woodlite to be struck by a runaway carriage, killing him and leaving Turner as the only available candidate for the job.

Moriarty had been pleased to take on work for a member of the police and had waved away payment, telling him instead that if the time arose when Moriarty needed his particular services, he would call upon him. That had been a good eight months back, and they'd thus far parted ways without any contact, though with the attempt on his life, Moriarty now saw need for him.

When he came to the row house in which Turner lived, he gave three solemn raps on the door, and then waited a few moments before repeating the action when he heard no movement from within.

He imagined Turner and his family were still asleep upstairs, though that was no concern of his. He needed a job done and he expected his wishes to be attended to posthaste.

Finally, the door opened, revealing a sleep-rumpled Turner, his short blond hair tousled and sticking up on end. He was still in pyjamas and a plain navy blue cotton dressing gown, the sash of which he was still tying as he opened the door.

Upon seeing Moriarty, his posture immediately changed, eyes widening first in recognition, then apprehension, back straightening as though he were a marionette whose strings had suddenly been jerked. "Professor . . . ." he trailed off, seemingly at a loss, before swallowing thickly. When he spoke again, his voice was hushed. "It's early, what can I do for you?"

177

Moriarty made no mention of the time, though he was pleased to see the immediate deference and subtle hint of fear Turner gave off at the sight of him. "You can invite me in, for a start."

Immediately, Turner stepped back, allowing Moriarty into his home. "Can I get you anything?" he asked. "Tea?" He hesitated and added, "My wife and child are still asleep upstairs," by way of explanation for his lowered voice.

Moriarty took no care to lower his own tone, speaking instead in the same cold commanding note as ever. "No tea. This isn't a social call. We have business to discuss."

"Right." Turner nodded, his Adam's Apple bobbing again as he swallowed apprehensively, taking Moriarty's coat and hat before leading him into a sparsely decorated parlour. He immediately set about starting a fire in the fireplace while he beckoned Moriarty to take a seat on the sofa. "What can I do for you?"

Moriarty perched on the edge of the sofa, noticing the stitching worn threadbare in places. His lip curled up in a sneer of distaste, the lack of sleep he'd suffered only serving to make him all the more impatient and demanding. He explained the events of the previous evening in few words before arriving at the point of his visit. "I believe my assailant will try again. I'll need you to tail me over the next few days and keep an eye out for anyone else who might be doing the same."

He spoke the words to Turner's back, watching him stoke the fire with a poker before the man finally stood, turning to face Moriarty again. "Have you filed a report on it? I could try my best to get assigned to your case."

Moriarty's head swiveled on his neck, turning from one side to the other slowly, as if to stretch his muscles, though his eyes never left Turner's. It gave the appearance of a snake sizing up a rodent it was about to devour. "I'm not interested in filing a report," he answered at length, his tone clipped. "When my pursuer is apprehended, I'll not be handing him over to the police. I'd far prefer to *deal* with him myself."

The threat within those words were unmistakable, and Turner, of anyone, should know just what sort of things Moriarty did when he'd decided to deal with someone on his own terms. Turner nodded again, though he still looked unsure, his hands toying once more with the sash of his dressing gown. "Westminster isn't in my division. I'm not allowed to patrol whichever part of London I choose. Perhaps there is something else I could – "

Moriarty had heard enough and cut him off before he was able to get another word out. "The man pursuing me is clearly dangerous. Is it not your job to make London a safer place for all citizens?" he inquired.

"With a wife and child, I'd imagine you'd want our streets to be free of murderers."

Turner swallowed again. "I – "

"It's just that it would be a shame," Moriarty continued smoothly, as if the Inspector hadn't spoken, "if something were to happen to your child. An infant girl, am I correct? Rebecca." He hummed the name out, a slow smile spreading his severe, bloodless lips even thinner.

Colour bloomed high on Turner's cheeks; anger and fear making him gawp at Moriarty wordlessly for a moment, before he reached up to run a shaking hand through his unkempt hair. "I – I can start as soon as you need me to."

"Glad to hear you've come around to the idea. Get dressed, Inspector. You have a long day ahead of you."

Moriarty's pursuer was more intelligent than he'd originally given him credit, because after employing Turner to tail him, he saw neither hide nor hair of anyone following him or acting suspiciously.

He would have assumed the soldier had given it up as a bad job now that Moriarty had an Inspector watching out for him, if not for the fact that the last three men he'd had appointments with had turned up murdered.

The first, a Mr. Jonathon March, a banker who had a case of sticky fingers and decided he'd wanted to start pocketing some of the money from his bank's safe, had been found dead in his home. Nothing from his residence had been stolen, but a single bullet had pierced his chest, straight through his heart.

After March had neglected to show up for his appointment, Moriarty decided to pay him a visit, because people did *not* back out on their appointments with him without consequence. When he arrived, he saw a swarm of policemen at March's residence and turned back, not wanting to get himself involved in a police matter in which he didn't control all the players. In the evening paper, he read of the murder, and though such a thing could be discounted as a coincidence, after having just survived an attempt on his own life, it didn't seem likely.

His assailant was clearly still on his tail and watching him close enough to know with whom Moriarty did business. Yet, why kill one of his clients? Beyond the minor inconvenience of it, Moriarty cared little for their lives, and the loss of money from March's business was minimal.

He shrugged it off as a desperate attempt on the soldier's behalf to rile him, and continued on as usual, instructing Turner to keep following him in case the soldier decided to show himself again.

179

Then, his next client was murdered three days later, and another two days after that. The papers started calling it the work of a deranged killer, though they were unable to find any connection between the murders. Each man was killed with a single shot through the heart, without any other assault or robbery of his person and an absolute lack of evidence as to who had done it.

It was starting to become . . . inconvenient. One murdered client didn't bother Moriarty overmuch, but if the murders continued, it would be only a matter of time until a connection between the men led back to him, and word would get around that anyone who hired him wound up dead.

Not to mention that the police, even as incompetent as most of them were, would eventually find the connection, and while he had Turner in his pocket and didn't doubt his ability to find weaknesses in the others to bend them to his will, it would take an amount of effort in which he did not wish to partake.

As ambitious as he was in things that interested him, he didn't appreciate feeling as though someone else was forcing his hand, and as Turner was proving worse than useless as a tail, Moriarty decided to approach this from a different angle. It was about time he did something to draw the solider out.

First thing the next morning, he invited Turner in and gave him a rundown of their new goal, before walking him to his door to dismiss him. He waited until the Inspector was on his doorstep in plain view of the street before arranging his features into his a scowl; brows knitted together, dark eyes narrowed in cool dissatisfaction, mouth curled into a sneer, as he informed the Inspector in a clipped tone, "Since you've been unable to find the man who attacked me, I have no choice but to relieve you from your duty."

Turner gave a nervous jerk of his head, Adam's Apple once again bobbing as he swallowed reflexively in fear. The sheer terror on the man's face amused Moriarty. Though this playacting was part of his plan, the Inspector looked genuinely terrified at Moriarty's cold fury.

When Turner spoke, his voice was hesitant and wheedling. "I'm sorry, Mr. Moriarty. I've been following you day and night as requested. I just haven't seen anyone that I'd consider suspicious, I – "

"I'm not interested in your excuses," Moriarty interrupted. "I made myself quite clear when I told you what I expected."

Turner's pallour faded almost to Moriarty's own near paper white tones. "Yes, but – "

"No." Moriarty gave a jerk of his head, cutting off any more excuses before they could issue from the Turner's lips. "I believe I told you what the price would be for your failure."

Turner's eyes widened. "Please, sir, don't hurt my family . . . ."

Moriarty watched the man dispassionately, tilting his head to one side and then the other slowly, stretching his neck out. "Then catch my assailant, Inspector." He reached into his pocket, withdrawing a small leather-bound appointment book and handing it to the other man. "In here you'll find the addresses of my clients and the dates of our appointments. Catch this man before he can kill another one of them. You have twenty-four hours."

He watched Turner take the book and then continue standing there, gripping it so hard that his blunt nails left small indents in the leather.

"Well? Off you go," Moriarty prompted, jerking Turner into action again.

He gave a start and then nodded, pocketing the book. "I won't let you down again," he promised, fitting his hat on and all but fleeing from the house.

"See that you don't." Moriarty smirked, watching him hurry off, before stepping back and shutting the door after him with a decisive click. Everything was going to plan so far. He'd just hoped the soldier had been lurking out of sight to witness that performance.

Most people's motives, Moriarty found, were easy to suss out – greed, malice, simple stupidity – they all drove men to act in ways that were tiresomely predictable, and this soldier of his was no different, he assumed. Greedy, yes, as he'd likely been hired to do this job and was therefore motivated by money. Malicious? Perhaps. The pattern of the bullets made for a quick death, and the use of a rifle meant he preferred to work from a distance, though Moriarty assumed that to be from his military training more than from any preference to not get his hands dirty.

As for stupidity? There'd been a surprising lack of it, thus far. The man had been careful not to get himself caught by police, nor noticed by Turner, and he'd been patient enough not to fire off another shot at Moriarty too soon after his failed first time.

Truth be told, he was the sort of man who Moriarty wouldn't mind having in his employ himself. Though Moriarty relished in his own intimidation tactics, usually needing little more than a few discrete, well-placed threats and a narrowing of his eyes, even he could admit that sometimes more drastic measures had to be taken. Having a trained muscle that was proficient with a gun had its advantages.

It really would be a pity for his assailant to be shot as Moriarty's plan came to fruition, but sometimes these things couldn't always be planned for. He was perfectly willing to pull the trigger if he deemed the man unreasonable after having a proper chat, but first he had to lure him in. Getting rid of Turner had only been the first step. Now to put the rest of the plan in motion

The soldier hadn't shot a single person in public thus far, preferring to take them down in their homes. As his first long range attempt had failed, Moriarty could only assume this time it would be something a little more close and personal.

So, to give the man time, Moriarty left his home quickly as if he had business with which to attend, immediately setting off for Regent Street. In his purported haste he neglected to turn the lock on his front door. If this soldier were to break into his home to await his return, he'd much rather there be as little destruction upon his property as possible. He didn't fancy another boarded up window.

Once on Regent Street, he allowed himself to get lost in the flow of pedestrians clamouring in and out of shops. His upper lip curled in distaste at the mass of swirling humanity around him; the cacophony of voices, the clomping of horses' hooves as carriages passed by, and a squeaking out-of-tune piano-organ ground by a boy looking for change. The boy gained nothing but a withering look from Moriarty as the professor passed by him.

A glance to his pocket watch told him it was barely nine in the morning; if this soldier were any sort of criminal at all, he'd surely wait until nightfall to make his move. He had hours upon hours to waste before then.

While it had been his plan to lose himself in the press of bodies along Regent Street, making it impossible to murder him without someone seeing, he quickly found being among that many people intolerable.

Surely, risking a bullet to the chest would be preferable to being amongst that much constant braying humanity, and after barely an hour he'd returned to Conduit Street once more, heading for Saunders, Otley & Co., a circulating library not too far from his home.

In addition to frivolous dramas and works of poetry, the library also had a large collection of practical and scientific texts. The professor whiled away the rest of the morning and much of the afternoon reading up on the management and keeping of bees, while pondering just how many stings it would take to overload a man's body, forcing it to shut down. It would be a waste for the bee to die as well, however inefficient

182

insects that they were. He made a mental note to research the keeping of wasps instead.

When it was approaching dusk, he ate at a local pub before checking his pocket watch once again and meeting Turner outside. At precisely their agreed meeting time, Turner made his way through the crowd, a subdued expression making his cornflower blue eyes appear dull.

"Hello, Mr. Moriarty," he inclined his head in greeting. Despite his many shortcomings, at least he was punctual. That was a trait Moriarty valued highly. Men who kept him waiting tended not to live long.

"Mr. Turner," Moriarty answered, voice cool. "I take it you've brought the cuffs I requested?"

Turner nodded, reaching into the pocket of his overcoat to pull out a set of silver handcuffs. He produced a small revolver as well, which he dutifully handed over to Moriarty.

After a cursory glance, Moriarty slipped both items into the pocket of his own coat and then shrugged the garment off, handing it over to Turner along with his top hat. Turner followed suit and soon Moriarty pulled on the other man's coat, looking down in brief distaste at the poor quality of the fabric compared to that which he was used to. He nodded for Turner to lead the way while he kept back at a discrete distance.

The plan was simple enough; Moriarty was banking on his assailant waiting for him in his home, and though Turner lacked Moriarty's tall, slim stature, in the poor light, Moriarty assumed the soldier would mistake Turner for him. Once the solider made a move, Turner would disarm and cuff him. He had explicit instructions not to fire upon the soldier unless absolutely necessary, but it would be foolhardy to not at least have brought a gun in preparation.

Moriarty watched Turner's back as they walked in silence toward his home; the professor taking care to keep well back and into the shadows. Turner walked up to his front door, opening it as if he were the owner of the place and stepped inside.

Moments later, Moriarty saw the light in his library shine through the curtains; Turner obviously had lit the gas lamp once he was inside. All was silent and he resolved to give the Inspector a few minutes before approaching the house himself to see how he was getting on. As soon as the thought had entered his mind, the unmistakable crack of a gunshot pierced the air.

Moriarty's head snapped up in attention. He hurried toward the house, hoping that Turner had been wise enough to follow his instructions. Had he killed the soldier before Moriarty himself could get his hands on him, there would be consequences.

As Moriarty's hand reached for the doorknob, he saw it turn before he could grasp it and the door was pulled open from the inside. The gestured revealed a man a bit shorter than himself but nearly twice as wide, compact with solid muscle. The man's sandy blond hair was cut in a short military style and smoothed down with wax, and he had a bushy moustache the same colour; it twitched as his lips pulled up into a smile. The gesture of amusement didn't reach the man's hard green eyes.

"Professor," he addressed Moriarty, stepping back so Moriarty could enter. "You've proven difficult to hunt down."

The smell of gunpowder was pungent in the air. Behind the soldier laid Turner, a spreading red stain across the front of his vest, soaking into his white cotton shirt. He drew in a shallow breath, moaning as he exhaled.

Moriarty's eyes slid from Turner's body on the floor back to the solider and he stepped inside. The man was still holding his military issue Webley revolver, though Moriarty just tilted his chin up in defiance, unafraid.

"And you've proven a nuisance," he answered dispassionately, stepping over Turner. "How disappointed you must be that you've still not taken me down. I'll bet your employer is most displeased."

The soldier laughed, raising his gun at Moriarty. "What makes you think I won't shoot you right now and be done with it?"

Moriarty watched the silver muzzle of the revolver point directly at his chest, though if he felt any sliver of fear it didn't show on his face. He just slowly tilted his head from one side to the other, stretching his neck out in his usual serpentine movement. "You could," he agreed, "But then you'd never hear my business proposition, and you'd be the poorer for it."

He watched the soldier cock his weapon, finger sliding to the trigger, though the man then hesitated a beat and Moriarty took advantage of the hesitation, adding, "I'm not sure what your employer has told you about me, but just by this brief meeting, I can gather a few things about you. Judging by your posture and the type of weapon you carry, you are a military man. Your skin is far too tan for someone who has spent much time recently in London, which means you've been abroad. Perhaps in Kabul, the Battle of Sherpur? Yet your decision to dabble in crime is a curious one. Maybe you've been recently discharged and found yourself unsuitable for a life which doesn't include wielding a gun."

As Moriarty spoke, the cruel, self-satisfied smile slid from the soldier's face, to be replaced with a look that was first weary, then

184

begrudgingly bordering on awe. "You've deciphered all that from just looking at me?"

Moriarty inclined his head in agreement. "I have. Yet I find one thing about your methods very curious."

Despite the look of awe on the soldier's face, his revolver didn't waver from Moriarty's chest. "And what's that?"

"If you've been hired to kill me, what purpose did the murder of my clients serve?"

The soldier's smile returned, and he let out a hearty laugh as though Moriarty had just told a particularly funny joke. "That, Professor, was just for my own amusement. You've proven more difficult to get to than I'd planned, and instead of trifling with the Inspector tailing you, it was far more entertaining to follow home the men you had meetings with and dispatch of them. I knew you'd eventually grow tired of the damage it was doing to your business and try to lure me out."

He let out another small chuckle, shaking his head, "It was quite a nice touch with the Inspector wearing your overcoat as well. Perhaps a lesser man might've fallen for the gag, but I recognised his gait the moment he walked up to your house."

As if on cue, another moan of pain issued from Turner on the floor. Without taking his eyes off Moriarty, the soldier turned his revolver on the Inspector, delivering a fatal shot.

The heartlessness of the action impressed Moriarty, as did the soldier's cleverness. Though he clearly wasn't as good at reading people as the professor himself, he was a great deal smarter than most men Moriarty employed. Moriarty could use someone skilled with a gun, since Turner was now no longer drawing breath.

"I have to commend you on your work," Moriarty told him. "You're far from the first man hired to take my life, but out of them all, you've got the closest."

"*Closest?*" The solider echoed with a raise of his brows. "My good sir, between the two of us I'm the only one with a weapon in hand and I've just ended another man's life. Whatever makes you think that I won't be successful in ending yours?"

It was a fair point and a lesser man might've conceded defeat and started to beg for his life, but Moriarty was not a lesser man. He only watched the solider intently, reaching up to remove the top hat he'd not had the chance to divest himself of earlier, what with the commotion he'd met upon entering his home. His overcoat was shed next and he took his time, drawing out the silence between them. He enjoyed the way the soldier's attention never left him as he waited for Moriarty's reply.

Whether the man realised it or not, he was already in Moriarty's thrall, and when Moriarty felt the tension in the room increase to such a level that the solider was about to speak again, Moriarty opened his mouth to reply. "I suppose you *would* be successful in your objective, if that's what you so choose, but you've just killed someone of use to me, and as such, a job opening has become available.

Whatever the solider had been expecting him to say, that clearly was far from the mark. He gaped at Moriarty, brows rising again this time nearly to his hairline. Slowly, he lowered his gun to his side. "Are you telling me you're looking to hire me?"

"I am," Moriarty confirmed.

"What makes you think I'd betray my boss to work for you?" he scoffed, though he didn't raise the gun again.

This time, Moriarty didn't even pretend to draw out the silence before answering. He already knew he'd won. The solider having lowered his gun was as good as a yes already. "It's steady work, and whatever you're currently being paid, I'll double it."

The solider stood motionless for a breath, thinking it over before slipping his gun back into its holster.

Moriarty added, "You can start by disposing of the Inspector's body. Then pay a little visit to your boss and bring him to me. Do we have a deal?"

He put out his hand to shake on it, like the start of all gentlemanly agreements. The soldier's brows knitted as he looked down at that hand, as though shaking it would be akin to making a pact with the devil.

"I'll even triple your pay, if you manage to impress me," Moriarty added, and the man's hand met his in a firm grip.

After they shook, Moriarty spoke once more. "Another thing. If you're going to work for me, I'll need to know your name."

The man nodded, reaching up to stroke his moustache before standing up straighter, heels clicking together. It was the move of someone used to standing at attention in front of a superior officer. "Of course. It's Colonel Sebastian Moran, sir. At your service."

The Case of the
Vanishing Stars
by Deanna Baran

My friend Holmes was never happier than when his formidable intellect was captivated by some abstruse problem. Contrariwise, ennui was abhorrent to him. October of 1885 was an intense month for Holmes. After the adventure of the cyclist's cipher came quick upon the heels of the problem of the change-ringers' society and the Armenian carpet affair, the comparative sluggishness of November left him morose and dissatisfied. Only so many hours could be filled by cutting articles from the papers and updating scrap-books. Although the weather was hardly conducive to such outings, and my wound ached at every change in the glass, I found myself taking wholly unnecessary turns through Regent's Park to escape the oppressive atmosphere of Baker Street, as the steely November skies had nothing on the gloom of a Holmes without a challenge. He had work, mind you, for rarely a day passed without the page admitting some colorful individual or another to our sitting room, but the parade of petty problems that beleaguer humanity did little to stimulate his mental machinery.

Thus it was, when I descended to breakfast early in December, that I was pleasantly surprised to find Holmes in better spirits than I had seen for several weeks. The night before, we had taken an evening's entertainment at St. James's Hall, and he was anxious to resume conversation on the subject.

"Mind you," he said, "I don't care much for Gallic glitter. Give me German introspection on the program any night. Still, that was rather a unique interpretation. Berlioz clearly specified *agitato*. One might even tread towards *vivacci* territory. Yet to give his *Fantastique* such an *andante* delivery – the character of the piece was completely transformed, and I doubt Berlioz would have thanked him for it."

The succeeding meal consisted of his humming of passages from four or five different interpretations of the piece in question, punctuated with approving or disapproving comparative analyses of the varying approaches. While I enjoy music, I have not the musician's brain that permits one to reduce a concert piece from its whole into its parts, as though there were no difference between the performance hall and the dissecting-room, and I found the majority of his criticisms too technical to appreciate. Still, I was heartened by this spark of enthusiasm on an

187

otherwise dreary morning, and I did all I could to encourage his exuberant opining.

So it was, that after the meal was cleared away, and he had substituted his violin for his egg-spoon for the purpose of illustrating his points, and the subject of conversation had meandered into the influences of French Romanticism upon Wagner, and from there upon programme music versus Gesammtkunstwerk, that when the bell rang to indicate a caller, he was visibly annoyed at this check upon his discourse. But he was ever the gentleman, and by the time our visitor had been shown into the room, she would never have suspected her timing was unwelcome or inconvenient.

She divided a cautious smile between the two of us. As I made my greeting and offered her a seat by the fire, it occurred to me that she must have been quite the beauty in her day. Holmes gave her fashionable appearance his customary swift analysis. "Watson and I were just discussing programme music," he said amicably. "How serendipitous to find someone who has trod the boards in our midst. Although now, perhaps, you seem to busy yourself with costuming, although that is not your primary occupation?"

Just as the jackdaw cannot maintain its charade once it speaks, neither could her charming appearance survive speech. For all the expense of her costume and the glitter of her ornaments, she possessed the harsh metallic twang of a costermonger.

"I toured the Continent and America in the '60's and '70's," she said. "Perhaps you remember 'Daddy, If You Love Me.' It was my big hit on the music-hall circuits, though some prefer 'The Big Noise at Brighton'. I don't mind taking a turn onstage to give the audience a treat, though I've run my own music hall these last ten years. I've worked both sides of the lights, and I knows what things belongs. A woman must always have an eye for tomorrow, what 'as no one's showered with diamonds forever."

It was hard to imagine this woman as a chanteuse, showered with jewels by an adoring public. But Holmes's cordiality didn't waver. "That is a very practical mindset – "

"Mrs. Hughes," she supplied. "The posters say another, and my Jimmy's gone to glory, but it's Mrs. Hughes all the same."

"Perhaps you can tell us what has brought you so far from Mile End on such a chill morning, Mrs. Hughes?"

Our guest's visible surprise confirmed the accuracy of his statement, but, never one to deny an audience's request, she launched upon her narrative. She possessed the singular inability of her class to relate a sequence of events in linear fashion. Yet Holmes was patient with her,

188

permitting her to drift into side channels of expository, but always drawing the threads of narration back towards their original point, here summarized for expediency.

Having spent the better part of fifteen years on stage, Mrs. Hughes determined to yield the limelight to a younger generation of performers. Although she had married a stolid, sensible stockbroker, she wished to additionally secure her future. She discovered a song-and-supper room for sale in Mile End, whose owner wished to forsake the overcrowding of the East End in favor of market gardening in Fulham. She purchased the premises, and between the depth of her purse and her considerable experience, launched a successful business providing cheap edibles and entertainment for the immigrants and laborers of the area.

There was a fire and a subsequent renovation. Her husband passed away one winter of double pleuro-pneumonia. The economic depression that began five years ago took its toll on the box office receipts. Overall, however, business proceeded as normally as it could for several years.

On the other hand, life was never ordinary when one's business model involved the employment of a motley variety of artistes. Just in the last fortnight, she'd dealt with the acrobat who'd attempted to climb the walls, the conjuror who lost his pigeons, prowlers at the basement window, and the police-whistle that interrupted a canine act. There were other peculiar things, like the matter of the drapers who had come to measure the curtains, yet she had placed no orders; or the gasfitters who had come to fix the lights, yet the lights were in perfect condition and no one admitted to having summoned them. But nothing ever happened that would require the services of a consulting detective.

However, around Martinmas, abnormalities began to accumulate. Her faithful right hand, Mr. Jacobs, who was had been with her a decade to schedule talent and oversee the technicalities of stage management, had passed away from blood poisoning at the beginning of the month. The new manager was competent enough, and had arranged for a number of intriguing performers, yet the performers themselves tended to be chronically unreliable. It was common in the business for an artiste to book his little ten-minute act, leave home fully made-up to take his turn, receive his pay, and then rush off to repeat the process at three or four establishments in one night. Despite this ambitious schedule, she rarely had a problem with individuals who failed to fulfill their contract. Recently, however, as many as a full third of the advertised "turns" on her program would fail to report for the curtain, much to the chagrin of her paying customers. Word was going around, and attendance, usually consisting of five to six hundred heads per night, had plummeted in response to the wagging of critical tongues. In a matter of weeks, she had come to a point where she was hesitant to advertise a particular program ahead of time, for fear of not being able to fulfill the audience's expectations.

The Christmas pantomime season was normally a busy and profitable time of year, and although *harlequinades* were no longer as fashionable as they had been mid-century, and she herself rarely ventured into dramatics due to licensing issues, those who patronized her hall would "never say 'no' to a good piece of business with a policeman and a string of sausages," as she expressed it. Although she had made some small economies by doing much of the costume design and tailoring herself, she still had invested a not-insignificant sum into costumes and set-pieces. Yet just last night, the entire cast of "Harlequin and Cinderella" had reported for the curtain, then without a word, vanished! Neither Harlequin nor Columbine nor anyone had remained to take the stage. The audience was in an uproar at her attempts to make substitutions for the climax of the night's program, and she'd had to refund the entire evening's receipts. If she'd known that her reputation would be in shreds, she would have sold it at a tidy profit to the stranger who had offered to buy her music hall back at Hallowtide.

"How many marriage proposals have you received since the beginning of autumn?" inquired Holmes.

This was not the question Mrs. Hughes was expecting. "Three," she said. "One, by letter, from an admirer who claimed to remember me from my 'Daddy, If You Love Me' days, but who never actually spoke to me in person. One from my new manager, about two weeks into his employment, but he was only fishing, and I told him what was what. One from a friendly rival from down the road. Mr. William Ferguson, of Bill's Cyder Cellar." She hesitated a moment. "I handed them all the mitten, of course. Not a one of them has a head on his shoulders, including the manager, and I intend to give him notice after Christmas."

"And, apart from those three, the rest of the year?"

"I had my share of fortune hunters after I lost Jimmy. I made things clear enough then. It's got around that it's not worth the effort, so it's rare what as I have to deal with unwanted attentions these days. I generally keeps to myself and my scrapbooks and don't pay much attention to the other places."

"Splendid. And, pray tell, when did the fire occur?"

"I bought the Aoede in January that year. It was late February. Someone placed a candle too close to the curtain. My plan was to space things out, so as it could pay for its own fix-up, seeing as the previous owner hadn't kept up with the place at all. It cost me a pretty sum, what with the painters and the carpenters and the plasterers and half of London

190

crawling over the place. We got the scaffolding out by March's end, though, and was back in business by the beginning of April."

"Half of London?"

"More like one person. He was a relative of the former owner, by name of Tull, but didn't know the place had been sold. Came running in there with the police on his heels one day. Caused a lot of trouble."

Holmes rose. "Thank you for your information, Mrs. Hughes. Who is generally around, and when?"

"I live in rooms onsite, sir, so it's rare what as I'm over a moment away. I had enough of the fast life back in my day, and the fizz don't taste so good when it's your own shilling. The manager interviews performers on Mondays. Meals are available daily, though most grab a bun through the window as they pass. We offer a program of music and entertainment four nights a week, and a matinee on Saturday, so there's the hands and the performers then, as well as the kitchen staff and the waiters."

"Most excellent. I hope to bring your problems to a tidy end before a week is through."

Mrs. Hughes looked disappointed. "I don't know if the Aoede's reputation can survive another week, especially after 'Harlequin and Cinderella.'"

"Even a conjuror needs time to collect his pigeons," said Holmes, with perfect tranquility. "There are at least nine different explanations for your recent events, and it will take a small amount of investigation to determine the cause at its root. If fortune is on your side, you may be able to make up most of your losses before Christmas. One piece of advice before you depart, however: even should a position come vacant, whether cook or waiter or anyone else, I beg you leave it unfilled for at least the week."

The door had scarcely shut on our mystified client before I turned to Holmes. "Surely, Holmes, that was going a bit too far. You know the artistic temperament for what it is. It's rather ungentlemanly of you to give her hopes, when you can't possibly do a thing to transform what is undoubtedly an unreliable segment of the population into sober and dependable human beings."

"And yet she has spent the last ten years with a perfectly sound business built upon the entertainment they provide, and had spent previous decades moving in those selfsame circles herself. She 'knows what things belongs', as she so quaintly put it."

"Speaking of which, how on earth did you know she was on the stage? It seemed a charitable guess, between the expense of her clothes and her dreadful accents, yet you had her labeled before she said a word."

"Surely you remarked upon her complexion, my dear Watson. Years of greasepaint for the stage will have an effect on the pores in a way mere powder never could."

"And the costuming? Yet you knew she was not a seamstress?"

"Surely you spotted those stray threads which clung unheeded to her skirts, Watson. One could hardly walk around a room where sewing activity is taking place without some of the materials adhering to one's hems, and she was distracted enough to not notice. Then there was the consideration of her cuffs. They were made of quite the extravagant silk plush, and are most excellent for retaining impressions. From the patterns of wear, one could spot the marks of long hours at the sewing machine upon the left cuff, but not both, as one would expect with, say, a professional typist. Add to that the fact that such a walking dress is unlikely to be found for less than fifty guineas, and, judging by the shape of the bustle, is quite the latest, and you have a woman far more affluent than most hirelings, especially with the economy in its current straits."

"And Mile End?"

"I had briefly considered Bethnal Green. Even the most recent newcomer to London could not have failed to place her in the East End, merely on the strength of her abuse of phonetics and idiom. But you know I've made a study of the unique characteristics of the various soils to be found in the districts of London. It is the rare person who does not have crusted dirt clinging to their boots at this time of year, with the rainy days of winter upon us."

"What do you propose to do?"

"Right now? I propose to peruse the papers. This afternoon, however, I intend to travel to Mile End."

"To lay eyes upon the Aoede?"

"Rather, to lay eyes upon Bill's Cyder Cellar. Would you care to come along?"

The odors of tobacco, perspiration, and onions mingled in a poisonous miasma at our destination. There was not a drop of decent wine upon the premises, but the waiters mingled through the crowds in the pauses between turns, noisily advertising the availability of gin, whiskey, and rum. Although it was presumably a supper-club, the only foods that appeared to be available were common breakfast foodstuffs: sausages, fried ham and eggs, kidneys. There were perhaps one hundred persons, of mixed company, crowded around tables, all eating and drinking with vigor and conversing loudly. A handful of infants

192

slumbered or nursed through the proceedings; the number of children present was shocking. Most of the company present ignored the entertainment at the opposite end of the long, narrow gallery, where a stage had been erected. A pair of violinists – one blind, the other with a wooden leg – and a pianist accompanied a vocalist whose song, or as much as I could catch of it, was more crude than comic. A placard on a stand beside him suggested that this was the fifth act of the evening; I did not feel as though I had missed much by arriving late.

Holmes had tasked me with discovering what information I could from the masses, while he pursued his own separate inquiries. Disguised, he had entered the premises a full ten minutes before I did, and I felt quite out of place alone amidst this raffish crew. I sidestepped a waiter peddling the sheet-music that had accompanied Number Five's performance and settled down in a vacant seat. I had changed my customary garments for shabbier clothing, but was uncomfortable in the knowledge that I had no place amongst this society. I ordered a whiskey for which I had little desire, just as Number Six took the stage, coughed for attention, and the waiters scuttered from the floor. There was a slight decrease in the din, and he commenced an act whereupon he juggled an assortment of loaded pistols. I found I could not take my eyes from the foolhardy spectacle, and all thoughts of striking up conversation with my neighbors fled for the duration of his act. Soon enough, however, he finished his performance, relinquished the stage, and the waiters buzzed through the room once more, calling for orders, while the few whose attention had been captured by his turn resumed conversation with their neighbors once more.

Fortified by a draught, which I suspected of having been somewhat watered, I turned to my own neighbors and attempted to make conversation with them. Yet what would have proven a singularly difficult undertaking under ideal circumstances proved nigh impossible amidst the noise and smoke of this crowded hall. Realizing I would get little insight from the party of cabmen I had originally sat next to, I circulated around the room in the hopes of attaching myself to some lone individual who would be amenable to casual conversation. But my approaches were generally received without encouragement, forcing me to move on, and thus I passed my time through a series of performing cats, an American comedian, and a Scotsman in kilt and sporran.

"Buy me my liquor?" I was approached by a very free and forward woman, and I automatically acquiesced to her request – gin, neat. "Out slummin', are we?"

"Perhaps," I said, not a little discomfited. "In fact, I had heard of Bill's Cyder Cellar, and I wished to see it for myself."

"It's a far cry from the Alhambra," said the woman, with a braying laugh, "but it's all the same at the bottom."

"I had also heard of the Aoede," I pressed. "And I wished to make a comparison of the two."

"Writing for the guidebooks, what?" joked a male neighbor, who had ignored me until this point.

"Er. More like, an investment," I said. "Suppose I wanted to invest in a music hall or a supper club. Is the Cyder Cellar an example of a successful enterprise?"

"Comic singers do best on stage," said the woman promptly, "but the music halls would be empty if it weren't for the people what comes to them."

"Yes, I believe that's rather self-evident," I began.

Another braying laugh.

"Take this act, for example," I pressed on hurriedly, indicating the one-legged dancer who capered onstage. "Suppose he has booked himself in three different venues on one night, one of which was mine. How can he be relied upon to faithfully make his appearance at all three locations? That's rather a hectic schedule. Surely the Cyder Cellar must have an appreciable number of no-shows, merely due to unavoidable obstacles that life places in one's way."

The woman appeared unconcerned. "We all like to eat, don't we? If he don't perform, he don't get paid, and if he don't get paid, he don't eat."

"My brother did turns in music halls for years," said the man. "The stories he had! The problem was, the music halls don't pay enough to keep body an' soul together, so you needs to stack 'em. The music halls complain that the same turn appears three times on the same street. They needs to pay more if they wants an exclusive."

Once the conversation had started upon this path of remuneration and employers, there was no retrieving it, despite numerous attempts. It was with relief that I escaped from the oppressive atmosphere of the hall to the chill of the overcast winter night and met Holmes outside the coffee house two blocks away at our designated time. Yet again, he had transformed himself with his usual deftness. Slouching about in a suit of third-hand clothes, his accent as unintelligible as any other in that shabby den, I felt a pang of envy at the realization he was always at ease, whether in the midst of kings or costermongers.

"All I could determine was that Bill's seems to have no trouble with irresponsible artistes," I reported. "I could find no instances of turns listed upon the programme, where the artiste failed to appear."

"Of course not," said Holmes. "You'll find this specific trouble is endemic to Mrs. Hughes' establishment, and will not be found plaguing her neighbors."

"Then I can't say I see the point of this wasted evening," I said, with some asperity. "Unless you discovered something you would care to share."

"We'll see how the Aoede is on Monday," he replied, "and that will give me a better idea of the facts in play."

By "we", Holmes obviously meant "I". He emerged from his room before dawn, this time dressed as one who had seen former affluence, but had come down in the world. He disappeared, violin case in hand, not to be seen again until the lamps had been lit.

"Congratulate me, friend Watson," he said, "for I am to make my stage debut on Friday evening at the Aoede. Or rather, congratulate James Gray, if all goes well."

"Whatever for, Holmes?"

"A simple experiment which may help us determine what outside forces may be meddling with the Aoede's contracted artistes, or if, perhaps, there is an explanation closer to home for Mrs. Hughes."

"And if nothing comes of it?"

"Then perhaps the labourers of London will enjoy ten minutes' worth of Mendelssohn, or what they can hear of it, and then I shall be followed by an adagio act and quickly forgotten," came the tranquil reply. "I spent several hours of my time observing the day's auditions and contracts. Next, I visited a jeweler's shop. Then, I placed an advertisement for the services of a reliable wall-paperer. The remainder of my day was spent investigating records of the area's criminal activity. Matters proceed in a satisfactory manner."

Contrary to expectations, however, by Friday afternoon, nothing had interfered that would cause any cancellation of plans. Holmes, under his alias, took the stage as Number Eight on the evening's bill, and executed his piece with much gravity. As Holmes is in the indulgent habit of compensating my patience with flurries of Mendelssohn and other favored melodies, I privately sorrowed over the indifference that met his performance.

The Aoede, even in its current state of disfavor, still held more than treble the number of patrons that Bill's Cyder Cellar had boasted. The atmosphere, with its high ceilings and glittering chandeliers and heavy velvet drapes, held pretensions of affluence which contrasted sharply with the dinginess of the Cellar. The ventilation was also distinctly superior, although the class of individuals who frequented the hall were

195

still of the poor and humble sort, and crudity and double entendre abounded throughout the evening's entertainment.

Three of the twenty billed performers were unable to make their advertised appearances: Sevastyanov the Russian illusionist; the Barzotti Brothers, who performed feats of strength; and "Hamlet in Eight Minutes, performed with the greatest possible success" by Henry Jones. They were all key pieces, and despite the audience's apparent lack of attentiveness, the subtraction of these three turns from the programme was met with great hostility. Although I had little fondness for music halls, it saddened me to see our client's livelihood in such unfavourable straits.

It was quite late by the time the hall closed and the crowd dispersed. The staff was left to clean and tidy. Holmes gestured for the manager and Mrs. Hughes to join him in conference, and we all seated ourselves around a table. He introduced the manager as Mr. Munby; Mr. Munby seemed quite at a loss as to why Number Eight had called a meeting, but despite his bull-like appearance, he followed his employer's lead with docility.

"I hope things have been quiet these last few days? No intruders?" inquired Holmes.

"Nothing's come to my attention," said Mrs. Hughes, glancing at Mr. Munby for affirmation.

Holmes nodded his approval. "One will find, with observation, that there has been an increase in the foot-traffic around your establishment these last few nights. It cost but a trifle and makes prowlers cautious. Have you had any defectors amongst your staff?"

"Wednesday, one of the waiters quit without notice," said Mr. Munby. "We've been shorthanded as a result, but I was instructed to leave the vacancy until further notice."

"Most excellent," said Holmes. "If you don't mind, I believe half of your problem could be solved by fresh wall-paper. I have taken the liberty of advertising around, and am in communication with four wall-paperers. They will come by in the morning, take measurements, and give their price. We will be here at nine in the morning to meet them."

"That's absurd!" exclaimed Mr. Munby. "We'll shut our doors before Christmas at this rate; this is no time for foolish spending."

"I believe the other half of the problem," continued Holmes, unperturbed by this interruption, "would be solved by the immediate termination of your employment, Munby."

Munby turned quite pink. "I've been here a month and am doing my best under the circumstances."

Holmes directed his conversation to Mrs. Hughes and myself, with the occasional gesture towards Mr. Munby as though he were some scientific specimen of mild interest. "You will recall that Mr. Jacobs passed on at the beginning of November. Concurrently with his illness and passing, you received an offer from an anonymous purchaser, which you refused. By midmonth, you had hired on Mr. Munby, and from the moment Mr. Munby took the reins, your artistes have begun to fail to appear in ways they had not hitherto."

"I say, that's not – " interrupted Mr. Munby.

"And not just small artistes who would be easily missed. Not a sentimental singer, or one juggler who is very much like another. Intriguing artistes with acts that capture the imagination, such as, say, a Russian magician, or an amusing interpretation of The Bard, or a comic skit. It is my assertion that there never was a Sevastyanov; there never were any Barzotti Brothers; and while I'm sure London is full of Henry Joneses, I doubt any of them is capable of performing 'Hamlet in Eight Minutes' with the greatest possible success. Certainly, none of them auditioned on Monday. I posit to you that all of these acts were fictions, created with the sole purpose of disappointing the audience by their failure to materialize."

"What of 'Harlequin and Cinderella'?" demanded Mrs. Hughes. "Surely I didn't wear my fingers to the bone stitching costumes for no one."

"Oh! Surely they were real enough flesh-and-blood humans. Perhaps they even had acquired a genuine script to rehearse. But they were mere confederates, and there was never any intention of bringing their *harlequinade* to opening night. You yourself said they had reported for the curtain, yet had turned around and promptly disappeared moments later. If merely Pantaloon had turned up missing, or you had mislaid a policeman, one might consider the possibilities. But to have your entire cast vanish into the night minutes before taking the stage! How can that be anything but deliberate? Especially when occurring as part of a pattern that has continued for a month now? London has its share of the criminal class, but I doubt there's much profit in the chronic kidnapping of stage magicians and songsters, especially when it's only from one stage on one street."

"I don't see – "

"Which brings us to motive," continued Holmes. "Mrs. Hughes lives a quiet, isolated life. She is content to focus on her business, which thrives under the care she and Mr. Jacobs had invested in its success. There are other similar businesses as well. All know the Alhambra, the Argyle, the Barnes – but they are geographically remote and may be, for the moment, disregarded. Looking within the immediate neighborhood, who would benefit if the Aoede closed its doors? There are numerous victuallers, of course, but Bill's Cyder Cellar is the only local establishment in direct competition for the cheap dining-and-entertainment crowd.

"Having visited the Cyder Cellar earlier this week, it was easy to tell that it is doing a poor business these days. At the peak of the evening, there were hardly a hundred individuals upon the premises, and of those, a tenth or more were children and infants! The spirits were adulterated; the food was lacking; the atmosphere was fetid; the cleanliness left everything to be desired. Bill is not the proprietor of a successful establishment; Bill is the captain of a sinking ship.

"Mrs. Hughes has told us she has no interest in marriage and is content to live quietly, yet she has received three propositions for marriage in the last six weeks, each, presumably, from a man who knows little or nothing of the woman to whom he proposed. One anonymous letter-writer; one from Mr. Ferguson himself; and one, as it happens, from you, Mr. Munby. When a man proposes marriage to a woman who is nearly a stranger, it is rarely from honorable motivations. Perhaps it is cynical of me, but ninety-nine times of a hundred, it is to gain access and control of whatever property she might bring to the union. And Mrs. Hughes is a prosperous, practical widow, having cultivated the diamonds of her youth into a tidy income. When Mr. Ferguson sensed his competition's vulnerability, upon Mr. Jacobs' illness and death, he attempted to buy her out for whatever pittance he could. When that failed, he attempted to again play upon the abandonment and isolation of a widow who has lost a trusted friend. And when that approach was rebuffed, he sent you in, Mr. Munby, to destroy from within as a ship-worm sabotages a ship. You made a halfhearted effort at a proposal yourself, but as that had failed twice before, it obviously did not work the third time it was tried. Instead, you concentrated your attack on her purse-strings. You advertised creative, inventive acts which could not possibly appear on stage, and attempted to destroy the credibility of her establishment, in the hopes that it would drive more patrons to Bill's Cyder Cellar, which, I've discovered, is unlikely to keep its doors open more than three months. He has enough bills from creditors to paper his office."

"It sounds plausible, but why should Mr. Munby go through all that effort?" I asked.

"Watson, you know that the study of physiognomy is just as important to me as the study of tobacco-ash or soil particles," said Holmes. "I had the opportunity to observe Mr. Ferguson himself earlier this week. He possessed a strong forehead with very square eyebrows. His earlobes were quite attached to the side of his head; he has a very square jaw; and there were seven or eight other unique points about his appearance. Looking at our friend Mr. Munby, you can easily observe that same phenotype, suggesting hereditary characteristics."

"He has no children. I'm not his son," said Munby sullenly.

"Perhaps. Perhaps not. You may be a nephew of his, or something else, but the pair of you certainly share the same blood," said Holmes. "I wonder what he could have offered that made you think it prudent to partake in such an infantile scheme."

Munby arose abruptly and stalked past three waiters, who had spent the last ten minutes rubbing down tables nearby with more care than was strictly necessary. "I'll not take this abuse any longer. Unfounded, that's what it is," he shouted over his shoulder as he departed the room.

"Of all the − !" exclaimed Mrs. Hughes, who was still processing the torrent of explanation. "What can I do about it?"

"Munby may or may not be his real name," said Holmes. "And there's no physical evidence, of course, to bring him to a court of law. No phonograph recordings of him and Mr. Ferguson plotting against you, or a useful outline of 'Steps to Destroy One's Competitor' in their own hand. Still, I believe you can take solace in the fact that Bill's shall be a distant memory soon enough. The wicked do not always prosper. Now, this shall suffice for tonight. Let us retire, as the wall-paperers will be here soon enough."

"The wall-paperers! Surely that was a joke," said Mrs. Hughes.

"As I said, ridding yourself of Munby was only half your problem," said Holmes. "This has been slow enough to play out, but things must be done in the proper order."

It seemed like no time before we were back at the Aoede, the chilly grey mist swirling through the streets. Mrs. Hughes was instructed regarding her part, and Holmes and I stationed ourselves behind the heavy drape of the closed curtain, where we could see but not be seen in turn.

Three different wall-paperers arrived in succession. Each time, Mrs. Hughes would go up to her office to take care of some papers while they and their assistants took measurements of the room. Mrs. Hughes would return after an interval. They conversed with Mrs. Hughes; she thanked them and they took their leave. Holmes sat quietly and made no movement.

With the fourth set of wall-paperers, however, it was different. As soon as Mrs. Hughes had departed, he scooted his ladder from its station by the wall, and dragged it to the center of the room while his assistant stood watch near the door. The one with the ladder then commenced a thorough investigation of each of the large chandeliers which depended from the ceiling. He gave a muffled cry of excitement as he found something. Holmes stepped calmly from behind the curtain, stick in hand, and said, "Don't get too excited, friend. It's only paste."

The wall-paperer nearly fell from his ladder, but quickly recovered himself. He looked at the glittering handful he had pulled from the profusion of crystal swags, then tossed it across the room in disgust. His companion had already bolted from the scene.

"I presume you're looking for the jewels that Philip Tull hid there ten years ago," said Holmes. "I assure you, they have been found and are returned to their lawful possessor."

Mrs. Hughes had re-entered the room during this exchange. "What, and diamonds, too?"

"While you were explaining your initial problem, I couldn't help remarking upon the additional oddities that had plagued you of late. Not just the prowlers, but the acrobat. The gas-fitters. The drapers. In each of those cases, random outsiders were finding every excuse to investigate the very ceilings of this particular room. Yet it didn't make sense to lay it at Mr. Munby's feet, as he had perfect access to this room 'round the clock, and had no reason to make elaborate excuses to investigate it with either acrobats or sham drapers. Therefore, there seemed to be a second issue at play, and it was my task to separate the threads of two independent problems.

"Imagine, if you will, ten years ago. You are a young man named Philip Tull, who has recently involved himself in some sort of criminal activity involving the possession of stolen property. With the police hot on your trail, you run to seek refuge on the premises belonging to a relative, but you are unaware that relative has relocated, and sold the property to another. You enter the premises; you see scaffolding has been erected for the post-fire renovation. You scramble up the scaffolding and hide sparkling jewels amongst a chandelier full of sparkling crystals. By the time the police capture you, 'the goods' are no longer in your possession, and they cannot arrest you on that . . . but there are other excuses for your detainment, as your existence has not been an honest one, and you find yourself in prison, where you die of influenza a few years into your term." Looking at the wall-paperer, he added, "I presume that is where you heard of the diamonds?"

"He knew he wouldn't make it out alive," said the wall-paperer gruffly. "There was three of 'em, and not as careful as they could be. His companions were caught with the goods on 'em, and met their ends on the scaffold. The jewelers got back everything in the end, excepting that

200

piece. Its secrets would have died with him, if it weren't for his bragging."

"A collet necklace of considerable value," said Holmes, retrieving the dummy and pocketing it. "An odd subject to contemplate upon one's death-bed. Now that you know Philip Tull's ill-gotten goods have been returned to their rightful owners, and you have no further reason to pester this establishment, I will give you three minutes' head start before I call the nearest policeman."

The wall-paperer did not require a second suggestion. He fled the scene. Mrs. Hughes was more interested in examining the substitute necklace, which Holmes permitted.

"Holmes! You seem to have had a good grasp of the situation before you left your arm-chair!" I said.

"Although the main points were relatively straightforward, it was merely a matter of filling in the details," said Holmes.

"These ain't paste!" exclaimed Mrs. Hughes, looking up from the diamonds in her hands.

"Indeed, they are not," said Holmes, retrieving them gently. "Just as our friends had difficulty in accessing premises which were so heavily occupied 'round the clock, I, too, would have had difficulty in hunting these down and performing a substitution without exciting attention. And I especially did not want to do anything that would make Munby suspect anything was afoot. It was easier to leave them in place and allow others an opportunity to direct us to their location. Come along, Watson. I noted a German seller of sheet-music the next street over. Perhaps he may have something of interest for solo violin."

The Song of the Mudlark
by Shane Simmons

Before you says a word, I'll tell you I know. My writing ain't so pretty as what Doctor Watson puts down on his pages, but then I'm not a learned medical man, am I? So why's he not writing up this adventure of his friend and fellow, Sherlock Holmes, you're likely to say. Well he don't know half as much about it as I do, and even Mister Holmes don't know all the details, smart as he is, knowing everything as he usually does. But me, I know the whole lot. I was there from the start and to the finish. Who am I then, to be so well informed? If you say, as people do, that Doctor Watson's always been Mister Holmes's right-hand man, I expect that makes me his left-hand man. Or boy. There's a few years to go yet before people see me as a man, even though I've been on my own, taking care of myself and my mates, since I was old enough to walk and run the streets of London.

The name's Wiggins. I'd tell you my given name, but then we ain't so well acquainted, you and me. I'm writing up this here story, and you're reading it, which is all well and good. But if I don't know your name, you only get "Wiggins" for mine and that'll have to do.

I might have writ this tale earlier, only my words weren't so good then as they is now, which is to say they was a whole lot more horrible back when these events first happened and was fresh to me. Nah, don't you worry. I remember all the whys and wherefores just fine, like it were only yesterday. I remember because nobody ever forgets the time they brought a big mystery to the doorstep of the great Sherlock Holmes. How big a mystery? Well, let's just say it was so mysterious a mystery, Mr. Holmes agreed to look into it right away, and that don't happen much. It's got to be quite a teaser to get him interested, otherwise he'll take one look and solve it, quick as a fiddle, and where's the fun in that, I ask you.

It was early one morning when me and the boys dropped by Baker Street. Mr. Holmes had a package come in on one of the ships at the dock, and he had sent me, personally, to fetch it. As it so happens, it was two packages I brought back – the one he was so anxious about, and another I hoped he would take on once I explained the situation.

I left the rest of the boys waiting in the lane out back. Mrs. Hudson was the name of the landlady, and she didn't much care for any of us tracking dirt inside and all over her nice clean floors. She was always claiming she'd just mopped them, even though I never saw her lay a hand to a mop or a broom except to chase us out of her rooms.

"He's upstairs and he's in a mood," she said when she saw it was only me coming in and my shoes weren't in such a sorry state.

She pointed the way, like I didn't already know it, like I hadn't been up there a hundred times before.

"Enter!" I heard Mr. Holmes shout after my first knock on the door.

He didn't sound none too patient. I didn't bother announcing it was me who'd come up. He would've already deduced that ages ago.

"Ah, Wiggins, at last," he said when he saw the wrapped bundle tied up under my arm.

"The package you been waiting on, Mr. Holmes," I announced.

He took it from me right off and tossed a shilling I had to grab out of the air.

"What package is this, then?" Dr. Watson wanted to know as he looked up from the morning paper.

"Oh, merely something for my chemistry experiments," Mr. Holmes told him. "A perplexing puzzle in its own right, and something to occupy my mind while London is beset with this wave of inexorably dull, unimaginative crime."

He cut the string on the package with a pair of scissors and brought it over to his work bench that was stacked high with all sorts of glass bottles and tubes filled with who-knows-what for reasons I couldn't guess at.

"All the way from South America is what the cabin boy told me," I said.

"Barring one side trip to Germany for refinement, but yes, quite right."

Mr. Holmes looked in one of his drawers and came up with a small leather case. He opened it and I spotted a needle inside, the kind I'd expect to see in a doctor's hand, not a consulting detective's. I figure maybe he swiped it from Dr. Watson without asking first because he seemed to not want the doctor to see what he was up to.

"Off you go, Wiggins. You have your shilling. I will send word if I have anything else for you."

I nearly left right when he told me to, but stopped in the door. I didn't want to waste his time, but then I weren't so sure if what else I brought him was a waste or not, was I?

"Mr. Holmes, there's something more."

"Is there? Well, out with it, Wiggins. What do you want?"

"It ain't what I want. It's what I have for you. A mystery."

I saw Mr. Holmes swap a look with Dr. Watson, and for a moment I thought they might laugh at me. But then Mr. Holmes must have seen how I looked so serious, and knew it wasn't any childish riddle I was on about.

"Best I introduce you in person," I said to them.

I stepped out of the room, to the top of the stairs, and whistled loud as I could. The back door opened and I could hear footsteps stomping on up, with Mrs. Hudson complaining about each one. I led my guest inside and shut the door so we didn't have to listen to the landlady no more.

"Another one!" said Dr. Watson, not at all happy when he saw who I'd brought into their home. "Well, better than him leading in the whole lot as he usually does."

It was another young urchin to be sure, even more ragged than the ones he'd seen Mr. Holmes deal with before. I was about to explain what was special about this one, but Mr. Holmes was ahead of me.

"Now there's an irregular Irregular!" he said. "The ranks swell and diminish, Watson, lads come and they go, but this one is quite different. Not your usual recruit I would say, Wiggins."

"No sir, you're right there."

"How so, Holmes?" said Dr. Watson. "He seems to fit right in with the other street Arabs."

"Several factors exclude him from the rest," said Mr. Holmes, looking the child next to me up and down. "Firstly, this lad is at least a year or two younger than the rest. The jacket, cap and trousers are considerably rougher than what Wiggins and his crew wear, as though salvaged further down the line of poverty and despair. And there has been some grief of late, I perceive. The tears are not flowing this moment, but the last ones carved twin ditches down those dirty cheeks too recently to have been filled in by fresh dirt. Though the dust is no different than what might be routinely kicked up in a busy London street, the mud on those shoes is another matter. That is not from any puddle or pit in the city. It comes from the banks of the river. I should say this is one of the mudlarks of the Thames standing before us."

The mudlarks were the lowest of the low, and children the lot of them, either with no parents at all, or mothers and fathers too drunk or worse to take care of them. They worked the banks of the Thames when the tide was out, picking through the muck for anything they could sell for a ha'penny. Scraps and rubbish mostly, but worth something to someone somewhere, if only a farthing or a bite to eat. Compared to the mudlarks, we street urchins were the tip-top of high society.

"Right you are, Mr. Holmes," I said, "though you've missed out on one detail."

204

"Have I? Do enlighten us then, Wiggins."

"She ain't no lad."

Mr. Holmes raised my companion's cap off her head and studied the face more closely.

"I do believe you are correct," he said at last. "An easy enough detail to miss under so much filth."

"Her name is Beth," I said. "I've seen her working down by the water before, but today I found her in such a state."

"Me da's been killed!" Beth cried out when she couldn't keep silent any longer. "Washed up in the Thames and bleeding money like he were made of it!"

Fresh tears carved new ditches through the dirt on her face.

"Bleeding money, you say?" said Mr. Holmes, picking out the one detail that weren't all too common. Poor folks drowning in the Thames was hardly worth a mention otherwise.

"The girl is imagining fairy stories, Holmes," said Dr. Watson and made to stick his nose back in his paper.

But Mr. Holmes, he didn't look so sure.

"Wiggins, have you seen this yourself?"

"No sir," I said. "But word is out that a body's been spat out of the river with the low tide and's lying on the banks. The mudlarks all know it, but the police haven't come 'round for a look. Not yet at any rate. And I figure since you seem to always know so much about dead bodies . . . ."

I had told Beth I knew a man who might help, but I didn't want to push my luck too far and endanger my job. Without Mr. Holmes paying us a regular salary, The Baker Street Irregulars would have a hard time of it, I know that much.

Mr. Holmes looked back to his work bench and his new experiment and I knew we was losing him.

"No, Wiggins. There is nothing to it for me. Best let the police sort the matter out. It sounds like a routine drowning, or perhaps an altercation that ended in the river."

Regular wages or not, I didn't let it stand there.

"Show it to him," I nudged Beth and she dug deep into her one pocket that didn't already have holes in it.

"Show me what?" Mr. Holmes wanted to know.

"A clue," I said.

Beth came up with a small hunk of metal, not unlike the old bolts and nails she scavenged along the water's edge. At first glance it looked like any other scrap, but Mr. Holmes took it in hand and saw what was so special about it at once.

"Where did you get this?" he asked Beth.

"It was stuck in Da. I shook him and it fell out."

"What do you make of this, Watson," said Mr. Holmes, handing the thing over.

"Why, it's a gold sovereign!" Dr. Watson declared after having his look.

"Yes, I can see that for myself," said Mr. Holmes. "But what does it tell you?"

"Well, it is certainly mangled. Not the usual wear and tear I would expect to see on such a denomination. And it is far more money than some unfortunate mudlark could ever make."

"Not in a year or more of hard labour, even if they should they live long enough to procure a better occupation," agreed Mr. Holmes. "What else?"

Dr. Watson had another look because Mr. Holmes was suggesting he missed something. Something important.

"It's all rusty," he said at last.

"No Watson, not rusty, but imbued with the stuff. Gold neither rusts nor tarnishes, yet this piece is absolutely caked with both."

"So what does that tell you?" asked Dr. Watson of his friend.

"What indeed?" was all Mr. Holmes had to say on the matter.

That got him interested. It made him stop and think for a moment, at any rate. And when he didn't come right back with an explanation, I dared figure I might have him.

"You'll have a look, though, won't you Mr. Holmes?"

Mr. Holmes had always done right by the Irregulars, and he gave me a bit of a nod and a smile and agreed.

"Watson, be the good doctor and see to our new client. If Mrs. Hudson has a soup on the stove, pour some into her. She's all skin and bones. Wiggins and I will take a hansom down to the water and see what we shall see."

After I dismissed the rest of The Irregulars for that day, me and Mr. Holmes caught ourselves a cab that took us straight down to the spot Beth had told me about. Once we were there, we saw the crowd that had gathered along the embankment. Somebody other than a mudlark had spotted Beth's dead father, and now the police were there, keeping everyone back.

It only took a word from Mr. Holmes to get past the two Bobbies blocking off the steps to the river. If they didn't know his face, they knew his name and reputation and that was enough. A third was standing at the water's edge, next to a fellow lying face-down on the rocks. The man on guard was a big peeler from The Yard – the kind what runs the likes of The Irregulars off the street if they get a notion we's up to

206

something they don't approve of. He would have chased me off right quick if Mr. Holmes hadn't vouched for me.

"My name is Sherlock Holmes," he said, "and this is my associate, Mr. Wiggins."

I tipped my hat at the introduction, polite whenever I must.

"Mr. Holmes," said the officer in charge of the scene, "always a pleasure to hear you're on the job. Though what interest this sort of vagrant might have for you is beyond me."

"Even the lowest among us may suffer an intriguing demise that warrants investigation."

"Take a look as you care, but he seems just another drowned shoreman to me. If anyone's at fault, I would point at the man who poured him his last drink."

It didn't take Mr. Holmes more than a moment to disagree with the policeman once he stooped down and began making all those deductions he's so good at.

"He is quite soaked through, but not drowned," he concluded. "No water has been inhaled. Dead men do not gasp for breath, above or below the water."

The man in charge didn't look so in charge once he heard it was a killing he was standing over.

"Hello, what have we here?" said Mr. Holmes, brushing aside the sopping tangle of hair at the back of the dead man's head. Beth had been right. Her father was bleeding money.

There, sticking out of an ugly hole punched through the back of his skull, was a tidy sum of money, all clumped together in a rusty chunk, with every coin stuck to their mates like they was all minted that way.

Mr. Holmes began the messy task of picking the pieces out as they would come. Some coins were loose, but most were massed in groups, with as many as a dozen at a time joined together. You'd need a hammer and long hours to break them all apart to spend. There weren't no more gold sovereigns like the one Beth had plucked out, but every other coin of the realm, copper or silver, made an appearance. All told, Mr. Holmes figured it to be at least three pounds worth – enough to have bought the eyes and ears of The Irregulars for a good long time, I'll tell you.

When he was done, the wound lay open and bare and it was sure as anything that that was what killed him. The bobby looked confused, and I'm not one to see eye-to-eye with the police most times, but it didn't make no sense to me neither.

"Who would kill a man and then, rather than stealing from him, deposit a sum of money in his body before throwing the corpse into the water? Surely he wasn't trying to sink it."

It was a foolish notion, but Mr. Holmes let it pass.

"Many a murdered man has been weighed down and sent to the bottom of the Thames. But not with only a handful of pocket change. And certainly not stuffed into a wound in his head. I would expect to see stones or perhaps heavy scraps of metal in his pockets, but there is nothing."

"What's the truth of it then, Mr. Holmes?" I asked.

"He was a shoreman most certainly, a tosher more specifically, but this has only been his occupation in recent years. The configuration of the callouses on his hands tell me of the tools he worked with. Not a long hoe, as a tosher might employ, but more likely shovels and picks. You can still see the discolouration in his skin from the coal dust to this day. He quit the mines after an injury left him with a broken arm that never set right, and came to the city to pursue a better life he failed to find. Fallen on hard times with a young child to support, he turned to toshing and may have come to more success at it than he wished."

Toshers were like mudlarks, all grown up but after bigger stakes. Their scavenging took them to much more dangerous, awful places. There were rewards to be had, sure enough, but it took a desperate man to try his hand at it.

"Was it murder?" was all the peeler wanted to know.

"I cannot say for the moment. Another man was involved at least. Of that much I am certain. Observe the heels of his boots, scuffed to the point of very nearly being worn through. The man was dragged here, pulled through the streets by his arms, and deposited along the banks of the Thames by someone in the middle of the night. He is wet, true, but from the morning rain, not the river. And the muck that covers his boots and trousers – how foul and fetid! I know every variety of mud than can be trodden in and tracked anywhere in London. I can tell you precisely which district a sample of soil is from and how fresh it is. But this! This I have never encountered. I am not acquainted with it nor, I suspect, do I wish to be. And yet, it shall be key to discovering the precise location where this man met his demise."

"What can my men do to help?" asked the policeman.

"Nothing at all. It is the assistance of young Wiggins I need now. As for the concerns of Scotland Yard, you may remove the body. It has told me all it can."

Mr. Holmes took me aside as the police prepared to carry the dead fellow to the wagon that had only just arrived. Beth's father would be filling a pauper's grave before another day had passed.

"We shall need a finer nose than mine to detect one scent amongst the myriad of fragrances we will face in the city streets," Mr. Holmes said to me. I knew straight off who he was talking about.

"Take a cab and have it wait for you," he said, giving me another shilling to cover expenses. "Pick up our mutual acquaintance and be back here as quick as you can. The longer we delay, the more the trail will be obscured by the regular traffic of London. I shall ask after any witnesses while you are gone, but our greatest hope lies with you and the best nose in England."

"Number Three, Pinchin Lane in Lambeth," was the address I gave to the first cab that would stop for me.

The journey wasn't a long one, and I soon found myself outside a row of shabby houses, picking out the one on the street filled with the calls and cries of a whole menagerie of animals.

"Can I borrow your dog?" I asked the man who came to the door.

I knew the reputation of this man who fancied himself a trainer of any beast he could lay his hands on, but he didn't know me from any other beggar.

"My dogs are not for rent," he said and tried to shut the door in my face. Only my foot in the frame kept him from kicking me out.

"Did I say anything about paying? No, I'm here to borrow on strict orders from Mister Sherlock Holmes."

And it was like I had said a magic word.

"Sherlock Holmes, you say? Then it must be Toby in number seven he's after."

It certainly was. Toby, ugly as sin, a shaggy mess if I'm completely honest, was the finest tracker dog to be had. Not that I had much cause to compare, but Mr. Holmes always swore by him, and we were soon reacquainted once his owner handed me the leash.

The hansom driver I left waiting didn't like carting around a boy of the street, even though I paid him good money. He liked it even less once I brought an unkempt mutt into his cab. Grumbling all the way or not, he got us back to the water in a short enough time.

Mr. Holmes took the leash from me as soon as we joined him and let the dog have a good sniff around. The body was gone, but the stink of his boots lingered and Toby soon had the scent. Didn't much care for it neither. Never did I see a dog recoil from a smell like that. For a dog what made it his business to put his nose to all sorts of dreadful things, this was one odour that seemed to outright offend him.

"I know, Toby," said Mr. Holmes. "Not the most pleasant aroma I have ever set you to follow, but follow it we must. There's a boy!"

209

Mr. Holmes's words of encouragement were enough to spark the dog's interest and he put his nose to the ground and hunted for which way the trail might lead. Through walkways and streets, around corners and down alleys we went. Toby kept us on the path that was invisible to the human eye but plain as day to the nose of an expert tracker dog.

Toby was so sure of himself as we wove our way into the city, it was a surprise when he started zigging and zagging, suddenly not so clear which way to go next.

"The trail splits in two, it seems," said Mr. Holmes. "The man who dragged Beth's father to the river may well have doubled back on his own path and then on to a new destination. Whether we trace this to the man himself or the origin of his crime will have to be Toby's decision."

At last, Toby picked a branch and on we went for a few blocks more until we came to an east-end pub that was a short-walk local to anybody within a few doors. Anyone much farther away would have picked a better place to drink their worries away. It looked to be a rough place, home to nightly bare-knuckled matches, scheduled or not, but all of them bet on just the same. Mr. Holmes walked right on in like he belonged there, so I followed in case he needed my protection.

"You there! Get that dirty little mongrel out of here!" the barkeep shouted at us as soon as we stepped inside.

"I assure you, sir, he is very well trained, devoid of fleas, and will refrain from relieving himself indoors," said Mr. Holmes.

"I weren't talkin' about the dog! I meant the boy."

"As did I."

"Beggars and thieves, the lot of them!"

"He is with me, and neither of us will be staying long."

The barkeep made no move to toss us out on his own. You don't give the bum's rush to a gentleman like Sherlock Holmes.

"I won't serve him," he growled instead.

"We won't be drinkin' the piss you serve," I informed him.

Mr. Holmes looked down at me, pardoned my French, and agreed. "Quite."

He led Toby around the pub, from table to table, seeing which one the dog liked best. It didn't take him a moment to bring us to a man sitting at a booth in the corner, working his way through a pint glass I'd wager had been refilled a few times already.

Toby seemed pleased to have come upon a pair of boots that matched the smell he'd been tracking, but he still took a step back when he caught a whiff of the fresh muck crusted there.

"What have you trodden in, I wonder," said Mr. Holmes to the man.

"What business is that of yours?"

210

"I am Sherlock Holmes and this is Mr. Wiggins. The dog's name is Toby, if that is of any concern to you. Where you have been and what you have been up to is very much our business when you leave corpses lying about in public places."

The man made a move like he might bolt, but Mr. Holmes stood in his way, blocking him in the booth.

"You can talk to us, or you can be arrested for murder. It is entirely up to you."

That settled the man down a bit. Mr. Holmes handed me Toby's leash and sat down across from him.

"We have introduced ourselves. Who do we have the pleasure of addressing?"

"The name's Seaver. Edward Seaver."

"And the dead man?"

"That would be Albert Ewart. A good friend, he was."

It was the first time either of us had heard Beth's father called anything other than "Da."

"A tosher of late," said Mr. Holmes, "but formerly a coal miner, was he not?"

"Aye, he was in the mines. And it was coal in the end, once the ore mine he was in ran dry and closed. Mining is dark, dangerous work any way you look at it. But ore don't give you the black lung like coal does. Old Bert couldn't take it more than two or three years before he got out and came here."

"Tell me, did Mr. Ewart keep in touch with any of his fellows?"

"He did. One of them came through town only a few days ago."

"Bringing more than news from the mines, I expect. You were partnered with Mr. Ewart?"

"We'd do some toshing together from time to time."

"Last night, for instance. Until it all went horribly wrong. Of course, that means you no longer need to share, and what a windfall Ewart's death must be to you!"

Mr. Holmes and that Seaver fellow both seemed to know what they was talking about, but me, I was lost.

"It was an accident, I swear it!" Edward Seaver blurted out before he ran.

Mr. Holmes went right after him, with me and Toby on his heels, shouting and barking for him to stop. It were no use. There was a tiny window up on the wall in the back room and Seaver wormed his way through it like he was greased. I could have fit just fine and offered to go after him, but Mr. Holmes stopped me.

"No use in it, Wiggins," he said. "Seaver will not drift too far astray from the object of his desire. Blood has already been spilled for it, accidentally or not. And he has risked exposure in order to move a body far from it. He will not leave it be now. Especially since he has no idea we have the means to discover it for ourselves."

"Discover what, Mr. Holmes?"

Mr. Holmes laughed and put a hand on my shoulder.

"Treasure beyond your wildest dreams, young Wiggins."

Mr. Holmes had us out on the street again, retracing our earlier steps. His eye weren't on the path, though. He was looking up at the dark sky. Storm clouds were rolling in over London.

"We must follow the other branch of the trail while time remains. More rain is coming, much heavier than last night. Even Toby's talented nose has its limits. The last of the scent will be washed away before the day is done."

Back at the spot where the trail had split, Mr. Holmes set Toby on the second branch. That one didn't lead very far at all, taking us into a flophouse nearby. The place was brimming with poor souls trying to scrape by on whatever work they could get. If they couldn't afford a room, they might at least rent one corner of a room, shared with as many as ten others.

Invited inside, we were glad to get out of the downpour that was just beginning. One of the tenants confirmed this was where Beth and her father spent their nights between days clawing a living out of London's castoffs. Nobody had seen Albert Ewart leave, dead or alive, during the night, but he could well have been spirited away down the hall while everyone else in the building was asleep behind closed doors. We were offered to be shown to the upstairs spot where they kept their bed rolls, but Toby insisted the trail led down to the basement instead. Mr. Holmes didn't argue and followed the dog.

The foundation weren't dug very deep, and it was more of a crawlspace than a basement we found at the bottom of the steps. Even I had to duck down, and Mr. Holmes had to crouch and support himself on his fingertips as we made our way along the earth floor. A lantern had been left at the bottom of the stairs and we used it to light up the black space for a look. The only thing down there other than a lot of cobwebs was a squat punt, tied to a support beam as though someone thought it might drift away, even on dry land.

"Why tether a boat in a basement, so far from the water's edge, I wonder?" said Mr. Holmes, though I suspect he already had a notion.

There were a series of loose boards set across the floor that looked like they had been left behind by workers when the house was first built.

When Mr. Holmes started to set them to one side, he revealed the large hole they had been covering. Someone had tunnelled their way out of the basement.

"Where do you think they was digging to, Mr. Holmes?" I asked.

"Apparently our deceased miner was keen to go mining under the city in tunnels already dug out for him."

Mr. Holmes held the lantern over the dark hole so we could peer down into it. I could see the excavation went straight down through the dirt and broke through an arch of brickwork, offering entry into the sewer line that ran right under the building.

"This is the sort of vandalism toshers have been reduced to since the new London sewer system was completed. Rather before your time, Wiggins, but access used to be a far simpler matter when it ran freely into the Thames. Now such intrusions are forbidden by law, and if they're caught in the act, they face fines they can ill-afford to pay."

"What's so worth the risk and the stink of rummaging down there?"

"We shall see in short order," said Mr. Holmes, bidding me to help him lower the punt into the stream of filthy water below us.

The climb down was precarious, but we were cautious every foothold of the way, making sure nobody took a dip we'd long regret. Mr. Holmes carried Toby down in his arms, mangy but manageable in size as he was. We were soon all aboard the punt. A long pole tucked inside let Mr. Holmes push us off the side and set us down the slow-moving stream.

"Let us ascertain what befell Albert Ewart while he was seeking his fortune. Here is a new scent for you, Toby. See if you can sniff it out amongst all the other odours down here."

Mr. Holmes took a thumb-sized item from his pocket and held it under Toby's nose.

"What's that?" I asked him.

"Something the dead man had tucked under his belt. It is a vital tool in the mining industry, and was recently supplied to Beth's late father by his visiting friend. Undoubtedly he wrote to request it and several more just like it. It is called a blasting cap."

"What does it do?"

"Why, it explodes, of course. Not as grandly as dynamite, for instance, but it offers a smaller controlled charge to set off its more devastating cousins when much stone needs to be moved. Used on its own, it can still produce quite a powerful bang."

Drifting on a punt, Toby couldn't put his nose to the ground, yet he seemed able to catch the scent of recently detonated powder in the tunnel

213

as he perched on the bow. It lingered in the still air, even hours later, and I thought I could smell it mixed in with the strong ammonia stink myself.

When Toby seemed excited about a certain bend in the tunnel, Mr. Holmes poled us in that direction, taking us down a split lane. The current seemed to be picking up as the rain water from above filtered down into the sewer. Mr. Holmes had to work the pole harder to keep us from being swept along too quickly to give the tunnel a thorough search by lantern light.

After Toby's keen sense directed us to make a couple more turns, we happened upon a dark mass jutting out of the water. I might have missed it entirely, but Mr. Holmes seemed to know what he was looking for.

"There it lies, Wiggins. Riches more than we could hope to have to our names combined and multiplied. Who would have thought that such a treasure trove would be found in so foul a place!"

I leaned in for a closer look by the light of the lantern. There was more money in front of me than I ever dreamt existed, all fused together into one rusted mass – an entire boulder of it, jutting out of the sewage like a monument a madman might have sculpted for no one to ever see.

"I don't understand, Mr. Holmes. How could such a thing even exist?"

Mr. Holmes had an explanation, sure enough. He always had everything figured out.

"Think of all the coins that are dropped and lost in the streets of London each day. Some are discovered and picked up again, but many others are washed away into the gutter, down drains and into the sewers. All it takes is for one or two of them to get their edges caught in the gap between bricks under the waterline and they will collect others, like silt in a steady flow. They gather and rust together there for years, even decades, until they create a vast structure like this one, tempting to the toshers who come down here looking for lost valuables, but impossible to move. Such a waste."

"I'll not waste a penny of it! That you can be sure of!"

There was a lamp approaching us from down the tunnel, with footsteps splashing through the water beneath it. We couldn't see the face behind the bright light, but we recognized the voice of Edward Seaver.

"It's not the first lump of rusted coinage toshers have come across down here, but it's the grandest. And can we ever profit from any of them? No! Even if we could break them free, they're too heavy to drag up top."

Mr. Holmes was expecting he'd turn up, and turn up he did.

214

"Albert Ewart had a solution, did he not? A certain expertise that came from his mining days."

Closer now, I could see Seaver had the lamp fixed to his coat to light his way no matter where he turned or bent. He had his tosher's hoe with him, but had no plans to go raking for lost valuables ever again if he could come away with the pile of money that didn't want to go anywhere.

"He thought we could break it up, blow it into smaller pieces we could carry off," he said.

"With a number of these," said Mr. Holmes, holding up the blasting cap for Seaver. "As you can see, you failed to pilfer all of them from your fallen friend."

"It were his poor luck the one piece he blew loose came right at him when the fuse burned too quick and he couldn't run far enough. Shot down the tunnel like a bullet it did, with only his head to stop it. I couldn't leave him down here for the rats, but I couldn't leave him in the flophouse neither. Not looking like that for his own daughter to see. So I dragged him down to the river to let the tide take him away. A long, heavy trip it was, in the dark and rain. By the time we made it to the banks, the rain had let up and the morning sun was coming out. People would spot us, I was sure, and think I done it."

I looked at the mass of coins again. Near the top, you could see the spot where the charge went off. It looked like a bite had been taken out of it, but only a nibble compared to how much remained.

"If you want your proof I weren't the one that killed him, the piece that struck him down must be here somewhere," said Seaver, turning this way and that, shining his light around the water and walls.

"Your evening might have been more profitable if only you had bothered to examine Albert Ewart's wound," said Mr. Holmes. "I found a fair sum imbedded there this morning."

"Oh, I see now," Seaver hissed suspiciously. "You come to take the rest for yourselves! Well it's mine, I tell you, and I'll have at it by hammer and chisel till I'm old and grey if I must!"

Seaver came at us with his hoe raised as if he might try to beat us away from his treasure. Even as he pushed forward through water up to his knees, he seemed to make hardly any progress.

Mr. Holmes had his punting pole jammed into the side of the mound of money, keeping us anchored in place even as the flow of water picked up its pace. I'd hardly noticed the lazy current go from a steady trickle to a rapid river while the two men talked, but when Seaver, standing right in the middle of the flow, started to lose his footing, I knew something was wrong.

215

"The water's gone quick on us, Mr. Holmes, and I can see it rising up the walls!" I said, suddenly frightened. "We don't want to get caught in here come high tide!"

"No, it is far too early for high tide," said Mr. Holmes, seeing the same danger as me. "This is rain water. A deluge, in fact!"

With a terrible shout of anger and terror, Seaver tipped back into the flood and was swept away down the tunnel and into darkness. The last I saw of him was the tiny point of light from his lamp that blinked out once water pushed through the glass.

"Perilous occupation, toshing," declared Mr. Holmes. "It will see the end of us next if we aren't quick!"

Mr. Holmes cast off from the monument of lost money and tried to keep the punt weighed with himself, me and Toby from getting turned over in the swell. We flew down the tunnel at a quick pace and I kept counting and recounting the layers of brick between the surface of the water and the top of the sewer. That number kept getting smaller.

"The water's rising fast, Mr. Holmes!" I cried over the gushing cascade. Pointing out the obvious to Sherlock Holmes is a waste of his time and yours, but I was scared silly.

"We are too close to the river!" he said. "All the water flowing into the sewers uphill is converging here. The entire tunnel will be filled to the top in moments."

Mr. Holmes soon had to duck his head to keep from scraping it across the arched brick ceiling. I was sure the rising water would squash us to jam against the roof before spilling over the sides of the boat and dragging us to the bottom. We'd be drowned for certain.

"This is what we are looking for!" Mr. Holmes announced, jamming his pole into the wall and turning us towards a dead-end route that was capped with a huge iron door, sealed shut with no means to be opened. "The river lies just beyond."

"I thought you said sewer water don't flow into the Thames no more!"

"It does, but away from the city and too many miles down river to save us now. We must rely on the emergency overflow outlets. They are designed to open when the sewer is over capacity to prevent flooding in the streets."

Mr. Holmes lay down at the bottom of the punt next to me and Toby. I gripped on tight to Toby's long, tangled mane and whispered to him, "Don't you worry, Mr. Holmes will see us through." But I wasn't so sure as the edges of the low boat floated high enough to touch the very top of the tunnel.

216

Just when I was certain we were all done for, there was a loud clatter that echoed through what bits of the tunnel weren't already under water. The next thing I knew, we were thrown forward and blown through the door as it flew open under all the pressure. I knew then what it was like to be fired out of a pistol. We were soaking wet in an instant, but not by sewer water sinking our little boat. It was rain, pouring down on us in sheets, and when I realized that I knew we were outside again.

I dared look up and saw we were adrift in the Thames. It was almost as dark out as it had been by lantern light in the tunnel, so black were the skies. Flashes of lightning lit up the shore enough for me to judge we'd been pushed all the way out to the middle of the flow, the tiniest ship on the whole river. Mr. Holmes stood up and surveyed our situation.

"We shan't be punting through waters as deep as the Thames," said Mr. Holmes, casting the useless pole down into our boat. "Make yourself useful, Wiggins, and help me flag down a passing vessel that might throw us a line."

I did as I was told, and it weren't too long before we was rescued, the three of us, and brought to the docks by a passing pusher tug. None were spared a thorough drenching, and me and Mr. Holmes had to return a stinking wet dog to his owner in Lambeth. We didn't tell him Toby might have ended the day smelling much worse had our venture into the London sewers gone badly.

"How has our houseguest been?" Mr. Holmes asked Dr. Watson back at Baker Street, once he'd gotten out of his wet clothes and into his robe.

"Ravenous," reported Dr. Watson. "I think we may go hungry in the coming week. Mrs. Hudson's pantry is down to crumbs."

Beth was sitting quietly by the window, humming softly to herself, trying to put the bad memories of the day aside with song.

"And how did your investigation go?" Dr. Watson asked.

"Well," said Mr. Holmes. "Wet but well."

"Back early enough to see to your chemistry experiments then, Holmes?"

Mr. Holmes took a long look at his work bench and then waved it away with his hand.

"No, Watson. I have had enough stimulation for the day. Perhaps tomorrow. At any rate, there is the girl, Beth, to attend to. Although I have solved the questions related to her father's death, she is too young to appreciate the case history, and there is no comfort for her to be had in the details. All that matters to her is that he is gone. "

"We should see about returning the girl to her mother," agreed Dr. Watson.

"Alas, there is no mother, Watson. Albert Ewart was a widower. A strip of clear skin around one finger told me of a ring that was there during his coal mining days, protecting that lone spot from the dust. It seems to have vanished years ago. Hard times or not, no living wife would let her husband pawn his wedding band."

Beth came out of her humming stupor and spoke up. "Mum's been dead so long, I can't hardly remember her."

"Another lost soul in London," said Mr. Holmes of the girl. "So many much too young for such a fate."

"I would say you already employ half of them, Holmes."

Dr. Watson was referring to me, standing out on a rug in the hall where I'd been told to stay, still dripping wet from the day, so I wouldn't stain the floorboards.

"Ah, if only that were so, Watson," said Mr. Holmes, giving me a grin. "Not a criminal in the city could lift a finger without my knowing of it."

"A single sovereign is hardly an inheritance that will keep her forever," said Dr. Watson. "Inquiries will have to be made at London orphanages to find one that can take her in,"

I had to raise an objection to that suggestion straight off.

"Some of the lads have been in and out of those places, and horrible they are. Like a prison for children whose only crime is being on their own."

"I am afraid it is the best we can offer her, Wiggins," said Mr. Holmes, even though I could tell he agreed with me.

"I understand," I nodded. "It's the best you can offer."

I, on the other hand, figured I could do better.

"Do not be so downtrodden, boy," said Dr. Watson. "She may yet be adopted."

But when Dr. Watson turned to address me, all he found were wet footprints across the floor to the window and back again.

"I believe she already has been," I heard Mr. Holmes say upstairs as I led Beth out the back door and away from Baker Street.

The rest of the lads were waiting for me at our usual spot, in an empty lot out behind a tanner's shop, just a few blocks away. The rain had let up and it looked like the weather had decided to behave itself again.

"Meet our new recruit," I said to them as I approached. "You can call him Ben."

"Ben," I repeated to Beth, making sure she understood her new name, "these are The Baker Street Irregulars. You're one of us now."

Not all of them were so quick to accept new faces. Mullin was the first to protest.

"He's not one of the boys. He don't even look like a boy."

"He's one of us because I says so," I told him, "and he's a boy if I says that, too. You want to argue with me, open wide so's I can knock out a tooth or two while I'm knocking some sense into you."

Mullin backed down as soon as he saw me make a fist, but some of the others weren't so easy to bend.

"You been playin' a little too thick at bein' the boss of late, Wiggins," another dared to say.

"Yeah? Well how many of you have gone on an adventure with Mister Sherlock Holmes and helped him solve a big mystery? None, that's right. Because there's Dr. Watson and then there's me."

And that seemed to settle it. I didn't mention Toby in the list of Mr. Holmes's partners, just in case they thought I might rank third behind a dog. Once the matter of expanding our ranks was decided, I felt Beth tugging on my sleeve.

"What do I do?" she wanted to know, now that she'd given up a life of mudlarking to become an Irregular.

"You do as the rest of us does," I instructed. "You watch and you listen. We're the eyes and ears of London, we lot. And whatever we know, whatever we learn, it's Sherlock Holmes who'll put it to good use."

She was young, the youngest we'd ever taken in, but she understood straight away. I couldn't honestly say that meant she had a bright future ahead of her, but she had a future with us, and that was something.

The Tale of the
Forty Thieves
by C.H. Dye

In perusing the records of the many adventures I shared with my extraordinary friend Mr. Sherlock Holmes, I am reminded how often the problems came to us in waves. Holmes might go weeks without a case, and then have several appear hard on each other's heels. So it was in the spring of 1887, when it seemed for a time that my friend might never get a chance to rest. I attempted to procure him a few days respite in the country after the months he spent in France, untangling the threads of the Netherland-Sumatra Company scandal, but as I have written elsewhere, that visit was interrupted by murder. We were not even a day back from Reigate when he was petitioned by Stephen Grice-Patterson to unravel the apparent haunting and thefts on the island of Uffa, in the Firth of Clyde. It was as well that I accompanied him to Scotland, for it took the both of us to lay the "ghost" after three night watches and a mad chase across the heather. By the time we set sail for Glasgow, all my medical instincts were aroused once more on my friend's behalf, but he insisted on returning to London by the night train, rather than taking a hotel and embarking in the morning.

We arrived at Euston Station at an hour when the dairymaids were still portioning out their wares to sleepy scullions, and the great metropolis had just begun to stir itself. We had just emerged into the light of the early morning sun and were casting about in search of a hansom when we were hailed by a familiar voice. Inspector Gregson of Scotland Yard was waving to us from the door of a growler on the street. "Mr. Holmes!" he called again. "Doctor Watson! Cabbie, draw us alongside those two gentlemen." We waited until the cab had parked beside us to give the Inspector our good mornings, and he returned them with alacrity. "You have no idea how glad I am to find you back in London."

I cannot say that I returned the sentiment with enthusiasm. A new case held little appeal. I have never quite lost the knack of sleeping under uncomfortable circumstances, thanks to my time in the Army, but I had spent most of the last fifteen hours travelling in an overcrowded railway compartment. I wanted nothing more than a bath and my breakfast. And I was concerned about Holmes, whose normal pallor was underlain with grey and whose eyes lacked their usual spark. He had forestalled a black mood by taking cocaine whilst we were awaiting our train in Glasgow, but had paid for the respite with restlessness. While I had dozed, he had fidgeted and read, restocking his pile of newspapers whenever opportunity presented. Still, he greeted the policeman with a nod and gladly accepted Gregson's offer of a ride to Baker Street.

No sooner were we on our way than the Scotland Yard detective asked Holmes, "Did you read about the Cartier bracelet while you were out of London?"

"A chain of diamonds and sapphires, stolen from a courier in the Strand last Friday. The company has offered a reward for its return."

"Yes. The courier, Hammond, didn't even realize he'd been robbed of his goods right away. He'd been jostled once or twice in the crowd, but he swears each time he checked his pocket and felt nothing amiss. But when he came to his destination, the bracelet was gone from the case. As neat a job as I've ever known."

"An ordinary crime," I interjected, hoping to keep Holmes from taking interest.

"Ordinary enough," Gregson agreed. "Were it not that the Foreign Office has become involved. They won't say why the recovery of the bracelet is so important, and I shan't speculate, but every man in the Yard is looking. And now a possible clue to the matter has come up near Elephant and Castle in Southwark. Do you know the area?"

"Tolerably." Holmes said, his fingers tapping against the pocket where he kept his cigarette case. It was empty, I knew, and so was mine, victim of his long sleepless night. "It is the intersection of several roads and a railway line. Not the richest of London's districts nor the poorest, although the Walter's Almhouses are home to more families than they were built for. The Baptist Tabernacle is the landmark most think of, although the area derives its name from a coaching inn mentioned by Shakespeare. They are building an underground station there, I believe."

"They are indeed, and there are two rival gangs which have stepped up their efforts to keep or take control of the nearby streets. It's made for a good many fights, a few robberies, and an increase in all sorts of other crime, particularly shoplifting and pickpocketing." The inspector tapped his bandaged leg. "Two nights ago Lestrade was on Brook Drive investigating a robbery when he came across one of the fights. He managed to blow his whistle and summon the nearest constables, but he got his shinbone cracked by a heavy belt buckle."

"Were the miscreants apprehended?" I asked, for I did not like to think of our frequent visitor being injured.

"Three were. Five escaped," Gregson said. "It would have been six, but for three constables, Hopkins, Madison, and Gambit, who gave chase. They cornered the third man, Jack Porter, in a rathole off of Lamlash Street. But along the way there, Porter ran through a room full of women and children sitting down to their dinner, and the constable nearest his heels, a young fellow named Hopkins, noticed as he tried to follow that the woman nearest the fire took one look at his uniform and thrust a paper in her hand towards the flames. Then Porter overturned the table for a distraction, and went out the window. Hopkins lost his footing and fell amidst the beans, and it was left to Madison and Gambit to catch Porter and tuck him into a Black Maria. Hopkins, meanwhile, realized that he recognized the woman who was berating him for destroying her supper – a pickpocket well known to the force by the name of Nettie Hannigan. Do you know of her?"

Holmes tapped his steepled fingers against his chin and nodded. "She is sometimes called 'Red Nettie', is she not? Not because of her hair, which is brown when she has not been using henna, but because of the strawberry mark which shows on part of her left ear and down her neck."

"That's right. She was caught with the goods a time or two when she was younger, but she's grown more canny since. Pretty enough, in her way, and does piecework, apparently, for a manufacturer of ladies accoutrements. Hopkins reports a sewing machine in the corner of the room, among other things." Gregson reached into his pocket for a sheaf of handwritten papers.

"Is there a connection between Miss Hannigan and the Cartier theft?"

"Nettie was apprehended on suspicion of shoplifting three hours after the theft near Charing Cross, though the female searcher found nothing and she was released. But here, let me read you what Hopkins reported. 'The force of wind from the table overturning blew the burning paper out of the center of the fire before it could be entirely consumed, and it fell under my eye. I saw the word 'police' and the word 'reward', in the portion already blackened, and a moment later one of the women poured the firebucket over me and the paper. I saw that three small pieces were unburnt and was able to recover them by putting my hands on them as I got back to my feet. The wet paper stuck to my hands, and I was able to preserve it within my handkerchief as I pretended to clean myself off and made my apologies to the women. Once back at the station, I investigated the scraps. All three bore typewritten letters. The smallest one had ' *H U F R M* '. The second largest ' *O W S L* – full stop – *X P Q* ', and the largest, ' *C E L E T in the paradol chamber until it is safe to C O L* '. Now I ask you Mr. Holmes, what can that be other than

222

an order to keep a bracelet in the paradol chamber until it is safe to collect the reward?"

"The paradol chamber?"

"Yes. '*P A R A D O L*'. Have you ever heard of it?"

"Are you certain that was what was written? Could it be that the *l* was rather an *x*?"

"It was typewritten. There was no mistaking one letter for another."

"Ah." Holmes scowled, but I could see that he was intrigued by the puzzle. "I should like to speak to Constable Hopkins directly, if possible."

"He's due to testify on another matter this morning," Gregson said, "but I'll let his sergeant know. The sooner the better. Hammond's company plans to treble the amount of the reward tomorrow. They're pressed by the Foreign Office too, and are far less concerned with bringing the thief to justice than they are in recovering the lost gems. But if we can find this mysterious chamber before morning, we might not have every treasure hunter in the city getting in our way."

Holmes shook his head. "I know London as well as any man alive, and I have never heard of a Paradol Chamber."

"And what does 'paradol' mean?" I wondered, foreseeing a long morning consulting our dictionaries and other reference works. "It sounds like the name of a patent medicine to me."

"Or a chemical compound," Holmes said, thoughtfully. "The *-ol* suffix points to an organic substance or an extract of some kind. But I associate the word with music. I believe it may be a family name, if not here, then on the Continent."

"I was thinking more along the lines of a secret society," Gregson admitted. "And I hoped you'd have heard of it, Mr. Holmes."

"If it is a secret society, it has kept its secret well," Holmes said. "Were there no other marks upon the page? No other words Hopkins might have seen?"

"None that he mentioned in his report." The Inspector passed over the pages to Holmes to read as the cab pulled up outside of 221b Baker Street. He absorbed the material quickly and quietly as I retrieved our luggage and went to unlock the door, and then handed the report back to Gregson.

"I see that Hopkins was careful to write the letters out in capitals, to avoid any confusion, but he doesn't say whether the typewritten letters were also capitals. Still, it does eliminate the possibility that the word was paradox."

"Then we'll have to keep looking." Gregson tipped his hat to us and got back into his cab. "I truly hoped you would have the answer at your fingertips, Mr. Holmes. But that's neither here nor there. Perhaps one of our informers has heard the name. I'll head in to Scotland Yard, and have Constable Hopkins sent round to Baker Street once he's done in the courts. Good day, gentlemen."

We made our way upstairs, after asking our excellent landlady Mrs. Hudson to provide us with coffee at her earliest convenience, and soon traded our outer layers for dressing gowns and slippers. Holmes lit a pipe, of course, and began to sift through the newspapers which the boy had collected for him during our absence. "Here is the first mention of the bracelet," he reported after a moment. "It was made for a Slavic princess, and was to be delivered to her embassy when it was stolen. That, no doubt, is the reason why the Foreign Office is involved."

"Do you think it was stolen deliberately then, as an affront to the lady?"

"Not if Red Nettie had anything to do with it," Holmes said. "She is an opportunistic thief, like most shoplifters and pickpockets. Which should be a comfort to the Foreign Office, since I doubt she has any notion of the value they place upon the bracelet."

"So we could leave the mystery to the police?" I asked, torn between my desire to see my friend take a proper rest and my uneasiness over the intervention of the Foreign Office.

"We could," Holmes said. "Except that the word 'paradol' has intrigued me. Take a look at our bookshelf, my dear fellow, and I'll see I can discover anything in the agony columns."

The coffee came, and then our breakfasts, but of the word "paradol" we could find no trace. Our reference works having failed us, Holmes decided to consult an expert, or several. "There is nothing which the researchers at the British Museum like better than to clutter their brain attics with irrelevancies. No one man can know everything," he said, as he dispatched the boy with a stack of telegram forms. "And it is as well to admit it." He sat down at the table and spooned some kedgeree from the salver onto his untouched plate.

My own plate had been filled and emptied again, but I poured myself another cup of coffee. "Especially not if he has the habit of sweeping away the facts he thinks of as clutter. Although given the reputed tidiness of your own 'brain attic', I cannot help but wonder what it was that made you ask if the word could be 'paradox'."

Holmes grimaced. "Even the best broom can't reach every cobweb. Were the word 'paradox' and not a 'paradol', I would have directed Gregson to Professor Martin Hoffmanstall, and his cabinet of curiosities near Hampstead. He had, as I recall, a gravity defying room in the garden

224

of his former establishment at Brighton, and 'Can you solve the paradox?' was a prominent line in the banner above the door."

"I take it that you did," I said, for it was evident in my friend's manner that the memory was a personal one.

"Any child could, once aware of the basic principles of optical illusion. The room is set an angle, and all means of comparing it to the horizon obscured. In it, water appears to run uphill and persons to change size, depending on where they stand. I thought it well worth tuppence, even knowing how the trick was done, and the trick was easy enough to duplicate. I'm sure it wasn't the only one."

"It's a shame then, that we cannot substitute one letter for another," said I. "Such a chamber sounds more than adequate as a hiding place."

Holmes poked at his breakfast and then set down his fork. "We'd still have to find it, and even then we might be doing little more than chasing a wild goose. For all we know, the paper which Constable Hopkins collected has nothing to do with the missing bracelet."

"What other word ends in ' *C E L E T* '?"

"Princelet?" Holmes suggested, and then leaned his elbow on the table and rested the bridge of his nose against his fingertips. "Not that a princelet held in any sort of chamber would be less urgent a matter."

"Eat something, Holmes," I said. "It will ease the headache."

"I haven't time."

"You do, you know. You'll have to wait here for Hopkins to arrive and for any responses to your telegrams. You will have time for your breakfast. You will have time for another pipe. You might even have time for a bath and a shave."

That earned me a smile, as Holmes rubbed thoughtfully at the growth upon his chin. "You know me too well, Doctor. Very well. I will take the rest you are urging upon me, since nothing can be done until we know more. And how will you fill the hours? A nap, perhaps?"

A nap sounded like an excellent idea. But I knew that Holmes would be more likely to take the rest he needed if he knew that the case was proceeding. And there was at least one task that was well within my capabilities. "I thought I might go over to the Public Records Office and see if I can find the name 'Paradol' anywhere. It is quiet and cool in the reading rooms there, and whether I succeed or not, it will still narrow our search."

"Better yet, try the churches of Southwark," said Holmes. "Begin with the Baptists and go on to St. Mary's of Newington. Gregson can set a constable trolling through the records of the nation. Let us concentrate our energies where we might have the greatest success. Tell them you've come across the name in a family Bible. And don't forget to ask the vergers. They'll know their gravestones off by heart."

I nodded. "Will you place advertisements in the newspapers as well?" I asked, thinking of the many occasions when he had done so in the past. "There must be someone in London who knows the word."

"If Gregson's theory about a secret society is correct, that would instantly inspire the criminals to move the bracelet," Holmes said. "No, Watson. If we're to find the 'Paradol Chamber' while it still contains the bracelet, we must exercise some discretion and limit ourselves to reliable sources."

I took a hansom cab. It was unusually warm for May, and I remembered that the day was as long now as it would be in late July, and the sun as high. As the cab went along Piccadilly, I noticed Professor Robert Bentley approaching the headquarters of the Linnean Society. I realized this was an opportunity I should not forego. Bentley had also trained as a surgeon, and was a member at my club. I had seen him there on several occasions, his bald head rising from the wild disarray of his sidewhiskers like a mountain beset with an overgrowth of untamed shrubbery. I doubted he knew my name, but my face might be familiar. And a more reliable source of information about organic compounds than Bentley and the other fellows of the Society I could not imagine.

I had the cab driver stop and approached the great botanist with my question, and much to my surprise, he nodded when he heard the word 'paradol'. "It's a fairly obscure reference," he said, "But I believe it is the pungent principle of the spice derived from *Aframomum melegueta.*"

I tugged my notebook from my pocket. "*Afromomum . . . .*" I began to write, and Bentley interrupted me.

"You might know it as Guinea pepper, or 'grains of paradise'. It's the latter name, I believe, from which the word 'paradol' is derived."

"I couldn't find it in the dictionary," I admitted.

"I would be surprised if you did," Bentley said. "Come inside and see if our library can do you better."

My excitement waned when I discovered that the word 'paradol' had been coined just three years prior, when the substance was identified in a paper by a chemist called J.C. Thresh. Still, I had discovered something, and when I emerged from the Linnean Society, I went to the nearest post office to send the information to Holmes. The reply came within half-an-hour. "Paradol also a name in France. Lucinde Paradol sang in Paris Opera. Proceed to parishes, I will research importers of grains of paradise."

So now, instead of a single thread, we had two. And at least we knew that the word could be a name. I set off for Southwark again, feeling hopeful.

By early afternoon, I was feeling much less hopeful. If anyone named Paradol had ever been born, married, or buried in Southwark, they had done so without the knowledge of the churches nearest Elephant and Castle. I had even gone as far afield as the nearest Catholic establishment, that being the most likely religion of an immigrant from France. I stopped to telegraph Holmes for further instructions, and was gratified by how quickly came the reply, telling me to meet him at Simpson's in the Strand at my earliest convenience.

Being much closer, I reached the restaurant well before Holmes, and decided to take my luncheon in the upper room, where I could observe the street below. But once seated, I allowed myself to close my eyes for a moment, and I was quite asleep when I was found by Holmes and PC Hopkins. A touch on my shoulder roused me.

"May we join you, Watson?" Holmes asked, although he was already taking the seat beside me and waving Hopkins into the chair opposite. "This is PC Hopkins. Constable Hopkins, my friend Dr. Watson."

"I'm pleased to meet you, sir," Hopkins said. He was a well-set up young fellow of about twenty-three, his bright blue eyes trying to take in the entire restaurant at once.

"And I you," I said absently, reaching for my now tepid cup of coffee. "I'm sorry I fell asleep, Holmes."

"It's hardly surprising after the past week. After we eat you can head back to Baker Street, and I will take the next shift of hunting," Holmes replied. He looked much better than he had in the morning, although there were still shadows beneath his eyes. "There's an importer in Rotherhithe who specializes in spices from Africa, and given your lack of success in the churchyards, it must be worth a try."

"I don't see how it could be, sir," Hopkins interjected deferentially. "I mean, I can't imagine anyone from the gangs at Elephant and Castle taking orders from the gangs at Rotherhithe. They're natural enemies."

"Improbable, I grant you, especially given that Red Nettie is an up-and-comer in the Forty Thieves. Nevertheless, we must eliminate the possibility," Holmes said.

"The Forty Thieves?" I asked.

"A gang of women who operate out of the Elephant and Castle district." Hopkins said, as if he were reciting from a manual. "A majority of them are widows and orphans at the moment, although some of the

227

senior members are married. In plain view, they teach girls skills they might use for legitimate trades, like dressmaking. But they practice Faginy as well, teaching the younger girls the arts of picking pockets and shoplifting and other petty crimes."

"They're frequently out on the Strand," Holmes added, "which is why I wanted to meet you here."

I looked out the window, down onto the passing pedestrians. The sun was beating down and the awnings were out, and most of the women passing had put up sunshades to protect their complexions. "I don't know how we'll recognize them," I said. "I can't see past the umbrellas."

Holmes paused in the act of signalling the waiter to clap his hands together, his whole demeanor changing with the strength of a new thought. "Hopkins," he said urgently, "Show me again the evidence you brought with you."

"All right, sir," Hopkins said, bewildered, but he brought out an envelope with the three scraps of charred paper carefully preserved between cards. I looked at them as Holmes examined them, his fingers tapping on the table as if it were a piano keyboard. They were just as the report had described them, other than a broader gap than normal between the words "is" and "safe". Holmes clearly saw more than I, however, and he chuckled as he indicated that Hopkins could put away the envelope once more.

"Watson, I've changed my mind. When we finish eating, would you care to join me in a stroll along the Strand?"

"If I can be of assistance," I said, curiosity as always overcoming any hesitation. I knew the signs of Holmes on the right track, even if he seldom vouchsafed his reasoning beforehand.

"Constable Hopkins, I would ask you to join us, but I think your uniform would alarm our quarry, and she'd no doubt recognize your face. Go and send word to Inspector Gregson that we are very likely going to be able to retrieve the bracelet this afternoon. Then find the constables patrolling this beat and ask them to be certain that, if we do confront Red Nettie, none of her acquaintances take to their heels with any of her accoutrements."

"Yes, sir, of course, sir, excuse me, sir," Hopkins practically leapt to his feet and departed with a vigour I could only envy.

Holmes watched him go with an indulgent expression. "I have hopes that that young man will make a detective in time," he said. "He shows a distinct talent for observation."

"And he listens to you, the way the older detectives don't," I observed.

Holmes shrugged, but I could see that he was pleased. "It is always easier to work with someone when they have little reason to cling to preconceived notions. I can only hope to live up to his expectations. In the meantime, let me turn the tables upon you, Doctor. You need to eat," he said, and raised his hand once more to summon the waiter. "It will help to dispel your headache."

Coffee and sandwiches refreshed me, and while I cannot say that I was at my best when Holmes and began our promenade along the Strand, I was alert enough to spot Nettie Hannigan before my friend had a chance to tug my sleeve. She wore a dress of light pink organdy, cut according to the most recent fashions, and her hair was swept up defiantly to reveal the mottled red mark on her neck, which explained the pugnacious expression that marred her otherwise attractive features. I would never have guessed her to be a thief, and would have placed her instead amongst the young wives and hopeful maiden daughters of shopkeepers or tradesmen, that class which was rising by an application of hard work. Her umbrella was exceptionally large, made of silver silk, with a heavy bamboo shaft and handle. It sheltered both her and the younger girl by her side, whose dress betrayed its self-made origins by an uneven hem and a crooked seam.

"Do you remember when I fell at the Cunningham's?" Holmes murmured, just loud enough for me to hear and nod in reply. I remembered his ruse very well indeed, for it had alarmed me greatly at the time to see him take such a nervous fit. "Do you think you can do that? And fall against the ladies as you pass?"

"I can try," I said, for there was little time to demur. Holmes bid me good afternoon and headed into the nearest shop, and I acknowledged him and kept walking forward. I did not think I could mimic his entire performance, but it was easy enough for me to place my cane badly and let my bad leg collapse. I fell, as I intended, against Nettie Hannigan, and to give her credit she did her best to catch me, though she had to let go of what she was carrying to do so. We tumbled down together, and once fallen I did not have to pretend to be in pain, for my knee struck a protruding cobblestone, and it was all that I could do not to disgrace myself with bad language.

Miss Hannigan's exclamations were not so discreet, though she kept her voice low. When she saw that my pain was genuine, she dispatched her companion to fetch a glass of water, and then helped me to the kerb where I could sit and massage my leg. She stayed by me, too, offering her handkerchief for the tears that had started from my eyes at the sudden blow. A moment later, Holmes appeared through the growing crowd, my cane in one hand and Miss Hannigan's umbrella and parcels in the other. "Watson?" he said, aping concern. He hadn't had time to change his attire, but he'd rearranged his hair so that it came down over his forehead, and his expression was that of a far more ingenuous man.

"I'm all right," I growled, even as I wondered what he was up to. I carefully extended my leg, checking to see what I'd done to myself. "I think it's just a bruise. Thanks to this lady, I didn't strike the ground with my full weight. I apologize, ma'am. I should have placed my cane more carefully."

She waved aside the consideration with an unexpected graciousness that made me feel ashamed of my pretense. "There's worse reasons for landing in the gutter," she averred, with a laugh. "Here's Lucy with some water for you, and good thing too. You're red as a parson's nose."

I mumbled something about the day being hot, and accepted the water. I was flushed from embarrassment, not heat, and I knew it, and the thrill of attempting the ruse was giving way to the realization that I had not the skill to maintain it. At that moment, Holmes stepped in, offering the parcel and umbrella to Red Nettie. "It was awfully good of you to help, Miss. but are you sure you're not hurt? You fell too," he said, in a voice much higher than his usual pitch and with a distinct Newcastle accent.

"I'm all right, but my dress isn't," she said, pointing out the large tear at which had parted the flounce from her hem. I flinched, remembering that my foot had come down on the edge of the fabric.

"I'm so sorry." This time my apology was more sincere, but I was still startled when Holmes pulled out a five pound note and pressed it into her hand.

"This should cover the damage, shouldn't it?" he asked, bouncing nervously on his toes. "I'm afraid I don't know what ladies dresses cost in London."

"This should be plenty," Miss Hannigan said, and coquetted her lashes at him. "Perhaps you and I can meet again, once it's mended?"

Holmes tittered, "Oh, I'd like that," he said, fluttering his hands nervously in a manner that had me ducking my head to keep from staring. "Shall I give you my card?" He dove a hand into his pocket and then frowned. "Oh, dear, I've left the case at the hotel. But you can call there, at least until Tuesday. At the Northumberland. Ask for Henry. Stephen Henry."

"Stephen Henry," she repeated, taking his hand for a moment.

"And now I should get my friend into a cab. Oh! There's one. Cabbie! Oh, cabbie!" Holmes dashed off to intercept a nearby growler.

I kept my head down, rubbing at my face with the hand that wasn't pressed against my knee, and beginning to shake with both the reaction to the pain and the laughter I dare not indulge at Holmes's antics. I didn't know why he didn't just confront the lady, but I was grateful enough for the opportunity to cease making a spectacle. A small crowd had gathered, and several hands helped me up into the cab, but I managed to wave and say thank you again, to the air in the general direction of the two ladies I had discommoded.

As soon as the cab turned a corner and the Strand was out of view, Holmes gave a great shout of laughter and buffeted me on the shoulder. "Well done, Watson! I didn't know you had a career in the theater." He tapped the roof. "Driver, wait here a moment."

"I don't," I said, trying to turn up my trouser leg so I could examine the bruise that was forming over my patella. His exuberance would have been welcome were it not that I was feeling rather misused.

"What was all that in aid of, Holmes?"

"A moment, Watson." Holmes leaned out the window and whistled. Not a minute later, Constable Hopkins had joined us, and Holmes had told the driver to go on to Baker Street. "There," he said as he settled back against the seat. "Now we can be comfortable."

Hopkins, perched opposite, looked at my friend with a puzzled mien. "I thought we were going to arrest her," he said. "And now you've just let her go."

"With five pounds in her purse," I added.

Holmes shrugged. "It was the only note I had with me," he said. "And I had not intended that she would damage her attire. Very clumsy of you, my dear fellow."

I took the admonishment in the spirit in which it was being given and merely raised an eyebrow at my effervescent friend. "So what is the result of our encounter with Miss Hannigan, Holmes? I have a bruised patella, she has five pounds, and you . . . what do you have?

"This," Holmes said, passing his hands across each other like a stage magician before pulling a glistening chain of gems out from his sleeve.

"The Cartier bracelet!" I exclaimed, the pain in my leg forgotten.

Hopkins applauded like a schoolchild at a Punch and Judy show. "Where was it?"

"In a hidden compartment in the bamboo handle of her sunshade," Holmes said. "In other words a . . . ."

"*Parasol* chamber," I finished, groaning with the realization of how much of the day I had spent in chasing wild hares.

"Precisely." Holmes could not have been more pleased with himself.

"How did you know?" Hopkins asked, and I echoed the sentiment.

"When Watson mentioned the umbrellas, just after you informed us that the older women of the gang were teaching 'dressmaking and the like', I considered how easily a dedicated seamstress could also make an umbrella. Then I remembered that amongst the respectable occupations open to unmarried females, typewriting is one of the most easily learned. I confirmed my supposition by comparing the letters on the scraps of evidence against the arrangement of keys designed by Mr. Sholes for the Remington typewriters most commonly available. The scraps were not code, as I originally thought, but finger exercises to train typewritists in using the machine without having to look at the keys. As the *s* and the *d* keys juxtapose, I assumed a simple keyboarding error. Inspector Gregson was wrong, it was indeed possible to substitute one letter for another."

I laughed. "Brilliant, Holmes. But why not have Miss Hannigan arrested?"

He put the bracelet into my hand. "I meant to. But she seemed kind enough to a gentleman who was injured on the street, and since I was able to retrieve the jewels without raising the alarm, I thought better of it. Miss Hannigan, should she be foolish enough to use her doctored sunshade to conceal ill-gotten goods again, will be caught and sentenced for some less perilous trinket. But in the meantime, we shall make back my small investment fivefold, and still have time for a nap."

The Strange Missive of Germaine Wilkes
by Mark Mower

London – Monday, 25th May 1891 – It will come as no surprise to many of you who have long followed the exploits of my dear friend and colleague, Sherlock Holmes, to learn that one of the most frequently asked questions I am now faced with is, "When did you first learn of Professor James Moriarty?" It is a query to which I have given much thought and some speculation in recent days, imagining that the name had first come to my attention only a month or so ago. But yesterday, while looking back over a sheaf of notes I had retained from the late summer of 1887, I was finally able to pinpoint with some uneasiness the moment when Holmes first alerted me to the existence of his arch-nemesis.

I had called in at Baker Street just before ten o'clock on a bright and sunny Saturday morning in August to find Holmes in an ebullient mood. Apart from looking somewhat tired and pallid, he appeared to be in reasonable health and was quick to jump up from his favourite armchair to greet me as I entered the upstairs room at Mrs. Hudson's direction.

"Watson, my dear fellow! What a pleasant surprise, and such perfect timing. I am currently awaiting the arrival of Inspector MacDonald, whose earlier telegram informs me that he has a conundrum that Scotland Yard cannot solve. I trust that will serve as a sufficient inducement to get you to linger a while and share a fresh pot of tea with me. I am sure that my wife will not begrudge you a couple of hours in my company – especially now that you have purchased the birthday present she has wanted for some time."

"Indeed Holmes, that sounds splendid," I replied, "but I am at a loss to know how you could possibly have ascertained the nature of my earlier errand."

I could see the glint in his eye as he realised that I was, as ever, confounded by his powers of deduction. "A simple case of pulling together the discernible clues into a workable hypothesis, my dear fellow. A couple of months ago you mentioned to me that my wife was keen to fill your newly-decorated parlour with a suitable piece of furniture. You joked about how much that was likely to cost and how much time you had already spent trying to find an ornate chair or couch

233

that would suffice. When we were last together – less than two weeks ago – walking back to 221b, we passed Druce's Furniture Showroom on the corner of Baker Street. I noted that your eyes dwelt a little too long on the stylish chaise longue that Mr. Druce has positioned very cannily in his window display. And armed with the knowledge that my wife's birthday falls in early September, I had thought at the time that you were minded to buy the piece and had hesitated only because of the hefty price tag."

"You are not wrong there," I admitted, disappointed that my thoughts and thriftiness had been so transparent. "But how did you know that I went back today to purchase the couch?"

"A few tell-tale observations to add to what I already knew," he continued. "As you always do, you carry your cheque book in its leather case in your inside top pocket. The case is slightly too big for the pocket and has a habit of poking out occasionally. Realising that this is a Saturday, and your bank is therefore closed, I can only speculate that the cheque book has been used to make a significant purchase. And reflecting on the fact that Druce's Showroom lies less than two-hundred-and-twenty yards from here, it seems reasonable to assume that you have already purchased the chaise longue and thought you would call in to see me while you were so close to your old haunt. Furthermore, your obvious smile and upbeat humour this morning suggests that the transaction has not been too damaging, by which I mean that you successful haggled with dear old Druce to give you a discount on the item in question."

I could not hide my astonishment, but was happy to point out a minor blemish in his otherwise comprehensive account. "Holmes, you clearly do not know Druce well at all. A discount was out of the question. What I successfully negotiated was free delivery of the piece on my wife's birthday!"

We both laughed as Holmes poured the tea and then raised an eyebrow at a further knock on the front door, before exclaiming: "Excellent, MacDonald is as punctual as ever."

Having poured another cup and exchanged some pleasantries with the man from Scotland Yard, Holmes was keen to get on with the business at hand. The amiable detective was happy to oblige.

"Aye, it's a puzzle alright. For some time, we've been aware that a gang of bank thieves has been planning some raids in the city. They are led by a one-time banknote forger called Germaine Wilkes, an American by birth. Late last night, one of my men spotted Wilkes walking through Westminster and promptly arrested him. We now have him under lock and key at the Yard, but he is proving to be most uncooperative and saying very little. At some point we will have to release him."

234

I was the first to interject. "Surely, you have sufficient evidence to hold him. Was he carrying anything that could incriminate him or provide a link to his known accomplices?"

MacDonald looked crestfallen and explained that he had spent all night interrogating Wilkes without success. He then reached inside his tweed frockcoat and drew out a folded sheet of paper. "The only piece of information we managed to find on him was this," he added, handing the opened note to my colleague. "The difficulty we have Mr. Holmes, is that we can't make head nor tail of it. And knowing that you're a man who's accomplished at solving all manner of riddles, we thought it might be one for you."

Holmes had fallen silent as he gazed intently at the page before him. His eyes rapidly scanned the missive and then he broke off, looked across at me and held out the note. "What do you make of it, Watson?"

I held in my hands a single sheet of foolscap paper, on which was printed the following:

Right 2, Left 3, 1, Right 3, 3, Left 2 – NO HIDE BIRDIE ID

Eager to make some sense of the seemingly unintelligible message before me, I thought of Holmes's methods and began to apply the same degree of scrutiny. "It seems to me that we have two parts to this message," I ventured. "The first few words suggest an instruction of some kind; perhaps a marching sequence, a map direction or even the coding sequence required to open up a safe or bank vault. The second part, in capital letters, may well be the substance of the communiqué, the real point that the author wishes to convey."

Holmes was unusually enthusiastic in his response. "Bravo Watson! I concur with you completely. The message does indeed appear to have two distinct parts and it would seem logical that the first is some form of instruction or direction-marker for the reader. What else?"

Egged on, I then suggested that the form of the note seemed significant. "Why bother to have this typeset and printed when it could so easily have been handwritten?"

This time is was MacDonald who replied with some eagerness. "My thoughts exactly, Dr. Watson. And if you look at the back of the note you will see that the imprint of the type has gone through the page, which tells us that the message was hand-typed rather than printed."

"Indeed it was," concurred Holmes. "A fact that we can take to be highly significant, I suspect. So, do you know who sent the note, MacDonald?"

The Inspector looked bemused. "No, how could I possibly know? Wilkes has refused to say anything about the note and where it came from."

"My dear Inspector. I thought your intelligence on Wilkes and his cohort of bank thieves might have extended as far as the knowledge that, while they are believed to be operating as a discrete gang, they have much broader connections to a large criminal network operating across London, parts of Europe, and as far as North America. It should come as no surprise that Wilkes hails from the other side of the pond. My contacts tell me that he was chosen specifically for his role by the real puppet-master in the criminal fraternity."

MacDonald tried to hide his frustration, but realised that Holmes had the upper hand. "So, Mr. Holmes, who do *you* believe sent the note to Wilkes?"

Holmes looked at him directly, and addressed him without a hint of conceit: "I have no doubt whatsoever, that this message was sent by the very person who directs all of the major operations of the criminal network I have described. That person is none other than Professor James Moriarty. I have it on good authority that Wilkes had previously been Moriarty's favoured lieutenant in a counterfeiting ring that once operated out of Cincinnati."

"How can you be so sure Holmes? And who is this Professor – I've never heard you mention him before?"

Holmes turned his gaze towards me, and for a split second a look of fear passed across his face. "That is because I had hoped to spare you, indeed protect you, from the knowledge that we now have a criminal mastermind operating with relative impunity from a base in London – a man who is more than a match for any of crime agencies which exist in New York, Paris or London itself. He is cunning and formidable and exceedingly dangerous. By day, he masquerades as an academic, eminent in his field, mentoring the very brightest student minds. By night, he casts off the gown – operating under a different cloak – and directing the endeavours of a very different class of followers. Make no mistake, Watson, Moriarty is behind this, and the less you know of him, the better it will be for your sake and your wife's."

The casual reference to my beloved wife had the desired effect and I offered no further challenge. I could see also that MacDonald had been listening intently, taking in this new information and looking slightly awestruck at Holmes's assertions. In the silence that followed, it was he who spoke first.

"So, where does all that leave us with this note, Mr. Holmes? Are you able to tell me what it means and whether I should continue to hold Wilkes?"

"I am sure I can crack the meaning behind this communication and set you on the right path. But I will need some time and your indulgence for a short while yet, as I need to make a short excursion into town. It is now half past ten. Could I suggest that we reconvene back here in Baker Street in two hours' time? I will instruct Mrs. Hudson to have waiting for us a light luncheon of bread and cold ham."

MacDonald was visibly relieved. "That sounds wonderful! I am very grateful to you, Mr. Holmes, and will take my leave. I will be back promptly at 12.30, as you suggest."

When MacDonald had gone, I took the opportunity to try and get Holmes to talk more about the enigmatic Professor Moriarty, but all of my gentle questioning brought little by way of a response. "I can tell you nothing further at this stage Watson. I really do have to go into town. A short spell of shopping should do the trick. I should then be in a position to tell you the substance of the message from Moriarty."

Without further explanation he was off, heading down the stairs of 221b, through the front door, and out into the street before I could even think to ask if he wanted me to join him. I resolved to await his return and find out whether he really could make sense of the strange note to Germaine Wilkes.

In Holmes's absence, I read the headline features in *The Times*, keen to find out if there was anything in the press that might shed some light on Wilkes's activities or the shadowy network of crooks that were being directed by Moriarty. The big news of the day was that a major financial fraud had been uncovered in a provincial bank in the south of England. There was also news that a cruise ship had run aground off the coast of Cornwall, with the loss of ten lives. Equally disturbing was the announcement that the previous evening a British politician had been found dead, close to Westminster Bridge. The report said that Augustus Waldringfield, the Member of Parliament for Chippenham East, had been found stabbed to death. It speculated that his death may have been linked to his much publicised opposition to the Irish Home Rule bill which had been defeated in the Lords the previous year. The article went on to say that it was well known that Waldringfield had been a fierce critic of the Fenian Brotherhood, the group thought most likely to have carried out the attack.

A little over an hour after he had departed, Holmes was back in Baker Street, clutching a large box which I imagined was the result of his mysterious shopping expedition. I was quick to express my surprise at his behaviour.

"Holmes, in all the time that I have known you, I cannot recollect another occasion on which you have left an active case in order to spend time purchasing something for yourself. Please tell me that this is some curious aberration on your part!"

"Watson, your instincts have not deserted you. This was no routine purchase, my friend."

He began to unpack the box, revealing a black mechanical instrument, along the front of which were positioned numerous keys, marked by different letters of the alphabet and other recognisable symbols. With care, he set the instrument down on his writing desk, and stepped back to admire its appearance.

"I have here a marvel of the modern age. A Sholes and Glidden patent typewriting machine, manufactured by the American firm of E. Remington and Sons. It was first produced in 1875, and is becoming more popular on both sides of the Atlantic, replacing the need for costly typesetting, and enabling even the most humble of offices to produce their own printed stationery. The arrangement of the keys enables the typist to adopt a standard finger position in order to use the machine. With experience, practice and dexterity, I am told that a regular operative can type out at least 40 words a minute."

He had heartfelt enthusiasm for this mechanical contraption and proceeded to insert into it a single sheet of paper taken from the drawer of the desk. I felt I had to express my obvious confusion. "I'm sorry Holmes, but I don't see what this has got to do with the note we are trying to decipher?"

"Well, let us return indeed to that very note, before MacDonald reappears. We shall look at it afresh." He spread the note out before us to the right of the typewriter. "Let us consider first its form. The page has been typewritten and deliberately so. Moriarty is telling Wilkes something by the mere fact that he has typed the missive. I believe that the "right, left, right, left" reference and the associated numbers are instructions related to the use of a standard typewriter. To that we will return in a moment."

He now pointed specifically to the second part of the message and read out "NO HIDE BIRDIE ID." "I believe there is a clear message here. Moriarty is saying: 'We can now expose the person who has to date been undercover, unrecognised or otherwise hidden from the public gaze.' 'BIRDIE' is his code for the mole, spy or agent he is referring to."

"But what about this word 'ID', Holmes, what does that suggest?"

"The term 'I.D.' has a certain American ring to it – a slang term for *identification*. It is not one which our British policing colleagues have yet adopted with any great enthusiasm, but the Police Department of New York has been pioneering in its work to provide I.D.'s for all of the major felons it wishes to apprehend. Inspector Thomas Byrnes' *Professional Criminals of America* was published in September last year and provides both written descriptions and photographs of the offenders concerned. I only know this because I was asked by the capable Inspector to contribute intelligence to some of the descriptions used in the book. For the purposes of our note, Moriarty is saying to Wilkes that the target's identity can now be revealed."

I was still confused. "So, who is the subject of the note? How could Moriarty be sure that Wilkes would know exactly who to target without risking detection if the note was intercepted?"

"A good point, Moriarty needed to be specific. But this is a clever piece of subterfuge. Alongside the main communication, there is a second, hidden message, which precisely answers your question. Let us now turn to that."

His pointed his long index finger at the main body of the text. "I thought at first that the hidden message was a simple process of letter substitution, with each different character of the 'NO HIDE BIRDIE ID' line representing an alternative letter in a traditional cypher. I was quick to discard the thought though, as there were no obvious solutions and it would have been unlikely that as a mathematical genius Moriarty would have relied on such an obviously easy code."

"Would the message be an anagram in that case?" I interjected, realising instantly that a straightforward anagram was also unlikely. "After all, the number sequence '2, 3, 1, 3, 3, 2', contained within what we believe to be the instructions, do add up to fourteen, the number of letters in the main message."

"That is true, but try as I might, Watson, I could think of no sensible anagram from the letters in the sentence. I did, however, come up with one line that I thought you might like as a medical man – 'I'd bid heroin die.'" I ignored the jibe, resisting the temptation to castigate him as I had so often for his casual drug use. Holmes returned to the subject of the typewriter.

"I am convinced that the keyboard will provide the solution to this puzzle," he said, placing his hands in the correct position for typing. "The sales assistant was most insistent that the fingers be positioned accordingly. Now, following the instructions in the note, we move our finger position one key to the 'right' and type the first two letters out as if we were routinely typing the word 'NO'. His fingers struck the keys accordingly and the letters "MP" appeared on the paper. He then tapped a long key at the bottom of the keyboard which he informed me was the "spacebar".

"Now we are instructed to move to the 'left.'" He repositioned his fingers to the left of the standard typing position and typed what would have been "HIDE", being careful to use the spacebar to separate the letters into two words – one of three letters, the second of just one. On the paper, the newly typed words read "GUS W." At this point I remained unconvinced that Holmes" experiment would bear any useful fruit.

Following the same logic and procedure, Holmes finished typing out the short sentence. Having done so, he pulled the newly typed page from the typewriter and retrieved an ink pen from the desk drawer, adding a few words atop the typed sentence.

"Let us see what we now have Watson! Put together, two sentences read: 'No hide birdie ID – MP Gus W not for us.'"

Recollecting the earlier article in *The Times*, the message now made perfect sense to me. "The dead politician Holmes! The MP for Chippenham East, Augustus Waldringfield – he was found murdered last night!"

"So it would appear, dear fellow. And his demise was at the hands of Wilkes and not the Fenian Brotherhood. That invention was most likely promulgated by Moriarty himself to throw the suspicion off his criminal associates. What you might not yet have read, Watson, is that Waldringfield has also now been linked to the major fraud case involving the Surrey Shires Bank, of which he was one of the directors. I think we can take it that Moriarty or one of his associates had found out about the bank's fraudulent activities, and had then tried to blackmail the MP with the information, threatening to reveal both the crime and the politician's link to it, if he did not bend to Moriarty's will. The outcome of the matter suggests that Waldringfield had refused to yield to the Professor's demands, and Wilkes was therefore instructed by this note to go public with the information about the MP's nefarious activities. Whether or not Moriarty had gone as far as to sanction murder we may never know."

At that point, a heavy footfall on the stairs alerted us to the return of Inspector MacDonald. When he entered the room, the detective looked tired and dejected. "I have bad news, I'm afraid. It seems that sometime this morning, after I had left him to come here, Wilkes received a visit at Scotland Yard from someone purporting to be his legal representative. Having spent just a few moments with Wilkes, the man asked to be released from the holding cell and left the building. The supervising officer said that Wilkes had appeared to be fine at that point and had expressed his confidence that he would soon be released from custody. However, when the same officer returned to check on Wilkes some twenty minutes later, he found the banknote forger in the last throes of death. It seems his visitor had dispensed some form of poison to the hapless prisoner and Wilkes died shortly afterwards. I guess that puts an end to our speculation about the puzzling note, Mr. Holmes."

It was Holmes's turn to look dejected. "That is troubling news, MacDonald, and I can only apologise for having underestimated the extraordinary lengths that Moriarty would go to in covering his role in this sad state of affairs. Doctor Watson will no doubt convey to you over lunch the full details of what we have uncovered, having deciphered the note, and our speculation as to its links to some of the recent stories which have appeared in the press. For my part, I will leave you in his excellent company. I find myself suddenly without an appetite and in need of some fresh London air."

With no further explanation, Holmes left us to the fine spread which Mrs. Hudson had prepared, and we spent the next hour discussing the meaning of the note and the ramifications of the case.

In the two weeks that followed, I saw very little of my colleague, immersed as I was in the celebrations for my wife's birthday. That, at least, had been a great success – the chaise longue being considered a most perfect centrepiece for our new yellow parlour.

When I did eventually feel comfortable to bring up the subject of the Wilkes note, Holmes was demonstrably reticent to discuss the matter in any further detail. With a dismissive shake of the head, he requested only that I promise him two things – firstly, never to make public the strange case of the typewritten missive, and secondly, to never let him forget that Moriarty might one day be the cause of his undoing. It is with more than a tinge of sadness that I convey to you, dear reader, as I sit here reflecting on the terrible events that have occurred at the Reichenbach Falls, I fear I have let Holmes down on both counts.

The Case of the Vanished Killer
by Derrick Belanger

It was a late Saturday morning on the first of October when I heard word of the double murder of the Smith siblings, a crime which held the attention of all of England for a few brief weeks in the waning months of 1887. Although the case is now well known throughout the Commonwealth, the role my friend played in solving the crime has been ignored and credit given to our own Scotland Yard. While England's brave officers deserve their fair share of credit for assistance on this adventure, I believe the murder would still be an unsolved crime, possibly one as famous and with as many outlandish theories as that of Jack the Ripper, if it weren't for Sherlock Holmes bringing the case to a swift conclusion.

The tale begins with me stirring bleary eyed in my bedroom at 221b Baker Street. My wife was overseas visiting her mother in Missouri, and I moved back in with Holmes for a few weeks to spend extra time with my dear friend. I had difficulty sleeping the previous evening as the weather was excessively chilly, and I awakened to find frost on my window and the sun already high in the morning sky. I joined Holmes in the dining room, where he had already imbibed two cups of Darjeeling tea and completed the morning edition of *The Times*.

"Good morning, Watson," Holmes said while folding up the paper. "You have risen just in time for a breakfast certain to warm you on this frigid autumn day."

Mrs. Hudson had prepared a fine meal of poached eggs on toast, grilled ham that was slightly crispy, and browned tomatoes. We drank orange juice with our breakfast and talked briefly about the recent cold spell which had enveloped all of England. This pleasant start to the day was interrupted by a ringing of the doorbell and Mrs. Hudson delivering Holmes a note.

I could tell by Mrs. Hudson's wide eyes and slight smile that this was no ordinary visitor.

Holmes looked at the note and handed it back to Mrs. Hudson. "Well, Watson," he stated, "it looks like we have a celebrity in our midst. Please, Mrs. Hudson, show the gentleman in."

It did not take Holmes's powerful reasoning skills to know the identity of his guest. Mrs. Hudson opened the door and a man in a rather dour black suit entered. Even out of costume, his notorious Van Dyke beard and long, flowing brown hair clasped back in a ponytail would leave any Londoner no doubt as to the gentleman's identity.

"Thank you for seeing me, Mr. Holmes," the man started in a drawl only spoken by natives of the American West. He turned to me and offered his hand. "Hello, my name is – "

"Buffalo Bill Cody," I said rising from the table and meeting his hand in a firm grip. "Thank you, my name is Dr. John Watson."

"Ah yes," Mr. Cody said as we shook hands then released our grip. "Heard about you. You're the guy writing that novel about this fella dealing with those Mormons," he said, referring to my forthcoming book, *A Study in Scarlet.*

"Let me assure you," Holmes responded, "that the actual solving of the case was not as dramatic as its portrayal in Dr. Watson's telling. Now, please have a seat, and let us know what brings a famous entertainer such as yourself to my residence."

Mr. Cody sat down in an easy chair, and we three pulled our chairs around in a circle. "First off, let me apologize for bothering you on the weekend. Know that I wouldn't be here if it weren't mighty important."

Holmes silently motioned with his wrist for Mr. Cody to get to the point.

"Anyway, I need your help sir, very much sir. You see, this Inspector Lestrade is threatening to keep my whole show from going on tonight. I can't afford to have a cancelled performance, but without my Indians, I'm not sure what to do."

At the mention of Lestrade, Holmes's ears perked up and the detective leaned forward clearly interested in the cowboy's tale.

"Mr. Cody, before I can tell you if I can help you, I must know the details of why Inspector Lestrade, a man I can assure you I know quite well, and a man I have, on many occasions, shown the error of his ways, is interested in keeping your Indians from performing."

"Well sir, did ya'll hear about the murder committed last night?"

"Murder?" I said raising my eyebrows in surprise.

"Yes, Watson," Holmes calmly informed me. "It is the headline of this morning's *Times*. As usual, the article includes all the grisly details, but none of the important aspects of the crime. Last night, or should I say, early this morning, a brother and sister with the last name of Smith were brutally murdered in their tenement building. The building is on Old Montague Street, in the Whitechapel district. There was no apparent sign of a break in. No money was stolen. The brother was found dead with a hatchet in his head, and the sister was found on the fourth floor landing, stabbed to death. At the time of the newspaper's publication, the police had no witnesses and no suspects. I assume that has changed."

"Right you are," answered Cody. "At just about dawn this morning, this Inspector Lestrade and half of Scotland Yard comes bursting into my Indians' sleeping quarters. They're hollering and screaming that one of my performers is guilty of killing these Smith siblings in cold blood. Fortunately, Red Shirt was there and was able to keep the peace. With all that at six in the morning, after my troop had rightly stayed up late celebrating, we're lucky no fights broke out, and no one got arrested."

Red Shirt was the name of the famous Lakota-Sioux leader who was part of Bill Cody's Wild West show. The press loved the Indian, and he was almost as famous as the cowboy before me. I was baffled as to why Mr. Cody was telling us about how Inspector Lestrade connected the Indians to the murder, and said as much to the gentleman.

"Well, apparently it wasn't no ordinary hatchet that killed that Smith boy. It was a tomahawk they found in his head, and that's not all. They also claim they found a few arrowheads on the floor of the apartment. That was what led the inspector to jump to the conclusion that an Indian had killed the Smiths. And, of course, where else to find an Indian but at my Wild West show?"

Holmes leaned back in his chair for a moment, taking in the description of Mr. Cody's situation. "Lestrade," the detective stated, "does have some rationale for his actions. Can you vouch for the location of all of your Lakota members?"

Mr. Cody's spine stiffened, and I feared my friend had insulted the celebrity, but when he spoke his voice was quiet and serious. "Mr. Holmes, I assure you that there ain't a one of my tribesmen who would commit such a crime. After last night's performance, as I said, they celebrated something fierce. I don't see how any of them would have had the capabilities to trek halfway across London, commit a murder, and return back to camp without anyone, including Red Chief, knowing they had gone missing."

"You admit there was a celebration that evening. In the general mood of celebrating, one could – "

"On my honor, sir!" Buffalo Bill interrupted my companion sternly, and he placed his right hand upon his heart. "On my honor, my men are innocent."

Holmes was silent for a moment. Then he nodded his head. "I cannot guarantee that my conclusion will satisfy you, nor that I will have solved the crime within your allotted time frame; however, I will be happy to provide my full attention to this matter."

The long haired cowboy gave a solemn nod of his head and the two men shook hands.

After bidding Mr. Cody *adieu*, Holmes and I quickly dressed and hailed a cab. We moved swiftly through the streets of London from Baker Street to Old Montague. Holmes was quiet at the beginning of the ride, his elbows resting on his knees and his hands resting, palms together before his face, as if my friend were in a meditative prayer. I knew he was deep in thought, preparing himself for the case at hand.

"The details of the case," the detective suddenly began, "do have some points of interest, at least as far as their description in *The Times* and by that of Mr. Cody. A brother and sister in a fourth floor apartment, murdered. The brother was killed with an axe; the sister with a throwing knife.

"The sister, a Miss Olivia Smith," Holmes continued, motioning me to be silent, "managed to stumble out into the hallway and call for help. As she lay dying, she pointed up the stairs, indicating that her accoster had escaped by ascending. The murderer fled to the roof, a seeming dead end, yet when some tenants climbed the stairs and searched the roof, they could find no trace of anyone. How does one ascend a set of stairs to the roof of a building and simply disappear?"

"Why, Holmes," I started, "it boggles the mind."

"Indeed," Holmes continued. "But we have not had a chance to visit the crime scene ourselves. My only hope is that ten hours after the crime was committed, the constables have left enough clues untrampled for my assistance to be of value. Aaahhh, Watson, we have arrived at our destination," Holmes said as the coach came to a stop in front of a large tenement building. Holmes paid the cabbie and we were greeted by the constable out front. He ushered us into the building, and we climbed the stairs to a front room on the fourth floor.

Waiting outside the door was a bleary eyed sergeant, reflecting on his notes, and shifting his eyes nervously about. Two other constables were wandering around, making sure no residents approached the crime scene. When the sergeant saw Holmes, he stepped back in surprise. "Sherlock Holmes, so glad to see you!" the sergeant warmly greeted my friend. "Has Inspector Lestrade sent you?"

Holmes merely nodded. "Sergeant Rousseau, I understand you are having issues with finding a suspect for this case. While Inspector Lestrade is interviewing the Indians at Earl's Court, I have been asked to look into the crime and view the crime scene."

I had to hold back a chuckle as I noted that Holmes did not tell the sergeant who had asked him to investigate.

"It is a rather odd case, indeed," the white haired sergeant stated, and he scratched at his whiskery chin. "Usually my men and I can solve our own crimes, but there are parts to this case that are perplexing." The sergeant gave out a loud yawn and apologized. "I was covering for Constable Stevenson last night, and I was the first officer at the scene of the crime. With everyone running about now, I'm not sure when I will be relieved of my shift."

"Why not tell me the details, and I will do my best to assist you in whatever way I can," Holmes explained in a humble manner.

Sergeant Rousseau recounted the details Holmes had read in *The Times*, but he filled in many of the story's gaps. The gaunt faced man explained, "As I'm sure you know, we have had a terrible time keeping members of our force. I was covering for Constable Stevenson who has come down with a severe case of the flu. While walking the rounds at approximately one a.m., I overheard cries of murder from a fourth floor window of the building in which we are standing. Upon my arrival, I found several residents cradling the dying form of Olivia Smith. After seeing that her wound was mortal – indeed, the life had already fled from the poor girl – I ascended the stairs in pursuit of the criminal. He was easy to track, as I noted a trail of bloody footprints that continued along the stairwell to the roof. On the roof itself, a flat style, the footprints mysteriously vanished. There was no trace of the murderer. I searched every corner of the roof and noted the buildings and alleys surrounding the tenement. There was no movement that caught my eye, no sign of a fleeing suspect.

"I then returned to the Smith's front room," he said, motioning to the area he was currently guarding, "and discovered the body of Donald Smith, the younger brother of Olivia. His body was slumped over the sofa. At this point, more officers arrived at the crime scene, in response to the calls for help. The residents also were beginning to come out of their corners to see what all the fuss was about."

"I suppose you let them trample all over the stairs and the crime scene," Holmes stated sternly.

"The officers did their best to hold back the curious and helpful, to keep evidence from being disturbed. I think you'll find they did an exceptional job," Rousseau said coolly. He did not appreciate Holmes questioning his police work.

"A search of the apartment left no clue as to the motivation of the crime," Rousseau continued. "There were no missing jewels. A locked safe box was discovered and appeared undisturbed. There was no sign of a break-in. The door to the living quarters was unlocked," Rousseau finished.

Holmes thanked Rousseau for his information. "I believe it is time for us to have our own look at the Smith residence, aye Watson," Holmes said to me, and then he whispered, "Despite Rousseau's assurances, let us hope the constabulary did not do too much damage to the crime scene."

Rousseau led us into the Smith's sparsely decorated lodging. The room consisted of a rather shabby, single bed; a sofa coated in the blood of Donald Smith; a central pine table, with a repaired, oak left side leg; a chiffonier adorned with family photos; and a small safe in the corner, with the door now open; yet, as Rousseau had reported, with no valuables missing.

"Rousseau and I will inspect the room," Holmes instructed, "I'd like you to read over the preliminary autopsy report on the Smith siblings."

The detective and sergeant wandered about the room. Holmes lifted the family photos, checked the blood stains on the floor, and inspected the contents of the open safe. I read the report on the Smith siblings. Both had been murdered in a most grisly fashion. Olivia Smith had been mortally wounded with a stab to her chest. The knife entered deep, penetrating the thoracic cavity. A pneumothorax developed, causing both lungs to collapse. For Donald Smith, the hatchet had been deeply rooted in the skull and had pierced the brain, rendering death instantaneously. I looked down at the sofa, coated in the man's blood, and I noted thick gobs that had dried upon the right sofa cushion, clearly indicating this is where the man's head had slumped when he died.

When Holmes joined my side, I could tell he had seen much more than the sergeant and his police force.

"Well, Holmes and Dr. Watson, have you learned anything that has escaped us?" asked Rousseau. I handed Holmes the police report on Donald Smith, and he examined it closely, then responded, "We still have much more of the crime scene to investigate; however, I can assure you that Donald and Olivia were not brother and sister. They were lovers."

"Lovers?" Rousseau asked astonished.

"Yes, if you look closely at the family photos you will notice both Donald and Olivia Smith together, holding hands in some of the photographs. The family portrait of all the matriarchs of the family has Olivia's left hand slightly concealed behind her dress. Even so, the edge of a diamond ring is clearly visible. Lastly, while the bed is a single, clearly it has the impressions of two bodies. Yes, indeed Sergeant, the Smiths were not only lovers, they were husband and wife."

As my friend explained his reasoning, I could see the truth behind the words dawn upon Rousseau's face as his look went from one of astonishment to one of being dumbfounded. I sympathized with the sergeant, as I had the exact same feeling, one I've had on many occasions with Mr. Holmes.

"That is truly astonishing, Mr. Holmes. I'm not sure how we could have missed it. Does that have any bearing on the case?"

I awaited a sarcastic quip from Holmes, but he was in a serious state, and merely responded. "I'm not sure as of yet. Come Watson. I'd like your opinion of the bloody footprints."

As we left the Smith residence, I started seeing the faint outlines of the bloody prints. It was just the left foot, in fact just the tip of the left foot. I couldn't make out much more than the man had stepped in a bit of spilled blood which had remained on his foot. Holmes stopped on occasion and observed the footprints with his magnifying glass, while Rousseau complained about the lack of officers on the force. Apparently, one constable sprained his ankle in all the rushing around the previous evening, leaving the Yard with one less patrolman. Eventually, we climbed onto the roof and were met with a burst of sunlight.

The roof was nondescript, except for one fact. The buildings surrounding this tenement were several floors taller than the current one. An alleyway separated the building on the northeast and southeast sides from the next closest residences. Even if a thief could make the leap across the alleys on either side, they would surely smash into the brick walls of the neighboring buildings. The southwest side of the building was close to another tenement, though this one had an exceedingly steep thatched roof. For one to leap onto this roof and work one's way down to the ground seemed difficult. To do so without being observed, impossible.

"Our prey is a skilled devil," Rousseau cursed.

"These are dark dealings, sergeant," Holmes agreed. I noted that Holmes was looking at a scuff mark on the northeast side of the building. What it could mean, I knew not, but I did notice a glimmer of recognition in my friend's eyes.

"It's a shame," Rousseau lamented. "If Lestrade isn't able to crack any of the savages at that circus, then this case may never be solved."

Holmes glared at Rousseau, his mouth turning into a deep frown. "If, by savage, you mean an Anglo man of approximately five feet in height, of a particularly strong and limber body, who is undoubtedly from America, probably New York, and who was associated with the Smiths, then yes, I'd agree with you. As far as the Lakotas from Mr. Cody's Wild West show are concerned, they are completely innocent."

After Holmes's tongue lashing of the sergeant, we made our way back out of the tenement building. "To me, this killer has done the impossible. Yet you are onto something, aren't you?" I asked my friend.

"Remember, cases that seem impossible often have the simplest conclusions. I have noted four possible solutions to the case, but I still need more facts before I can deduce the resolution. For now, I need my Boswell's gift of observation."

"Whatever I may do to assist you, Holmes."

"There is a tavern there," said Holmes pointing to a dingy, dilapidated ground floor establishment almost directly across the street. "I would like you to interview the barkeep and see if he had any notable customers yesterday evening. Take copious notes, and then send them to me when you are finished."

"Where will you be?" I asked.

"Why, at Earl's Court, attempting to show our dear friend Lestrade some semblance of reason."

I nodded and said goodbye to my friend. I expected him to hail a cab, but I was surprised to see Holmes instead enter the building neighboring the northeast side of the Smith's tenement.

The pub across the way had seen better days. The bar was stained different colors in several areas, crude attempts at covering up its missing chunks of wood. The furniture was a mix of different style tables and chairs from the last thirty years. The lighting was dark, the establishment drab, and the bloated barkeep with three shabby customers were the only people present. I noted that the customers kept their coat collars up and their heads face down in their ale. Not to stay hidden from me, but to stay hidden from the world. Such was the glum life of the alcoholic.

The barkeep, ruddy cheeked and with a crooked smile, lit up when he saw me enter, possibly because of my dress and obvious station in life. I joined the rank group at the counter, ordered a pint, and struck up a casual conversation with the gentleman, who introduced himself as Daniel Spitzer. It was my good fortune to discover the man was not only of jolly spirits but quite a talker. After discussing London's cold spell for a moment, I turned the conversation towards the Smiths.

"That's a terrible business, mind you, what with all that hullabaloo last night. Who would have thought that could happen to a nice couple like that?"

"Couple?" I inquired. "The *Times* said they were siblings."

"Oh, they claimed that they were brother and sister. Not sure why, not sure what they were fleeing from, really. Oh, don't look surprised. If a couple is pretending to be siblings, you know that they are hiding from someone. It always puzzled me, but I never asked, though I've got an inkling as to what they were running from. You see, the death of the Smiths is terrible for them, but it's also terrible for me," he added with a wink.

"What do you mean terrible for you?"

"No shame telling you that the bar is only a portion of my income. A good chunk of my money also comes from the track, and the Smiths were some of my best clients. You see they bet big, but often lost just as big. I'm not sure where all their money came from, but between you and me, I bet they were swindlers. Nice folks here, always stayed out of trouble, but they had something about them, always looked a little haunted, if you ask me."

Mentioning the tracks and horses led to a separate discussion on the prospects of the thoroughbred Ocean Breeze in the upcoming afternoon race. After placing a small wager with Spitzer, I turned the conversation back to the previous evening, and I was surprised to discover that he had been working during the time the crime was committed. "Yes, sir, I pretty much live here. I have to leave to go down to the tracks on occasion, but there isn't a day that goes by where I'm not here at least fourteen hours. Anyway, last night, guess it would have been after one, people started flooding in. Some even had blood on their clothes. One poor officer looked stunned and shaken, same with two of the men, their clothes covered in blood. I'm guessing they were kicked out by the police before they had a chance to even change their clothes."

"Did you know the two men?" asked Watson.

"I know one of them, Abe Bruder, a jeweler near the Black Lion. Can't miss his flowing beard. Even that had streaks of blood in it. The man badgered on and on with a group of my people. Talked about holding the poor body of Miss Smith as she breathed her last breath. They were most upset, with good reason."

I pondered this information for a moment. Old Montague Street was known as having a predominantly Jewish population. I wondered if I would need to seek out a translator to assist with the Hebrew of the residents.

Finally, I pressed Spitzer again about anything else unusual that evening. He shrugged. "Nothing more than you'd expect. Lots of wailing and crying about the neighborhood and our lot in life. No one struck me as standing out. Everyone was shaken from the murder."

I finished my ale and began to say goodbye when suddenly a thought occurred to me. "Do you know of any Americans who frequent your establishment?" I asked.

Daniel's eyes lit up. "Course I do, know of one man in particular who hails from New York. He's in here all the time."

I was surprised by this bit of good luck and asked for this man's name.

"Course you can have his name. You've been speaking to him for the better part of an hour," Daniel beamed.

Puzzled, I inquired what Daniel meant.

"It's me, you fool. I'm originally from Buffalo, New York."

After my interview with Spitzer, I had my notes sent to Holmes, and returned to our residence. Relaxing, I enjoyed a glass of brandy and continued reading of Miss Nellie Bly's adventures in the book, *Ten Days in a Mad-House*, an appropriate title to reflect upon while sorting this case. Here was a girl voluntarily going undercover to expose the mistreatment of women in Blackwell's Island Asylum in New York. I wondered how many monsters lived in that American colony, and in my mind cursed our luck that Britain hadn't squashed General Washington's rebellion over a century ago. In due course, the brandy worked its effects, and I dozed off only to be awakened by Holmes shaking me a few hours later.

"Wake up, Watson," Holmes insisted. "We are to be guests at Mr. Cody's Wild West Show this evening. Mrs. Hudson is preparing a dinner of roast beef for us, and we should have just enough time to sup before our carriages arrive."

"Holmes, really," I started. "Do you have the solution to this dastardly case? Was it one of Mr. Cody's Indians?"

"I almost certainly do have the solution, and I assure you Mr. Cody's Indians had nothing to do with the crime."

"Well, out with it man," I demanded. "What happened?"

"You will accept my apologies Watson, as I cannot quite tell you the solution yet. There is still one last piece of the puzzle which I shall put in place tomorrow when one of Lestrade's men will join us. I believe he will identify the killer."

"But how?" I insisted. "How did the man pull this off?"

"In due time, Watson," Holmes answered mysteriously. "I believe you will find this evening's performance most enlightening. It took some convincing on my part, but once I assured Lestrade I'd have the murderer behind bars by tomorrow afternoon, he agreed to let Cody's show go on. Personally, I think the inspector just wanted an excuse to go home and finally catch up on much needed sleep."

After a delicious dinner of roasted beef and stewed vegetables, Holmes and I descended the stairs and waited for our coach to arrive. I was taken aback to see not one but three carriages stop in front of our home. Puzzled at why three carriages were needed for two men, I was about to ask Holmes when the answer came round the corner. Jostling towards us was a group of street urchins, dressed in dirty rags and making all sorts of noise as they tramped and jumped excitedly.

Holmes lit up at seeing the rag-tag army marching towards us. "Hello, Thaddeus, hello Barney," he addressed two of the older boys in the front. "Is this everyone for the Wild West performance?"

"Yes, Mr. Holmes," answered Thaddeus, a tall lad, thin – not from his body type but from his lack of nourishment. "There's a dozen of us, sir." He paused then quietly added in a tone of astonishment. "Golly, are we really gonna meet Mr. Cody?"

"Of course you are, lad, as long as we make the show on time. Plus, Mr. Cody has agreed to treat everyone to all the snacks they can eat."

A grand hurrah went up from the children, and then they scrambled into the growlers. I noted how one of the drivers scowled at seeing his passengers, but he kept his mouth shut, and with a crack of the reins, we were all off to the show. Holmes looked rather cheerful. "I wonder Watson, what will be more entertaining, seeing the show, or seeing the expressions of awe on the Irregulars' faces when they see the performances?" I heartily agreed, but inside I wondered what Buffalo Bill Cody would think of his special guests for the evening.

Fortunately, Mr. Cody was as gracious and kind as the stories in the adventure books make him out to be. When we arrived at the fair ground, Cody was there to meet us, dressed in his stage costume, with his gray cowboy hat, tan shirt with fringe, dark riding boots, and his arms filled with a dozen bags of peanuts for the irregulars. After handing out food and shaking hands with the children, the showman led us to our seats. While the giddy children oohed and awed at the spectacle of the show grounds, Holmes asked Mr. Cody, "Did you honor my request?"

"I sure did, Mr. Holmes. Not exactly an authentic portrayal, but I doubt the audience will mind. I reckon you folks are in for one great show. Now, here are your seats. I best get ready."

After the showman had left, I asked Holmes about their side conversation. The detective was distracted, beaming with pride at seeing the boisterous excitement of the irregulars.

"It is tragic, Watson, that my investigative team of children so rarely get to act like children," Holmes lamented.

The irregulars always left me a bit unsettled. The unsupervised children had a wild edge about them, but I conceded that Holmes was correct. It was nice to see all of them excited about a spectacle, not about a morsel of food to alleviate their growling stomachs.

"As to your question, Watson, I asked Mr. Cody to add an act to tonight's performance that I had the pleasure of viewing during rehearsals this afternoon. I believe you will find it both entertaining and of the most interest."

I was taken aback by Holmes's coyness, but I could see he wanted me to show patience. I simply nodded in understanding and left the detective to gaze upon the happiness he brought to our loyal street urchins. Before long, the Wild West show began. It was just as marvelous as the news reported, perhaps even more so.

Cody came charging out in the center of the stage, riding Old Charlie, the famous twenty-one-year-old horse noted as Cody's favorite, who seemed to enjoy the attention as much as his human companion. "Ladies and Gentlemen," Mr. Cody grandly called with a wave of his hat and a bow, "this evening you are in for a feast of the eyes, as you journey thousands of miles across the sea and over the lands, past the Florida swamps and the Adirondack Mountains, to land in the true heart of America, that of the Wild West. Tonight, my friends, you will marvel at the sharp shooting of Annie Oakley, spy an Indian attack on a pioneer stage coach, gasp at the acrobatic feats of Buck Taylor, and witness man conquer nature as a recreated wildfire appears before your very eyes. But enough talking from me – On with the show!"

A huge roar of approval and applause thundered from the audience as a herd of Buffalo rumbled onto the fairgrounds. Both cowboys and Indians worked together to corral the beasts and show a simulated hunt of the now almost extinct symbol of America. This act was followed by the great Annie Oakley. The sharpshooter known as "Little Sure Shot," threw two clay pigeons into the air. She then hurled herself toward a table where two rifles lay in wait. I expected the dame to pick up the nearest Winchester and shatter one of the fake birds. To my astonishment, the lady leaped over the table, grabbing both rifles and let off two shots even before her feet hit the ground. The pigeons shattered in the air, and the crowd went wild. Holmes was applauding and laughing, but I could see his eyes were on the raucous Irregulars.

After the great Annie Oakley came the stagecoach robbery. The wild Indians, adorned with war paint, whooping and hollering, riding horses bareback, launched a full attack on the circled wagons. The coachmen tried their best but were no match from the overwhelming onslaught of Indian arrows. The actors did a magnificent job falling over, pretending to be dead, and, for added effect, with an arrow emerging from their backs. Just as all seemed lost, a trumpet call came from off stage and the cavalry, led by Buffalo Bill himself, came charging out and drove the Red Men away.

Again the audience seemed to lose their sense of decorum as they called, hollered, and cheered in a way to rival the whoops of the defeated Sioux. Next up came the cowboys. Buck Taylor and his compatriots held races, rode bucking broncos, reenacted daily voyages of the Pony Express, leaped over fallen coaches, and picked up sombreros from the ground while their horses continued at full gallop. Mr. Cody joined the group, riding his faithful companion. He had audience members toss baseballs into the air which he shot from the sky with his Colt army revolver, never slowing Old Charlie who continuously raced around the grounds at a furious pace.

Next came the astounding acrobats of John "The Ranger" Billings. "Ladies and Gentlemen," Cody dramatically started, "you will now witness mankind fighting that most monstrous beast of nature, that terrifying creature which consumes whole towns in its jaws, that horror known as the wildfire." The stage was set at a logging camp in the Rocky Mountains. A ranger station was on one side of the stage and on the other was a tower adorned with a bell to ring at any sign of danger. Two show hands set a pile of brush in the center of the stage and set it ablaze. Suddenly, Mr. Billings, in full ranger gear, burst out of the ranger station. He attempted to get to the bell tower, but the flames blocked his path. He showed concern with his flailing arms and tried several different pathways around the flames but to no avail.

The audience was absolutely silent, and I began to worry that perhaps the act had gotten out of hand, that the fire had shown a life of its own, and perhaps we would be evacuating the building. I looked at the faces of the children in front of me and even scanned the audience to find most faces showing at the very least concern, if not absolute fright.

Just as I was about to suggest to Holmes we move towards the exits to help disperse the crowd, I witnessed the most staggering gymnastic skills my eyes had ever seen. The Ranger grabbed a long, thin yet sturdy, piece of lumber. A cry came up from the audience as Mr. Billings then sprinted straight for the flames in the center of the stage. I felt my heart pounding, *What*, I wondered, *was this fool doing? Would he commit suicide before thousands?*

Then, the miracle occurred. Just as Mr. Billings was about to reach the flames, he jabbed the pole into the ground and used the stick to vault himself over the wildfire and land at the top of the bell tower. The sound of the bell ringing was drowned out by the raucous roars from the audience. We were all on our feet, hooting and screaming for more, and we did not stop our applause even as the fire brigade entered the stage and extinguished the flames.

Our cheers must have sounded for a good ten minutes when, suddenly, what I witnessed, truly witnessed, dawned upon me. "Holmes!" I shouted. "The killer!"

It was about two in the afternoon that following day when an elegant landau arrived in front of 221 Baker Street and both Mr. Cody and Mr. Billings arrived at our doorstep. We warmly greeted the entertainers who made a contrasting pair. Cody with his long hair and whiskers, Billings with his shaved face and closely cropped hair.

"Do you really think you've got the varmint behind this fiasco?" Cody asked. Before Holmes could respond, a wagon pulled to the curb behind where Mr. Cody's landau had just departed, and out stepped Lestrade, and three of his constables. There was a fourth man the group, assisted in removing from the carriage, who had a lame foot and a crutch. The men helped their crippled companion through the front door, and we heard them struggling up the stairs.

"We should help that young man," said Billings.

"Actually, I have a rather unusual request for you," said Holmes and he opened the door to his bedroom. "Please stay here, gentlemen, and await my call to come out. You will hear the conversation I am about to have with the officers of the law, but I ask that you remain silent and do not reveal the fact that you are here until told to do so. As you know, Mr. Cody, I can be trusted."

"If that's what you'd like Mr. Holmes, well, okay then." Cody assented, and the two men entered the bedroom after which Holmes closed the door behind them.

Shortly thereafter, the constables finally reached the door to our sitting room. Holmes warmly welcomed them in and offered a couch for the lame officer to lay upon. After they entered, I noted that Holmes closed and locked the door behind them.

Rousseau was one of the men present. The other two affable men were introduced as Constables Holly and Tiller, both young officers whose forms didn't quite fill out their uniforms, giving them an unintended comic charm. The lame officer on the couch was introduced as Constable Fowler, a man closer to my own age with coal black hair and a crooked nose.

"Really, Holmes," Lestrade complained, "I don't know why you couldn't have gone to Constable Fowler's residence. Forcing him to climb those stairs is beyond my reasoning."

"As I find is almost always the case," Holmes muttered, but Lestrade did not respond, either because he ignored my friend or did not hear him.

"Constable Fowler, like Rousseau, was an officer at the scene of the crime Friday evening. Watson, if you recall, he is the officer that Rousseau informed us had sprained his foot that night. I believe that Fowler witnessed the murderer as he fled from Old Montague Street."

Fowler shook his head. "Mr. Holmes," he replied, "if I can help in any way, I will. It was the dead of night, and I did not see anyone flee from the crime scene. I only arrived quickly because I reside on Old Montague myself. There were quite a few people running about, but I can't say I saw someone fleeing from the area."

"Fowler, please look over these photographs of members of Mr. Cody's troop. I believe there is someone you will recognize," Holmes insisted and handed a pile of promotional photographs from Cody's show to the officer.

The constable took the photographs from Holmes and began looking them over. The collection was a menagerie of men, both Red and White. With each turn of the pictures came a shake of the head from Fowler. Finally, he reached the end of the pile and held aloft one picture of a bald strongman. "Possibly him, although he would have had a wig on, but there's something familiar about him."

Holmes looked crestfallen. "That man is Melvin Brady, a former member of Mr. Cody's troop, who never made the voyage to London. I did not mean to include his picture in the mix. Ah," Holmes perked up. "There is one more photograph." He removed a small, folded paper from his pocket and handed it to the injured man.

Fowler looked at the photo and his eyes bulged from his face. With a swift motion, the invalid was on his feet and dashing towards the door. He grabbed at the handle, attempting to turn it, and finding it locked.

Realizing his situation, the fiend turned towards Holmes. Wild eyed, teeth clenched like a wounded animal, he sprang at Holmes with an inhuman growl. He made it but three steps before Rousseau, Lestrade, and the other constables had grabbed him and thrown him to the floor.

"Holmes, what on earth is going on?" asked Lestrade, after the officers had restrained Fowler with some rope.

"Cody, Billings please come out now," Holmes called. "I believe you will recognize Mr. Wendell Finke, a former employee of the Wild West show."

Lestrade was stunned to see the two showmen step out of Holmes's private room, and I noted a slight reddening of his features, tightening of his jaw, and clenching of his fists. "Really Holmes!" Lestrade growled. "Did we need these theatrics?"

Holmes did not answer the Inspector's question. He waited as both Cody and Billings looked over the still struggling form of Finke. I saw a slight recognition in Wild Bill's face, but Billings clearly knew the man before him. "Finke," Billings gasped. "What have you done to yourself?"

"Only what needed to be done to give what those two had coming to them!" spat Finke.

"Mr. Finke was a member of Mr. Cody's Wild West show," Holmes explained to Lestrade and the other officers. He handed them the last photograph he had shown to Finke which revealed the man in full cowboy regalia, but with blonde hair and a straight nose. "He was the assistant to Mr. Billings and a noted acrobat. After the troop arrived in London in the spring, Mr. Finke was part of the show until the end of April, when he abruptly quit."

"That's right," Finke blurted, then held his tongue. The man was fuming, and we were not sure whether he would speak more, yell at us, or struggle against his bindings, or perhaps do all three at once.

Finally, with a heavy sigh, Finke seemed to decide that since he was caught anyway, he should tell his tale and explain his actions. "I had finally tracked down those Smith crooks. I had stumbled upon them in London. They had taken everything from me, the devils. I met them in New York, at my mother's funeral, though they weren't called Smith then. Then it was Roger and Mary Corbin. Roger claimed to be a stockbroker, claimed he could double my inheritance by investing in a horseless carriage company. I fell for it. I was the rube, I was. They took everything and fled. That was ten years ago almost to the day.

"Finding myself destitute, I sought out work, jobs that allowed me to move around as I tried to track down the Corbins. I almost caught up to them once in Chicago, but they disappeared again before I could find them. They always left rich men poor in their wake. Roger was a gambling man of the worst kind, the kind that does not know when to stop and always loses.

"Finally, in the fall, I joined Mr. Cody's troop. I had given up on tracking down the Corbins. Their trail had gone stale, and I had moved on. Then, as fortune would have it, one day I was exploring London and ended up in a tavern on Old Montague. Who should I see making a wager with the barkeep? Why, Mr. Roger Corbin. I saw him, but he did not recognize me. I followed the man, found out where he lived, who he was, that he hadn't stopped his wicked ways."

"That's when you decided to murder them?" Lestrade demanded.

"No. It had been years since I had seen them. I tried to put them out of my head. Tried my best, but I couldn't stop thinking about what they'd done, how they were still swindling people. After a few weeks, I decided to seek my revenge. I quit Mr. Cody's show and became a constable. It was easy enough. There's quite a shortage of us." He motioned to the other officers present. "Anyway, I took lodging in the building next to the Corbins, now Smiths. I dyed my blonde hair black, and even got my nose smashed in a proper tavern brawl. I needed to make sure the couple wouldn't recognize me. As an officer, I occasionally entered their tenement building. I noted how tight the hallways were, how crammed the stairwells. If I were to kill the couple, I most surely would be seen fleeing, especially if I was wearing my police outfit."

"But," Holmes interrupted, "you were an acrobat, a skilled knife thrower, and a man who knows how to walk a tight rope, or vault across a pit of fire. You will recall, Watson, that after inspecting the home of the Smiths, we wandered up to the building's roof, and I noted a scuff mark in the in the roofing overlooking the northeast side of the building. My first thought was that someone had laid a pole or thin ladder across the two buildings and that there were even possibly two assailants, one to hold the pole while the other scurried across it. The person who scurried to the other building would have to be someone who was extremely athletic. From the bloody footprints I noted the man's gait and knew he had to be about five feet in height, the exact height of Mr. Finke. I also deduced that the man who killed the Smiths was someone that they knew, most likely from America, as one of the photographs of the couple in front of The Statue of Liberty, was crumpled slightly and off to the side, as if the killer had stared long at the image before discarding it. I also knew that the man had to be Anglo. Otherwise, someone would have noted a man of a different race, especially a Lakota Sioux, approaching or fleeing the tenement building.

"Extraordinary, Mr. Holmes," remarked Rousseau. "Still how did you find that Finke was our man?"

"Ahh, well after Watson and I left the Smiths, I went to the tenement on the northeast side of the building. If the assailants had escaped via the rooftop, there was a good chance they would have been seen returning down the stairs to their lodgings. I inquired with the building supervisor about the building tenants. He mentioned Officer Fowler. It dawned on me that a constable would have the means of committing the murders, return down to the street level, and cover up his tracks. I knocked on the officer's door, pretending to be a reporter for *The Times*. I noted the man's features and when I visited Mr. Cody's grounds I stumbled upon Mr. Billings practicing his wildfire act. After seeing the pole vaulting, I realized one man could easily have committed the crime. I inquired with Mr. Billings about current and former members of the Wild West show capable of completing the pole vault. When he showed me the picture of Mr. Finke, gentlemen, the case was closed."

"But how on earth did Finke get a vaulting pole?" Lestrade inquired.

"The missing pole!" suddenly Billings called out in shock then turned to the bound Finke, "You stole it!"

"That's right," Finke snarled. "I returned to the showground as an officer of the law. I stole the pole and returned to my building, then the next day, I went to the roof of the Smith residence and stashed the pole, ready to finally enact justice."

"But the pole?" Lestrade puzzled. "How did you transport such a large pole?"

"I believe Mr. Billings can answer your question," Holmes interjected.

"Yes," answered Billings. "The pole is an invention of my own. I found bamboo bends quite easily and can achieve greater heights than hard wood; however, it is still difficult to transport an eight foot piece of wood. I created a five piece version where the pieces screw together to make the pole, quite similar to the newer cue sticks."

"Then everything was set," continued Holmes. "Finke entered the building in his police uniform. The Smiths, seeing a constable at their door, invited him in. Finke then dispatched the Smiths, climbed to the roof, removed his shoes, tossed them into the alley below, vaulted over to his own building, and then descended the stairs to his room where he put on new shoes. The accoster quickly went to the alley where he gathered the bloody shoes and the stick, which he disassembled, hid them in a bag or beneath his uniform, and then stashed them away in his own apartment. I would not be surprised, constables, if you were to find the materials still inside Finke's residence."

Lestrade looked stunned at all that had been revealed before him. "I assure you Mr. Holmes, that my men will search his room after we bring him back to the Yard."

"Before you take Mr. Finke away, I do have one question for him. Why did you set up Mr. Cody's Lakota-Sioux?"

"I know those men, barbarians they are," grumbled Finke. "I figured there wasn't nothing I did to the Smiths that those warriors hadn't done a thousand times over to settlers. If an Indian hanged for the crime, so be it. There's a saying in America, that the only good Injun is a dead Injun."

Holmes's face was filled with absolute revulsion at Mr. Finke. "I believe in your country, just as ours, all people are created equal, and all people are equal in the eyes of the law. You chose to take the law into your own hands. You committed a crime and now must face the punishment."

Finke lashed out with harsh words at my companion, words I cannot repeat in the confines of this narrative. My dear friend just stood quietly as the constables hauled away the murderer.

"I'm glad that's over," I said to my companion as the wagon took Finke away.

"I agree, Watson. Finke believed he was serving a perverse form of justice. In the end, he was actually a worse criminal than that of the Smiths. I believe he will learn true justice when he hangs from the end of a rope. And now, Watson, onto another puzzling dilemma," my friend stated.

"I hope it is not another grisly murder," I stated in astonishment.

"No, no, I was deciding whether I should order the quail or the flounder at Simpson's this evening."

The Adventure of the
Aspen Papers
by Daniel D. Victor

*Nine-tenths of the artist's interest in [bare facts]
is that of what he shall add to them
or how he shall turn them.*
— Henry James, *The Art of the Novel*

I

Mrs. Hudson recognized a man of noble bearing when she saw one. Those were the visitors she most often reserved for herself to introduce, leaving to the boy in livery the task of announcing the guests she deemed less important. As a consequence, when she appeared at the door of the sitting room one morning in late October of 1887, both Sherlock Holmes and I looked up with great expectation. Sensing the drama her presence created, she smoothed down her skirt, cleared her throat, and proclaimed, "Mr. Henry James."

It wasn't that I thought she'd actually recognized the cerebral American author of *Roderick Hudson* and *The Portrait of a Lady*. Rather, it was the man himself who presented quite the authoritative figure. He appeared to be in his forties, with piercing light-grey eyes, a high forehead, and thin dark hair at his ears that accented a balding pate. Combined with his short grizzled beard and sensitive mouth, his features conveyed a sense of dignity, perspicacity, intelligence. What's more, having recently moved to London from the States, he was attired in a smart, three-piece English suit, a gold chain stretched taut across his waistcoat. Taken as a whole, his was an image destined to command respect from anyone, even those like Mrs. Hudson, who had never heard of him – let alone his reputation.

"Mr. Sherlock Holmes?" said our visitor to my friend, somehow aware of which of us to address.

Holmes bowed slightly, introduced me, and indicated that James take a seat.

No sooner had we settled ourselves than he addressed us. "Gentlemen, I come to you – I come to you – with a problem."

Let me say from the start that for so accomplished a writer, Henry James had the startling tendency to hesitate and repeat – almost to stutter

261

– when he spoke. His manner of speech seemed less a bumbling with words, however, than the rehearsing of finely-tuned sentences. To spare the reader superfluous repetition, I have striven to minimize this characteristic.

In point of fact, James' voice was rich and melodious, almost mesmerizing; and I was pleased to observe that Sherlock Holmes was immediately engaged. As I have reported elsewhere, the previous spring had been a difficult time for my friend. He'd been worn down by the months he'd devoted to resolving the matter of the Netherland-Sumatra Company, not to mention the unpleasant business near Reigate in Surrey where ironically he'd gone to regain his strength. To see him devote his complete attention to Henry James was most reassuring indeed.

I hoped it would be equally reassuring to James; for as he sat drumming his fingers on the velvet arm of the chair, he certainly looked in need of some sort of aid.

"You don't mind if I smoke," said Holmes. It was more of a statement than a question, and it left to me the obligation of offering James a cigar.

"Not today, Doctor," said he, waving off the suggestion. "I'm – I'm in need of quick answers. This is not a social call."

Holmes flashed a smile as he filled his briar with dark shag. "How can I be of service?"

"It's a moral issue, Mr. Holmes," said James and immediately got to the point. "An acquaintance of mine has gone missing. Since I'm the one responsible for having gotten him into a sticky situation, I feel responsible for finding out what's become of him." He placed one hand on top of the other, interlocking his fingers in the process. It was as if he was signalling the complexity of the story he was about to tell.

"Pray, start at the beginning," said Holmes, blowing a blue cloud upward.

"The acquaintance in question, gentlemen, one Thomas Warren, arrived in London from New York at the end of the summer. He's an aspiring young academic, though a bit headstrong and compulsive. He's a professor – an instructor – at the University of Virginia, and the two of us have exchanged some correspondence. He hopes to advance his career through a biography of the American poet, Jeremy Aspen – Jeremy Bishop Aspen."

"Jeremy Aspen," I repeated. It was a name unfamiliar to me. Holmes, who took little interest in poetry, showed no recognition at all.

James pulled at his beard. He resembled a frustrated instructor, annoyed that his students had not remembered his previous lecture. "Aspen was famous for the romantic poetry he composed at the turn of

262

the century. His devotees call him 'The Orpheus of the New World'. A few months ago, I learned through my arcane literary connections that a former paramour of Aspen, a woman named Olivia Borden, is rumoured still to be living in London. I forwarded this information to Professor Warren, and so great – so intense – was his interest that he dropped everything he'd been doing and immediately sailed to England."

"Quite the dedicated scholar," I chuckled.

A frosty glare quieted me. "I thought so too, Doctor; but he's gone beyond so benign a description. He considers Aspen a veritable god. More to the point, he's obsessed with the idea that Miss Borden will further his career. He believes that not only could she be a fountain of knowledge regarding Aspen, but that she might actually possess letters of an intimate nature from Aspen himself. Such a find – such a discovery – would elevate Warren's career in an instant."

"The paramour of a poet who wrote so long ago?" said I. "She must be well advanced in years."

"Close to ninety, I should imagine," said James, waving away Holmes's smoke that had begun to envelop us all. "Her age explains Warren's haste. He rightly fears that she could die at any moment, in which case *his* moment would dissipate as well. Little is known of the years Aspen spent away from his home in New York, you see. Oh, we're well aware that he lived for some time in England – but nobody knows the details. The scholar – the researcher – who furnishes such information would certainly receive grand honours, and now Warren – thanks in great part to ·my encouragement – believes he can get the answer from this old woman, a lady with whom Aspen supposedly fell in love over seventy years ago. Warren thinks she must be the reclusive muse that scholars have been seeking for years."

"If these letters exist," I observed, "I imagine they'd be worth a fortune."

"To be sure, Dr. Watson," said James. "Thomas Warren's quite right. The discovery of such a woman would go far to establish his career. He can't afford to miss out."

"And how well has he succeeded?" Holmes asked.

"That's just it. I don't know. Not long after he got here, he wrote me a lengthy letter. He said he'd established that the old woman really does exist and that he'd been able to track her down to a run-down manor house in Southwark called The Hollows. She lives in rented rooms there with her niece."

Holmes exhaled another blue cloud. "You're a literary man yourself, Mr. James. Hasn't this singular information from Warren sparked a similar curiosity in *you*? Why haven't you met the woman yourself, for example?"

"A fair question, Mr. Holmes. Aspen, you see, is Warren's province. It's true that I did go there – to The Hollows – once – but only after Warren had gone missing. That's when I met the niece, a middle-aged spinster type, quite plain and matronly. I learned very little. Indeed, most all that I'm telling you I gleaned from Warren himself."

"Pah!" Holmes snorted. "Little comes from second-hand tales."

Henry James arched his eyebrows. Accomplished writer though he might be, I was certain he was unused to people discounting his narratives.

Nonetheless, he ran his hand across his balding head and continued. "Warren wrote me about an overgrown garden within the grounds. Apparently, he managed to convince the niece of his love for flora. More important, he convinced her of his need for seclusion. He told her he was a writer, you see, and required peace and quiet in order to compose. It was the grotesqueness of just such a garden, he told her, that soothed his soul. And I should imagine that she believed him."

"Quite so," murmured Holmes, the pipe clenched firmly between his teeth.

"The niece told him that her aunt craved money; and in the end, he offered the old woman much of his life savings for two rooms. He paid for three months the amount it might have cost him to stay in an exclusive flat for a year – that's how important the Aspen papers are to him. She agreed; and he delivered the money to her in gold in a bag of *chamois*-leather. Or so he told the story. Accompanied by his manservant, he moved in soon after and seemed to be getting along. I myself had just returned from a lengthy stay in Italy – Venice and Florence, in particular – and have been quite busy with my own writing. Quite frankly, I didn't think much about not having heard from him."

"How long has it been?"

Henry James looked to the ceiling the way some people do when they calculate sums. "It's three months since he moved into the house, the Hollows. But when I received no answer to a letter I sent him a few weeks ago, I myself went down there – to Southwark. That's when I encountered the niece. Rita Borden – Miss Rita, she's called. At first, she sounded worried. She said that she didn't know what had become of Mr. Warren – that he seemed to have disappeared. And that was all. Then she said she didn't want to talk to me. It was quite strange, really. She seemed both reticent and direct at the same time. All around, I must tell you, it was not too inviting a place."

"And the old woman – she still lives?"

264

James flashed a quick smile. "Yes – as far as I know. Though I for one never got to see her."

"And the Aspen papers?" Holmes asked, taking the pipe from his mouth. "I assume that while Warren was living at The Hollows, he never stumbled across them. If he had, I suspect he would have shared that knowledge with you."

"I don't know, Mr. Holmes. At the beginning of all this, I would have expected him to tell me of his discoveries. Now I'm not so sure. When I asked Miss Rita about his work, she shut the door in my face. That's when I thought of turning to you."

Sherlock Holmes put down the briar and smiled at Henry James.

Good fortune was smiling upon the writer as well. Appealing to my friend's talents was a sure-fire method of engaging his services.

"I would like it very much, Mr. Holmes, if you could go to Southwark – to the house – and find out what's become of Thomas Warren. It was I, after all, who set him off on this course; and it will be I who'll feel culpable should something tragic have happened to the poor fellow."

James reached into his inside coat pocket and produced a wallet.

"Let us see what I can uncover before we talk finances, Mr. James. Perhaps there will be very little mystery at all. What say you, Watson? Are you set for a drive to the Borough in search of a missing scholar this afternoon?"

I readily agreed. The pageboy could take a message to my wife, who was more than understanding when it came to matters involving Holmes. As for my surgery, I had no patients scheduled for the next day and could easily be spared.

"Dr. Watson and I will look into this matter, Mr. James. It seems quite the curious puzzle."

Shaking hands with Holmes and me, Henry James offered a formal nod. Then he turned and marched down the seventeen stairs to the outer door, his footfalls ringing steady and certain.

II

A hansom carried us to London Bridge and over the river into Southwark. As per James' instructions, we took the specified turnings below Long Lane and soon found ourselves in a low, wooded area where the abundance of foliage obliterated the afternoon sun. A final bend in the roadway brought us to the aging manor house known as The Hollows. Draped in darkness by the shade of the massive oaks that surrounded it, the structure appeared to be a single square – its two tall chimneys rising like bookends at each side; its once honey-coloured walls turned black by a century of soot, grime, and neglect. The curtained windows looked dark; many on the ground floor were barred. A rusting metal fence framed the primordial landscape, presenting to the unlucky visitor a tangle of gnarled and overgrown hedgerows.

Our driver pulled his horse up before the access road. The metal gates, mired in damp soil, might gape wide for eternity.

"Do you know this place?" Holmes asked the man.

"Aye," said he, pulling down the front of his cap as he surveyed the gloomy scene, "but just to pass by. Nobody in there but a pair of daft old ladies. There's some what calls 'em witches, but that's just a tale. They live in a couple of rooms downstairs; the rest of the place stays empty."

Holmes nodded and instructed him to wait: paying for the added time would be far easier than trying to hail another cab on this deserted road.

With a dank, cloying smell attacking our nostrils as soon as we set foot on the broken flagstones, Holmes and I quickly negotiated the irregular pathway through the unruly grounds. It came as no surprise to encounter neither bell nor knocker when we reached the entrance to the house, and Holmes pounded on the massive oak door with his fist.

After a few moments, it was opened but a few inches by a short young woman dressed in a blouse and skirt of white linen. She stared out at us suspiciously from beneath a single eyebrow extending above both eyes. Her black hair hung in a plait down her back to her waist.

"*Si?*" said she in Spanish through the small gap.

"Is your mistress in?" Holmes asked, but already we could sense someone else approaching behind her.

"Yes?" this latter asked, stepping in front of the maid and opening the door a few inches wider. She was a heavy-set, middle-aged woman draped in a formless dress of navy blue. "Rosa doesn't speak much English. What do you want?" She wore her dark hair tightly wound in a bun, its severity accenting her aquiline nose; and she stared at us with wide-set eyes. This was obviously the matronly niece, Rita Borden, about whom Henry James had spoken.

"Yes?" she asked again.

"You are Miss Borden? Miss Rita Borden?"

"I am Miss Rita. And who are you, I should like to know?"

"My name is Sherlock Homes, and we're looking for a gentleman who lodges here, Mr. Thomas Warren."

"Oh," said she. "He's gone. Left suddenly, he did, without even taking his man. I haven't seen him in days – though it seems much longer."

266

There was sadness in her voice. But suddenly, just as Henry James had forewarned, she countered, "And what's it to you?"

"I'm a colleague of Mr. Warren," Holmes lied.

"You're another book critic then?" said she with a touch of venom.

"Not exactly. But we haven't heard from him in months, and we are concerned about his welfare."

She smirked. "He said he was interested in our garden. That's what he told my aunt. He said he wanted to rent a room, but she told him no."

"And yet I understand that he did secure lodgings here. What changed your aunt's mind?"

"Money, of course. Lots of it. Say, you do ask a lot of questions. I don't know why I should be telling you all this."

"To help find Mr. Warren, of course."

Holmes seemed to be offering hope, and she brightened a bit at his response. "My aunt gets a trifling amount each year from someone in America – hardly enough for us to live on. That's why she accepted a lodger. She wants the money for *me*."

During the course of this discussion, Miss Rita had allowed the door to open wider, and it was through this larger gap that I gazed upon the ancient woman herself. The maidservant had pushed towards the door a three-wheeled Bath-chair. Staring up at us from its brown, wickerwork seat was a decrepit little figure cloaked in black – or in what must have at one time been black; her dress was now a faded dark-grey, worn shiny by many years of wear. Sitting hunched over like that, she could have been a hundred years old.

Henry James' estimate, however, was probably nearer to the mark. She had to be close to ninety – infirm, frail, desiccated. Breathing seemed to be a chore as well. But it was not her cadaverous form that caused the most alarm. That distinction fell to a black veil of tightly drawn lace that covered the upper half of her visage, leaving visible only her withered lips and skeletal jaw. It was as if she was wearing a ghastly mask. Worse, in the darkness of the room, though you could barely discern her eyes, you still had the sense that they were boring right into you.

"Who's there, Rita?" she called in a grating voice. "Who's come to disturb our afternoon?"

"Two men looking after Mr. Warren." Her tone was matter-of-fact.

"Show them in, dear. *They* might have money as well."

Miss Rita led us into a large sitting room, the thick green-velvet curtains pulled shut before a row of French windows. Heavy crossbeams ran across the ceiling, and oak panelling lined the walls. Although white sheets covered most of the furniture, a few wooden chairs and a low mahogany table stood open in a far corner, illuminated by a pair of yellow candles. One got the feeling the room had looked like this for ages.

The old woman leaned forward and gestured for us to sit down.

"We're looking for Thomas Warren, Miss Borden," Holmes said as soon as we were seated. "We know that he roomed here for months and has now disappeared. We were hoping you might shed some light on the matter."

Below the unyielding vizard, the old lady worked a small smile – a sort of smirk, actually.

"He came here under false pretences," she rasped. "He said he valued our old garden. He said it was exactly the kind of quiet place he was looking for in which to do his writing. He said he'd seen it through the fence and wanted to revive it. All it needed was some work, he said. He promised to find some geraniums or 'Jack Frost' that would flourish in the shade. He festooned the house with flowers. For weeks on end he played his game, and only lately did he show his hand."

"He talked to me of plants and nature as well," added Miss Rita. "At first. Then he moved on to art and books. It took him months to get round to talking about the research he did on writers. And when I asked if he knew about Jeremy Aspen, he said he didn't know the name. Didn't know Aspen was a poet, he said. The rogue was lying, of course. In point of fact, he knows lots about Aspen. But it was only last week that he finally began asking about him. He said that since he did research on other writers, he might as well enquire about Aspen. He wanted to know if my aunt might have some papers or letters concerning the man."

"As if I would leave Mr. Aspen's papers lying about," the old lady said. "Once I realized that's all he was interested in," she added in a confidential whisper, "I told him he would *never* get them from me." In a sudden burst of energy, she hissed, "*If* I had any such papers to give, that is." This last utterance seemed to have tapped all of her strength; for after saying the words, she dropped back in her wickered chair and appeared to fall asleep.

Miss Rita gestured sympathetically at her aunt. "It's late," said the niece, rising and moving towards the entrance hall.

When she opened the door, we could see a finger of late-afternoon sunlight poking its way through the leaves. "I fancy you won't be nosing round here again," she said, her wide eyes registering a degree of triumph as she closed the door.

"That was no great help," said I as we walked along the broken flags. "Not only did we learn nothing about Warren, but we haven't even determined that the Aspen papers are real."

"Did you not notice, Watson, how Miss Borden spoke of the poet as *'Mr.* Aspen'? When one refers to public figures that one *doesn't* know, one generally calls them by their surnames only."

"I've never thought of the matter."

"Well, please do. We say, 'Shakespeare wrote' or 'Shakespeare said'."

"Of course, now that you mention it."

"But when one speaks of an acquaintance, one employs a title like 'Mister'."

"And the old woman called the poet *'Mr.* Aspen'."

"Precisely, old fellow. I'd be willing to wager that a relationship between Miss Borden and Jeremy Aspen is more fact that fiction."

"Then how do you explain Warren's disappearance? If she's the right lady, why would he have left?"

"Since I expect him to return, the reason doesn't concern me. No doubt, he was frustrated. He'd spent months cultivating his relationships with the two women and saw nothing come of it. As long as the papers are here, however – not to mention his manservant – he'll be back. The Aspen papers are too important for him to abandon."

The hansom stood where we'd left it; the sorrel horse was impatiently pawing the dirt.

"Back to Baker Street, if you please," Holmes instructed the driver as we climbed into the cab. To me he said, "I shall speak to the Irregulars." He was talking of the young street Arabs whom he frequently hired to provide information from the byways of London. "They can keep an eye on The Hollows for us. That way, when Warren does return, we shall know."

The carriage took off with a jolt, and Holmes leaned over to me. "After I instruct the boys, Watson, I think a dinner in the Strand might be in order."

I smiled in agreement, but Sherlock Holmes was already staring out the window submerged in thought. I don't imagine he noticed the pink and purple swirls of sunset painting the sky.

III

"Dead!" came the cry as the street urchin burst into our sitting room the next morning. We were just finishing breakfast when he gave us the news. "There's somebody in that house what's died! Popped their clog, didn't they? Hopped the twig!"

Sherlock Holmes put down his coffee and rose to meet the lad. "Who?" he demanded.

"Dunno, do I?" said the boy, brushing a lock of dirty brown hair from his eyes. "But I seen the wagon arrive. Only there was no black feathers on the horses. And no coffin inside. Just a bloke in a tall hat and black togs. He went into the house."

Sherlock Holmes was already donning his coat.

"Come, Watson! There's not a moment to lose! We must get to the body before it's taken away. That was the undertaker the boy saw – come to make final arrangements with Rita Borden."

Thomas Warren must have kept his own watch on The Hollows. For no sooner had the old lady died than Warren returned. In all probability, it was his manservant who'd informed him of her death. In any event Warren was already there when we arrived.

Rosa admitted us, and Holmes and I introduced ourselves in the sitting room. In black suit and sombre mien, Warren certainly dressed the part of a concerned mourner. Attired for a funeral, he had obviously packed his luggage for England contemplating the possibility of bereavement. Yet with those dark, penetrating eyes and black hair combed straight back, he appeared more dashing young suitor than heavy-hearted scholar.

"We're here at the behest of Henry James," Holmes told the professor. "Mr. James is concerned with your whereabouts and the progress of your business."

"I'll contact him when it's appropriate," Warren said without much concern. "'*Comme il faut*', as the man himself likes to say."

Holmes and I exchanged glances, but fell in line behind Warren as he crossed the sitting room and, passing through the door to the ground-floor sleeping quarters, made his way to Olivia Borden's inner sanctum. It was there that Miss Rita stood beside the bed, the diminutive body of her aunt lying before her.

The late Olivia Borden commanded the centre of an anachronistic tableau. With her veil no longer in place, one could see the prominence of her aquiline nose and the roundness of her skull. Wrinkled hands folded on her chest, she was clothed in luminescent white, a dress most probably kept hidden away for this particular occasion. The threadbare quilt upon which she rested had yellowed over the years; and the bed itself, of Regency design, might have come from another century. Redundant hairbrushes and depleted unguents adorned the dressing table, and a mirror replete with spidery cracks presided over the futile homage to vanity. Atop the nearby chest of drawers, a japanned wooden box that could have contained any number of rings or necklaces or letters stood conveniently open – open and empty. With dusty white drapes covering the windows, the whole scene, illuminated as it was by floor-candelabras on either side of the bed, seemed a setting from some antique mystery play.

Warren had positioned himself next to Miss Rita and bowed his head. Despite his show of sympathy, I felt certain that his concern dealt less with the dead woman than with the papers she'd been suspected of possessing, the same papers presumably now in the custody of her niece.

We took our cue from Miss Rita and, following a decent period of respect, prepared to exit. I made one last visual sweep of the chamber, hoping I might detect evidence of someone's final frantic search for the missing papers. But there appeared no signs of disruption.

As I turned to leave, however, Holmes caught my arm. "Watson," he whispered. "Engage the others in conversation. I need time in here to examine the scene."

"I wonder," he now said to Miss Rita, "if you'd mind giving me a moment alone with your aunt. Many people will tell you that I am a private person who prefers to keep his personal thoughts strictly between the deceased and himself."

"You hardly knew the woman," she scoffed, but Holmes seemed sincere; and fortunately Miss Rita, no great master of recognizing deceit, needed no further convincing. For his part, Warren seemed eager to talk. Indeed, no sooner did we find our places in the sitting room than he began discussing what he knew of the elder Miss Borden and Jeremy Aspen.

"Looking at that old woman," said he, "you wouldn't think her to have been a beautiful, vivacious, even rebellious young lady. But she must have been *all* those things. It would explain why Aspen was attracted to her. For that matter, I often wonder how they met."

Miss Rita shrugged. "He came calling on her."

"But that's my point," said the professor. "Aspen was an aristocrat; Miss Borden's background was more modest. My guess is that she must have been connected to someone with whom the poet had dealings here in England. She could have been a governess to a child of one of Aspen's friends. Or the daughter of someone he'd employed – a secretary, perhaps, or a portrait painter. Americans love to have their images immortalized by English artists. Whatever the circumstances, she attracted the man – so much so that she became the object of his love. She was, after all, *'l'ange'* in his cycle of love sonnets."

I shrugged my shoulders, hoping that the conversation would prevent the others from wondering what Holmes was up to.

Suddenly, Warren's eyes flashed, and he changed the subject. "I think she hid the papers somewhere." He pointed at a tall mahogany secretary's desk with brass fittings. "That was my first choice. I'd always suspected it was locked, but I couldn't be sure. Not that I would ever steal them, mind you; but a few weeks before her death, I finally worked up the courage to see if the desk would open. I was just about to test the lock when the old lady interrupted me."

"Why," Rita cried, "that must have been just before you left."

"In truth," Warren said, "she gave me quite the fright. 'Stop that!' she'd rasped while teetering on a cane in the doorway – all those months and I didn't even know she could walk. In such a fury was she that she tore off that infernal mask and threw it to the floor. That was when I saw her magnificent eyes."

"My word," I barely whispered.

"They were wide and deep and full of hatred. And yet, strange to say, they also filled me with a kind of comfort. For looking into those extraordinary orbs, I somehow felt closer to Aspen. Her rage at me was a short-lived imitation of the torrid flames that must have burned so brightly when she was in his arms, a fiery passion that I thought had been all but extinguished."

Warren's own eyes were wide open now, a man staring full-on into a vibrant past.

"'I know what you're looking for,' the old woman screeched, ' – why you've come here.' She nodded at the secretary desk. 'Go ahead and look inside, if you must.' Reluctantly, I tried the lid and, discovering that it was unlocked after all, lifted it open. I expected to discover nothing, and nothing is precisely what I found. The old woman stared triumphantly at me. It was when she turned and hobbled back to her room that I realized she would never be giving me the letters. Only when they passed to Miss Rita might I have a chance of securing them. Mortified – and not a little angry – I left the house the next day."

Miss Rita sat open-mouthed. There was obviously a lot about her aunt she'd apparently never got to know.

Just then Rosa entered the room with two large vases of Calla lilies.

"I ordered them," Warren said.

A look of admiration appeared in Miss Rita's wide-set eyes. I couldn't say whether she'd ever had a social engagement with a man, but she was certainly appreciative of Warren's gesture.

I, on the other hand, was more cynical. With the papers as Warren's goal, I couldn't help regarding all of his acts as empty motions. They were designed to get Miss Rita to share her aunt's literary trove with him. In fact, I was beginning to suspect that the letters had motivated the behaviours of everyone in that house. Perhaps the old woman had been dangling them in front of the professor to unite him with Miss Rita. Or

272

perhaps the middle-aged spinster herself was hoping to inherit them and use them to entice the man.

Holmes's return interrupted my thoughts. He arrived in the sitting room just as Miss Rita was rising to help Rosa set up the flowers.

"It's a bit stuffy in here," he observed, striding to the green-velvet drapes. Drawing one of them aside, he opened the French window an inch or two. Then he turned back to Miss Rita. "One last question, if I may. Did your aunt write a will?"

Miss Rita looked down. "No. She had nothing to leave me."

"Except for the papers," Thomas Warren muttered.

Holmes glared at the professor, but all he said was, "Don't fail to let Henry James know that you're safe." Then he motioned for us to leave, and once more we expressed our condolences to Miss Rita.

"If you don't mind my asking," Holmes said to her as we were about to exit, "should I want to pay my respects yet again, when will the undertaker come for your aunt."

"At nine o'clock tomorrow morning."

With Holmes nodding at the information, we left that frightful house and hurried back to our waiting hansom. I climbed in as under darkening skies my friend exchanged a few words with the driver. Then Holmes joined me, and we began our journey back to Baker Street. Or so I thought.

IV

After we'd made the first turn that hid us from The Hollows, the cab came to an abrupt halt. The horse whinnied in protest, but Holmes stepped out and bade me follow. He dropped a healthy number of coins in the driver's hand, and the two of us stood out in the road listening to the clink of the horse's hooves diminish as the hansom disappeared in the darkness.

"Should anyone be watching," he explained, "I wanted it to appear that we'd left. The old woman was murdered, Watson; and I fear there may be more violence yet to come."

"Murdered?" I cried. "But she looked so peaceful, Holmes. What makes you say such a thing?

"You know my methods, old fellow. As soon as I was alone with the body, I drew my lens and examined the corpse. It was absurdly simple to discover the bits of down in Miss Borden's nostrils, the tiny feathers she must have inhaled gasping for her final breaths with a pillow held down over her face."

"Who committed this heinous act?"

273

"That is what I hope to confirm tonight."

"But, Holmes, surely we must inform the police."

"We don't have the time," said he, shaking his head. He then motioned me to follow, continuing his explanation as we moved down the dark road towards The Hollows. "We know that Olivia Borden's body will be collected by the undertaker tomorrow morning at nine. I fear that the immediacy of that appointment may precipitate some harmful action."

"You think that Miss Rita is in danger then?"

Holmes smiled. "On one level, I think not. The death of the old woman leaves the niece as the sole link to the papers. Anyone seeking the papers would be foolish to silence her."

"Unless," I added, "the miscreant has already acquired them."

"If he had acquired them, Watson, he would no longer be here." We were approaching the house now, and Holmes lowered his voice. "When I searched the old woman's room, I spied some sheets that appeared dishevelled on the far side of the bed. I immediately ran my hand beneath the upper mattress."

"Did you find anything?"

"A single scrap of very old foolscap containing a few strokes of faded ink. But even so small a morsel was enough to suggest that somehow the withered old woman had mustered the strength to hide the papers between her mattresses."

"Surely such a hiding place could not be secure. When Rosa changed the bedding, she'd discover the cache."

"You're right, of course," replied Holmes. "Perhaps Olivia Borden had originally kept them in the secretary desk just as Warren suspected or even in the japanned box so conveniently left open for us. But move them she did, and somehow – maybe with Rosa's help – hid them beneath her mattress. In any case, I suspect that by now Rita has found her aunt's hiding place – or may even have been given the papers. In any case, Rita's probably the only one who knows their current location."

I was about to respond; but we had reached the metal fence, and Holmes put his finger to his lips. In the darkness, we slipped through the open gates and tiptoed to the garden at the side of the building. It was here that we encountered the French window that earlier Holmes had so presciently left open. Although we could see nothing of the sitting room through the curtained glass, we could hear quite clearly the conversation that was going on inside.

"I thought that you *liked* spending time with me," Miss Rita was saying to Warren.

"Of course, I do," said the professor. "I enjoy your company. Remember those summer evenings out in the garden?"

"Yes," she sighed. "They were grand." You could hear the longing in her voice. "For years I've been imprisoned here with my aunt. And then you came round, someone who took an interest in me."

There was a moment of awkward silence. I imagined Warren dwelling on her final few words. "Now listen," he said at last. "I don't believe I've ever acted in an ungentlemanly manner towards you."

"I thought that the flowers – "

"They were intended for your aunt as well as for you."

"So *you* might get the papers. Perhaps that's what my aunt was thinking all along. In the end, bringing the two of us together must have meant more to her than spending her final hours with her niece."

Warren wouldn't give in. "I should imagine that all along her plan had been to give me the papers."

"No!" said Miss Rita firmly. "She never wanted outsiders to get their hands on them." There was a pause of a few moments during which Miss Rita must have been fashioning her most convincing smile and most flirtatious voice. "Now if you were a *relation* . . . ."

The word could have but one meaning.

"Me – and *you*?" Warren spat out.

"I've liked our time together."

"But for the rest of our lives? Not even the receipt of *all* your aunt's papers would be worth such misery!"

We heard her gasp and then the rustle of clothing and the stomp of heavy feet. Warren had obviously stood and was about to make a grand exit up the stairs to his room. "I'll be leaving in the morning!" he shouted. "Early!"

Muted sobs filled the silence.

Sitting on the damp ground by the open window, we managed to stay awake through an uneventful night. With only the routine activities of nocturnal creatures to distract us – mice scrabbling among the tree roots, crickets drumming their songs, an owl hooting his displeasure at our presence – we had to wait until the next morning for human passions to become enflamed.

Sometime before dawn, Holmes reached inside the window and, adjusting the green-velvet curtains that had blocked our view, created a gap of about half-an-inch through which we could peer. The morning activities in the house played out before us as if we were attending the theatre. Off-stage, the clatter of dishes and clanging of pans announced that Rosa was preparing breakfast in the kitchen. At half-seven, Miss

Rita made her entrance from the sleeping quarters on the ground floor. Dressed in austere black, she was prepared for her meeting with the undertaker. At almost the same moment, as if he'd been waiting, Thomas Warren emerged from his chamber and hurried down the stairs. Despite his threat to leave before the removal of the body, he wore the same black suit we'd seen the previous day. Miss Rita turned at his approach, a melancholy look colouring her down-cast face.

"I'm sorry," Warren said, reaching for her right hand. "I've been cruel. I should have taken your proposal more seriously last night."

She raised her head.

"In fact," he said, sounding full of contrition, "I've given myself the chance to examine your offer once more, and I believe I now see much wisdom in its implementation. I owe my career to the securing of those papers; and while I did all I could in the most proper way to obtain them from your aunt, I believe she never seriously appreciated my efforts. I think that for as long as she lived, she intended to use those papers as bait to bring me closer to you."

Miss Rita's wide eyes looked even wider. And more melancholy. Perhaps she sensed what Warren was about to suggest.

"In fact, I believe we should honour your aunt's wishes and agree to such a union. I believe she intended for you to do with them exactly as you had proposed to me last night. I am, you see, quite prepared to accept your aunt's papers – the Aspen papers, if you will – as a dowry."

At some point during Warren's last few words, Miss Rita's left hand had begun a slow journey upward until it was covering her now open mouth.

"Why, what's the matter?" asked Warren. "I know it's what you want. Everyone will be pleased. You will get a husband; I will get the letters; and your aunt's memory will be honoured."

Miss Rita lowered her head.

"What's the matter?" Warren asked again. His eyes signalled fear; his tone had grown desperate.

"Oh, Thomas," she said slowly, "I burned the papers last night. Once you refused me, I saw no point in keeping them."

"You *burned* them? The key to my life's work?"

"I was going to have them buried with my aunt," she explained, realizing that she'd also destroyed any future she might have envisioned with this man. "But you made me so angry last night that I burned them one by one. It took a long time."

Warren's eyes began to bulge. "After what I've already done?" he muttered, his face turning dangerously red.

"What?"

276

"And to think," he snarled, "I almost found you charming."

"We can still marry," Miss Rita urged. "You'll see. I can make you a good wife."

Thomas Warren glared at her. The silence seemed interminable. In the end, he threw back his head and laughed. It was a loud, raucous laugh, but it slowly transformed itself into a maniacal shriek. Suddenly, he was upon her, his white fingers tightly gripping her throat.

Without a word, Holmes sprang up, jerked open the French window and raced towards the struggling pair. Wrapping an arm around Warren's neck, he yanked him off the poor woman, who fell heavily to her knees on the hardwood floor.

In an instant, I had joined Holmes; and between us we managed to wrestle Thomas Warren onto one of the sheet-covered armchairs. Rosa ran out from the kitchen to see what the trouble was. She helped her mistress to stand, and Holmes ordered her to go out in the street to find the nearest constable.

"*La policía!*" he instructed.

Soon we heard the blast of a police whistle, and within the hour Inspector Gregson arrived at The Hollows.

Not long thereafter, we had the satisfaction of seeing Thomas Warren charged with the murder of Miss Olivia Borden – whom he confessed to smothering after he'd secretly returned to the house – and the attempted murder of Miss Rita Borden. Between two uniformed officers, he was marched to the police van, which immediately drove off in the direction of Scotland Yard.

As it clattered down the road, it passed the undertaker's hearse, which was just then approaching the house.

V

The following afternoon, Henry James joined us for tea at Baker Street. Holmes had sent a request to the writer at his rooms in De Vere Gardens following Warren's arrest, and James eagerly accepted. In addition to the tea, Mrs. Hudson set out small chocolate biscuits and a few of the sugary doughnuts James was known to enjoy.

Sherlock Holmes reported the details of the case to our guest as we sampled our tea.

"Good Lord," said James, when Holmes had finished. "I had no idea my letter regarding Jeremy Aspen would create – would weave – such a tangled skein."

"More tangled than you can imagine, Mr. James," Holmes observed. "For it is my conjecture that the Aspen papers contained more value of a

277

personal nature than even your world of *belles-lettres* could estimate. I have no valid proof, you understand; but judging from my own observations – the similar facial structures, the widespread eyes, the curved nose – not to mention the concern that Olivia Borden expressed regarding her niece's welfare – I can only conclude that a major topic of the correspondence between Jeremy Aspen and his mistress was the welfare of their child – a daughter I believe to be Miss Rita Borden."

At this revelation, the doughnut Henry James was poised to devour fell onto his plate.

"And does Miss Rita know of your conjecture?" I asked.

"Only if she read the letters before she burned them – and, of course, only if my supposition is accurate. Based on so little evidence, it is certainly nothing I would share with her."

James took a small bite of the doughnut he'd dropped. "So," he said after finishing the morsel, "in addition to the tale – the mystery – surrounding the Aspen papers, we also have a story dealing with the secret love-child of a writer and his mistress. Not to mention the cunning machinations of a so-called scholar."

"Just so, Mr. James," said Holmes.

The author didn't respond for a moment. Staring off as they were, his grey eyes suggested his mind was somewhere else. If my own writing experiences were any model, I imagined him already at work, composing in his head some sort of novel dealing with the bizarre triangle of old woman, forlorn niece, and obsessed academic.

"One writer to another, Mr. James," I dared to say, "quite a story, is it not?"

"Indeed, Dr. Watson. Perhaps one we might both attempt to record – each in his own fashion, of course."

"An excellent suggestion," said I, already devaluing my factual narrative when compared with the intimate psychological embellishments so typical of James' fiction. His ornate and methodical style could perfectly reflect the labyrinthine twists and turns of a mind diseased.

"I would, of course, purge the story of obvious references," said he. "And shift the scene of the adventure to somewhere outside of London. Maybe even outside of England." Suddenly, he clapped his hands together, the notion of subterfuge obviously gaining in appeal. "Who knows?" he cried. "Perhaps I'll even fudge or doctor my notebooks – change Jeremy Aspen to Byron. Or Shelley."

Holmes nodded in appreciation. He often worried about the inadvertent but harmful revelations that occasionally found their way into my own accounts of his cases.

278

"I shall walk – no, I shall drive – to the National Gallery this very afternoon and look at landscapes for inspiration. Turner's watercolours of Venice might be just the thing!"

Sherlock Holmes poured himself more tea. "I envy you, Mr. James. The world of detection offers no such escape. *My* boundaries are limited by the rules of logic and the confines of reality. The detective cannot go willy-nilly where inspiration calls him."

"Ah, yes, Mr. Holmes," said Henry James. "But it is the claustrophobia created by such rules that leads the literary artist to the world of fiction. Imagination trumps reality every time."

Such abstract arguments usually make my head spin. But on this occasion, I was ready to do battle. "I – I take your remark as a challenge, sir," said I to Henry James. "Let us each report the story of the Aspen papers in our own manner and leave it to posterity to judge who has rendered the stronger case."

With a smile, Holmes pointed first at the gasogene and then at the spirit case. I understood his gestures and, producing three glasses, mixed the sparkling water with brandy. Once everyone was served, we hoisted our drinks.

"To the judgment of posterity," proclaimed Sherlock Holmes.

"Hear, hear," Henry James chimed in, and then the three of us emptied our glasses.

The Ululation of Wolves
by Steve Mountain

The wolf howled.

He knew when his leader was dead. The crisp, red, warm smell of life was becoming tinged with the acid, blue, icy smell of death, creeping like a snake through the early spring air. Ahead lay a time of uncertainty – a new leader would have to be chosen.

One by one, more wolves joined the mournful lament.

Sharing accommodation with Holmes was never dull. We had been at Baker Street for seven years, and yet still I could rarely predict at the start of a day what would have come to pass by that day's end. One day would perhaps herald the start of a protracted adventure, another would end having resolved a seemingly intractable problem in a matter of hours due to Holmes's genius. My least favoured, of course, were those days when nothing happened and which led to monotony and depression, and the inevitable arguments over his use of various substances to ward off the effects. But whether with work or without, Holmes had become a rare attraction, no part due to my efforts (I felt) once my reports of his successes had started to be published.

This day had started typically enough; Mrs. Hudson had brought our breakfast and Holmes was settling down after reading the newspaper when we heard a commotion in the street. Holmes rose to see what was unfolding below.

"Someone in a hurry!" he exclaimed, returning to his seat. "I wonder what he wants of us?"

"Perhaps nothing at all," I replied. "It is entirely possible for people to have business of their own without conferring on them the need to make use of your services."

He smiled, a slight look of pity on his face. He seemed to be counting under his breath.

Shortly there was a violent knocking at the door, which we heard Mrs. Hudson open. Holmes looked to me and rubbed his hands. "Adventure?"

"How did you know – as if I should dare ask?"

He passed me a telegram as he rose. "This was delivered earlier, whilst you were getting dressed."

I read it quickly, and gave it back. "Adventure indeed, Holmes. Mr. Reynolds appears in desperate requirement of you."

"I think perhaps his desperation stems from an understandable lack of progress with more conventional means of investigation."

Shortly afterwards, our guest was sitting in the chair facing me, flushed and breathless from his exertions in reaching us from the station in under ten minutes. Holmes stood over him.

"Brandy?"

Reynolds politely accepted Holmes's offer and took the glass with trembling hands. He seemed to relax slightly. I made to offer a cigar, but was declined. Holmes walked back to the window and looked down onto the late morning bustle of Baker Street. The spring sunshine was streaming through the bay, against which he then half drew the curtain and returned to his seat. Dust hung in the air. Our visitor drew a deep sigh.

"So," said Holmes, "Tell me what brings you from Ellington House. Your telegram spoke of great urgency."

"Nothing less than murder, Mr. Holmes," replied our visitor. "But the local force are at a loss," he added. "So they have sent in the Metropolitan force, led by an Inspector Lestrade I believe – " Holmes coughed quietly – "but all I know is that from the good Doctor's account, we need *you*, Mr. Holmes, to solve this." Holmes raised an eyebrow.

My pride was short lived. "The good Doctor's account paints my successes in an overly dramatic light which I fear the reality may fail to live up to," replied Holmes. "There have been situations in which I have had to admit defeat or error."

Reynolds laughed. "Not so, Mr. Holmes! I know some of those with whom you have had dealings. We gentlemen's gentlemen share many secrets, I can assure you."

Some colour came to Holmes's cheeks. "Pleasantries aside, then, tell me what troubles you. From the beginning." He sat back in his chair and lit his pipe as Reynolds started to recount his tale.

"I am – was – Sir Cedric Wolfe's valet."

"The Director of the London and Colonial Bank," interrupted Holmes.

"As you say, Mr. Holmes. I have been in my post these past eleven years and can vouchsafe my master as being a man of honour and deserving of total respect."

"The perfect master, then," I opined.

"In many ways, yes, Doctor," replied Reynolds. "He was seen by some to be a hard man, cold even, but fair. He had responsibilities which he took very seriously, and sometimes I felt these weighed heavily on him. Like all of us he had his ways but, indeed, a better master I have not served in twenty years. He was always the gentleman to me."

"We all know about little ways, don't we, Holmes?" I said. Holmes waved my comment aside impatiently, although I caught a glimpse of a wry smile.

"When you say, 'ways', what do you mean?" Holmes enquired. "In detail, please."

Reynolds thought for a moment, as if marshalling his thoughts. "He was a pedant, Mr. Holmes. Everything he used had to be under his control – stamped, embroidered or engraved with the family crest, even down to the linen, crockery, cutlery; the curtains were made specially with the crest within the woven design. Visitors have to sit at specific places at table. You could set a clock by his routines.

"I have started rather negatively I fear – please forgive me. Mr. Holmes, my master was a great man, rich of course through his work, but generous in equal measure to those to whom he chose to show liberality. Always on his terms, though! The Ellington estate is only small, some two hundred acres of Buckinghamshire park and farmland, and so has only a small number of house and estate staff. He cared passionately for the good of the estate, which he inherited from his father some eight years ago, and he his father before that – six generations in all, Mr. Holmes." He paused; Holmes drew quietly on his pipe.

"Perhaps he cared for the estate more than he cared for those closer to him in familial ties – but that was the measure of him. As to his 'ways', well, as I said everything had to be just so, and he was unnerved and became anxious and upset if anything was different or out of place. He was an insecure man, Mr. Holmes, and afraid of the dark. Not insecure in his profession, of course," he added quickly, "in which he was peerless; but he oft spoke to me of various fears. And . . . ." He paused again. When he next spoke, I thought I detected a slight air of reserve in his voice. "He kept the menagerie his grandfather started half-a-century ago."

"A zoo? What animals?" I asked.

"Only one species now, Doctor. In former times it included big cats, for the old man spent long in Africa. But now, only wolves, and they unpenned. I think it is supposed to be a play, a poor one in my humble opinion, on the family name. I must admit to that collection being the one distasteful feature of my life serving him. One becomes almost a prisoner in the House and estate, there being a high wall running the full length of the boundary, and just the one gate as entrance, from the Bicester Road. A second wall surrounds the House, closer in, and the wolves have free run between the twin circuits of the walls."

"That would certainly play well to a fear of anything out of the ordinary," mused Holmes. "He would feel secure knowing he was so well guarded . . . ."

"Indeed, Mr. Holmes," continued Reynolds. "I am not being disrespectful of my late master when I say that his bond with them was almost unnatural. He spent long hours studying them, and walking alone in the fields in their company. I believe they accepted him as one of their pack, or even the leader – they were all hand reared of course, so tame to a degree. But only with him, Mr. Holmes. Any stranger, or other member of the household who went out there without precaution, was in some danger. And that is what has got the local force so lost as to a solution to his murder. Despite the walls, despite the wolves running free. How could anyone have got in and done the deed? So the constabulary consider the murder must have been committed by someone already in the House. Inspector Lestrade concurs with this view."

"I expect he does," said Holmes. "It makes eminent sense. But it cannot be as simple as that, for otherwise you would not be here. Now, although I have of course read the account of the affair in the newspaper after I received your telegram, I would like to hear it in your own words."

Over the next hour, Reynolds explained to us the events of that fateful night at length. Holmes stopped him at a number of points to clarify details, whilst I made hurried notes.

Two days earlier, on the evening of the 22nd March (so Reynolds recounted), all had seemed tolerably well. His master had followed all his usual habits, although he seemed troubled, by what he would not share. After dinner at six he had taken leave of the household – his wife Lady Elizabeth, their teenaged son Thomas and daughter Sarah, together with their guests – a Mr. Wilson, who was an old school friend; Mr. Graham, a neighbour from the village; and Mr. Turner, a business associate who had been dealing with a land transaction on the Estate. Sir Cedric had gone straight to his room and, as was his custom, locked the door to conclude business affairs for the day in solitude.

For the rest of the evening, they had all retired to the Games Room. From about seven, the gentlemen, including Thomas, were left to continue whilst the two ladies took their leave for the kitchens to plan with the staff the meal for the following day – a special luncheon to be given to welcome Colonel Sir Jerome Russett to the village upon his return from the colonies. This concluded, the ladies had retired to the Drawing Room where they were later joined by Thomas, and passed the rest of the evening sewing, the boy reading quietly in a corner.

At nine, Reynolds had himself withdrawn to his chamber – a room next to that of Sir Cedric, and through which anyone wishing to communicate with his master would have to pass. At about eleven, it was reported that the children had retired to their rooms and Lady Wolfe to hers, and come midnight the rest of the household and their guests were in their beds. The Butler, Maddison, had reported that when he did his final rounds of the House all the doors and windows were secure.

"At seven yesterday morning, I rose and started to prepare my master's clothes and breakfast. As by usual custom, it was Lady Wolfe who, at eight, went to her husband's room with the breakfast I had prepared, and . . . ." At this point Reynolds' voice broke. My further offer of brandy was gratefully accepted. Holmes drummed his fingers on the arm of his chair whilst the man regained his control. ". . . They couldn't open the door. Normally my master unlocked it when he awoke."

"Did you check it was unlocked when you arose?" asked Holmes.

"I admit I had not checked whether it was locked or unlocked. I do not check it every day by rule, for there is no need to do so. That is how the house works, Mr. Holmes – he always unlocks it. That is the routine. We had to break down the door. He was sitting in his chair facing the fireplace, back to the window. The fire was dead . . . and so was he. He had been stabbed. My mistress was hysterical and took to her bed. "

"That tallies with the newspaper account," said Holmes. "Unusually accurate for a change. Please, describe the room. Just so I can clearly picture the setting."

Reynolds seemed taken aback. "Well, Mr. Holmes, it's just an ordinary bedroom, simply furnished. On the ground floor; my master worked and slept in that room all the time I have been in service. A large fireplace, which was prepared and lit at five-thirty each evening at this time of year. A writing desk. A bedside table, with his supply of candles for when the nights are dark – the House will be late getting an electricity supply, for he did not hold with it. French windows to the gardens, which are locked out of use, even in the summer. Curtains always half drawn; he would sometimes watch the wolves roaming the grounds before retiring to his bed. Please believe me when I say that nothing was out of the ordinary to any previous day."

"So what has got our professional friends so baffled?"

"We know he was alive for some time after ten. But everyone in the house was accounted for at and after that time. And no-one could get in from outside without falling prey to the wolves; or at the very least, rousing them, which would have been heard. I was in the room next door, and heard nothing. No-one came through my room."

"Ten?" I asked. "How do you know?"

"He lit a candle after that time. His candles are custom made to burn for exactly . . . ." He saw Holmes's quizzical glance, so he corrected himself. "Near enough, give or take maybe ten minutes, for ten hours, and the candle was burning low as we entered the room at eight yesterday morning. We know no-one entered his room – it was locked and his key was on the bedside table. No-one went through my room once I settled down to my end of day tasks at nine. No-one was out of sight of anyone else at any time when he could have been killed. And yet, he is dead."

"There is no duplicate key?" asked Holmes.

"Only one that I hold, in case of emergency. I can vouch it was not away from my person all night."

"Could not someone have got into the room from the window?" I asked. "He slept on the ground floor, you say." Almost as soon as the words were out of my mouth, I knew the mistake I had made.

"Locked and bolted out of use, as I said, and all the glass intact. And of course the wolves . . . ."

"Keep up, Watson!" interrupted Holmes impatiently. Then to our visitor, "What do you know of the three guests?"

"Turner has been dealing with matters of the Estate – land sales, lettings, purchases – for as long as I have been at the House. His father before him held the same station, with the elder Mr. Wolfe. My master looked after him and his family well. Graham owns the lodge next to Ellington House, and has been a family friend for many years. He is a regular visitor and takes great interest in the well-being of the children. I admit I don't know much about Wilson, but he and my master seemed to get on very well. They had not met up these past twenty years, evidently. He was fascinated and frightened in equal measure by the wolves."

"What did your late master think of Mr. Graham's interest in the children?" I asked.

"I have never detected any concern on his part."

Holmes turned to me with a twinkle in his eye. "Your thoughts?"

I took a deep breath, and looked to Reynolds with a resigned smile. "He does this, just to show how good he is. Inevitably, whatever I say will be wrong."

"Far from it, my dear fellow!" interrupted Holmes. "But I do value your often refreshing views."

"Very well. We know nothing about this man Wilson. What brought him to the House just at this time? Surely suspicion has to fall first on him. Somehow he got into Wolfe's room and did the deed during the night."

285

"Very well; but how, Watson? That is what I am after."

"That's your job, Holmes," I replied. "You will draw me no further."

"Well, a fascinating diversion awaits us," said Holmes, suddenly warming to the task. "I think we will return with you to Ellington House. Let's see if we can help the local constabulary – and our friend Lestrade – make some progress. But first, gentlemen, I need to spend a little time making use of *'Who's Who'* and see if my library holds any clues. You may order a cab to the station for one hour's time, Watson. And there will be a telegram to send shortly."

Ellington House was reached by a short ride from the village station. The afternoon sun was starting to set behind the trees as we were driven along the curving driveway through park lands until the House came into view. It was not a large house, as such houses go, but, reflecting the reported character of its pedantic owner, not a blade of grass seemed out of place. Nonetheless, and perhaps unsurprisingly, an air of gloom seemed to hang over it. Off to the left, I noted we were being watched – two wolves lay under a stand of trees. Other shapes moved furtively in the bushes away to our right. On the light wind a single howl echoed around the gardens.

We came to a second gate, which was unlocked by Reynolds. A short ride onwards, and we were greeted at the front door of the house by Maddison. Most of the other staff had been given leave of absence, so only the family, their three visitors, and a young policeman from the local constabulary were about, along with Lady Wolfe's maid and the cook. Lestrade, or anyone else from the Metropolitan force for that matter, was no-where to be seen.

Holmes was led into the Games Room and had a short conversation with each of the three guests in turn. Turner was open and affable, but I thought the man Graham looked uncomfortable on questioning about his interest in the family; his statement that such interest was only made in light of Sir Cedric's coldness towards them, and his concern over their future education and well-being, seemed forced and unlikely to me, whilst Wilson seemed a most disagreeable sort, furtive and secretive.

"It's those blasted wolves, Mr. Holmes!" he exclaimed. "I'm sure one of these days no good will come of keeping them so unnaturally. Howling and calling to one another as they do, it's enough to put anyone off their game. Or their meal." The glass of whisky he held betrayed the shaking of his hand.

"Well, no good *has* come, Mr. Wilson. They seem quiet enough now," replied Holmes.

"Yes, I suppose so," he blustered. "But they frighten me, and I'm not sorry to say it. How anyone could go wandering about after dark knowing those things were around is beyond me. Only a ghost would want to do so."

The man who had been introduced as Turner sighed. "I tell you, no-one else saw it."

"What did you see?" asked Holmes sharply.

"I saw a figure moving across the lawn, after dark, whilst I was taking a break from the game. I'm convinced it could not have been anything from this world."

"No-one else saw it, Mr. Holmes," replied Turner, "even though he called me to the window. I think it was the drink playing tricks."

"I was as sober as any man!" exclaimed Wilson. "I did see it I tell you! A ghostly figure, making quickly towards the outbuildings."

"Come, my friend," soothed Graham. "Take no heed. If you say you saw it, well, I believe you."

Turner snorted. "You were trying to put me off my game," he retorted to Wilson. "The boy was slowing us down, and you could see how that was affecting me."

"Gentlemen, please!" exclaimed Reynolds. "We have all suffered a great shock, and Mr. Holmes is here to help. Have respect, please!"

Holmes seemed satisfied of his enquiries. Wilson looked especially discomforted, and my suspicions of him grew. This story of his seeing a figure outside was clearly meant to distract attention, and once we were out of the room I shared this with Holmes.

His only reply was, "It may be of interest, Watson." I decided not to tempt Holmes's disapproval further by repeating my growing conviction that Wilson was somehow involved. Holmes would get to the truth, I knew.

Holmes spent a few minutes talking to the cook, and then, the interviews seemingly complete, spent the next half hour or so subjecting Sir Cedric's bedroom to a minute examination. The room had been sealed by the police as soon as they had arrived. On hands and knees, or even on occasion almost lying flat, he worked his way across the floor; and as he went he picked up various small items that had fallen on the carpet; here a few hairs, there a short piece of string. All went into an envelope. When he had finished he went to the window, checked the lock and bolts, and stood quietly looking out over the lawn towards a lake as the sun set, the curtains half drawn as usual across the French windows. He was seemingly in a world of his own. At one point he looked again at the contents of the envelope. Reynolds and I waited patiently.

"Was there anything – anything, mark you – out of the ordinary that night that you have not shared?" he asked at length. Reynolds thought long and hard. "I don't think so, Mr. Holmes," he replied. "There were the three guests of course in the house, so the routine was different in that respect . . . . Ah, there was one thing which they commented on. Especially our Mr. Wilson. The wolves broke into howling at about eight. Only for a short time – I remember thinking they must have caught a deer, perhaps."

Holmes eyes were suddenly bright. "That is most suggestive, is it not, Watson?" he said. Regrettably the mystery was lost on me. He fell into silence again. "I would like to speak with her Ladyship, please," he then continued.

A few minutes later the lady was duly ushered into the room. Her eyes were red with crying; with her, her daughter also came for support. They sat together on the edge of the bed, holding hands.

"Please accept our sympathy in your sad loss," I said. I caught Holmes's sideways glance. "*I know you wouldn't say it,*" I mouthed silently to him.

"Indeed," added Holmes. "Please, Lady Wolfe, I will not keep you a moment. I have but one question, just to clarify my thoughts you understand – you were with your daughter all evening once you had left the gentlemen to their games, yes?"

"Yes."

"*All* evening?" There was a definite emphasis on the 'all'.

"As I said, yes."

"Oh. Then that is very sad," replied Holmes.

She looked at him in shock – and I likewise. "What do you mean by that, Holmes?" I muttered quietly. "Of course it is sad. This dear lady has lost her husband, and the young lady her father, in the most awful circumstances."

Holmes ignored my protestations. "Thank you, that will be all," he said, and dismissed them with a wave of his hand. When they had left, I addressed him angrily. "Do you really not understand the effect your thoughtless behaviour has on people, Holmes? The ladies need our sympathy and support, not your rudeness!"

"Perhaps they do," said Holmes. "But the case is all but solved nonetheless. I know who, and I know the when and broadly the why. I just need a few moments to determine the how." He produced a telegram from his pocket. "This is the response to the telegram I asked you to send whilst we were in Baker Street."

"Yes, I know it full well," I replied. "It came as we were leaving."

"It holds some interesting information about Colonel Sir Jerome Russett."

"You mean, he did it? But how? He wasn't seen in the house that night."

Holmes sighed. I could feel the approach of another assault on my already battered pride. "Watson, sometimes your inputs are most valuable. Other times – No, he did not do it, but he is the reason for why it was done."

"Pray, then, tell us," said Reynolds.

"First I must have a quiet word with the constable," said Holmes. He left the room; Reynolds and I exchanged glances whilst we waited. He returned a few minutes later, smiling broadly. "Capital! So, now, let us join the others. We have an old friend joining us as well."

Lestrade had just arrived, and was having his coat taken by Maddison as we entered the Great Hall. "Well, Mr. Holmes," he said, "I heard that you had been engaged, and I have to say that on this occasion I would be somewhat grateful of any assistance you can offer."

"This is a change, Lestrade!" I exclaimed.

"Come, come Watson," replied Holmes, "Do not be so harsh on our friend. Do not worry, Lestrade, I will not take this as a sign of your desire for regular use of my meagre talents. I am always ready and willing to help, as you well know, should help be requested. The story Mr. Reynolds has unfolded today merely piqued my interest."

"And I am glad of it, Mr. Holmes," replied the policeman. "I cannot make head or tail of how the deed was done. From ten in the evening no-one was out of sight of anyone else, and yet murder was committed. After I was summoned, I spent most of yesterday and again today trying to see how it could work, but . . . ."

"Have no fear, Lestrade," continued Holmes. "I believe I can help you with the solution, although of course the credit will be to the Metropolitan force. I have no desire for fame." I coughed quietly. "Beyond what has already been thrust upon me by the good Doctor of course," he continued, barely breaking his stride. "But first, a quiet word please."

Holmes and Lestrade left the room for a few moments and I heard snatches of a whispered conversation outside the door. "*Arrest . . . walking . . . ghost . . . .*"

They returned and Lestrade took the constable aside as Holmes started to speak. "Key to the solution is that the murder did not take place when you think it did. Not at or after ten. It took place earlier. And if you ignore the supposed time of the murder, other opportunities present themselves. What I needed was a motive. Once I had that, then I merely had to construct the events of the night to place the murderer in the right place at the right time."

"So what is the motive, Holmes?" I asked.

"It is the oldest motive, I am afraid, Watson. But we will come to that."

"But, Mr. Holmes, I don't understand." Reynolds' voice was flat, shocked. "We know the murder could not be earlier than ten. The candle. It had not yet gone out as we broke the door down at eight in the morning. It is a ten hour candle. Even allowing for a few minutes' variation in the manufacture, I'm sorry, but you can't get the murder to happen earlier than when I was in my room next door to Sir Cedric. There just is not the variation in the candles to do that. I tell you, Sir Cedric was a man extremely upset by anything out of its usual routine. Samples were regularly tested. A candle burning longer than ten hours would have driven him mad."

"Nevertheless it had to be so," retorted Holmes. "Watson is familiar with my methods. Test everything. What is left after disregarding what does not fit the facts has to be the truth. The murder took place at about eight, not ten."

"How so precise?" asked Lestrade.

"The wolves," replied Holmes.

"I'm sorry, Holmes," I interrupted. "Are you saying that you can pinpoint the time of a murder by the actions of the wolves?"

"Most certainly. Both Reynolds and your cook report that they broke into a veritable ululation of howling at eight. They knew their pack leader – for that, in effect, was what Sir Cedric was – had met his end."

"You are going to have to explain this, Mr. Holmes." Lestrade was clearly at the same time both impatient to know the solution, yet clearly in awe of Holmes's intellect.

"First, may I say that Master Thomas of course is totally innocent of any involvement in this sad chain of events." He turned to Thomas. "You joined your mother and sister in the Drawing Room when?"

"About eight thirty, sir. After our 'best of three' on the billiard table was concluded."

"So you see, the murder could have been committed at any time between the ladies leaving the Games Room at about seven, and eight thirty. By nine you were in the room next door to Sir Cedric, and would have heard if anything amiss was going on." He saw Reynolds' blank expression. "You see, between the time the ladies left the cook and until Master Thomas joined them in the Drawing Room, the two ladies were on their own."

Reynolds was shaking his head. "No . . . ."

290

"But yes," replied Holmes. "You asked for a motive. Lady Wolfe loves the Colonel. But there is more to it than that. Have you noticed how alike Master Thomas is to his father, but Miss Sarah is not, nor strongly to her mother?"

"Yes, but that is common, Holmes," I responded.

"But *'Who's Who'* did lead me to a *Times* article about the Colonel. An article which includes an illustration."

"Stop! Enough!" exclaimed the lady.

"No, it must be out," replied Holmes. "Did you never tell your daughter that the Colonel was her father?"

The room was in turmoil for a moment. The young constable standing behind the chaise longue on which the ladies were sitting moved closer to it on a motion from Lestrade. Holmes waited for us to settle. Reynolds was shaking his head.

Lady Wolfe did not speak for a long time. Her daughter fixed her in her gaze, whilst the son sat groaning on a chair and buried his head in his hands. Finally it was the younger woman who spoke. "Mother told me the night my . . . father died. Just after dinner."

"When I learned the Colonel was coming back to the village," Lady Wolfe interrupted, "it was all I could do to plan for our future life together. I knew eventually my husband would find out about us, and thus we would be in danger. I have not loved him for many years, Mr. Holmes."

"So you killed him," said Holmes.

"He could be a brute if roused," she answered simply. The daughter nodded. "If once he had found out about us, please believe me, I knew it would then be my body you would be finding. I had to kill him before the Colonel arrived."

"That's not the master I know!" protested Reynolds. "He would never have acted in such a way!"

"But he would, Reynolds," replied Lady Wolfe simply. "He was not the saint you believe him to be. Not a bad man of course – I loved him once – but cold and dismissive to me, and others. You must have seen that. He loved his wolves more than any of us."

"I have hated him for years," added the young woman, "and I'm glad I am free to say that now." Reynolds gasped.

"To others outside the family, Reynolds, your master was caring and attentive," said Holmes. "But it is sometimes the way. To those closest to him all he had left was a coldness, leaving them starved of love and affection . . . ." He let the words tail off, and then continued sadly. "It does happen in families, sometimes . . . ."

"No!" continued Reynolds. "It will not do. Even if the ladies were on their own between seven and eight-thirty as you say, you forget the candle. There is no way you can possibly get it to be alight at that time. I'm sorry, Mr. Holmes, but on this occasion I believe you are in error."

Holmes's response was measured. I knew from experience he did not like his deductions to be questioned in such a manner, and saw his knuckles whiten slightly. "So how did the night's events unfold, I ask?" he said quietly. "Well, when the ladies left the gentlemen to their game, we know they went to the kitchens, ostensibly to discuss the meal arrangements for the Colonel's visit. Doubtless as a result of my more informal questioning, Lestrade, the cook now recalls that Lady Wolfe went outside for a few minutes, complaining of a headache and needing to walk in the fresh air. You missed that, and I am afraid as a result you made your enquiries more difficult than necessary, for on that one piece of information the whole matter rests.

"Lady Wolfe merely needed an excuse to go outside. Her route took her along the north side of the House, the same side as the Games Room. She was the so-called 'ghost' seen by Mr. Wilson, although he did not recognise her because of the lack of light. But note, she was seen walking with purpose and speed, not with leisure, towards the outbuildings. There is only one building along that frontage that can be reached without venturing into the wolves' enclosure – the ice house. That was the point at which I started to realise how she had committed the murder of her husband."

"She may have wished to choose a joint for the meat course," I responded. "I know that's what my mother used to do."

"But in an establishment such as this, Watson, that is the cook's job – to choose the joint of meat for approval. Lady Wolfe went to the ice house for a very specific reason, did you not, madam?" The lady nodded. "You then made your way to your husband's room, whilst your daughter went to the Drawing Room. You had agreed to act as alibi for each other. So sad; involving your daughter in your crime."

"I'm not sorry," the daughter said quietly.

"But Sir Cedric's room was locked, Mr. Holmes!" exclaimed Reynolds. "I have the key, here." He held it up. I understood his motive, for I would do the same; trying to find a way of upholding the family honour in the face of what were becoming overwhelming odds.

"I had a copy made," whispered Lady Wolfe, "from my husband's key." Reynolds was crestfallen.

"So," continued Holmes, "you entered his room and killed him. He was sitting by the fire, back to the door and the window, and probably didn't hear you or see you coming. When the deed was done, you locked the door behind you, hid the key, and joined your daughter in the Drawing Room before Master Thomas arrived." She nodded. "Which brings us to the time of death. The evidence is most compelling for eight."

"Probably," she replied. "I didn't really look. All I knew was that I had to be back in the Drawing Room before Thomas came to join us. I knew they were playing best of three, so yes, perhaps eight was the time."

"Remember too," continued Holmes, "that the heat of the fire would have kept the body warm, so we cannot rely on that for an accurate assessment of the time of death. And we have evidence provided by the wolves."

"But the candle, Holmes," interrupted Lestrade. "We come back again to the candle. With respect, this scheme just does not work. It was still alight at eight in the morning."

"To which I reply, the ice house."

Lestrade looked blank, but all suddenly became clear to me. I remembered, almost from nowhere, something that Holmes had spoken about some years ago, in the early days of our acquaintance. "Of course!" I exclaimed. "Why, that's wonderful, Holmes!"

"Come, Watson, explain to our friends!" said Holmes. "You have spent long enough complaining about the experiments I undertake in our lodgings. Now you see why I invest my time thus."

My chance to redeem myself had come. "If you freeze a candle, it slows the rate of burn. So a ten hour candle could easily burn for a couple of additional hours."

"Splendid, Watson!" exclaimed Holmes. "I knew I could rely on you. Lady Wolfe had previously secreted a packet of candles in the ice house, which although is outside the main house is within the second wall and so safe from the roaming wolves. That is why you thought Sir Cedric was unsettled on the night of his death, Reynolds; he became aware somehow of the theft and being the kind of man he was, this would weigh on his mind. His security had been broken; how could that be? No doubt he started to suspect everyone of some hand in it.

"So armed as I was with that knowledge, I tested a scheme of events whereby the time of lighting the candle now moves earlier, to eight or thereabouts, and found no lack of supporting evidence. The final proof I needed was in what I picked up from the carpet." He took the envelope from his pocket and shook out the contents onto a side table. He showed a short piece of string to Reynolds. "You see here, a trimmed candle wick."

"I'm sorry . . . ?" breathed Reynolds.

"To ensure a slow burn, the trick is to trim the wick close to the candle. The flame burns small and slowly, and together with the frozen wax gives plenty of time for the murder to take place whilst young Thomas was together with your visitors, and before you went to your own room, Reynolds."

I suppressed the urge to clap, but doubtless my face displayed enough of my emotions.

"But I am very disappointed nonetheless, in everyone," continued Holmes abruptly.

"Why, Holmes?" I asked, now suddenly unsure of what had been missed.

"Simply the candle itself," he replied. "It was obviously intended to mislead our professional colleagues into thinking that the time of death was after ten when Lady Wolfe was in others' company. And yet, two nights ago the moon was full and the weather was clear. We know the curtains were half drawn. So what with the firelight and the moonlight, why would he even need a candle? There would be enough light in the room to not need any other, even for someone scared of the dark."

"Of course!" said Lestrade. "How did we miss it?"

"Because you take what you see on face value. Let that be a lesson, especially to your colleagues in the local constabulary. As soon as I verified that the room was as it had been found, and seeing it faced full south, I knew the candle was the key to solving the case."

Lady Wolfe gave a cry and buried her face in her hands.

"It is a great irony, of course, but oftentimes it works thus. If the candle had not been lit," continued Holmes, "it would not have been so easy to solve this case. But now it seems you have another account to add to your collection, Watson. A good day's work, if I may be so bold."

The Case of the Vanishing Inn
by Stephen Wade

From time to time in these memoirs of my life with Sherlock Holmes, there emerges a case which has been eclipsed and consequently forgotten. This may be the result of accidental omission, or perhaps by an oversight by my good self, a man as fallible as the next, in spite of my desire to be meticulous in the chronicling of the remarkable detective work effected by my singular friend. This case is exactly that: it was a pleasure to discover my notes when revising some of my stray papers, and I assemble the narrative now, not without a little sense of personal pride at my part in it.

Holmes was away at the time. It was in early June, 1888, soon after the business with the King of Bohemia, and I firmly believe that the encounter with Irene Adler had been a strain upon Holmes's normally robust constitution; he had, of course, performed exceptionally well in that case. Whatever the reasons for his absence throughout that month – and I forget what called him away – the result was that I was left in sole charge of matters at Baker Street. The strange and challenging events of that month return vividly to my memory now that the writer in me attempts to retrieve them from the great backward and abysm of time, as the poet said.

It began with Inspector Lestrade arriving. Now I am aware that in the pages of my memoirs this little man tends to be depicted with less than flattering descriptions, and with some rather demeaning imagery. But to a certain extent he excelled himself in this adventure, and I value him a little more highly now.

I saw him arrive in a hansom cab across the road, as I was finding it hard to settle without the comforting presence of Holmes, silent though he would have been, at the breakfast table. I was staring out of the window, with no other motive than to relieve the tedium of being the sole inhabitant of that wonderfully intriguing lair of the great mind that was Sherlock Holmes.

A bare minute later Lestrade was shown in, and he was not alone. Behind him was a thin, athletic young man with a mere shadow of hair on his face where a beard would eventually flourish, given time. He was almost twice the height of Lestrade and crouched somewhat when addressed, so as not to seem distant and overbearing. He had rich brown hair, as I saw when he doffed his hat on being introduced, and a winning smile, conveying the optimism and joy of youth.

"Ah, good morning Dr. Watson. The sun is out and the day bodes well . . . and I must introduce you to Detective Constable Lees." The little man turned and nodded upwards. Lees shook my hand as Lestrade began an encomium on myself and my friend. "Lees, I want you to remember this place. Fix this address in your bobby's memory, and look upon it as your most fruitful resource in times when failure rears his ugly head. This is the office of Mr. Sherlock Holmes, a man whose talents have helped me solve a few complex cases, though I had done the hard work myself . . . yes . . . he has stepped in and offered a contribution."

A *contribution*, I thought, but held my tongue. Why, the little rogue was claiming to be far more than he was. He had the cheek to press the point. "Now, Dr. Watson, I have a special role just now. I have been given the task of teaching young Lees the ins and outs of trapping the bad 'uns of this great city of ours . . . and there are bad 'uns a plenty, as the doctor knows . . . ." He looked at me and added, "Dr. Watson is not averse to firing his pistol at a desperate villain if extreme action is needed, oh no, a good man in a fight is your doctor. He's played his part in my cases, haven't you, Doctor?"

I had planned to offer them tea and crumpets, but I changed my mind after that last statement. The rat-faced upstart was playing the lead part in a sordid little farce, particularly to impress the young man who stood there, mouth almost dropping in awe as Lestrade gave his most audacious falsehood, "Now Lees, Holmes and Watson have more than once been behind me in some shadowy den of evil as I led the way, anxious to protect my civilian charges, useful though they sometimes prove to be."

That was too much. There was a rage building in me and I fought for self-control as I hinted that they must be very busy men and so on. But the little man smiled at me and said, "Oh, not before I tell you how I wish to recruit you for a mysterious appointment tomorrow."

"Do go on," I droned, expecting some ridiculous monologue of lies.

"Dr. Watson . . . read this if you please." He handed me a sheet of paper which had been crumpled and creased in his coat pocket. It read:

Esteemed Inspector Lestrade,

There is an instance of danger to a royal personage. Your talents are required. Be at the Old Charger Tavern, Poland Street, at seven tomorrow.

You must come alone.

One who cares for Britain

He searched my face for a response and asked, with a note of swelling pride, "What do you make of that, sir?"

I decided to pander to his self-regard merely to have some sport. "Now, Inspector, this person asks particularly for you . . . not any Scotland Yard detective you see, but yourself! That is mighty complimentary. Of course, we know who the royal person is . . . ."

He winked at me. "It's the Prince of Wales o'course. He loves to go down with the common people . . . he'll be in disguise, and creep in there for some female company . . . ."

"He's right, Lees, listen to the man!" For what seemed like several minutes he beamed and then put his hands to his coat-lapels and swaggered so unashamedly that he needed a dash of normality, but I kept a straight face.

"Now Dr. Watson, I'm not going alone – I'm taking young Lees here, aren't I?"

"You are, sir, Mr. Lestrade, sir. I'll be there . . . to learn."

The young man, who had minded his manners and said nothing so far, had a broad northern accent, probably from Yorkshire. Holmes would have known which town he hailed from, and perhaps even how long he had resided in London.

"Nobody knows Lees, you see. He can come along and be . . . well, be invisible, I reckon!"

"I can step into a crowd and hide, in a trice, Mr. Lestrade. He's taught me everything about being a detective, Dr. Watson. He is a . . . well, He's an *eminence grise*!"

Lestrade was not sure whether or not he was being insulted. But he decided to pretend to understand and put on a false smile. "Yes, I am . . . one of those. See, Dr. Watson, these young Bobbies now, they've done more school now . . . see, He's quoting Latin. Now me and my mates down Lambeth, when we was learning, we had the school of the street."

Amused though I was with all this, I had to make a point. "Inspector . . . there's just one little detail about that letter . . . I have never heard of a public house called the Old Charger. Though it is some time since I was in Poland Street."

"Oh yes, well now there's a job for young Lees. Lees . . . go and find the place in Poland Street now . . . immediately, and report back to me at the Yard. Doctor Watson, I will see you there tomorrow at seven, right?"

Young Lees left in some haste, muttering the name of the inn, and then Lestrade did a little bow before putting his hat on again and saying, "Oh, and . . . bring your revolver, would you, old mate?"

The truth is that, after Lestrade left, I pondered the letter and I decided that it was probably written by some deranged anarchist, or perhaps a drunken poet, some person of that category. After all, why would a member of the royal family visit a rough place in that part of the city? I was not convinced by Lestrade's thoughts on the Prince of Wales. The thought of the Prince turning up there was ludicrous. But whatever the truth of the situation, I could not let him down; he was an old and valued acquaintance, when all said and done.

At five minutes to seven the next day, I turned into Poland Street off Oxford Street and looked around for the Old Charger. I thought I knew most London drinking-places, but that was a new name to me. However, to my surprise, after a steady walk of a few hundred yards I stepped across the road, having seen an inn-sign, and there it was: a splendid though well-worn picture of a grand old black horse swinging in the breeze.

The main saloon was packed with what were clearly the flotsam and jetsam of society: most were dishevelled and loud, some of them swaying around as if already worse for a superfluity of alcohol in their ravaged bodies. One or two young women were ensconced by the one long window, and a gaggle of stolid old men, ruddy faced and miserable, sat in one corner. Nobody appeared to notice me at all, and I ordered a glass of beer, with a polite enquiry to the landlord, who was a fat, happy soul with a greyish apron swathed around his middle and a wet beard. I asked if there was another room.

"Oh yes, upstairs of course, sir . . . we tends to get the more better types of coves what sits up there." As I listened, I could see no Lestrade or Lees anywhere in the mass of people milling around. "Tonight, as a matter of fact, it's occupied by a private club of gentlemen . . . leisure after their labours, as you might say."

"This must be a new establishment?" I asked. Holmes would have wanted facts, so I emulated his approach.

"You're quite right, guv'nor. We been here just free weeks. Is it free weeks, Lizzie?"

He addressed the question to a beautiful young woman who was serving a man with a pint of best mild. "Yes, about that father. Seems longer."

"You're very popular," I followed up, "Do you own the place?"

298

"Oh no . . . a foreign gentleman has it. German cove . . . Kurs . . . Kust . . . what's he called, Lizzie, the German mister?"

"Kunstlich" she said, with a smile that would have been alluring to the most steadfast gentleman out for a frisk, as Dr. Johnson would have put it. "Maurice . . . He's Maurice to me anyway. A very pleasant man he is, cultured!" In fact, I could have been out for a frisk, as there seemed to be nothing to disturb the gaiety of the place. It hardly appeared to be a site for an assassination.

I sipped my beer and started to look around when a bearded, middle-aged man came next to me and gave his name, holding out his hand as he spoke. "Good evening, sir . . . I am Harry Devaney!" He was square and solid, every inch the well-to-do city type, I thought, and it was strange to see him in a rough-house like that. His handshake was strong and firm, and as his drew back his hand, I noticed some inky stains on the fingertips. For a second, I felt a thrill of satisfaction as I considered that I had produced a Holmesian deduction. He would have been proud of me. Ink stains on the finger tips would suggest a literary man perhaps, or a man in a clerical position in the City of London; but surely, I recall reflecting, an investor would not tend to acquire such black marks. He was not, I concluded, what he seemed to be. I was a little discomfited and at that moment, thoughts of some kind of threat to a royal personage appeared to be a little more possible.

I gave my name. "Oh, a doctor . . . well, I feel comfortable in the company of a medical man . . . I have a weakness of the heart, sir. Too much strenuous work in my youth, when I was a railway manager . . . out in the shire I was. But now I'm not so active . . . ."

"What is it you do?" I asked, determined to make a mental note of it, in case there were to be developments. If any criminality was to emerge, then, as experience told me, it was the more educated characters one had to watch closely.

"Oh I'm an investor. I now invest in the locomotives, rather than arrange for their tracks and their routes across this fair land!"

That was an elusive nomenclature, I reflected. An investor could be anyone, from a member of the new rich to an outright swindler. But he talked volubly and entertainingly, and I listened, and in the course of that conversation, I spotted Lestrade and Lees. They came in separately, Lees perhaps ten seconds after his superior. The young man melted into the crowd, and Lestrade walked to the bar and had to force his way to a spot where he could order a drink.

Mr. Devaney still wanted our talk to continue, and I was struggling to think of a reason why. Surely, I thought, such a man would be drawn to other men of finance in his out-of-office time, and not to a medical man. He continued with his talk of the time when he organised the extension line from East Grinstead to Lewes, and he had no thought that I might find that subject tedious. However, as he spoke, I scrutinised his features further, and it struck me that his beard and full moustache were a deep grey everywhere except for a strange hue across the tips of his moustache which suggested black, wiry texture, as if frayed or damaged. I pondered on what activity might cause such a strange shade and banding across the hairs.

Here was a man who appeared to be a penman of some kind, and indeed also a man whose mouth and lips were subject to some kind of discolouration. He was, in short, a puzzle.

Then my reflections were disturbed by an almighty commotion, as there was a crack as a table overturned and crashed onto the floor-tiles, and there were shrieks of anger. Someone called out, "Hands off my gal, you young scab!" I looked across, to see a bullish, squat man grabbing hold of Lees' collar, though he had to stretch somewhat, being a foot shorter. He then let go and swung back an arm ready to strike. But Lees blocked the jab and the man was pushed back. A young woman squealed, "Jim . . . he touched me . . . He's a foul swine he is . . . you get him!"

I went over, but hands held me back and someone shouted, "Let 'em fight!" The crowd moved back and created a space large enough for the two men to face each other. I couldn't see Lestrade anywhere, and I assumed he was stuck fast in the crowd, as I was. Voices screamed encouragement and insults, and the muscled man, who looked like a navvy, squared up to Lees, who crouched a little and put up a guard with his arms and fists. I could see immediately that the young detective was familiar with the pugilist's skills, and my surmise was soon shown to be correct. As his opponent approached, looking fearsome and swinging another punch at his man, Lees again blocked, but this time he brought an uppercut to the man's jaw and the fellow reeled back, with a scream of pain.

A voice called out, "Four to one the bull!"

Another echoed, "Even money the tall one . . . even money!"

I was disgusted at the corruption and depravity of mankind that they could take bets in such a demeaning situation, but of course, it was nothing new; I had seen such despicable low behaviour out in Afghanistan, and my time with Holmes had confirmed my opinion that there is a degenerate class beneath any scrap of decency and right-thinking in our dear Queen's realm.

Another assault from the shorter man ended in his taking a fist directly in the face and blood spouted from his nose. He yelled like a stuck pig, and a crowd of men gathered him up and restrained him from

300

any further injury; he was patently second-best. A tall man was elected to go to Lees and raise his arm. "I declare this young fellow the winner!" he shouted. Everyone needed more drinks and there was a press against the bar. As this happened, I saw Devaney go to a door and walk through, with Lestrade by his side. The latter looked back and he saw me. I could tell by his demeanour that he wanted me to follow.

But this was followed by a deep frustration; the landlord saw me and stood in my way. "No, sir, as I said, there's a private party up there. The German gentleman has the room."

"But I have just now seen two men go through, and I assume walk up the stairs!"

"They are his friends, sir . . . now please . . . have a drink on the house!"

Terrible fears infested my imagination then. He ushered me to the bar, and he poured me a drink. Not far from me now, Lees was being offered drinks by a dozen men, and he had to refuse. I could see that he also wanted to be upstairs, knowing his Inspector was up there, and perhaps in trouble.

I put my mind to work, and thought more upon the man, Devaney. My poor brain battled to apply the ratiocination Holmes had spoken of when I first met him, in his talk of the writer Poe. What would stain a man's fingers and make that mark on his moustache? I pictured the moustache and the odd colour on the band through it, and the realisation came, like a rising sun. By heavens, he was a scientist . . . the marks were burns! A man who had such ink stains permanently on him, and burn-marks on his facial hair – well, that man experimented with something dangerous. He could be the anarchist, I concluded. He had to be stopped. He would be, logic suggested to me – a man who manufactured bombs!

As I determined on drastic action, I was aware that the landlord had been called over to the window by one of his friends, and I moved smartly to the door again, only to find that, as I opened it and walked through, there was a large, sturdy man in my path.

There is a slight shiver of regret when I record this in this account of such a difficult and testing case, but at that instant I had to make a quick decision to apply some violence. This is not my habit of course, but I was sure that Lestrade was in danger. I took my revolver from my side-pocket and brought up the stock heavily on the man's temple. He fell over, and I struck him once more, so that he was unconscious.

Behind me, to make the atmosphere of fear and disquiet even worse, I heard another furore, as if a second fight had ensued. But I could do nothing but run upstairs. My heart thumped so that I felt the beat in my throat, and as the gun was still in my hand, a part of me felt certain that I may have to use it, and perhaps do so to save a life.

However, when I reached the top of the stairs, the door was partly ajar and I heard conversation. My immediate impression was that the talk was civilised, and so I stopped to listen and to observe through the space between door and jamb. A handsome, tallish man was speaking, and with a German accent. That was, I concluded, the Herr Kunstlich the young lady had spoken of. He was speaking to someone nearer to the door, at the side of my vision, and I squinted, just able to make out that the man was Devaney, and he was bending over a tripod on which was perched a photographic camera.

As my eyes switched to see the right-hand side of the room, I felt a start of astonishment as I saw Lestrade with a man by his side who pointed a gun at the detective's head. Between them, sitting on a couch, was a woman with long, rich, black hair and bared breasts, slouched in a most indecent position. Why, I thought, she could be one of the worst harlots who haunt the Haymarket, and here she is, involved in a group of characters who want to kill Lestrade.

"Mr. Lestrade, my offer is a generous one. I am the sort of man who buys everything he wants, and on this occasion I wish to buy a policeman. In fact, I wish to buy you. My dear friend with the camera here, now he will take this picture. It will be a very tasteful *carte de visite*, showing your good self having a little recreation . . . and enjoying it of course. If you don't act at your ease and give this young lady some of your favours . . . for our lens . . . then I'm afraid tonight will be your last night on this earth, and a bullet will despatch you into eternity."

"No, you can't do it! This is wrong . . . I'm an officer of the law!" Lestrade was hardly presenting the most gallant and admirable qualities of the British gentleman who gained an empire for us. "Who the devil are you anyway, you German fiend!"

"Ah, no matter," the man said, walking gracefully a few steps away from Lestrade. "Let's simply say that your friend Mr. Sherlock Holmes knows very well who I am . . . he is, in fact, the one person in the world I most wish to see flourish, for he brings the kind of excitement that life very rarely offers one . . . this kind of excitement I would say, *naturlich*, a scene in which Death flutters his black cape and makes the shivers of fear run through your intestines, *nicht wahr?*"

I recall the devil's words most perfectly. My mind worked hard to try to define who he was, and why he spoke of Holmes. I still clutched the gun, but I expected at every second to have someone rushing behind me to clutch at my legs and drag me back, away from any opportunity of saving poor Lestrade from his imminent fate.

"Inspector, all I ask for is a little information. This is a very big city, and any businessman such as I has to have feelers out in every little back alley, as well as in the grand thoroughfares. You would be the perfect man to supply such information. So, my friend, if you wish to live, and walk into Scotland Yard tomorrow in this beautiful June weather, you must vow to be one of my little purchases, and this gentleman here will take a picture of you with Lisette here, my little female entertainer. She spends all her time learning how to please sporting young men, the sons of lords . . . oh yes, your fate will be in safe hands. *Lestrade and the Siren Lisette.* That will be written under the picture. '*Lestrade and the Siren Lisette enjoying each other's charms*', it will be written. All the world will know, Inspector . . . time for you to decide now!"

The German voice, precise and menacing, was eating into my sensibility now, and I was caught between action and sheer paralysis. As he spoke, he was moving more and more to the left, well away from my line of sight.

There was a cacophony behind me, in the downstairs room, and then I heard shouts indicating that there was another fight in progress. I distinctly heard Lees's name shouted yet again. At this stage in my account, I must confess to a certain degree of dithering on my part, but when there was the sound of footsteps behind me on the lower stairs, necessity dictated my action, and I burst into the room. At that very instant, there was a horrific explosion and a dazzling spasm of light across the room, emanating from my right. I lifted one hand to protect my face and the other was free to pull the trigger of my revolver.

The second I saw Lestrade dive to the ground and the gunman beside him move, I fired; astoundingly, in the moment it took to make that decision, someone grasped my legs in a rugger tackle and down I went, hitting the floor hard.

I must have passed out momentarily, because when Lestrade's face was above me, shaking my shoulder and asking if I could see him, I sensed that all was comparatively tranquil again. When I managed to sit up, I looked around and asked the officer where the people were.

"Oh, they hopped it out. The German . . . he went downstairs, and the others went after him . . . the lady is still cowering behind the couch, and she's sobbing, sir . . . if you're up to it, you should attend to her, like."

The transformation was beyond belief. The room was bare except for a camera and tripod and the couch. I managed to look at the young woman, and happily she was merely in a state of shock and nervous alarm – not at all surprisingly. When she was sitting up and relatively calm, I saw that Lestrade had gone downstairs and I followed him.

In all my days working against the criminal fraternity of our great capital city, I have never been so astounded. The room downstairs was completely empty, except for Lestrade bending over Lees, who was severely injured, lying on the floor by the window. "Dr. Watson, come and have a look at the boy, quick!" Lestrade called.

The young detective was badly bruised and cut about his face, but I could detect no evidence of fractures; he had been, as I was, unconscious, and was muttering about there being "three of them . . . in the fighter's gang. Too . . . too much for me . . . ."

I insisted that Lees be taken to hospital, and Lestrade went to find constables and attend to that. I looked around, and it was as if there had never been a human presence in the place; where there had been the bar, there was simply a wall and a table; the seats and small tables by the window were gone also; I ran outside and expected to see the sign, indicating the Old Charger, but there was nothing to see. There was Poland Street, as it always was, except for the inn I had visited the previous night.

Lestrade came back with several policemen, and Lees was carried outside to a cab. Lestrade directed one of the policemen to go upstairs and comfort the young woman.

"He was a regular hero, our Detective Constable . . . should be commended!" Lestrade said.

"Inspector," I asked, still dumbfounded at what was around me, "Who was the German?"

"Wish I knew, sir . . . him and that photographer cove, they was very close. My God, Dr. Watson, the man said he wanted to buy me . . . oh by Heaven! The camera . . . ."

His face had the appearance of a man in sin who had seen the revelation of some mighty truth, and he ran upstairs. I followed, full of curiosity to see what had alarmed the man.

"Here we are. The camera . . . there's still the plate in it! What relief, Dr. Watson. "

I inspected the camera and when I looked around I saw what had been the source of the blinding light. It was the flash powder of course, and that explained Devaney's inky fingers and singed moustache. I explained that to Lestrade.

"Oh yes, I seen these before today, sir, the flash powder is very dangerous. Burns you, it does. This is a most risky business, this picture-making. I don't hold with it." He went to the machine and slid out a plate. "On this fiendish thing there's a picture of me with that . . . that young lady over there." We looked at her, now wrapped in the constable's cloak and trying to smile.

"To think . . . I could have been . . . what's that word . . . ."

"Compromised?" I ventured.

"Ruined, I think, puts it more exactly, Doctor."

"Who on earth was the German? " I asked, expecting no answer.

"Well, one of 'em called him Maurice . . . well, *Mauritz,* German variety of Maurice."

"What about that plate? What's on it?" My question caused a stir on Lestrade's face. "Well, nothing now guv." He hurled it to the floor and stamped on it.

My mind was now working hard, turning over all the facts, and trying to assemble them as Holmes would have done. Maurice Kunstlich . . . what or who was he? "How's your German, Inspector? Mine is very feeble I'm afraid . . . I recall a problem with the word *Rache* at one time . . . ."

He called the constable across. "My ability with other tongues is limited, but Hesslam here has a German dad . . . ."

"The man was given the German name," he said, with instant understanding, "Well, that would be Maurice Arty in English, sir. Ridiculous name, sir"

Maurice Arty . . . Moriarty. My God! At that moment, I had the awful realisation that I had been in the presence of the fiend himself, the deadly enemy of my dear friend Holmes. Worse still, the thought struck me, there had been a picture of him on that plate, now shattered and useless, at our feet. Holmes was never to know that fact. I persuaded myself that there would simply have been a blur, as the man had stepped out of the picture before I shot at his minion.

I rather think that my losing the notes of this case is perhaps the result of my embarrassment at missing a unique opportunity of trapping an image of the man whose machinations often gave Holmes and myself sleepless nights, and more than acceptable amount of worry.

Then, something dawned in my mind that night, as I sat in my armchair, working out the amazing disappearance of that inn. I said the words aloud. Moriarty knew that Holmes was away! My brooding, cerebral friend would have seen through his German identity in a second. As for Lestrade: well, I never saw him stretch the truth of his life in front of younger officers again. He reverted to his usual crass, thoughtless self, but it has to be said that he behaved with courage and self-control.

I have only once walked along Poland Street since that strange evening. I recall stopping to look at the wall on which the inn-sign hung. I blinked, took stock of who and where I was, and for a second I heard the sound of laughter and drunken jollity behind that solid stone. One day, I resolved, I shall relate the whole affair to Holmes. But for now, let it lie.

The King of Diamonds
by John Heywood

Sir William Voigt, owner of a quarter of the world's diamond mines, was not a man to hide his light under a bushel. He wore diamond-encrusted jewellery with the flamboyance of a Maharajah, and so great was his wealth that it earned him the sobriquet of The Diamond King among the English press. It can have surprised nobody that when such a man lost his life in a wood on a Norfolk estate, the tragedy was recounted in the greatest detail. But interest in the sad event was not to last: before the week was out, new tales of death and scandal were vying for the attention of the public, and curiosity about the millionaire's murder withered away as suddenly as it had sprung up. Soon, perhaps, Sir William will be quite forgotten, and against that day I wish to record here a brief sketch of the events surrounding his death. The newspaper reports at the time were partial and misleading, for it is seldom within the powers of the reporter to delve under the surface of the disaster he recounts and unearth the twisted complexities beneath. My friend and colleague Sherlock Holmes, however, has made it his life's work to shine a light upon these dark secrets, and he seldom did so to greater effect than when looking into the death of the King of Diamonds.

The summer of '88 had lasted long and late; in early October of that year, the streets through which I passed on my way home to Baker Street still glowed warm in the light of the setting sun. Within a day or two, however, the season turned, and the golden light of summer was replaced by morning mists and darkening afternoons. Now, instead of strolling home in comfort, I and a thousand others like me hurried homewards through the damp streets, each of us huddled in his great-coat against the biting air. It was on one such evening that the case I am about to relate began. I had returned home to find that the landlady Mrs. Hudson had set a fire, the first of the autumn. Sitting by it was Holmes, his heels resting upon the coal-scuttle, so absorbed in some black-letter tome that he continued to read without so much as a glance at me or a word of greeting. Not that I had the least objection to my friend's unclubbable ways. After a busy day at my practice, I was looking forward to a few hours of quietness, and so I was happy to settle myself in the other chair by the fire and read the paper. The evening proved as pleasantly uneventful as I had hoped. From time to time a few words of conversation would flare up between us, much as a few flames would occasionally shoot from a log, only to die down again into a steady glow. One of us might shift to a more comfortable position in his chair, and then settle again, as the burning logs once or twice collapsed into the embers and then continued to burn quietly in their new arrangement. The lines of print swam before my eyes, the paper fell from my hand, and I was drifting into sleep when my drowsy reverie was interrupted by a knock at the door.

"Come in!" I heard Holmes cry. The door opened to reveal a lady dressed in a most curious manner; heavily veiled, she wore a broad-brimmed hat trimmed, as was her collar, with silver astrakhan, while the skirts of her dark top-coat were so low and full that they brushed the floor. After hesitating for some seconds in the doorway, the lady rushed impetuously into the room, only to bridle suddenly and stop dead in her tracks again. She lifted her veil, and her glance, flickering between us, finally alighted on my friend: "Mr. Sherlock Holmes, detective?" she asked. Her manner of speech was as curious as her appearance and behaviour. It was evident that she was not a native of this country. Stepping up to Holmes, she clasped his hand in both of hers. "Mr. Holmes, help me, I beg you. My brother's life is in jeopardy. The Diamonds King is dead! And they say – "

"You are very disturbed, madam. Please calm yourself," said my friend, guiding her to a chair and bidding her sit. "The *sal voltile*, if you would, Watson. Now," he said, turning back to her, "when you are ready, you will tell me about the Diamond King and your brother, and what danger it is that brings you here." He gestured in my direction. "This is my friend and colleague, Dr. Watson, and my name you know. There, of course, you have the advantage of us."

The lady sat upright, grasping her bag in her gloved hands and clenching her teeth as she struggled to control her feelings.

"Good evening, Dr. Watson and Mr. Holmes. I am Miss Maria Oblonsky."

"Good evening, Miss Oblonsky," I answered. "It so happens that I have just been reading about the Diamond King. It's a bad business. Have you heard the news, Holmes?" I asked, retrieving the paper from the floor.

"No. You had better enlighten me. If you will read out the report, Watson, I shall be much obliged, and Miss Oblonsky will then tell us what she knows of the matter, and how she and her brother come to be involved."

I turned to the page headed "A Dreadful Murder at Carre Castle" and read aloud from it.

308

A tragic event has taken from us one of the Empire's greatest men. Sir William Voigt, better known to many as the King of Diamonds, was as familiar a figure on Change as he was at Monte Carlo, and was also a fine sportsman, who bagged, it is said, more head of game than any man living. It is our sad duty to report that "The King of Diamonds" is dead.

Sir William Voigt met his death shortly after midday today on the Norfolk estate of the Marquess of Ambleside, during a weekend shooting party. Among the exalted guests were the writer Mr. Peake Aubrey, General Sir Arthur Lamb, General Oliphant, and other prominent public figures. This morning's shoot started after an early breakfast and was to continue into the early afternoon, with the marksmen taking their luncheon in the field. Sir William ate with his fellow hunters, and soon afterwards complained that he was unwell. It became evident that he was in great pain, but all attempts to help were in vain; within a few minutes he was dead.

It was immediately suspected that the luncheon he had just ingested was the cause of his death, and we are informed by Inspector Shaw of the North Norfolk constabulary that poisoning, accidental or deliberate, has not been dismissed as a possibility. "An inquiry is in hand," said that officer. "The circumstances surrounding Sir William Voigt's death will be investigated fully, and I am confident that if there has been foul play we shall find it out."

We have little doubt that Inspector Shaw is correct, and that further details of this dreadful event will come to light over the next few days, details which are yet shrouded in much darkness. Readers may be assured that this journal will be second to none in laying before them all the circumstances behind this unhappy event as they emerge.

"Now, Miss Maria Oblonsky," said Holmes, "perhaps you will be kind enough to tell us about yourself. Beyond the obvious facts that you have only been in this country for a few weeks, that you work as a seamstress, and that you and your family have seen better days, I know little about you.

She looked at him in astonishment. "How do you know these things? How do you know that I am seamstress? How that my family were once more rich?"

A smile of satisfaction briefly passed over Holmes's features at the amazement that his powers of observation and deduction had produced. "The signs are obvious enough to the practised eye. You have pronounced marks around the tips of your index and middle fingers," he observed. "They are the marks, common amongst seamstresses, made by the constant use of a thimble. Incidentally, that the marks are on your right hand proclaim you to be left-handed. If you wish to preserve your secrets from the eyes of men, you would do well not to remove your gloves. The hands have much to tell those who can hear."

"And my family? That we are not rich now as before?"

"There are many signs. These gloves, for instance," he answered, picking them up from the table. "They are of fine kid, and fitted to your hands by the glove-maker." Holmes rose and took the lady's hand in his own, splaying the fingers as though she were a patient in a public ward. "I observe that the index finger is slightly longer than the fourth; a most unusual proportion." He held the glove against her hand. "Precisely the same proportion here, you see," he pointed out. "This glove was certainly made to fit that hand."

"You are as clever as they say, Mr. Sherlock Holmes; but how does this tell you that my family fell from fortune?"

"It is simple enough. The glove, though of excellent quality, is now old and worn. See here, where scratches on the surface have been carefully dyed, and here, where a break in the seam has been mended in thread of the matching colour. Bespoke gloves of the best quality, many years ago, but not enough money to buy new ones now when they are needed, although the owner," he added with a nod towards the lady, "still has proper pride in her appearance. What else can that mean, but a reversal of fortunes?"

Not unnaturally, she seemed downcast by this reminder of her present state. "It is quite true. I have lost all I once had."

"Not all, Miss Oblonsky. As I said, you have not lost your pride." Holmes dropped her glove on to the table and resumed his chair. "Now, let us concentrate on the matter in hand," he said. "Pray be kind enough to tell me about you and your brother, and what brought you to this country."

"My brother Peter and I have good education, and we come from good family, very old family, but, as you see, not rich like in the days before Uprising. Little by little we lose everything, and then we have no money. My brother Peter Oblonsky comes to your country since fourteen

310

years. It is very difficult for Peter. He pulls cart at market, but still he sends some money home for us. Then he works footman, and because we come from good family, he knows to be footman and to wait at table. He does not serve port in sherry-glass and so. Then he is manservant to one man, which is for two years, and now he is valet to Sir William Voigt."

"When did your brother Peter enter Sir William's employment?" asked Holmes.

"This is three years ago, in the same year that Mother dies. In Warsaw, I am lucky to find work. You know already that my job is seamstress. Peter writes to me that there is work for seamstress in London and also for domestic staff, like he is. He thinks that there will be place for lady's maid, or perhaps I find position as governess. So two months ago I come to England. Peter finds for me small room in Covent Garden, which is not garden, but streets and alleys."

"You have given me a very clear account of your background, Miss Oblonsky. Now, tell me what happened in these last few days."

"Last Wednesday afternoon, Peter and I meet. We meet on Wednesday afternoons, because they are his afternoons off work. Peter tells me that he will go with Sir William to Norfolk, to the castle of Lord Ambleside. Then on Sunday, they will return to London. Peter wants me to see England, which he says is in many parts very beautiful, not like Covent Garden, so he pays for me to take train to Norfolk, and he pays for room in the inn so I may be near him in Norfolk. One day, Peter has free time, so I meet him and we go for walk near where he stays with Sir William. He is right, the country is most beautiful. That day is Thursday. The next time I will meet him is Saturday. Two o'clock we will meet, at the South Lodge gate, but when I come to gate I see another man is there waiting instead. He asks me if I am Maria, and he tells me that there is something wrong. He says that Sir William Voigt is dead and Peter cannot come to meet me. He tells me that Peter is in police prison for killing Sir William. This I cannot believe. I ask how Sir William dies, and he says that he is poisoned. Sir William eats sandwich and dies. The person who makes sandwiches for Sir William is Peter. And they search Peter's room and find hidden there jewels of diamonds that belong to Sir William, the Diamond King.

"No mention of an arrest in the paper," Holmes said to himself. "So the theft was discovered and Oblonsky arrested after the newspaper reports were despatched. Now, Miss Oblonsky, tell me about your brother's relations with his late employer. Do you know of any difficulties between them?"

"My brother was very pleased to have his position with Sir William."

"He never complained to you about his master?"

"But yes, I must tell you that he did sometimes tell me that Sir William was a difficult person to please, and demanded much of him, but then also Sir William can be very generous and kind. You must understand that Peter is gentle man, very good man, and I know that he will never, never try to hurt or kill, never. Please, Mr. Holmes, you must help save my brother. I know that he is not guilty of this death. I know it. Please, will you help?"

"I will see what I can do, Miss Oblonsky. But you must understand that I am not in the position of a lawyer who represents his client's interests. My task, if I undertake to investigate this matter, will be to find out the truth, whatever it may be. I ask you to bear in mind these points: that your brother, apparently, prepared the sandwiches that poisoned his employer; that very valuable property of the dead man was found hidden in your brother's effects. If I should find the truth about Sir William's death, it may not be what you believe and wish it to be. You do understand that?"

Miss Oblonsky rose from the chair and stood straight, her back straight and head high.

"I ask no more than that, Mr. Holmes," was her reply, given with something of the pride to which my friend had alluded. "Your words are great relief to me. I have no friends in your country except my poor brother, and if Sherlock Holmes is investigating this death, I know all that may be done is being done."

Holmes acknowledged her words with a shallow bow. "I shall look into the matter, Miss Oblonsky, and see what I can find. If I have any news for you, you shall hear it within a day or two. You have done well to come to me, and there is at present no more that you can do. Leave matters in my hands, and try to set your mind at rest. In the meantime, I wish you a safe journey back to Covent Garden."

Closing the door behind the lady, Holmes stepped briskly over to the book-case, pulled out Bradshaw and the atlas, and carried them over to the table. He spread them open and turned up the lamp. "Let me see – Carre Castle . . . it is rather off the beaten track . . . Brailston Thorpe will be the station." He turned to Bradshaw and ran his finger down the column: "A train leaves Liverpool Street at 8.48. Will you be accompanying me, Watson?"

"If you wish. I have nothing planned for tomorrow."

"Capital! I shall tell Mrs. Hudson that we breakfast at seven."

From the station at Brailston Thorpe, we took a four-wheeler, and across the flat landscape we saw, far away in the distance, the turrets of

312

Carre Castle rising from the low-lying mists. It was a further half-hour's drive before we reached the South Lodge, where we turned in and drove on to the main gates. The castle, which we had seen floating in the distance like a vision of Camelot, now loomed heavily over us, massive and grey, its turrets and mullions rising far above our heads. As we entered the Great Hall, we seemed to be in another age, for suits of armour stood sentinel by the doorway, and tapestries and old weapons of war hung upon the walls. They brought to my mind fabled days of yore – "old, far off, unhappy things, and battles long ago." I said as much to Holmes, but the romance of the past had no place his heart, and in response he merely asked a maid who was working nearby where Inspector Shaw was to be found. "The police are working from the gun-room, sir," she answered. "Down that corridor there and to your right."

We found the gun room easily enough, but our knocking went unanswered, and when we entered we found ourselves in an empty room. There were no guns to be seen; they were, no doubt, behind the stout locked cupboards that lined one side of the room. Nor were there any people in the room. An aged dog approached us, slowly wagging its tail, and, having made itself known to us, wandered off again to slump down in its basket. We saw no other sign of life.

"The enquiry does not appear to be proceeding at full pelt, does it?" said I. But I spoke too soon, for at that very moment a door on the opposite side of the room flew open and two men strode in.

"Monstrous!" cried the first man. "How am I to make a report when half the witnesses have fled to the four corners of the earth? 'Tis beyond me."

"Yes, sir," answered the other, leaning forward to brush some cartridges off a rough table with his sleeve. The first slammed down a heavy ledger onto the table and, looking up, caught sight of Holmes and myself. He glared at us across the room.

"How may I help you gentlemen?" he asked, in no very friendly tone of voice. We introduced ourselves. "Inspector Shaw, of King's Lynn," he responded. "We're honoured, I'm sure, to have you here, Mr. Holmes, but I'm afraid you've missed the boat this time. We already have our man, safely under lock and key in the station."

"Yes, so I heard," replied my friend. "Commendably speedy of you. However, I am privately retained to look into this case. I hope it will not inconvenience you if I do so?"

"Not at all, I'm sure," was the muttered answer.

"Thank you, Inspector. I suppose you have little doubt that it was the prisoner Oblonsky who killed Sir William?"

313

"No doubt of it."

"Poisoned the sandwiches, I hear. The police surgeon examined the body?"

"He did. Found enough arsenic in the body to kill a horse, and enough in what were the rest of the sandwiches to kill another horse. Now, a good supply of arsenic is kept in a locked cupboard in the scullery, as rat poison, and what would you think? Most of it is missing."

"Has the cupboard been forced?"

"I don't think so – Constable?"

The constable pulled a notebook from his pocket and consulted it. "No, sir. 'Cupboard door locked, remaining powder on shelf.'"

"Any idea as to the motive?" continued Holmes.

"Motive? There's no mystery there – theft. The greater part of Sir William's personal jewellery was missing, and we found several pieces hidden in Oblonsky's bag – some shirt studs and a tie-pin. All set with diamonds, of course. Sir William was no fool, and when he missed his jewellery he would guess who had taken it. Oblonsky had to silence him."

"And the other stolen jewels?" asked Holmes. "Where were they?"

"We haven't found them yet. We've searched the man's room, of course. It's my guess that the sly fellow has hidden them in some other part of the castle. We may never find them."

"I wonder why he did not hide all the jewellery in that way, then."

"Because he didn't have time. He had to leave his room to prepare for the morning shoot before he had finished hiding the jewellery. Or perhaps in his hurry he simply overlooked them."

The inspector shot Holmes a knowing glance. "I can guess what you're thinking, Mr. Holmes. You're thinking, 'This is all well and good, but it's just supposition. Where's the proof?'"

"Ah! You are right, Inspector Shaw. I was thinking something along those lines."

"'Tis a question of access," explained the Inspector. "You'll be wanting to make your own enquiries, of course, but here's my advice. We have three vital items in this murder: the arsenic, the jewellery, and the sandwiches. Who had access to all three? A simple question, but 'tis sometimes the simple questions that count.

"Now, I'll be getting back to my report. 'Tis a shame you weren't in time to catch your man. We beat you to it this time, Mr. Holmes!"

"Nonetheless, I'd like to have a word with Oblonsky. Perhaps you'll be good enough to write an order to your man at the station.

"But before we go to the station to see Oblonsky," said Holmes as we left the gunroom, "there are one or two other people here I'd like to

314

speak to. It would be as well to hear what the butler can tell us, first of all. He's likely to be as well informed as anyone about yesterday's arrangements."

The butler was in his pantry, a stout, dignified silver-whiskered man named Meades. Holmes had guessed rightly, for although the butler had remained in the castle during the shoots, he was, nevertheless, aware of the whereabouts of the guests and servants at all times. The sport for that day, he told us, had taken place in the lower Midden woods, a part of the estate that lay at such a distance from the castle – some twelve or thirteen miles – that it had been decided that the guests would not return for their luncheon, but would take a light meal in the woods, and return to the castle late in the afternoon. The eight guests and their host, Lord Ambleside, formed three groups of three Guns for that morning's shoot, stationed some two or three furlongs apart. Sir William's group also included the novelist Peake Aubrey, and Lord Henry, Lord Ambleside's son.

Oblonsky had prepared Sir William's food in the kitchen in the morning, and then accompanied him on the shoot. It was not unusual, Meades explained, for a valet to prepare his master's outside meals in this way, as he would know better than the castle staff the gentleman's requirements. The regular staff did, however, prepare the food for Mr. Aubrey and Lord Henry, who were not accompanied by a manservant. Oblonsky used the same kitchen as the regular staff, but on being asked exactly where the various servants were working, Meades regretted that he was unable to say. Nor was he well placed to give first-hand information about the arsenic, advising us to apply to Mrs. Olds the housekeeper on both these subjects.

He did, however, give precise information about the times at which events took place. He assured us that Oblonsky must have gone to the kitchen before nine o'clock to prepare the sandwiches required by his master, the shooting party having left the castle at ten past nine in the morning. As to the time and circumstances of Sir William's death, the butler, having been at the time in the castle itself, twelve miles from the scene of the tragedy, was able to give us only an indirect report. He had been informed, however, and had no reason to doubt, that nothing out of the way had occurred within the Voigt threesome until Voigt ate the sandwich served him by his valet. Shortly after eating the sandwich, he had fallen to the ground in pain, and within less than a minute was dead. There was little doubt that it was the sandwich that had poisoned him, for one of the dogs, in the confusion, snapped up one of the fallen

315

sandwiches, wolfed it down, and quickly met the same fate as Sir William.

The dreadful event had, of course, brought to a premature end the weekend's sport, and many of the guests had already left or were on the point of leaving. The two Guns who had been of Sir William's party, however, remained; Lord Henry and Mr. Peake Aubrey.

"Those two," asked Holmes; "are they still at the castle?"

"They are, sir. I am given to understand that Lord Henry will be staying for some little time. Mr. Aubrey will leave us this afternoon."

"At least are still here. Many of the guests seem to have left already. Indeed, a carriage on its way out passed us as we came in."

"Yes, sir. That would have been General Oliphant and his party. You will readily understand that the misadventure has brought the sport to an unexpectedly early end. Only Mr. Aubrey, Sir Lumsden Grey and General Lamb are still at the castle."

"And Lord Henry?"

"Indeed so, sir. I was thinking of the guests only."

"Where am I to find Lord Henry and Mr. Aubrey?"

"Mr. Aubrey, I believe, is in the library. As for Lord Henry, I cannot say with any certainty, but he is often to be found in the billiards-room at this time of the day."

In the billiards-room, we found two young men in the midst of a frame, one stretching over the table to play a shot, the other leaning against the back of a chair with his hands in his pockets, watching his opponent. The onlooker identified himself as Lord Henry and his friend at the table as Mr. Walter Willoughby. "Fire away with your questions, Mr. Holmes," he said. "We have plenty of time, I'm sorry to say. Willoughby's well into his stride, and once he gets going like this there's no stopping him."

Although he responded willingly enough to Holmes's questions, Lord Henry's answers were something of a disappointment, for they told us nothing we did not already know. I shall, therefore, not weary the reader with every question and answer that passed between Sherlock Holmes and Lord Henry. Suffice it to say that the young man's account of events only confirmed what we had heard before.

Mr. Aubrey, who, as the butler had predicted, was to be found in the library, had, at first, equally little to tell that was new. After the morning's shooting, Sir William, he said, had settled himself on his shooting-stick in a clearing and taken a sandwich from the little hamper presented by his valet, Oblonsky. He had offered to share the sandwiches with his fellow Guns. "A dashed close shave," as Aubrey put it, for had the sandwiches not contained mustard he would have accepted Sir

William's offer, a decision which would surely have proved fatal. Soon Voigt complained of feeling unwell. A minute later he was grimacing in pain and wavering on his seat; and then he crashed to the ground, clutching his stomach. Within a minute he was dead. In these matters, Aubrey's answers, like Lord Henry's, served only to corroborate those accounts of the morning's events that we had already heard, but on the topic of his fellow guests, Aubrey was more informative. Asked to describe them, he pondered a moment, pushed back a lock of hair from his forehead, and settled back in his chair.

"I have no interest in tittle-tattle," began the novelist, "but as a simple spinner of tales, I take a keen interest in the foibles of my fellow creatures; and I may say that I am a seasoned traveller in the ways of the human heart. Of course," he added, "you gentlemen understand that these observations are not to be repeated willy-nilly. They are of a private nature.

"Youth first: Lord Henry. I've known him since he was a boy, and he's become a very pleasant young man, though whether he'll measure up when he becomes Marquess, I don't know. Well, that day is a long way off, we all hope. Perhaps he's rather in his father's shade at present. I know nothing of his friend, Willoughby, I'm afraid.

"Two other young men, the Mainwaring brothers. Hugo is a charming fellow, but his brother Ralph is quite another kettle of fish. He was drunk most of the time. In fact, he had to cry off the shoot. Rude to the servants, too. To be frank with you, he's a blackguard of the first water. Why Ambleside keeps inviting him I cannot imagine.

"Now, General Lamb. I hadn't seen him since Majuba, but he's the same as ever: a fine old soldier. He fell out with Voigt after dinner, you know. I don't know what it was all about, but voices were certainly raised. The port was flowing rather too freely, I dare say. There was another General, too, Oliphant. He was quite unlike one's idea of a military man. Very quiet. I could scarcely get a word out of him, and he looked as if he'd spent his life at a desk. Rotten shot, too. He kept himself to himself." Aubrey counted off the guests on his fingers.

"That's six. There were ten Guns in all. Well, poor Voigt, of course. I was with him and Lord Henry, you know. Saw him die." The writer's flow of words dried up for a few moments. "We spoke about that. As to the man himself, I hadn't met him before, but of course with a man like that, his reputation precedes him. He was a touch vulgar, it must be said, red of face and loud of mouth, though one doesn't wish to speak ill of the dead. He was very friendly and gregarious, though. You couldn't help yourself liking the man. Now, who else? Your humble servant, of course, and there's Ambleside, our host. I have no secret information for you

317

there, I'm afraid. Just a very fine gentleman of the old school. That's nine. Who else?" He rubbed his jaw as he tried to call the last Gun to mind. "Grey!" he cried. "Lumsden Grey. How could I forget? I was at school with him. He's in the Privy Council now, if you can believe me. I let him have a few home truths about his damned government, and he had to admit I spoke a good deal of sense."

"Thank you, Mr. Aubrey," said Holmes. "Tell me, do you know if any of these men had some quarrel with Sir William? Or of any other enemies he may have had?"

"Enemies? A man like that probably has enemies in three continents. He won't have built up the world's biggest diamond business without treading on a few toes. And I'm not only talking about personal enemies. There are those who can't bear to see a man do well – anarchists, socialists, nihilists – they hate to see any man make his way to the top."

"You think this was a murder motivated by envy?"

The writer shrugged his shoulders.

"Why not? We all know of the outrages these monsters perpetrate. They are not above killing innocent people, Mr. Holmes. Indeed, they glory in murder. The fouler their misdeeds, the louder they boast of them. You know who I mean: anarchists." He moved a little closer and lowered his voice. "Oblonsky is one of them!" he hissed.

If Lord Henry had given too little information, Mr. Peake Aubrey had perhaps given too much.

"What do you make of it all, Watson?" Holmes asked me as we left the library. "Who might have been enemy enough of Voigt to kill him? Any idea?"

"Well, perhaps if Oblonsky is indeed an anarchist – or if Voigt has made an enemy who crossed his path here – or – dash it, Holmes, I don't know. It all seems so vague and confusing; I'm afraid I'm quite in the dark."

"I'm with you there, old man; all this seems to be leading nowhere," he said, shaking his head. "Let us hope that a talk with Oblonsky will shed some light on the matter. But before I speak to him, I'd better have a word with Mrs. Olds, the housekeeper. I'd very much like to see her poison cupboard and find out who had access to it."

Mrs. Olds was in her scullery, in a cap and apron, sitting at a plain deal table on which was heaped a score or so of freshly shot birds. A kitchen maid stood by as the housekeeper ran a thick finger down the columns of the game-book that lay open before her, no doubt checking that the records and the bag matched. At our approach, she pushed the book aside and rose to her feet.

318

"The arsenic? I wish I'd never set eyes on it, that I do. It's kept in that cupboard in the corner there."

Holmes strode over to it and bent over the lock, running his fingertips over it and examining it through his pocket lens. He turned to the housekeeper.

"The key, if you please."

She took a key from her apron pocket and unlocked a wall-cupboard. From the row of keys inside she selected one and handed it to Holmes. He glanced at her keenly.

"Is this key always kept there?"

"Yes, sir."

"And who has a key to the key-cupboard?"

"Mr. Meades and myself."

"And the key to the poison cupboard is always kept locked in there?"

"Oh yes, Mr. Holmes!"

"On no, Mrs. Olds!"

She looked at him in astonishment.

"Now tell me the truth," he continued. "Why was the arsenic cupboard left unlocked yesterday?"

His certainty and hawk-like gaze were more than a match for her feeble protests, and she gave up her pretence. "I can't say, sir, really I can't. It was locked first thing yesterday, but on these busy days a person can't always keep an eye on everything at once. All I can tell you is this; when we were cleaning up after luncheon yesterday, there was the key left in the cupboard door."

Holmes and I left the kitchen and came back up the stairs. I was still struggling to make sense of the case.

"So anyone in the kitchen could have slipped into the scullery when it was empty and taken the arsenic, with no-one any the wiser."

"Exactly," Holmes agreed. "We have not narrowed the field much. In fact, I don't seem to be making much progress at all."

"What do you intend to do?" I asked.

"I intend to see Oblonsky. Perhaps he will be able to cast some light on this murky business."

A two-wheeler awaited us at the stables, and soon we were rattling along the misty lanes to the village of Carre and its police station.

The sergeant in charge carefully wrote our names in his ledger and walked with us down to the cell, locking the door behind us once we had entered. Oblonsky was a small man with thick hair greying at the temples. He was neatly dressed, but his jaw told me that he had not shaved since his imprisonment the previous day. He was sitting on a bench that jutted from the wall, his hands clasped before him. On our entrance, he jumped briskly to his feet and gave a short bow. Holmes explained that we were there at his sister's behest, at which the prisoner expressed his gratitude and assured us of his innocence.

"In that case, Oblonsky, there is good reason to hope that in a few hours the charges against you will be dropped, and that you will walk from here a free man." So said my friend; but his words brought little cheer to Oblonsky, who received them with a weary shake of the head. "I have held back nothing from the police, I assure you, and yet here I am," he said, indicating the walls around him, "a prisoner, to be tried for murder." Again he shook his head and cast his eyes to the floor of his cell.

"Come now, do not be downhearted," insisted Holmes. "Although things seem black from your police-cell here, the case against you is much weaker than it appears. There is every chance that you will soon be free. But if that is to happen, you must give me the information I seek as fully and accurately as you can. It is of the first importance that you do not pass over some detail because you think it trivial. You must allow me to judge what is germane to your case, and what is not."

Holmes pulled up his chair and leaned forward, so that he was looking his man squarely in the face. "Firstly; are you a member of any political society?"

Oblonsky looked somewhat taken aback by the question, and I confess that I shared his surprise. "I gave my word that I would tell you the truth," he said, "and so I will. Yes, I am a member of a group for progress in the world."

"The name of your group?"

"That I cannot tell you, because we have no name. It is safer thus, and more in keeping with our beliefs."

"Well, would you say your group is nihilist? Anarchist?"

"No, not nihilist, no!" Oblonsky spoke with passion. "We abjure them, their despair, their violence, their bombs and killings. We are not nihilist. Anarchist?" He inclined his head one way, then the other. "Perhaps. We oppose ourselves to violence, whether done by the greatest nations or by the meanest person. We hope for a day when there will be no money, no property, no distinctions of rank, no need for prisons and armies. We meet to discuss how this may be achieved."

"So you look forward to a day when there will be no man and no master?"

"We do, Mr. Holmes."

"I take it that you kept your views on social matters from your master."

"But no, I told Sir William my beliefs. One day he found some papers recording our discussions, and he asked me about them. He was insistent that I tell him. So I told him."

"What was his response?"

"He laughed loudly and slapped me on the shoulder. 'You're a rum bird, Oblonsky,' he said."

Homes then turned his attention to the events of the fatal morning, beginning with the point-blank question, whether Oblonsky had introduced poison into the sandwiches. The valet repudiated the suggestion categorically, swearing that he had no idea how the poison had been put into the sandwiches, except that he had not done it himself.

"Well, somebody did it," was Holmes's blunt reply. "Now, what can you tell us about the diamond jewels that were found in your bag? Did you steal them?"

"I did not," he assured us.

"Do you have any idea how they came to be there?"

"None."

"Somebody put them there." Holmes got to his feet and paced the little cell two or three times. He turned to the prisoner: "You understand, I'm sure, that these two questions are at the crux of this case. If we can answer them, you will be a free man. If not, your life will be forfeit. So let us do all we can to find the answers. I believe you and Sir William arrived at the castle three days ago, did you not? What rooms were you given?"

"We arrived on Thursday evening and were put in the East wing, Sir William on the second floor, and I on the third."

"Who else was in the East wing?"

"General Lamb occupied the room next to Sir William."

"I see. Was anybody else on the third floor with you?"

"Yes, General Lamb's manservant Griggs. He was on the upper floor, as I was. Our rooms were opposite each other on either side of a narrow passage. His room looked out on to the parterre, mine on to the courtyard.

"At first, Griggs and I did not hit it off very well. He held himself deliberately aloof, not acknowledging my presence at all. It was uncomfortable. But soon he became more friendly towards me, helping me in my duties at times. We were on good terms in the end."

"When did you first notice this change of attitude in Griggs towards you?" asked Holmes.

The prisoner glanced upwards as he tried to recall events to his mind. "It was the day before yesterday, in the evening, when he and I were both in our rooms, preparing for the following day. I was fetching Sir William's hip-flask and luncheon case, which would be needed in the morning. Griggs was also busy preparing for the day ahead. He had left his door open, and as I left my room I glanced through the open door and caught his eye."

"What was he doing?"

"Exactly what, I cannot tell you. There are a thousand little things that a manservant must attend to in good time if everything is to go smoothly. Just which of these so many tasks occupied Griggs at that moment, I do not know. Unpacking some piece of equipment or clothing, I should say, for when I saw him he was kneeling at a small open case. My sudden appearance at his doorway surprised him and he gave a start. I made a remark to the effect that we both alike had much to do in our line of work. He fully agreed, and for a few moments we shared our experiences. It was from that time that relations between Griggs and me became warm. The bond between men who work side by side is naturally strong. Many laugh at this truth, but I believe this bond has a place in every heart, and the warmth that briefly grew up between myself and Griggs is an example of it."

"Cast your mind back to that moment when you caught sight of Griggs and spoke with him. Was there anything remarkable about it?" asked Holmes. "Please think carefully."

The valet frowned, thinking over the question. "No, sir," he finally answered. "Nothing at all unusual. I had gone into Sir William's room first, and then into my own, to fetch what was needed for the next morning. I left my room hurriedly to return to Sir William's room, and it was then, as I was hurrying to the stair, that I saw Griggs and spoke with him. When I was finished in Sir William's room, I went down to the servants' hall to complete my tasks."

"And then?"

"And then I returned to the East wing. As I came up the stairs, Griggs, hearing me return, opened his door, and we had some talk before retiring. He had been giving my earlier words much thought, he said, and they had given him a new understanding. Nothing must stand between two comrades; not the power of law, nor of wealth, nor of social degree. However strongly these chains might bind a man, he should never betray his fellow.

"I was touched by his sincerity in these new-found beliefs, and we clasped hands and swore loyalty to each and all our fellow men. So we parted as brothers."

322

"The next morning, I rose at half past six and made Sir William his coffee. I laid out his clothes and equipment for the shoot, and at about a quarter past eight went down to the kitchen. A table was set aside for the use of us visiting staff, where I was able to make a luncheon for Sir William and for myself."

Holmes closed his eyes and frowned in concentration.

"I entered the kitchen," continued Oblonsky, "and went to the cupboard and safe, whence I took what I needed for the luncheon sandwiches."

"You did not bring your own supplies?"

"No, I took what I needed from the castle provisions. For instance, there is at all times a pat of butter in the dairy safe, from which I helped myself. I also cut the bread for the sandwiches from the loaf in use at the time; there is always a loaf available. And so with the ham, salt and pepper, and parsley. Only the mustard I prepared myself. Sir William liked a particular mixture."

"I see," said Holmes. "You say that you visiting servants had your own table, but shared the general supplies?"

"Exactly so, sir."

"Were you alone in the kitchen?"

"Not at all. The kitchen was a busy place, with people passing to and fro, fetching and carrying constantly."

"Let me see," said Holmes, his eyes still closed as he painted in his mind's eye a picture of the kitchen that morning. "You were sitting at the table, others bustling around you on various errands. Did you stay at your table all the time?"

"No, I had to leave the table several times. I had to fetch the bread, the butter, the ham, and the mustard ingredients."

"Were you alone at the table?"

"No. Wilkins, General Oliphant's man, was there too. He left before me, but I was soon joined at the table by Truman, Sir Lumsden's man, and Griggs, my neighbour. We were quite a party!"

"While luncheon for many of the Guns was being prepared by the castle staff?"

"That is correct, and of course luncheon had to be prepared for those not at the shoot, for the family, and for the castle staff too. It was a very busy morning in the kitchen. We at our table had to speak up to be heard above the noise and chatter."

"Some of that chatter coming from your table, I suppose. What did you talk about? The day's duties?"

"No; our duties were all decided, and gave little opportunity for debate. Sporting matters, as I recall, were the topic of much of our talk –

323

the prize-fighters of this country and America, and the St. Leger. Two at the table having recently been successful in their bets on the race. We talked about the Whitechapel killings, too, as do people up and down the country; although surely you, Mr. Holmes, know more than any about those ghastly murders?"

"And where else did your conversation lead you?"

"Our conversation turned from the murders to the perfect sandwich, and how it should be made. It is strange, is it not, how talk at a table flows, twisting this way and that?"

"What was your view on the sandwich question?"

"I favour ham sandwiches," replied the valet. "There I am at one with my employer – or was at one with him, I should say."

"Tell me about the sandwiches you made, that killed Sir William. Where did you put them?"

"I wrapped them and put them into Sir William's small hamper."

"Where did you put the hamper? Is there any way that the luncheon could have been interfered with?"

Oblonsky shook his head. "The hamper went into my satchel, which I carried at my side until I offered it to Sir William. I have been sitting here in this cell racking my brains, but for the life of me I cannot think of how anyone could have tampered with those sandwiches.

"What am I to do, Mr. Holmes? I swear to you that I did not kill Sir William, and yet I prepared the food that poisoned him. The police think me an anarchist, a man who would kill for his beliefs. How can I hope to escape the gallows? What will become of my sister?" Oblonsky's head fell forward and he covered his face in his hands.

"The outlook is not so bleak as you fear," my friend answered. "Do not despair; many men have been arrested only to be released later without facing a charge. Assure yourself that though you languish here, I shall be doing what I can to discover the truth behind Sir William's death." Holmes stood up and buttoned his coat. "Come, Watson. There is no time to waste. I must be back at Carre Castle before the last of the guests have gone."

The mists we had seen earlier in the day drifting around Carre Castle had now quite vanished, and the enchanted England of King Arthur had vanished with them, leaving in its place the real England of today: gardeners working in the grounds, a pair of bays being harnessed, and, strolling between the hedges of the parterre, the figure of Lord Henry's friend, Mr. Willoughby, smoking a cigar. Holmes did not wait to admire the view, however, but entered the castle immediately, and strode briskly down to the gun-room, where we found Inspector Shaw. "Ah, 'tis

Mr. Holmes!" said he. "How was your talk with the prisoner, sir? Did he confess?"

"He did not."

"He'll maintain his innocence to the end, I dare say."

"I dare say he will."

The inspector glanced shrewdly into Holmes's face. "You still believe that man to be innocent, do you not? I should like to know how you propose to clear his name. I must warn you, Mr. Holmes, that once we have our man, we're not quick to let him go. We may not be flashy, but we are dogged."

"An admirable virtue, inspector."

"We like to think so. May I ask you, Mr. Holmes, as you don't think Oblonsky was responsible for Sir William's death, who the devil was?"

"I prefer not to air my suspicions until they are confirmed."

"That's all very fine, but when might that be? You know, don't you, that half or more of the guests have left already, and the ones still here will be leaving this afternoon? No good having your suspicions confirmed after the bird has flown, I'd have thought."

"There I agree with you, inspector, and I assure you that the question will be decided, one way or the other, this afternoon."

"And how do you propose to arrange that?"

"Before I answer your very pertinent question, let me first put a question to you: what is the most damning evidence against Oblonsky?"

"There's a deal of evidence against him; but the diamonds found in his bag seal it for me. Circumstantial, you may say, but I'd call that a powerful circumstance."

"You agree, then, that the thief of Sir William's diamonds is in all probability the murderer?"

"Certainly I do. Why do you think we have Oblonsky in custody?"

"Well, then," said Holmes, "you will surely agree that we would do well to find the missing jewels, for when we know who has the diamonds, we will know who is behind Sir William's death."

A smirk of complacency appeared on the policeman's face. "I'm afraid you've not quite grasped the facts, Mr. Holmes. The missing diamonds, as you call them, are no longer missing. They were found in the effects of the man Oblonsky and are now in police custody in Carre station."

"Some of them were found, as you say, but others are still missing."

"The fact remains that diamonds belonging to Voigt were found in Oblonsky's bag. That's the fact, whatever your theories say. Oblonsky says he doesn't know how they came there. Well, I do."

"Perhaps you're right, Inspector. Still, I shall carry out my simple plan: I shall make a search of the luggage before it leaves the castle today. I don't want to miss the opportunity while I have it."

"I wish you good fortune hunting for those other jewels, Mr. Holmes," said the policeman. "You'll need it."

"Thank you, Inspector. Come, Watson, let us take a turn outside. The cold air may sharpen my wits."

So we left the inspector muttering about needles in haystacks. For a few minutes we walked in silence, the gravel crunching under our boots and our breath hanging like smoke in the cold air. I was the first to speak: "Are you still in the dark, then?"

Lost in thought, he walked on for a good many paces before answering with the distracted air of a man suddenly woken from sleep. "What? No, there's little mystery about how and why the Diamond King met his death. My problem now is to prove the matter to the satisfaction of the police, so the real murderer can be taken and Oblonsky released. As the inspector kindly reminded us, time is not on our side."

"How did you find out what took place yesterday?" I asked him. "Was there some clue I missed? I can't fathom this business myself, I freely admit."

"My dear fellow, I found out by asking Oblonsky, who obliged by telling me. Though the importance of what he said was not apparent to the man himself – nor to you, I gather," Holmes added, with a sly sidelong glance at me.

"I'm sorry to say it was not. Tell me, what – "

Holmes stopped and put his hand on my arm. "Hush! Do you hear that?"

It was a faint rasping sound, repeated regularly every second or so.

"I think the help I'm looking for may be close at hand," said Holmes, and sped off at such a brisk pace that I could scarcely keep up. We were hurrying alongside a bank of tall hedges that hid the castle from view. Rounding it, we found ourselves in a large yard, on three sides of which the stables were ranged. In a corner, smoke was rising from a pile of damp leaves, and beyond it I spied the source of the noise we had heard: a man in the doorway of one of the stables, sawing wood to repair the shaft of a cart that stood by.

"Excellent!" exclaimed Holmes. "There's the fellow I need. Now, Watson, it is of vital importance that the servants of the remaining guests attend me in the gun-room in twenty minutes from now. Will you ensure that? Thank you. Do not fail me. I shall meet you there in twenty minutes."

I carried out Holmes's instructions, and at the appointed time the following people were assembled in the gun-room, besides myself: Inspector Shaw and his constable, Griggs, valet to General Lamb, and Truman, Sir Lumsden's man. We were an awkward, silent group, not knowing what to say to each other, and the few minutes we were together there passed painfully slowly. It came as something of a relief when the door was flung open and Holmes strode into the room. Throwing down his coat and hat, he perched on the edge of a bench and began to question the servants about their movements and those of their masters. The answers he received were not very enlightening, serving merely to confirm what we had already heard, and offering, so far as I could tell, no new information to throw light on the mystery. After a few minutes, Holmes turned to Shaw.

"Do you have any questions for the men, Inspector?"

Shaw shrugged and shook his head.

"Nor I. Bye the bye, Inspector," he added, as we left the room, "I'll be carrying out that search of the rooms in a quarter of an hour or so. Just the servants', I think, don't you?"

Shaw darted an angry glance at Holmes, and moved his hand side to side in a furious gesture of negation, demanding immediate silence. I could well understand the inspector's anger, for it was most likely that the servants, only a few yards behind, had heard his words, and a search would be rendered quite pointless were they alerted to it. But my friend failed to notice the inspector's warning, and indeed made matters worse by continuing, "Watson, you'll help me, won't you? I'll start with Truman's room, and then we can go on to Griggs'."

I, too, tried to signal to Holmes to remain silent, although by then any harm was already done. Once we turned the corner in the corridor, however, Holmes changed utterly. The absented-minded Holmes who had strolled down the passage with us suddenly tautened in every sinew. Throwing at us a glance of the fiercest concentration, he put his finger to his lips, and, whispering in a hiss, "Follow me!" sped down the corridor. He turned, raced through a dining-hall, and then into another corridor. I realised, as I struggled to match his pace, that we were now in the East wing, at the foot of the stairs. Up he galloped, we following him as close as we could, when we met the carpenter with his tool-bag coming down, the same man whom I had seen half-an-hour ago in the stable yard. "Is it done?" asked Holmes.

"All done as you asked, sir."

"Good man!" he said, and hurried on. We ran up the second flight of stairs and found ourselves in the narrow passage Oblonsky had spoken of, with doors on either side. Holmes opened one of them. He stepped inside first, and, again enjoining us to silence with a finger to his lips, ushered in the three of us: myself, Inspector Shaw, and his constable. The room we entered was as dark as a cupboard, and not much larger, its ceiling sloping down almost to the floor. It smelt of staleness and dust, and was full of boxes, trunks, upturned chairs and other jumble. The floor was of rough planks. There was no window, but the darkness was pierced by a single beam of light in which motes of dust swirled as we disturbed the air. Holmes beckoned us over to show us its source: a hole freshly cut in the wall at about four feet from the floor. I bent down and peeped through. I saw a small room, plainly furnished, lit by a dormer window in the slope of the ceiling. Under the window was a narrow bed, and a small table with a candle and a box of vestas upon it. A fireplace stood in the opposite wall and a cupboard in the alcove. On the floor lay two cases, the lids closed.

"Griggs' room," whispered Holmes. "He will be returning to it at any moment. Absolute silence is essential! The creaking of a floorboard might be enough to alarm him. Constable, do you stand by the door, and be ready to block his escape when I give the signal."

We did not have long to wait before we heard footsteps coming up the stairs and along the passage towards us. The steps ceased, and we heard a door-handle turn. I peered into the bedroom. At first I saw nothing, only hearing the sounds of hurried movement and a step on the wooden floor, for the door was not visible through the peep-hole. Then a figure came into view; it was the manservant Griggs. He glanced about him. Had he seen or heard something to arouse his suspicions?

For a few moments he hesitated. Then, crouching down to the floor, he plunged his hands into one of the cases and started flinging out clothes left and right. He pulled out a small packet which he pushed into his coat pocket, and then returned to the search, rummaging frantically until he pulled out another packet. I felt a touch on my shoulder. Holmes was signing me to let him watch. I moved aside, and he bent down to the spy-hole, too dark a figure to make out except for where the light shone in a bright circle on his predatory eye. His hand was up, ready to give the constable the signal. We waited breathlessly, not daring to move.

Suddenly Holmes dropped his hand, and the policeman rushed out, followed by the rest of us. He flung open the door, and over his shoulder I saw Griggs leap to his feet and snarl like a cornered animal. Griggs rushed to the little window, flung it open and, to my unspeakable horror, leapt out before the constable could stop him – out into a sheer drop of forty feet to the ground. I could scarcely believe what I saw when the constable immediately dived out of the window after him, and was gone.

I ran to the window and saw the manservant and the policeman running away from me down a roof valley six feet below the window-sill, the roof sloping up on one side and on the other side a crenellated parapet. The policeman was gaining on his quarry, but before he could catch him Griggs scrambled up the roof towards its apex, grasping at a chimney-stack to help pull himself up the steep slope. The constable seemed about to follow when Griggs' feet above him, scrabbling desperately to grip on the slippery roof, dislodged several slates. The policeman shielded himself from them with his arm as they slid and clattered down the roof and over the battlements. Griggs managed to grasp the ridge and began hauling himself upwards. I was about to climb out to help when, with a cry of, "The other side, man!" Holmes dashed out of the room and across the passage into the opposite room, Oblonsky's.

We opened its window and I started to clamber out when I instantly froze; on this side the roof had no parapet, but only a gutter and the forty foot drop to the courtyard. I glanced sideways up; silhouetted against the sky was the figure of Griggs, perched on the ridge of the roof. He held something in his hand, which with a vile oath he flung down at the policeman on the other side of the roof. He reached down to pick up another missile and aimed again, but this time leaned so far back for his throw that he lost his balance; waving his arms and clutching wildly at the air he slowly toppled backwards towards us and, with a hideous wail, slithered head-first down the roof, over the guttering, and out of sight.

We stood in the courtyard. On the ground behind us lay the body of Griggs, covered by a blanket, with the constable standing guard over it until the police surgeon should arrive. Inspector Shaw, showing little of his earlier hostility, was discussing the case with Holmes.

"We were convinced at first that Oblonsky was our man, I'll grant you," he admitted. "Of course, we would have got round to Griggs soon enough, have no doubts on that score. But you were the quicker, Mr. Holmes, I won't deny it. When did you first have doubts about Oblonsky?"

"I never thought him a suspect. From the outset it seemed most unlikely to me that Oblonsky was the culprit."

The inspector twisted the end of his moustaches as he tried to make sense of this remark. "But it was he who poisoned the sandwiches," he said.

"Was it?"

"Well, he prepared them. Much the same thing."

"Not quite the same thing, but I grant you that everyone must have known that, as Sir William's valet, he was the one who prepared those sandwiches."

"Exactly."

"As you say, exactly. Tell me, Inspector, if you wished to murder a man, would you do it in the one way that you knew would immediately establish your guilt in everyone's eyes?"

The inspector frowned thoughtfully. "Well," he continued, "but what about the diamonds in his bag?"

"There again, is it likely that a murderer would leave such incriminating items in his own luggage? No, they were placed there by somebody else.

"So I started with the likelihood that Oblonsky was not the murderer. Was there anyone else I could eliminate? Well, the guests were unlikely suspects. The theft of the poison from the scullery cupboard pointed to a servant. In the bustle of the kitchens, a servant might have found his way into the scullery without attracting much attention, but not a guest. One can hardly imagine General Lamb or the Marquess appearing in the kitchens unnoticed. So, a servant other than Oblonsky was indicated.

"But further than that, I was at a loss. It was not until Oblonsky told me of the singular change in Griggs' behaviour that I had my first positive clue. Griggs' coldness, even hostility, had turned to an astonishingly warm friendship in an instant, it seemed. When had it changed so suddenly? When Oblonsky had looked through the doorway and seen Griggs rummaging in a suitcase. It was from that moment that Griggs had sworn undying loyalty to the principles so dear to Oblonsky's heart. Oblonsky himself was clearly unaware of the significance of that moment. He had seen Griggs rummaging in a suitcase and, naturally enough, thought little of it. Yet it was evidently of the greatest importance to Griggs, if he changed so suddenly from the moment he was spotted. What was his secret? I asked myself.

"Someone had stolen the diamond jewels from Voigt. Suppose that person was Griggs, I wondered, and that what Oblonsky had seen unawares was Griggs secreting the stolen jewels in his case. Griggs, surprised in his guilty act, did all he could to placate Oblonsky for the time being by claiming a kind of brotherhood with him. For the time being only, for while Oblonsky lived, Griggs was unsafe, as he thought. When the conversation in the kitchen turned to sandwiches, and Oblonsky announced his preference for ham sandwiches, Griggs leapt to the conclusion that Oblonsky was preparing ham sandwiches for himself. Here was an opportunity to silence Oblonsky permanently, he thought.

Seizing his chance, he used the confusion of the kitchen to make his move, adding the arsenic to the mustard when Oblonsky had stepped away from the table. He was lucky enough to find the rat poison in the cupboard that should have been locked. He prepared the lethal mustard, with what results we know, and put some of the less valuable jewels he had stolen into Oblonsky's case to incriminate him.

"No other hypothesis fitted the facts, but proof was lacking. The other diamonds beside the tie-pin were, I guessed, hidden somewhere in Griggs' effects. I therefore announced a search of the servants' rooms, making quite sure that Griggs, in particular, heard me, and I waited for him to lead us to the hidden jewels. A crude stratagem, perhaps, but it served its purpose."

"Ah, now I see!" exclaimed Shaw. "You had me there, Mr. Holmes, I can't deny it." He smiled as understanding dawned, but a moment later he was frowning again and pulling on his moustaches. "Wait a moment," he said. "Why bother to use any of the jewels at all to implicate Oblonsky? Although the poisoned food didn't kill the intended victim, the fact that Oblonsky prepared it was enough to have him arrested and out of the picture."

"We'll never know now," said Holmes, with a nod towards the body under the blanket, "but my guess would be that he was simply trying to be clever. He held in his hand more wealth than he could dream of, so he could afford to use some of the lesser jewels to add to Oblonsky's apparent guilt."

Shaw shook his head in despair. "The Diamond King, they call him, one of the richest men in the world. They say an army of thousands protects his diamond trade. And what becomes of him? Another man's servant steals his beloved diamonds from under his nose and then kills him by mistake."

Our trap drove up. Opening the door, Holmes turned to the inspector.

"I take it you'll be releasing Oblonsky without delay?"

"I will indeed."

"Then my business here is finished."

Holmes and I climbed in, the driver flicked the reins, and we set off for Brailston Thorpe. As we turned into the main drive, I saw a group of four or five men gathered under one of the vast elms that lined the drive on either side. Two of the men were on horseback. One of those on foot gave a signal to the driver to pull up, and walked over to us.

"Mr. Sherlock Holmes?"

"That is my name."

"Perhaps you would be good enough to step over here. Lord Ambleside would like to speak with you."

As he approached the group, the man on the tallest horse turned towards him and looked down. "Mr. Holmes, the detective! You have been looking into the death of my friend Voigt."

"I have, my Lord."

"It was his servant, they tell me."

"It was General Lamb's servant."

"Another one? What a damnable business! Is he under arrest?"

"He is dead, my lord."

"No, the servant, the one who killed Voigt."

"He is dead. He fell from the roof not an hour ago."

"The roof? What was he doing on the roof?" He raised his hand to forestall an unnecessary answer. "Well, it doesn't much matter now. I won't keep you any longer, Mr. Holmes. Rat poison!' he sighed. "What a beastly way to go!"

The Marquess turned back to his group, leaving Holmes and me to continue our journey home.

The Adventure of
Urquhart Manse
by Will Thomas

"Mr. Holmes," our visitor said, "I must ask you to listen to my story in its entirety, without question or comment until it is done. Afterward, I will readily answer anything that you may ask. If you can accomplish this feat, I assure you, you will have succeeded already where Scotland Yard has failed."

Sherlock Holmes raised a brow in her direction, and eyed her speculatively. She was a comely young woman, almost too young to have the word *Mrs.* in front of her name.

"Very well, madam," he said.

"And you, Doctor, do I have your word as well?"

"You have it most readily, Mrs. Urquhart. Now pray tell us your story."

"Very well," she said, and sat back in the basket chair in our sitting room. She was petite, and smartly dressed, but there were dark circles under her eyes signaling sleepless nights. Something of significance was troubling her.

"First of all, I grew up in Tunbridge Wells, the daughter of a merchant sea captain, Daniel Cavell, who went down with his ship in the Indian Ocean off of Borneo when I was six. Since then I have lived with my mother, or did until I was married last year.

"I met Alexander Urquhart at the garden party of a friend, which he admits to having been dragged to by his brother, Andrew. Alec and I were attracted to each other immediately, and within a month our courtship began. The family lives in an old estate named Urquhart Manse, on the Old Kent Road, outside of town. It is set back among trees, and has fallen on better days. Alec invited us there for lunch one day. It was a gloomy old pile, in need of a woman's touch. While we were there, mother and I had the chance to meet Andrew, his younger brother. He must have been younger by mere minutes, for the two were twins."

So far, Holmes was keeping his promise to her, but was writing furiously upon his cuff with a small, silver pencil.

"Alec works in London as a stock-broker, but Andrew – I'm afraid he doesn't do much of anything. He claims to be an actor, but on most days he makes small repairs on the estate which, frankly, he has no skill

333

in making. Both he and Alec are tall and red-haired, but while Andrew is clean-shaven, Alec has a becoming moustache.

"We were married before Christmas, and I moved into the manse. Sometimes I think there is an air of tragedy about the place. Alec admitted to me that he had assumed he and Andrew were the last of the family in his line, but that my arrival had given him hope for the future. I took the house in hand, trying to brighten it up a bit, but I have been aided in no way whatsoever by the housekeeper, Mrs. Petrie. She is a dour old Scotswoman, who seems to resent my presence in the house. She used to be the boys' nanny, however, and Alec wouldn't think of getting rid of her. She has a wing all to herself, the east wing, which Andrew claims has been water damaged by holes in the roof which he hopes to eventually patch. That is how matters stood until last week."

Holmes cleared his throat. I had at least a dozen questions, and I was sure his must approach the century mark at least. However, he had made a promise. He gestured for her to continue.

"Monday morning I arose early, intending to look over the kitchen accounts before Mrs. Petrie arrived. I found Andrew dead at the foot of the stairs. The staircase is old and worm-eaten, and some of the boards are loose. I have tripped on them myself, and had taken Andrew to task for not tending to them. Obviously he had come down in the middle of the night too quickly, and fallen. I woke everyone with my cry. Mrs. Petrie made some rather rude remarks in her grief. She claimed she knew my presence in the old house would bring tragedy.

"Alec was beside himself with grief. He ran into the hall in his dressing gown and held his brother's stiff body until the police and an inspector arrived. Of course, I cannot say what it must be like to lose a twin brother, but my husband was more broken up than I have ever seen him.

"Since then he has been very polite, but distant. When I taxed him about it, he told me it was grief. He seems very distracted, and once or twice he has barked at Mrs. Petrie, which I've never seen him do before. It's obvious he has been under a great deal of strain. I suggested he take a few days off from his firm to grieve properly, but he dismissed the idea out of hand. Two nights ago, I awoke to find Alec standing in my bedchamber, glaring at me. I almost cried out, but he merely turned and left the chamber. It gave me a strange, unsettled feeling. I almost wished I had never come there. That's all, I'm afraid. Yesterday I called our solicitor and asked for the name of a good detective, and he gave me yours. I made the appointment and here I am."

"Good?" Holmes asked.

"Well, competent rather. He said you were the best in London."

334

Holmes gave a thin-lipped smile.

"That is a pretty little story. May I ask questions now?"

She gripped the hand rails of the basket chair.

"Ask away, Mr. Holmes."

"Did you immediately suspect the man dead at the foot of the stairs was your husband, or did that come later?"

I suspect some women would have fallen apart at the bluntness of the question, but she swallowed and answered.

"It wasn't immediate, no, but his manner was so different afterward that I began to think he might not be Alec at all."

"Did Andrew Urquhart give you any indication that he might be attracted to you?"

"I fear he did. He watched me all the time. Sometimes I found him standing in a doorway just watching me. At meals he was very loquacious, quite unlike Alec, and he tended to flirt, even in front of his own brother. Twice he told me he wished he had been the first to meet me at the garden party."

"I assume Alec is the heir."

"Yes, Mr. Holmes. Alec owns all the property, such as it is, but he is also responsible for it. He provides the sole income we all live upon."

"May I take it Andrew had no knowledge of stocks and bonds or brokerage?"

"Not a whit," Mary Urquhart said. "Or so I assume."

"The only physical difference between them was the moustache your husband wears? There was no birthmark or other feature which might help you determine which brother is now living with you?"

"None, I'm afraid. I wish it were that simple."

"Perhaps it is that simple. Why not simply ask him if he is Andrew?"

"I've wanted to for ages, but if I did, and he actually is Alec, it would crush him. He is having a difficult time enough dealing with his brother's death."

"And if he is Andrew?"

"Then he could simply lie. He was an actor, and never as honest in his speech as my husband."

For a moment she shook, and I was concerned, for Holmes abominates emotion during a case. However, she mastered herself, and bade him continue.

"Do you think you could recognize a false moustache?"

"I think so, but Andrew was very good at such things. He kept a make-up table for his creations."

"Kept or keeps, Mrs. Urquhart? In your heart of hearts, do you believe he is or isn't your husband?"

"I'm not saying I believe, Mr. Holmes, but I very much suspect he is not. If it is so, has he killed his own brother in order to possess everything, all of it, including me?"

"That is what Watson and I intend to find out. Did Andrew Urquhart seem in any way prone to violence?"

She considered the matter carefully, tapping at her lip in thought.

"He was not normally as forceful as Alec in speech, but he was more guarded. Who really knew what he was like privately? I will say this, he was not without strength. Some of the repairs he made required lifting heavy wood and rock. Just because his interest was in theater did not mean he was physically weak."

"How did Andrew die, if, indeed, it was Andrew? What was the coroner's verdict?"

"It was ruled an accident. Misadventure was the term he used. He fell coming down the staircase and broke his neck."

Holmes turned to me and raised his eyebrows.

"Yes, a fall down stairs can frequently result in a broken neck. The head is thrown into all kinds of contortions by tumbling against hard surfaces," I told them.

Holmes turned back to our guest and tented his fingers in front of him.

"And when you say you woke to find your husband staring at you, how exactly was he staring? Did he seem menacing, or troubled, or did he appear angry? What was your impression?"

"It was really remarkable. First of all, his nightshirt and hair were rumpled from sleep. The look he gave me I can only describe as fierce. I almost feared for my life. I would have tried to soothe him, but he suddenly turned and left the room, as if in a dream."

"I see," Holmes responded. "Tell me, Mrs. Urquhart, since you first met your husband, up until your arrival here today, did you find the inhabitants of Urquhart Manse to be secretive? Are they, for example, cut off from all their neighbors? Did you suspect that they were colluding together to keep some fact or facts away from you?"

"Oh, very much so, Mr. Holmes. That is exactly how I felt, and feel even now."

"Then Mrs. Urquhart, I accept your case. How amenable is the man you live with to accepting visitors?"

"Not at all, sir. As Mrs. Petrie says, 'we keep ourselves to ourselves.' However, the Old Kent Road is often used by hikers. I believe there are guides for walking in the area."

"Capital! Do not be surprised if a pair of tired and footsore travellers suddenly appear at your door this evening."

"I shall look forward to it. What of your fee?"

"I shall send a billet afterward. Nothing calamitous, I assure you."

"Thank you, Mr. Holmes. Dr. Watson."

I showed her to the door. When I returned, Holmes already had the Baedecker in hand and was looking up the railway time tables to Tunbridge Wells.

"Have you anything pressing in your surgery this afternoon or tomorrow?" he asked.

"Would it matter if I did?"

"I'm sure it would to someone."

He rubbed his hands in anticipation of an interesting case. Then he stuffed shag tobacco into his old oily clay and lit it.

"Surely this fellow can't think he can kill his own brother in order to take his wife, pretty as she was," I told him.

"Did you find her pretty? I hadn't noticed. I'm sure there is far more to it than wife-stealing, Watson, but it is no good theorizing before the facts. Let us have a good lunch and then prepare for a journey to Kent."

After lunch we changed into clothes more fitting for the country, along with stout walking shoes. We loaded a pair of rucksacks with enough clothing for a few days, and I chose a stout blackthorn stick and my old service revolver, just in case. We were at Charing Cross Station near one, in order to catch the South Eastern Railway commuter train south. I had no scruples about abandoning the hot, torpid city for rural Kent on such a beautiful May afternoon.

Arriving in Tunbridge Wells, Holmes purchased an ordinance map and a copy of A WALKING GUIDE TO HISTORIC KENT. Holmes does not take exercise, but he had a nervous, energetic constitution that was stimulated by a walk of a few miles. As for myself, my war wound was always aided by a marathon walk in the country, and my lungs invigorated by the air of the south coast.

We took an omnibus out of the old royal town and alighted again in the country a couple of miles from Urquhart Manse. Rather than growing tired, we were both enervated by the walk, and the anticipation of what we would find when we got there. Finally, we spotted the house, set back from the road by a tall wrought-iron fence. Its yard had been let go to ruin. The building was a horseshoe shaped affair, with both wings facing the back, and a portico in the front. The bones of the old house were still strong, but the surface had been weathered by years of neglect. It nearly had the look of an old haunted house. I could see how a new bride brought to such a house would find it daunting.

"This I where you turn up lame, old fellow," Holmes said.

I gave a cry of pain and removed my left shoe. Holmes leant me a shoulder and helped me to the front door, where we knocked loudly. After a few minutes a small, sharp-faced woman answered, looking at us with suspicion.

"I say," Holmes began. "My friend has just turned an ankle in the rut in front of your house. I think he needs medical attention."

"Away wi' ye!" Mrs. Petrie cried. "We need nane of your kind here!"

"Who is it?" a voice I recognized as our client's asked.

"A pair of vagabonds by the look of 'em," the housekeeper replied.

"My friend is hurt!" Holmes called out. "He needs a doctor!"

"Oh, dear," Mary Urquhart said, and a moment later appeared at the door behind the housekeeper. "What has happened?"

"He has turned an ankle, ma'am," Mrs. Petrie said. "He can walk back to town well enough. It's probably a scheme to bilk us for money."

"What is it?" a man asked, appearing behind both women. He was tall, with a head of red hair and blue eyes. He wore a moustache. It could only be Urquhart, though which one was still a matter of dispute.

"This poor man has fallen and injured himself. I think he must get off his ankle."

"We don't take visitors here," Urquhart replied.

"But he has injured himself, probably in one of the ruts in front of the house. You really must do something about them, Alec."

"No visitors," he repeated.

"Such nonsense!" Mrs. Urquhart said. "Come in, gentlemen, and rest yourselves. No doubt you have walked for miles. Mrs. Petrie, bring some tea."

"I doubt there is much call for that," the housekeeper said.

"Mary," Urquhart warned.

"Alec," she implored. "They are guests in our home, our very first, in fact. I hope you will see that they are given proper hospitality. I would not want to be embarrassed in my own home."

Confronted by an obstinate wife and two strangers expecting him to do the right thing, he finally relented.

"Very well. Come in, gentlemen. Forgive my rude country manners. I'm Alec Urquhart."

"Sherlock Holmes," my friend said, pumping his hand.

"John Watson."

I limped forward and fell into a stuffed chair.

338

"We were taking a Kentish tour, with the aid of a guidebook," Holmes said. "Watson and I are solicitors in London. My friend just had to get out of the City, you know."

"Fresh air," I muttered, as I slowly raised my "injured" ankle to a hassock. "I don't think it is broken."

"Then you'd best be on your way!" the housekeeper called from the doorway.

"Tea, Mrs. Petrie!" Mary Urquhart insisted.

Grumbling, the woman complied. She was a dour looking older woman, thin and bony, but with a will of iron. Obviously she had been given the run of the house, and had no problem offering her opinions. Mrs. Urquhart was challenged to keep her in her place.

"I work in the City," Alec went on.

"Oh, really? Where?" Holmes asked.

"Carr and Threadgill, in the Commercial Road."

"A stockbroker!" Holmes said to me. "We must be careful with this one, Watson. A canny firm by its reputation."

"It is. How far did you hope to get today?" Urquhart asked.

"Wadhurst."

"As far as that? I'm afraid you wouldn't have reached it unless you walked all night."

"You disappoint me exceedingly. Is there an inn nearby?"

"Not within five miles, I'm afraid."

"Alec!" Mary Urquhart cried. "Invite them to spend the night! We have plenty of rooms."

"I don't think that would be appropriate, being in mourning for Andrew as we are."

"But Mr. Watson is injured! He cannot walk anywhere, and there is no way to hire a vehicle at this time of night."

Urquhart looked about to argue, but after staring into the eyes of our client for a few moments he finally relented.

"I shall have to inform Mrs. Petrie."

"I'll do it," Mrs. Urquhart said. With a twinkle in her eye she left the room.

"We regret imposing ourselves upon you, sir," Holmes stated, after she was gone. "Watson and I could pay – "

"I'm sure that will not be necessary," came the reply. Urquhart's pale features colored.

Mrs. Petrie showed us to our rooms with as little grace as she dared. Dinner consisted of overcooked beef and undercooked potatoes. Afterward, our host treated us to whisky-and-sodas.

"Have you lived here long, sir?" Holmes asked.

"For generations, Mr. Holmes. My ancestor came south among the Sassenach with James 1st. Our family has been here even since."

"These old houses require a good deal of repair. There is always something breaking or needing to be fixed."

"You have no idea. It seems at times that the house is falling down about our ears. My dear brother Andrew was doing his best to maintain the house, but alas, he is gone now. He met with an accident on the staircase."

"We are sorry to hear that," Holmes said.

"Yes, he is gone, right when we needed him most."

Urquhart seemed disinclined to discuss the matter further. We left him brooding and staring into the fire.

"What are your impressions, Watson?" Holmes asked, when we were in our room.

"If the man is a villain, he is a better actor than I would have credited. What did you think of the moustache?"

"It appears genuine, but a trifle sparse. He could have grown it in under a false one within a week."

Holmes raised his arms to the ceiling and formed fists in frustration.

"How I wish I could have seen the brothers together, side by side. They say twins can be identical, but really, no two people are exactly alike. The smallest blemish, spot or mole can distinguish one from the other."

"That housekeeper is a bit of work," I said. "I wonder if she is naturally averse to strangers, or whether there a reason she wants us out of here."

"Let us not forget Mrs. Urquhart waking to find a man glaring at her, no matter which brother it was."

"You know, Holmes, I suspect it might be somnambulism. If so, I suspect her life is in danger. Such cases can lead to violence, particularly if disturbed. If his brother tried to wake him on the stair, for example, just such an outcome might occur. But what are we to do?"

"We must wait until the family settles for the night, then go exploring."

"The East Wing!" I cried, rubbing my hands together.

"Yes, Watson, I am particularly interested in the East Wing."

Holmes and I were old hands at waiting for the stroke of midnight. We slipped off our shoes and made our way slowly up the grand staircase to the first floor. Holmes went ahead, feeling for every creaking stair in our path, while I brought up the rear with my "twisted ankle". We were taking a risk of being caught, but I knew I had my trusty revolver with me, if worse came to worst.

The East Wing was a shambles, with falling plaster, peeling wallpaper, and moldy old carpets. All the rooms, which numbered four to a side in this wing, were dark, save for one at the far end. The floor was ancient and dusty, but I noticed several footmarks going back and forth. Holmes measured his foot against one.

"Size ten," he said. "Very near the size of the Brothers Urquhart. One of them must have come here recently, but for what purpose I cannot say."

We began to open the various doors in the wing. All were unlocked. Some were bedrooms untenanted, and smelling of damp and wood rot. A few were in need of repair, and one had tools and paint tins on the floor. Holmes stepped forward and ran his finger across a lid, it came away covered in dust.

"So far, Mrs. Urquhart's opinion of her brother-in-law's carpentry skills have been confirmed. But hush!"

We heard a voice coming from the one room in the wing with light gleaming from under the door. It was at the far end, the farthest from the staircase. Why would a housekeeper want to be so far from her kitchen, I asked myself. I could not mistake Mrs. Petrie's shrill and peevish tone coming from the room. To whom was she speaking? From what I could make out, she was giving someone her litany of complaints about the new visitors and the lady of the house. I strained my ear but could hear no response whatsoever. Was it herself she was speaking to, or a dog, or was someone else in the room? I began to imagine all sorts of things. Something was very wrong in this house that Mary Urquhart had come to. It was far from the ideal home a bride expects upon her marriage.

We were progressing down the hall, in order to press our ears against the wall of the housekeeper's room, when I accidentally trod upon a board that squeaked. Holmes nipped behind an old standing clock, while I jumped back into the dark recess of a door frame. We were just in time. Mrs. Petrie stepped out with a raised candle and looked about her. She had a shotgun broken open over her arm. Our seeming advantage evaporated.

"Who's there?" she cried. "No tricks, now!"

We dared not move. She looked about and raised her lamp higher, but did not come further into the hall. If it were a dog she was speaking to, she might unleash it, and if the rest of the house was any indication, it would not be a border collie. However, she closed the door and apparently did not give us a second thought. After a moment or two

341

Holmes stepped from behind the clock and gestured for me to follow him.

"That was a close call," I said, when we were out of the wing again.

"Quite," Holmes said. "The last thing I expected was that Mrs. Petrie would be so heavily armed."

"What do we do now? Go back to our room?"

"No. We'll be forced to leave in the morning, so we must use our time wisely. I wish to examine the stairs where Alec Urquhart's body was found."

So saying, he pulled a small dark lantern from his pocket and lit it with a pack of vestas. Then he carried it with him and led the way to the staircase.

"Don't you mean Andrew Urquhart?" I asked.

"Do I? That remains to be seen.

Reaching the bottom of the stairway, Holmes immediately went down upon his hands and knees, examining the carpet with the aid of the candle. At one point he crawled down the steps like a tomcat, examining the decayed wood of the steps. When he reached the floor where the body came to rest after the fatal fall, he even went down upon his stomach, examining the floor with a pocket lens. Finally, he sniffed the carpet thoroughly.

"What is it?" I asked.

"Soap," He answered. "Scented with bay rum."

"Shaving soap!"

"Precisely. I think we can both conjecture how it got there."

"I'm surprised the local inspector didn't notice it."

"I'd have been surprised if he had," Holmes said.

"Where do we go from here?" I asked, as he stood and stretched his lean frame.

"To our beds. If you will play watchman for the first few hours, and listen for any movement in the house, I will stay awake until dawn. We must be ready when Mrs. Petrie comes down for breakfast."

"Ready to do what?" I asked.

"Oh, I have a small diversion planned, but in order for it to work, we must separate the housekeeper from her rifle."

My three hour watch was uneventful, and after I shook Holmes awake, I lay down upon my bed and dozed while fully dressed. I was awakened at dawn by a rooster somewhere nearby, reminding me how far we were from the cosmopolitan streets of London. When I sat up in bed, I found Holmes sitting in a chair with his knees drawn up, tobacco burning in his clay pipe.

"Are you ready?" he asked eagerly.

"Is Mrs. Petrie stirring?"

"She has just gone to the kitchen to light the stove. Shall we explore the East Wing without her presence?"

"By Jove, yes!"

We climbed the stairs again, I with my hand on my revolver and he armed with a set of skeleton keys. Holmes was a match for any burglar. We reached the housekeeper's door, and while he picked the lock, I put my ear to the door, listening for any sound within. There was no whining from a dog that I could hear, or any cry, human or animal. The room appeared to be deserted.

"That's got it," my friend said, but before I could respond the door flew open in our faces and we were knocked to the ground. Something sailed over my head. I had just enough time to turn my head and glare after it.

"What was it?" Holmes asked, for I had a better look at whoever had knocked us over than he.

"It was most definitely a man," I stated.

"Did you recognize him?"

"How should I have recognized him?"

Just then there was a scream from the corridor. It sounded like Mrs. Urquhart. We leapt to our feet and ran down the hall as quickly as possible. In the hall we passed Mrs. Petrie, armed with nothing more dangerous than a spatula. She glared at us scornfully as I ran past on my injured ankle.

Mary Urquhart wailed again, and as we neared her door we could hear the sounds of furniture being upended. As we entered, we saw Alec Urquhart locked in a desperate struggle with another man. Both were ginger haired, and when the other fellow turned his head I saw he was his double in every way, down to the very moustache on his upper lip.

Sherlock Holmes did not hesitate, but jumped upon the back of the combatant who was dressed, Alec Urquhart still being in his nightshirt. I joined the fray as well, seizing the man's muscular arm and trying to keep him from strangling Urquhart. Was this Andrew returned from the grave, I wondered, or had Alec set up this up to trap his brother into revealing his jealousy?

Whoever we were wrestling with, he was uncommonly strong, and seemed to have little difficulty tossing all three of us about the room. Holmes had an arm wrapped about the fellow's throat, but he had little effect against his bull neck. This version of Urquhart seemed larger and stronger, with a deep chest and apelike arms. With one shake of his arm he set me flying against the wall. Mrs. Urquhart, cowering in a corner, shrieked again.

343

"Archie!" I heard Mrs. Petrie's voice behind me. "Put the man down immediately!"

In answer, he swept the air with one of his long arms and knocked the poor woman senseless. Then he tore Holmes from his shoulders and flipped him over onto his back with a jarring crash. Having done that, he closed his hands about the throat of the last of the Urquharts, and began to squeeze the life from him.

Alec Urquhart's face was already pale, but now it turned chalky white, and his lips looked blue. I tried to remove the fingers from his fragile throat, but they were like steel. The poor man could not take much more of this. As a medical man, I feared he was approaching death.

"Archie!" Mary Urquhart barked. "What do you think you're doing? You put him down this instant!"

The muscular attacker suddenly looked up, his concentration broken. His face looked perplexed, and possibly even ashamed.

"Did you hear me?" she continued. "Am I going to have to repeat myself? Take your hands away now.'

The thick, ruddy fingers began to pull away from Urquhart's throat, leaving him coughing and gasping for air. The intruder looked down sheepishly.

"You know this man?" I asked.

"I believe he is the man I found staring at me that night. He looks very much like my late husband. He can only be another brother!"

"Thank you, Archie," she continued, using the name the housekeeper had supplied. "I'm very proud of you. Now can you come over here and sit beside me? I shall let you hold my hand if you do."

A feint smile grew on the fellow's lips and he crossed the room to her. I saw an expression on his face which explained everything. This brother was mentally slow.

"So," I said. "The Urquharts weren't twins at all. They were triplets."

"Precisely," Holmes said. "Watson, would you be so good as to see to Mrs. Petrie?"

I crossed to the old woman. She was in her sixties and the blow had sent her sprawling. I helped her up and nothing appeared broken, but she there was a dark bruise upon her cheek.

"My god," our host finally choked out.

"Do I have the honor of addressing Mr. Andrew Urquhart?" Holmes asked.

All of us leaned forward for the answer. Mary Urquhart hand even squeezed the hand that had been choking our host a few minutes earlier.

"You do," he finally muttered.

344

The young bride burst into tears. I handed her my handkerchief, while the strange doppelganger patted her hand with mute concern on his face.

"You mustn't think I killed him, Mary," Urquhart went on. "I was genuinely happy for Alec, even if I admired you myself. The morning I found him dead at the foot of the stair was the worst of my life, but I could tell no one."

"You shaved your brother's corpse, fashioned a false moustache, and took his place," Holmes said.

"I did. I'm afraid I panicked. We had always been trained to keep the family secret, you see, and to never let anyone know about Archie."

"Did he kill your brother?"

"I wish I knew, Mr. Holmes. Archie has a temper, and afterward he doesn't remember things. The truth is he has been very curious about Mary since the wedding. I warned Alec that it was time to move Archie to a proper facility, where he could be looked after properly, but he wouldn't hear of it. We'd had several arguments both before and after the wedding about how Archie was handling all the changes that had occurred, but Alec took all my suggestions as an affront to his abilities. He was head of the Urquhart clan, you see, and he would make all the decisions."

"You understand these events put you in a bad light," Holmes said. "You are the chief suspect in a murder investigation."

"I begin to suspect, sir, that your being here is no accident. Just who are you, really?"

"Mr. Urquhart, I am a consulting detective hired by your sister-in-law to look into the matter of several curious events that have happened since she arrived at this house. I cannot keep the matter hidden, you understand. A man has been slain."

"I understand that, sir, and I am ready to take any punishment the courts find necessary. I loved my brother, and a day hasn't gone by that I haven't regretted his death. I've made several mistakes, but only to try to rectify the large one Alec made when he brought Mary here, yet refused to tell her about Archie."

"I understand there are loose boards upon the staircase. Have you formed a conclusion as to what happened?"

"No, sir, I haven't. I mean, he could have fallen in the middle of the night. The stair was loose and I intended to fix it. However, Archie was agitated the night when Alec fell, but then he is often agitated without causing trouble."

"Many men in your situation would have taken advantage of the situation. Why didn't you?"

"I'd like to think that Mary's arrival awoke in me new possibilities. I wanted to be a better man to please her, not a worse one."

"So, you became a stockbroker," my friend, a thin smile playing on his lips.

"Actually, I rather enjoyed that part. Alec always talked about his work, so I knew the names of his partners, and what he did there. I was terrified on my first day, but I found I enjoyed the work."

"And what was Mrs. Petrie's part in all this?" Holmes continued.

I looked over and saw that the woman had begun crying, the tears rolling down her withered cheeks.

"I was the children's governess before I became housekeeper," she said. "We knew within a few years that something was wrong with Archie. Mr. Urquhart put it about that he had died of diphtheria, then sought out the best medical care. All of them suggested Archie be put away, because of his violent tendencies, but the old master refused. 'A family must look after its own,' he said."

"You kept the secret to this day," Holmes said.

"Aye, and I warn't Mr. Alec he had no business bringing a bride home to this old manse. Nothing but tragedy would e'er come of it. I've naught against you, ma'am. You've a good soul, but I knew the secret would come out one way or the other, and not for good."

There was a silence in the room for a moment or two.

"So, what happens now, Mr. Holmes?" Andrew asked. "According to the courts, I am a dead man."

Holmes turned to me.

"Watson, what is your opinion of Mr. Urquhart's actions?"

I considered the matter. Sometimes Holmes would saddle me with the responsibility for an entire case, almost on a whim.

"It would have been better if he had revealed what had occurred immediately, rather than keep it to himself. However, he did not take advantage of his circumstances by placing demands upon another man's wife. I believe he was merely trying to contain the mounting problems in order to keep a secret that was not his."

"I believe you are 'off the hook', sir," Holmes told Urquhart. "I cannot fault Watson's logic or judgment."

"Thank you, Mr. Holmes, but what do we do now? According to the law, I am a dead man."

"You want an opinion, sir? Very well, I shall give it. You must resign your position on some pretense and sell this tragic old building. Archie must go into a proper facility with doctors to watch over him. Mrs. Petrie should be given a proper severance, if he wishes to leave. I suggest you move away and change your name."

I thought it a harsh sentence, but the only one under the circumstances.

"And what of Mary?" Andrew Urquhart asked.

"That is a decision she must make for herself."

"I shall go home to my parents' house for a while. I have some thinking to do."

"And what of Archie?" Andrew went on. "He might be innocent of the crime."

"Perhaps, but your brother must be put away in either case, whereas if you are found responsible, you will surely hang for it."

Holmes turned and regarded our client.

"Mrs. Urquhart, do you consider this matter concluded?"

"Yes, Mr. Holmes. Thank you."

"Watson and I must return to London, then. Our continued absence encourages mischief among the Underworld."

We gathered our few possessions and made our way back to the station. Holmes did not speak about the case again until we were on the platform.

"A family secret causes all sorts of mischief, Watson. It is a conspiracy as much as any governmental plot, and the one whom is hurt the most is often the most innocent."

Some cases end with a timely resolution, while others we don't hear about for months or even years later. One day during the holiday season a couple entered our consulting rooms in Baker Street unannounced. They were a fashionably dressed couple living in Paris, where intrigue was not unknown. They were a Mr. and Mrs. Anderson of the 18th Arrondissement. He was a stockbroker, with a shock of red hair and a nice looking imperial. His wife, "Marie", looked quite content. As a medical man, I suspected she was expecting a child. Perhaps there would be more Urquharts after all.

The Adventure of the
Seventh Stain
by Daniel McGachey

Preface: The Identity of Cases

Such does his celebrity continue to grow that, despite his retirement to his bees and his studies in Sussex, many are the letters that still arrive daily for Sherlock Holmes, and in particular since my friend finally granted permission that I might share with an admiring world the details of his return from that watery grave in which my published accounts had left him a decade earlier. This, naturally, is a source of considerable pride to the humble narrator of Holmes's adventures; the satisfaction further bolstered by the fact that the post brings me almost as many letters, gifts and requests for a reply or souvenir as are received by my celebrated associate.

Rather, it is *usually* a source of pride. Yet there is little to crow over when a goodly proportion of the day's mail is devoted to messages proclaiming one a liar, a fraud, or a charlatan. There have admittedly been prior accusations that my works are not entirely truthful records, not least from Sherlock Holmes himself who was never shy of offering a detailed critique, whether one had been invited or not. Yet opening a ninth, then a tenth missive in succession to accuse me not simply of the "embellishments" that were the basis for Holmes's disapproval, but of outright deception against my loyal readers, is not a situation for which I was remotely prepared.

The source of this unheralded epidemic of disapprobation lies with the latest edition of *The Strand Magazine,* in which I fulfilled what I considered a long-standing obligation in presenting the adventure I had dubbed "The Second Stain". This title had prompted its own flow of missives requesting further details, since I first made passing mention of it in certain earlier accounts. And it is these fleeting allusions that now cause such ire, for the details I had previously let slip and the particulars in my recently published tale bearing that designation do not tally. So, far from rewarding the curiosity excited by those teasing hints, I have succeeded only in provoking the wrath of those in whom curiosity has turned to frustration.

Revisiting those earlier references to a "Second Stain", I see that in one instance I have it listed as an episode in which Holmes failed to

348

conclude his case satisfactorily, while in the other I have referred to an incident involving some of the most powerful houses in the land. And while, as in my now published statement, the household of the Right Honourable Trelawney Hope may surely be regarded as noble and powerful, certain of the international players initially mentioned are missing from the scene, and Holmes's return of the document that threatened not only his client's political career but also the fate of nations could in no way be regarded a failure. Thus, the public cry of "substitution" or "fake" is not so readily dismissed. So I readily admit that this case is neither of those to which I so recklessly alluded in the past. Yet nor is it a fiction to obscure the true events. It is without question the story of "The Second Stain". However it is not the *only* adventure of Sherlock Holmes to bear this title!

In truth, amongst my notes there exist details of no fewer than *seven* separate cases to which the appellation has been applied; though on delving into those files, closer examination of my occasionally unintelligible handwriting reveals one of these actually to be labelled "The Second *Strain*", dealing as it does with the misappropriation of a brace of bacillus cultures, each harmless unless brought into contact with the other. It was only due to the rapid action of Sherlock Holmes that half of London narrowly avoided catching a fatal bout of cold. Thus we reduce the total to six, and the affair of the Trelawney Hope document diminishes the number yet further.

Of the others, the case previously referred to as unresolved falls into that category in which Holmes was unable, as in his customary maxim, to entirely eliminate the impossible, herein with relation to a chamber in which a supposed "phantom bloodstain" refused, after more than two centuries, to dry. Holmes was swift in finding the cause of a second, more recent bloodstain and, in turn, the murderess who sought to mask her crime with an ancient curse. But my friend's determination to dispel the far older mystery of the original, livid splash was to remain frustrated, and my report of the venture lies sealed with those other apparently impossible cases that may one day find their solutions in science, yet which, for now, remain within the province of superstition and the supernatural.

Two further sets of notes refer to acts of vandalism which were easily resolved and offer little to excite the reader's interest, while the sixth I find listed involved a celebrated Renaissance painting in a prominent gallery whose discoloured layers of three-hundred year old varnish artfully disguised its far more recent genesis on the easel of an illiterate flower-seller in the cellar of a Soho gin-house.

349

Which leaves us with one outstanding case, and this, indeed, is that which my readers have been clamouring for. But they must clamour in vain, for it remains one which discretion still stays my hand from signing over to the public gaze. But record it I will, for an undefined future reader, which is a nobler reason than – by documenting the events they are so curious about in papers which must still remain sealed away from their gaze – to spite all those who have taken time to put pen to paper and stamp to envelope to libel my name. Petty? Even if so, by the time other eyes peruse these pages, my pettiness will be long forgotten and posterity will have benefited, whatever my motive.

I. Three Callers at 221B

I had been married little under half-a-year and, as the bright summer days lengthened, my time was divided between the domestic comforts of the marital home and my efforts to establish my new practice. I had not forgotten my good friend, of course, nor would my dear Mary have allowed me to do so, and I endeavoured to make myself known at my former lodgings as often as my schedule permitted. The last such visit had seen our reminiscences cut short by the sudden arrival, and yet more sudden collapse, of Captain Gideon Blackhall of the *S.S. Genevieve*, and a leisurely few hours stretched dramatically into those several tense days in which we strove to uncover the reason behind the captain's sudden lapses into prolonged stretches of fearful, nightmare-haunted sleep. Now, having just received a much revived Blackhall in my surgery, I was able to confirm that the opiates he had been surreptitiously fed, so that his first mate and crew might tend to the practicalities of their thriving smuggling trade undisturbed, would soon be out of his system. So it was with the intention of relaying this good news to Holmes that I ascended the well-worn stairs to my old sitting room.

"Please, calm yourself," said Sherlock Holmes soothingly to the young woman who started from her seat as I bounded into the room. "You have no cause for alarm with Dr. Watson. He may have forgotten his manners as regards knocking on doors in houses where he no longer resides, but in other regards he is quite the gentleman."

"My apologies, Holmes," I stammered. "I shall call again at a more convenient time. I'm deeply sorry if I startled you, Miss . . . ."

"Miss Lodge had just begun telling me her most interesting story, Watson. I'm sure you won't mind my friend sitting in while we conclude our meeting, Miss Lodge. Besides being a gentleman, as I said, there is no man better to have at one's side in a time of crisis."

350

As grateful as I was for Holmes's endorsement, I was still more gratified to see the panicked expression on the young woman's face relax into a somewhat bashful smile. "I'm pleased to meet you, Doctor." She offered me her gloved hand, but as I bent to take it she froze indecisively, as if caught in mid-curtsey and, both rather flustered, we straightened up and parted.

Before I could return any pleasantry, Holmes cut in, declaring, "Seat yourself and stop distracting my client from the statement of her case, if you would, Watson." The face of mock chastisement I pulled at this command saw the lady put a handkerchief to her mouth to stifle a laugh, and even Holmes permitted himself a thin smile. "Well, as we all seem to be comfortable in one another's presence, let us continue. Miss Lodge, if you would briefly summarise what you have already told me for my friend's benefit?"

She turned to me, still too self-conscious to look me fully in the eye, and thereby allowing me the opportunity to inspect her more closely. She could have been no more than seventeen, neatly but plainly attired, though both the heaviness of her clothing and the thickness of her gloves were vastly unsuited to the summer's warmth. Her face was scrubbed and pink, her eyes bright, but with a puffiness around them that spoke of recent tears. "My name is Florence Lodge, sir, and my problem is my whole family's problem, for it is our poor older sister who has been taken from us." My eyes must have darted upwards, as if to the Heavens, for she shook her head firmly. "Taken by the law!" She paused, addressing the sudden rise in her voice, her tone as she resumed remaining studiedly polite. "Your pardon, but she has been taken from us by the police, Dr. Watson. She is a good, decent woman who would break neither the law of God nor man! And she would never betray one as has been so good in offering her a generous paying situation, and who has been the very soul of kindness itself to her those years she's been there! But still, she has lost that situation, and lost her liberty, and we don't know what is to be done to help her. For the police say there is proof against her, and she will not tell even us who she loves one word about what has brought her to such a pitiful plight. But I've read enough about you both, sir, to know that if anyone can see through false proofs to find the truth, then surely these are the men I speak to now."

"Oh, surely," agreed Holmes with a quick smile, waving the young lady to continue.

"I can offer you five pounds if you will help free my unfortunate sister. I would gladly give more, but those are all I have set aside. Though if poor Mathilda isn't cleared and allowed her position back, that fiver isn't going to go far in keeping us lot – my mother and little

351

brothers – off the streets. Mathilda's been our chief support since Dad went, and though I try to chip in when I'm earning, someone has to help with the little ones, so it's not as often as I'd like. I'll be able to go to ten, fifteen even, if you can wait a little for the balance."

I was moved by the composure with which Miss Lodge set out her circumstances, with humility but no hint of pleading, and I was further touched by Holmes's simple reply of, "You need not trouble yourself over my fee."

His prospective client, on the other hand, appeared markedly less touched than I by the gesture, replying sharply, "We don't expect anyone's charity."

"Nor do I offer it. If an injustice has been done, my reward will be in seeing it righted. And I have little else to occupy my time at the moment." This latter was said with an edge of asperity, and I scarcely needed to follow Holmes's glance to confirm that it fell upon the pile of newspapers threatening to spill off the table, and the topmost headline – matching that which nestled discreetly in my bag and which was being yelled by every paper vendor in London – proclaiming, "Continent's Foremost Specialists Consulted in Marleigh Towers Tragedy". I could not have declared which was the most likely basis of Holmes's annoyance; that he himself had not been consulted in that matter which had gripped the city for days, or that there were others regarded as closer to the forefront of criminal investigation than he.

What then followed is one of those coincidences that would appear on the page as fanciful and farfetched if it were not absolute fact. My eye had no sooner lit upon that newspaper report than my attention was diverted by the rattle of carriage wheels drawing to a halt below. Having followed one of Holmes's manoeuvres in sitting with my back to the window in order to view his visitor's every change of expression while leaving my own features and the direction of my gaze partially obscured in shadow, it required a mere turn of my head to see that the carriage bore a coat of arms made instantly recognisable by its repeated presence in those news reports. Hurriedly gathering up the overflowing newspapers, I hissed, "Holmes, Lord Sternfleet of Marleigh Towers is on your doorstep."

I had expected these words to galvanise the languid detective, but before even he could spring, alert and energised, from his seat, his young guest was on her feet and at the sitting room door. "I must go! I cannot meet . . . No, I will not meet . . . ." The chiming of the doorbell cut across her words, and she threw the door wide and rushed from the room.

"I have your address, Miss Lodge," called Holmes. "I shall call on you there to hear the remainder of your account, and so establish how best I may assist you."

The young lady paused at the head of the stairs, snapping heatedly in response, "You shan't find me there, for I'll be waiting vigil outside that place they're keeping her. I can see I wasted my time coming here, and that my sister's troubles and her story are much too petty for you, Mr. Holmes! You'd do us both a kindness in forgetting I ever was here."

"I cannot forget, nor would I wish to!" But my friend was left addressing an empty landing, as the rapid din of her receding footsteps on the stairs was followed by a deep, masculine voice letting fly an exclamation of startled annoyance, and Mrs. Hudson's concerned call after the hastily departing visitor, just as the front door slammed with some finality.

"Such an extraordinary change of demeanour," I shrugged. "Was she perhaps too embarrassed to meet such a distinguished figure?"

"Because she is merely a scullery maid or char and he a peer of the realm? No, there is more to it than that."

But before I could establish what Holmes meant, or how he had known the girl's mode of employment, his landlady hastily entered wearing a flustered look – one which turned rapidly to a grimace of mortification on sighting the cluttered mess of her upstairs front room – and announced severely, "A distinguished gentleman to see you, Mr. Holmes."

"Thank you, Mrs. Hudson, that will be all. My, my; a third caller since the clock chimed the hour? It is as well I am without ego, or such unforeseen popularity might turn my head! Lord Sternfleet, do come in."

"You know me, sir?" demanded the tall, stylishly garbed but grim faced gentleman who strode impatiently into the centre of the room, his dark eyes peering suspiciously from behind a swirling wreath of smoke from the cigar clamped in his gritted teeth; then, glancing at the newspapers I still held in my hands, gruffly adding, "Of course you know me, Mr. Sherlock Holmes. How foolish a question."

"Of course, your Lordship," replied Holmes, with the merest hint of a sly smile in my direction. "Alas, Watson, gone so soon are the days when our noble guests arrived masked and aliased, allowing us a scant few seconds' intrigue at least."

"There can be no intrigue over my visit, I trust," glowered our eminent caller, "as my unhappy circumstances are the most talked about scandal of the summer."

"A prominent foreign gentleman found in his bed with his throat cut while a guest under the roof of one of the nation's most highly esteemed

353

diplomats, and another guest so traumatised by the discovery that she has taken to her own bed, while her renowned husband is torn between his official duties abroad and his husbandly duties toward his stricken wife.''

"You encapsulate in a few words what the press has devoted yard upon yard of column inches to in these past dreadful days,'' muttered Lord Sternfleet darkly, seating himself stiff and alert on the sofa toward which Holmes gestured, before he too sat, drawing deeply upon his pipe so that the combined smog from it and his guest's cigar threatened to fill the room.

"Already you have the pre-eminent experts of both affected countries en route to forage the ancestral grounds for traces of an assassin. I am sure your judgement in awarding these specialists *carte blanche* will eventually prove sound. They say that Herr von Waldbaum has the tenacity and stamina to turn entire households on their head in pursuit of his prey, while Monsieur Dubuque is more inclined to probe within the actual heads of those inhabiting the households." If it were possible for the nobleman's expression to darken any further, these words provided just cause. "I would have been most interested in studying these gentlemen at work, but as you observed from my now disrupted previous appointment, I am already engaged on a case.''

Lord Sternfleet's eyes bulged in their sockets. "That unruly child who practically dashed me over on your doorstep?''

"My client,'' said Holmes blandly. "Yes.''

"But you surely realise the enormity of my situation, Holmes! My family's long-established name lies in hazard. My cousins are the Earls of Shardsmere. My own sister is married to a Duke! What affects my reputation also overshadows some of the noblest houses in Britain! And as this ghastly business has taken place on British soil, a British agency must take charge of these enquiries.''

"And on whose advice do you approach me? Not on the say-so of Scotland Yard, for the official charged with taking the case over from your local constabulary – Inspector Godfrey Highford? Thank you, Watson – is not one that has consulted me in the past.''

"Nor did he wish you consulted here, for what his approval matters. Yet your suitability and availability for this commission were vouched for by an utterly reliable source within those circles my position makes my own, Mr. Holmes. From any other, I would have suspected favouritism in the recommendation, but knowing my advisor's precise and logical nature, such a factor would, I believe, be absolutely incidental.''

Hindsight now leaves it clear to me that this nameless advisor could only be Mycroft Holmes, yet at this time I had encountered Holmes's remarkable older brother but once, and the scant information I held on him gave no indication of the supreme levels of authority or trust he held within the government, nor, of course, of his influence in murkier, shadowed areas of power. And as such things were yet unknown to me, so too was the reason this reply appeared to nettle Holmes, who coolly responded, "Your advisor's cast-iron reputation for reliability must suffer a unique dent, for I remain otherwise engaged."

"Then, Holmes, you must disengage yourself! Before God, I promise five hundred guineas to the one who untangles this frightful affair. No? A thousand! More, if you would but name your price! And what can that wretched girl offer?"

"Your Lordship could lose the sums he speaks of a hundredfold and only notice the loss if it meant switching to a less exclusive brand of cigar. That 'wretched girl' offered to the very limit of what she can give – beyond even that – and only the direst need would inspire such a sacrifice. Therefore her needs are more urgent, and my services are hers."

Fearing that my friend's pique had prompted him to act rashly, I spoke urgently. "Miss Lodge's case is no doubt important, but the matter at Marleigh Towers is the only crime being spoken of anywhere."

His Lordship turned an appraising eye on me, as if noticing my presence for the first time. "Lodge, do you say?"

"The name has some meaning for you, Lord Sternfleet?"

"A triviality, Mr. Holmes. A damn servant girl my wife imprudently trusted was caught taking advantage of these appalling events to cover her own petty thievery. She is rotting miserably in a cell now, but if only that cell held the malefactor who brutally did to death a guest to this nation as well as to my home! There are international implications here, sir. My guests were in this country for more than a mere holiday. Not that this is known save by those under orders of the strictest confidence."

"Then, as you have clearly decided to take me into your confidence, I had better hear the full particulars," said Holmes, mildly.

Lord Sternfleet rose to his full, considerable height, the steely look returning to his eyes. "Then it would be better for you to hear the account at the site of these grim events, if you would be good enough to accompany me."

"Well, Watson, will your good lady wife miss you dreadfully if you were gone a few hours? You have no objection if my friend, Dr. Watson, joins me, your Lordship? He is an invaluable ally and frequently highlights angles to a situation that I may have failed to consider."

Whether either my wife or Lord Sternfleet objected or not, Holmes did not wait to learn, as, throwing his dressing gown aside in favour of a light jacket, he led our procession downstairs and into the waiting carriage, although he did recall his manners long enough to permit Lord Sternfleet the task of instructing the driver to convey us to Marleigh Towers.

II. Guests of His Lordship

What was recounted during the drive to that stricken house was in keeping with the news reports. Lord Herbert and Lady Verity Sternfleet – herself the daughter of an illustrious house, whose elderly patriarch was said to be gravely affected by the possible scandal – had opened their home to a gathering consisting of Monsieur Francois Lefalque, the French industrialist and magnate, and his near neighbours on the far side of the much disputed Franco-German border, the Graf and Grafin Rupert and Natascha von Schellsberg. "This was a reunion of longstanding friends, you understand, who have often played host to one another, be it in manor house, chateau or schloss. Yet in recent years there had been a cooling in our kinship, and my dear Verity urged me to allow her to extend an invitation before we good companions had drifted irretrievably into the status of mere former acquaintances. To our great elation, the invitations were enthusiastically accepted, and the dining hall of Marleigh Towers rang with happy laughter, while the jovial discussion of old times led freely into plans for further reunions and a strengthening of bonds grown fragile due to neglect. The happy group that parted long after midnight was one fully expecting to reconvene over breakfast in a similarly joyful frame of mind. Yet all joy was dashed aside by the terrible discovery of that morning.

"We had, I suppose, dined and drank rather too well. Consequently none of us was notably early in rising, or else Francois Lefalque's brutal fate would have been detected far sooner. And when those horrified screams rang out and set bedroom doors crashing and footsteps hurtling along corridors, I had to forego dressing, throw on my dressing gown, and race from my room to discover the outcry's source. I almost collided with Verity, looking so pale and anguished as she grasped my hand for courage, and we both rushed to find the maid – Tanner is the name my wife cried out – standing shuddering and whimpering in the open doorway of Lefalque's bedroom, while Rupert von Schellsberg's swift arrival and efforts to discover the cause of the snivelling girl's alarm were hampered by the fact that, in his rudely awoken perplexity, he addressed her in his native German.

"At our approach, Tanner nearly threw herself into my wife's arms, such is the devotion and esteem in which the staff holds Lady Verity.

356

'Your Ladyship, the gentleman asked me to wake him, but the door wasn't locked nor even closed properly, because it opened at my knock, and I saw . . . Oh, it's too horrible, your Ladyship! You mustn't look!'

"The Graf, already left looking green and drawn by his consumption of claret the previous night, had now glimpsed what Tanner had seen, and he echoed her words. 'Your wife should not see this, Sternfleet. Nor any woman. My God, if Natascha had witnessed such a thing!' And he lurched to his wife's bedchamber, his hurry partly fuelled by his wish not to be seen looking so shaken as servants began swarming into the upper corridor, drawn by those cries. My wife instructed her lady's maid – that despicable girl I spoke of earlier, Lodge or Hodge – to give the gravely shaken Tanner something warming for the shock, and she wrapped a coat around her and took her down to the kitchens. Then, ignoring all warnings and my own attempts to prevent her, Lady Verity strode past me and into that bloody chamber."

So gripped was I by the account, I was startled back into the reality of our carriage by the raising of Holmes's hand. "Sir, you are lapsing into melodrama, and such is best left the province of the good doctor. My understanding is that what blood was visible was confined to the victim, his bedding and night attire, not slathering the walls of some gore-streaked horror chamber. I appreciate that emotions have run wild, but as it has been left too deplorably late for me to witness the scene for myself, I must ask that you are as accurate as possible in your report so that I may reconstruct the setting in my mind."

Plainly unused to being interrupted in anything, Lord Sternfleet even so acknowledged the reasoning behind Holmes's rebuke, nodding tersely before continuing. "I feel I have told this story a thousand times over, to a veritable parade of policemen of all ranks, and to my superiors and advisors within Parliament. I will attempt to be as precise with you as I was with them. But when I cast my mind back, the room and its contents recede, and all I clearly see is the glassy-eyed glare of my old friend and a monstrous quantity of blood! Francois was propped up in the bed, pillows at his back, and his nightshirt and sheets were soaked through. It can only have been a cowardly sneak attack as he had slept, for he had the strength of a bear. Once, as a younger man, I saw him tackle and best two men far larger than he, purely because he overheard them make some remark about a lady in our company. But here he had no time to fight back, and his throat was cut clean across."

"So, even if he had attempted to cry out," I mused, "he would have been unable to raise more than a choking gurgle."

"Thank you for that medical viewpoint, Watson," murmured Holmes. "I wish you had been allowed to extend your skills to an examination of the wound while fresh, but a coroner's report will have to suffice. Pray continue, Lord Sternfleet."

"I instructed one of the servants lurking in the corridor to assemble the male staff in the entrance hall. One was to ride out to summon the police, the others to secure the house and patrol every inch of the park."

The groan this elicited from Holmes was no doubt in response to the idea of a troop of butlers, footmen and stable-boys trampling across the grounds and efficiently obliterating any valuable trails underfoot. However, rather than voicing a complaint I had heard him level at many a police inspector over similarly unthinking carelessness, he prompted, "You believed it was murder from the first instant?"

"If it had been suicide, then where was his instrument of self-destruction? His hands were free of any blade or shard. My wife refused to consider that a murderer may have stalked within our home as we slept, insisting some terrible act of despair must have caused our friend to end whatever woes may have beset him. I had actually to restrain her from dropping to her knees in search of a weapon that might have fallen under the bed. It was only the return of the Graf that brought her to herself, his shock now equally matched by concerns for the Grafin, who had practically fainted in her bed at the news and entered that state of profound shock in which she remains. Rupert was naturally inclined to take her immediately back to Germany but, even had Inspector Highford been of a mind to let him leave the country, Natascha's condition forbids it. Not that any suspicion falls on such a noble visitor, of course, and his continued presence is a mere courtesy. But it is for this reason he has summoned the specialist from Dantzig to hasten the progress of the enquiry."

"If you incline toward notions of an intruder or assassin, your Lordship, you must feel that Monsieur Lefalque was a man whose death would benefit some other agency. Was anything stolen, from his room or his belongings? No documents of a private and confidential nature?"

Lord Sternfleet released a long plume of smoke as he slowly exhaled, before shaking his head. "I do not understand, Mr. Holmes, what you may be insinuating."

"Come now, we have no time for game playing. The death of a minor visiting dignitary with no connection to government – or should I stress no *visible* connection? – is embarrassing, indeed painful, but unlikely to cause the international crisis you protest of. But if it has set so busy a man as Fritz von Waldbaum scurrying through the facts of the man's life, and has also caught the lofty attention of your – ha! – advisor, there is more to it than is being said. Plainly put, was Lefalque carrying any clandestine document that others may wish to either obtain or suppress?"

"There you go wildly astray, Mr. Holmes. Francois was no spy, nor would I use my own home for such sordid goings on as you imply. It is where I live, sir! It is where my wife and family should feel safe."

"Well, as family has been invoked, what of Madame Lefalque? It is she who summoned the feted Dubuque to take charge of discovering how she comes to be a widow, I believe? Was she not invited to this friendly jamboree?"

"Claudine Lefalque prefers to summer in the South of France, and has invariably done so for many years."

"But the marriage was still a viable one, with no estrangement? No? And Madame's relations with the rest of the party? Your wife, for example?"

"Amicable. Agreeable! Friendly! We were all of us friends, Mr. Holmes!"

Holmes nodded in silent acknowledgement of Lord Sternfleet's grim insistence, and that silence persisted as the bustling, cramped streets thinned around us to the outlying tranquillity that abides beyond the city's overflowing heart, with even these charming byways becoming less crowded with their pleasant terraced houses and gardens. I viewed as much of this as I could through yet another fog of tobacco fumes, eventually giving in and, at risk of ending up as cooked and wrinkled as one of Mrs. Hudson's breakfast kippers, I produced my own pipe and puffed merrily away until the gates displaying that same coat of arms that adorned our transport came into view, and beyond it the great wooded parkland that held Marleigh Towers in green seclusion. On spying our approach, from slouching as wilted as the rapidly drying out flowers in those suburban gardens, a constable stationed at the gates became as stiffly formal as any Palace guardsman, marching swiftly to open the way, before no doubt slumping once more the instant our carriage was out of sight along the tree-lined driveway whose verdant abundance shielded from the outside world that house whose unwelcomed notoriety had made it a beacon for the morbidly inquisitive.

III. Inside the Murder Room

Marleigh Towers' renown had not, of course, commenced with this recent outrage. Its stables have at various times housed several champions – including a particular thoroughbred whose best remembered victory had, in my bachelor days, brought me winnings enough to finance a holiday in Margate that was itself memorable for several happy reasons that shall not be divulged here – while I had long nurtured a wish to view the great clock whose hands famously remained frozen at the hour and minute its tower was struck by lightning in 1827, at the precise instant General Sir Hartford Sternfleet fell drunkenly under a carriage outside his club and was trampled to death. It was from high atop this tower that, on hearing the grave news, his young wife threw herself in her urgent desire to be reunited in eternity with the general. Perhaps unfortunately for her, she survived the plunge and lived to a greatly advanced age, though with injuries so awful to behold they eventually earned her the cruelly whispered title of "The Red Widow"; thus she remained confined both to her wheelchair and to a house that had become a constant reminder of all she had lost, and which she chose to spend her remaining years filling with her bitter, impotent rage, which some say has never quite fully dispersed. The disappointing truth, however, was that this infamous landmark looked like any other stopped clock, while the enduring grandeur of the house itself was something I observed but fleetingly, as Lord Sternfleet set a brisk pace in marching Holmes and me indoors through a pillared portico, past deferential servants and constables alike, and straight up the magnificent main staircase.

"You are taking us directly to the murder room?" enquired Sherlock Holmes, keeping step easily with his Lordship's long strides.

"I was given to expect that this is where you would prefer to begin. Now, you there, Constable Whoever-you-are, is Inspector Highford still skulking somewhere?"

The uniformed officer seated outside the bedroom door scrambled to his feet, apologetically replying, "He's down our local station, your Lordship. Said he reckoned that maid wasn't telling all she knew."

"Damn fool! She can wait," grunted our host. "The stupid child has nothing to do with this."

"Of course the poor girl has nothing to do with it!" The imposing voice that chimed down the corridor was followed by my first equally imposing sight of the striking and elegant Lady Verity Sternfleet. She strode with a gliding step to her husband's side and, as he discreetly extinguished his cigar, she slipped a fond arm comfortably round him, insisting, "We are allowing our own horror and suspicion over poor Francois to make us vengeful. You must instruct that inspector to stop hectoring her and let the poor, bewildered creature go free."

"My sweetest Verity, you are altogether too soft-hearted. The girl took advantage of this, was too brazen or foolish to not get caught, and must pay the cost of her own greed and stupidity. Now, now, do not upset yourself. No, do not argue, for I felt you shiver. Shall I have Tanner make you up another fire?"

"A fire? In this summer heat, would that not be rather excessive?" remarked Holmes.

"Exactly so, Mr. Holmes," agreed Lady Verity. "Indeed, such a fuss, but my husband found me shivering before a freshly-lit fire in my bedroom on that awful morning, and since then he has been trying to bundle me in blankets and shawls, as if I might shudder myself into pieces."

"Shock can have profound and pronounced effects," I warned, delicately. "If you would like me to perhaps prescribe something for your nerves . . . ."

"My nerves are perfectly all right, Doctor, merely jangled."

"But you are recovered enough to go out, I perceive."

As Lady Verity looked down at her own fashionable if sober dress, her pearls, and her long silken gloves, a pained look crossed her gentle features, and her poise momentarily deserted her as she wrung her hands together. But her natural grace asserted itself swiftly, as she tightly smiled. "Oh, Mr. Holmes, this costume is not for going out. I cannot go out, but instead I must face a daily procession of strangers in my home, and even now – particularly now, with so many eyes upon us – one cannot allow appearances to slip. If I am to be peered at and queried, I shall ensure it is on my own terms."

"Not the attire to go crawling about the floor searching for weapons," Holmes murmured sardonically, but if his words had been meant solely for my ears, they also reached Lady Verity's, and her genteel tone sharpened in response.

"If it helped discover who had done this terrible thing, I would crawl through the undergrowth clad in a ballgown and diamond tiara! I admit that I was not thinking clearly when first we found Francois. But perhaps I was clearer in my thoughts than it appeared, for the blade I sought was later found."

Holmes turned keenly, his eyes flashing at this fresh data. "I had not read of this."

"We have managed to keep some secrets back from the press. Here, I will show you the very spot. No, Herbert, I am not a weakling, and keeping me out of the room will not erase what I have already seen. Follow me, if you will, gentlemen."

The bedroom was spacious and comfortable, with expansive windows letting golden light flood in. A wardrobe lay open, its contents on display, the cut of a wealthy man's suits unmistakeable even here. A jug and bowl sat on the sideboard, pen and paper on the bureau, and all

361

seemed so normal it would have appeared that the occupant had stepped out mere moments before, had it not been for the stark memorial the bed made to the violence that had been committed here. Stripped of its bedding, and with the stains already dried to a darkening brown, the mattress looked better suited to an abattoir than a bedroom; wings of blood apparently stretching out around the corpse my mind's eye placed in the bed. That blood had dripped and dried in rivulets down the side close by the door and an awkwardly placed bedside cabinet that nestled between door and bed, leaving powdery burgundy puddles on the polished floorboards, and a deep crimson crusting to the tufts on the rug.

"Inspector Highford claims the discovery of it, yet in a way I helped. No, not crawling on the floor. That officious little fellow had asked my description of that morning's events. Rather than repeating what I had already told his colleagues, I felt it easier to show him. But I fear I overestimated my own courage, for no sooner had I entered than I felt terribly faint. I reached wildly for support, forgetting this bedside cabinet was on casters. It slid easily across the floor and almost brought me sliding down with it. The inspector, in an attempt at gallantry I suppose, moved to assist me. But just as he had steadied me he very nearly knocked me aside again, crying, 'What's this I spy here?' And from the floor he scooped up Francois' razor, with its blade and ivory handle still red and wet from his blood."

"You knew it was Lefalque's own razor?"

"At that moment? No, of course. But I assumed it to be so – whoever else's razor would I expect? – and an inspection of Francois' shaving kit showed this to be true."

"And was there any indication of how it found its way underneath the cabinet?" asked Holmes, crouching smartly to run his slender fingers in the gap between the base and the floorboards, before narrowly examining the floor around both cabinet and bedside.

"We believed that Francois must, in his death throes, have dropped or thrown it."

"But the angle at which he would have had to release or propel it counts against that, otherwise why should I be summoned?" As he spoke, Holmes paced the room, his grey eyes prowling over every surface, fingers prising lightly at the window locks, knuckles rapping softly on wood panelled walls as if some secret means of access might be revealed, before his attention turned once more to the floor, prompting a tut-tut of disapproval. "This morass of foot-scuffs are evidence of nothing more than the British bobby at work. But since the floor was recently scrubbed, as you would expect before a visitor's arrival, and there has been no recent rain, no trail in the dust nor muddied footstep

362

could be expected in any case. Yet if murder had been the intent, why would the culprit have required the victim's own razor? Surely any killer worth the label carries their own weaponry?"

"Unless the murderer wished the crime to look like suicide," I exclaimed.

"Without placing the instrument of death in Lefalque's hand to strengthen the illusion?"

"A burglar, then? An opportunist, taken unawares, who grabbed the first item that came to hand? Then, in their panic at the horror they had perpetrated, they threw down the razor wildly, before fleeing without whatever spoils they had come for?"

My hypothesis prompted only a noncommittal grunt from Sherlock Holmes, but I had expected no more, knowing well his preference to leave any clear statement of events until he had gathered and analysed all data available to him. His eyes and attention now seemed transfixed by that fearful stain, practically as if it drew him to it. So closely did he lean in to inspect the grisly markings, angling his neck so that he alternately peered down at the ruined mattress and then up at the wall above the head of the bed, while stretching out his long frame and lightly describing arcs in the air with his thin fingers, that for a mortifying instant I believed he might lay at the centre of those bloody angel wings in an attempt to view the scene as if through the eyes of the murdered man. "If I may call on your expertise again, Watson; a cut throat would not produce a steady flow of blood?"

"Not necessarily," I advised, glancing apologetically at Lord and Lady Sternfleet before responding to Holmes's impatient gesture to elaborate. "If the carotid artery were severed, as I believe was the case here, then it would spray outwards . . . in gouts."

"I should desist from occasionally chiding your mastery of words, Watson. 'Gouts'! Exactly!" He sprung upwards, like an impatient jack-in-the-box. "Where are these gouts? We see the leakage of the life force, but where is the stain of that initial spray? Unless something obstructed its projection before it could spatter."

"You imagine that the killer, who would necessarily be close to him to strike, was that obstruction? Good God, Holmes, they would be coated all over in his blood!"

"And a fleeing, blood drenched murderer would leave a trail in their wake. Yet there is no red footmark nor handprint, and not even the tiniest crimson droplet to be found anywhere else in this room, or in the halls beyond."

"If you must continue with this barbarous talk, Holmes," barked Lord Sternfleet, "can we not at least get out of this charnel room?"

Sherlock Holmes, as if deaf to these protests, laid a finger absently against the lip of the water jug on the cabinet, murmuring, "With nothing removed apart from the corpse and bedding, who emptied the water jug? Ah, but he had drank heavily, so would have been thirsty." His distracted air dispersing with an abrupt clap of his hands, he continued, "Without the late occupant's presence, there is little more to be learned here. Besides, I must carry out my next interview in less distressing surroundings."

"If you would wish to interview me, Herr Holmes, it makes no difference if you do so here or anywhere else," announced the man who stood stiffly in the doorway. Here was a rugged fellow, made all the more so for the darkening growth of stubble on a strong, determined chin, which stood at odds to his smart suit, across whose jacket breast I could picture a row of medals, and yet smarter bearing and intonation. "My wife, however, if you wish to speak with her, must to be given time to prepare herself, and cannot be pressed on these dark matters."

"It has clearly been a strain, Graf von Schellsberg," said I, noting the shadows around his eyes, "for both of you."

"The Grafin is most upset, Herr Doctor," he replied, a polite nod acknowledging my concern. "She it was who introduced me to Francois Lefalque some twenty years ago, while I was merely a student, and he seemed so worldly. I learned from him how to live life and celebrate the living of it." A far-off look stole across his features, a shadow of a smile raising the tips of his moustaches. "Ha! Live? He could have been the death of us both. I remember now, to impress a woman he claimed to be wooing in secret, he stole some gaudy trinket from a hotel we had found ourselves supping in, then paraded his prize until the gendarmerie threw us both in a cell for the night to sober us up. Yet when he was told the next morning to expect a fine, he produced twenty times what the bauble would have cost. 'I could have paid for it, of course, but this experience with you, friend Rupert, I could never have bought.' Where he led the way, I followed, but when I was wed to my glorious Natascha and put such wildness behind me, it was he who quickly followed me, marrying Claudine but months later. We had become, you might say, respectable. If I may be glad of anything from these past days, it is to have a final memory of how he assisted me to my room, both of us staggering and laughing, as if we were become for an instant those youthful, drunken rogues once more.

"Yes, there had been some strain in the friendship. But purely in matters of business. Francois inherited many factories and dealings in his province, which you must know runs side by side with my own region. Between us there is the border, marked by the great river, across which our friendship has built bridges to match those tangible bridges of stone and timber. One signifier of this alliance was always the free flowing of workers from my region into his factories, and of rural labourers from his territory into the farmlands of my own. Of late, however, more and more of my people were informed they were no longer required, while his tenants were discouraged from taking up work in our fields. Francois was more business-like about it than I had ever seen. 'The factories become automated, Rupert, and it is but correct that my own people be first to learn these new technologies.' But if you think this a reason for vengeance, I would bear a very bloody hand if I took such revenge against all who inconvenienced me in affairs of business."

"I thank you for your statement, my Lord Graf," said Holmes with a slight bow, "which I would undoubtedly have sought. But if we may remove ourselves to the downstairs area, I wish to speak to the unfortunate servant who raised the alarm."

IV. A Rival of Sherlock Holmes

Though Lord Sternfleet objected to Holmes interviewing a lowly member of his staff before his guests, with his wife's calming influence brought to bear he bit down on his objections, as he also did when my friend requested that he might speak to Miss Tanner alone. So we were soon seated at the table in the large, white-tiled kitchen, with a healthily plump, tousle-headed girl of some twenty years, uncomfortable in an ill-fitting lady's maid's uniform, seated apprehensively on the very edge of a kitchen chair opposite us. "Will this take long, sir? Only with everything that's happened and us being short, and all, I can't neglect my new duties. Thank you, sir. But you won't make me describe it again, will you, sir?"

"We have already heard all about that, and you have been very brave," said Holmes with one of those placid smiles he would conjure up when dealing with excessively nervous witnesses. "But you said that the late gentleman asked you to waken him early."

"Most particularly early, sir. 'You will knock at five of the clock, and if I do not answer you are not to hesitate a moment, but to come in and waken me.' Only the master's party stayed up so late that by the time we'd cleared after them it was after two, and I near overslept myself and forgot until breakfast was nigh served up. You . . . you don't think, sir, that if I had been on time, the gentleman might still be alive? Or," and here her hand flew to her throat, "Or might I have opened the door on the killer swooping over the bed with the bloodied blade still at work? Oh, sir! Now I'm moved up there, next door to her ladyship, I don't sleep hardly any, knowing what happened just a few doors along."

I was quick in reassuring her that she had no call for guilt over failing to waken Lefalque on time, or to fear that she had narrowly escaped his fate. She displayed clear relief at this, and also that Holmes steered his questioning to events prior to her appalling find. "Any other requests from the gentleman, sir? Only, before dinner, for ink and paper. No, he sent no letter that I know of, sir, as it would have been me or one of the footmen sent out to post it."

"I saw both ink and paper on the bureau, but nothing written," mused Holmes.

"He might have put off writing whatever it was to the morning," I suggested. "Indeed, that may have been why he wished to rise so early."

"Or perhaps what he wrote never left the house. But surely, Miss Tanner, it's not a lady's maid's task to deliver mail. Oh, but you have been recently promoted, I gather, in place of that shameful rogue, Hodge . . . ."

The maid's rosy cheeks reddened further and the quaver fled from her voice. "Lodge is her name, sir, and Matty isn't no rogue, sir, and whatever she done must have been because her family needed the money, or someone forced her to it, but not for her own self! She weren't like that."

"I thank you, Miss Tanner, as I am certain your friend would for your spirited defence and your loyalty."

"If any was loyal, it was she to me, and to the mistress, sir. If she done the thing she's accused of, she must have had reasons."

"Greed is as good a reason for theft as any wretched excuse I've heard over the years," snapped the diminutive, grimacing, fellow whose gingerish beard failed to conceal his weak chin, and who strode into the kitchen on the balls of his feet as if hoping to gain height, circling around us with all the purpose of a bull in fervent pursuit of a china shop. "We haven't met, Mr. Sherlock Holmes, but I've heard a very great deal of you from my colleagues, and how you have a knack of getting wound up in those cases of theirs that might attract public notice for your vaunted methods."

"Inspector Highford, I presume. Forgive me; I have heard nothing of you from your fellow officers. And I can assure you that gaining notice for my methods will not be the case here."

"No, sir, it is I who offer you that assurance! But as you have been called in by his Lordship, I will let you proceed, even if you do not have the same courtesy to wait until the regulars are present to begin your inquisition." Then, making abundantly clear his intention to monitor whatever may follow, he scraped a chair noisily across the tiles and sat, fixing Holmes with his pale and narrow gaze.

"Matty was proper shaken," the maid, after a nervous glance at the scowling policeman, continued. "Though she was more concerned about Lady Verity than her own self, I'd swear. A real kind gentlewoman the mistress is. She gave me as many days off to get over the sight of that poor gent's throat as I may need; only I've no family near nor anywhere to go, so I stayed here where there was folks about. And Matty, who had been so good and looked after me in my fright, she let go for the day to see her people."

"Which was more kind than sensible, as we had not had time to question everyone," opined Highford. "But she can't have expected me to still be here in my vigilance. These local boys aren't much, and it took a proper professional turning up before we even had the weapon, but with our Mathilda acting suspicious by the shrubs near the path, even this lot had to notice. And with her wrestling with a bag she tried to drop as soon as she saw the constable's approach, I had her. Yes, I can show you what the bag contained, for it is still here." And with an impatient cry he summoned a constable, before sending the man rushing off again to fetch the confiscated item. "We've had no time to take it to the local station, as I've more important matters to attend to here. But you be sure that when they're settled, I'll be taking Miss Mathilda Lodge and her bag of spoils back with me to the Yard and teaching her how those who abuse the trust of their betters are dealt with there. Come on, let's have them here, lad." The garments Highford wafted out across the kitchen table, as if laying a delicately embroidered table cloth, were a pair of women's nightdresses, the one of them plain but of the finest cotton, the other more feathered and lacily decorated than anything one might see in any but the most stylish and exclusive clothing shop.

"In all things feminine and fashionable I bow to your considerable knowledge and experience, my old friend, yet your blush tells me that this is not a common garment." I protested that, as a recently married man, I should keep my own counsel in such matters, provoking a barked laugh from Holmes. "But it is at least as uncommon in London as a maker's label declaring its origin in a deluxe continental boutique would make it."

"And worth a penny every bit as pretty as these ribbons and laces. Though not worth nearly as much as this," gloated Highford, tossing a large and sparkling ruby brooch onto the topmost nightdress, where it redly glistened like a fresh bullet wound to the heart of the garment's unseen wearer. "Lord Sternfleet confirms it as property of his wife, and the girl has no good explanation for why she would be in possession of it. For cleaning and polishing, she claimed, yet she could give the name of no jeweller to whom such a task had been assigned. No, there was nothing noticed as missing previously, but that simply tells me that after some petty pilfering the likes of these fine garments, she'd grown bold, and thought nobody would pay any heed to a missing jewel when there was murder on every mind."

"Matty isn't like that, I've told you already!"

"Mind your place and hold your tongue, Miss Tanner! If she's so innocent, how is it that when we took ourselves round to her old mum's address, we found towels enough to fit some nice gaps in the linen closet here, all fresh from the copper and hung out to dry in her back yard? Ha! Just as they've hung her out to dry? The mother doesn't even know what day it is, chasing after those nippers of hers, and I doubt she'd ever seen anything so clean and white hung there since her wedding day. If then! I would still have brought her in and got something out of her. Leastways suggesting that such an action might just be my next step, with the mum in the next cell and the little ones to the poorhouse, got Miss Mathilda talking, and she's admitted, finally, that she took them. And that the murder was the cause!"

"Did she, indeed?" responded Holmes, an eyebrow sharply rising. "How so?"

"Folks, as I've long-since learned, are ghoulish. They were lining up outside the gates here the instant word was out someone had died nasty inside. Or maybe the mob just smelled the blood! Fine fabrics and the like will fetch a price anyway, as you'd know if you'd to deal with every dipper who'd hooked himself a pocketful of silk hankies. But as souvenirs of the murder house, she saw they'd double or treble in price. And this is the girl whose innocence everyone pleads? The depths to which some will sink to make money from misery. Unbelievable!"

"The exact word," replied Holmes. "And so you have left this frightened girl to fret and stew, and await her punishment as a common thief, while you scrabble to locate the clues to a killer you have not the slightest trace of, before your field of enquiry is invaded by private investigators from all across the continent."

As the inspector rose abruptly, glaring down at Holmes, I was put instantly in mind of one of those awful, spoiled lapdogs one sometimes sees snapping and growling defiantly round the heels of a much larger hound, oblivious to the fact that one single flash of teeth and snap of a jaw from the mightier beast would quickly silence its yapping. "And fretting and stewing has finally produced results, for her confession will be all I need when her time in the dock comes round."

368

Holmes leapt smartly to his feet, and I did likewise, if less nimbly, and followed as he strode towards the kitchen door. "Then you merely prolong her agony as you do your own. And we waste valuable time here."

Highford's unconvincing mien of superiority could not survive his awkward stumbling trot as he came clattering up the stairs and barging through the green baize door into the marbled hall in our wake. "What do you mean by that? If you know something, you'll tell me, Mr. Holmes!" These squawked demands brought a halt to the urgent conversation taking place by the foot of that great staircase we had earlier ascended, as Lord and Lady Sternfleet and the Graf von Schellsberg turned their combined scrutiny upon us.

"I cannot know, only suspect, while one who gains nothing from withholding what she does know is not being asked the proper questions, since, in your eagerness to arrest someone for anything, you treat her as a mere pilferer instead of a vital witness who may know exactly why Lefalque died and who it was that applied the killing blade." The instant these words passed Holmes's lips, Highford snapped his instructions for a constable to ride to the station and fetch the prisoner. Sherlock Holmes, lighting a cigarette, raised a concerned eyebrow. "You are surely not leaving such a valuable witness to the care of a fresh-faced constable?"

"The Dickens I will," cried Highford, storming toward the door, while Holmes drew the constable momentarily aside, murmuring a few quick words to him and eliciting a nod of assent before the policeman hurried off in pursuit of the inspector.

The echo of the constable's footsteps had barely been replaced by the rattle of the police wagon's wheels when a door slammed directly above. I looked to the top of the stairs to see a swaying apparition, hair awry around a pale and staring face, a clawed hand tugging her dressing gown around her while she grasped the railing with the other, as if dragging herself forward with every step. "You know. You know! No use now in hiding it," she shrilled, her words halting the Graf's ascent toward her, before he addressed her in urgent German. The distressed woman, so clearly his wife, replied in that same tongue. The language was lost on me, yet still the shifting expression on the Graf's face spoke eloquently of his shock, anger and finally utter sadness, while his refusal to accept his wife's proffered hand as she passed him was answered by a glance of such sorrow and regret that my heart was moved to both of them.

"Thank you for saving me the trouble of summoning you, Grafin von Schellsberg. The inspector will be back as if the devil himself was on his tail, so keen is he to have the experts repelled at the ports. Therefore, we have little time to piece this story together."

"Natascha, you are not well, and do not know what you are saying," pleaded Lady Verity, gripping her friend by the shoulders as if trying to calm a hysteric. But the Grafin had become calmness itself, brushing back her unkempt hair from her weary but striking face, and summoning up every inch of poise in her reserves.

"I know exactly what I am saying, Verity," she said, her English faultless and clear. "I should have said it all from the beginning, and saved all of you these dreadful days."

"And will you leave your friend to speak alone, your Ladyship?" asked Holmes. "Or would you have me speak for your part in the tragedy?"

"You impertinent swine," roared Lord Sternfleet, his eyes savage with uncomprehending fury.

"Mr. Holmes is correct. I must speak along with Natascha," said her Ladyship. "No, please, Herbert, do not look at me like that, as if I were a stranger. Just listen, and try to find it in your heart, if not to forgive, then to understand that we did only what we thought was for the best." Lady Sternfleet then placed her hand in Grafin's, and the women faced their dumbstruck husbands with an air of desolate nobility, before politely requesting that we move elsewhere so that they might relate their sad tale.

V. The Statement of the Crime

The clear blue day seemed to dim and the shadows lengthen, while the clouds beyond the windows of the vast drawing room in which we now gathered converged and loomed, darkening the heavens and betokening storms as if in sympathy with the events taking place inside that room. "You knew of my part in this from the outset, Mr. Holmes," said Lady Verity, "but may I know how?"

"I should also like to know this," snapped Lord Sternfleet, his temper as hot as the glowing tip of blazing cigar, "and also why you kept these monstrous accusations to yourself while sending the inspector off after trifling matters."

My voice echoed loudly in that vast room, as I snapped, "A defenceless woman's liberty is not a trifle!"

"Well said, Watson! I knew because, while the inspector and I both regularly encounter the worst and most depraved examples of humanity, I have also learned to listen when innocence is protested and where loyalty is invoked; for what purpose does it serve to pursue justice if we

370

cannot believe there exists good in this world, despite its vices, temptations and ills?"

"You evidently mean the innocence and loyalty protested by Miss Lodge's sister," I surmised, finally slotting the pieces of that incomplete statement I had heard on my arrival in Baker Street into place within the larger puzzle of the day.

"Lord Sternfleet's brusque arrival interrupted a resourceful young visitor in the telling of her story, yet the dramatic reaction his imminent presence provoked was to provide me with two of the most vital missing parts of that tale. I now knew the household involved, and also that the 'good' and 'kind' employer spoken of could not be a reference to his Lordship; a supposition his very clear attitude to anyone not his social equal rapidly proved. This is why I did not instantly expose her Ladyship's involvement, for to earn the loyalty she has been shown, she must be a formidable woman, and my subsequent discoveries of the day have only confirmed that deduction. Why else would an innocent, facing imprisonment, remain silent for another's sake? To whom was she loyal, if not the mistress whose kindness and honour she has praised, not only within this household where deference would be expected, but beyond and with those she most trusts? And with that honour so highly spoken of, I could reasonably conclude that you, Lady Verity, had not been the late Lefalque's mistress.

"It is not prurience that causes such an allegation, so put aside your outraged sensibilities, your Lordship! That this soiree was arranged to coincide with Madame Lefalque's traditional absence was suggestive, and there have been too many coincidences along the way to allow the strange wanderings of nightdresses to be counted as such. We then have the possibility of notes being written that do not pass outside this house, and, as your Lordship assures me Lefalque was carrying no secret papers, what other kind of incriminating item might more easily require a fire to hasten its disposal than some indiscreet communication? Ah, talk of secret papers surprises some of you? But there has been little innocence to this gathering, and while your Ladyship was fostering intrigues and affairs of the heart, affairs of an equally delicate nature were the ultimate goal of other parties."

"Rupert, this is nothing but speculation and exaggeration," protested Lord Sternfleet.

But if the Graf even heard him, it was impossible to tell, for his focus remained on his wife, who quailed on seeing the pleading in his eyes. Even so, she shunned the chair I offered her. "I shall stand, if you please. I have been nesting in that bed upstairs for days, afraid to come out. I now stand before you all, and I admit that, yes, I once was the paramour of Francois Lefalque. Before you and I ever met, my dearest Graf, when I was but a reckless, imprudent girl, and he a wildly charming fellow. But the charm masked spite and jealousy, and when I met a decent man, an honourable man, I recognised that what I had thought of as love with Francois was as shallow an approximation of that sensation as his charm was an approximation of goodness. This was again the mask he wore when he vowed we could remain friends, even if no longer lovers. And, it tears at my heart to admit, it was the charm he used those shameful times when I forgot my own goodness – until he reminded me by his lack of warmth what it was I risked losing. He persisted, playfully, slyly, but I was strong, and finally he saw that his patience was never to be rewarded. I see this only now, after what I heard and saw when last I was alone with him. But before, I had not known that his passions burned so cold, and in this coldness was born that distancing between us as friends."

"Natascha had confided, long ago, of the excitement and danger of her affair," offered Lady Verity. "Two overgrown schoolgirls giggling in the dark over forbidden confidences. When Herbert spoke of the growing distance between us, I was reminded of this thrilling affair. I realised that a dash of spice might be added to entice Francois from his chateau, and perhaps a rekindling of old flames may have been what was necessary to thaw our cooled friendship. So I used my letter of invitation to suggest to Francois how keenly our mutual friend anticipated his affirmative response."

"You used my wife as bait?" hissed Graf von Schellsberg coldly.

"Rupert, I knew nothing of this insinuation," insisted the Grafin. "I believed Francois to have forgotten our past. We were the friends we all once were. You drank and sang together, and then, when you tired, he helped you to your room, and I was delighted to see the young friends of happy memory still peering out from within those more careworn, mature faces. Yet it was not until I was in my own room and dressing to retire that I saw the message someone had pushed beneath my door. The opening lines puzzled and then chilled me, for they were words I had written, so long ago, in a private letter. I shall not tell you what these innocent words were, or how they read when removed from their setting, but beneath these were written, 'I have kept the originals all this time, and they are even now close to my heart. We will discuss these long departed sentiments – and establish whether they truly are departed? If you do not call on me in my room, I shall know you await me in yours, and you will hear my knock before the clock strikes the next hour.' The scheming devil had left me little choice but to face him and find out for myself what mischief he meant.

"Almost as I closed the door to his room, the sly, smiling welcome was gone from his face and he was upon me, grabbing at my shoulders, at my wrists, tearing my dressing gown from me and dragging me to him, an all the while pleading, 'Why did you ignore me so over dinner? Since when were your glances only for your husband? Is it a game to you, to hold my heart in your hand like one of the trinkets I won for you? Do you feel it pound for you?' His strong grip pressing my hand to his chest. His face red and looming over mine, the alcohol fumes of his breath filling my own breathing! 'This heart beats for you, the blood it pumps is for you, and if you have no use for my heart, what use have I of my blood?' And then the blade was in his hand, weaving so close to my face I still feel the chill of its passing on my skin. I beseeched him to think of his own Claudine, but he used such words to describe her, how little she truly meant to him, and how it should have been us who had made our match! I told him that my husband was a hundred times the man he was. 'Then, as his is the knife within my heart, let his blade be the one to still it, and let my blood forever stain what is his.' And when I saw the razor's handle and Rupert's crest emblazoned there, I understood that the purpose of his supposed kindness in helping Rupert to his chamber had been to steal this deadly thing. He meant to ruin us both, for who would believe the husband innocent when his wife is found covered in his rival's blood, and his razor is in that rival's throat?"

"I would have wielded it myself, had I known the kind of man he was," swore the Graf, moving rigidly to his wife and placing an uncertain arm around her.

The rush of anger instilled by this dreadful testimony giving way to a surge of protectiveness that made me wish only to be by my own beloved wife's side, and I grimly admitted, "There are many who would feel you justified!"

"No, you should not wish this," cried his wife, pulling him tighter to her. "You saw him dead, but I saw the life leave his eyes as they grew as wide as his mouth and his throat grew wider yet. Then I was only aware of such heat soaking through me, and the warmth on my face. As his grip loosened and I saw the blood upon me, I thought it was I who had been killed! Then he fell, and I cannot now remember what was in my mind as, even while he lay in that spreading darkness on the floor, I propped his head on pillows lest he choke on his own blood, and tore sheets and blankets from the bed to wrap round him and bring warmth back to his cooling body. But to no avail! Those white sheets so quickly bloomed dark and red. Perhaps his strength and madness had poured into me, for I dragged and heaved him across the room in his scarlet shroud and onto that bed, as if hoping to make comfortable what no longer had any

373

sensations. I sat for long minutes, turning over and over what might have been had I just surrendered to his demands. His game won, he would have bored of his quarry easily in his satisfaction. None but I would have been the wiser, and I would have crept back to my own room to deal with my own guilt, so my beloved Rupert would never have been hurt by the knowledge of what I was."

"You must not consider that any alternative, Grafin. Not ever! Nor should you torture yourself with any possibility you may have spared your husband pain," I insisted, finally grasping Lefalque's instruction that the maid, Tanner, was to simply walk in to rouse him at so early an hour and what scene he had wished witnessed. "He intended your private shame to be discovered and shared, no matter what."

"You sat traumatised, only gradually comprehending that he was dead," said Holmes gently. "But the floor was awash with his blood while he sat up in bed. Even in your dazed condition you understood this was no natural scene. Whose notion was it to mop up the blood on the floorboards to ensure it looked like he had ended his life where he lay?"

"When I was wakened by a figure sobbing quietly at my bedside, white-eyed and scarlet from head to foot, I genuinely believed in that moment that the legends of the Red Widow of the Sternfleets were true after all. How I wish now that it had been that malicious old ghost!" declared Lady Verity. "Natascha confided all that you have just heard, and it was plain that neither the Grafin's reputation and marriage, nor whatever standing our late companion had once enjoyed, even undeservedly, would be served by deeper investigation of these matters."

"Thus the empty water jug, as I'm sure the jugs and basins from your rooms saved traipsing up and downstairs with pails. Also the ransacked linen closet, for towels to scrub those floors as clean as you hoped your consciences might appear."

"My own maid, dearest sweet Mathilda, was roused from her sleep in the antechamber next to my room. On seeing Natascha's pitiable state she fetched one of her own shifts to replace that ghastly sullied nightdress. As I helped my poor friend wash away the traces of that man, the precious girl did the same on the floorboards, even having the vigilance to wipe clean those spatters that had followed Natascha along the hall to my door. I would have burned the towels and the nightdress, and my own which now bore his blood. But none of us are calculating criminals with any notion of what might betray us, and it was clever Mathilda who realised that the loss of the towels might be noticed and queried, while the disappearance of so singular a nightdress might alert the Graf to some irregularity. Any tiny thing might be our downfall. The towels might go unnoticed for days, but if we were to turn Natascha's very genuine shock to serve us, she need only stay bundled up in bed for a day or so while Mathilda stole the items away to wash and then quietly return them. I would not send a girl scurrying into the night with a sack of blood-soaked garments, but it was her notion and her insistence. I was so grateful I pressed my dearest treasure – the ruby brooch Herbert had given me when first we were engaged to marry – on her. I wanted her to know how grateful I was for her loyalty, and though she tried to refuse it and to wave it away, it was this token, truly meant, that damned her when she sought to return it."

"Yet it may well provide her salvation," said Holmes. "I watched you plead your devoted servant's case, and I have no doubt your winning ways would have inspired your husband eventually to relent in his judgement. But ponder on this, your Ladyship. Such a case as this could be the making of a man like Highford, and well he knows it. But what only we know is that he will never find his murderer. So when there is none to be found, he may look closer at the bird already in his cage, and if he looks closely enough, he might just find that one speck of blood on those towels that her hands failed to wring out, and then he will have found as good a murderer as any. The thieving maid, caught red handed stealing from her betters, who strikes back at her wealthy, noble captor and murder is done? What use would it then be for her to plead her convoluted case?"

"If it had come to that, I would have spoken for her."

"And brought the Grafin the infamy she had sought to escape? An old friend, or a loyal servant? I wonder if the choice would have been so easily made."

With a chastened look settling across her fine features, her Ladyship sighed, "You do not think much of us, Mr. Holmes."

"On the contrary, you have created a situation I never had encountered before, and one which may be unique – a suicide which has all the appearance of a murder which is attempting to disguise itself as a suicide. Now, looking out I perceive the approach of the police carriage in the drive, so little time remains. I will summarise what I believe to have then occurred, and you must correct any deviation from the truth.

"The maid smuggled the stained garments home, soaking and scrubbing them and leaving them to dry, before creeping back just as the horror was exposed. If your late night revels had not caused Miss Tanner to sleep on, the alarm may have found a missing lady's maid, but she slipped back in the confusion and it was only her kindness in offering her coat that might have betrayed her nocturnal departure and return. You two, meanwhile, having transformed the room to how you imagined a suicide scene should look, removed the last items which might incriminate you, such as the razor bearing the von Schellsberg coat of arms."

The nobleman raised a trembling hand to his stubble-flecked throat. "No wonder you clung to me, Natascha, calling me back when I attempted to leave you to make myself presentable! If it were not that my hand shook so much at the thought of putting a blade to my skin, I would have caressed my own neck with the very steel that pierced his!"

"As to the letters Lefalque had brought with him that spoke so charmingly of this past entanglement, your Ladyship concealed them in her own chamber. But when it dawned on you that there may yet be a search, you chose to burn them, hence the unseasonal fire in your grate. I have missed nothing so far, I think, but even in your thoroughness it was you that missed something."

Lady Sternfleet nodded solemnly. "I had Lefalque's own razor, but had not summoned the courage to put it in his hand. After settling Natascha, I found myself poised at the door of her room, my hand on the handle, my nerves steeled, when that scream went up. I ran out, hoping to reach that room before anyone else, but it was too late! My husband never saw that the chamber I had come from was not my own, but it was also he who prevented my placing the concealed razor into the blood beneath the bed, where it may plausibly have fallen. I had to bide my time, hoping my pounding heart would not burst as I awaited my chance to slip into the room and hide the bloodied blade somewhere it could then be found, for I could not simply leave it in plain view where it had not been before."

"And the blood that was on the blade when it finally was found?" I asked.

"Her own. A few drops, easily spilled. Watson, I recall your puzzled glance as I identified my earlier visitor as a char. It was her gloves that made it a likelihood. While she had scrubbed her face and donned the most respectable clothing she owned in order that she not be found lacking in our company, the gloves in such weather were too much. Thus she was concealing her hands, and the reddened, raw ravages of the hard work they were put to. And while her ladyship may also strive to maintain a respectable mode of dress, the gloves too are misplaced. You wince now as you wring your hands, Lady Verity." Removing her left glove in silent reply, she revealed the bandage wrapped inexpertly around the heel of her hand. With her nodded assent, I quickly examined the cut, confirming that it had not become infected, before reapplying the dressing. "You concealed the razor as close to the bed as you could, then arranged to stumble and bring about its revelation. But it was clear that this was not the only time that cabinet was moved, and it certainly was not to dust the floor, as there were several recent tracks from the casters in the dust still lying below it. This may also have occurred to even Highford in his murder hypothesis, and this too should be to our advantage."

"You hint repeatedly of salvation and advantage," protested Lord Sternfleet, "but what can you mean? Where is our advantage, and what salvation can we expect?"

"You alone, between yourselves, can decide how these events shall affect you, and if the deceptions and betrayals now brought to light are to be punished or absolved. But there is no good purpose served by staining your names as a consequence of an atrocious and selfish act by one who has deceived and betrayed you all in turn. However, this is not the only stain that must be lifted, and this one may not be as easily washed away as blood from a garment! While you may decline in your social standing, perhaps finding your official duties diminished, your places lost at a few dinner tables and functions, I talk of a deeper, darker stain which threatens absolute destruction of an innocent's future and a blight on the lives of those closest to her. Now, here is the inspector and his prisoner. Co-operate, and all will be as well as can be, but go against me and nothing is more certain than that which you most fear."

VI. The Adventure of the Second Statement

The anxious young lady escorted brusquely into the room by Inspector Highford was unmistakably kin to the girl who had fled from Baker Street scant hours before. There was the same clear complexion, the same sharp but pleasant features, and, alas, the same bright eyes rimmed red through the rubbing away of tears. As Holmes indicated that this Miss Lodge be seated, it struck me that even so simple an act as her sitting in this drawing room, surrounded by what society declared as her betters, was one that would be impossible under any other circumstance. It was evidently a prospect that caused her no little unease, although Holmes's generous smile and courteous tone swiftly eased most of her nerviness. "Now, Miss Lodge, you have no need to look so frightened, or to fear that we are going to bombard you with more questions than you have already endured, for all is known. No, you need not look to your mistress. She has told all. We know that you are guilty of no more than loyalty, and of putting this before the truth, and before your own best interests."

The girl was struck silent by incomprehension, yet the same could not be said of Inspector Godfrey Highford, who blazed around the room, issuing demands to know "what everyone else obviously damn well

377

does!" His impatient outburst drew forth quiet, shuddering sobs from the utterly wretched maid, though these sobs subsided as my friend wove his chain of detail and event. I have on many occasions watched Holmes silence a room while he used every aspect of his innately theatrical soul to present the facts in a case with a clarity made startling by his dramatic emphasis on each salient point. Yet here was a performance beyond even those, for he delivered the steps toward his conclusions with so little artifice or guile that they took on the banal solidity of a grocer's list or railway timetable, rendering each detail mundanely realistic, even to the ear of one who already knew the truth.

There were, of course, truthful elements to this statement, as he spoke of Francois Lefalque's occasional streaks of violence and instability, and of a simmering, unfathomable resentment that he had nurtured for his erstwhile friends, weaving these facts seamlessly toward the moment when, to her horror, Lady Verity had discovered her trusted guest stealing from her home. Why would such a wealthy man do such a thing? That was for an expert on mental disorders to establish, but Holmes insisted that a perusal of the gendarmerie records from Lefalque's home province may show a history of similar acts. There had come a confrontation, with Lefalque declaring his intent to leave at the earliest opportunity in the morning. Yet, alone in the fastness of night, in all likelihood contemplating his loss of honour and the estrangement of his friends, he had opted to make a more drastic departure.

"But the razor, Mr. Holmes," insisted a smugly grinning Highford, "could not have been found below the cabinet if he had inflicted this upon himself. Surely that undermines your whole argument?"

"Place yourself in Lefalque's position. Your path is set, your anger and shame guiding you, and the mortal blade is in your grasp. But your drunkard's hand is shaking so badly you cannot hold the blade straight. No, neatness of the cut does not come into it. It is not an aesthetic qualm, but Dr. Watson may tell you of the results that are inflicted when a straight razor does not deliver the finishing stroke."

"Certainly," said I, gravely, and while I spared the most awful details in deference to those others present, what I briefly described left Highford looking as grey and crumpled as his suit waistcoat.

"He lays the razor down on the cabinet by his bed as he gulps down water to revive his senses. But that shaking hand drops the blade. To reach it, he merely has to slide the cabinet out on its casters. He sees no need to then reposition it against the wall as he commits his last hopeless act, and the killing blade falls once more to the floor. You will have observed, I've every confidence, those multiple marks of the casters in the dust. This is because the door, when her Ladyship burst into the

378

bedroom that morning, struck the displaced cabinet and sent it rolling smoothly back into its usual position, inadvertently obscuring the razor and allowing a tragedy to appear an outrage."

"And the girl?" cried the inspector, gripping fast to the one thing he still held while the remainder of his case seemed to drift away quicker than the smoke from Holmes's cigarette.

"Mathilda Lodge acted out of loyalty to protect the reputation of one powerless to do so themselves. Petty though most of them were, had those stolen items come to light, what chance would Lefalque's posthumous honour have stood? In her overwhelming grief, Lady Verity asked her most trusted servant to remove them, but with the police trampling hither and yon, there was little prospect of returning the objects unseen, as was proven when she was so suddenly apprehended. But her sense of loyalty to her mistress would not allow her to plead her own innocence, while Lady Verity's horror of bringing dishonour to the name of her beloved friend stilled her from speaking up in her saviour's defence. Thus two well-intentioned acts of mercy resulted in an unfortunate stalemate."

I fought to suppress my grin as the Scotland Yarder whined, "Can this be true?" It was evident that he wished to rail and shout at someone, but like many bullies I have seen, his tyranny of those unlucky enough to rank below him was matched only by his terror of offending those of a higher station.

"Indeed, it is so," replied Lady Verity. "And we are so deeply, desperately ashamed of our deceit, no matter how pure the motives."

"And Monsieur Dubuque and Herr von Waldbaum are coming all this way for a murder enquiry where no-one has been murdered?" A hard gleam of pleasure appeared in the miserable official's eye, and he became noxiously confidential. "If I may speak with them first, Mr. Holmes, sir? You have somehow spirited my entire murder case away defter than an Oriental conjuror at The Alhambra, so you could at least allow me that. I understand the Parisian has been searching out suspected mistresses on the say-so of Madame Lefalque, while the German has been investigating underhand political aspects. It would be good to tell them that while they've chased these side issues, we've used British common sense to lay the case to rest."

"I shall leave you to explain how *we* did so, Inspector. And I shall prepare my own full statement, should these visitors need any clarification on the points you will present. If, of course, that is what my client wishes."

"By all means, it is, Mr. Holmes, thank you," insisted Lord Sternfleet.

379

"Forgive me, Lord Sternfleet, but while I appreciate the courtesy you have shown in inviting me into your home and confidence, you, sir, are not my client."

Leaving the nobleman to choke on his cigar, my friend beckoned to the young constable who had returned with the inspector. "Yes, Mr. Holmes, the person was there, outside the jail where you said, and I delivered your instructions, and an honour it has been, sir, to assist. And here, now, is the wagon I ordered to bring her."

"As I informed your Lordship on numerous occasions this morning, I already have a client, and this is she." Just then, the young lady I had encountered briefly in my old sitting room walked in, looking warily around each face, as if suspecting her every footfall carried her further into a trap. Yet when her eyes fell on her sister she broke into the most dazzling grin and rushed to embrace her.

"When I saw them take you from the station I was set to follow, even if I had to run every mile of the way, but then the copper said Mr. Sherlock Holmes was waiting for us here and called on a wagon to bring me to you."

"I'm free, Florrie!" cried her sister, laughing and sobbing all at the same time. "I don't know how you managed it, but I'm free!"

"Without the valuable testimony of this young lady to her sister's circumstances, and her statement of the character of both your former servant and of your wife, I may not have found the thread needed to unravel this case, your Lordship. Yes, 'former servant', for I believe that while loyalty is said to be its own reward, you swore on oath a considerable sum – one thousand guineas? What a memory you have, Watson! – to any who would resolve this matter. That reward rightly belongs to my client. Minus, of course, the sum of five pounds, which I shall remit to cover my fee."

VII. A Brief Retrospection

I may be seen as sentimental, but as I look back on those closing moments in the drawing room, it is not the wary, uncertain glances and uncomfortable, unvoiced questions that hovered over the family and guests of that house which remain most vivid in my recall, but the simple joy and warmth of those two loyal sisters, celebrating their togetherness, and not yet even aware of the fortune that was soon to be theirs. And here the distance of time allows me to report that the money was invested well, and was only the seed that grew into a great family business and also benefited many a charity that seeks to improve the lot of the supposed lower orders. And if I suppress this other tale of a "Second

Stain" – that being the insidious stain of suspicion, prejudice, and guilt – it is not for the sake of preserving any clandestine espionage route, nor to protect the confidences and tribulations behind the noble façade of those influential families whose affairs lay at the heart of it. It is, instead, out of loyalty to that faithful servant and her devoted sister, whose part in events beyond their control is best left unspoken until such times as the information can have no unhappy result for them.

I am confident that these past secrets are as secure as is the sisters' continuing bright future, but in that July of fifteen years past, there remained one last obligation before any who knew the truth in the case might consider security remotely possible. I was present the next morning when the famous European crime specialists called at Baker Street seeking, as Holmes had predicted, some clarification of whatever coup de théâtre had occurred to render their services redundant while they were still in transit, since the account presented to them by a preening Inspector Highford on their arrival in London had singularly failed to illuminate much beyond the Scotland Yarder's inexplicably high opinion of his own talents.

To this day I still retain the almost verbatim report I transcribed of that demonstration, and it is this transcript that has proved invaluable in allowing me now to recall and accurately record the tangle of truths, half-truths and outright fabrications that have long-since supplanted the true facts of the case. And as I watched those gentlemen as they, in turn, closely watched Sherlock Holmes faultlessly recreate that same sequence of betrayal, tragedy, and sheer chance that he had woven the previous day – Monsieur Dubuque, large eyes peering unblinkingly over the rims of his pince-nez like a peevish, professorial owl rather than a police officer; Herr von Waldbaum alternately tut-tutting and chuckling to himself as, with a tiny pencil clamped in his huge hand, he jotted the salient points in his little notebook, before drawing a line under them with some decisive finality – a growing reassurance dawned that, as far as the various authorities whose minds had been turned to it were concerned, the Leflaque problem could now be relegated to a dossier sealed and stamped as "Resolved with no further inquiry necessary".

If there was any ill feeling that their energies or journeys had been wasted, neither let it show, nor allowed it to sour a sense of mutual admiration amongst the best brains each respective country had to offer. It was, after all, Marcel Dubuque who would petition his own government to secure Holmes's assistance in prising apart the grip of fear in which Paris was held in the summer of 1894 by the notorious Boulevard Assassin, Huret; while my abiding memory of Fritz von Waldbaum shall forever be those few deadly seconds when he and I

381

faced one another over the barrels of our revolvers until, with a timely warning cry from Holmes and a booming laugh of startled recognition from the German, each party realised that the other was skulking in that labyrinth of tunnels below the streets of Vienna on the self-same mission to prevent the ancient terms of a blasphemous covenant from being horribly fulfilled.

There is little more to relate with bearing to the Marleigh Towers incident, although you, my dear future reader, are no doubt asking the question that did not occur to me until I was seated with Holmes in a carriage bearing us back towards Baker Street. "In my sheer admiration at watching as you masked a suicide that had been mistaken for a murder that appeared to be disguised as suicide as an actual suicide after all, but one committed for completely different reasons – I believe I managed to get that right, but I cannot swear to it, or repeat it – I entirely forgot about these international implications that were the source of much talk whose ultimate meaning I quite failed to grasp."

"My boy, I had begun to wonder if you had lost interest," smiled Holmes from behind his pipe, "but you do not disappoint. Simply put, where an easy back and forth of workers and labourers exists across borders – and particularly borders as fractious and troubled as those in the very heart of the cauldron of nations across the narrow Channel – there lies an easy passage for all manner of others, whose work may be more enigmatic, and whose labours are decided in private rooms and silent chambers nearby. Yes, my dear fellow, a virtual open door with a 'welcome' mat on either side for certain covert agencies, for where man can travel freely, so too can what he holds in his pocket, his luggage, or simply in his mind. Well, I shall have our driver deposit me in the city, where I shall take my turn to play the reliable advisor in suggesting that a new route be found, be it over the Alps by elephant, or down the Rhine in a barrel. I rather think Lord Sternfleet may be delayed in relaying the news, as other, more delicate explanations must take precedence."

"That there should be such lack of trust and honesty between man and wife," I mused, sorrowfully, "and such betrayal and secrecy amongst friends."

"I shall not let it trouble me," said Holmes. "I have very few friends, and the best of them I trust implicitly, while I shall, of course, never marry, so need have no fear of the many dangers of that dubious arrangement. Ah, and here we are at Pall Mall, and I must leave you. And what shall you do now?"

I cast a stern eye in his direction and murmured, "Oh, I shall armour myself against those many dubious dangers, and go back home to my new wife."

"Ah, Watson, you forgive me, I'm sure? There, you try to hide a smile, so you do. But if I may paraphrase the recent utterances of an individual who holds you in the highest regard, and who is therefore a wise man indeed; what purpose does it serve to pursue justice – and deserved happiness is most surely only a specific form of justice – if we cannot believe there exists good in this world? Goodbye, my dear fellow, until fate or fortune brings us together again."

The Two Umbrellas
by Martin Rosenstock

On a cloudy autumn evening, a young man in a Chesterfield coat crossed the courtyard of a Georgian-style office building and approached its gate onto Whitehall. In his right hand, he carried a satchel; an umbrella was tucked under his left arm.

"Have a good evening, Mr. Ferguson," called out the sentry in a wooden coop by the threshold.

"Thank you, Palmer. You too."

"Oh, and enjoy your holidays, Mr. Ferguson," the sentry remembered.

"I am sure I will."

Ferguson stepped onto the footpath. He passed a brass plaque affixed to the building's façade: *Admiralty House – British Royal Navy.* Taking his umbrella, he began to swing it, not quite in rhythm with his gait, as he headed down the street towards Charing Cross. The noise of cabs and coaches, delivering passengers to their supper destinations, filled the air; newspaper boys cried the evening editions. Men in suits and overcoats were moving determinedly away from their places of employ. Twice, Ferguson lifted his silk top hat in greeting and received an identical salutation in return. His features during these exchanges were controlled; the brown eyes behind a pince-nez widened briefly with practiced geniality. Once in a while though, when unobserved, a twitch passed over his face, and he would then press his lips together so as to reestablish an appearance of nonchalance.

Ferguson was slight of build. His shoulders did not fill his coat, and the legs of his trousers flapped loosely with each step. His face, at first glance, appeared nondescript, the face of a man who had gone, or perhaps rather had been propelled, through life without encountering major discomfitures, let alone obstacles. The features were fine and suggested schooling and cultivation. One could imagine him conversing on a Turner exhibition or the quality of a tenor's interpretation of a Verdi aria. Yet one would have been hard pressed to imagine him taking a paintbrush or stepping onto a stage. On closer inspection, though, this air of comfortable staidness appeared forced, yet perhaps not consciously so. A tightness sat around his jaws, as if his teeth were constantly on the verge of clenching in anticipation of pain. His head was fixed at a light upward angle, conveying a blend of fancy and ambition.

He pulled out his watch, looked at it, then increased his pace, now swinging the umbrella with more gusto. He did not hear the bicycle which, swerving between pedestrians, was approaching him from behind. At the last moment the rider shouted a warning, but too late. He hit Ferguson's shoulder at almost full speed. The umbrella slipped from his grasp, described an arc through the air, and landed clattering by the entrance of a whitewashed house that stood unimpressively next to Admiralty Arch. The satchel fell in front of him. As Ferguson's outstretched hands struck the footpath to either side of the satchel, it luckily prevented his face from hitting the pavement. His pince-nez detached itself, glanced off the satchel, and slithered two yards across the stones before coming to rest on the curb.

A middle-aged gentleman in a rumpled beige suit, who was emerging from the entrance in front of which the umbrella came to the ground, rushed to the victim.

"Are you all right, Sir?"

"Yes, yes. I . . . I think I am . . . ." The middle-aged gentleman helped Ferguson to his feet, who, on rising, gripped his satchel.

He exhaled loudly, then surveyed the footpath in alarm. Some pedestrians slowed their steps, but as the crisis had already passed they continued on their way.

"Can you see my spectacles, by any chance?"

"Oh dear. I'm afraid not . . . ."

"I am rather dependent on them, unfortunately."

"These ruffians on their bicycles. They are a menace. The police need to do something about these newfangled things," muttered the man, gripping the edges of his suit and looking around. "There they are," he exclaimed and stepped up to the curb. He settled down on his haunches with a wheeze. "And you're lucky. They are not even broken." Having retrieved the pince-nez, he stood up. "A little scratched merely." He wiped the spectacles clean against the arm of his jacket.

Ferguson had remained immobile, staring into the distance. On now receiving his accoutrement, he hurriedly squeezed it onto his nose. "Thank you, Sir. Much obliged."

"You are most welcome. And the umbrella." The middle-aged gentleman picked it up from the footpath in front of the entrance. "I say, you were rather lucky, all things considered."

"I believe I was," agreed Ferguson, taking the umbrella and giving it an anxious glance. Apparently satisfied, he assumed his former expression, chin lifted, his features showing determined equanimity. "Thank you again, Sir. You have been most kind." He looked ahead to the corner where the bicycle must have disappeared and shook his head in anger. "Well, what can one say . . .? I must be on my way. I am in a bit of a hurry . . . ." He pointed to a line of hansom cabs that stood waiting at Charing Cross, then raised his hand in good-bye and resumed his walk.

The crowd absorbed Ferguson's figure. The man in the rumpled suit remained behind, a few waxy blotches forming on his jowly face. Finally, he stepped back through the door out of which he had emerged. It had only been leaned to. Inside the foyer was another man. He had a cigar in his mouth and stood bent over a walnut table on which lay an umbrella whose handle had been detached as well as a few sheets of tracing paper. These the man held pressed down on the edges. The top sheet showed what appeared to be a construction plan of a warship.

"Looks as if everything were here, Mycroft," said the man around his cigar. "As you had expected."

The middle-aged gentleman approached the table. "Well," he said with stern contentment, "now things are back where they belong. And Ferguson is our deliveryman."

"Are you certain he will not mention his accident to his friends? They might form a suspicion."

"Rest assured, he will not. He was able to brush himself off. Vanity will seal his lips."

"Look at these!" The man turned to another page, and the ash shook precariously at the tip of his cigar. "As good as the originals! I'd love to wring his thin neck! The cab will follow him?"

"Don't worry, it's waiting at Charing Cross," smiled the man called Mycroft. "If we're lucky, he will board it. If he takes another one, ours will follow the one he takes. All is going according to plan."

The man with the cigar voiced another doubt: "What if Ferguson looks at the new version and realizes it's not his . . . ?"

"That is conceivable, but not likely. They will be in a hurry. We had to take that risk."

"I see." The man exhaled a thoughtful puff of smoke. "No more news about this character behind all this?"

"Not really. As I told you the other day, he only appeared a few months ago as if out of nowhere. One thing, he seems to be a mathematician by profession, of all things . . . ."

"I never liked math." The man chuckled. "Bane of my school days. Let us make sure his career is short-lived. We should get underway, I suppose. If you are sure Ferguson is heading to the East End."

"I'm sure about the East End. Where in the East End I don't know, unfortunately. But I've seen to it that we'll have word once he reaches his destination."

The man with the cigar rolled up the papers. "Very good. I'll follow your lead, Mycroft; this is your operation."

Unbeknownst to the two men now leaning over the documents from the umbrella, the little drama on the sidewalk had had an observer. After Ferguson emerged from the office building, a stout man with a gray walrus moustache appeared from the inside of a black coach that stood idle on the opposite side of the street as if waiting for an important personage. The man wore the thick, double-breasted dark jacket of coachmen during the cold season. He now clambered onto the box, apparently having concluded a nap inside his vehicle, and began readying himself for a resumption of his duties. While Ferguson walked down Whitehall with measured steps, swinging his umbrella, the coachman nestled with the reins. His head jerked briefly to the side as a young man with a cap pressed down upon his forehead suddenly appeared on a bicycle, heading in the same direction as Ferguson. The coachman's head remained lowered, but his fingers became motionless. From a distance of almost a hundred yards, he watched the collision between the bicycle rider and Ferguson and the appearance of the middle-aged gentleman from the house door. The coachman waited until Ferguson took leave of his helper and resumed his walk towards Charing Cross, then maneuvered the coach into the street with a smack of the whip.

The coach maintained a slow pace, and the man with the walrus moustache watched Ferguson approaching the line of hansom cabs. One cab driver accosted the young man and tried to steer him towards a vehicle, but Ferguson ignored the imprecations and selected another cab. The coachman increased his speed as the cab with Ferguson inside pulled into the busy traffic of Charing Cross. Immediately, the cab whose driver had failed to receive the young man's business followed. The two cabs, the coach behind them, now made a half tour of the circle, passing under Nelson's Column, which pierced the gray sky like a barren mast, and headed down Northumberland Avenue towards the river. On reaching the Thames, they turned west along the Embankment, before finally crossing Westminster Bridge. The water lay dark in the evening light, emitting an odour of seaweed and dead fish. From down the river came the braying of a steamship's horn; the paraffin lamps of the cabs and coaches bobbed yellow in the dusk.

The man with the walrus moustache allowed other vehicles to insert themselves between his coach and the two cabs, but never lost sight of his quarry; the second cab followed the same practice with regard to the first one. A keen northwest wind blew towards the Channel, but could not dispel the pall of clouds and smoke over London. The cold air brought a flush to the coachman's heavy round features, crisscrossed on the cheeks by a spider's web of capillaries. The three vehicles passed through Lambeth into the Borough and crossed the river again on Southwark Bridge. They then turned east on Thames Street and made their way through the City towards Whitechapel. The buildings on either side began to take on a derelict aspect; some passers-by moved furtively, as if reluctant to be seen.

As the two cabs and the coach turned into the thoroughfare of Fenchurch Road, the coachman let his horse's croup feel the whip. The animal broke into a faster trot and passed the cabs. He did not look left. Another touch of the whip, and he had soon left the two vehicles far behind. He reached a three-storey redbrick building with Old Forge Hotel painted over the entrance in peeling verdigris letters. Turning into an alleyway, he followed it for fifty yards, turned into a lane, then into another one, and after thirty yards gingerly steered his coach into a walled courtyard. He jumped from the box with an agility surprising for a man of his bulk and walked back out of the courtyard, pulling a heavy gate closed behind him. Having secured it with a padlock, he retraced his way to the hotel and entered the building through a side door that led into a hallway. Down it ran a carpet of indeterminate colour. A man who looked like a prize fighter stood, arms before his chest, in front of a door. He now moved hastily aside and knocked, three raps followed by a pause and another single rap.

A rustling sound could be heard, then a bolt slid back. The door swung open and revealed a woman. She was tall and dressed in a mauve silk Caraco jacket whose top buttons were open. It set off her décolletage and slim waist advantageously. The frosted lustre of a string of pearls circled her slender neck. A flush was just receding from her cheeks, leaving her skin with a lightly rouged porcelain complexion. The room behind her lay in half light; thick curtains sealed the windows. The flame of a single gaslight on the wall imparted a copper glow to her wavy auburn hair. She had a thin nose that sloped upward towards the point. A hard clarity lay in her eyes and belied the expression of girlish ingenuousness on her features. At least two decades and a half had been hers on this earth, and some of those years had been rich in experiences. She now opened her lips to reveal a line of white teeth and was about to speak, when a voice from the shadows cut her off:

"Moran, come in. What is the news?" The voice was low and almost without inflexion, yet commanding. "Beatrice, shut the door."

The woman did so, after Moran had stepped inside.

388

"As you had expected, Professor," said Moran, a grin under his moustache. "They staged the accident while Ferguson was walking towards the cabs."

"Mycroft Holmes had to strike. This was his last chance. Are they following Ferguson?"

"Yes, there's a cab behind his."

"When will he be here?"

"In three, four minutes."

The man who elicited these quick replies sat reclining in an easy chair. His right calf dangled comfortably over his left knee.

"Pour yourself a drink, Moran." The Professor rose and gestured towards a decanter and some glasses on a sideboard. His hands were large, with long fingers, pianist's hands. A signet ring with a dark blue spinel gleamed on his left hand.

He took a glass of gin that stood on a side table and crossed the room with long steps. He was over six feet tall, yet appeared of only a little above average height. His back was slightly bent, as if he had spent too much time hunched over a desk. Yet a closer look revealed that in fact his entire frame was coiled in wiry expectancy. He was middle-aged in an ill-defined manner. He had thin, metal gray hair, combed back straight from his forehead. His features were taught and unlined. The shadow of a beard covered sallow cheeks and a bony chin. The only feature that bespoke the body's fleshly substance was his lips. They lay full and sensuous on his face as if painted on, displaying a prominent Cupid's bow.

He took up station by the window and with index and middle finger pushed the curtain an inch aside. Every once in a while, he took a sip from his glass, rolled the liquid in his mouth, and then swallowed with an expressionless face.

"Professor Moriarty." The woman's voice had the modulation that comes with years of training. Yet now she spoke a little unsteadily, and a hint of a Yorkshire accent flattened her vowels, while her fingers played with the antimacassar on the chair behind which she was standing. "I've asked you this before, but what will happen when . . . things don't go as he hopes?"

"And as before, my dear, I tell you he will be heartbroken."

"That is all?"

"You will never hear from him again. There are two types of men, Beatrice, those who are capable of revenge and those who are not." She seemed to be considering this when Moriarty turned. "But you *must* leave with him tonight."

She looked into the Professor's strangely unblinking gray eyes.

"I never renege on a bargain."

"Good." He passed an appreciative glance down her figure, as if beholding a fine piece of artisanship he had created. Then he turned back to the window.

"Here they are . . . ." he announced after a minute.

"Shall I go into the lobby?" asked Moran, who had settled down with his drink on a sofa next to a cold fireplace.

"No, someone is already there."

The familiar knocking signal came after half-a-minute. Her dress rustling, Beatrice crossed the carpet to the door. Ferguson entered with all the aplomb of a schoolboy tiptoeing into the classroom after the bell has rung. Yet in the presence of the woman his appearance changed rapidly. He straightened up, and his chest appeared to broaden. His pupils expanded behind the pince-nez, lending him an air of determination and focus. A ruddy colour crept into his cheeks, and a smile that betokened a belief in assured well-being spread over his thin face.

He leant forward awkwardly. Both his hands were full; in his right he held his satchel and top hat, in his left the umbrella. "Miss, Miss . . . J-Jones." He recovered himself and brushed her cheek with his lips. "Sorry I'm a little late – "

"I was becoming worried for you, Henry." Her voice had acquired a playful lilt and had risen by half an octave.

"Nothing to worry about," he assured her. "All went well . . . ."

She pushed the door closed, then slipped his hat from his fingers and hung it on a hook in the wall. Turning, she gestured towards the man who had crossed the room behind her.

"As the Professor told you it would. He is rather good at anticipating events."

Ferguson switched his satchel into his left hand, and Moriarty took the young man's right. There was a grasping quality to the Professor's motion, as if he were laying claim to a coveted object.

"Good evening, Mr. Ferguson."

"Good evening, Sir."

"No surprises. I am glad."

"It happened almost exactly as you had expected. A cyclist hit me."

Moriarty lifted both hands, palms up, to indicate his invariable correctness in such matters. "These are the clumsy ways our friends in the government mount their efforts."

"We took quite a risk," Beatrice observed. "I am relieved."

Ferguson shrugged. "It was nothing, really. And I did put on a good show, even if I say so myself."

390

Moriarty gave a short, rasping laugh. "I am sure you did. Now to our business," he added, steering Ferguson by the elbow to a desk in the corner.

Moran and Beatrice joined as the young man placed his satchel on the desk and took the umbrella in both hands.

"First, the wages of my accident," he said with an emphatically wry smile, unscrewing the wooden handle.

Moriarty bent forward to inspect the umbrella. "They produced a nice duplicate, I have to say."

"I left mine in the office occasionally, so they would have enough time." Ferguson pulled a role of tracing papers from the shank and held it out to the Professor.

"So," said Moriarty, his long fingers closing around them, "this is what Mycroft Holmes would have me pass on to my clients." He unrolled the papers and eyed the top one, head tilting left to right and back. Then he repeated the procedure with the remaining sheets. A lopsided grin formed on his full lips. "Not bad at all. Every number, angle, curve is wrong, but believably wrong. One must appreciate dedicated work." He laid the papers on the desk and pointed at the satchel. "That contains the genuine plans."

"It does. Hidden in plain sight, so to speak. As you suggested."

"Oh, not my idea." The Professor raised a modest hand, the spinel shining dully. "Some years ago, I read a story about a detective in search of a stolen letter. I forget the title, but the story was rather good. The idea was that the most obvious places are never searched."

"It appears Henry has kept his side of the bargain," Beatrice interjected now.

"Indeed he has," agreed Moriarty. His left hand closed on the satchel's grip, while his right pulled an envelope from his jacket. "And I never renege on one, Miss Jones." The envelope passed into Ferguson's sheepishly outstretched hand. "The sum we agreed upon in government bonds. You are a wealthy man now, Mr. Ferguson."

The young man held the envelope mutely between thumb and index finger.

"Please, do have a look inside." The Professor gestured invitingly.

Ferguson fingered open the envelope, Beatrice by his side. Her lips parted as her lover's thumb grazed the edge of the bills. Then her large blue eyes quickly rose to meet his glance, and with a smile he slipped the envelope into his coat. His left arm passed around the small of her back and pulled her against him.

"Wouldn't you like to have a look at the genuine plans?" He pointed at the satchel.

Moriarty shook his head. "That will not be necessary. I trust you, Mr. Ferguson. And now we must see to it that you have a chance to enjoy your newfound wealth. Mycroft Holmes appears to bear . . . enterprising government employees somewhat of an animus. Even the ones he believes to have been useful. A pity, isn't it? This hotel has more exits than are readily visible, Mr. Ferguson," he continued. "If you were to leave by the front door, you would be pursued, I am afraid, and would not see the end of it . . . until the end. Happily though, I've been preparing for such eventualities."

He gave Moran a nod, who set to work moving the chairs and table to the edge of the room. The others watched, as he bent down and rolled up the carpet until a trap door became visible in the wooden floor. A handle was set into the door's boards in such a manner that the surface was flush. Very carefully, Moran took the handle between thumb and forefinger of his left hand and lifted the metal half moon into an upright position. In the handle's centre the nub of what looked like a screw became visible. A penknife appeared in Moran's right hand and with a click a stiletto blade sprang out of the handle. He proceeded to push the blade's tip under the metal nub. Once he had dislodged it, he laid aside the knife and pulled a thin splint from the centre of the handle. The splint was just long enough to traverse the body of the handle to the inside. The splint's tip would inevitably puncture the skin of anyone who gripped the handle without being aware of this hidden danger. Moran rose from his knees, walked over to the side table, and placed the splint in the table's centre. Then he returned and with one swift movement yanked open the trap door.

Moriarty approached the gaping black hole. A few steps of a ladder where visible before darkness closed in.

"You see, Mr. Ferguson. Everything is prepared. This passage leads to a house some distance away. My associate here, Colonel Moran, will take you. You can trust him implicitly; he has worked aside me for many years. From this house, you will all three travel by coach to a spot somewhat east of the docks. A boat will be waiting. I understand you have given some valuables for transport to your charming lady here. You will find them stowed in your cabin. You will be in Calais by tomorrow morning, Mr. Ferguson. There, Colonel Moran will take his leave from you. Our customer does not reside in your place of destination. I'm afraid the crossing might not be comfortable tonight, but such is the lot of us who travel light."

Moran had lit an oil lantern and now descended the ladder. The hole was not as deep as it had initially appeared, somewhat over eight feet. The entrance to a side passage became visible; the passage was a little under six feet in height and a foot and a half in width. A wooden beam, the first in a long line one might conjecture, supported the entrance. Having reached the bottom, Moran stood in the centre of a dirty three-by-three foot square and held up the lantern.

"Please," said Moriarty, looking at the pair. "Don't worry. I assure you, it's quite safe."

Beatrice nodded, but first went over to the hook in the wall and took Ferguson's hat. She placed it in his hand as if to say that he would forget his own head if it were not attached. Then she pulled up the hem of her dress, turned her back to the hole, and placed a dainty shoe on the first rung. In a few seconds she was below, Moran gallantly raising a hand to assist her with the final steps.

"Our ways part here, Mr. Ferguson," said Moriarty. "I wish you good fortune. Remember, you must never again set foot in this country, no matter how homesick you become. And beware of Her Majesty's many agents; the reach of their arm is long."

Ferguson paled at these words, yet nodded as if to intimate that he had considered his choices long and carefully. Moriarty did not extend his hand. In his left he held the papers, in his right the satchel. Ferguson turned and slowly descended the steps.

"We're ready," Moran's voice called from below after a few seconds.

"Don't forget the merchandise." The Professor lowered himself on one knee and extended his arm holding the satchel downward. A careful observer might have seen that one of the satchel's two straps, both of which had been closed, now hung half open and dangled outside the loop.

"Thank you," came Moran's voice from the hole, and the Professor retracted his arm, hand empty, and rose.

Without further ceremony, he closed the trapdoor.

Beside him on the floor lay a manila folder of exactly the size that fitted snugly into the satchel. Moriarty took the folder and laid it on the side table. He picked up the splint Moran had placed there. Holding it between his fingertips, the Professor retraced his steps. He kneeled down and fitted the splint into the hole in the handle, before carefully settling the handle into place. Then he went over to the sideboard and poured himself a gin. Thoughtfully, he emptied the glass. He finally set it down and returned to the trapdoor. Unlike Moran, he used a fingernail to dislodge the splint before pulling it out. He held it up towards the gaslight. On the tip, an oily sheen was visible. Moriarty pulled out a handkerchief and wiped the splint clean with a few vigorous motions. He looked at it critically, then nodded. A sting, yes, for sure, but no longer a deadly one. He replaced the splint in the handle, stood up, rolled back the carpet, and moved the pieces of furniture to where they had stood before.

His work complete, he crossed the room and opened a wardrobe. Inside hung a tattered black pea coat, a pair of patched trousers, and a collarless shirt. A shelf held a false gray beard and some other items that might be found in an actor's dressing room. On the wardrobe's inside door was a mirror. He took off his dark lounge coat, while pulling a silver comb from its inside pocket. He threw the coat over the wardrobe's door and then proceeded to smooth back his hair. Smiling approvingly at his image, he unbuttoned his satin waistcoat. He would walk out the front door. An old salt on shore leave could afford this place. Maybe he would be swaying a little; old salts on shore leave generally did.

Mycroft Holmes was walking along the gas lit streets of Billingsgate towards London Bridge. He had thrown on a brown Newmarket coat over his rumpled suit, but had neglected to close either. A woolen scarf hung uselessly around his neck. His hands were rammed into his trouser pockets. The large man carried his head bent; wisps of hair hung into his high forehead. His steps had a discontented, stomping quality. A few times, he almost bumped into another pedestrian, who invariably was the one to swerve so as to avoid the collision.

A thin rain began, whipped into sheets by the wind, and Holmes raised his collar and quickened his steps. He passed a pub, halted, walked back, and entered the premises. He blew his nose on a well-worn handkerchief, then approached the bar and settled down on a stool at the corner of the short side. Closing time was less than an hour away. The pub was half empty. Its regular patrons were the merchants of the City, and on a Friday night many of those gentlemen had more fashionable or disreputable venues to attend. A group of men sat chatting by a fireside; some of them held instruments on their knees, but only one occasionally scratched at a violin. A few tipplers lined the bar. Tobacco smoke hung under the ceiling, immobile and as if it had always been there and always would be.

Holmes ordered a stout, and sat with it, hands circling the glass. Every once in a while, his eyebrows would crease or he would press his teeth against his upper lip as if in response to a thought that had come to an end. Then he would take a sip of beer.

He did not notice the figure slipping onto the stool perpendicular to his own. The next time Holmes emerged from his thoughts, he saw a bearded man across the edge of the bar. He was wearing a tattered black pea coat and a cap from under which protruded a mass of gray hair – an old salt on shore leave. He seemed familiar to Holmes in a vague way, one of the thousands of faces he had encountered, none of which he ever forgot. The man's left hand was closed around a glass of gin; his right hand lay invisible below the bar.

"Yer looked like yer were woolgatherin' there, guv'nor," said the old salt and gave a good-natured, hoarse laugh.

"It has been an interesting day."

"Mine too, mine too."

Holmes lifted a tired eyebrow.

The sailor took a gulp of gin, then said, "I got me 'ands on sumthing, guv'nor, sumthing I been after for a while."

"A nice coincidence . . ." mumbled Holmes.

"'Ow so, Sir?"

"I lost sight of someone today, someone I've been after for a while."

"That's a rum thing, guv'nor." The sailor's eyes twinkled with cold merriment underneath heavy brows. Then his voice changed, losing any trace of Cockney and acquiring a mocking, imperious tone. "But there are no coincidences, only excuses of a lazy mind."

The two men looked at each other. Slowly, Holmes began to rise.

"Sit down, Mr. Holmes. A gun is pointed at your stomach. And you never carry a weapon yourself, I know."

Holmes settled back on his stool, his hand closing tightly around his glass. "What do you want, Moriarty?"

"To meet, at last," smiled the Professor. "After all these months of circling each other like two backyard tomcats. Have you discovered the tunnel from the Forge Hotel yet, Mr. Holmes?"

"We have. I'm sure your hands were calloused after all the digging."

"Please, Mr. Holmes. Why so acerbic? We both know, some do the digging, some think for the diggers. Our two institutions are much alike in this regard. And anyway, what could you have done? Arrest Ferguson? Would that not have suggested he was under observation?"

"We would have waited a while."

"Even then, would an arrest not have cast doubts on the genuine nature of Ferguson's documents? I might have become suspicious, thought you might have exchanged them for false ones at some point. Who knows, even my clients might have developed second thoughts – "

Holmes's lips thinned.

"Speechless, Mr. Holmes? Did you really think I'd fall for your fakes? I'm rather hurt, I must say."

Holmes's mouth opened, but Moriarty waived him to be silent.

"Please, Mr. Holmes. Who cares about boring details?"

"We will find him. He will stand trial for high treason."

"Maybe you will, maybe you won't. Maybe he will, maybe he won't," Moriarty said flatly and sipped from his gin. He glanced at the bandaged middle finger of Holmes's right hand. The Professor's face appeared perfectly expressionless, but Holmes could not be certain. An urge to rip away Moriarty's false beard welled up inside Holmes, yet at the same time he feared that he would behold a triumphant grin, perhaps worse, a pitying smile.

"Is he together with that tart you placed in his way?" he asked.

"An ugly word, Mr. Holmes! Miss Beatrice is a thespian, an artist! And yes, I believe he is sharing her company, blissful as a child at Christmas."

Holmes snorted. "You know what will happen, Moriarty. One morning, he will wake up, and your thespian will have danced out of his life, with the money."

"My good Holmes, Ferguson is a young man. These are the mistakes young men make. He will learn. Yet for now he is happy because he acted upon his desires. Thus it should be. I merely gave him the opportunity for happiness." After a pause, he leaned conspiratorially over the bar. "Really, my enterprise is to make people happy, Mr. Holmes."

At the other man's raillery, the colour rose in Holmes's cheeks. His fingertips turned white around the glass. Moriarty had been watching closely. He lifted a hand as if to suggest one last moment of reprieve before the inevitable fight. The spinel still gleamed on his ring finger, out of keeping with his modest attire.

"You may not believe this, Mr. Holmes, but even your happiness has been on my mind." He slipped his hand into his jacket's side pocket, brought out a folded sheet of tracing paper, and pushed it across the bar. Holmes did not take his eyes off the other man's face. Finally, he reached for the sheet and unfolded it. He studied it for close to half-a-minute, his skin turning ashen.

"This is from the genuine document . . ." he whispered.

"It is," confirmed the Professor. "But don't you worry. I sent Moran on his way with the false version you provided us."

Holmes swallowed.

"How did . . . ?" His voice deteriorated into a croak, and he cleared his throat. "How did you get this?"

"Immaterial, Holmes. Immaterial. But there are things I like to keep for myself. I am a bit of a collector. Who knows, perhaps I am even a patriot. And my clients will be satisfied. Your version is compelling enough. They will not notice the difference. You may keep that," he said, pointing to the paper. "A memento, if you will." Moriarty slipped from his stool. He placed some coins on the bar. "Allow me, your drink is on me. I had ever such a pleasant conversation this evening. I will also leave you this." He hung an umbrella by its handle on the bar's edge next to Holmes. "You should be more careful, Mr. Holmes; otherwise you'll catch a cold."

With that, the old salt turned, crossed the room with long, silent steps, and disappeared into the night. Holmes eyed the umbrella that was swinging lightly. He recognized its somewhat widened shank. The urge to break the blasted thing rose from his stomach like acid. He looked at his bandaged middle finger. The wound stung, but the pain was not physical. An odd chill seemed to emanate from the empty place across from him, as if a void had been left there. He had played the game too loosely, but they would meet again, many times, he had a sense. The next round would find him better prepared, much better prepared.

Holmes's eyes fell upon the gin glass Moriarty had left standing upon the bar. Holmes stared at the glass for a while as if trying to impose order on a string of inchoate thoughts. After a while he reached over and carefully picked the glass up by its rim. He turned and held the glass in the direction of the fireplace. Moriarty's fingerprints were clearly visible. Raising his eyebrows, Holmes turned back to the bar and set down the glass. He looked at it, occasionally rubbing his chin. It was time to come up with some new ideas. Slowly, he finished his pint.

Beatrice let her head fall back against the rear of the coach and closed her eyes. The sound of the horse's hooves and of the wheels on the cobble stones was soothing. She felt tired, but her heart beat rapidly. Everything had worked as planned. They were already outside Calais. A few hours to Amiens and tomorrow on to Paris! She would see Paris, finally! She would do more than see it; she would make it her own!

She opened her eyes and brushed a strand of her auburn locks behind her ear. Henry Ferguson lay slunk into the corner, his mouth half open, producing chortling noises. His complexion was still greenish. Moriarty had been right about the Channel crossing. She reached over and pulled two envelopes from the inside pocket of Ferguson's coat. Placing them on her lap, she passed her fingers over the top one. She could feel Moriarty's government notes inside. Laying it on the upholstery, she took the other. The envelope bulged slightly. She unsealed it and pulled out a folded set of tracing papers. They made a low crackling sound as she smoothed them out on her knees. She inspected them for close to a minute. For all she could tell, they showed boats and their parts. Men were such fools! All this intrigue for some drawings, of which one could tell one's lover to make as many copies as one pleased! Oh well, if this was what they considered worth spending money on, who was she to tell them otherwise? She folded the papers and replaced them in the envelope. Then she slipped both envelopes back into Ferguson's coat. She had an idea who might be interested in this set of copies.

Her eyes rested on Ferguson. Despite his complexion, his sleep appeared happy. Oddly, she had found of late that she rather liked him. His presence was comforting. He would never leave her, never make demands. What to do with him? Time would tell. She turned to look at the green hills of the French countryside. The storm had blown itself out over night, and now the drops on the yellow leaves of the beech trees sparkled in the late morning sun. A pink hue lay on her chest. She felt like laughing, but she preferred her lover to remain asleep, and so she only smiled.

The Adventure of the Fateful Malady
by Craig Janacek

A quick reference to my journals confirms that the year 1889 was a very busy one for Mr. Sherlock Holmes. Notwithstanding the fact that marriage had precipitated my departure from the flat at 221b Baker Street, I called upon Holmes regularly, and he was kind enough to include me in several of his more peculiar adventures. I have already set down for public consumption such strange tales as that of the false beggar, [1] and the woman's wit that foiled both a king and a genius. [2] But other problems, such as the mystery of Mr. Philip King, the famous inventor, who boarded the Flying Scotsman at King's Cross Station and was never seen again, [3] cannot be told until the principals of the matter have passed beyond the ken of human existence. These cases must be safely locked away until a new day has dawned, and the terrible events depicted in the following narrative are just such an example.

It was during one of my visits to Baker Street that autumn when Holmes found himself engaged by a client of no small renown. We were sitting in front of the afternoon fire where I had reclaimed my former arm-chair, while Holmes was animatedly describing to me, in minute detail, my movements of the day. Despite having repeatedly been on the receiving end of Holmes's series of logical deductions, it nonetheless amazed me when he inquired whether my trip to Hatton Garden had been a successful one.

"I fail to see, Holmes, how you could possibly know precisely which street I visited today?"

"It was simplicity itself, Watson. The first observation is the faint sparkle of gold coming from the distal right sleeve of your coat."

I reflexively glanced downwards and verified his inspection. "What of it?"

"Why, Watson, how many methods exist for a man to obtain gold dust upon his sleeve? Surely very few, especially when that fellow is a practicing physician and not an artisan? When you add to the chain of logic the facts that this man was married almost a year ago, but at the time was rather deficient in his pocket-book, it suggests that he was engaged upon the errand of buying a gift for his wife. And where else in London does a man go to purchase jewelry other than Hatton Garden?" [4]

I laughed appreciatively. "Guilty as charged, Holmes."

399

He smiled back. "I think in this case, you are literally wearing your heart upon your sleeve, [5] Watson." He paused and listened for a moment. "Ah, if I am not mistaken, the sound of a brougham stopping outside our door suggests that we are about to be visited by a client." He rose and peered out of the bow-window towards the street below.

I had little time to be pleased that Holmes had automatically involved me in the case, for the door was swiftly opened. An austere man entered, his springy steps communicating a great energy. His iron grey hair placed him at a shade over fifty years of age, though his cleanly-shaven face was unlined. His nose and chin were angular, and his features as grave as a sphinx, though his eyes shone with vitality and shrewdness. As to his dress, his double-breasted woolen frock coat and cashmere-striped trousers were of the highest cut and quality. He removed his top hat and perched stiffly in the basket chair that Holmes had indicated.

"My name is Sir James Saunders," [6] began our visitor, but he was forestalled by Holmes.

"If I may, sir? You recognized, of course, Watson, that Sir James is a fellow medico. However, rather than a general practitioner, he specializes in dermatology. You are engaged at the highest levels of a hospital, and it is upon their business that you come."

"You are correct, Mr. Holmes. For the last six years I have had the honor of being the Director of the Charing Cross Hospital. [7] But you must know these facts already, to be so familiar with my history."

"Not at all, Sir James. The simple method to distinguish a dermatologist from other medical men is to compare their hands and face, one rough from constant washing, the other smoother than is typical for their age. Your career has been successful, for how else would you afford such a fine brougham? But it is plain from your horses, which are hardly fresh and glossy, that your practice is not located in the vicinity of the nearby Cavendish Square, where the most eminent physicians hang their lamps. [8] Therefore, I reasoned that you are most likely the head of a hospital, and so it proves to be."

Sir James nodded. "That is excellent, Mr. Holmes. This is precisely why I have consulted you." He paused and studied Holmes for a moment. "I have been informed that you are a man whose discretion can be trusted absolutely."

"I am glad that it is so said," replied Holmes mildly.

"It is of critical importance that no word of this matter spreads to the public. If Fleet Street [9] hears of this, the reputation of the Hospital will suffer a mortal blow, from which it could never hope to recover."

"Perhaps if you told me of your problem, Sir James?"

The man sighed. "Very well. I am afraid, Mr. Holmes, that the Black Death is once more upon us." [10]

"Indeed," said Holmes, his lids drooping over his eyes.

Sir James appeared dismayed that his dramatic words had such little effect upon the demeanor of my friend. "I am not certain that you understand the gravity of the situation, Mr. Holmes," said he, urgently. "The Great Plague of London may have been two hundred years ago, [11] but nothing that caused such a massive upheaval is ever truly forgotten. As the harbinger of a terrible comet appeared in the sky, [12] a hundred thousand died in London alone. [13] Of course, that was small fry compared to the Black Death pandemic itself. [14] Over a million souls dead, Mr. Holmes, up to a third of the entire population of England! Imagine if such a horror was to return?"

"Surely this is a matter for the authorities, Sir James?" I interjected. "How have you succeeded in keeping this quiet?"

"This was not a decision that I came to on my own, Dr. Watson. The Board of Health has been notified. The Necropolis Railway [15] has refused to take the bodies, for fear of spreading the contagion, and it was the Board that secretly approved the extraordinary measures of permitting us to cremate them *in situ*. [16] Mr. Holmes, I assure you that the matter is dire."

"I recognize, sir, that you believe that a great pestilence has descended upon your hospital. However, I fail to perceive of what service I could be to you? Your particular problem seems to be more along the lines of Dr. Watson here than that of a consulting detective. I am no physician." He sank back into his arm-chair, his interest clearly waning.

"I don't require for you to help the patients, Mr. Holmes. A team of skilled doctors, ably assisted by caring nurses, is laboring night and day to accomplish that herculean task. What I ask of you is to determine from where the plague is originating. We have isolated every patient, and yet new cases continue to occur, almost every day." [17]

Holmes frowned. "It was my understanding that such miasmas have been mainly eliminated in no small part due to the sewers engineered by Sir Joseph Bazalgette?" [18]

"But, Holmes, the plague is mainly spread via rats," [19] I interjected.

"That is indeed the accepted hypothesis, Dr. Watson," replied Sir James. "It is believed that the Black Death first descended upon Europe via grain ships originating from China, which unwittingly harbored the infected rats."

"Surely you must have a mechanism in place to safeguard against such an infestation?" asked Holmes.

401

"Indeed we do, Mr. Holmes. Like many hospitals, we kept a clowder [20] of Manx mousers, descended from a cat that legendarily sailed about the HMS *Ajax* at Trafalgar. [21] However, three weeks ago all of our Manx were suddenly found dead."

Holmes sat up again. "That is most remarkable."

Sir James shrugged. "Is it? I thought it a coincidence, perhaps one that initiated the infestations. So we have taken pains to rectify the situation. We brought in a famous rat-catcher from Shadwell, by the name of Dick Whyte." [22]

"But the results have not been satisfactory?"

"Mr. Whyte continues to catch large numbers of rats, Mr. Holmes, but it has made no impact upon the spread of the contagion."

"Then what is your theory?"

"I came to seek a theory, Mr. Holmes, not to suggest one. However, Dr. Edward Purcell, who we brought in this summer to help us combat London's outbreak of cholera, suspects that it might have been introduced to the hospital by a coolie from Wapping or Rotherhithe." [23]

Holmes glanced at his pocket watch. "The hour is getting late," he noted, "but hospitals never sleep and rat-catchers are nocturnal beings. Let us waste no more time here, but rather see what we can ascertain tonight."

Sir James insisted on driving us to the hospital in his brougham. On the way, I mentioned how odd it was to find a disease typically associated with the history books now stalking the streets of London.

"Not really, Dr. Watson," said our new employer. "As you well know, the plague has never entirely vanished. The Ottomans battled it until a few decades ago, and China continues to experience outbreaks. [24] As our means of transportation grow ever more rapid and our world shrinks, diseases long thought past, or even those yet to be discovered, will spread ever so much faster."

"So this outbreak is affecting all of London?" inquired Holmes.

"No, Mr. Holmes, the Board of Health tells me that Charing Cross Hospital is the only one seeing cases so far. They are monitoring it closely, to ensure that it does not spread beyond our walls."

"Most singular! When exactly did the outbreak begin?"

"It was roughly two weeks ago. Dr. Purcell was the first to note the symptoms. The patients all developed high fevers, flushing, blackened tongues, tarry excreta, and finally fits [25] before they died. In the beginning, only those who were already ill seemed to catch it. The first several victims had severe cases of cholera. Dr. Purcell thought that perhaps it was some never-before-seen variant of that great scourge. But

402

as this year's cholera outbreak waned, our plague persisted. It struck down a man with consumption, [26] another with an inoperable tumor on his liver, and a woman with severe dropsy. [27] And then the most tragic thing of all happened. It struck down one of our physicians."

"An elderly practitioner?"

"Quite the opposite. Dr. Alfred Taylor was but a few years out from his degree at the University of London. [28] He was in the prime of health. A great loss, for his career was considered to be very promising. He was researching the pathology of chorea, [29] and was due to win the Golding prize."

"Ah, and will someone else be awarded the prize in his stead?" asked Holmes, mildly.

Sir James shook his head sadly. "Certainly not! It will be awarded posthumously. Still, we have been fortunate, really, given the history of the medieval plague doctors. Most of them survived little longer than their patients. Every member of the hospital staff has been exemplary in their bravery, for none have deserted their posts."

I thought about the costume of the plague doctors, with its heavy waxed overcoat, brimmed hat, glass-eyed mask, and cone-shaped beak, and shook my head at the terror that might be unleashed were such signs of imminent death to make a return to the streets of London. These grim ponderings were cut short by our arrival at the hospital.

Although it had once been situated near the similarly-named railway station, the building now lay just off the Strand on Agar Street. The ionic capitals flanking the front door and gleaming white façade inspired confidence, and gave little hint of the terrible pestilence that currently ravaged the inhabitants. As we were about to mount the front steps, Holmes placed a hand on my shoulder. "Watson, there is no need for you to go any further. I will gladly report back to you what I discover."

I frowned. "Whatever are you talking about, Holmes?"

"Death might stalk these halls, Watson. There is no need for you to expose yourself."

"Do not be ridiculous, Holmes. I have faced greater dangers than this, and I still have the Jezail lead in my shoulder to prove it."

He shook his head. "But you had no other to think of when you braved those perils. Now you do."

I nodded in sudden comprehension. "Ah, I see, Holmes. But Mary understands who it is she married. The Reaper may walk in the door of my consulting room at any moment. Should I bar it as well?"

Holmes smiled. "Capital! Well, I must admit that I am glad to have you at my side, Watson. I am somewhat out of my element, but we are very much in yours." He turned to his client. "Now, Sir James, if you will be so kind as to point us in the direction of Mr. Dick Whyte, we will begin our investigation with him. We will look for you in your office when we are finished."

The hospital director reminded us that Mr. Whyte had not been entrusted with the true reason for his sudden employment. He then indicated that the rat-catcher's wagon could be found parked by the side entrance off William IV Street, named in honor of our great Queen's father. Holmes nodded and turned his steps in that direction. The four-wheeler proved to be easy to identify, for it was a ramshackle affair whose weathered boards looked as if they were on the verge of utter collapse. A sorry nag, far past the time when it should have been put out to pasture, was harnessed to the front, slowly grazing from a feed bag. The conveyance was deserted when we arrived, though we could hear rustling and squeaking sounds coming from within the locked compartment, which suggested that the man's outings had thus far been successful.

We had not long to wait before the owner made his appearance. Mr. Whyte was a middle-aged man with huge black whiskers, and his mouth was only visible from where his beard parted to permit the blackened stem of a pipe. He wore an eccentric scarlet topcoat, waistcoat, and breeches, with a huge leather belt from which hung a series of small cast-iron cages. The rodent occupants of these cages were clearly terrified by a small black and tan terrier that nipped at them constantly. As the man drew nearer, he seemed alarmed to find us inspecting his wagon.

"What gives, Guv'nor?" he cried, briefly removing the pipe from between his lips.

"You are Mr. Dick Whyte, I presume?"

"I give my name only in return for another, Mister Questioner."

"My name is Sherlock Holmes, and this is my associate, Dr. Watson."

He shrugged. "What of it?" he asked in a surly tone.

"I have been retained by Sir James Saunders to inspect the hospital for potential sources of contagion. You have a very dangerous profession, Mr. Whyte."

"No more than some. I've a mate who lost his leg working the rails, and another who drowned off Gravesend. But my beauties rarely bite, Mr. Holmes." The pipe rapidly returned to his mouth between sentences, such that I doubted that he ever took a breath directly from the air.

"Are you not concerned about disease?" inquired Holmes.

His face twisted in disdain. "Nah, I am well protected from that."

"Really?" said Holmes, his eyebrows rising. "How so?"

The man stared at Holmes for a moment, and then shrugged again. "I guess there is little harm in letting you onto my little secret. Do you know, Mr. Holmes, the occupation of the only people to uniformly survive the greatest malady of them all, the Black Death, which some have blamed on my beauties?"

"No, I am afraid not."

"It is said that none who kept a tobacconist shop died, Mr. Holmes. Thus, the finest Virginia leaf is my charm," said he smugly, emitting a great cloud of blue smoke.

Holmes burst into a hearty laugh. "Then I too must have little to fear, Mr. Whyte, for Dr. Watson here has often accused me of poisoning myself with a surfeit of tobacco. [30] Now then, perhaps you might deign to show me your catch for the evening?"

Whyte's brusque manner appeared to have vanished after the discovery of this shared habit, and he proudly displayed for us his rats. From a distance, I gazed at the pack with some revulsion, but Holmes bent close and stared at them with his singular intentness. Finally, he straightened up, a gleam in his eyes which suggested that he had seized upon some irregularity.

He turned to the rat-catcher and glanced at his terrier. "That is a fine dog you have there, Mr. Whyte. It is a fortunate thing that you brought a canine to assist you, given the sudden deaths of all of the cats that once lived on site."

Whyte grinned broadly. "Tommie here is a grandson of the famous Jacko himself. [31] There has never been a finer ratter, Mister. A far sight better than some mangy cats!"

Holmes nodded. "You may have noted, Watson, during the period when we shared our lodgings, that there were some nights when I would never return home?"

I was surprised by this sudden *non sequitur*, but managed to stammer a response. "I have so remarked, upon occasion."

His face lit up with a whimsical smile. "I have several small retreats scattered about London, most of which can be found in less than salubrious locales. [32] It may surprise you to learn that one such refuge lies over a boxing den in Cambridge Circus which, in its former life, served as a rat-baiting pit. The denizens of that spot are still to be found in great numbers."

"I fail to comprehend your point, Holmes."

He shook his head. "That is because you see, but do not fully observe." He turned to the rat-catcher. "Tell me, Mr. Whyte, these are old English rats, are they not?"

The man's expression turned wary. "That's right."

Holmes smiled. "Also known as the black rat, or ship's rat? Where exactly did you find them, Mr. Whyte?"

"In the hospital, of course."

"Indeed? For black rats are nigh impossible to find in urban London now that they have been replaced by the Norwegian, or brown, rat." [33]

Whyte suddenly turned a ghastly color and looked from one to the other of us like a hunted creature. "I don't know what you mean," he stammered.

"I submit," said Holmes in his sternest tone, "Mr. Whyte, that you poisoned the clowder of Manx that once lived in this hospital so that the Director would be forced to hire you to take over the business of keeping it free of rats. And that you introduced a pack of ship's rats, collected by you on the wharfs, to this building, thereby introducing a terrible contagion. I am afraid that you will procure a charge of manslaughter, at the very least."

Whyte was shaking his head violently. "No, Mister, I swear it's not true. I never killed no cats! You are right about the black rats, but they were never set free in the hospital. I just bring them along for show, pretending that I caught them here, since they pay me by the rat. Truth be told, this place has no rat problem. It's as clean as a whistle. If I didn't pad my catch, I wouldn't make a shilling in this gig."

Holmes stared at the man intently for a moment, and then laughed sharply. "I believe you, Mr. Whyte. I suggest that you terminate your employment forthwith and return to your former haunts of Shadwell. I shall inform Sir James of your departure."

"Whatever you say, Mister!" the rat-catcher exclaimed. Within moments, he and his terrier were planted upon the wagon's seat and his nag was being whipped into motion.

Holmes watched them go for a moment and then turned to me with a chuckle. "I have been pursuing a red herring, Watson. Given the veritable den of thieves that constitutes greater London, it is perhaps of little surprise that there should be two villains in this case, a small one in the form of our Mr. Whyte, and somewhere else a much more important one. William of Ockham would be much displeased. [34] Still, we have learned a few facts of note from Mr. Whyte."

"We have?"

"Oh, yes, Watson. We shall docket those for the time being and see what additional matters will bear upon it. What steps would you propose to take now, Watson?"

"I would inspect the medical files of the victims in an attempt to find some common link."

"Excellent, Watson! The same thought had occurred to me. Let us rejoin Sir James and have him grant the necessary access."

In the office of the Director, Holmes quickly recounted what had transpired with the rat-catcher. Sir James absorbed this news with little expression other than a small frown, and then agreed to show Holmes the records of the stricken patients. "They are all in Dr. Purcell's office. If you will follow me, gentlemen?"

The place in question proved to be a good-sized chamber, half of which was lined with bookcases, while the other portion was set up as a chemical laboratory. In the former sat a heavy oaken desk upon which lay several theatre playbills and a stack of manila folders filled with handwritten papers. The broad, low tables of the laboratory side were littered with curved retorts, test-tubes, measures, litmus-paper, glass pipettes, and a formidable array of bottles filled with all manners of solutions and dry materials.

Holmes surveyed the place quietly. "What exactly is Dr. Purcell working on in here, Sir James?" he asked, waving his hand towards the chemical apparatus.

"Ah, yes, well, the man is a veritable genius. When he is not directly attending to patients, Dr. Purcell is always experimenting on new compounds which might help alleviate the suffering of our patients. When he first arrived, he was working on developing anti-cholera agents, but he has since shifted his aims towards trying to find some vaccine against the plague. His work is being supported by our great patron, Miss Vivian Crawford, heiress to the Crawford paper fortune."

"Is such a thing really possible?" I inquired. [35]

"Dr. Purcell believes so. He has taken for his inspiration the fabled 'Four Thieves Vinegar.'"

I shook my head. "I am not familiar with that particular medicinal."

"It was the secret recipe of a medieval gang of burglars from Marseille who used it to protect themselves from the plague while they plundered the homes of the sick and the dead."

"Dr. Purcell clearly believes that it is composed of vinegar, wormwood, marjoram, sage, cloves, rosemary, camphor, and several other herbs which I do not immediately recognize," [36] said Holmes as he inspected the contents of the tables. He turned back to the Director. "Well, Sir James, Watson and I will now spend some time perusing these charts in order to determine if we can find some common thread that binds these victims together."

With that dismissal, Sir James left us to this work, which proved to be exceedingly dull. Hours of attempting to decipher the nigh illegible scrawl of a hurried physician strained my eyes mightily, and at one point

I closed them for a minute of rest. The next thing I knew, Holmes was shaking me awake.

"My dear Watson," said he, smiling. "Let's return you to your home. There is nothing more to be learned here tonight."

"I am very sorry, Holmes," I replied, stretching. "Did you learn anything of note?"

"No, but the hour is early, metaphorically-speaking. I have hopes that tomorrow will bring some progress."

The following morn, my wife and I were breaking our fast when the clang of the bell announced the arrival of an early visitor. At this hour, I presumed it to be a patient and put on my coat so as to be ready to receive them. To my surprise, it was Sherlock Holmes who stood upon my step.

"Good morning, Watson. How long is your docket of patients this morning? Do you think Jackson or Anstruther would handle them for you?"

"Yes, certainly. Have you solved it, then?"

He shook his head ruefully. "Not yet, Watson, not yet. But I think it possible that Dr. Purcell might have something interesting to tell us, and I knew that, having begun upon a case, you would be loath to not see it through to the end."

"Of course. I would be happy to accompany you."

"Very good. He lives not far from here, in Harley Street, but in the interest of time, I have engaged a hansom."

The residence of Dr. Purcell proved to be one of the somber, flat-faced, ochre-colored brick townhouses wherein the great specialists of the age practiced their arts. The door was answered by Dr. Purcell's valet who, at the presentation of our cards, admitted us into the well-appointed sitting room. There we were soon joined by a middle-aged woman. Even in the long-past bloom of youth she could not have been considered handsome, for she had a thin pointy nose, protuberant eyes, obstinate chin, and the deep lines of her cheeks suggested that the frown that lay upon her face was perpetual. The cut of her gloomy black dress harkened from many seasons ago, and from her neck dangled a pair of silver pince-nez upon a brown silken cord.

"How do you do, gentlemen?" she began, her tone cold. "I am afraid that my husband is resting after a long night. He is engaged upon a medical matter of the utmost urgency."

"Indeed, Mrs. Purcell, it is upon this same matter that we come. We were brought into the case by Sir James Saunders."

"Oh, I see." She raised the pince-nez to her eyes and peered again at our cards. "But only one of you is a doctor. You, Mr. Holmes, are a detective?"

"That is correct, Mrs. Purcell. I hope to determine how this plague is entering Charing Cross Hospital."

"Ah, then my husband will be most interested in talking with you."

Holmes smiled. "Thank you, Mrs. Purcell. By the way, you must be a great enthusiast of music to share the name of England's greatest composer. [37] I once heard Foley singing his *Dido and Aeneas* at the Royal Opera House. It was exquisite." [38]

Mrs. Purcell shrugged. "I care little for frills such as music. If you excuse me, Mr. Holmes, I will rouse my husband now."

Once she left, Holmes smiled and nodded slightly, as if she had confirmed some theory of his, though I could little see how a three-hundred-year-old Baroque opera had anything to do with the pestilence stalking Charing Cross Hospital. He turned to me and raised his eyebrows suggestively. "Do you have any views upon the case, Watson?"

I shook my head. "I am baffled, Holmes. I read through the same charts as you last night, but failed to see any clue as to the origin of this plague."

Holmes raised his finger as if to elaborate upon some point, but paused as we were joined by our host. I knew him to be closer to fifty than forty, but the slight flecks of grey at his black temples lent him a distinguished appearance rather than an aged one. His face was square, with a firm jaw and heavy eyebrows, from which penetrating brown eyes studied us. His finely cut suit was of the newest fashion, which indicated to me that his practice was remuneratively successful.

After introductions were made, Dr. Purcell waved us to the settee, as he sank into one of the armchairs. "So Sir James has asked you to help me find the source of the plague?" said he, with some measure of haughtiness in his voice.

"Just so, Dr. Purcell," replied Holmes, agreeably. "I expect that Sir James felt you might be near the point of exhaustion, and could benefit from a fresh set of eyes."

"Yes, of course. You have heard, gentlemen, that we lost another man, Mr. Garrett the emphysemic diamond-cutter, to it just last night? It shows no sign of relenting. At the moment my hypothesis is that it was brought in by some fool who was mingling with one of those damnable Lascars down by the docks. [39] But I am having the devil of a time determining how exactly it continues to spread from patient to patient."

"Have you identified the index case?"

"No, I have been too busy trying to find some ward or vaccine against the plague itself. I don't have time to be traipsing around town interviewing relatives of the deceased. But, now that you are here, Mr. Holmes, that might be just the job for you?"

If Holmes was offended to have some tedious task foisted upon him, his face did not show it. "Indeed. My thoughts were proceeding along the same lines as yours, Dr. Purcell. Tell me, the plague miasma is typically a summer malady, is it not? Do you find it unusual that it continues to linger into the autumn?"

Dr. Purcell shook his head. "Not at all. It has been unseasonably warm, don't you think?"

"Certainly. By the way, what do you think happened to your colleague, Dr. Taylor?"

"What do you mean?" Purcell asked, sharply.

"Just that the plague had, for the most part, struck down only those already enfeebled by some other illness. Dr. Taylor was the only strong man to fall."

The doctor shrugged. "I cannot say for certain, Mr. Holmes. No autopsy was performed in our haste to minimize spread of the contagion. Perhaps Taylor had some hereditary weakness of his heart?"

"Ah, yes, I had not considered that possibility," said Holmes, mildly. "Well, I shall waste no more of your time, Dr. Purcell. Watson and I will begin by investigating the antecedents of the victims."

Once we had departed the house and walked some distance in the direction of Baker Street, Holmes emitted a sharp laugh.

"What is it Holmes? I heard nothing out of the ordinary."

"Again, Watson, that is because you heard, but did not listen. But do not concern yourself, for in this failing you are joined by nearly every other person in London, and the world, for that matter."

I shook my head at the extent of Holmes's pride, but recalled that his powers of observation were extraordinary. I had not forgotten how Holmes had once solved the shocking affair of the Chadwick murder simply by noting that her afternoon tea was a full ten degrees cooler than it should have been. [40]

"So, are we now going to interview the relatives of the deceased?"

"Not at all," Holmes snorted with amusement. "I have another tactic in mind. I think that for now, Watson, you can safely return to your patients. I have a few experiments planned, and the smells may be particularly malodorous. If you would be so good as to call upon me in the morning, I expect to have all of the answers that I require."

I arrived at Baker Street as the sun was rising, and was therefore much surprised to find the Director already present. Sir James's composure seemed much shaken. "I am afraid that we have no choice now, we must close the hospital completely," said he, a hint of despair in his voice. "We cannot continue to put lives in danger."

"What has happened?" I asked.

"I received this telegram from Dr. Purcell this morning. He has identified what he believes to be the source of the contagion."

"Indeed?" said Holmes, mildly. "And what was it?"

"Dr. Purcell believes the index case was a patient, Arthur Bryant Collier, who was treated by Dr. Taylor on the ninth of August. Mr. Collier was an explorer for the Royal Geographic Society, known for his travels amongst the Berbers of the Atlas Mountains. Collier died of apoplexy two days later, but having re-reviewed his charts, Dr. Purcell noted that there were some of the same features found in the other victims. Purcell's note speculates that Collier's clothing accidentally carried a mutated form of microbe back from Africa. Likely via the unhatched eggs of a sand fly, and it is now being transmitted via the bite of those now emerged flies. [41] That must be how it has spread so readily around the hospital!"

"Dear me!" said Holmes, his shining eyes and lively tone suggesting that he was much amused by this development. "Then you have no further use for me, I presume?"

"I am sorry for wasting your time, Mr. Holmes. I assure you that you shall nevertheless receive your full fee."

Holmes held up a hand. "If you would refrain from closing the hospital for another few hours, Sir James, I think that I may still be of some assistance. In fact, I highly doubt that you shall see any more cases after today."

Sir James appeared little mollified by this. "You have yet to hear the worst of it, Mr. Holmes. This morning, Dr. Purcell himself was struck down."

"Indeed," said Holmes, mildly. "This plague strikes quickly. Why just last night, Dr. Purcell and I both happened to attend the premier of Grieg's latest violin sonata, [42] and he looked to be in the prime of health."

"I fail to see . . . ."

"I assure you, Sir James, that I can explain in more detail later today. But time is of the essence if we are to ensure that this scourge ends with Dr. Purcell."

"Very well," agreed Sir James, with obvious reluctance.

Holmes and I were soon seated in a cab, whose driver was given orders to proceed to Harley Street with all haste. Holmes appeared both merry and concerned at the same time. I could certainly understand the latter, as we rolled towards a house which contained a pestilence that could prove to mean our deaths, but the source of the former emotion was an enigma.

"I cannot fathom your attitude, Holmes. You seem most happy that Dr. Purcell has contracted this terrible disease. The man is likely to die!"

Holmes chuckled. "Well, I cannot help but take some enjoyment over this development, Watson. It has transpired almost precisely as I predicted it."

"What?" I exclaimed. "You knew that Dr. Purcell would fall ill?"

"I thought it highly probable."

"And the records of Mr. Collier? How did we miss those the other night?"

He smiled broadly. "We did not. In fact, I looked quite carefully through the notes on the last days of poor Mr. Collier."

"So you already knew that he was the index case?"

"Not at all, Watson," said he, shaking his head. "I am afraid that Dr. Purcell has made a grievous error, for no such symptoms were recorded in Mr. Collier's chart two nights ago."

With a confused brain I considered this new information. When we arrived at Harley Street, it was a morose Mrs. Purcell herself who eventually opened the door. "I am very sorry for the delay, gentlemen. You see, the staff has all deserted us. They learned that the Doctor had fallen ill, and did not wish to risk contracting it."

"And yet you remain, madam?" asked Holmes.

She shrugged indifferently. "Someone needs to watch over him until he gets better."

"What makes you so confident that he will pull through?"

"He told me that he perfected his anti-plague vaccine last night. He assured me that it will reverse his symptoms. He also gave me a dose to protect me."

"Have you taken it?" asked Holmes suddenly, his tone sharp.

"Oh, yes. Just now. The taste is far from pleasant, so I followed it with some tea."

Holmes dug into his coat-pocket and extracted a small phial. "If you value your life, Mrs. Purcell, I entreat you to take this immediately," said he, gravely.

"What is it?" she exclaimed, her eyes widening.

"It is the syrup of ipecac. [43] It will cause you to violently expel the contents of your stomach. I am afraid, Mrs. Purcell, that there was an error with your husband's formulation."

"Oh," she said, looking stunned. "But what of the Doctor? He too has taken it."

"My colleague, Dr. Watson, here, will attend to him at once. Please, Mrs. Purcell, look to yourself."

"Very well," she agreed, clearly persuaded by Holmes's commanding manner. She swiftly departed into the water-closet.

"Come, Watson, it is past time for us to have a little discussion with the Doctor," said Holmes, gravely.

It was a pitiable sight that awaited us in the room at the top of the stair. Despite the fine autumn day, the drawn grey curtains of the sick-room cast a melancholy atmosphere. A rubicund, feverish face peered at us from beneath a thick quilt. His mouth hung slightly open, and his parched tongue was as black as coal. From a distance I had little doubt that the man was close to death. But he stirred as we entered.

"Ah, Mr. Holmes, Dr. Watson, I would stand back if I were you. I do not wish for you to fall ill as well," said he, feebly.

"That is most kind, Dr. Purcell," said Holmes. "But I do not think we are in much danger. In fact, I think you may rally soon." He took one of the seats at the side table, while I maintained my place by the door.

"What do you mean?" the doctor croaked.

"It is a strange plague that you have contracted, Doctor. For one, the tarry stools. In your experience, Watson, what does such a thing indicate?"

"Why, bleeding in the intestines, of course," I answered.

Holmes turned to me. "Do you recall, Watson, when Stamford first introduced us at the laboratory of St. Bart's? I had at the time just perfected my chemical re-agent which is precipitated only by the presence of hemoglobin. [44] And yet, when I tested a sample of effluvium taken from the unfortunate Dr. Taylor, it was strangely negative for blood."

Dr. Purcell pushed himself up in the bed, and wearily swung his bare legs over the side. "Perhaps the sample had degraded?" he postulated.

"Yes, that is an interesting suggestion, Doctor," said Holmes agreeably. "And, pray tell, what is your explanation for this?" He opened his left hand and revealed a shiny bit of metal slag.

The man sighed heavily and shuffled over to the table. He picked up the curious metal and rolled it between his fingers. "I really cannot say, Mr. Holmes," Purcell replied, sinking into the other chair.

"Ah, but I can. It took me several hours yesterday afternoon, but I finally isolated the key ingredient in your medicine to be the subsalicylate of bismuth. [45] This agent can have extraordinary benefits at treating the flux. [46] I suspect you learned as much during your research into methods to fight cholera?"

"I have long sought an adequate remedy for that terrible disease," Purcell replied, mildly.

"Bismuth is the only known medicine to leave behind a metal slag after being heated by a Bunsen burner."

"Is that so?"

"But that is not the only remarkable property of bismuth, Dr. Purcell. It also is very toxic to felines."

"Truly?"

"And when given repetitively to humans, it has one very unusual side-effect. It turns the tongue and excreta black."

Dr. Purcell sat silently, staring at Holmes. "What of it?"

"Do you not think it strange that these are two of the key features of the plague that has descended upon Charing Cross Hospital?"

The doctor shrugged. "It is an interesting coincidence, Mr. Holmes, to be certain. But if you are implying that my medicines are causing the plague, then you are clearly mistaken. For bismuth is not associated with either fevers or fits."

"No, you are absolutely correct, Dr. Purcell. To produce such an effect you would need to mix it with something else. Say the leaf of the belladonna which, as you may be aware, contains high levels of the alkaloid known as atropine?" [47] Holmes pulled from his coat pocket one of the bottles that I had seen in the doctor's office and set it upon the table.

A fire flared in the man's eyes. "What are you implying, Mr. Holmes? That I have poisoned myself?" cried he, motioning to his feverish countenance. "That would be mad!"

"Not if you had carefully worked out the precise dose that falls below the fatal range. Perhaps by poisoning a series of already terminal patients?"

"And why would I want to do that? What would I have to gain?"

"From killing the patients? Nothing. But by removing your hated rival, Dr. Taylor, you now have the attentions of Miss Vivian Crawford all to yourself."

"Who?" he stammered.

"Come now, Dr. Purcell. It will do you no good to deny it. I was not the only one to see the two of you in the box at St. James's Hall last night. [48] Many witnesses could be found should you care to continue with your protestation of innocence."

"You were there?" he croaked. "I did not see you."

414

"That is what you might expect when I am watching you. I had little concern that you would penetrate that particular disguise." Holmes turned to me. "You must have noted, Watson, that Dr. Purcell is a great aficionado of classical music and opera. Hence the playbills upon his desk at work. His dour wife does not share his enthusiasms, and he eventually decided to eliminate her in favor of a younger replacement who, it should be noted, also commands a considerable fortune. And what better way to ensure that no questions are raised than if the ill-fated Mrs. Purcell died from the very same plague that struck down so many others? I imagine she would have been the last victim, is that not so, Dr. Purcell? You would then dose everyone with your harmless compound of 'Four Thieves Vinegar' and declare the plague cured."

The man sneered. "You have no proof."

Holmes smiled. "Yes, your clever plague scare ensured that the bodies were rapidly cremated. I suspect that you first noted that your cholera treatment had the unusual side-effect of a blacked tongue. But your great inspiration occurred at the symphony, did it not? A quick perusal of the past performances at St. James's Hall demonstrates that on the twenty-first of August they performed the *Danse Macabre* of Saint-Saëns. [49] It was during that medieval allegory on death that the full formulation of your plan came together."

Dr. Purcell shook his head defiantly. "No, you are terribly mistaken, Mr. Holmes. Perhaps you yourself are manifesting the initial symptoms? Delirium is quite common. I forgive you for these accusations."

"And will your wife forgive you, Dr. Purcell?"

"What do you mean?" he asked, sharply.

"I assure you that Mrs. Purcell will be quite fine. While she had indeed just taken the dose that you gave her, my ipecac will prevent it from proving fatal. She will not go the way of your poor patients."

As his shoulders collapsed, the fight seemed to drain from his body. "They were dying anyway."

"Not Dr. Taylor." Holmes shook his head. "There are scarlet threads of life running through the bright tapestry of the universe, Dr. Purcell. What gives you the right to cut a man's thread?" asked Holmes, severely.

Dr. Purcell stared blankly at the tabletop. "It was a mercy," he whispered, clearly still thinking upon the innocents who fell during his care.

Holmes stared at him silently for a moment and then pushed the bottle towards the Doctor. "So is this."

Holmes rapidly turned and strode out of the room. I followed him silently, my thoughts morose. When we reached the sitting room, he turned and studied my face. "Do you disagree with my methods, Watson?"

I considered this for a moment. "I am not certain," I finally replied.

"Well, I for one cannot say that it is likely to weigh very heavily upon my conscience. Dr. Purcell literally took upon himself the role of Atropos." [50]

"Atropos?" I asked.

"I learned of her when reading about the effects of atropine in the first volume of the *Encyclopedia Britannica*. [51] She is the eldest of the Three Fates. It is her abhorred shears that ends the lives of us mortals."

"And have we overstepped our roles, Holmes? Are we not acting as judge, jury, and executioner?"[52]

"Not at all, Watson. We merely offered him the choice. It is up to him whether he meets his destiny in his own bed, or at the end of a hangman's noose."

After a moment, I nodded. "Then let us hope he chooses wisely."

"Indeed. Do you have any other thoughts upon the matter, Watson?"

"You know, Holmes. I never really thought it was the plague."

"And why is that?" he asked, clearly puzzled that he may have missed some clue.

"Because there was no comet to herald its coming."

Holmes smiled grimly and shook his head. "Good old Watson. Come, we have waited long enough. Let us learn the decision of Dr. Purcell."

It was a singular scene which met our eyes when we re-entered the bedroom. On the table lay the bottle, its cap off and the contents emptied. Beside the table, upon the wooden chair, sat Dr. Edward Purcell, his cravat loosened. His chin was slumped upon his breast, and his eyes were fixed with a horrible vacant stare at the floor. His tongue protruded slightly from his mouth, and it was still stained that deep black color. He made neither sound nor motion, and had surely passed beyond the veil to the bourn of that undiscovered country. [53]

Such are the true particulars of the death of Dr. Edward Purcell of Charing Cross Hospital. It is not necessary to prolong this narrative in order to tell of how Holmes broke the news to Sir James Saunders. Suffice it to say that Holmes spared Mrs. Purcell the public ignominy of having been wed to a murderer, and Sir James thanked Holmes warmly for his professional service. The official verdict, as carefully directed by my friend, came to show that the Doctor had met his doom at the hands of a brief but terrible outbreak of the Black Plague, which fortuitously burned itself out after the death of that once-renowned specialist.

When we had finally settled back at Baker Street, my friend sighed heavily and shook his head while gazing at the fire. "As I have said before, when a doctor goes wrong, he is the first of criminals. The ways of destiny are difficult to comprehend, Watson. Is the world nothing more than some ugly beast against which we must wage eternal battle?"

"Perhaps the madness exists so that you have something to combat?"

Holmes glanced at me and laughed. "I never get your limits, Watson. Very well then, I suppose that we shall embrace the madness. By the way, Watson, I have a small gift for you." He reached into his coat pocket and extracted a small book, which he proceeded to hand over to me.

I was greatly surprised by this unexpected act from a man whose paucity of expressed sentiment led so many to regard him as a little more than a cerebral automaton. [54] "I believe this is a first, Holmes." I studied the volume, which proved to be a compact edition Boccaccio's *Decameron*. Flipping it open, I found the name of Joseph Stangerson upon the fly-leaf, and smiled broadly at the recollection of our initial adventure together. [55]

"Have you read it?" he inquired.

"When I was a school-boy. It's been over twenty years."

"And do you still remember the premise?"

"A group of young aristocrats of Florence tell a hundred ribald stories, if memory serves. A sort of Italianate *Canterbury Tales*, is it not?" [56]

"Ah, but there were not *in* Florence, were they, Watson? They had fled to a villa in the hills in order to escape the Black Death. I found Boccaccio's description of it quite illuminating: *'The form of the malady . . . black spots or livid making their appearance in many cases on the arm or the thigh or elsewhere, now few and large, now minute and numerous.'* If I recall correctly, Watson, you on one occasion, in the very early days of our association, demarcated the limits of my knowledge in a detailed list."

"Your memory is precise, as usual, Holmes," said I, chuckling.

"At the very top of that list you rated my knowledge of literature as 'nil.'"

"Well, until you quoted Boccaccio at me just now, I would have sworn that was still the case."

"Indeed, for during my training I could see no purpose to cluttering my little brain attic with words written centuries ago, save only when they were a description of crimes, of course. But you see, Watson, if I had but read Boccaccio earlier, I would have realized much sooner that

417

Dr. Purcell's supposed plague was a fraud. The blackness was all wrong. His patients' tongues may have been black, but they had no spots upon their skin, for he could find no method to simulate them. If I had not limited myself, Mr. Garrett might still be alive, and Mrs. Purcell would not have come within minutes of her death, saved only by our fortuitous arrival," he concluded, solemnly.

"You cannot blame yourself, Holmes. You are but a man. You cannot know everything."

"But why not, Watson?" he shook his head, grimly. "That is my profession after all. To know things. There is no reason I should not add to my mental resources, for who can tell when some rare smidgen of knowledge might mean the difference between life and death. It is possible, Watson, that I have made a mistake. But it is perhaps better to learn wisdom late, than to never learn it at all. I therefore promise you that this is a deficiency which I plan to rectify straightaway." [57]

It was then that I understood that the pocket-edition of Boccaccio was not Holmes's gift. The gift was, in fact, a brief glimpse into the all-too-human soul which lurked, carefully hidden, behind the façade of that cool reasoning machine.

NOTES

1. This is clearly a reference to the events recorded in "The Man with the Twisted Lip".
2. Certainly, this denotes Irene Adler and "A Scandal in Bohemia".
3. This problem sounds similar to the cases of both James Phillimore ("The Problem of Thor Bridge"), but also Louis Le Prince, a French motion picture pioneer who boarded the Dion-Paris Express on 16 September 1890, and mysteriously vanished. His case is still unsolved.
4. Hatton Garden is a street in the Holborn district of London which has been London's jewelry quarter since medieval times.
5. The famous line of Iago, from Shakespeare's *Othello* (Act 1, Scene 1).
6. Many years later it is Holmes who enlists the aid of Sir James Saunders in "The Adventure of the Blanched Soldier".
7. Charing Cross Hospital is where Dr. James Mortimer trained (*The Hound of the Baskervilles*, Chapter 2) and is where Holmes is taken after he is beaten by thugs in the employ of Baron Gruner ("The Adventure of the Illustrious Client").
8. Cavendish Square is the historic home of London's medical specialists, where Dr. Percy Trevelyan hoped to one day have his

418

practice ("The Adventure of the Resident Patient"), while a red lamp is the usual sign of the general practitioner, such as Dr. Barnicot ("The Adventure of the Six Napoleons").

9. Fleet Street was the traditional home of the British national newspapers until the 1980's, and as such it is a metonym for the British press.

10. In 1889, the exact cause of the plague was not yet known. Five years later, Alexandre Yersin of France was credited as the primary discoverer of the bacterium that eventually became known as *Yersinia pestis*.

11. The Great Plague of London (1665-1666) and was the last major plague epidemic in England. It has been hypothesized that the coincidental Great Fire of London (1666) was responsible for putting an end to the epidemic, as the rebuilding of London did away with many of the previous conditions that fostered the spread of the plague.

12. Comets have long been considered heralds of doom and omens of world-altering change.

13. This was fifteen percent of the population of London.

14. The Black Death pandemic hit southern England in 1349.

15. The London Necropolis Railway opened in 1854 to transport cadavers and mourners between the Necropolis Railway Station in London (near Waterloo Station; this was destroyed in an air raid during World War II) and Brookwood Cemetery (built to replace central London's squalid and overcrowded historic cemeteries).

16. Cremation was not legal in Great Britain until 1885, but the practice took a long time to catch on. In all of 1888, only 28 cremations took place in the UK, though the number increased greatly after this method was chosen in 1905 by the famous Shakespearean actor Sir Henry Irving, whose company manager was Bram Stoker, and who staged the play *Waterloo* in 1894 for Arthur Conan Doyle.

17. The incubation period of bubonic plague is two to five days, with the septicemic form being even shorter.

18. Sir Joseph Bazalgette (1819-1891) was the chief engineer of London's Metropolitan Board of Works who, in response to the Great Stink of 1858, set out to create the sewer network that resulted in the cleansing of the Thames and relief from recurrent cholera epidemics.

19. The connection of rats to the plague has long been recognized, for whenever large numbers of rats were found dead, an outbreak

was sure to follow. However, the link to the rat's fleas was a more modern discovery. Of note, only one other unrecorded story details Holmes and Watson dealing with rodents: The giant rat of Sumatra ("The Adventure of the Sussex Vampire").

20. A clowder is one of the accepted terms for a group of cats.
21. The tail-less Manx cats from the Isle of Man are prized as hunters, and a strong preference for them as ship's cats is thought to be responsible for the world-wide spread of what originated as a very insular breed.
22. Classic rat-catchers were still active into the early 1900's in many parts of the world. The most famous was an eccentric character named Jack Black, appointed Her Majesty's Ratcatcher.
23. A "coolie" was a cheap and unskilled laborer from Asia. They congregated in the London docklands, where they were feared to be spreading disease. Holmes blamed them for his fictitious Sumatran fever ("The Adventure of the Dying Detective").
24. The Black Death ravaged much of the Islamic world until at least 1850. The Third plague pandemic (1855–1859) started in China, and eventually spreading to all inhabited continents. It killed 10 million people in India alone. Even in "civilized" North America, the plague struck San Francisco in 1900-1904, followed by another outbreak in 1907-1908.
25. Americans would call these "seizures".
26. Also known as tuberculosis.
27. Dropsy is an archaic term for edema, principally of the feet, and most often caused by congestive heart failure.
28. Where Watson also got his degree (*A Study in Scarlet*, Chapter 1).
29. Sydenham's Chorea (historically known as St. Vitus' dance) was a disorder characterized by rapid jerking movements of the face and hands, and was a common sequelae of Streptococcal infections in the pre-penicillin era.
30. Watson condemned Holmes's excessive tobacco consumption in both "The Adventure of the Five Orange Pips" and "The Devil's Foot".
31. Jacko was a black and tan Bull Terrier that set the world record in 1862 for the time it took him to kill a pack of sixty rats. The sport of ratting was not formally banned in England until 1912.
32. Watson also noted the presence of these refuges in "The Adventure of Black Peter".

33. This is true, but clearly unknown to Holmes or Watson was that only black rats are potential carriers of the plague, another possible reason why it has largely died out over time.

34. William (c.1287-1347) of Ockham (or Occam) was an English medieval philosopher whose maxim on the law of parsimony states that "entities should not be multiplied unnecessarily." This "Razor" competes for fame with the maxim of a later Englishman: "When you eliminate the impossible, whatever remains, however improbable, must be the truth."

35. Indeed it was soon to be. Waldemar Haffkine, a doctor working in Bombay, India, was the first to invent and test a vaccine against the plague in 1897.

36. Four Thieves Vinegar was a legendary ward against the Black Death. One recipe from Marseille states: "Take three pints of strong white wine vinegar, add a handful of each of wormwood, meadowsweet, wild marjoram and sage, fifty cloves, two ounces of campanula roots, two ounces of angelic, rosemary and horehound and three large measures of camphor. Place the mixture in a container for fifteen days, strain and express, then bottle. Use by rubbing it on the hands, ears and temples from time to time when approaching a plague victim."

37. Henry Purcell (1659-1695) was considered the premier English-born composer until the late 1800's, when he was supplanted by Edward Elgar (1857-1934), and later Ralph Vaughan Williams (1872-1958).

38. Holmes was not feigning his interest in the opera. In the Canon he can be seen attending it at the end of both "The Adventure of the Red Circle" and *The Hound of the Baskervilles* (Chapter 15).

39. "Lascar" is a now archaic term indicating non-white (typically Indian) sailors aboard British ships. The most famous Lascar was the confederate of the beggar Hugh Boone ("The Man with the Twisted Lip").

40. Unfortunately, a more complete account of the Chadwick murder, and how exactly the temperature of her tea played a role, has yet to be discovered.

41. It was not until 1896 that the rat flea, *Xenopsylla cheopis*, was identified as the vector of *Yersinia pestis* from rats to humans, so at the time, Dr. Purcell's theory would not be implausible. In fact, the North African sand fly is capable of transmitting a terrible disease, *leishmaniasis*, also known as *kala-azar* or *dum-dum fever*, which remained a major problem until the advent of the antibiotic era in the 1950's.

42. Edvard Grieg (1843-1907) was the greatest Norwegian composer. His Sonata No.3 was written in 1887. Holmes's familiarity with it may have influenced his later choice to adopt the guise of the Norwegian explorer Sigerson ("The Adventure of the Empty House").

43. Known to Western medicine since the root was brought back from Brazil in the 1600's, but no longer on the market, for many decades it was recommended that ipecac be kept in every house in case of accidental poisoning.

44. As noted in *A Study in Scarlet* (Chapter 1).

45. Bismuth salts have been used as an antidiarrheal agent since the 1700's, but were not sold directly to consumers until 1901. The black-colored salts can have the unintended side-effect of turning the tongue and stool black.

46. The flux is an archaic term for dysentery, itself a catch-all term for various severe intestinal infections caused by bacteria, parasites, or viruses. Dysentery was historically a great killer, taking the lives of such famous individuals as King John Lackland (1216), King Henry V (1422), and Sir Francis Drake (1596).

47. Holmes himself was familiar with the use of belladonna, which he used to dilate his pupils in "The Adventure of the Dying Detective". Atropine was isolated in 1831, but knowledge of the effects of the various plants from which it may be derived is ancient. In addition to *Atropa belladonna*, mandrake and henbane can also produce the typical symptoms, which may be remembered as "hot as a hare (or Hades), dry as a bone, red as a beet, mad as a hatter."

48. The Royal Philharmonic Society moved to St. James's Hall on Great Portland Street in 1869, where it remained until 1894, when they moved to the Queen's Hall. The Hall was a neo-Gothic masterpiece, whose cavernous interior imitated the Moorish palace of the Alhambra. Holmes also heard both Norman-Neruda (*A Study in Scarlet*, Chapter 4) and Sarasate ("The Red-Headed League") play there. Dickens gave his last public reading there shortly before his death in 1870. In 1902, St. James's Hall was bought by the owner of a rival concert hall, who had it demolished in 1905.

49. Camille Saint-Saëns (1835-1921) was a great favorite of English audiences of the 1880's, where he was considered the greatest living French composer. In 1874, he wrote his *Danse Macabre*, his take on the medieval allegory on the universality of death,

which originally arose out of the terrible horrors of the Black Death.

50. Atropos one of the three *Moirai*, or Fates. She was known as the inevitable, for she cut the thread (woven by Clotho and measured by Lachesis) with her abhorred shears.

51. The first volume of the Encyclopedia also played a significant role in the false employment of Mr. Jabez Wilson ("The Red-Headed League").

52. Holmes often took matters into his own hands when he thought he could serve the spirit of justice more readily than a British jury. Some of the most famous examples include his pardoning of James Ryder ("The Adventure of the Blue Carbuncle"), Captain Croker ("The Adventure of the Abbey Grange"), and Dr. Sterndale ("The Adventure of the Devil's Foot").

53. From Hamlet's great soliloquy in Act III, Scene 1: "Who would these Fardels bear, / To grunt and sweat under a weary life, / But that the dread of something after death, / The undiscovered Country, from whose bourn / No Traveller returns, Puzzles the will, / And makes us rather bear those ills we have, / Than fly to others that we know not of."

54. Watson compares Holmes to a machine in several other places in the Canon, most notably in "A Scandal in Bohemia": "He was . . . the most perfect reasoning and observing machine that the world has seen;" and "The Adventure of the Crooked Man": "[the] composure which had made so many regard him as a machine rather than a man."

55. Holmes must have acquired this from Gregson after the successful conclusion of the events of *A Study in Scarlet*.

56. This is a typical example of an English-centric world view of the Victorian era. *The Decameron* of Boccaccio (1313-1375) was completed in 1353, while *The Canterbury Tales* of Geoffrey Chaucer (1343 – 1400) was not published until 1483, and was almost certainly inspired by the earlier work.

57. Holmes certainly did so, for soon after this adventure he could be found reading a "pocket Petrarch" (one of the great Italian Renaissance poets) upon the train to Ross ("The Boscombe Valley Mystery").

About the Contributors

The following contributors appear in this volume
The MX Book of New Sherlock Holmes Stories
Part I – 1881-1889

Hugh Ashton was born in the UK, and moved to Japan in 1988, where he has remained since then, living with his wife Yoshiko in the historic city of Kamakura, a little to the south of Yokohama. In the past, he has worked in the technology and financial services industries, which have provided him with material for some of his books set in the 21st century. He currently works as a writer: novelist, copywriter (his work for large Japanese corporations appears in international business journals), and journalist, as well as producing industry reports on various aspects of the financial services industry. Recently, however, his lifelong interest in Sherlock Holmes has developed into an acclaimed series of adventures featuring the world's most famous detective, written in the style of the originals, and published by Inknbeans Press. In addition to these, he has also published historical and alternate historical novels, short stories, and thrillers. Together with artist Andy Boerger, he has produced the *Sherlock Ferret* series of stories for children, featuring the world's cutest detective.

Deanna Baran lives in a remote part of Texas where cowboys may still be seen in their natural habitat. A librarian and former museum curator, she writes in between cups of tea, playing *Go*, and trading postcards with people around the world. This is her first venture into the foggy streets of gaslit London.

Kevin David Barratt became a fan of Sherlock Holmes whilst at school. He is an active member of the *The Scandalous Bohemians*, a group who meet regularly in Leeds and for whom Kevin has contributed an essay on *Sherlock Holmes and Drugs* (which can be read at *www.scandalousbohemians.com*). Kevin is also a member of *The Sherlock Holmes Society of London.* He is married with two grown-up children and lives in Yorkshire.

Derrick Belanger is an author and educator most noted for his books and lectures on Sherlock Holmes and Sir Arthur Conan Doyle, as well as his writing for the blog *I Hear of Sherlock Everywhere*. Both volumes of his two-volume anthology, *A Study in Terror: Sir Arthur Conan Doyle's Revolutionary Stories of Fear and the Supernatural* were #1 best sellers on the Amazon.com UK Sherlock Holmes book list, and his *MacDougall Twins with Sherlock Holmes* chapter book, *Attack of the Violet Vampire!* was also a #1 bestselling new release in the UK. His novella, *Sherlock Holmes and the Adventure of the Peculiar Provenance,* is forthcoming from Endeavour Press. Mr. Belanger's academic work has been published in *The Colorado Reading Journal* and *Gifted Child Today*. Find him at *www.belangerbooks.com.*

Sir Arthur Conan Doyle (1859-1930) *Holmes Chronicler Emeritus.* If not for him, this anthology would not exist. Author, physician, patriot, sportsman, spiritualist, husband and father, and advocate for the oppressed. He is remembered and honored for the purposes of this collection by being the man who introduced Sherlock Holmes to the world. Through fifty-six Holmes short stories, four novels, and additional Apocryphal entries, Doyle revolutionized mystery stories and also greatly influenced and improved police forensic methods and techniques for the betterment of all. *Steel True Blade Straight*

C.H. Dye first discovered Sherlock Holmes when she was eleven, in a collection that ended at Reichenbach Falls. It was another six months before she discovered *The Hound of the Baskervilles*, and two weeks after that before a librarian handed her *The Return*. She has loved the stories ever since. She has written fanfiction, but this is her first published pastiche.

Steve Emecz's main field is technology, in which he has been working for about twenty years. Following multiple senior roles at Xerox, where he grew their European eCommerce from $6m to $200m, Steve joined platform provider Venda, and moved across to Powa Technologies in 2010. Steve is a regular trade show speaker on the subject of mobile commerce, and his time at Powa has taken him to more than forty countries – so he's no stranger to planes and airports. He wrote two novels (one bestseller) in the 1990's and a screenplay in 2001. Shortly after he set up MX Publishing, specialising in NLP books. In 2008, MX published its first Sherlock Holmes book, and MX has gone on to become the largest specialist Holmes publisher in the world, with around one hundred authors and over two hundred books. Profits from MX go towards his second passion – a children's rescue project in Nairobi, Kenya, where he and his wife, Sharon, spend every Christmas at the rescue centre in Kasarani. In 2014, they wrote a short book about the project, *The Happy Life Story*.

Mark A. Gagen BSI is co-founder of Wessex Press, sponsor of the popular *From Gillette to Brett* conferences, and publisher of *The Sherlock Holmes Reference Library* and many other fine Sherlockian titles. A life-long Holmes enthusiast, he is a member of *The Baker Street Irregulars* and *The Illustrious Clients of Indianapolis*. A graphic artist by profession, his work is often seen on the covers of *The Baker Street Journal* and various BSI books.

Jayantika Ganguly is the General Secretary and Editor of the *Sherlock Holmes Society of India*, a member of the *Sherlock Holmes Society of London*, and the *Czech Sherlock Holmes Society*. She is the author of *The Holmes Sutra* (MX 2014). She is a corporate lawyer working with one of the Big Six law firms.

Bob Gibson, graphic designer, is the Director at Staunch Design, located in Oxford, England. In addition to designing the covers for MX Book publications, Staunch also provides identity design and brand development for small and medium sized companies through print and web for a wide range of clients, including independent schools, retail, financial services and the health sector. *www.staunch.com*

John Atkinson Grimshaw (1836-1893) was born in Leeds, England. His amazing paintings, usually featuring twilight or night scenes illuminated by gas-lamps or moonlight, are easily recognizable, and are often used on the covers of books about the Great Detective to set the mood, as shadowy figures move in the distance through misty mysterious settings and over rain-slicked streets.

Dr. John Hall has written widely on Holmes. His books includes *Sidelights on Holmes*, a commentary on the Canon, *The Abominable Wife*, on the unrecorded cases, *Unexplored Possibilities*, a study of Dr. John H. Watson, and a monograph on Professor Moriarty, "The Dynamics of a Falling Star". (Most of these are now out of print.) His novels include *Sherlock Holmes and the Adler Papers, The Travels of Sherlock Holmes, Sherlock Holmes and the Boulevard Assassin, Sherlock Holmes and the Disgraced Inspector, Sherlock Holmes and the Telephone Mystery, Sherlock Holmes and the Hammerford Will, Sherlock Holmes and the Abbey School Mystery,* and *Sherlock Holmes at the Raffles Hotel.* John is a member of the *International Pipe-smoker's Hall of Fame,* and lives in Yorkshire, England.

John Heywood (not the author's real name) was born in Gloucestershire in 1951, and educated at Katharine Lady Berkeley's Grammar School and Jesus College, Cambridge. After graduating, he supported himself in many different ways, including teaching, decorating, house-sitting, laboring, and mowing graveyards, while at the same time making paintings, prints and drawings. He continues to make art, and his work is now in collections in Europe and America, and is regularly exhibited. He currently lives in Brixton, South London, and works as a painter and as a teacher of art and English in adult education. In 2014, his first book, *The Investigations of Sherlock Holmes,* was published by MX Publishing. It was enthusiastically received by the critics, and has recently been issued in India.

In the year 1998 **Craig Janacek** took his degree of Doctor of Medicine at Vanderbilt University, and proceeded to Stanford to go through the training prescribed for pediatricians in practice. Having completed his studies there, he was duly attached to the University of California, San Francisco as Associate Professor. The author of over seventy medical monographs upon a variety of obscure lesions, his travel-worn and battered tin dispatch-box is crammed with papers, nearly all of which are records of his fictional works. To date, these have been published solely in electronic format, including two non-Holmes novels (*The Oxford Deception* and *The Anger of Achilles Peterson*), the trio of holiday adventures collected as *The Midwinter Mysteries of Sherlock Holmes,* and a Watsonian novel entitled *The Isle of Devils.* His next project is the short trilogy *The Assassination of Sherlock Holmes.* Craig Janacek is a *nom de plume.*

Roger Johnson BSI is a retired librarian, now working as a volunteer assistant at Essex Police Museum. In his spare time he is commissioning editor of *The Sherlock Holmes Journal,* an occasional lecturer, and a frequent contributor to the Writings About the Writings. His sole work of Holmesian pastiche was published in 1997 in Mike Ashley's anthology *The Mammoth Book of New Sherlock Holmes Adventures,* and he has the greatest respect for the many authors who have contributed new tales to the present mighty trilogy. Like his wife, Jean Upton, he is a member of both *The Baker Street Irregulars* and *The Adventuresses of Sherlock Holmes.*

Leslie S. Klinger BSI is the editor of *The New Annotated Sherlock Holmes* and many other books on Holmes, Watson, and the Victorian age.

Luke Benjamen Kuhns is a crime writer who lives in London. He has authored several Sherlock Holmes collections including *The Untold Adventures of Sherlock Holmes* (published in India & Italy), *Sherlock Holmes Studies in Legacy,* and the graphic novel *Sherlock Holmes and the Horror of Frankenstein.* He has written and spoken on the various forms of pastiche writing, which can be found in the *Fan Phenomena Series: Sherlock Holmes.*

Michael Kurland has written over thirty novels and a melange of short stories, articles, and other stuff, and has been nominated for two Edgars and the American Book Award.

427

His books have appeared in Chinese, Czech, French, Italian, German, Japanese, Polish, Portuguese, Spanish, Swedish, and some alphabet full of little pothooks and curlicues. He lives in a Secular Humanist Hermitage in a secluded bay north of San Francisco, California, where he kills and skins his own vegetables. He may be communicated with through his website, *michaelkurland.com.*

David Marcum first discovered Sherlock Holmes in 1975, at the age of ten, when he received an abridged version of *The Adventures* during a trade. Since that time, David has collected literally thousands of traditional Holmes pastiches in the form of novels, short stories, radio and television episodes, movies and scripts, comics, fan-fiction, and unpublished manuscripts. He is the author of *The Papers of Sherlock Holmes Vol.'s I* and *II* (2011, 2013), *Sherlock Holmes and A Quantity of Debt* (2013) and *Sherlock Holmes – Tangled Skeins* (2015). Additionally, he is the editor of the three-volume set *Sherlock Holmes in Montague Street* (2014, recasting Arthur Morrison's Martin Hewitt stories as early Holmes adventures,) and most recently this current collection, *The MX Book of New Sherlock Holmes Stories* (2015). He has contributed essays to the *Baker Street Journal* and *The Gazette*, the journal of the Nero Wolfe *Wolfe Pack.* He began his adult work life as a Federal Investigator for an obscure U.S. Government agency, before the organization was eliminated. He returned to school for a second degree, and is now a licensed Civil Engineer, living in Tennessee with his wife and son. He is a member of *The Sherlock Holmes Society of London, The John H. Watson Society* ("Marker"), *The Praed Street Irregulars* ("The Obrisset Snuff Box"), *The Solar Pons Society of London,* and *The Diogenes Club West (East Tennessee Annex),* a curious and unofficial Scion of one. Since the age of nineteen, he has worn a deerstalker as his regular-and-only hat from autumn to spring. In 2013, he and his deerstalker were finally able make a trip-of-a-lifetime Holmes Pilgrimage to England, where you may have spotted him. If you ever run into him and his deerstalker out and about, feel free to say hello!

Daniel McGachey Outside of his day job – which, over the past quarter century has seen him write extensively for comics, newspapers, magazines, digital media, and animation – Scottish writer Daniel McGachey's stories first appeared in several volumes of *The BHF Book of Horror Stories* and *Black Book of Horror* anthology series, and *Filthy Creations* magazine. In 2009, Dark Regions Press published his first ghost story collection, *They That Dwell in Dark Places,* dedicated in part to M.R. James, whose works inspired the creation of the collected stories. Since 2005, he has reviewed television and radio adaptations of James's stories for *The Ghosts and Scholars M.R. James Newsletter,* while his sequels to several of James's original tales appeared as the Haunted Library publication *Ex Libris: Lufford* in 2012. Moving from M.R. James to his other lifelong literary hero, his 2010 Dark Regions Press collection pitted Sir Arthur Conan Doyle's rational detective against the irrational forces of the supernatural in *Sherlock Holmes: The Impossible Cases.* His radio plays have been broadcast since 2005 as part of the mystery and suspense series *Imagination Theater,* including entries in its long-running strand of new Holmesian mysteries, *The Further Adventures of Sherlock Holmes.* He is working on a new "impossible case" for Sherlock Holmes and Dr. Watson in the novel, *The Devil's Crown.*

Adrian Middleton is a Staffordshire born independent publisher. The son of a real-world detective, he is a former civil servant and policy adviser who now writes and edits science fiction, fantasy, and a popular series of steampunked Sherlock Holmes stories.

Steve Mountain is a "born and bred" native of Portsmouth in the UK. Married with two grown-up children, he works for a local Council as a civil engineer, trying to retro-fit cycle riding facilities into roads not originally built for the purpose. This is usually, but not always, successful. Seeing his name in print is nothing new, although to date this has been mostly in articles in the local newspaper complaining about the effect of said cycle facilities on other road users. Having helped his daughter solve a problem with one of her Holmes pastiches, he caught the fiction writing bug himself. He has self-published one of his early stories with *Lulu*.

Mark Mower is a crime writer and historian and a member of the Crime Writers' Association. His books include *Bloody British History: Norwich* (The History Press, 2014) and *Suffolk Murders* (The History Press, 2011). His first book, *Suffolk Tales of Mystery & Murder* (Countryside Books, 2006), contained a potent blend of tales from the seamier side of country life – described by the East Anglian Daily Times *Suffolk* magazine as ". . . a good serving of grisliness, a strong flavour of the unusual, a seasoning of ghoulishness and just a hint of the unexpected . . . ." Alongside his writing, Mark lectures on crime history and runs a murder mystery business.

Sidney Paget (1860-1908), a few of whose illustrations are used within this anthology, was born in London, and like his two older brothers, became a famed illustrator and painter. He completed over three-hundred-and-fifty drawings for the Sherlock Holmes stories first published in *The Strand* magazine, defining Holmes's image forever after in the public mind.

Summer Perkins is a film student who lives in Portland, Oregon, and has been a fan of the various incarnations of Sherlock Holmes for many years. Though no stranger to writing in the world of Holmes, this is Summer's first published piece. In addition to writing, Summer can be found reading, watching films, and studying various eras in history.

Martin Rosenstock studied English, American, and German literature. In 2008, he received a Ph.D. from the University of California, Santa Barbara for looking into what happens when things go badly – as they do from time to time – for detectives in German-language literature. After job hopping around the colder latitudes of the U.S. for three years, he decided to return to warmer climes. In 2011, he took a job at Gulf University for Science and Technology in Kuwait, where he currently teaches. When not brooding over plot twists, he spends too much time and money traveling the Indian Ocean littoral. There is a novel somewhere there, he feels sure.

Shane Simmons is a multi-award-winning screenwriter and graphic novelist whose work has appeared in international film festivals, museums and lectures about design and structure. His best-known piece of fiction, *The Long and Unlearned Life of Roland Gethers*, has been discussed in multiple books and academic journals about sequential art, and his short stories have been printed in critically praised anthologies of history, crime and horror. He lives in Montreal with his wife and too many cats. Follow him at *eyestrainproductions.com* and *@Shane_Eyestrain*

Denis O. Smith's first published story of Sherlock Holmes and Doctor Watson, "The Adventure of The Purple Hand", appeared in 1982. Since then, numerous other such accounts have been published in magazines and anthologies both in the U.K. and the U.S. In the 1990's, four volumes of his stories were published under the general title of *The*

Chronicles of Sherlock Holmes, and, more recently, a dozen of his stories, most not previously published in book form, appeared as *The Lost Chronicles of Sherlock Holmes* (2014), and he wrote a new story for the anthology, *Sherlock Holmes Abroad* (2015). Born in Yorkshire, in the north of England, Denis Smith has lived and worked in various parts of the country, including London, and has now been resident in Norfolk for many years. His interests range widely, but apart from his dedication to the career of Sherlock Holmes, he has a passion for historical mysteries of all kinds, the railways of Britain and the history of London.

Amy Thomas is a member of the *Baker Street Babes* Podcast, and the author of *The Detective and The Woman* mystery novels featuring Sherlock Holmes and Irene Adler. She blogs at *girlmeetssherlock.wordpress.com*, and she writes and edits professionally from her home in Fort Myers, Florida.

Will Thomas is the author of seven books in the Barker and Llewelyn Victorian mystery series, including *Some Danger Involved*, *Fatal Enquiry*, and *Anatomy of Evil*. He was nominated for a *Barry* and a *Shamus*, and is a two time winner of the Oklahoma Book Award. He lives in Broken Arrow, Oklahoma, where he studies Victorian martial arts and models British railways.

Daniel D. Victor, a Ph.D. in American literature, is a retired high school English teacher who taught in the Los Angeles Unified School District for forty-six years. His doctoral dissertation on little-known American author, David Graham Phillips, led to the creation of Victor's first Sherlock Holmes pastiche, *The Seventh Bullet*, in which Holmes investigates Phillips' actual murder. Victor's second novel, *A Study in Synchronicity*, is a two-stranded murder mystery, which features a Sherlock Holmes-like private eye. He is currently completing a trilogy called *Sherlock Holmes and the American Literati*. Each novel introduces Holmes to a different American author who actually passed through London at the turn of the century. In *The Final Page of Baker Street*, Holmes meets Raymond Chandler; in *The Baron of Brede Place*, Stephen Crane; in *Seventeen Minutes to Baker Street*, Mark Twain. Victor, who is also writing a novel about his early years as a teacher, lives with his wife in Los Angeles, California. They have two adult sons.

Stephen Wade has a special interest in crime history, having published widely on regional crime. His book, *The Girl who Lived on Air* (Seren) was a Welsh Book of the Month for Waterstones last year. He was formerly a lecturer in English, and also worked as a writer in prisons for six years. His latest book is a short story collection, *Uncle Albert* (Priory Press). The current fiction project is a collection of crime stories featuring Lestrade.

The following contributors appear in
The MX Book of New Sherlock Holmes Stories
Part II – 1890-1895 *and* Part III – 1896-1929

Mark Alberstat, BSI, has been a Sherlockian based in Nova Scotia since his early teens, when he began reading the stories from his father's two-volume Doubleday edition. When he discovered the wider world of Sherlock Holmes, he was fortunate enough to become a regular correspondent with American John Bennett Shaw, who encouraged Mark to start a local club, which he did while still in high school. That club, *The Spence Munros*, continues to meet and is the Sherlockian achievement of which

430

Mark is most proud. In addition, Mark, and his wife, JoAnn, edit *Canadian Holmes*, the quarterly journal published by *The Bootmakers of Toronto*. At the January 2014 Baker Street Irregulars dinner, Mark was given the investiture name of *Halifax*.

Peter K. Andersson is a Swedish historian specialising in urban culture in the late nineteenth century. He has previously published a collection of Sherlock Holmes stories, *The Cotswolds Werewolf and Other Stories of Sherlock Holmes*.

Claire Bartlett is a writer and journalist who has worked extensively in comics and magazines. With her regular writing partner, Iain McLaughlin, she has worked on several radio and audio series, including *Doctor Who* and *UNIT* for Big Finish Productions and Imagination Theater's horror anthology series, and *Kerides the Thinker*, which she co-created and co-writes with McLaughlin. They have also written novels for Big Finish Productions, Telos Publishing, and Thebes Publishing. She is currently working on a non-fiction book for publication in 2015. Claire lives in Dundee, Scotland.

Matthew Booth is the author of S*herlock Holmes and the Giant's Hand*, a collection of Sherlock Holmes short stories published by Breese Books. He is a scriptwriter for the American radio network *Imagination Theatre*, syndicated by Jim French Productions, contributing particularly to their series, *The Further Adventures of Sherlock Holmes*. Matthew has contributed two original stories to *The Game Is Afoot*, a collection of Sherlock Holmes short stories published in 2008 by Wordsworth Editions. His contributions are "The Tragedy of Saxon's Gate" and "The Dragon of Lea Lane". He has provided an original story entitled "A Darkness Discovered", featuring his own creation, Manchester-based private detective John Dakin, for the short story collection *Crime Scenes*, also published by Wordsworth Editions in 2008. Matthew is currently working on a supernatural novel called *The Ravenfirth Horror.*

Bob Byrne was a columnist for *Sherlock Magazine* and has contributed to *Sherlock Holmes Mystery Magazine* and the Sherlock Holmes short story collection *Curious Incidents*. He publishes two free online newsletters: *Baker Street Essays* and *The Solar Pons Gazette*, both of which can be found at *www.SolarPons.com*, the only website dedicated to August Derleth's successor to the great detective. Bob's column, *The Public Life of Sherlock Holmes*, appears every Monday morning at *www.BlackGate.com* and explores Holmes, hard boiled, and other mystery matters, and whatever other topics come to mind by the deadline. His mystery-themed blog is *Almost Holmes*.

Peter Calamai, BSI, a resident of Ottawa, was a reporter, editor and foreign correspondent with major Canadian newspapers since 1966. For half those years he has worked five minutes' walk from the Rideau Canal and the Commissariat Building. When editor of the Ottawa Citizen's editorial pages, Calamai had the good fortune to spend an afternoon interviewing canal historian Robert Legget. He has been an active Sherlockian since the mid-1990's, concentrating on Holmes and the Victorian press. Honours include designation as a Master Bootmaker by Canada's leading Sherlockian society and investiture in the *Baker Street Irregulars* as "The Leeds Mercury", a name taken from *The Hound of the Baskervilles*.

J.R. Campbell is a Calgary-based writer who always enjoys setting problems before the Great Detective. Along with his steadfast friend Charles Prepolec, he has co-edited the Sherlock Holmes anthologies *Curious Incidents*, *Curious Incidents 2*, *Gaslight Grimoire: Fantastic Tales of Sherlock Holmes*, *Gaslight Grotesque: Nightmare Takes of Sherlock*

Holmes, and *Gaslight Arcanum: Uncanny Tales of Sherlock Holmes*. He has also contributed stories to Imagination Theater's Radio Drama *The Further Adventures of Sherlock Holmes*, and the anthologies *A Study in Lavender: Queering Sherlock Holmes* and *Challenger Unbound*. At the time of writing, his next project, again with Charles Prepolec, is the anthology *Professor Challenger: New Worlds, Lost Places*.

Catherine Cooke BSI is a Librarian with Westminster Libraries who divides her time between maintaining and developing the Libraries' computer systems and the Sherlock Holmes Collection. She is a Fellow of the *Chartered Institute of Library and Information Professionals*, Joint Honorary Secretary of the *Sherlock Holmes Society of London*, a member of the *Baker Street Irregulars*, and of the *Adventuresses of Sherlock Holmes*. She won the Baker Street Irregulars' *Morley-Montgomery Award* for 2005 and the Sherlock Holmes Society of London's *Tony Howlett Award* in 2014.

Leslie F.E. Coombs is a true polymath whose interests include the writings and work of Conan Doyle, and he is a Holmes devotee. He has a keen interest in the social and technical history of Victorian Britain, and has extensive knowledge of military weaponry and ergonomics, and of naval, military, aviation and transport technologies. In addition to his writing of books and articles for magazines, he has written extensively on aviation and steam locomotion, and he is an editor and publisher's reader. Leslie Coombs's fictional writing has already produced two collections of Holmes short stories, and "The Royal Arsenal Affair" is one of a number of short stories which will appear in his third collection, to be published shortly.

Bert Coules wandered through a succession of jobs from fringe opera company manager to BBC radio drama producer-director before becoming a full-time writer at the beginning of 1989. Bert works in a wide range of genres, including science fiction, horror, comedy, romance and action-adventure but he is especially associated with crime and detective stories: he was the head writer on the BBC's unique project to dramatise the entire Sherlock Holmes canon, and went on to script four further series of original Holmes and Watson mysteries. As well as radio, he also writes for TV and the stage.

Bill Crider is a former college English teacher, and is the author of more than fifty published novels and an equal number of short stories. He's won two *Anthony* awards and a *Derringer* Award, and he's been nominated for the *Shamus* and the *Edgar* awards. His latest novel in the Sheriff Dan Rhodes series is *Between the Living and the Dead*. Check out his homepage at *www.billcrider.com*, or take a look at his peculiar blog at *http://billcrider.blogspot.com*.

David Stuart Davies BSI is a long time Sherlockian. He is a member of *Sherlock Holmes Society of London* and an invested *Baker Street Irregular*. He is a writer and editor and author of six Sherlock Holmes novels – the latest being *Sherlock Holmes: The Devil's Promise* (Titan), and two books on the films of the Great Detective. He has also penned two plays about Holmes and *Bending the Willow*, a volume about Jeremy Brett playing Sherlock. David is a member of the national committee of the *Crime Writer's Association* and edits their monthly magazine, *Red Herrings*. He has edited various collections of mystery & supernatural fiction and is the author of two crime series: one set in the Second World War featuring the detective Johnny One Eye, and another based in Yorkshire in the 1980's with DI Paul Snow. The latest novel in this series is *Innocent Blood* (Mystery Press).

C. Edward "Chuck" Davis was born and raised in New Jersey, and has lived in Colorado since 1993. He worked for over forty years as a draftsman and technical illustrator for AT&T, Sikorsky Aircraft, Exxon Engineering and Research, and Lockheed-Martin/Federal Aviation Administration. Additionally, he provided research, editing, illustrations, and technical advisory services for a number of publications, and is currently working on several projects, including *The Lunarnauts: The Rescue of Professor Cavor* (A sequel to the 1901 H. G. Wells novel *The First Men in the Moon*), *The Years of Infamy: The Japanese Invasion of Hawaii*, and *The Lion of the Sea (Il Leone di Mare)*, a historical fictional novel based upon the experiences of his late father-in-law who served in the Italian Navy during World War II.

Carole Nelson Douglas is the author of sixty New-York-published novels, and the first woman to write a Sherlock Holmes spin-off series using the first woman protagonist, Irene Adler. *Good Night, Mr. Holmes* debuted as a *New York Times* Notable Book of the Year. Holmes and Watson have been Douglas' "go-to guys" since childhood, appearing in a high school skit and her weekly newspaper column. Seeing only one pseudonymous woman in print with Holmes derivations, she based her Irene Adler on how Conan Doyle presented her: a talented, compassionate, independent, and audacious woman, in eight acclaimed novels. ("Readers will doff their deerstalkers." – *Publishers Weekly*) Those readers pine in vain for a film version of the truly substantial and fascinating Irene Adler that Holmes and Sir Arthur Conan Doyle admired as "The Woman." Now indie publishing, Douglas plans to make more of her Irene Adler stories available in print and eBook. *www.carolenelsondouglas.com*

Stuart Douglas runs Obverse Books *www.obversebooks.co.uk*, a small genre publisher. He has written short stories for many imprints, and his debut novel, *Sherlock Holmes: The Albino's Treasure* has just been released by Titan Books.

Séamas Duffy lives and works in Glasgow. His areas of interest are crime fiction, historical fiction, social history, and London writing. He has contributed articles to the London Fictions website and to the *Baker Street Journal*, and wrote the Foreword for *The Aggravations of Minnie Ashe* by Cyril Kersh, published by Valancourt Books in January 2014. His first collection, *Sherlock Holmes In Paris* was published Black Coat Press in February 2013, and in May 2015 *Sherlock Holmes and The Four Corners of Hell* was published by Robert Hale of London. A third novel *The Tenants of Cinnamon Street* will be published in autumn 2015. This is historical crime fiction set in 1811, centred on Aaron Graham – a real Bow Street Magistrate – who investigated the Ratcliff Highway Murders. Séamas Duffy is also a musician and composer with an interest in Irish Language and History, and has produced *Tairngreacht Na nDraoideann* ("A Druid's Prophecy") in Irish and *Ó Ghartan Go Ghlaschú: Odaisé Colm Cille* ("From Gartan to Glasgow: Odyssey of Colm Cille") in Irish and Scottish Gaelic – both suites of Celtic music and song celebrating aspects of early Celtic culture, the latter emphasising the shared cultural heritage of Scottish and Irish Gaels.

Matthew J. Elliott is the author of *Lost in Time and Space: An Unofficial Guide to the Uncharted Journeys of Doctor Who, Sherlock Holmes on the Air* (2012), *Sherlock Holmes in Pursuit* (2013), *The Immortals: An Unauthorized Guide to* Sherlock *and* Elementary (2013), and *The Throne Eternal* (2014). His articles, fiction and reviews have appeared in the magazines *Scarlet Street, Total DVD, SHERLOCK*, and *Sherlock Holmes Mystery Magazine*, and the collections *The Game's Afoot, Curious Incidents 2, Gaslight Grimoire*, and *The Mammoth Book of Best British Crime 8*. He has scripted over 260 radio plays, including episodes of *The Further Adventures of Sherlock Holmes*, *The Classic Adventures of Sherlock Holmes*, *Doctor Who*, *The Twilight Zone*, *The New Adventures of Mickey Spillane's Mike Hammer*, *Fangoria's Dreadtime Stories*, and award-winning adaptations of *The Hound of the Baskervilles* and *The War of the Worlds*. Matthew is a writer and performer on *RiffTrax.com*, the online comedy experience from the creators of cult sci-fi TV series *Mystery Science Theater 3000* (*MST3K* to the initiated). He's also written a few comic books.

Lyndsay Faye, BSI, grew up in the Pacific Northwest, graduating from Notre Dame de Namur University. She worked as a professional actress throughout the Bay Area for several years before moving to New York. Her first novel was the critically acclaimed pastiche *Dust and Shadow: An Account of the Ripper Killings by Dr. John H Watson*. Faye's love of her adopted city led her to research the origins of the New York City Police Department, as related in the Edgar-nominated Timothy Wilde trilogy. She is a frequent writer for the *Strand Magazine* and the Eisner-nominated comic *Watson and Holmes*. Lyndsay and her husband, Gabriel Lehner, live in Queens with their cats, Grendel and Prufrock. She is a very proud member of the *Baker Street Babes*, *Actor's Equity Association*, *Mystery Writers of America*, *The Adventuresses of Sherlock Holmes*, and *The Baker Street Irregulars*. Her works have currently been translated into fourteen languages.

James R. "Jim" French became a morning DJ on KIRO (AM) in Seattle in 1959. He later founded *Imagination Theatre*, a syndicated program that is now broadcast on over 120 stations in the U.S. and Canada, and also heard on the XM Satellite Radio system all over North America. Actors in French's dramas have included John Patrick Lowrie, Larry Albert, Patty Duke, Russell Johnson, Tom Smothers, Keenan Wynn, Roddy MacDowall, Ruta Lee, John Astin, Cynthia Lauren Tewes, and Richard Sanders. Mr. French states, "To me, the characters of Sherlock Holmes and Doctor Watson always seemed to be figures Doyle created as a challenge to lesser writers. He gave us two interesting characters – different from each other in their histories, talents and experience but complimentary as a team – who have been applied to a variety of situations and plots far beyond the times and places in the Canon. In the hands of different writers, Holmes and Watson have lent their identities to different times, ages, and even genders. But I wanted to break no new ground. I feel Sir Arthur provided us with enough references to locations, landmarks, and the social conditions of his time, to give a pretty large canvas on which to paint our own images and actions to animate Holmes and Watson."

Wendy C. Fries is the author of *Sherlock Holmes and John Watson: The Day They Met* and also writes under the name Atlin Merrick. Wendy is fascinated with London theatre, scriptwriting, and lattes. Website: *wendycfries.com*.

Dick Gillman is a Yorkshire-man in his mid-sixties. He retired from teaching Science in 2005 and moved to Brittany, France in 2008 with his wife Alex, Truffle the Black Labrador, and two cats. He still has strong family links with the UK, where he visits his two grown up children and his grandchildren. Dick is a prolific writer, and during his retirement he has written fourteen Sherlock Holmes short stories and a Sci-Fi novella. His latest short story, "Sherlock Holmes and The Man on Westminster Bridge" was completed in July 2015, and is published for the first time in this anthology.

Jack Grochot is a retired investigative newspaper journalist and a former federal law enforcement agent specializing in mail fraud cases. He lives on a small farm in

434

southwestern Pennsylvania, USA, where he writes and cares for five boarded horses. His fiction work includes stories in *Sherlock Holmes Mystery Magazine*, *The Sherlock Holmes Megapack* (an e-book), as well as the book *Come, Watson! Quickly!*, a collection of five Sherlock Holmes pastiches. The author, an active member of *Mystery Writers of America*, can be contacted by e-mail at *grochot@comcast.net.*

Phil Growick has been a Sherlock Holmes fan since he watched a black and white Basil Rathbone and Nigel Bruce on his grandparents' TV when he was five. His first Holmes novel was *The Secret Journal of Dr. Watson*. It has a surprise ending that no one, as yet, expected, and left everyone demanding to know what happened to all the major characters; primarily, of course, Holmes. Ergo, he wrote the sequel, *The Revenge of Sherlock Holmes*, which answered all the questions the readers of the first book were asking. His greatest joys are his wife, his sons, his daughters-in-law, and his grandsons.

Carl L. Heifetz Over thirty years of inquiry as a research microbiologist have prepared Carl Heifetz to explore new horizons in science. As an author, he has published numerous articles and short stories for fan magazines and other publications. In 2013 he published a book entitled *Voyage of the Blue Carbuncle* that is based on the works of Sir Arthur Conan Doyle and Gene Roddenberry. *Voyage of the Blue Carbuncle* is a fun and exciting spoof, sure to please science fiction fans as well as those who love the stories of Sherlock Holmes and *Star Trek*. Carl and his wife have two grown children and live in Trinity, Florida.

Mike Hogan writes mostly historical novels and short stories, many set in Victorian London and featuring Sherlock Holmes and Doctor Watson. He read the Conan Doyle stories at school with great enjoyment, but hadn't thought much about Sherlock Holmes until, having missed the Granada/Jeremy Brett TV series when it was originally shown in the eighties, he came across a box set of videos in a street market and was hooked on Holmes again. He started writing Sherlock Holmes pastiches about four years ago, having great fun re-imagining situations for the Conan Doyle characters to act in. The relationship between Holmes and Watson fascinates him as one of the great literary friendships. (He's also a huge admirer of Patrick O'Brian's Aubrey-Maturin novels). Like Captain Aubrey and Doctor Maturin, Holmes and Watson are an odd couple, differing in almost every facet of their characters, but sharing a common sense of decency and a common humanity. Living with Sherlock Holmes can't have been easy, and Mike enjoys adding a stronger vein of "pawky humour" into the Conan Doyle mix, even letting Watson have the second-to-last word on occasions. Mike is British, and he lives in Italy. His books include *Sherlock Holmes and the Scottish Question*; *The Gory Season – Sherlock Holmes, Jack the Ripper and the Thames Torso Murders* and the Sherlock Holmes & Young Winston 1887 Trilogy (*The Deadwood Stage*; *The Jubilee Plot*; and *The Giant Moles*). He has also written the following short story collections: *Sherlock Holmes: Murder at the Savoy and Other Stories*, *Sherlock Holmes: The Skull of Kohada Koheiji and Other Stories*, and *Sherlock Holmes: Murder on the Brighton Line and Other Stories*. *www.mikehoganbooks.com*

Jeremy Holstein first discovered Sherlock Holmes at age five when he became convinced that the Hound of the Baskervilles lived in his bedroom closet. A life long enthusiast of radio dramas, Jeremy is currently the lead dramatist and director for the Post Meridian Radio Players adaptations of Sherlock Holmes, where he has adapted *The Hound of the Baskervilles*, *The Sign of Four*, and "Jack the Harlot Killer" (retitled "The Whitechapel Murders") from William S. Baring-Gould's *Sherlock Holmes of Baker*

Street for the company. He is currently in production with an adaptation of "Charles Augustus Milverton". Jeremy has also written Sherlock Holmes scripts for Jim French's *Imagination Theatre*. He lives with his wife and daughter in the Boston, MA area.

Paul D. Gilbert was born in 1954 and has lived in and around Lindon all of his life. He has been married to Jackie for thirty-eight years, and she is a Holmes expert who keeps him on the straight and narrow! He has two sons, one of whom now lives in Spain. His interests include literature, ancient history, all religions, most sports, and movies. He is currently employed full-time as a funeral director. His books so far include *The Lost Files of Sherlock Holmes* (2007), *The Chronicles of Sherlock Holmes* (2008), *Sherlock Holmes and the Giant Rat of Sumatra* (2010), *The Annals of Sherlock Holmes* (2012), and *Sherlock Holmes and the Unholy Trinity* (2015). He has just started work on *Sherlock Holmes: The Four Handed Game*.

Kim Krisco, author of three books on leadership, now follows in the footsteps of the master storyteller Sir Arthur Conan Doyle by adding five totally new Sherlock Holmes adventures to the canon with the recently released *Sherlock Holmes – The Golden Years*. He captures the voice and style of Doyle, as Holmes and Watson find themselves unraveling mysteries in America, Africa and around turn-of-the-century London that, as Holmes puts it, "appears to have taken on an unsavory European influence." Meticulously researched, all of Krisco's stories read as mini historical novels. Indeed, he traveled to the UK and Scotland in May of 2013 to do research for his most recent book. The five novellas all take place after Holmes and Watson were supposed to have retired. *Sherlock Holmes – The Golden Years* breathes new life into the beloved "odd couple," revealing deeper insights into their protean friendship that has become richer with age . . . and a bit puckish. Krisco's diverse career fashioned a circuitous route to his becoming a full-time writer. He has taught college, written and directed TV and films, and served in corporate communications. He has two writing desks: one in a travel trailer on a river in the Rocky Mountains of Colorado, and the other in a *pequeña casa* on an estuary in La Penta, Mexico.

Andrew Lane is a British writer with thirty-odd books to his credit, a mixture of fiction & non-fiction, Adult & Young Adult, and books under his own name and ghost-written works. Most recently he has written eight books in a series (sold in translation to more than twenty countries at the last count) imagining what Sherlock Holmes would have been like when he was fourteen years old. The third of these books, *Black Ice*, is referenced in passing in his story for this anthology. *A Study in Scarlet* was the first book that Andrew Lane bought with his own pocket money. He was nine years old at the time, and the purchase warped his life from that moment on.

Ann Margaret Lewis attended Michigan State University, where she received her Bachelor's Degree in English Literature. She began her writing career writing tie-in children's books and short stories for DC Comics. She then published two editions of the book *Star Wars: The New Essential Guide to Alien Species* for Random House. She is the author of the award-winning *Murder in the Vatican: The Church Mysteries of Sherlock Holmes* (Wessex Press), and her most recent book is a Holmes novel entitled *The Watson Chronicles: A Sherlock Holmes Novel in Stories* (Wessex Press).

James Lovegrove is the author of more than fifty books, including *The Hope, Days, Untied Kingdom, Provender Gleed*, the *New York Times* bestselling *Pantheon* series, the *Redlaw* novels, and the *Dev Harmer Missions*. He has produced three Sherlock Holmes novels, with a Holmes/Cthulhu mashup trilogy in the works. He has also sold well over forty short stories and published two collections, *Imagined Slights* and *Diversifications*. He has produced a dozen short books for readers with reading difficulties, and a four-volume fantasy saga for teenagers, *The Clouded World*, under the pseudonym Jay Amory. James has been shortlisted for numerous awards, including the Arthur C. Clarke Award, the John W. Campbell Memorial Award, the Bram Stoker Award, the British Fantasy Society Award, and the Manchester Book Award. His short story "Carry The Moon In My Pocket" won the 2011 Seiun Award in Japan for Best Translated Short Story. His work has been translated into over a dozen languages, and his journalism has appeared in periodicals as diverse as *Literary Review*, *Interzone* and *BBC MindGames*. He reviews fiction regularly for the *Financial Times*. He lives with his wife, two sons, cat, and tiny dog in Eastbourne, not far from the site of the "small farm upon the South Downs" to which Sherlock Holmes retired.

Bonnie MacBird has loved Sherlock Holmes since breathlessly devouring the Canon at ten. She has degrees in music and film from Stanford, is the original writer of the movie *TRON*, won three Emmys for documentary film, studied Shakespearean acting at Oxford, and divides her time between her home in Los Angeles and a hotel room in Baker Street. She runs *The Sherlock Breakfast Club* and a playreading series in Los Angeles, where she also teaches writing at UCLA Extension. Her first novel, *Art in the Blood* (HarperCollins 2015) features a kidnapping, murder, and an art theft, and challenges Holmes's artistic nature and his friendship with Watson to the limits.

William Patrick Maynard was born and raised in Cleveland, Ohio. His passion for writing began in childhood and was fueled by early love of detective and thriller fiction. He was licensed by the Sax Rohmer Literary Estate to continue the Fu Manchu thrillers for Black Coat Press. *The Terror of Fu Manchu* was published in 2009 and was followed by *The Destiny of Fu Manchu* in 2012 and *The Triumph of Fu Manchu* in 2015. His previous Sherlock Holmes stories appeared in *Gaslight Grotesque* (2009/EDGE Publishing) and *Further Encounters of Sherlock Holmes* (2014/Titan Books). He currently resides in Northeast Ohio with his wife and family.

Lyn McConchie began writing professionally in 1990. Since then, she has seen thirty-two of her books published, and almost three hundred of her short stories appear. Her work has been published to date in nine countries and four languages, which she says isn't bad for an elderly, crippled, female farmer. Lyn lives on her farm in the North island of New Zealand where she breeds coloured sheep, and has free-range geese and hens. She shares her 19th century farmhouse with her Ocicat, Thunder, 7,469 books by other authors, and says that she plans to write forever or die trying.

Iain McLaughlin has been writing for a living since 1985. He has worked on numerous comics in the UK, and was editor of the *Beano* for a time. He has written novels, short stories, radio plays, and some TV episodes, often working with regular writing partner Claire Bartlett. He wrote several stories in the "Doctor Who" universe, beginning with 2001's *The Eye of the Scorpion*, which introduced the character of Erimem. He has also written audios for *Blake's 7*, and radio plays of legendary sleuth Sherlock Holmes. Additionally, he has written numerous horror radio plays, and created and wrote every episode of Imagination Theater's *Kerides The Thinker* radio series. His *noir* novel, *Movie Star*, was released by Thebes Publishing in 2015. He was born and still lives in Dundee on the east coast of Scotland.

Larry Millett worked for thirty years as a newspaper reporter in St. Paul, where he lives, while building a parallel career as a mystery novelist and architectural historian. He has written seven mysteries featuring Sherlock Holmes, all but one of them set in Minnesota. His first novel, *Sherlock Holmes and the Red Demon*, appeared in 1996. His second novel, *Sherlock Holmes and the Ice Palace Murders*, was adapted in 2015 into a play that performed to full houses at a theater in St. Paul. He is now working on a new mystery featuring Holmes that will be published in 2016 by the University of Minnesota Press.

Chris Redmond, BSI, is editor of the website *Sherlockian.Net*, and the author of *A Sherlock Holmes Handbook*, *In Bed with Sherlock Holmes*, and other books, as well as many Sherlockian articles. He is a member of the *Baker Street Irregulars*, *The Bootmakers of Toronto*, *The Adventuresses of Sherlock Holmes*, and other societies. He lives in Waterloo, Ontario, Canada.

GC Rosenquist was born in Chicago, Illinois, and has been writing since he was ten years old. His interests are very eclectic. His eleven previously published books include literary fiction, horror, poetry, a comedic memoir, and lots of science fiction. His latest published work for MX Books is *Sherlock Holmes: The Pearl of Death and Other Stories* (2015). He works professionally as a graphic artist. He has studied writing and poetry at the College of Lake County in Grayslake, Illinois, and currently resides in Lindenhurst, Illinois. For more information on GC Rosenquist, you can go to his website at *www.gcrosenquist.com*.

Geri Schear is a novelist and short story writer. Her work has been published in literary journals in the U.S. and Ireland. Her first novel, *A Biased Judgement: The Diaries of Sherlock Holmes 1897* was released to critical acclaim in 2014. The sequel, *Sherlock Holmes and the Other Woman*, will be released by MX Publishing in November 2015. She lives in Kells, Ireland.

Carolyn and Joel Senter ("Those Sherlock Holmes People in Cincinnati") were the founders of *Classic Specialties*, which they operated for more than a quarter century, as "North America's leading purveyor of items appertaining to Mr. Sherlock Holmes and His Times." After retiring *Classic Specialties* in 2014, the Senters have maintained their contact with The Sherlockian Community via membership in several scions and Sherlockian societies, continued participation in numerous Sherlockian gatherings and, primarily, through their monthly (almost) internet newsletter, *The Sherlockian E-Times*. Their previous contributions to the world of Sherlockian printed literature have included the compiling and editing of *The Formidable Scrap-Book of Baker Street*, the publication of three full-length Sherlockian books, and the authoring of articles for various Sherlockian periodicals.

Robert V. Stapleton was born and brought up in Leeds, Yorkshire, England, and studied at Durham University. After working in various parts of the country as an Anglican parish priest, he is now retired and lives with his wife in North Yorkshire. As a member of his local writing group, he now has time to develop his other life as a writer of adventure stories. He has recently had a number of short stories published, and he is hoping to have a couple of completed novels published at some time in the future.

Tim Symonds was born in London. He grew up in Somerset, Dorset, and Guernsey. After several years in East and Central Africa, he settled in California and graduated Phi Beta Kappa in Political Science from UCLA. He is a Fellow of the *Royal Geographical*

Society. He writes his novels in the woods and hidden valleys surrounding his home in the High Weald of East Sussex. Dr. Watson knew the untamed region well. In "The Adventure of Black Peter", Watson wrote, "the Weald was once part of that great forest which for so long held the Saxon invaders at bay." Tim's novels are published by MX Publishing. His latest is titled *Sherlock Holmes and The Sword of Osman.* Previous novels include *Sherlock Holmes and The Mystery of Einstein's Daughter, Sherlock Holmes and The Dead Boer at Scotney Castle,* and *Sherlock Holmes and The Case of The Bulgarian Codex.*

Sam Wiebe's debut novel *Last of the Independents* was published by Dundurn Press. An alternative private detective novel set in the Pacific Northwest, *Last of the Independents,* won the 2012 Arthur Ellis Award for Best Unpublished First Novel. Sam's short fiction has been published in *Thuglit, Spinetingler, Subterrain,* and *Criminal Element,* among others. Follow him at @sam_wiebe and at *samwiebe.com.*

Marcia Wilson is a freelance researcher and illustrator who likes to work in a style compatible for the color blind and visually impaired. She is Canon-centric and her first MX offering, *You Buy Bones,* uses the point-of-view of Scotland Yard to show the unique talents of Dr. Watson. She can be contacted at *gravelgirty.deviantart.com*

Vincent W. Wright has been a Sherlockian and member of *The Illustrious Clients of Indianapolis* since 1997. He is the creator of a blog, *Historical Sherlock,* which is dedicated to the chronology of The Canon, and has written a column on that subject for his home scion's newsletter since 2005. He lives in Indiana, and works for the federal government. This is his first pastiche.

MX Publishing

MX Publishing is the world's largest specialist Sherlock Holmes publisher, with several hundred titles and over a hundred authors creating the latest in Sherlock Holmes fiction and non-fiction.

From traditional short stories and novels to travel guides and quiz books, MX Publishing caters to all Holmes fans.

The collection includes leading titles such as *Benedict Cumberbatch In Transition* and *The Norwood Author* which won the 2011 *Tony Howlett Award* (Sherlock Holmes Book of the Year).

MX Publishing also has one of the largest communities of Holmes fans on *Facebook*, with regular contributions from dozens of authors.

www.mxpublishing.co.uk (UK) and *www.mxpublishing.com* (USA).

CPSIA information can be obtained at www.ICGtesting.com
Printed in the USA
LVOW11*0723090915

453317LV00002B/23/P